Mike Ashley is a leading authority on horror, fantasy and science fiction. Since 1974 he has written and edited over thirty books, including *Weird Legacies, Souls in Metal, Mrs Gaskell's Tales of Mystery and Horror, Jewels of Wonder, Best of British SF* (2 vols.), *Who's Who in Horror and Fantasy Fiction, The Mammoth Book of Short Horror Novels, The Pendragon Chronicles* and *The Camelot Chronicles*.

He has also contributed widely to fantasy magazines and encyclopedias in Britain and America, including *Amazing Stories, Locus* and *Twilight Zone Magazine*. In 1993 he published the first "Chronicles of Crime", *The Mammoth Book of Historical Whodunnits*, which has proved tremendously popular.

The Mammoth Book of
HISTORICAL DETECTIVES

Edited by
Mike Ashley

Robinson
London

Robinson Publishing
7 Kensington Church Court
London W8 4SP

This collection first published in the UK by Robinson
Publishing 1995

ISBN 1–85487–406–3

Printed and bound in the EC

10 9 8 7 6 5 4 3 2 1

Contents

Sources and Acknowledgements

The compilation of this anthology and the publication of the previous volume (*The Mammoth Book of Historical Whodunnits*) seem to have encouraged much response. My thanks to all of those who responded to the previous volume with ideas and suggestions (all, I might add, of a positive nature), some of which have borne fruit in this book. My thanks to Robert Adey for once again loaning some rare volumes, to Jack Adrian for likewise providing some rare texts, to Lawrence Schimel for alerting me to Charles Ardai's story (I only wish Lawrence himself could be present in this volume), and finally to all of the authors who have been so receptive and encouraging to my ideas.

Acknowledgements are accorded to the following for the rights to publish the stories in this anthology. Every effort has been made to trace the owners of copyright material. The Editor would be pleased to hear from anyone if they believe there has been an inadvertent transgression of copyright.

"Death in the Dawntime", © 1995 by F. Gwynplaine MacIntyre. Original story, first published in this anthology. Printed by permission of the author.

"Death Wears a Mask", © 1992 by Steven Saylor. First published in *Ellery Queen's Mystery Magazine*, July 1992. Reprinted by permission of the author.

"The King of Sacrifices", © 1995 by John Maddox Roberts. Original story, first published in this anthology. Printed by permission of the author.

"The Three Travellers", © 1975 by Edward D. Hoch. First published in *Ellery Queen's Mystery Magazine*, January 1976. Reprinted by permission of the author.

"The Case of the Murdered Senator", © 1950 by Wallace Nichols. First published in *London Mystery Magazine*, October 1950. Unable to trace the author's representative.

reprinted in *Cork of the Colonies* (New York: International Polygonics, 1984). Reprinted by permission of the author.

"The Scent of Murder", © 1958 by Theodore Mathieson. First published as "Captain Cook, Detective" in *Ellery Queen's Mystery Magazine*, October 1958, and reprinted in *The Great "Detectives"* (New York: Simon & Schuster, 1960). Reprinted by permission of the author.

"The Inn of the Black Crow" by William Hope Hodgson. First published in *The Red Magazine*, October 1, 1915. Copyright expired in December 1965. No record of copyright renewal.

"The Spirit of the '76", © 1976 by Lillian de la Torre. First published in *Ellery Queen's Mystery Magazine*, January 1977. Reprinted by permission of the author's agent, David Higham Associates (UK) and Harold Ober Associates (US).

"Deadly Will and Testament", © 1995 by Ron Burns. Original story, first published in this anthology. Printed by permission of the author and the author's agent, The Mitchell J. Hamilburg Agency.

"The God of the Hills" by Melville Davisson Post. First published in *Country Gentleman*, September 1927, and reprinted in *The Methods of Uncle Abner* (Boulder, Colorado: The Aspen Press, 1974) and *The Complete Uncle Abner* (San Diego, California: University of California, 1977). Copyright expired, December 1980. No record of copyright renewal.

"The Admiral's Lady", © 1995 by Joan Aiken Enterprises Ltd. Original story, first published in this anthology. Printed by permission of the author.

"The Eye of Shiva", © 1995 by Peter Berresford Ellis. Original story, first published in this anthology. Printed by permission of the author and the author's agent, A. M. Heath & Co.

"The Trail of the Bells", © 1985 by Edward D. Hoch. First published in *Ellery Queen's Mystery Magazine*, April 1985. Reprinted by permission of the author.

"Murdering Mr Boodle", © 1995 by Amy Myers. Original story, first published in this anthology. Printed by permission of the author and the author's agent, the Dorian Literary Agency.

"The Phantom Pistol", © 1989 by Jack Adrian. First published in *Felonious Assaults*, edited by Bill Pronzini and Martin H. Greenberg (New York: Ivy Books, 1989). Reprinted by permission of the author.

"The Adventure of the Frightened Governess", © 1995 by Basil Copper. This is a complete and unabridged version of the story originally published in an edited version in *Some Uncollected Cases of Solar Pons* (New York: Pinnacle Books, 1980). This version is printed by permission of the author.

Introduction
THE SECOND BOOK
OF CHRONICLES

Here is a second helping of the chronicles of crime. The reaction to the first volume, *The Mammoth Book of Historical Whodunnits*, has been very favourable, and this volume allows us to explore and enjoy an even wider set of stories.

This time you will find not only stories set in ancient Rome, the Far East, medieval England and the American colonies, as in the first volume, but you'll also be taken as far afield as the Pacific Ocean on the voyages of Captain Cook and as far back as Australia in 35,000 BC, in what must be the earliest ever setting for a murder mystery. There is also a story by Edith Pargeter (Ellis Peters) that has been unreprinted for over forty years, and a long-forgotten story by William Hope Hodgson not reprinted for eighty years. And because some readers were surprised that I drew the cut-off point in the last anthology at 1900 (with one exception), I've extended the coverage to introduce at least one story set in the 1920s. This volume thus contains detective stories spread over 37,000 years! There are twenty-nine stories, of which twelve are new and were specially written for this anthology and a further seven have never been published in book form before.

One of the pleasures of researching for and compiling an anthology like this is the thrill of discovery. I was delighted at the feedback on the first volume where readers suggested new names to me. In addition, historical detective stories and novels are now starting to appear regularly with scarcely a month passing without some new series beginning.

Some of these discoveries are included in this anthology. Steven Saylor is a young American writer who has produced several stories and novels about his Roman detective, Gordianus the Finder, and one of those early stories is reprinted here. Kate Sedley, whose books about the fifteenth-century pedlar Roger the Chapman have been appearing since 1991, has contributed a brand new story about his adventures. Keith Heller, who produced three novels about parish watchman George Man, has also written a couple of short stories, one of which is reprinted here. And Amy Myers has contributed a totally new story featuring her master chef, Auguste Didier.

In addition to these I have made other discoveries, and although the following authors are not represented here, you may be interested to learn about their books. (Similarly, if you have made any discoveries that I haven't mentioned in either this book or the last one, then I would be very interested to hear from you, c/o the publisher.)

I was grateful to Mr R. F. Glayzer, who wrote to draw my attention to the works of Raymond Foxall, who wrote a series of novels about the Bow Street Runners, based on the real life of Harry Adkins, one of the cleverest of the runners and sometime spy. The books are set around the year 1800. They began with *The Little Ferret* (1968) and include *The Dark Forest* (1972) and *The Silver Goblet* (1974).

Edward Marston, whose books about Elizabethan investigator Nicholas Bracewell I listed in the previous volume, has now started a new series about the investigations of Ralph Delchard and Gervase Bret set during the compilation of the Domesday Book in the reign of William I. So far I have seen two books, *The Wolves of Savernake* (1993) and *The Ravens of Blackwater* (1994).

For those who like the mysteries of ancient Egypt there is *Murder in the Place of Anubis* (1994) by Lynda S. Robinson, set during the reign of Tutankhamun. And in the medieval era, there is a new series set in fourteenth-century York by Candace Robb. This began with *The Apothecary Rose* (1994) followed by *The Lady Chapel* (1994). Set just twenty years after those novels, at the time of Chaucer's *Canterbury Tales*, is *Death is a Pilgrim* (1993) by Gertrude and Joseph Clancy, which came from a Welsh publisher, Northgate Books, in Aberystwyth, so may easily have been missed. This brings us on to the Elizabethan period, with *A Famine of Horses* (1994) by P. F. Chisholm, set in the Scottish borders in 1592.

Finally, I was interested to acquire a further anthology of historical detective stories, *Once Upon a Crime* (1994), edited by Janet Hutchings. This reprints thirteen stories from the pages of *Ellery Queen's Mystery Magazine*, with their settings ranging from ancient Rome (Steven Saylor's "The Lemures") to 1937 New England ("The Problem of the Leather Man" by Edward D. Hoch). None of the stories is duplicated in either of my volumes.

Those then are some of my discoveries since the last book, in addition to others revealed within this anthology. It seems that the historical detective story is thriving, and long may it continue to do so.

So, let's roll back the mists of crime . . .

Mike Ashley

PART I
The Ancient World

DEATH IN
THE DAWNTIME
F. Gwynplaine MacIntyre

When I was compiling The Mammoth Book of Historical Whodunnits *I was searching high and low for a detective story set in
pre-history. I knew I'd seen one somewhere in a turn-of-the-century
magazine, but no matter how I searched, I couldn't find it. I still
haven't. But while working on this volume, I mentioned the idea to F.
Gwynplaine MacIntyre. He instantly took up the challenge. In fact, he
did more than that. He set the story in the ancient aboriginal culture
of Australia, allowing a chance to explore the origins of some of their
language and thinking.*

*F. Gwynplaine MacIntyre (b. 1948), "Froggy" to his friends, was
born in Scotland but was raised in Australia, hence his knowledge of the
native culture. He has since lived in England and Wales but currently
resides in the United States. He has been appearing in the science-fiction
magazines since 1980, and drew upon his Australian background for
one of his first stories, "Martian Walkabout" (Isaac Asimov's SF
Magazine, March 1980), but "Death in the Dawntime" is his first
published mystery story. It's set around 35,000 BC and I'm sure that
makes it the earliest setting ever used for a detective story. Can anyone
prove me wrong?*

The screaming came at sunrise, three dawns after the wet.
Nightwish had been asleep at the outer edge of the *ngurupal*,
the portion of the campsite reserved for initiated males – not inside
it, for at twelvesummers age he had not yet undergone the *kurini*,
the ritual of manhood – but as close as he dared to the edge
of the privileged area. Now the screaming awakened him, and in
the wide outback dawn he got up and ran towards the sounds of
the agony.

The screams came from the redstone caves. Other males of the
Wuradjeri had heard the screams too, for as Nightwish ran towards

the caves he saw men – Speartouch and Dauber and Rainspeak – running ahead of him, towards the same destination. Even lame old Toegone, with his mangled foot, had got here ahead of Nightwish and was limping briskly towards the caves. Yet by now the screams were silent. The red-ochre clay was still damp here, from the long days of wet, and the mud splattered the men's naked feet and bare legs as they ran through a clutter of wombats' mounds amid the grass and hurried on towards the caves.

There were four redstone caves here; two reserved for ritual purposes, one empty. The fourth cave was sealed with a large round boulder; sealed imperfectly, with a thin vertical aperture remaining. The screams had come from within.

With the sharp end of his boomerang, Speartouch rapped the boulder. "*Ei! Lungah!* Anybody in there?"

The boulder gave no reply.

Other men from the *ngurupal* were here now, as well as several women from the she-ground. Speartouch tapped three of the strongest men. "*Duku.* Help me move this thing." Someone caught his attention: the young Nightwish, eager to help. "You too, boy. Push."

As they bent to their task, Nightwish sang thoughts in his head. This cave was Grabtake's. Five days ago, when the nomad people Wuradjeri first made camp at this site, Nightwish's clan-brother Grabtake had been content to sleep in the privileged *ngurupal* space with the other elder males. But two days later he had suddenly claimed this cave as his personal residence – the cave with the boulder inside that was larger than the mouth of the cave – and Grabtake had walled himself inside every night by pushing the boulder up against the cave's mouth. And now he . . .

The boulder suddenly gave way, rolling backwards and into the cave. Speartouch pushed past it, with Dauber and the eager Nightwish just behind him. Dauber held the tribe's picture-magic; it would be his task to make the picture showing whatever had happened here.

Grabtake was dead. He lay sprawled on his side, in the dust at the cave's rear. His eyes, unblinking, gazed lifelessly upward towards the realm of Baiami the Skygod. His dead hands were claw-shapes, clutching at something invisible.

Healchant fingered the body. "*Paraka!* Get up! Awaken!" If any clevering in the world could bring this corpse back to life, Healchant was the one member of the Wuradjeri who would surely find it. But now Healchant paused and shook his head. "*Warai.* He's dead."

Speartouch prodded the corpse with his boomerang so that

Grabtake fell over on to his back. "*There* is what killed him. *Ngana!*" There was a spear through Grabtake's heart. The lower half of the shaft had broken off and was missing. There were no other entrances to the cave, and no niches or hollows inside the cave large enough to make a hiding-place.

The dead man had been murdered in a cave that had been sealed from the inside. And no one had come out; the men of the tribe would have seen the murderer escaping in the first light of dawn as they ran towards the cave.

"What do *you* want, boy?" asked Speartouch, annoyed, as Nightwish pressed forward to look at the body. "*Minja wontu ngana?* What are you looking at? A man is dead. There is nothing to see."

"Oh?" Nightwish pointed at the dead man's hands. "LOOK!"

The dead man's fingertips were *changed*. Some unknown god-thing had altered the flesh at the ends of his hands, turned it black with a foam of white blisters.

Healchant went pale beneath his ritual body-paint. "Something has . . . something has *bitten* his hands," was the only explanation he could clever at the moment. Then, in an awed whisper: "A god-thing has done this."

"I think," said Speartouch, "that we should call a council."

The council talked much and decided little, which was often the way with councils. Old Toegone suggested that the dead man had been slain by a *dzir* or a *buginja*; since they were invisible evil spirits, they could easily pass through solid rock, kill a man, and escape without being seen. Speartouch unclevered this by pointing out that the dead man had been slain with a spear, a man-weapon. *Dzir* and *buginja* were evil enough to kill men, aye, but everyone knew that they possessed death-magic far more weaponous than spears.

This was no spirit-death: it was a murder. And the murder had occurred only two quickspans before the men arrived, Speartouch reminded his council-brothers. They had *heard* the dead man's screams with their own ears, and then the men of the tribe had reached the murder scene barely two quickspans later. But how could any man kill another man inside a sealed cave, and then escape unseen in such a brief fragment of time?

And how came it that Grabtake's fingertips had been *transformed*, changed in some manner that no member of the Wuradjeri had ever seen before? Healchant believed that Grabtake must have touched a thing that was taboo, and the taboo had bitten his fingers. Could this be why the murderer had slain him?

At the far edge of the *ngurupal*, Nightwish stood bursting with desire to speak. He had his own ideas for how to investigate the murder. But Nightwish had not yet done walkabout or undergone *kurini*; if he dared to speak, his words would fall dead and unheard at the border of the warrior-place.

A hand touched Nightwish's shoulder. "Have the beardfaces finished babbling yet?" whispered a soft voice in his ear.

Nightwish turned. Tinglesweet stood there behind him. She was a twelvesummers female, the same age as Nightwish, yet already her breasts had ripened and she had undergone the bloodflow that proved she was a full woman of the Wuradjeri people. Nightwish was attracted to her, and he had privately sung dreams of coupling with her . . . dreams that he dared not sing aloud, because his *jarajuwa* totem-beast was Maruwai the Red Kangaroo, while Tinglesweet's *jarajuwa* was Kuru the Bandicoot. Most incompatible. Now, seeing the ripe evidence of Tinglesweet's female adulthood, Nightwish hastily put one hand over his own genitals, hoping she had not noticed that he lacked the *burumalwu*, the ritual cord of emu's sinew that men of the Wuradjeri bound about their testicles to signify man-status.

Tinglesweet saw the gesture: she slapped the boy's hand aside from his naked genitals, and she laughed when she saw the proof of his immaturity. "So the boy is not a man yet! I had wondered why you stand outside the council-ground."

"D'you know about the murder?" Nightwish asked her.

Tinglesweet nodded at the council. "The beardfaces are babbling, while somewhere a murderer dances. *Kala*, why don't you and I go to the murder-place? We can hunt for cleverings that might sing to us the killer's name."

Nightwish glanced back at the *ngurupal*. Rainspeak was arguing with Dauber, and other men were shouting theories. Clearly, nothing would be settled here in any handful of time. Nightwish reached over, and shyly touched Tinglesweet's hair. "*Bilaka*. I will show you the death-place."

The dead man had not walked away. This was good, for it proved that the spirit Jaruta – who likes to dress himself in dead men's bodies and walk about in their flesh – had no desire to inhabit this particular corpse. After glimpsing the dead man, Tinglesweet flinched, and she looked away hastily. Nightwish felt secretly pleased, for surely Tinglesweet would be impressed that Nightwish could look upon the corpse without flinching.

The boulder that had blocked the entrance to the cave was too heavy for Nightwish to move by himself. With gestures, he showed Tinglesweet how it had been wedged tightly into the cave's mouth when he and the others arrived. "*Ngana tu?* D'you see?" Nightwish demonstrated, shouldering aside a phantom stone. "Inside the cave each night, Grabtake pushed the stone so that it blocked the cave's mouth. Then, in the morning, he pushed the stone to one side so that he could get out."

"Push to come, and push to go." Tinglesweet slapped at a sandfly, then studied the boulder. "Could a man *pull* that stone into position, behind himself, on his way out of the cave?" she asked.

Nightwish frowned, and then he tried to pull the stone. But the boulder was made of psammite, soft yellow sandstone; when he tried to get a solid grip, clumps of the boulder came away in his hands. Finally he gave up. "This stone can only be pushed, not pulled," he deduced. "And because of its position when the murderer screamed, the stone must have been pushed into place from the *inside*. By the dead man, before he was murdered. Or else by the killer."

Tinglesweet nodded. "So there are two eithers. Either a murderer *outside* the cave somehow sent a spear *inside* – through solid rock – or else a man *inside* the cave did the killing, and then he got *out* – through solid rock – without disturbing the boulder at the entrance. And in either case the killer got away unseen, even while men were running towards the cave."

Nightwish clevered his thoughts, hoping that one of them would sing the answer. Suddenly he remembered something: "*Tungani!* I saw it! The shape of the stone did not truly match the shape of the cave's mouth. There *was* an opening . . . but it was too small for a man to pass through." With his hands, Nightwish fashioned a vertical slit in mid-air: barely more than a spear's width.

"That's it, then," said Tinglesweet. She began a dance, taking the various roles. "The murder happened at dawn, yes? Because old Kapata-the-Moon does not give enough light for men to kill by." As she danced, Tinglesweet became the murderer: glancing up at Kapata-the-Moon, stumbling in the dark because there was not enough moonlight. Now she was Kapata, the moon in the sky, looking down at the murderer's vigil. "And the cave's entrance faces the sunrise, yes? *So!* The murderer waited outside until dawn . . ." – she was the murderer again now, dancing warily – ". . . and, as soon as he had light to do his dirty work, he flung a spear through that narrow crack between the boulder and the cave. *Whishshst!*" Now, with hands clasped over her head, Tinglesweet *became* the spear. She mimicked its flight, dancing through the cave and whizzing towards the dead man. "*There!* The spear found its prey, and killed this man."

"That is *warai*. Impossible," said Nightwish, glad to have a chance to impress Tinglesweet with his knowledge of weaponry. As a young male preparing to undergo *kurini*, he knew more about spears than any she-one could know. "The cave's opening was a narrow slit. No man could throw a spear through such a tiny hole . . . not *accurately*. See? You can place a spear against the hole, but then the arm must be drawn *back*, to have power to hurl the spear, and it must come forward again quickly, so quickly that there is no time to make sure that the spear meets the hole."

As Nightwish spoke, Tinglesweet glanced downward at his bare genitals, unadorned by the *burumalwu* man-cord, and then she swiftly glanced away again. Nightwish clevered what the female was thinking: since Nightwish had not yet undergone the male hunt-ritual of walkabout, Tinglesweet was unwilling to consider him an expert witness on the subject of spears. Quickly, he added the biggest clever to his argument: "Besides, the other men and I, we would have seen the killer running away."

Tinglesweet mocked his words: "The *other* men and you? One boy and some beardfaces, you mean. And the murderer *did* escape, while you were running towards the cave." She stood up, and brushed yellow sand from her brown thighs. "Let us hunt for cleverings. Something within this cave may sing the murderer's name."

The two younglings searched the cave for clues. This was difficult, since neither knew precisely what they were looking for. Suddenly Nightwish cried out: "*Ngai!*"

"You have found something?"

"I have found a thing that is not here," Nightwish said.

"Your words jump like a kangaroo," said Tinglesweet.

"I mean, a thing that *should* be here is missing, and its missingness sings a piece of the mystery," Nightwish explained.

"What is missing, then?" Tinglesweet was eager.

"Look." Nightwish pointed to the broken half-length of spear protruding from the dead man's chest. "The other half of the spear – the rear half, the part that a man holds when he aims – is not here. I saw that it was missing when we found the body, but I thought that it was somewhere in this cave. It is not."

"The murderer took it with him," decided Tinglesweet.

"*Warai*. Why would the murderer take half the murder weapon, and leave the other half?" Nightwish shook his head. "No. I am certain that *this* half of the spear – the front half – is all that was ever here. But how can a man aim *half* a spear through a narrow slit of rock? A broken spear is harder to aim than a whole spear."

"I have a more important question," said Tinglesweet. "*Why* did someone murder Grabtake? There had to be a reason."

Again, Nightwish felt that he should have more clevers than this girl had. Nightwish and Grabtake were both totem-born to Maruwai the Red Kangaroo, and had quartered together. Tinglesweet, born under the sponsorship of Kuru the Bandicoot, could not have known Grabtake very well. "Grabtake was disliked," said Nightwish, truthfully. "The elder males have told me that he always held back in the hunts, and did less than his share. At hunt's ending, when the day's meat was brought to the campsite, Grabtake always tried to get more than his fair claim, and he always tried to snatch the choicest portions."

"Hardly cause for murder," Tinglesweet observed.

Suddenly a thought sang loud in Nightwish's head. "I remember now! During the wet, Grabtake walked with all the other hunt-males and slept among them, in the *ngurupal*. When we reached our present campsite, he did the same. But three days ago, he suddenly awayed himself from the rest of us. That was when he started to sleep in the cave, shutting himself in at night." Another remembering sang in Nightwish's memory. "And during the last three days, Grabtake spent much time sucking his fingers, as if they were hurt."

Tinglesweet glanced at the corpse's peculiar blistered fingertips, and she shuddered. "Three days ago, you say? Then *that* must have been the day when . . . when the god-thing changed his hands. But that doesn't explain why someone murdered him."

Nightwish started to nod, then suddenly a great cleverness sang amid his thoughts. "I know! Grabtake must have *owned* something. Something the murderer wanted." Nightwish was certain of it now. "Three days ago, it must have begun: that was when Grabtake would no longer walk or sleep among us. He must have *made* a something, or *found* a something . . . a thing so special that he wanted it all for himself, and he would let no others of the Wuradjeri see it. But the murderer knew. He came into the cave while Grabtake slept, took the important thing, killed Grabtake, and ran away."

Tinglesweet sucked on a strand of her hair. "There's a hole in your clevering, boy. How did the murderer get out of a sealed cave? And how did he get away unseen while you and the men ran *towards* the cave?" She shook her head. "That's not the answer. Let us hunt for more cleverings, and hope that they will sing the killer's name."

They kept searching the cave. Nightwish sang a silent clevering: if *he* were Grabtake, and if he owned a thing so precious that other men would kill to own it, where would he keep it? He would keep it on his person every waking moment, and then place it nearby when he slept. *Look under the bed.* Quickly, Nightwish went to the gathered mound of dead grass and soft moss at the rear of the cave that must have been Grabtake's bedding-place. Beside it was . . .

"LOOK!"

Tinglesweet approached the corpse reluctantly, to see what Nightwish had found.

There was a thin vein of *kirapurai* – red-ochre clay – at the rear of the cave, in exactly the spot beside the bedding where a man would place his most precious possession, so that he could touch it in the middle of the night and assure himself it was still there. But the clay itself was not why Nightwish had cried out. Someone had pushed something *into* the clay, for safekeeping. Now the something was gone, but it had left its shape behind: an indentation in the clay. Tinglesweet saw it too, and she cried out in astonishment.

The indentation in the clay possessed a shape that the Wuradjeri people had no word for: *a perfect hemisphere*, absolutely round, its diameter about half of Nightwish's thumb. Some spherical object had been pressed into the soft clay. Now it was gone, but its circular image remained.

"A god-thing was here, and a god-thing was taken," Nightwish shuddered. His trembling finger traced the edges of the circle. "D'you see? All of its edge is the same distance from its heart."

"Only one other thing wears that shape," said Tinglesweet, with awe in her voice. "Kapata-the-Moon has that shape, but only for three nights out of every month. It is . . ." she tried to draw the moon-shape with her hands, and then – unable to describe the wondrous thing with all the clevers in her mouth – she made up a new clever that would sing its true nature: "It is . . . a *circle.*"

Nightwish let out a long whistling note, as he clevered this new concept. "A circle. Grabtake owned the only circle, and someone killed him for it. The murderer stole the only circle in the world."

All the way back to the campsite, Nightwish sang circles and Tinglesweet danced circles. By the time they reached the broad white chant-stone in the middle of the Wuradjeri campground, the two younglings had clevered a way to *make* circles. Nightwish explained to the elders what they had discovered. "Grabtake owned a circle. Someone else wanted it. The one who wanted the circle murdered him, and stole the circle."

"Very interesting." Speartouch rubbed his jaw. "What is a circle?"

Quickly, Nightwish borrowed an emu-cord from Healchant and a spear from Rainspeak. It was a prize spear, for its tip was a barb from a stingray's tail that Rainspeak had obtained in barter from a warrior whose tribal land bordered the northern sea.

Now men and women of the Wuradjeri watched curiously as Nightwish knotted one end of Healchant's cord round the shaft of Rainspeak's spear, then fastened the cord's other end to a sharp fragment of *karul*, transparent crystal quartz. "These have a circle," he explained.

Old Toegone, perched on a stone with his mangled foot thrust out in front of him, spat in contempt. "I see no circle, whatever a circle may be."

"All things have circles inside them," said Nightwish, putting words to the clever as it formed in his thoughts. "All things contain hidden circles . . . but we can sing the circles out, so that they can be seen."

With a shout, Nightwish thrust the spear's barb into the soft ground, burying it to the depth of a man's hand. Now Tinglesweet, gripping the sharp quartz, stepped as far from the spear as she could . . . until the cord that bound spear to quartz became *taut*.

Tinglesweet danced, chanting the song of the circle as she circuited the spear. She danced widdershins, anti-clockwise, in the same path as Ngunipinga-the-Sun . . . the Sun who was herself shaped like a squashed circle, and who now perched herself dusk-wise above the outback's western horizon. Tinglesweet's sharpened *karul* quartz bit the ground as she moved in her dance . . . but always and ever the same distance from the spear, so that the cord remained *taut*. Meanwhile, Nightwish gripped the spear. As the emu-cord approached his ankles he whooped, and leapt over it, so that Tinglesweet could finish her circuit.

"*There!*" she shouted triumphantly. "*Kalanduku!* All of you! Behold the circle!"

The first circle ever scribed by humans lay in the soft turf of the campground, with Nightwish in its centre and Tinglesweet at its border. The men and women pressed forward, to see this new shape.

Rainspeak reclaimed his spear, and made certain that Nightwish had not blunted its barb. "So that is a circle," said Speartouch. "What good is it?"

"It is pretty to look at," said Tinglesweet.

"But not pretty enough to kill for," said Speartouch. He jabbed a finger at the circle's rim. "You would have us believe that Grabtake was murdered for *that*?"

Rainspeak stood up. "Let me see this thing, then. *Kurana!* Show me!"

Hooting, jeering, the elders of both sexes followed Nightwish and Tinglesweet back to the murder scene. Even old Toegone, shouting at the others to wait for him, limped along at the procession's rear. At the mouth of the cave several women hung back; the sandflies had discovered Grabtake's corpse, and in the outback heat his scent was most unpleasant. Nightwish vaulted into the cave, and pointed to the indentation in the red-ochre clay. "There it is."

Speartouch looked, and for the first time in his life beheld *a perfect hemisphere*. "It is a god-shape!" he exclaimed.

"What, that mark on the ground?" Rainspeak pushed forward contemptuously, with a frown that warned Nightwish of danger.

"*Wari muluk!*" the boy shouted. "Someone stop him!"

Rainspeak thrust the butt of his spear into the soft clay, smudging the hemispherical indentation. "I see no god-things here," he spoke. "I see a mark on the ground." As he said this, Rainspeak fumbled with the emu-cord binding his genitals; he undid it, and he urinated on the smudge. "And now I see a puddle on the ground." He laughed. "No man would kill another man, and tempt the wrath of Baiami, for the sake of a mark on the ground. Let us go."

Laughing and jeering, the men and women of the Wuradjeri walked away, leaving Nightwish alone. Someone touched his fingers gently and he turned. Tinglesweet was there.

"I have thought of a clever," she told him. "Grabtake touched a god-thing that bit his hands, yes? And a god-thing – a circle shaped like the Moon – was stolen from his cave by whoever killed him. Perhaps the taboo that bit him and the thing that the murderer stole are both *the same object*."

The very same clever that Tinglesweet heard was now singing to Nightwish. "I see what you mean!" the boy whooped. "The god-thing bit Grabtake's hands when he found it. Someone has killed him, and taken the god-thing. But the god-thing bites whoever touches it. We must find someone whose hands are bitten like the dead man's. He who wears the bites, he is the murderer."

Tinglesweet nodded. "Let us search our totem-people, you and I. I will look at the hands of my Bandicoot people; you seek the hands of your Red Kangaroo-folk."

Nightwish felt a rush of excitement. "Then, if we have not found the killer, we will look among the other two clans of the Wuradjeri. I will search the hands of the people totem-born to Kilpatsha, the Black Kangaroo; you look among the hands of those whose *jarajuwa* is Jungkai the Grass Hen. I will meet you *ngaku*, afterwards at the chant-stone. Let the wind guide your feet! Hurry!"

For the next many timelongs, Nightwish looked at hands. Hunters' hands, chanters' hands, potters' hands, weaver-hands, gather-hands. Men's and women's and children's hands he examined, hoping to find the strange fleck of white blisters and black markings that he had seen on Grabtake's fingers: *the bite of the god-thing*.

By the time of twilight, he had examined the hands of every man, woman, and child born to two totem-clans . . . but found no trace of the god-thing. Tinglesweet was waiting at the chant-stone; by the look on her face, Nightwish knew that she also had failed.

"Perhaps the killer is not of Wuradjeri," Tinglesweet suggested.

"No. I am certain that the murderer is among us," Nightwish said. "Yet something is wrong. A man found a god-thing, and it bit his hands. *Why?* Another man killed him, and stole the god-thing, yet the god-thing did not bite the murderer. Why *not?* This is a mystery, and all my clevers in a heap can sing no answer."

Nightfall came, and the darkness and stars, yet Nightwish did not sleep. He sat awake, and wished for cleverthoughts.

He thought of Kalwaka, the ancient time, the time of his ancestors' ancestors. And before Kalwaka there was Ngurukanbu, the Beginning-of-All . . . a time so ancient that men and women had not yet been sung by their totem-beasts. At the time of Beginning-of-All there were no secrets, because Baiami came down from the sky and sang to the beasts, giving them the answers to all the world's mysteries. But that was long ago, and *now* the world was much more complicated, with so many more mysteries in it.

Kapata-the-Moon came out from a cloud over Nightwish's head, mocking him. On this particular night, Kapata's shape was a perfect circle, like the mark in the clay had been. The red clay inside Grabtake's cave had witnessed the murder, but it could no longer sing the killer's name because Rainspeak had defiled the clay with his essence. The clay that . . .

Suddenly Nightwish remembered a clever. The clay inside the dead man's cave was *kirapurai*, red ochre. And the clay on the ground outside the dead man's cave was the identical red ochre. So the two clays were one, and they owned the same song. Which meant that the clay *outside* the cave could sing Nightwish the answer to what had happened *in* the cave, during the murder.

Softly, silently, so as to awaken no-one, Nightwish got up and ran towards the cave.

There was moonlight, enough to see by. A shrub of *wilga*-wood, black willow, stood in Nightwish's path. He seized a branch of the shrub, bent it aside so that his body could slip past. The *wilga* branch, under tension, slipped out of his hand and shot back to its former

position with a whistling sound that Nightwish feared would awaken
the others. Nobody roused. He ran on.

When Nightwish got to the cave, he saw the hole in his own
cleverness. The clay outside the murder scene could not sing its true
chant, for it had been defiled. He could see the splattered footprints
of his own feet and the elder men's outside the dead man's cave. And
among these were the footprints of the women. And blades of grass,
amongst the footprints, everywhere.

It was interesting, Nightwish discovered, how each footprint had
its own especial song. The women's footprints were narrower than
the men's, and the footprints of the children were smaller and more
uncertain than the prints of their elders. And over there – *ngai!* –
there were the broken footprints of Toegone; the marks of his whole
foot deeper than the prints of his maimed foot, because he put more
weight upon the good one. And other men had left their footprints
here as well. It ought to be possible, Nightwish decided, to match
each footprint with its original maker, and . . .

Suddenly the moonlight sang the answer.

One set of footprints were different from all their brothers and
their sisters, in an unexpected way. Nightwish saw it: Yes. The other
footprints all sang truth, but one set of footprints sang lies.

Now Nightwish knew who had murdered Grabtake and stolen the
god-thing.

But he didn't know *how*. And the council would want proof.

Nightwish went back to the campsite. The elder males were asleep
within the *ngurupal*, which the boy Nightwish was forbidden to enter.
He selected a bed-likely spot in a patch of mossed grass, at the
warrior-ground's southern edge. As Nightwish lay down for the
night, he surreptitiously extended his arms across the border of
the *ngurupal*. He was not yet a man, but tonight his hands would
sleep among the warriors and hunters; perhaps some of the men's
hunt-magic might enter him through his fingers. In the morning,
Nightwish would need to wear a hunter's hands. For he would be
hunting a murderer.

Dawntime came, and the usual chores. Nightwish saw no sign of
Tinglesweet; the elder women must have put her to work performing
she-tasks. Nightwish had his own duties: as an apprentice warrior,
he was supposed to spend the day gathering tree-gum. Older men of
the Wuradjeri – males whose minds held hunt-knowledge but whose
bodies were too old to join the hunt – were sitting cross-legged in
the *ngurupal* and chipping flints into long pointed spearheads. Later,
these flintmen would use the sticky tree-gum gathered by Nightwish,

as well as sinew-cords reaped from dead emus and kangaroos, to bind the spearheads to shafts for the men of the hunt.

Nightwish disliked gum-harvesting, for the tree-gum was messy and smelt unpleasant. Sandflies were attracted to the stuff, and tended to trap themselves in it. Today Nightwish had no desire to trap flies. He was planning to trap a murderer.

Among the hunters of Nightwish's totem, any beast was fair game for their spears except their own *jarajuwa*: Maruwai, the red kangaroo. A black 'roo, or a grey, or any other beast at all was worthy prey. The men set out then, in groups and pairs, and there were three or four men of independent spirit each of whom preferred to hunt alone. Nightwish saw one of these men leave the campground, and then he followed him. This man was the murderer.

The lone hunter walked northwest, away from the campground and into a stand of *wilga* trees. Nightwish was pleased; here in the woods, with many trees to hide behind, he could easily stalk his quarry. He crept along behind the murderer.

As the forest deepened, Nightwish began to think that perhaps he had outclevered himself. The murderer carried a bundle of spears, and in his left hand he clutched a pouch of bandicoot-skin that might contain unknown weapons . . . perhaps it even contained the stolen god-thing itself. But Nightwish was unarmed. For a moment the boy considered turning back. No; if he turned away now, Baiami the Skygod would witness his cowardice, and Nightwish would be cursed forever. He kept stalking his prey, deeper into the woods.

The murderer walked on, beyond the forest, until he emerged into the bare outback desert. This was open ground, with few places to hide. There were a few red sandstone outcroppings, some shallow grass, and a single stand of leafy *koolibah*. If Nightwish confronted his quarry here, the murderer would see him coming from a distance and be ready for him.

Nightwish hung back, at the edge of the forest, while the murderer went on through the low grass towards the *koolibah* trees. In the shadows, Nightwish's hands tallied the murderer's footsteps: *Firstfinger, secondfinger, thirdfinger, fourthfinger, hand. A double hand, two double hands* . . . At last the murderer reached the stand of trees, and sat down: thirdfinger-many double hands plus one hand more of footsteps away; too far away for Nightwish to take him by surprise. Among the *wilga*, Nightwish watched as the murderer sat in the pale outback sand and rested his bundle of spears by his side. There was a log of dead eucalyptus nearby; the murderer placed this in front of himself. Then he fumbled with his bandicoot-leather, unwrapped it, and took out . . .

. . . the god-thing.

It must have come from the sky, from the place where Baiami the Skygod dwelt, for Nightwish sensed that no such thing could have been birthed here in the world of men. The god-thing glittered like Baiami's crystal wife, the goddess Kurikuta, who is made of living quartz. Yet this glittering god-thing was an alien colour such as Nightwish had never seen before. *Grass* was the nearest thing to it in colour, but the green of grass was very distant to the hue of this god-thing. And just as Nightwish had envisioned, this god-thing was the same shape as the moon. The god-thing slid out of the leather, and rolled into the murderer's hand.

Nightwish watched, but did not comprehend. The god-thing had bitten Grabtake's fingers when he touched it. How was it possible that the man who murdered Grabtake and stole the god-thing could now hold it without being harmed?

As Nightwish watched, the killer lifted the god-thing and raised it towards Ngunipinga-the-Sun. The god-thing glittered ever brighter, like a star. For a timelong, nothing happened. Then, suddenly, *another god-thing appeared*.

This thing too was an alien colour. Not quite yellow like the sun over-sky, nor red like the sunset at dusking. This was a colour between them. The god-thing danced across the eucalyptus wood, and as it danced it sang a song all coloured black. And as Nightwish watched, the dancing sun-bright god-thing's chant became so loud that he could hear the words although he could not understand them: "*Kricka tricka crack, cricka track . . .*"

And as it danced, the chanting god-thing grew. The killer, who at first had watched the dancing apparition quite calmly, seemed to grow more apprehensive as the thing grew larger. Now he took the first god-thing – the green sphere – and slipped it back into his leather bag. He scooped handfuls of sand and flung them at the second god-thing. The god-thing's black chant ended, and its dance became more subdued. The thing-like-the-sun shrank, as more and more sand overwhelmed it. Then suddenly the thing *vanished*.

Nightwish, watching from his hiding place, could feel the hairs prickling at the back of his neck. He had come here, unarmed, to catch a killer who was weaponed well with spears. Now it was clear that the killer also possessed two god-things . . . and could make them *obey* his commands. *My quarry has powerful weapons.* For a timelong, Nightwish thought of tiptoeing back to the campground. Then he realized: *No. I am here, I have watched, and the killer has not clevered my presence. He has a god's weapons . . . but not a god's eyes, or else he'd have seen me. Baiami the Skygod must be my protector, then. Yet if I turn back now, Baiami will abandon me.*

Among the people Wuradjeri, a male is a hunter . . . or else he is nothing. Nightwish, the boy on his man-brink – twelvesummers his age – had chosen his prey, and stalked his quarry to this place. Now he must prove himself a hunter, by catching this murderer. Or else he was nothing, forever. To catch a killer, or die trying: either path would bring honour and god-favour. To flee now would be to make himself nothing.

Nightwish took a deep breath. He stepped out from among the *wilga* trees, and advanced into the bare outback plain. The murderer saw him coming, and looked up but did not rise. He sat calmly, waiting, beneath the *koolibah*.

"You have murdered a man," Nightwish told him. "You have killed the man Grabtake, a brother of my totem-clan . . . and of *yours*, for you and I and the dead man shared a totem-dance. You have killed our clan-brother."

The man beneath the *koolibah* was Toegone. He sat calmly, with his crippled foot extended in front of him. He beckoned Nightwish to approach. "The boy speaks boldly to the man," said Toegone mockingly. "Have you forgotten, boy? When Grabtake was slain in his cave, I was in the campground nearby you. When his death-scream awoke us, you and I went, together, to the scene of the murder . . . you running, I limping. So! I could not have done the crime."

"That is what I thought at first," Nightwish nodded. "But now I remember: when I awoke and ran to the cave of the murder, you were *ahead* of me. How can a limping man outspeed a runner? There is only one answer: you were already awake, already there. You must have been at the dead man's cave before dawn, *before* Grabtake screamed. And then, when men came running, you pretended to be running also."

Toegone seemed amused as he reached for his bundle of spears. "Who clevered this for you, boy?"

"The clay told me," said Nightwish. "I saw your footprints in the clay outside the cave. The footprints sang lies, but the clay sang the truth." As he advanced towards the killer, Nightwish pointed over his shoulder to his own trail of footprints in the outback sand. "*Ngana tu!* Do you see? As I walk, my heels bite more deeply into the earth than my toes. And the blades of grass in my footprints bend forwards. But at the cave where death sang murder, Toegone, I found one set of footprints with toes that bit deeper than heels, and grass that bent backwards. *Your* footprints were else-made from all the others. I thought at first that your prints were different because you limped. No; your footprints were else-made because you walked away from the murder scene *backwards*."

"Very interesting." Toegone took a spear from his bundle, and examined its shaft. "Have the emus stolen your brain, boy? I could never have killed our clan-brother. The entrance to the dead man's cave was *sealed* by a boulder."

Nightwish stood his ground. "You killed Grabtake by sending a spear through the narrow opening between the boulder and the cave's wall. What I cannot clever is how you managed to aim a spear truly – *half* a spear, I mean, because the other half is missing – through such a small opening. But you killed, and then you walked away backwards so that no man or god would see your else-footprints – broken footprints, with a maimed foot – pointing *away* from the death scene."

Toegone lifted his spear in both hands, and squinted along down the length of its shaft, to be certain of its trueness. "You seem to have clevered it all, boy."

"Almost all." Nightwish nodded. "You killed a man who found a god-thing, and then you stole the god-thing. At first I wondered how the murderer could steal the god-thing from a sealed cave. Now I know: you killed Grabtake, and you left empty-handed. Afterward, when several of us were in the cave together and no man watched, then you took the god-thing from where it slept in the clay. Now I charge thee, murderer: by the law of Wuradjeri, you must return to the council-place with me. Come back to the *ngurupal*, and sing your crimes to the elders. They will judge your fate, and they will decide what to do with the god-thing that you stole from the dead man."

"The god-thing is *mine!*" Toegone sat bolt upright in outrage. "Grabtake and I hunted together, four days past, when we both saw the god-thing fall out of the sky. We ran to the spot where it fell . . . aye, but *he* arrived first, because I cannot run swiftly." Toegone ruefully eyed his maimed foot as he spoke. "Grabtake and I saw the god-thing fall into a river. And when it fell, *clouds* – white growing clouds that hissed like serpents – rose out of the water. Even the water itself seemed to dance, where the god-thing fell, as if bewitched. *Tungani*, I saw Grabtake wade into the river. He reached in with both hands, to snatch the god-thing. Then he screamed, for the god-thing had bitten him. I saw the blooding of his fingertips."

"Did the god-thing show its teeth?" Nightwish asked.

"No, but Grabtake whimpered that the green thing that fell from the sky was *hot*, like the desert at noon when the sun is over-sky. Worse than that: the thing was so hot that it bit Grabtake's fingers, and blistered his hands. After a timelong, when the water stopped dancing, and the hissing clouds no longer rose above the water, Grabtake tried again. This time he plucked the god-thing from the water, and it did not bite him with the heat of the sun."

Nightwish said nothing.

"The god-thing is mine!" said Toegone, clutching his pouch made of bandicoot-skin. "When Grabtake showed it to me, it was I who discovered that the god-thing contains a wondrous cleverness: it can steal a piece of the sun, and bring it *here*. But then Grabtake snatched back the god-thing, and would not share. He went into the cave, and sealed it so that none could share the new cleverness. So I killed him, and took what is mine by right."

Nightwish nodded. During Toegone's murder-chant the boy had gradually come closer to the murderer, so that now there were only a two hands' manyworth of footsteps between them. "You must come back with me, to the elders, and confess," Nightwish declared.

"*Kuriapu*." Toegone shook his head. "I would rather stay here, boy, so that I can do . . . THIS!"

Suddenly he flicked his spear. Nightwish dodged, just in time to prevent the spear from biting into his heart. But then he screamed, as he felt the sharpened flint impale his leg. Nightwish fell, and as he toppled he saw the hunter reaching for another spear. This one would find its prey . . .

Somehow Nightwish got up. He managed to run, with blood streaming from his wounded leg and the shaft of the spear still buried in his limb. The second spear whistled past him, and already his wounded leg betrayed him and he fell again.

"*Kalantu palu!*" The murderer's voice danced in Nightwish's ears. "You will die, boy! *Paraka!* Stand up and die like a man, then! *Kalantu palu!*"

Ahead of Nightwish was a crust of red sandstone, bulging up from the floor of the desert. And beside the sandstone outcropping, probably nourished by some underground spring, grew a small stand of black *wilga*-trees. Crawling, stumbling, desperately trying to escape, Nightwish managed to fling himself behind the temporary shelter of the sandstone. A tell-tale stream of blood from his wounded leg showed precisely where he had concealed himself.

"You cannot hide, boy! Get ready to die!"

Escape was impossible. Nightwish was in the middle of the desert, unable to run, barely able to walk. With this spear in his leg, he could not possibly outspeed the killer. Nightwish could hear Toegone's voice, taunting him, as the murderer came limping steadily closer: "I saw where you went, boy. Thank your god-luck that I cannot walk fast, or I would have caught you by now. When I reach the place where you hide, I will kill you."

A weapon! A weapon! Nightwish glanced upwards frantically, and saw that the uppermost ridge of the sandstone was *sharp*. Could he use this? Rising onto the knee of his good leg, Nightwish seized a piece of the ridge in both hands, and pulled. The brittle sandstone broke off easily . . . and then it *crumbled* into fragments in his hands. Useless! *Worse* than useless, because now there was a long vertical notch in the outcropping, showing Toegone precisely where Nightwish was hiding behind the notched sandstone.

"You will die, boy . . ." Through the notch, Nightwish saw Toegone lift another spear.

A weapon! *A weapon!* Nightwish's injured leg was throbbing. He looked down, and saw that the shaft of the spear was still embedded in the muscle of his leg. Already the sandflies were on him, licking at the blood, where . . .

No.

Only half the spear was in Nightwish's leg. The lower half had broken off, and was somewhere out there on the outback floor. With a grimace, Nightwish managed to pull the sharpened tip of the weapon out of his leg.

"*Paraka!* Stand up, then, and die!"

Half a spear. Could Nightwish use it as a weapon against the oncoming killer? No; the broken spear was too short to be aimed properly. Nightwish crawled backwards, felt the supple *wilga*-shafts bending as he thrust himself against the willow shrubs. Through the notch in the sandstone, he could see Toegone limping steadily closer. Any moment now, the time of Nightwish's death-chant would . . .

A cleverness, a cleverness sang loud inside his head.

The notch in the sandstone was the same width as the narrow opening in the mouth of Grabtake's sealed cave. The half-spear in Nightwish's hands was very nearly the same length as the half-spear that Toegone had used to murder Grabtake. Suddenly Nightwish knew the missing pieces of the clever.

"*Kalantu palu!* Now you die!"

Toegone was two hands' many footsteps away, and limping closer. Swiftly, Nightwish uprooted a supple shoot of willow. With the heel of his hand he flattened the butt of the half-spear, where it had broken off uncleanly.

"*Paraka!* Stand up!"

Quickly, Nightwish fitted the half-spear into the notch within the sandstone . . . the same way that Toegone must have fitted the murder weapon into the notch between the boulder and the wall of the cave while he had waited until dawn to murder Grabtake. The dawn had been a part of Toegone's murder scheme; he had needed the first light of Ngunipinga-the-Sun to show him his prey. Now, with his shortened spear fitted into the notched sandstone, Nightwish turned it towards his approaching enemy. It was unnecessary to *aim* the spear now; it was pointed towards its target, and the two sides of the notch would hold it steady just as the narrow slit between the boulder and the cave's wall had steadied the spear that murdered Grabtake. Gritting his teeth to ignore the pain in his throbbing leg, Nightwish fitted one end of the willow-shoot to the butt of the half-spear. Now he bent the *wilga* double in his hands, until the two ends of the willow bough touched each other. He could feel the tension of the willow, straining to unbend itself. If he released one end, the other end of his new invention would snap forward, and propel the spear to its target with far more force than Nightwish's own arm could summon.

"Now I kill you, boy!" The angry face of Toegone loomed above the sandstone ridge. He saw Nightwish, and the murderer grinned in triumph as he raised his spear to claim another soul. And now, at the very last possible moment, Nightwish discovered the flaw in his own improvised weapon: he would have to kill Toegone with the first shot, because there would never come a second chance . . .

The Horniman Museum, near the Lambeth district in southeastern London, is privately owned. Thus the objects within its glass cases are arranged according to the whimsies and moods of the museum's original owner. For example, one exhibit-case – in defiance of all biological order or taxonomy – contains the stuffed figures of a kangaroo, a cricket, and a frog . . . simply because all three creatures *jump*. Another exhibit places a porcupine and a sea-urchin alongside a thistle . . . because all three of them possess *stickles*. Any two objects beneath the same glass may be entirely unrelated, except in Mr Horniman's fancy.

On a rainy Sunday morning, after visiting the Horniman Museum's aquarium, I passed into a corridor that I had never noticed before, and here I discovered a glass case containing two peculiar objects. The one on the left was a long slat of carved wood, with a crude handle at one end and a notched device at the other. A brief inscription on a brass plate underneath explained its origin:

> The *woomera* functioned as a multi-purpose tool: as a chisel, as a blade to strip bark from trees, but especially as a spear-thrower. Used as an extension of the warrior's arm, the *woomera* increased the spear's range and speed, but made it more difficult to aim. The example here was made by aborigines of New South Wales, Australia.

The second object in the same exhibit-case was much smaller. It was a nearly perfect sphere, of bright greenbottle glass, about the size of a child's shooting-marble; what we Clydesiders used to call a *penker*. Again, a brass plate underneath explained:

> The *australite* (so named because they are found only in Australia) is a form of tektite, or glassy stone of high silicate content. Tektites originated in outer space and fell to Earth as meteorites. Most australites are spherical, but some take the form of spheroids, discs, and even teardrops. The specimen above was found in New South Wales, Australia. Its date of origin is approximately 35,000 B C.

It was afternoon when Nightwish managed to return to the encampment, hopping on his good leg and dragging his injured leg behind him. With a shout, Healchant rushed over and examined the boy's injury, so that he would know what medicinal paste to prepare. Waving onlookers away, Nightwish managed to reach the common-ground.

Tinglesweet was there. She and two of her clan-sisters sat cross-legged and holding ridged flints, which they were using to whittle the ends of willow-shoots into sharpened fish-spears. A small mound of wood shavings and curled bark had accumulated in front of the women. Tinglesweet saw Nightwish approach, and she nodded towards his injured leg: "A boy who went hunting caught more than he bargained for," she murmured.

"I have caught more than that." Nightwish fumbled within the bag of bandicoot-skin that he was carrying, and he brought out a small object. "Behold! I have brought you a god-thing!"

"*Ahhh* . . ." Women, children, and old men of the Wuradjeri gathered closer, to admire the bauble. Its perfect shape and its brilliant green colour were two qualities that they had never seen before. But the few warriors present, men back from their hunt, seemed unimpressed.

"A god-thing, you call this?" mocked Rainspeak, and beside him Speartouch laughed sardonically. "A pretty toy for babies, but otherwise useless. Only a toy god, a baby god would give such things. Never a warrior-god."

Nightwish ignored this. He held the bright god-thing aloft as he had seen Toegonc do, and he let it catch the bountiful rays of Ngunipinga-the-Sun. The sphere of silicate glass, acting as a convex lens, caught and refracted the sunlight. Within the pile of shavings and bark near Nightwish's feet, a bright pinpoint of light appeared. The light brightened. Smoke uncurled from the wood. And then . . .

"*Ahhh!*" A new thing, a wondrous new thing now appeared. For the first time in their history, the people of the Wuradjeri witnessed fire.

"Do not touch this thing," Nightwish warned, "or it will bite . . . no, a new word is needed. It will *burn* you, as it burnt Grabtake's fingers. If we feed this new thing, it will grow. If we respect it, it will serve us." He put the bright green sphere back into its bag. He took a twig from the ground nearby and fed it to the flame. The fire grew; its black smoke rippled and danced, and now the crackling fire sang its chant: "*Kricka tricka crack, cricka track.*"

"A mighty god-thing indeed!" said Tinglesweet, in utter awe.

Nightwish was pleased that he had finally impressed her. "It is a god-thing now," he said. "But when we tame it, and make it serve us, it will no longer be a god-thing. It will be *ours.*" He fed another piece of wood to the hungering flame, and the miracle grew. Others of the Wuradjeri, seeing this, ran to gather more wood.

And all that night the dark was bright as day, around the fire, as all the people danced their praises of the greatest cleverness that had ever come among them since the time of Beginning-of-All.

THE JUDGEMENT OF DANIEL

In the first volume I reprinted a detective story recorded by Herodotus in around 440 BC and suggested it may have been the earliest written historical detective story. Needless to say such statements are always open to challenge, which is exciting. I was reminded of several mystery stories in the Bible, particularly in the Book of Daniel. Daniel, one of the most famous prophets in the Old Testament, lived from about 630–536 BC. He is usually accepted as the writer of the Book of Daniel and technically it means any incident that he recalls is contemporary with him and not a historical story. I'm not sure, though, when the following extract was written. It doesn't appear in the authorized version of the Bible, having been excluded from the Jewish texts around the first century AD because it was not written in Hebrew. It may therefore be a later apocryphal addition, included to show the wisdom of Daniel. I am grateful to Richard Lonsdale of the Sacred Heart Church in Maine, who drew my attention to this episode, which is taken from the New Jerusalem Bible.

In Babylon there lived a man named Joakim. He was married to a woman called Susanna daughter of Hilkiah, a woman of great beauty; and she was God-fearing, for her parents were worthy people and had instructed their daughter in the Law of Moses. Joakim was a very rich man and had a garden by his house; he used to be visited by a considerable number of the Jews, since he was held in greater respect than any other man. Two elderly men had been selected from the people, that year, to act as judges. Of such the Lord had said, "Wickedness has come to Babylon through the elders and judges posing as guides to the people." These men were often at Joakim's house, and all who were engaged in litigation used to come to them. At midday, when the people had gone away, Susanna would take a walk in her husband's garden. The two elders, who used to watch her every day as she came in to take her walk, gradually began to desire her. They threw reason aside, making no effort to turn their eyes to Heaven, and forgetting the demands of virtue. Both were inflamed by passion for her, but they hid their desire from each other, for they were ashamed to admit the longing to sleep with her, but they made sure of watching her every day. One day, having parted with the words, "Let us go home, then, it is time for the midday meal," they went off in different directions, only to retrace their steps and find themselves face to face again. Obliged then to explain, they admitted their desire and agreed to look for an opportunity of surprising her alone. So they waited for a favourable moment; and one day Susanna came as usual, accompanied only by two young maidservants. The day was hot and she wanted to bathe in the garden. There was no one about except the two elders, spying on her from their hiding place. She said to the servants, "Bring me some oil and balsam and shut the garden door while I bathe." They did as they were told, shutting the garden door and going back to the house by a side entrance to fetch what she had asked for; they knew nothing about the elders, for they had concealed themselves.

Hardly were the maids gone than the two elders sprang up and rushed upon her. "Look," they said, "the garden door is shut, no one can see us. We want to have you, so give in and let us! Refuse, and we shall both give evidence that a young man was with you and that this was why you sent your maids away." Susanna sighed.

"I am trapped," she said, "whatever I do. If I agree, it means death for me: if I resist, I cannot get away from you. But I prefer to fall innocent into your power than to sin in the eyes of the Lord." She then cried out as loud as she could. The two elders began shouting too, putting the blame on her, and one of them ran to open the garden door. The household, hearing the shouting in the garden, rushed out by the side entrance to see what had happened to her. Once the elders had told their story, the servants were thoroughly taken aback, since nothing of this sort had ever been said of Susanna.

Next day a meeting was held at the house of her husband Joakim. The two elders arrived, full of their wicked plea against Susanna, to have her put to death. They addressed the company, "Summon Susanna daughter of Hilkiah and wife of Joakim." She was sent for, and came accompanied by her parents, her children and all her relations. Susanna was very graceful and beautiful to look at; she was veiled, so the wretches made her unveil in order to feast their eyes on her beauty. All her own people were weeping, and so were all the others who saw her. The two elders stood up, with all the people round them, and laid their hands on her head. Tearfully she turned her eyes to Heaven, her heart confident in God. The elders then spoke. "While we were walking by ourselves in the garden, this woman arrived with two maids. She shut the garden door and then dismissed the servants. A young man, who had been hiding, went over to her and they lay together. From the end of the garden where we were, we saw this crime taking place and hurried towards them. Though we saw them together, we were unable to catch the man: he was too strong for us; he opened the door and took to his heels. We did, however, catch this woman and ask her who the young man was. She refused to tell us. That is our evidence."

Since they were elders of the people and judges, the assembly accepted their word: Susanna was condemned to death. She cried out as loud as she could, "Eternal God, you know all secrets and everything before it happens; you know that they have given false evidence against me. And now I must die, innocent as I am of everything their malice has invented against me!"

The Lord heard her cry and, as she was being led away to die, he roused the holy spirit residing in a young boy called Daniel who began to shout, "I am innocent of this woman's death!"

At this all the people turned to him and asked, "What do you mean by that?"

Standing in the middle of the crowd, he replied, "Are you so stupid, children of Israel, as to condemn a daughter of Israel unheard, and without troubling to find out the truth? Go back to the scene of the trial: these men have given false evidence against her."

All the people hurried back, and the elders said to Daniel, "Come and sit with us and tell us what you mean, since God has given you the gifts that elders have."

Daniel said, "Keep the men well apart from each other, for I want to question them." When the men had been separated, Daniel had one of them brought to him. "You have grown old in wickedness," he said, "and now the sins of your earlier days have overtaken you, you with your unjust judgements, your condemnation of the innocent, your acquittal of the guilty, although the Lord has said, 'You must not put the innocent and upright to death.' Now then, since you saw her so clearly, tell me what sort of tree you saw them lying under."

He replied, "Under an acacia tree."

Daniel said, "Indeed! Your lie recoils on your own head: the angel of God has already received from him your sentence and will cut you in half." He dismissed the man, ordered the other to be brought and said to him, "Son of Canaan, not of Judah, beauty has seduced you, lust has led your heart astray! This is how you have been behaving with the daughters of Israel, and they have been too frightened to resist; but here is a daughter of Judah who could not stomach your wickedness! Now then, tell me what sort of tree you surprised them under."

He replied, "Under an aspen tree."

Daniel said, "Indeed! Your lie recoils on your own head: the angel of God is waiting with a sword to rend you in half, and destroy the pair of you."

Then the whole assembly shouted, blessing God, the Saviour of those who trust in him. And they turned on the two elders whom Daniel had convicted of false evidence out of their own mouths. As the Law of Moses prescribes, they were given the same punishment as they had schemed to inflict on their neighbour. They were put to death. And thus, that day, an innocent life was saved. Hilkiah and his wife gave thanks to God for their daughter Susanna, and so did her husband Joakim and all his relations, because she had been acquitted of anything dishonourable.

From that day onwards, Daniel's reputation stood high with the people.

DEATH WEARS A MASK
Steven Saylor

One of my most welcome discoveries following the publication of The
Mammoth Book of Historical Whodunnits *is the work of Steven
Saylor, whom I had somehow overlooked and had not listed in the
appendix. Edward Hoch first drew him to my attention. He is the
author of (at the last count) four novels and eight short stories about
Gordianus the Finder, set at the time of Cicero in the first century*
BC. *The novels run* Roman Blood *(1991),* Arms of Nemesis
(1992), Catilina's Riddle *(1993) and* The Venus Throw *(1995),
and they are an absolute delight. Gordianus is not a transplanted
twentieth-century investigator, but someone at home in the bizarre
world of ancient Rome. He has no connections to the ruling aristocracy
and must survive by his own wiles and cunning. Saylor was born
in Texas in 1956, and grew up near Cross Plains, where Robert
E. Howard lived and wrote his stories about Conan. He now lives
in California where he has worked as an editor and writer. His
first short story about Gordianus was "A Will is a Way" (Ellery
Queen's Mystery Magazine, March 1992). This following was the
second.*

"Eco," I said, "do you mean to tell me that you have never seen
a play?"

He looked up at me with his big brown eyes and shook his head.

"Never laughed at the slaves on stage who have a falling-out and
bludgeon each other with clubs made of cork? Never swooned to see
the young heroine abducted by pirates? *Never* thrilled at the discovery
that our hero is not the penniless vagabond we thought, but the secret
heir to a vast fortune?"

Eco's eyes grew even larger, and he shook his head more vigorously
from side to side.

"Then there must be a remedy, this very day!" I said.

It was the Ides of September, and a more beautiful autumn day
the gods had never fashioned. The sun shone warmly on the narrow
streets and gurgling fountains of Rome; a light breeze swept up from

the Tiber, cooling the seven hills; the sky above was a bowl of purest azure, without a single cloud. It was the twelfth day of the sixteen days set aside each year for the Roman Festival, the city's oldest public holiday. Perhaps Jupiter himself had decreed that the weather should be so perfect; the holiday was in his honor.

For Eco, the Festival had been an endless orgy of discoveries. He had seen his first chariot race in the Circus Maximus, had watched wrestlers and boxers in the public squares, had eaten his first calf's-brain-and-almond sausage from a street vendor. The race had thrilled him, mostly because he thought the horses so beautiful; the pugilists had bored him, since he had seen plenty of brawling in public before; the sausage had not agreed with him (or perhaps his problem was the spiced green apples he gorged himself on later).

It was four months since I had rescued Eco in an alley in the Subura, from a gang of boys pursuing him with sticks and cruel jeers. I knew a little of his history, having met him briefly in my investigations for Cicero that spring. Apparently his widowed mother had chosen to abandon little Eco in her desperation, leaving him to fend for himself. What else could I do but take him home with me?

He struck me as exceedingly clever for a boy of ten. I knew he was ten, because whenever I asked, he held up ten fingers. Eco could hear (and add) perfectly well, but his tongue was useless.

At first his muteness was a great handicap for us both. (A fever caused it – the same fever that claimed his father's life.) Eco is a skillful mime, to be sure, but gestures can convey only so much. Someone had taught him the letters – the widow Polia, perhaps, or the boy's father before he died – but he could read and write only the simplest words. I had begun to teach him myself, but the going was made harder by his speechlessness.

His practical knowledge of the streets of Rome was deep but narrow. He knew all the back entrances to all the shops in the Subura, knew where the fish and meat vendors down by the Tiber left their scraps at the end of the day. But he had never been to the Forum or the Circus Maximus or the hot springs at Tarentum, had never heard a politician declaim (lucky boy!) or witnessed the spectacle of the theater. I spent many hours showing him the city that summer, rediscovering its marvels through the wide eyes of a ten-year-old boy.

So it was that, on the twelfth day of the Roman Festival, when a crier came running through the streets announcing that the company of Quintus Roscius would be performing in an hour, I determined that we should not miss it.

"Ah, the company of Roscius the Comedian!" I said. "The

magistrates in charge of the Festival have spared no expense. There
is no more famous actor today than Quintus Roscius, and no more
renowned troupe of performers than his!"

We made our way from the Subura down to the Forum, where
holiday crowds thronged the open squares. Between the Temple of
Jupiter Stator and the Senian Baths, a makeshift theater had been
erected. Rows of benches were set before a wooden stage that had
been raised in the narrow space between the brick walls.

"Some day," I remarked, "a rabble-rousing politician will build
the first permanent theater in Rome. Imagine that, a proper theater
made of stone, as sturdy as a temple! The old-fashioned moralists
will be scandalized, of course – they hate the theater because it comes
from Greece, and they think that all things Greek must be decadent
and dangerous. Ah, we're early – we shall have good seats."

The usher led us to an aisle seat on a bench five rows back from
the stage. The first four rows had been partitioned by a rope of purple
cloth, set aside for those of senatorial rank. Occasionally the usher
tromped down the aisle, followed by some toga-clad magistrate and
his party, and pulled aside the rope to allow them access to the
benches.

While the theater slowly filled around us, I pointed out to Eco
the details of the stage. Before the first row of benches there was a
small open space, the orchestra, where the musicians would play;
three steps at either side led up to the stage itself. Behind the stage
and enclosing it on either side was a screen of wood with a folding
door in the middle and other doors set into the left and right wings.
Through these doors the actors would enter and exit. Out of sight,
behind the stage, the musicians could be heard warming up their
pipes, trilling snatches of familiar tunes.

"Gordianus!"

I turned to see a tall, thin figure looming over us.

"Statilius!" I cried. "It's good to see you."

"And you as well. But who is this?" He ruffled Eco's mop of brown
hair with his long fingers.

"This is Eco," I said.

"A long-lost nephew?"

"Not exactly."

"Ah. An indiscretion from the past?" Statilius raised a suggestive
eyebrow.

"Not that, either." My face turned hot. And yet, I suddenly
wondered, how would it have felt to say: "Yes, this is my son." Not
for the first time I considered the possibility of adopting Eco legally
– and as quickly banished the thought from my mind. A man like

myself, who often risks death, has no business becoming a father; so I told myself. If I truly wanted sons, I could have married a proper Roman wife long ago and had a houseful by now. I quickly changed the subject.

"But Statilius, where is your costume and mask? Why aren't you backstage, getting ready?" I had known Statilius since we both were boys; he had become an actor in his youth, joining first one company and then another, always seeking the training of established comedians. The great Roscius had taken him on a year before.

"Oh, I still have plenty of time to get ready."

"And how is life in the company of the greatest actor in Rome?"

"Wonderful, of course!"

I frowned at the note of false bravado in his voice.

"Ah, Gordianus, you always could see through me. Not wonderful, then – terrible! Roscius – what a monster! Brilliant, to be sure, but a beast! If I were a slave I'd be covered with bruises. Instead, he whips me with his tongue. What a taskmaster! The man is relentless, and never satisfied. He makes a man feel no better than a worm. The galleys or the mines could hardly be worse. Is it my fault that I've grown too old to play heroines and haven't yet the proper voice to be an old miser or a braggart soldier? Ah, perhaps Roscius is right. I'm useless – talentless – I bring the whole company into disrepute."

"Actors are all alike," I whispered to Eco. "They need more coddling than babies." Then to Statilius: "Nonsense! I saw you in the spring, at the Festival of the Great Mother, when Roscius put on *The Brothers Menaechmus*. You were brilliant playing the twins."

"Do you really think so?"

"I swear it. I laughed so hard I almost fell off the bench."

He brightened a bit, then frowned. "I wish that Roscius thought so. Today I was all set to play Euclio, the old miser – "

"Ah, then we're seeing *The Pot of Gold?*"

"Yes – "

"One of my favorite plays, Eco. Quite possibly Plautus's funniest comedy. Crude, yet satisfying . . ."

"I was to play Euclio," Statilius said rather sharply, drawing the conversation back to himself, "when suddenly, this morning, Roscius explodes into a rage and says that I have the role all wrong, and that he can't suffer the humiliation of seeing me bungle it in front of all Rome. Instead I'll be Megadorus, the next-door neighbor."

"Another fine role," I said, trying to remember it.

"Fah! And who gets the plum role of Euclio? That parasite Panurgus – a mere slave, with no more comic timing than a slug!" He abruptly stiffened. "Oh no, what's this?"

I followed his gaze to the outer aisle, where the usher was leading a burly, bearded man toward the front of the theater. A blond giant with a scar across his nose followed close behind – the bearded man's bodyguard; I know a hired ruffian from the Subura when I see one. The usher led them to the far end of our bench; they stepped into the gap and headed toward us to take the empty spot beside Eco.

Statilius bent low to hide himself and groaned into my ear. "As if I hadn't enough worries – it's that awful moneylender Flavius and one of his hired bullies. The only man in Rome who's more of a monster than Roscius."

"And just how much do you owe this Flavius?" I began to say, when suddenly, from backstage, a roaring voice rose above the discordant pipes.

"Fool! Incompetent! Don't come to me now saying you can't remember the lines!"

"Roscius," Statilius whispered, "screaming at Panurgus, I hope. The man's temper is terrible."

The central door on the stage flew open, revealing a short, stocky man already dressed for the stage, wearing a splendid cloak of rich white fabric. His lumpy, scowling face was the sort to send terror into an underling's soul, yet this was, by universal acclaim, the funniest man in Rome. His legendary squint made his eyes almost invisible, but when he looked in our direction, I felt as if a dagger had been thrown past my ear and into the heart of Statilius.

"And you!" he bellowed. "Where have you been? Backstage, immediately! No, don't bother to go the long way round – backstage, now!" He gave commands as if he were speaking to a dog.

Statilius hurried up the aisle, leaped onto the stage, and disappeared backstage, closing the door behind him – but not, I noticed, before casting a furtive glance at the newcomer who had just seated himself beside Eco. I turned and looked at Flavius the moneylender, who returned my curious gaze with a scowl. He did not look like a man in the proper mood for a comedy.

I cleared my throat. "Today you'll see *The Pot of Gold*," I said pleasantly, leaning toward the newcomers. Flavius gave a start and wrinkled his bushy brows. "One of Plautus's very best plays, don't you think?"

Flavius parted his lips and peered at me suspiciously. The blond bodyguard looked at me with an expression of supreme stupidity.

I shrugged and turned my attention elsewhere.

From the open square behind us the crier made his last announcement. The benches rapidly filled. Latecomers and slaves stood wherever they could, crowding together on tiptoe. Two musicians stepped onto the stage and descended to the orchestra, where they began to blow upon their long pipes.

A murmur of recognition passed through the crowd at the familiar strains of the miser Euclio's theme, the first indication of the play we were about to see. Meanwhile the usher and the crier moved up and down the aisles, playfully hushing the noisier members of the audience.

At length the overture was finished. The central door on the stage rattled open. Out stepped Roscius, wearing his sumptuous white cloak, his head obscured by a mask of grotesque, happy countenance. Through the holes I glimpsed his squinting eyes; his mellow voice resonated throughout the theater.

"In case you don't know who I am, let me briefly introduce myself," he said. "I am the Guardian Spirit of this house – Euclio's house. I have been in charge of this place now for a great many years . . ." He proceeded to deliver the prologue, giving the audience a starting point for the familiar story – how the grandfather of Euclio had hidden a pot of gold beneath the floorboards of the house; how Euclio had a daughter who was in love with the next-door neighbor's nephew, and needed only a dowry to be happily married; and how he, the Guardian Spirit, intended to guide the greedy Euclio to the pot of gold and so set events in motion.

I glanced at Eco, who stared up at the masked figure enraptured, hanging on every word. Beside him, the moneylender Flavius wore the same unhappy scowl as before. The blond bodyguard sat with his mouth open and occasionally reached up to pick at the scar across his nose.

A muffled commotion was heard from backstage. "Ah," said Roscius in a theatrical whisper, "there's old Euclio now, pitching a fit as usual. The greedy miser must have located the pot of gold by now, and he wants to count his fortune in secret, so he's turning the old housekeeper out of the house." He quietly withdrew through the door in the right wing.

Through the central door emerged a figure wearing an old man's mask and dressed in bright yellow, the traditional color for greed. This was Panurgus, the slave-actor, taking the plum leading role of the miser Euclio. Behind him he dragged another actor dressed as a lowly female slave, and flung him to the middle of the stage. "Get out!" he shouted. "Out! By Hades, out with you, you old snooping bag of bones!"

Statilius had been wrong to disparage Panurgus's comic gifts; already I heard guffaws and laughter around me.

"What have I done? What? What?" cried the other actor. His

grimacing feminine mask was surmounted by a hideous tangled
wig. His gown was in tatters about his knobby knees. "Why are
you beating a long-suffering old hag?"

"To give you something to be long-suffering about, that's why! And
to make you suffer as much as I do, just looking at you!" Panurgus and
his fellow actor scurried about the stage, to the uproarious amusement
of the audience. Eco bounced up and down on the bench and clapped
his hands. The moneylender and his bodyguard sat with their arms
crossed, unimpressed.

> HOUSEKEEPER: *But why must you drive me out of the house?*
> EUCLIO: *Why? Since when do I have to give you a reason? You're asking
> for a fresh crop of bruises!*
> HOUSEKEEPER: *Let the gods send me jumping off a cliff if I'll put
> up with this sort of slavery any longer!*
> EUCLIO: *What's she muttering to herself? I've a good mind to poke your
> eyes out, you damned witch!*

At length the slavewoman disappeared and the miser went back into
his house to count his money; the neighbor Megadorus and his sister
Eunomia occupied the stage. From the voice, it seemed to me that the
sister was played by the same actor who had performed the cringing
slavewoman; no doubt he specialized in female characters. My friend
Statilius, as Megadorus, performed adequately, I thought, but he was
not in the same class with Roscius, or even with his rival Panurgus. His
comic turns inspired polite guffaws, not raucous laughter.

> EUNOMIA: *Dear brother, I've asked you out of the house to have a little
> talk about your private affairs.*
> MEGADORUS: *How sweet! You are as thoughtful as you are beautiful.
> I kiss your hand.*
> EUNOMIA: *What? Are you talking to someone behind me?*
> MEGADORUS: *Of course not. You're the prettiest woman I know!*
> EUNOMIA: *Don't be absurd. Every woman is uglier than every other,
> in one way or another.*
> MEGADORUS: *Mmm, but of course, whatever you say.*
> EUNOMIA: *Now give me your attention. Brother dear, I should like to
> see you married –*
> MEGADORUS: *Help! Murder! Ruin!*
> EUNOMIA: *Oh, quiet down!*

Even this exchange, usually so pleasing to the crowd, evoked only
lukewarm titters. My attention strayed to Statilius's costume, made of

sumptuous blue wool embroidered with yellow, and to his mask, with its absurdly quizzical eyebrows. Alas, I thought, it is a bad sign when a comedian's costume is of greater interest than his delivery. Poor Statilius had found a place with the most respected acting troupe in Rome, but he did not shine there. No wonder the demanding Roscius was so intolerant of him!

Even Eco grew restless. Next to him, the moneylender Flavius leaned over to whisper something in the ear of his blond bodyguard – disparaging the talents of the actor who owed him money, I thought.

At length, the sister exited; the miser returned to converse with his neighbor. Seeing the two of them together on the stage – Statilius and his rival Panurgus – the gulf between their talents was painfully clear. Panurgus as Euclio stole the scene completely, and not just because his lines were better.

> EUCLIO: *So you wish to marry my daughter. Good enough – but you must know I haven't so much as a copper to donate to her dowry.*
> MEGADORUS: *I don't expect even half a copper. Her virtue and good name are quite enough.*
> EUCLIO: *I mean to say, it's not as if I'd just happened to have found some, oh, buried treasure in my house . . . say, a pot of gold buried by my grandfather, or . . .*
> MEGADORUS: *Of course not – how ridiculous! Say no more. You'll give your daughter to me, then?*
> EUCLIO: *Agreed. But what's that? Oh no, I'm ruined!*
> MEGADORUS: *Jupiter Almighty, what's wrong?*
> EUCLIO: *I thought I heard a spade . . . someone digging . . .*
> MEGADORUS: *Why, it's only a slave I've got digging up some roots in my garden. Calm down, good neighbor . . .*

I inwardly groaned for my friend Statilius; but if his delivery was flat, he had learned to follow the master's stage directions without a misstep. Roscius was famous not only for embellishing the old comedies with colorful costumes and masks to delight the eyes, but for choreographing the movements of his actors. Statilius and Panurgus were never static on the stage, like the actors in inferior companies. They circled one another in a constant comic dance, a swirl of blue and yellow.

Eco tugged at my sleeve. With a shrug of his shoulder he gestured to the men beside him. Flavius was again whispering in the bodyguard's ear; the big blond was wrinkling his eyebrows, perplexed. Then he rose and lumbered toward the aisle. Eco drew up his feet, but I was too slow. The monster stepped on my foot. I let out a howl. Others around me started doing the same, thinking I was badgering the actors. The blond giant made no apology at all.

Eco tugged at my sleeve. "Let it go, Eco," I said. "One must learn to live with rudeness in the theater."

He only rolled his eyes and crossed his arms in exasperation. I knew that gesture: if only he could speak!

On the stage, the two neighbors concluded their plans for Megadorus to wed the daughter of Euclio; with a shrilling of pipes and the tinkling of cymbals, they left the stage and the first act was done.

The pipe players introduced a new theme. After a moment, two new actors appeared on stage. These were the quarreling cooks, summoned to prepare the wedding feast. A Roman audience delights in jokes about food and gluttony, the cruder the better. While I groaned at the awful puns, Eco laughed aloud, making a hoarse, barking sound.

In the midst of the gaiety, my blood turned cold. Above the laughter, I heard a scream.

It was not a woman's scream, but a man's. Not a scream of fear, but of pain.

I looked at Eco, who looked back at me. He had heard it, too. No one else in the audience seemed to have noticed, but the actors on stage must have heard something. They bungled their lines and turned uncertainly toward the door, stepping on one another's feet. The audience only laughed harder at their clumsiness.

The quarreling cooks came to the end of their scene and disappeared backstage.

The stage was empty. There was a pause that grew longer and longer. Strange, unaccountable noises came from backstage – muffled gasps, confused shuffling, a loud shout. The audience began to murmur and move about on the benches.

At last the door from the left wing soundlessly opened. Onto the stage stepped a figure wearing the mask of the miser Euclio. He was dressed in bright yellow, but not in the same cloak as before. He threw his hands in the air. "Disaster!" he cried. I felt a cold shiver down my spine.

"Disaster!" he said again. "A daughter's marriage is a disaster! How can any man afford it? I've just come back from the market, and you wouldn't believe what they're charging for lamb – an arm and a leg for an arm and a leg, that's what they want . . ."

The character was miserly Euclio, but the actor was no longer

Panurgus; it was Roscius behind the mask. The audience seemed
not to notice the substitution, or at least not to mind it; they
started laughing almost immediately at the spectacle of poor Euclio
befuddled by his own stinginess.

Roscius delivered the lines flawlessly, with the practiced comic
timing that comes from having played a role many times, but I
thought I heard a strange quavering in his voice. When he turned
so that I could glimpse his eyes within the mask, I saw no sign of
his famous squint. His eyes were wide with alarm. Was this Roscius
the actor, frightened of something very real – or Euclio, afraid that
the squabbling cooks would find his treasure?

"What's that shouting from the kitchen?" he cried. "Oh no, they're
calling for a bigger pot to put the chicken in! Oh, my pot of gold!"
He ran through the door backstage, almost tripping over his yellow
cloak. There followed a cacophony of crashing pots.

The central door was thrown open. One of the cooks emerged on
stage, crying out in a panic, "Help, help, help!"

It was the voice of Statilius! I stiffened and started to stand, but
the words were only part of the play. "It's a madhouse in there," he
cried, straightening his mask. He jumped from the stage and ran
into the audience. "The miser Euclio's gone mad! He's beating us
over the head with pots and pans! Citizens, come to our rescue!" He
whirled about the central aisle until he came to a halt beside me. He
bent low and spoke through his teeth so that only I could hear.

"Gordianus! Come backstage, now!"

I gave a start. Through the mask I looked into Statilius's
anxious eyes.

"Backstage!" he hissed. "Come quick! A dagger – blood – Panurgus
– murder!"

From beyond the maze of screens and awnings and platforms
I occasionally heard the playing of the pipes and actors' voices
raised in argument, followed by the muffled roar of the audience
laughing. Backstage, the company of Quintus Roscius ran about
in a panic, changing costumes, fitting masks onto one another's
heads, mumbling lines beneath their breath, sniping at each other or
exchanging words of encouragement, and in every other way trying
to act as if this were simply another hectic performance and that a
corpse was not lying in their midst.

The body was that of the slave Panurgus. He lay on his back
in a secluded little alcove in the alley that ran behind the Temple
of Jupiter. The place was a public privy, one of many built in
out-of-the-way nooks on the perimeter of the Forum. Screened by

two walls, a sloping floor tilted to a hole that emptied into the Cloaca Maxima. Panurgus had apparently come here to relieve himself between scenes. Now he lay dead with a knife plunged squarely into his chest. Above his heart a large red circle stained his bright yellow costume. A sluggish stream of blood trickled across the tiles and ran down the drain.

He was older than I had thought, almost as old as his master, with grey in his hair and a wrinkled forehead. His mouth and eyes were open wide in shock; his eyes were green, and in death they glittered dully like uncut emeralds.

Eco gazed down at the body and reached up to grasp my hand. Statilius ran up beside us. He was dressed in blue again and held the mask of Megadorus in his hands. His face was ashen. "Madness," he whispered. "Bloody madness."

"Shouldn't the play be stopped?"

"Roscius refuses. Not for a slave, he says. And he doesn't dare tell the crowd. Imagine: a murder, backstage, in the middle of our performance, on a holiday consecrated to Jupiter himself, in the very shadow of the god's temple – what an omen! What magistrate would ever hire Roscius and the company again? No, the show goes on – even though we must somehow figure out how to fill nine roles with five actors instead of six. Oh dear, and I've never learned the nephew's lines . . ."

"Statilius!" It was Roscius, returning from the stage. He threw off the mask of Euclio. His own face was far more grotesque, contorted with fury. "What do you think you're doing, standing there mumbling? If I'm playing Euclio, you have to play the nephew!" He rubbed his squinting eyes, then slapped his forehead. "But no, that's impossible – Megadorus and the nephew must be on stage at the same time. What a disaster! Jupiter, why me?"

The actors circled one another like frenzied bees. The dressers hovered about them uncertainly, as useless as drones. All was chaos in the company of Quintus Roscius.

I looked down at the bloodless face of Panurgus, who was beyond caring. All men become the same in death, whether slave or citizen, Roman or Greek, genius or pretender.

At last the play was over. The old bachelor Megadorus had escaped the clutches of marriage; miserly Euclio had lost and then recovered his pot of gold; the honest slave who restored it to him had been set free; the quarreling cooks had been paid by Megadorus and sent on their way; and the young lovers had been joyously betrothed. How this was accomplished under the circumstances, I do not know. By some miracle of the theater, everything came off without a hitch. The cast assembled together on the stage to roaring applause, and then returned backstage, their exhilaration at once replaced by the grim reality of the death among them.

"Madness," Statilius said again, hovering over the corpse. Knowing how he felt about his rival, I had to wonder if he was not secretly gloating. He seemed genuinely shocked, but that, after all, could have been acting.

"And who is this?" barked Roscius, tearing off the yellow cloak he had assumed to play the miser.

"My name is Gordianus. Men call me the Finder."

Roscius raised an eyebrow and nodded. "Ah, yes, I've heard of you. Last spring – the case of Sextus Roscius; no relation to myself, I'm glad to say, or very distant, anyway. You earned yourself a name with parties on both sides of that affair."

Knowing Roscius was an intimate of the dictator Sulla, whom I had grossly offended, I only nodded.

"So what are you doing here?" Roscius demanded.

"It was I who told him," said Statilius helplessly. "I asked him to come backstage. It was the first thing I thought of."

"You invited an outsider to intrude on this tragedy, Statilius? Fool! What's to keep him from standing in the Forum and announcing the news to everyone who passes? The scandal will be disastrous."

"I assure you, I can be quite discreet – for a client," I said.

"Oh, I see," said Roscius, squinting at me shrewdly. "Perhaps that's not a bad idea, provided you could actually be of some help."

"I think I might," I said modestly, already calculating a fee. Roscius was, after all, the most highly paid actor in the world. Rumor claimed he made as much as half a million sesterces in a single year. He could afford to be generous.

He looked down at the corpse and shook his head bitterly. "One of my most promising pupils. Not just a gifted artist, but a valuable piece of property. But why should anyone murder the slave? Panurgus had no vices, no politics, no enemies."

"It's a rare man who has no enemies," I said. I could not help but glance at Statilius, who hurriedly looked away.

There was a commotion among the gathered actors and stage-hands. The crowd parted to admit a tall, cadaverous figure with a shock of red hair.

"Chaerea! Where have you been?" growled Roscius.

The newcomer looked down his long nose, first at the corpse, then at Roscius. "Drove down from my villa at Fidenae," he snapped tersely. "Axle on the chariot broke. Missed more than the play, it appears."

"Gaius Fannius Chaerea," whispered Statilius in my ear. "He was Panurgus's original owner. When he saw the slave had comic gifts he handed him over to Roscius to train him, as part-owner."

"They don't seem friendly," I whispered back.

"They've been feuding over how to calculate the profits from Panurgus's performances . . ."

"So. Quintus Roscius," sniffed Chaerea, tilting his nose even higher, "this is how you take care of our common property. Bad management, I say. Slave's worthless, now. I'll send you a bill for my share."

"What? You think I'm responsible for this?" Roscius squinted fiercely.

"Slave was in your care; now he's dead. Theater people! So irresponsible." Chaerea ran his bony fingers through his orange mane and shrugged haughtily before turning his back. "Expect my bill tomorrow," he said, stepping through the crowd to join a coterie of attendants waiting in the alley. "Or I'll see you in court."

"Outrageous!" said Roscius. "You!" He pointed a stubby finger at me. "This is your job! Find out who did this, and why. If it was a slave or a pauper, I'll have him torn apart. If it was a rich man, I'll sue him blind for destroying my property. I'll go to Hades before I give Chaerea the satisfaction of saying this was my fault!"

I accepted the job with a grave nod and tried not to smile. I could almost feel the rain of glittering silver on my head. Then I glimpsed the contorted face of the dead Panurgus, and felt the full gravity of my commission. For a dead slave in Rome, there is seldom any attempt to find justice. I would find the killer, I silently vowed, not for Roscius and his silver, but to honor the shade of an artist cruelly cut down in his prime.

"Very well, Roscius. I will need to ask some questions. See that no one in the company leaves until I am done with him. If I may, I would talk with you in private first. Perhaps a cup of wine would calm us both . . ."

Late that afternoon, I sat on a bench beneath the shade of an olive tree, on a quiet street not far from the Temple of Jupiter. Eco sat beside me, pensively studying the play of leafy shadows on the paving stones.

"So, Eco, what do you think? Have we learned anything of value?"

He shook his head gravely from side to side.

"You judge too quickly." I laughed. "Consider: we last saw

Panurgus alive during his scene with Statilius at the close of the first act. Then those two left the stage; the pipers played an interlude, and next the quarreling cooks came on. Then there was a scream. That must have been Panurgus, when he was stabbed. It caused a commotion backstage; Roscius checked into the matter and discovered the body in the privy. Word quickly spread among the others. Roscius put on the dead man's mask and a yellow cloak, the closest thing he had to match Panurgus's costume, and rushed on stage just in time to keep the play going. Statilius, meanwhile, put on a cook's costume so that he could jump into the audience and plead for my help.

"Therefore, we know at least one thing: the actors playing the cooks were innocent, as were the pipe players, because they were on stage when the murder occurred."

Eco made a face to show he was not impressed.

"Yes, this is all very elementary, but to build a wall we begin with the first row of bricks. Now, who was backstage at the time of the murder, has no one to account for his whereabouts at the moment of the scream, and might have wanted Panurgus dead?"

Eco bounded up from the bench, ready to play the game. He performed a pantomime, jabbering with his jaw and waving his arms at himself.

I smiled sadly; the unflattering portrait could only be my talkative and self-absorbed friend Statilius. "Yes, Statilius must be foremost among the suspects, though I regret to say it. We know he had cause to hate Panurgus; so long as the slave was alive, a man of inferior talent like Statilius would never be given the best roles. We also learned, from questioning the company, that when the scream was heard, no one could account for Statilius's whereabouts. This may be only a coincidence, given the ordinary chaos that seems to reign backstage during a performance. Statilius himself vows that he was busy in a corner adjusting his costume. In his favor, he seems to have been truly shocked at the slave's death – but he might only be pretending. I call the man my friend, but do I really know him?"

I pondered for a moment. "Who else, Eco?"

He hunched his shoulders, scowled, and squinted.

"Yes, Roscius was also backstage when Panurgus screamed, and no one seems to remember seeing him at that instant. It was he who found the corpse – or was he there when the knife descended? Roscius is a violent man; all his actors say so. We heard him shouting angrily at someone before the play began – do you remember? 'Fool! Incompetent! Why can't you remember your lines?' Roscius now claims he can't remember the incident at all, but others saw him and told me it was Panurgus he was shouting at. Did the slave's performance in the first act displease him so much that he flew into a rage, lost his head, and murdered him? It hardly seems likely: I thought Panurgus was doing quite well. And Roscius, like Statilius, seemed genuinely offended by the murder. But then, Roscius is an actor of great skill."

Eco put his hands on his hips and his nose in the air and began to strut haughtily.

"Ah, Chaerea; I was coming to him. He claims not to have arrived until after the play was over, and yet he hardly seemed taken aback when he saw the corpse. He seems almost *too* unflappable. He was the slave's original owner. In return for cultivating Panurgus's talents, Roscius acquired half-ownership, but Chaerea seems to have been thoroughly dissatisfied with the arrangement. Did he decide that the slave was worth more to him dead than alive? Chaerea holds Roscius culpable for the loss, and intends to coerce Roscius into paying him half the slave's worth in silver. In a Roman court, with the right advocate, Chaerea will likely prevail."

I leaned back against the olive tree, dissatisfied. "Still, I wish we had uncovered someone else in the company with as strong a motive, and the opportunity to have done the deed. Yet no one seems to have borne a grudge against Panurgus, and almost everyone could account for his whereabouts when the victim screamed.

"Of course, the murderer may be someone from outside the company: the privy where Panurgus was stabbed was accessible to anyone passing through the alley behind the temple. Yet Roscius tells us, and the others confirm, that Panurgus had almost no dealings with anyone outside the troupe – he did not gamble or frequent brothels; he borrowed neither money nor other men's wives. His craft alone consumed him; so everyone says. Even if Panurgus *had* offended someone, the aggrieved party would surely have taken up the matter not with Panurgus but with Roscius, since he was the slave's owner and the man legally responsible for his actions."

I sighed with frustration. "The knife left in his heart was a common dagger, with no distinguishing features. No footprints surrounded the body. No telltale blood was found on any of the costumes. There were no witnesses, or none we knew of. Alas!" The shower of silver in my imagination dried to a trickle; with nothing to show, I would be lucky to press Roscius into paying me a day's fee for my trouble. Even worse, I felt the shade of dead Panurgus watching me. I had vowed I would find his killer, and it seemed the vow was rashly made.

*   *   *

That night I took my dinner in the ramshackle garden at the center of my house. The lamps burned low. Fireflies flitted among the columns of the peristyle. Sounds of distant revelry occasionally wafted up from the streets of the Subura at the foot of the hill.

"Bethesda, the meal was exquisite," I said, lying with my usual grace. Perhaps I could have been an actor, I thought.

But Bethesda was not fooled. She looked at me from beneath her long lashes and smiled with half her mouth. She combed one hand through the great unbound mass of her glossy black hair and shrugged an elegant shrug, then began to clear the table.

As she departed to the kitchen, I watched the sinuous play of her hips within her loose green stola. When I bought her long ago at the slave market in Alexandria, it had not been for her cooking. Her cooking had never improved, but in many other ways she was beyond perfection. I peered into the blackness of the long tresses that cascaded to her waist; I imagined the fireflies lost in those tresses, like twinkling stars in the blue-black firmament of the sky. Before Eco had come into my life, Bethesda and I had spent almost every night together, just the two of us, in the solitude of the garden . . .

I was startled from my reverie by a tiny hand pulling at the hem of my tunic.

"Yes, Eco, what is it?"

Eco, reclining on the couch next to mine, put his fists together and pulled them apart, up and down, as if unrolling a scroll.

"Ah, your reading lesson. We had no time for it today, did we? But my eyes are weary, Eco, and yours must be, too. And there are other matters on my mind . . ."

He frowned at me in mock-dejection until I relented. "Very well. Bring that lamp nearer. What would you like to read tonight?"

Eco pointed at himself and shook his head, then pointed at me. He cupped his hands behind his ears and closed his eyes. He preferred it (and secretly, so did I) when I did the reading, and he could enjoy the luxury of merely listening. All that summer, on lazy afternoons and long summer nights, the two of us had spent many such hours in the garden; while I read Piso's history of Hannibal, Eco would sit at my feet and watch elephants among the clouds, or he would lie on his back and study the moon while I declaimed the tale of the Sabine women. He understood Greek, strangely enough, though he knew none of the letters. Of late I had been reading to him from an old, tattered scroll of Plato, a cast-off gift from Cicero. Eco followed the subtleties of the philosopher's discourses with fascination, though occasionally in his big brown eyes I saw a glimmer of sorrow that he could never hope to engage in such debates himself.

"Shall I read more Plato, then? They say philosophy after dinner aids digestion."

Eco nodded and ran to fetch the scroll. He emerged from the shadows of the peristyle a moment later, gripping it carefully in his hands. Suddenly he stopped and stood statue-like with a strange expression on his face.

"Eco, what is it?" I thought for a moment that he was ill; Bethesda's fish dumplings and turnips in cumin sauce had been undistinguished, but hardly so bad as to make him sick. He stared straight ahead at nothing, and did not hear me.

"Eco? Are you all right?" He stood rigid, trembling; a look which might have been fear or ecstasy crossed his face. Then he sprang toward me, pressed the scroll under my nose, and pointed at it frantically.

"I've never known a boy to be so mad for learning." I laughed, but he was not playing a game. His expression was deadly serious. "But Eco, it's only the same volume of Plato that I've been reading to you off and on all summer. Why are you suddenly so excited?"

Eco stood back to perform his pantomime. A dagger thrust into his heart could only indicate the dead Panurgus.

"Panurgus and Plato – Eco, I see no connection."

Eco bit his lip and scrambled about, desperate to express himself. At last he ran into the house and back out again, clutching two objects. He dropped them onto my lap.

"Eco, be careful! This little vase is made of precious green glass, and came all the way from Alexandria. And why have you brought me a bit of red tile? This must have fallen from the roof . . ."

Eco pointed emphatically at each object in turn, but I could not see what he meant.

He disappeared again and came back with my wax tablet and stylus, upon which he wrote the words for *red* and *green*.

"Yes, Eco. I can see that the vase is green and the tile is red. Blood is red . . ." Eco shook his head and pointed to his eyes. "Panurgus had green eyes . . ." I saw them in my memory, staring lifeless at the sky.

Eco stamped his foot and shook his head to let me know that I was badly off-course. He took the vase and the bit of tile from my lap and began to juggle them from hand to hand.

"Eco, stop that! I told you, the vase is precious!"

He put them carelessly down and reached for the stylus again. He rubbed out the words *red* and *green* and in their place wrote *blue*. It seemed he wished to write another word, but could not think of how to spell it. He nibbled on the stylus and shook his head.

"Eco, I think you must have a fever. You make no sense at all."

He took the scroll from my lap and began to unroll it, scanning it hopelessly. Even if the text had been in Latin it would have been a tortuous job for him to decipher the words and find whatever he was searching for, but the letters were Greek and utterly foreign to him.

He threw down the scroll and began to pantomime again, but he was excited and clumsy; I could make no sense of his wild gesturing. I shrugged and shook my head in exasperation, and Eco suddenly began to weep with frustration. He seized the scroll again and pointed to his eyes. Did he mean that I should read the scroll, or did he point to his tears? I bit my lip and turned up my palms, unable to help him.

Eco threw the scroll in my lap and ran crying from the room. A hoarse, stifled braying issued from his throat, not the sound of normal weeping; it tore my heart to hear it. I should have been more patient, but how was I to understand him? Bethesda emerged from the kitchen and gazed at me accusingly, then followed the sound of Eco's weeping to the little room where he slept.

I looked down at the scroll in my lap. There were so many words on the parchment; which ones had keyed an idea in Eco's memory, and what could they have to do with dead Panurgus? *Red, green, blue* – I vaguely remembered reading a passage in which Plato discoursed on the nature of light and color, but I could scarcely remember it, not having understood much of it in the first place. Some scheme about overlapping cones projected from the eyes to an object, or from the object to the eyes, I couldn't remember which; was this what Eco recalled, and could it have made any sense to him?

I rolled through the scroll, looking for the reference, but was unable to find it. My eyes grew weary. The lamp began to sputter. The Greek letters all began to look alike. Normally Bethesda would have come to put me to bed, but it seemed she had chosen to stay with Eco instead. I fell asleep on my dining couch beneath the stars, thinking of a yellow cloak stained with red, and of green eyes gazing at an empty blue sky.

Eco was ill the next day, or feigned illness. Bethesda solemnly informed me that he did not wish to leave his bed. I stood in the doorway of the little room and spoke to him gently, reminding him that the Roman Festival continued, and that today there would be a wild-beast show in the Circus Maximus, and another play put on by another company. He turned his back to me and pulled the coverlet over his head.

"I suppose I should punish him," I whispered to myself, trying to think of what a normal Roman father would do.

"I suppose you should not," whispered Bethesda as she passed me. Her haughtiness left me properly humbled.

I took my morning stroll, alone – for the first time in many days, I realized, acutely aware that Eco was not beside me. The Subura seemed a rather dull place without ten-year-old eyes through which to see it. I had only my own eyes to serve me, and they had seen it a million times before.

I would buy him a gift, I decided; I would buy them each a gift, for it was always a good idea to placate Bethesda when she was haughty. For Eco I bought a red leather ball, such as boys use to play trigon, knocking it back and forth to each other using their elbows and knees. For Bethesda I wanted to find a veil woven of blue midnight shot through with fireflies, but I decided to settle for one made of linen. On the street of the cloth merchants I found the shop of my old acquaintance Ruso.

I asked to see a veil of dark blue. As if by magic he produced the very veil I had been imagining, a gossamer thing that seemed to be made of blue-black spiderwebs and silver. It was also the most expensive item in the shop. I chided him for taunting me with a luxury beyond my means.

Ruso shrugged good-naturedly. "One never knows; you might have just won a fortune on a toss of the tiles. Here, these are more affordable." He smiled, laying a selection before me.

"No," I said, seeing nothing I liked, "I've changed my mind."

"Then something in a lighter blue, perhaps? A bright blue, like the sky."

"No. I think not – "

"Ah, but see what I have to show you first. Felix . . . Felix! Fetch me one of the new veils that just arrived from Alexandria, the bright blue ones with yellow stitching."

The young slave bit his lip nervously and seemed to cringe. This struck me as odd, for I knew Ruso to be a temperate man and not a cruel master.

"Go on, then – what are you waiting for?" Ruso turned to me and shook his head. "This new slave – worse than useless! I don't think he's very smart, no matter what the slave merchant said. He keeps the books well enough, but here in the shop – look, he's done it again! Unbelievable! Felix, what is wrong with you? Do you do this just to spite me? Do you want a beating? I won't put up with this any longer, I tell you!"

The slave shrank back, looking confused and helpless. In his hand he held a yellow veil.

"All the time he does this!" wailed Ruso, clutching his head. "He wants to drive me mad! I ask for blue and he brings me yellow! I ask for yellow and he brings me blue! Have you ever heard of such stupidity? I shall beat you, Felix, I swear it!" And he ran after the poor slave, brandishing a measuring rod.

And then I understood.

My friend Statilius, as I had expected, was not at his lodgings in the Subura. When I questioned his landlord, the old man gave me the sly look of a confederate charged with throwing hounds off the scent, and told me that Statilius had left Rome for the countryside.

He was in none of the usual places where he might have been on a festival day. No tavern had served him and no brothel had admitted him. He would not even think of appearing in a gambling house, I told myself – and then knew that the exact opposite must be true.

Once I set to searching the gaming places in the Subura, I found him easily enough. In a crowded apartment on the third floor of an old tenement I discovered him in the midst of a crowd of well-dressed men, some of them even wearing their togas. Statilius was down on his elbows and knees, shaking a tiny box and muttering prayers to Fortune. He cast the tiles; the crowd contracted in a tight circle and then drew back, exclaiming. The tiles had come up two black, two white.

"Yes! Yes!" Statilius cried, and held out his palms. The others handed over their coins.

I grabbed him by the collar of his tunic and pulled him squawking into the hall.

"I should think you're deeply enough in debt already," I said.

"Quite the contrary!" he protested, smiling broadly. His face was flushed and his forehead beaded with sweat, like a man with a fever.

"Just how much *do* you owe Flavius the moneylender?"

"A hundred thousand sesterces."

"A hundred thousand!" My heart leaped into my throat.

"But not any longer. You see, I'll be able to pay him off now!" He held up the coins in his hands. "I have two bags full of silver in the other room, where my slave's looking after them. And – can you believe it? – a deed to a house on the Caelian Hill. I've won my way out of it, don't you see?"

"At the expense of another man's life."

His grin became sheepish. "So, you've figured that out. But who could have foreseen such a tragedy? Certainly not I. And when it happened, I didn't rejoice in Panurgus's death – you saw that. I didn't hate him, not really. My jealousy was purely professional. But if the Fates decided better him than me, who am I to argue?"

"You're a worm, Statilius. Why didn't you tell Roscius what you knew? Why didn't you tell me?"

"What did I know, really? Someone completely unknown might have killed poor Panurgus. I didn't witness the event."

"But you guessed the truth, all the same. That's why you wanted me backstage, wasn't it? You were afraid the assassin would come back for you. What was I, your bodyguard?"

"Perhaps. After all, he didn't come back, did he?"

"Statilius, you're a worm."

"You said that already." The smile dropped from his face like a discarded mask. He jerked his collar from my grasp.

"You hid the truth from me," I said, "but why from Roscius?"

"What, tell him I had run up an obscene gambling debt for which a notorious moneylender was threatening to kill me?"

"Perhaps he'd have loaned you the money."

"Never! You don't know Roscius. I was lucky to be in his troupe to begin with; he's not the type to hand out favors to an underling in the amount of a hundred thousand sesterces. And if he knew Panurgus had mistakenly been murdered instead of me – oh, Roscius would have loved that! One Panurgus is worth ten Statilii, that's his view. I *would* have been a dead man then, with Flavius on one side and Roscius on the other. The two of them would have torn me apart like a chicken bone!" He stepped back and straightened his tunic. The smile flickered and returned to his lips. "You're not going to tell anyone, are you?"

"Statilius, do you ever stop acting?" I averted my eyes to avoid his charm.

"Well?"

"Roscius is my client, not you."

"But I'm your friend, Gordianus."

"I made a promise to Panurgus."

"Panurgus didn't hear you."

"The gods did."

Finding the moneylender Flavius was a simpler matter – a few questions in the right ear, a few coins in the right hands. I learned that he owned a wine shop in a portico near the Circus Flaminius, where he sold inferior vintages imported from his native Tarquinii. But on a festival day, my informants told me, I would be more likely to find him at the house of questionable repute across the street.

The place had a low ceiling and the musty smell of spilled wine and crowded humanity. Across the room I saw Flavius, holding court with a group of his peers – businessmen of middle age with crude country manners, dressed in expensive tunics and cloaks of a quality that only emphasized their wearers' crudeness. Closer at hand, leaning against a wall (and looking strong enough to hold it up), was the moneylender's bully.

The blond giant was looking rather drunk, or else exceptionally stupid. He slowly blinked when I approached. A glimmer of recognition lit his bleary eyes and then faded.

"Festival days are good drinking days," I said, raising my cup of wine. He looked at me without expression for a moment, then shrugged and nodded.

"Tell me," I said, "do you know any of those spectacular beauties?" I gestured to a group of four women who loitered at the far corner of the room, near the foot of the stairs.

The giant shook his head glumly.

"Then you are a lucky man this day." I leaned close enough to smell the wine on his breath. "I was just talking to one of them. She tells me that she longs to meet you. It seems she has an appetite for men with sunny hair and big shoulders. She tells me that for a man such as you . . ." I whispered in his ear.

The veil of lust across his face made him look even stupider. He squinted drunkenly. "Which one?" he asked in a husky whisper.

"The one in the blue gown," I said.

"Ah . . ." He nodded and burped, then pushed past me and stumbled toward the stairs. As I expected, he ignored the woman in green, as well as the woman in coral and the one in brown. Instead he placed his hand squarely upon the hip of the woman in yellow, who turned and looked up at him with a startled but not unfriendly gaze.

"Quintus Roscius and his partner Chaerea were both duly impressed by my cleverness," I explained later that night to Bethesda. I was unable to resist the theatrical gesture of swinging the little bag of silver up in the air and onto the table, where it landed with a jingling thump. "Not a pot of gold, perhaps, but a fat enough fee to keep us all happy through the winter."

Her eyes became as round and glittering as little coins. They grew even larger when I produced the veil from Ruso's shop.

"Oh! But what is it made of?"

"Midnight and fireflies," I said. "Spiderwebs and silver." She tilted her head back and spread the translucent veil over her naked throat and arms. I blinked and swallowed hard, and decided that the purchase was well worth the price.

Eco stood uncertainly in the doorway of his little room, where he had watched me enter and had listened to my hurried tale of the day's events. He seemed to have recovered from his distemper of the morning, but his face was somber. I held out my hand, and he cautiously approached. He took the leather ball readily enough, but he still did not smile.

"Only a small gift, I know. But I have a greater one for you . . ."

"Still, I don't understand," protested Bethesda. "You've said the blond giant was stupid, but how can anyone be so stupid as not to be able to tell one color from another?"

"Eco knows," I said, smiling ruefully down at him. "He figured it out last night and tried to tell me, but he didn't know how. He remembered a passage from Plato that I read to him months ago; I had forgotten all about it. Here, I think I can find it now." I reached for the scroll, which still lay upon my sleeping couch.

"'One may observe,'" I read aloud, "'that not all men perceive the same colors. Although they are rare, there are those who confuse the colors red and green, and likewise those who cannot tell yellow from blue; still others appear to have no perception of the various shades of green.' He goes on to offer an explanation of this, but I cannot follow it."

"Then the bodyguard could not tell blue from yellow?" said Bethesda. "Even so . . ."

"Flavius came to the theater yesterday intending to make good on his threat to murder Statilius. No wonder he gave a start when I leaned over and said, 'Today you'll see *The Pot of Gold*' – for a moment he thought I meant the debt Statilius owed him! He sat in the audience long enough to see that Statilius was playing Megadorus, dressed in blue; no doubt he could recognize him by his voice. Then he sent the assassin backstage, knowing the alley behind the Temple of Jupiter would be virtually deserted, there to lie in wait for the actor *in the blue cloak*. Eco must have overheard snatches of his instructions, if only the word 'blue.' He thought that something was amiss and tried to tell me at the time, but there was too much confusion, with the giant stepping on my toes and the audience howling around us. Am I right?"

Eco nodded, and slapped a fist against his palm: exactly right.

"Unfortunately for poor Panurgus in his yellow cloak, the assassin is also uncommonly stupid. He needed more information than the color blue to make sure he murdered the right man, but he didn't bother to ask for it; or if he did, Flavius must only have sneered at him and rushed him along, unable to understand his confusion. Catching Panurgus alone and vulnerable in his yellow cloak, which might as well have been blue, the assassin did his job – and bungled it.

"Knowing Flavius was in the audience and out to kill him, learning that Panurgus had been stabbed, and seeing that the hired assassin was no longer in the audience, Statilius guessed the truth; no wonder he was so shaken by Panurgus's death, knowing that he was the intended victim."

"So another slave is murdered, and by accident! And nothing will be done," Bethesda said moodily.

"Not exactly. Panurgus was valuable property. The law allows his owners to sue the man responsible for his death for his full market value. I understand that Roscius and Chaerea are each demanding one hundred thousand sesterces from Flavius. If Flavius contests the action and loses, the amount will be double. Knowing his greed, I suspect he'll tacitly admit his guilt and settle for the smaller figure."

"Small justice for a meaningless murder."

I nodded. "And small recompense for the destruction of so much talent. But such is the only justice that Roman law allows, when a citizen kills a slave."

A heavy silence descended on the garden. His insight vindicated, Eco turned his attention to the leather ball. He tossed it in the air, caught it, and nodded thoughtfully, satisfied at the way it fit his hand.

"Ah, but Eco, as I was saying, there is another gift for you." He looked at me expectantly. "It's here." I patted the sack of silver. "No longer shall I teach you in my own stumbling way how to read and write. You shall have a proper tutor, who will come every morning to teach you both Latin and Greek. He will be stern, and you shall suffer, but when he is done you will read and write better than I do. A boy as clever as you deserves no less."

Eco's smile was radiant. I have never seen a boy toss a ball so high.

The story is almost done, except for one final outcome.

Much later that night, I lay in bed with Bethesda with nothing to separate us but a gossamer veil shot through with silver threads. For a few fleeting moments I was completely satisfied with life and the universe. In my relaxation, without meaning to, I mumbled what I was thinking. "Perhaps I *should* adopt the boy," I muttered.

"And why not?" Bethesda demanded, imperious even when half-asleep. "What more proof do you want from him? The boy could not be more like your son if he were made of your own flesh and blood."

And of course, she was right.

THE KING
OF SACRIFICES
John Maddox Roberts

A contemporary of Gordianus, is Decius Caecilius Metellus, the creation of John Maddox Roberts. His adventures have appeared in the novels SPQR *(1990),* The Catiline Conspiracy *(1991),* The Sacrilege *(1992),* The Temple of the Muses *(1992) and* Saturnalia *(1993). Metellus has one advantage over Gordianus in that being a member of a noble Roman family, and a Roman official, he has access to people and places normally denied the plebians. That doesn't, of course, make his life any safer, as the fate of many noble Romans will attest, but it does mean Metellus can sail rather close to the wind at times. The following story, specially written for this anthology, takes place towards the end of Metellus's long life, in the early days of the reign of Augustus Caesar.*

Roberts (b. 1947), is probably better known in Britain for his novels continuing the adventures of Conan the Barbarian, although he is the author of nearly thirty sf, fantasy and mystery novels. His contemporary mystery novel A Typical American Town *was published in Britain in 1994. Perhaps it will not be too long before his novels about Metellus will also be available in Britain.*

The First Citizen rarely summons me. This may be because we detest one another so deeply. He has never bothered to have me killed because I am a relic of the old Republic he claims to have restored. As the oldest living senator I have a certain prestige. Besides, I am not that important. Once, my family controlled the most powerful voting blocs in the Senate, the Plebeian Assembly and the Centurionate Assembly. But that great generation of vigorous political men died in the civil wars and the remnants are scarcely worth my attention, much less his.

But I have certain talents that are unique, and there have been times when the First Citizen has had need of them. At such times he requests my presence, smiles his false smile, and seeks my aid. One such occasion occurred in my 73rd year.

I spent the morning dozing through a Senate meeting. As the power and importance of that august body dwindled, so did its speeches expand. One time-serving nobody after another got up to discourse windily upon trifles. My neighbors discreetly nudged me any time my snoring became obtrusive.

The session ended at noon, not a moment too early. I pushed myself to my feet with my walking stick and left the Curia. I didn't really need a stick, it just lent me an air of venerability. Once outside, I paused at the top of the steps to breathe the clean air and survey my City.

The sight was not altogether pleasing. There was still much in evidence that was ancient and familiar, but the spate of building that had been going on for more than twenty years had changed the City almost beyond recognition. Temples that had been simple, sober and dignified had become masterpieces of the confectioner's art, their facades tarted up with white marble and frothy carving and gilding. And some of the temples were new, erected not to honor the gods but to the glory of a single family.

There was, for instance, the temple of Venus Genetrix, the goddess from whom Caesar had claimed descent. A tenuous connection for the First Citizen, who was merely the grandson of Caesar's sister. And then there was the temple of Mars the Avenger. Mars had always had his shrines outside the City walls. Now he had been brought within, solely to remind everyone that the First Citizen had avenged (so he claimed) the murder of the great Caius Julius. Some of the new public buildings were begun by Caesar, but most bore the name of the First Citizen, or of his cronies: Agrippa and Maecenas. Somehow, the whole city had become his clientele.

I used to make fun of my father for indulging in this sort of good-old-days grumbling. Now that I am old I rather enjoy it.

My grumpy musings were interrupted by the arrival of my grandson, Decius the Youngest. He is nicknamed Paris for his exceptional looks. It is not good for one so young to be so handsome. It presages a life of trouble and a bad end. All the splendidly handsome men I have known came to a bad end: Milo, Marcus Antonius, Vercingetorix, they flourished briefly to great admiration and were gone. On the other hand, there is much to be said for dying young.

"Grandfather!" He ran up the steps, scattering senators and their hangers-on like chaff before a whirlwind. The boy had yet to dedicate his first beard and he possessed a commendable lack of respect for authority. He was breathing heavily and thrust a small scroll at me. "A letter from the Palace!"

I accepted it. "From Himself, I take it?" I said loudly, using the term his sycophants often used. Time was when only slaves used that term to refer to their master.

"How should I know?" he said, all innocence.

"Because you've read it, imp. The seal is broken."

He shrugged. "The messenger must have dropped it."

"What a liar. By the time I was your age I could lie far better than that. Let's see, now." I held the missive at arm's length and read loudly, as if I were hard of hearing:

"*From the First Citizen to the venerable Senator Decius Caecilius Metellus, greeting.*" Actually, here he employed the name which he illegally usurped from a better man and which I refuse to use. Recently, the Senate had voted him the title of Augustus. The Senate can give him any silly title it likes. He will always be sneaky little Caius Octavius to me.

"*The First Citizen requests the honor of your company in his home this afternoon, to confer upon a matter concerning the good of the Senate and People of Rome.*" I snorted. "Summoning me like some Oriental despot, is he? Well, that's just like him. Got himself into a tight spot again and needs me to get him out of it, no doubt!" All over the Curia steps, senators began sidling away from me, as if to clear a target range for Jove's thunderbolt. I love to see them do that.

"Father says you shouldn't talk like that," Paris said, quite unconcerned.

"Your father has grown disgustingly respectable these last few years. In his younger days there wasn't a professional criminal in Rome who could match him for villainy. Come along." I took him by the shoulder. "Let's go find something to eat and pay a visit to the baths and then we'll go see what the First Citizen wants."

On the waterfront near the Aemilian Bridge was a colorful little establishment called the Nemean Lion. That district of Rome is much devoted to Hercules and references to the demigod's legend are numerous. It was owned by a man named Ulpius who, in his youth, had been one of Milo's thugs. His daughter-in-law made the best pork sausage in Rome and each Saturnalia I gave them a nice present, so that they kept for me a reserve of fine, unwatered Falernian.

Since the day was fine we sat out front beneath the awning and watched the river traffic while Ulpius's granddaughters loaded the table with food and brought a flask of my private stock.

"Mother says you drink too early in the day," Paris said, lighting into the eatables. "She says you drink too much generally."

"She does, eh? Three generations of my relatives have said the same thing. I've presided at most of their funerals. I'm not going to face the First Citizen sober."

"Why do you hate him so much?" he mumbled around a mouthful of honeyed date cake.

"Because he destroyed the Republic and set up a monarchy and killed all the best men in Rome – all the true republicans."

"Then why didn't he kill you?" Precocious little bugger.

"By the time he got around to considering me, he'd decided to pose as the benevolent savior of the State. It's one of the political rules: Kill all your important enemies as soon as you seize power. The survivors will be so relieved that they'll forget all about it within a year. His great-uncle Julius Caesar neglected to kill his own enemies, and look what happened to him. Pretending respect and affection for me bolsters his image as the all-forgiving father of his country. It costs him nothing since I no longer count for anything, politically."

Truthfully, he didn't murder the Republic. It committed suicide. He just rearranged the carcass to suit him better. And most of the best men killed each other before Julian had a chance at them. No sense confusing the boy with political subtleties at so tender an age, though.

"So why are you willing to help him?"

"Why don't you finish your lunch?"

Thus fortified, and with the worst of my aches massaged from my bones at my favorite bathing establishment, I felt up to the long trudge up the Palatine and an interview with my least favorite Roman.

From the bottom of the steps we encountered guards. Caius Octavius makes a great show of being an ordinary citizen, living among his fellows without fear, and claimed that he never violated the ancient law against bringing armed soldiers into the City. The burly men who lounged around the residence wore togas, but they clinked as they moved and they studied me with an unsettling fixity.

A steward greeted me in the atrium and disappeared into the interior of the vast house to announce me. A few minutes later a splendidly handsome and stately woman appeared.

"Decius Caecilius, how good of you to come! And this must be the handsome grandson of whom I hear such brilliant reports!"

"I don't know who you listen to, Livia, but if you've heard that he's anything but a lazy troublemaker your spies should be crucified."

"But so many of them are your relatives."

"All the more reason to nail them up," I grumbled. Of all the many intriguing and dangerous women I have known in my long life, Livia was the most perilous, the subtlest, and the most intelligent by a tremendous margin, and I knew Cleopatra, who may have been the most powerful as well as the best educated woman who ever lived. I always accorded Livia the highest respect.

"Come along, my husband is in his study. I do hope you'll be able to help him. He has great confidence in you."

This should be good, I thought.

We found Octavius sitting at a desk attended by secretaries, apparently absorbed by weighty matters of state. At our arrival he stood and extended his hands.

"Ah, my old friend Decius Caecilius Metellus, I am so pleased that you've found time to visit me." With his spindly body and his large head with its unruly hair, he rather resembled a thistle.

"Always happy to be of assistance to the Senate and People," I said pointedly. The irony sailed right past him.

"As all good men should be. Please, sit down, Senator. And this would be the youngest to bear your ancient name? What a splendid example of Roman youth."

I was beginning to regret having brought Paris. The less these people noticed him, the better. I found myself falling into these lapses of judgement as I aged. Not that my discernment had ever been worthy of praise. I feigned creakiness as I lowered myself into a chair and sat with my hands resting atop my stick. A slave brought in a tray bearing a platter and cups.

"Please, take something, my friend. It's a long walk up the Palatine."

The platter held fresh figs. The cups held plain water. His pose of plainness and austerity had been concocted for him by Livia. Even his banquets were Stoic affairs, featuring only peasant food. I could easily picture him sneaking off afterward, to gorge in private upon imported delicacies and rare wines.

"Thank you, no. I must take a care for my digestion, you know." Paris kept a straight face. He showed real promise.

"I see." He nodded commiseratingly. "My own health is rather uncertain." He was famously cold and wore two tunics even in summer, three or even four in winter, all under a great blanket of a toga. I think his inability to get warm was the result of perpetual fear. Like all tyrants he lived in terror of plots and poison.

Livia hovered nearby, her eyes always fixed adoringly upon her husband. I wondered if she bothered to do that when there were no witnesses.

"My husband has worn himself out in service to the state and the people," she intoned.

To my credit, I did not gag. "It seems I am here to take some of that burden upon my own aged shoulders," I said. "What might be the nature of this difficulty?"

"Ah, yes, well – esteemed Senator, you are aware of my concern for the declining morals of the citizenry, are you not?"

I said nothing, just raised my eyebrows.

"Well," he went on, "things have reached a shocking state, Senator, just shocking. The Roman family is not what it was in the days of our ancestors and the strength of character that made Rome great throughout the world has reached such a state of degeneracy that the very best of our families are dying out – yes, dying out, because our young men prefer dissipation and foreign vices to marrying and starting families!"

"How could I fail to notice?" I said. "You made that speech to the Senate last month."

"Proving, if any proof were needed, the seriousness of the problem!" Pedantic little twit.

"I hope you will not think I am boasting," I said, "but my own life has not been one of perfect probity. In fact, the words 'scandalous,' 'licentious,' and even 'degenerate' have been bandied about in company where my name was mentioned."

"That was when you were younger, Decius," Livia said. "You have acquired the respectability of venerable years. The follies of youth are quickly forgotten." The woman's political acuity was astounding.

"I have not given up the habit of folly," I told her.

"Excellent," she said, smiling. I knew then that I had said the wrong thing.

"I am sure you are aware," Octavius told me, "that the position of *Rex Sacrorum* has been vacant for some time?"

"Naturally," I said. "It's been vacant for most of my lifetime." The King of Sacrifices is a very ancient office, tremendously honorable, but surrounded by as many taboos as that of the *Flamen Dialis*. Usually, the position went to some doddering senator too old to mind the restrictions on his behavior. Such a priest rarely lasted more than a few years and then the office was vacant again.

"I had a candidate, eminently qualified, together with the concurrence of the Senate and the pontifical colleges."

"So I heard. Some jumped-up new patrician of yours, isn't he? Scandalous thing, if you ask me; making new patricians for the first time since Romulus."

The First Citizen reddened. "Decius Caecilius, you are perfectly aware that this was a measure necessary to restore the State! By ancient law many offices and priesthoods require patricians, and there were no longer enough of them to go around! In the days of Camillus there were more than a hundred patrician families. By the time of my first consulship there were no more than fourteen. Something had to be done."

"You were yourself offered that honor," Livia put in, "and your descendants."

"The *gens* Caecilia Metella has been the greatest of the plebeian families for centuries," I said peevishly. "I would not change that status. It is no honor for me and it would shame my ancestors." He began to puff up like Aesop's bullfrog but just then a significant detail penetrated my age-and-wine-fogged mind. "Your pardon, First Citizen, but did you say you 'had' a candidate for *Rex Sacrorum*? I know that one as well trained in the arts of rhetoric as you are does not employ tenses haphazardly."

"The fellow's dead," Livia said.

"Ah, now we approach the heart of the matter." I leaned forward, chin atop my cane. "Am I safe in assuming this new-minted patrician did not choke to death on an olive stone?"

"He was murdered," Octavius said, seeming almost upset by it.

"No doubt you can find a replacement," I reassured him.

"Not as easy as you might think," he muttered, "even for me. However, replacing him is not the problem. It is the murder. It is going to cause a scandal!"

This raised my eyebrows. "Not only a murder, but a scandal, eh? I do hope none of your relatives are involved." I suppose it was rather unfair of me to refer, even obliquely, to his daughter's scandalous life, but when was he ever fair to anybody?

"No, for which I render the gods due thanks. But for years now I have bent my efforts toward restoring respect for the traditional Roman family, and now this!" He smote his fist upon his bony knee in vexation.

"And now what?" I prodded.

"We think it was somebody in his family who did him in," Livia said. "His wife, perhaps, maybe a daughter or one of the other relatives. There were things about him . . . we did not know when we chose him for the position." I did not miss the significance of the "we." Octavius made few decisions without consulting her and rumor had it that he never made a move without her permission.

At last this was getting interesting. "What sort of things?"

"I will not countenance slanderous hearsay," her husband said, primly. "Such rumors may be baseless and are no better than the anonymous denunciations during the proscriptions!" What a hypocrite.

"Senator," Livia said, "you are renowned for your expertise in these things. We want you to investigate this murder and report to us."

"I see. Has a praetor been assigned?"

"Not yet," Octavius said. "Should your investigation produce evidence sufficient for a trial before a praetor's court, I assure you that all the proper forms will be respected. I am, after all, First Citizen, not Dictator." Such piety.

I rose. "The name of the unfortunate gentleman?"

"Aulus Gratidius Tubero. He was discovered dead in his house this morning." His spoiled-brat mouth twisted at the sheer impertinence of this death.

"Then as a former praetor and many times a *iudex*," I said, "I will undertake this investigation." It was mealy-mouthed of me to pretend that I was duty-bound by constitutional tradition to do as he wished. I merely did not want to admit that I did Octavius's bidding like everyone else. One could not be long in his Senate without contracting this disease of pious political hypocrisy.

Livia saw me to the door, a fine-boned hand resting on my equally bony shoulder. "Decius, you know I would never seek to influence your investigation."

I was expecting this. "What do you want?"

"My husband and I would be *most* grateful if our family were to be kept out of this dreadful mess."

Uh-oh, I thought. "Not Julia again?" Between them, Livia and Octavius had a sizable brood. Most were turning out, strangely, to be fairly decent. Tiberius and Drusus, Livia's boys by a previous marriage, were making their names as excellent soldiers. Julia was another matter. Although only nineteen years old, she was already a widow, her husband and Octavius's designated heir, Marcellus, having died a year or two previously. She had a reputation for extravagance, overweening pride and a taste for liaisons with married men. This was a bit of an embarrassment, since Octavius, in his zeal to restore Roman family values, had declared adultery a crime; a laughable concept if ever there was one.

"I'm afraid so," Livia affirmed sadly. "I fear that someone has laid her under a curse."

More likely under every bush and ceiling in Rome, I thought, wisely refraining from chuckling at her unfortunate choice of words.

"However, she is now betrothed to Vipsanius Agrippa." Her lip curled only slightly. There was venom between Livia and her husband's loyal soldier-advisor.

"Agrippa? The man's near my own age!"

"Don't be ridiculous. He's the same age as my husband. She needs a mature man who can keep her on a tight rein. This marriage is important and we can't have her embroiled in some squalid scandal."

"I'll make no promises," I said. I did not fool her. It was why she put up with my show of insolence. She knew that I would not endanger my family to save my wounded Republican pride.

"Nor would I ask you to," she said, smiling. "Your first duty is to the Senate and People." My, how the woman did love to rub it in.

As we walked from the palace Paris said, "So that's the First Citizen. He's not much to look at, is he?"

"Neither is a dagger in the back," I told him. "But you'd be foolish to ignore either one."

The house of Aulus Gratidius Tubero was situated on a slope of the Aventine overlooking the Circus Maximus. In the riots following Caesar's assassination the area had burned to the ground and a number of fine houses were built on the very desirable sites thus provided. There was a splendid view of the beautiful temple of Diana to the north. In front of the gate stood a pair of the clinking men.

"No admittance by order of *Imperator* Augustus," one of them said. So he already had them using his new title. The effect was somewhat spoiled by the man's thick, German accent.

"I am here by order of that same person," I informed him.

"Who are you?" Clearly, Livia had not bothered to send a messenger ahead.

"I may be the man who killed your grandfather when Caesar was proconsul in Gaul. Let me pass, you Teutonic ox!"

The man reddened, but the other put a hand on his shoulder. "Don't you know a senator when you see one?" This one's accent was at least Italian, although certainly not from Rome. He gave me a perfunctory if reasonably obsequious smile. "Sorry, sir, but our orders were very strict. Are you the *iudex* assigned to investigate?"

"I am. I've come here straight from the palace, but if you want to explain to the First Citizen . . ." I made to go.

"Oh, I'm sure it's all right," the Italian said hastily. "Anyone can see that you are a most distinguished gentleman."

"I should think so," I said, passing between them. Behind me I heard the German grumble something. The other said, in a low voice: "How much trouble can one old winesack of a senator cause, anyway?" Nothing wrong with my hearing, although what I hear does not always please me.

The *janitor* was chained to the gatepost in the style affected by householders who espouse unwavering adherence to ancestral practices. I've never done it in my house. My *janitor* always has a hook on the end of his chain. He attaches it to the ring on the gatepost when visitors call. This one announced me and a plump, pleasant-featured woman appeared from within.

"Welcome, Senator Metellus," she said. "I wish your visit could have been at a happier time." She was remarkably composed for a widow of such recent bereavement, but Romans have never been inclined to the sort of extravagant mourning fashionable among barbarians. We have hired mourners for all the wailing and breast-beating. Still, a tear or two might have been appropriate.

"This is such a dreadful occurrence!" she said, actually sounding quite put out. "But I do believe that the First Citizen is being too severe. Those detestable guards out there won't even let the undertaker's men come in. I mean, really! There are rites to be observed, after all!"

This was sounding worse by the minute. If nothing else, Octavius was a stickler for the religious niceties. "So the body is still on the premises?" Since she wasn't grieving heavily, I saw no reason why I should not be blunt.

She shuddered, or pretended to. "Yes, in that disgusting . . ., well, you will see."

"Then please take me there. I wish to begin my investigation with its prime object." She led me through a courtyard where household slaves stood around looking confused but dry-eyed. When even slaves can't fake a few tears you know that the departed was not a beloved master.

"I was given to understand," I said in a low voice, "that a certain person of the First Citizen's household may be involved." With such circumlocutions did we avoid saying "royal family."

"Oh, that trollop!" she hissed. At least something could rouse her to a pitch of emotion. "She and my husband . . . The things they . . . Oh!" The woman had trouble completing sentences.

Somehow, I suspected that the two had been up to more than mere dalliance. I was right.

We approached a door at the rear of the house, an area usually given over to storage, pantries, slave quarters and the kitchen. This was an unusual door, double-leaved, of massive wood construction and strapped with bronze. One leaf was slightly ajar. The smell wafting from within was not agreeable, something like the sort of blood-and-incense aroma you get at a sacrifice, only not as fresh.

"I cannot accompany you within, Senator," the woman said, primly. "It is too ghastly."

I pushed the door open. It was too dark to see much. "I need light."

Hands folded modestly before her, she turned her head and bawled like a drunken market-woman: "Leonidas! Come here and bring lamps, you lazy wretch!" So much, I thought, for Octavius's new patricians. The menial thus addressed appeared, a few others in tow, bearing lamps.

"You go in first," I said to the slave with the brightest lamp. With a look of extreme distaste, the man passed within.

Illuminated, the room was about the size of a typical triclinium although decorated in a manner rarely encountered in dining rooms. First, there was the altar. Altars are common enough in Roman houses, usually dedicated to ancestors or the guardian genius. This one was not the usual sober, square block of white marble. It was in the shape of a huge, coiled serpent, black in color, and it stood before a statue of a crocodile-headed Egyptian deity. I recalled that his name was Sobek. Like so many of those addicted to foreign cults, Tubero liked to mix them promiscuously. In a wall-niche was a bronze hand from which sprung a small human figure as well as a number of tiny animals and other symbols. It is called, I believe, a Sabazios hand, and is emblematic of some disgusting foreign sect or other. There were many other such talismans: a deformed human skull, a mummified baboon, a basket full of colorful, polished stones. Beside a brazier, now cold, stood a bronze bowl heaped with frankincense. And, of course, there was the body.

The late Aulus Gratidius Tubero lay on his back amid the considerable disarray of his toga. Upon his features sat a perfectly corpselike expression, which is to say, no expression at all. There was a great deal of blood. The whole floor was sticky with it. Whatever wound had brought about such an effusion, it was not visible. I crouched by the body, pulling up my clothes a little to keep them out of the blood. Even above the smells of blood and incense I detected the sour reek of wine.

"Remove his toga," I ordered the slaves. They just rolled their eyes fearfully. They were afraid, like most of us, of the contamination that comes of touching the dead before the proper rites are performed. I rose on creaky knees and took a handful of the incense. "I am a pontifex," I said truthfully, "and I can carry out the lustrum," lying through my remaining teeth this time. I sprinkled the yellow crystals over the body while mumbling unintelligibly. "There," I said. "He is purified. Now do as I say."

Without further protest, one of the slaves lifted the toga, rolling the corpse over on his belly. The pale back was striped with furrows like that of a chastised slave. The stripes were nearly vertical, slanting very slightly from the right buttock to the left shoulder. They formed shallow gouges and lay atop older stripes. They were not sufficient to account for all the blood. I glanced at the toga. It was liberally smeared with blood, but not soaked.

"Turn him over," I ordered. They rolled him onto his back. "Ah, here's the fatal wound," I said as the slaves backed away in horror. Tubero's genitals were entirely missing.

The soles of my sandals made sticky sounds as I examined the room in greater detail. The statue of Sobek stood upon a circular base, but the base stood upon a square patch of floor that was free of blood. I ran a hand along the Egyptian god's arm and came away with a deposit of dust. A similar test of the coiled-snake altar proved it to be clean. I left the shrine and found the wife of Gratidius standing outside.

"You found him like this?" I asked her.

"Yes," she said. "That is, the slaves located him when he was not to be found in his bed this morning." She spoke as if this were not an uncommon occurrence.

"Why did you notify the First Citizen instead of one of the praetors?"

She looked uncomfortable. "Well, because that woman was with him last night. Julia, the First Citizen's daughter."

"I see. And this was not the first time?"

"I have heard gossip. They frequented the same licentious parties. But this was the first time he brought her into *my house!*" She packed a lot of venom into those last two words.

"When did she arrive and when did she leave?"

"She arrived a little after sunset. I did not see her. I kept to my own quarters for the whole evening. I did not want to set eyes on her. It is difficult to believe that she is the child of the savior of the Republic." I had grown so accustomed to this sort of twaddle that I no longer even winced at it.

"By the way," I said, "please accept my congratulations upon your new patrician status. I do not believe your husband's tragic demise will affect that."

"You are too gracious," she said, preening.

"It is unfortunate that he never got to be invested as *Rex Sacrorum*."

"Oh, yes. That would have been a wonderful privilege." She sounded utterly indifferent. This was a distinction she would not miss. As wife of the *Rex Sacrorum* she would have endured as many taboos as he. She would have become all but a prisoner in her own house, lest she glimpse some forbidden sight, like a black dog or a man working at his trade.

"I'll take my leave now, but I wish to speak with your steward."

The man was a Greek in his middle years and I knew at once I would get little from him. He had the look of one who knew how to keep the secrets of the household. I spoke with him as he accompanied me to the door.

"Did you admit the lady Julia yesterday evening?"

"I did, Senator. That is, the porter admitted the lady and the master."

"And when did she leave?"

"I did not see her leave. I questioned the porter but he must have been asleep. I shall have him flogged soundly." Like all good and trustworthy retainers he could lie with a perfectly straight face.

"As you will. I do urge you to search your memory, though. It may be that you and the rest of the staff shall be called to testify in court, and slaves can only testify under torture."

He shrugged. "One endures what one must."

I walked away, wondering why the worst masters always seemed to have the best slaves. I have always striven to be an exemplary master, and my slaves have always been lazy good-for-nothings.

My weary feet took me back to the house on the Palatine, where the clinking men conducted me to Livia.

"I need to speak with Julia," I informed her.

"Is it truly necessary?"

"Absolutely."

"Very well then, if you must." She guided me to a wing of the sprawling but ostentatiously austere mansion where the various children of the family had their quarters. Julia sat in a spacious room, carding wool by the light of the late afternoon sun. This is what Octavius expected Roman wives to do, however high their birth. Even Livia pretended to card, spin and weave wool. I suppose she might have directed her slaves at the work, when she could spare the time.

"Julia," Livia said. "I believe you know the distinguished Senator Decius Caecilius Metellus. He is *iudex* investigating the murder of Gratidius Tubero and needs to speak with you." With that, Livia took a chair and watched me with gorgonlike intensity.

"Have we your leave, Madame?" I asked. "I would prefer to confer in privacy."

"That would not be proper," Livia insisted. "Julia is a widow of a patrician family."

"I believe my venerable years constitute sufficient chaperone."

"Not if half of what is said about your past is true." Nonetheless, she rose. "I do, however, trust your well-demonstrated sense of self preservation." She left, her spine rigid with indignation.

"It's so refreshing," Julia said, "to see someone with the nerve to defy her."

"I am old," I said. "I won't live much longer whatever I do. You, on the other hand, infuriate her regularly. You are very young and have to live in the same house with her."

"It's not courage," she said. "It's desperation." I had to sympathize. I always rather liked Julia. She was a spirited, intelligent young woman forced to adopt the false Stoicism of the Julio-Claudian house and marry for the sake of political alliances.

"You may have carried your independence a little too far this time. Gratidius Tubero is dead and you seem to be the most likely suspect. I hope you can convince me otherwise."

"How did he die?" I told her and her fair skin turned even paler.

"How may I convince you?" she asked, greatly sobered.

"First tell me about the events of last night."

"I encountered Tubero at a dinner party given by the Parthian ambassador. I'd seen him a few times before, at similar occasions. We frequent the same circles."

"The high-living set. In my youth I was fond of the same milieu. In your position it is unwise."

She shrugged. "Exile or death from boredom. Which is worse. Anyway, by nightfall we were both the worse for the wine and he urged me to come to his home to see his collection of foreign cult objects. I've taken part in some of the Mysteries . . . only the lawful ones," she added hastily. "Anyway, it seemed fascinating at the time. But the trip from the embassy to his house was a long one, and by the time we arrived I was sober enough for second thoughts. In his atrium I begged off, pleading illness. He was still very drunk and wild-eyed. Besides, I could see a woman, probably his wife, spying on us from a side room.

"So I returned home and that was all until this morning, when I found myself under virtual arrest."

I stood. "Very well, I have noted your story."

"Don't you believe me?" I could hear the desperation in her voice.

"I will take your words into consideration." A good scare would do her a world of good.

"Well?" Livia said, when I left Julia's chamber.

"I must consult with some experts. I would like to meet with you and the First Citizen at Tubero's house this evening."

"But are you satisfied that Julia had nothing to do with this sorry business?" She was almost pleading. How I loved that.

"Not yet. Will you meet with me there?"

She fumed for a while. "We will." It was good to have the upper hand with these people for a change.

I left the mansion on the Palatine and went to the houses of two of my fellow pontifexes who were far more learned than I in religious matters.

It was already dark when I reached the house of Gratidius Tubero once again. Paris carried a torch before me, overjoyed at the prospect of messing about in a murder investigation.

I found a whole crowd of metallic-sounding men in togas before the door of the house, as well as a number of lictors shouldering their *fasces*.

"You stay out here," I ordered Paris. "This business is entirely too ugly for one as young as you."

"But you've always told me that when you were my age . . ."

"Enough. Times were different then. Besides, this looks like a dangerous enough crowd to suit even you."

I went inside and found the First Citizen seated by the pool in the courtyard, along with Livia and Octavius's right-hand man, the formidably competent Marcus Vipsanius Agrippa, whose future marriage into the house depended upon the result of my investigation. The widow Gratidius stood by, looking suitably awed by the presence of so many mighty persons. A chair was thrust under me and I sank into it gratefully. I was getting rather old for these long, active days.

"I have indulged you because I know you to be efficient at this sort of work," said the First Citizen. "I trust you have reached a satisfactory conclusion."

"By 'satisfactory' I take it you mean one that clears your family of scandal?" I enjoyed the sight of his reddening face for a while, then added, "If so, be at ease. Julia didn't do it."

"What do you mean?" blurted the widow.

"Silence, woman!" Octavius barked, a little of his real nature showing through. "Explain, Senator." Relief oozed from his pores.

"Will you accompany me into the room where the murder occurred?"

He raised a hand piously. "Senator, you know quite well that, as *pontifex maximus* of Rome I may not look upon human blood. Livia is under the same rule."

"Are we going to maintain that fiction?" I said, mightily vexed. "You attend the *munera* like everyone else. Gladiators bleed rather profusely."

"Those are funeral games and therefore are religious observances. It is different," he said.

"Oh, very well," I said. "Marcus Agrippa, will you bear witness on behalf of the First Citizen?"

"I will," he said. So the two of us went into the now extremely smelly shrine while the royal couple waited just outside the door. The body was quite stiff now. A number of lamps now illuminated the grotesque scene.

"You have all heard Julia's story and I find it to be true in all relevant details."

"I knew it!" Octavius said.

"Then who killed him?" Livia demanded.

"Bear with me. How did you ever settle on such a man to be *Rex Sacrorum*?"

"Senator," Octavius said, "have you any idea how difficult it is to get *anyone* to accept that office?"

"Just so. He must have been drunk when he accepted. It seems he was often in that state. In any case, while his wife was very pleased to be promoted to patrician status, she had no interest in being the wife of the *Rex Sacrorum*."

"Then a Roman wife has murdered her husband, with the collusion of the household slaves? Infamous!" A tragedian could not have done it better.

"No!" squawked the widow.

"Much as I hate to clear that woman of anything," I said, "I fear I must tell you that she didn't do it either. In fact, there was no murder."

"This should be a good one," Agrippa said. "What happened?"

"The silly bugger did it himself."

That raised Agrippa's eyebrows. "I've heard of opening your veins, but this . . ."

"You will notice the toga. It is smeared with half-dried blood. Had the man been wearing it when the wound was inflicted, it would be soaked. The wife and servants found him here, dead and quite naked, and they wrapped him in it to make the scene marginally less bizarre."

"The blood is as described," Agrippa reported to those outside the door.

"This statue," I indicated the crocodile-headed god, "is not the one that stood here last night. Its base is round and the blood was stopped in its sticky progress by a square pedestal."

"I can confirm that," Agrippa reported.

"Now this god has a fearsome aspect with his reptilian head, but he is actually a Nile fertility god and quite benevolent. I suspect he is left over from an earlier enthusiasm of the late Tubero, who had a taste for the exotic, not to mention the unwholesome. He has a coating of dust, whereas the altar is quite clean. If you will institute a search of the house, you should find a statue of Cybele, along with certain paraphernalia associated with the worship of that goddess: cymbals, a scourge studded with knucklebones, a sickle and so forth. You may even discover the . . . ah . . . items missing from the gentleman here."

"Find them!" Livia barked. There was a rustling and clinking from without.

"Why Cybele?" the First Citizen asked.

"Allow me to wax pedantic. Almost two hundred years ago, Hannibal was still romping about in Italy. Our ancestors were frightened by a shower of stones that fell from the heavens. The Sybilline Books were consulted and it was revealed that the danger would be averted by this Phrygian goddess. From King Attalus the Senate received certain cult objects and the goddess was installed in the temple built for her on the Palatine. Hannibal was duly driven out and her worship continues to this day, but only in a decorous and lawful form.

"However," I continued, relishing this part, "there is another side to her worship; an alien, oriental and wholly disreputable side. It has long been forbidden in Rome, but it enjoys a certain vogue among those bored by the decorum of the State religion. The *Corybantes*, the ecstatic followers of the goddess in her more daemonic aspect, are noted for practicing flagellation, hence the studded scourge. In their religious transports, candidates for priesthood castrate themselves and throw their severed members upon the altar."

"Barbarous!" Octavius muttered.

"Last night poor Tubero, spurned by Julia, solaced himself with a good session of holy flagellation. You notice the whip marks? They are almost vertical, quite unlike the horizontal and diagonal stripes one sees when a slave is whipped by a second party. This is because Tubero was lashing himself, slinging the thongs over his left shoulder."

"That's what it looks like," Agrippa affirmed.

"I suspect that Tubero was a man who liked these private games. He allowed fantasy to become reality. In any case, having drunk himself silly and then inflamed his senses with the dubious pleasures of self-flagellation, he performed the final rite. He probably intended merely to mime the actions. After all, the lack of an audience would deprive the ritual of half the fun. But he was not in a steady state of mind and he went too far. The expression on his face when he realized what he was holding must have been worth seeing. This was not a conventional orgy of Cybele, so no one was there to stanch the blood and he perished."

"Disgusting!" Octavius shouted. "And to implicate my family!" The widow was already bawling and begging for mercy. Nobody paid any attention.

"Actually," I said, "it was rather clever. Julia had conveniently placed herself on the scene, and everyone knows what a stickler you are for the purity of Roman family life. The woman did not want it to come out that her husband, the new-minted patrician, was an idiotic loon. She figured that, by implicating Julia, she would trick you into covering up the whole squalid mess."

"To suspect me of such perfidy! I'll search the law tables until I find a charge under which she can be executed!" The woman blubbered even more vociferously.

"That would mean a court trial," Livia pointed out. "You don't want your name associated with such a squalid mess. There was no murder and trying to put one over on you doesn't really constitute treason. You are *pontifex maximus*. Charge her with some sort of sacrilege – desecration of a corpse or something. Exile her to one of those dreadful little islands we keep for the ones we can't condemn to death."

"If you say so, my dear," Octavius grumbled. "It's better than the treacherous bitch deserves."

"You've never seen those islands," I told him.

We left the house amid much wailing, the formidable escort all around us. Octavius placed a hand on my shoulder. "I can't tell you how grateful I am, Decius Caecilius. You really must accept a promotion to the patricianship."

Another hand came to rest on my other shoulder. "Decius," Livia purred, "we *truly* need a new *Rex Sacrorum*."

I closed my eyes wearily. "I don't suppose you have another of those islands handy?"

These things happened in the year 734 of the city of Rome, during the unconstitutional dictatorship of Caius Octavius, surnamed Augustus.

THE
THREE TRAVELLERS
R. L. Stevens

It is not the best-kept secret that R. L. Stevens is a pen name of Edward Hoch (b. 1930), probably the most prolific writer of mystery short stories, of which he has published over seven hundred. Most of them fall into one of a number of series. The following story, though, is a neat one-off, set at one of the most auspicious moments in history. After all, if one of the Three Wise Men couldn't double as a detective, who could?

Now the three had journeyed several days when at last they came upon the Oasis of Ziza, and Gaspar who was the wisest of them said, "We will rest our horses here this night. It will be safe."

"Safe for horses and men," Melchior agreed. "But what of the gold?"

"Safe for the gold also. No one knows we carry it."

The sun was low in the western sky as they approached, and Gaspar held up a hand to shield his eyes. It would be night soon.

A young herdsman came out to meet them and take their horses. And he said, "Welcome to the Oasis of Ziza. Have you ridden far?"

"A full moon's journey," Gaspar replied, speaking in the nomadic tongue. "What is your name?"

And the herdsman answered, "They call me Ramoth, sire."

"Here is a gold coin for you, Ramoth. Feed and water our mounts for the journey and another will be yours on the morrow."

"Which way do you travel, sire?"

"Towards the west," Gaspar said, purposely vague.

When the young herdsman had departed with the horses, fat Balthazar said, "I am not pleased, Gaspar. You lead us, it is true, but the keeping of the gold is my responsibility. And travellers guided by the heavens would do well to journey by night."

"The desert is cold by night, my friend. Let us cease this bickering and settle ourselves here till the dawn."

Then Melchior and Balthazar went off to put up their tent, and Gaspar was much relieved. It had been a long journey, not yet ended, and he treasured these moments alone. Presently he set off to inspect the oasis where they would spend the night, and he came upon a stranger who wore a sword at his waist.

"Greetings, traveller," the man said. "I am Nevar, of the northern tribe. Do you journey this route often?"

"Not often, no. My name is Gaspar and I come with my two companions from the east."

Nevar nodded, and stroked his great growth of beard. "Later, when the sun is gone, there are games of chance – and women for those who have the gold to pay."

"That does not interest me," Gaspar said.

"You will find the companionship warming," Nevar said. "Come to the fire near the well. That is where we will be."

Gaspar went on, pausing to look at the beads and trinkets the nomad traders offered. When he reached the well at the far end of the oasis, he saw a woman lifting a great earthen jar to her shoulder. She was little more than a child, and as he watched, the jar slipped from her grasp and shattered against the stones, splashing her with water. She burst into tears.

"Come, child," Gaspar said, comforting her. "There is always another jar to be had."

And she turned her wide brown eyes to him, revealing a beauty he had not seen before. "My father will beat me," she said.

"Here is a gold coin for him. Tell him a stranger named Gaspar bumped you and made the jar break."

"That would not be true."

"But it is true that I am Gaspar. Who are you?"

"Thantia, daughter of Nevar."

"Yes, I have met your father. You are very lovely, my child."

But his words seemed to frighten her, and she ran from him.

Then he returned to the place where Melchior had erected their tent. They had learned from past encampments to leave nothing of value with the horses, and Gaspar immediately asked the location of the gold.

"It is safe," Balthazar told him. "Hidden in the bottom of this grain bag."

"Good. And the perfume?"

"With our regular supplies. No one would steal that."

Melchior chuckled. "If they did, we could smell out the culprits quickly enough!"

And then Balthazar said, "There is gaming tonight, near the well."

"I know," Gaspar replied. "But it is not for us."

The fat man held out his hands in a gesture of innocence. "We could but look," he said.

And Gaspar reluctantly agreed. "Very well."

Later, when the fire had been kindled and the people of Ziza came forth from their tents to mingle, the three travellers joined them. Almost at once Gaspar was sought out by a village elder, a man with wrinkled skin and rotting teeth. "I am Dibon," he said, choosing a seat next to Gaspar. "Do you come from the east?"

"Yes, from Persia."

"A long journey. What brings you this far?"

Gaspar did not wish to answer. Instead, he motioned towards a group of men with small smooth stones before them. "What manner of sport is this?"

"It is learned from the Egyptians, as are most things sinful." Then the old man leaned closer, and Gaspar could smell the foul odour of his breath. "Some say you are a magus."

"I have studied the teachings of Zoroaster, as have my companions. In truth some would consider me a magus."

"Then you journey in search of Mazda?"

"In search of truth," Gaspar replied.

Then he felt the presence of someone towering over him, and saw it was the figure of Nevar. His right hand rested on the sword at his waist. "I would have words with you, Gaspar."

"What troubles you?"

"My only daughter Thantia, a virgin not yet twenty, tells me you gave her a gold coin today."

"Only because I feared the broken water jug was my fault."

"No stranger approaches Thantia! You will leave Ziza this night!"

"We leave in the morning," Gaspar said quietly.

Nevar drew his sword, and Gaspar waited no longer. He flung himself at the big man and they tumbled towards the fire as the game-players scattered. Gaspar pulled Nevar's sword from his grip.

Then Thantia broke from the crowd, running to her father.

"This stranger did me no harm!" she cried out.

"Silence, daughter!" Nevar reached for a piece of burning firewood and hurled it at Gaspar, but it went wide of its mark and landed on a low straw roof nearby.

"The stable!" someone shouted, and Gaspar saw it was the herdsman Ramoth hurrying to rescue the horses. The others helped to quench the flames with water from the well, but not before a quantity of feed and supplies had been destroyed.

Then Gaspar and Melchior went in search of fat Balthazar, who had disappeared during the commotion. They found him behind the row of tents, playing the Egyptian stone game with a half dozen desert riders. He had a small pile of gold coins before him.

"This must cease!" Gaspar commanded.

The nomads ran at his words, and Balthazar struggled to his feet. "It was merely a game."

"Our task is far more important than mere gaming," Gaspar reminded him, and the fat man looked sheepish. "While you idled I was near killed by the swordsman Nevar."

"A trouble-maker," Balthazar agreed. "I will not rest easy until Ziza is behind us on our journey."

Then as they passed the burned stable on the way to their tent, old Dibon approached them saying, "This ruin is your fault, Gaspar. Yours and Nevar's."

"That is true, old man. We will stay here tomorrow and help rebuild the stable."

Dibon bowed his head. "A generous offer. We thank you."

But when they were alone, Balthazar complained, "This will delay us an entire day!"

"We will travel a distance by night, as you wished."

Now another surprise was waiting at their tent. As Melchior raised the flap to enter, there was a whimper from within. Gaspar pushed past his hesitating companion and lit the oil lamp. By its glow they saw the girl Thantia crouched behind a pile of robes.

"Please!" she gasped. "Please hide me. My father has beaten me and I fear for my life!"

"I fear for ours if he finds you here," Melchior said.

Gaspar held the oil lamp closer and saw the bruises on her face and arms. "We cannot send you back to him. Remain here with Melchior and Balthazar. I will return shortly."

Then he made his way to the place where old Dibon rested, and he told the elder what had happened. Dibon nodded and said, "My daughter and her husband will find room for Thantia until Nevar regains his senses. You were wise to come to me."

Gaspar and his companions delivered the girl to Dibon, and went with them to the dwelling place of Dibon's daughter. Later, in their tent, Balthazar grumbled again about the delayed departure. But they settled down at last to sleep, as the fires of the encampment burned low around them.

In the morning, by the first rays of the rising sun, Gaspar was awakened by Balthazar's panic-filled voice. "Wake quickly, Gaspar!" he pleaded, shaking him. "Someone has stolen our gold!"

Gaspar saw at once that the words were true.

The leather sack of grain contained only grain now. Though the tent showed no sign of forced entry, and though their regular supplies were untouched, the gold had vanished.

"I cannot believe it!" Melchior gasped. "How could a thief have entered while we slept?"

Gaspar agreed such a thing was impossible. "The gold was stolen before we retired last night," he reasoned. "We were away from the tent during the gaming and fire, and again while escorting Thantia. A thief could have entered at either time."

"What of the perfume and incense?" Melchior asked.

"Untouched," Balthazar said. "My special knot is still in place on the other bags."

"Only the gold," Gaspar mused.

"It is truly as if someone knew where to look."

"The girl!" Balthazar exclaimed. "We found her in here! She could have searched for the gold and found it."

"Possible," Gaspar admitted. "But I cannot bring myself to believe it."

"We cannot leave Ziza without the gold," Melchior said.

"Let us put our minds to the problem while we work at the stable," Gaspar said.

Now when they reached the stable Nevar was already there, toiling with the others. He paused in his labours when he saw the three, and shot an accusing finger at Gaspar. "You have stolen away my daughter. I will revenge myself!"

"Your daughter is safe, in the care of Dibon and his family."

His words quieted Nevar, but Melchior asked, "If he was so concerned, why did he not come after us in the night?"

Balthazar agreed. "Or did he come, and steal our gold away?"

Then presently old Dibon appeared, with the girl Thantia at his side. She cast not a glance in her father's direction, and he went about his work ignoring her. Gaspar laboured diligently through the morning, instructing Dibon and the others in Persian building techniques. He too ignored Nevar, not wanting more trouble.

Once, while Balthazar was off to the well for water, Melchior whispered, "Is it possible that our companion betrays us, Gaspar?

Might he have stolen the gold himself to cover his losses at the stone game?"

But Gaspar would hear none of it. "We must never doubt each other, Melchior. In my heart I know Balthazar is innocent, as I know you are innocent. And I remember the scene at the stone game. There were gold coins in front of him. He was winning, not losing."

"How will we recover the gold, Gaspar?"

"Through the power of our minds, Melchior. We are wise men, and we must use our minds to determine the thief's identity."

"But there is no clue to his identity!"

"Sometimes the lack of a clue can be one."

Balthazar returned with the water and they drank eagerly. Later as they ate of their supplies, Thantia came to them. "I thank you for helping me," she said. "The elders have spoken to my father and he has promised never again to beat me. I will return to him now.'

"We need no thanks," Gaspar assured her.

Then old Dibon came to join them. "How may we repay you for your work on the stable?"

"You may recover our stolen gold," Balthazar blurted out.

"Gold? Stolen gold?"

"It was stolen from our tent," Balthazar hurried on, before Gaspar could silence him.

"There are no thieves in Ziza!"

"There is one."

"I will summon the elders. We will search for your gold."

"No, no," said Gaspar. "We will recover it."

"But how?"

"By finding the thief. It is best to say nothing and catch him off guard."

Old Dibon bowed his head. "I will do as you suggest."

"One favour. Could you ask that our horses be brought to us? We must appear to be leaving."

Then, as they waited, Balthazar gathered their supplies. And Melchior said, "I have put my mind to the problem, Gaspar. But there are too many possibilities. The girl Thantia could be the thief, or her father Nevar. Or any of the game players."

"Or old Dibon himself," Balthazar added. "There are too many to suspect."

Gaspar nodded. "What is needed is an oracle."

"You mean to kill a beast as the Romans do?"

Gaspar shook his head. "My oracle will be a living animal." He saw the herdsman Ramoth leading their horses. "My steed will tell me who has our gold."

"Your horse?" fat Balthazar laughed. "Who learns anything from a dumb animal?"

Gaspar held out some grain for the horse. "You see how he eats? He is hungry."

"What does that tell us?" Melchior asked.

"That our gold was stolen by Ramoth!"

Then presently old Dibon appeared, with the girl Thantia at his side. She cast not a glance in her father's direction, and he went about his work ignoring her. Gaspar laboured diligently through the morning, instructing Dibon and the others in Persian building techniques. He too ignored Nevar, not wanting more trouble.

Once, while Balthazar was off to the well for water, Melchior whispered, "Is it possible that our companion betrays us, Gaspar? Might he have stolen the gold himself to cover his losses at the stone game?"

But Gaspar would hear none of it. "We must never doubt each other, Melchior. In my heart I know Balthazar is innocent, as I know you are innocent. And I remember the scene at the stone game. There were gold coins in front of him. He was winning, not losing."

"How will we recover the gold, Gaspar?"

"Through the power of our minds, Melchior. We are wise men, and we must use our minds to determine the thief's identity."

"But there is no clue to his identity!"

"Sometimes the lack of a clue can be one."

Balthazar returned with the water and they drank eagerly. Later as they ate of their supplies, Thantia came to them. "I thank you for helping me," she said. "The elders have spoken to my father and he has promised never again to beat me. I will return to him now."

"We need no thanks," Gaspar assured her.

Then old Dibon came to join them. "How may we repay you for your work on the stable?"

"You may recover our stolen gold," Balthazar blurted out.

"Gold? Stolen gold?"

"It was stolen from our tent," Balthazar hurried on, before Gaspar could silence him.

"There are no thieves in Ziza!"

"There is one."

"I will summon the elders. We will search for your gold."

"No, no," said Gaspar. "We will recover it."

"But how?"

"By finding the thief. It is best to say nothing and catch him off guard."

Old Dibon bowed his head. "I will do as you suggest."

"One favour. Could you ask that our horses be brought to us? We must appear to be leaving."

Then, as they waited, Balthazar gathered their supplies. And Melchior said, "I have put my mind to the problem, Gaspar. But there are too many possibilities. The girl Thantia could be the thief, or her father Nevar. Or any of the game players."

"Or old Dibon himself," Balthazar added. "There are too many to suspect."

Gaspar nodded. "What is needed is an oracle."

"You mean to kill a beast as the Romans do?"

Gaspar shook his head. "My oracle will be a living animal." He saw the herdsman Ramoth leading their horses. "My steed will tell me who has our gold."

"Your horse?" fat Balthazar laughed. "Who learns anything from a dumb animal?"

Gaspar held out some grain for the horse. "You see how he eats? He is hungry."

"What does that tell us?" Melchior asked.

"That our gold was stolen by Ramoth!" It was after Dibon spoke to Ramoth that the young herdsman confessed his crime and begged forgiveness. When the missing gold had been returned to Gaspar's hands, the others questioned him.

"How did you know it was Ramoth?" Melchior asked. "We barely spoke to the youth."

"My horse told me, as I told you he would. The horse was hungry, so had not been fed. You see, the thief never touched our other supplies, never unfastened Balthazar's special knot. How could he have found the gold so easily, without searching for it? But the gold was hidden in a sack of grain, and after the fire destroyed the stable, Ramoth came in search of feed for our horses. He came while we were away, and looked in only one place – the grain bag. Feeling the weight of it, his fingers reached through the grain and came upon the gold. He stole it, but then could not take the grain lest we realize he was the thief. So the horses went hungry."

"You are a wise man, Gaspar," Balthazar conceded.

"As we all are. Come, let us mount."

"It will be dark soon," Melchior said.

Gaspar nodded. "We will get bearings from the star."

Dibon was by the well to wish them farewell. "Ramoth will be punished," he promised.

"Show mercy," Gaspar said.

"Do you ride west with your gold?"

"West with gifts for a King. Gold and frankincense and myrrh."

"Good journey," Dibon said.

He watched them for a long time, until the three vanished from sight over the desert wastes.

THE CASE OF THE MURDERED SENATOR
Wallace Nichols

Wallace Nichols (1888–1967) is really the grandfather of the Roman detective story. His series about Sollius, the Slave Detective, began in the pages of the London Mystery Magazine *in 1950 and ran for over sixty stories. I reprinted the first two stories in the last volume. For the current selection, I've jumped over one story to present the fourth in the series, first published in the October 1950 issue.*

I

Gaius Sempronius Platorius was a tribune in the Danubian army. He had won promotion early in the frontier wars of the Empire, and had the reputation of being a young man of valour and headstrong character. He was a rake and a gambler – but all the Roman frontier officers were gamblers: what else could they do with their spare time in the wilds?

Now he was on a well-earned leave, and on his way to Rome. His great friend, a fellow officer named Torquatus, had left camp two days ahead of him, and they had promised themselves a festive meeting in Rome. Platorius had been away for six years, and wondered how he would be received in his father's house. He knew how he intended to be received if it lay in his power or determination to secure his rightful position there. He was a youth no longer, but a man of experience. The legions respected him. The Emperor himself had spoken approvingly of his service.

Would it be best, after all, to let bygones be bygones? He knew that in the past he had been an unsatisfactory son – but that was no reason why he should be ousted from his father's will by an adopted stepson: though it might be legal, it was against nature, and, as the son of his father's body, he stood for the rights of nature rather than for those of mere legality.

He did not feel forgiving towards his father, and certainly he felt enmity towards Quintus, the son of the second wife, and whom his father had made his heir. And to be heir to Sempronius the Senator was to be the heir to great wealth. Platorius was not reconciled to the loss of his patrimony; nevertheless, he was riding homeward with a certain sardonic pleasure in the situation, and as the milestones to Rome were notched off in his reckoning, he went over carefully in his mind what he intended to do.

Thus brooding and planning, he rode down Italy, and came one evening to the final resting-place before the last few miles to Rome. It was a ramshackle inn, but he had occupied worse quarters many a time during his military life, and he shrugged his shoulders with cynical indifference. He had ridden a certain distance beyond the usual posting-inn, a far superior hostelry in all respects, but this dark, lonely and lesser inn suited his requirements very well. It was some hours nearer to Rome.

He reached it at twilight, and saw to his horse's stabling the first thing.

"You have another traveller?" he asked, surprise in his tone, and pointing to a second horse in the stable, a riding-horse, and not the usual heavy farm-horse such as might have been expected there.

"No traveller," gruffly replied the innkeeper, "only his horse. He left it yesterday, and is visiting, I suppose," he added, with a leer, "some woman in a villa hereabouts. He will be back to claim it. 'Tis naught to me. I ha' been paid for stall and fodder – and if he never returns I have a horse that'll fetch a fine price anywhere. I know a good horse when I see it. I shall lose naught either way."

He tapped his nose with a fore-finger, and they returned indoors. Platorius ate a rough meal, and then pleaded fatigue, and was shown by the landlord to an uncomfortable bed. He was the only guest staying the night; the inn's other frequenters were but an itinerant thief and an old vagabond, and a few farm-slaves from the neighbourhood, and none of these remained for long after the full falling of the dark. It was not an inn of much evening custom, but rather a daylight halt for muleteers and country wagoners making to and from the Roman markets. Platorius congratulated himself.

He slept late – assuredly he had ridden far during the previous twelve hours – and had to be roused by the landlord. After a swift meal, he rode away. While saddling his horse he had noticed that the other horse was still in the stable. He had gone to its stall and patted its flank. He loved horses. It was a well-bred bay, and like an army horse.

He did not hurry himself on that last stage of his long journey. Perhaps he was a little uneasy, now that the time for his unexpected home-coming drew near – unexpected because he had deliberately sent no word of his intention. He had meant to surprise his father: in surprise should lie the best augury for success. He spun out his ride now rather than pressed it, and arrived at his father's great Roman house some little time after midday.

It was not at all the kind of home-coming that any man would ordinarily expect, for he found a crowd surging about the gates, and the house itself in a turmoil, with weeping slaves and a distraught step-mother. His father had been murdered during the night, and Quintus, the adopted son, had already been accused.

II

"It is terrible, terrible, Valeria; I have no words for it," said Titius Sabinus. "Is there anything I can do?"

The widow of Sempronius, who was also Sabinus's cousin, hesitated, and stared at him with a hard, tearless gaze, and her face was white and drawn.

"Your slave Sollius . . ." she breathed. "I wondered, Titius, whether . . . I know that my son did not do it, but everyone is convinced that he did! Perhaps your clever Sollius could discover the murderer?"

"Of course, Valeria, of course," Sabinus fussily assured her, a little put out of his stride by having his own offer of his astute slave forestalled. "I will send for him, and you shall take him back with you."

And so it came about that Sollius found himself committed to investigating the murder of his master's fellow senator, Sempronius. He did not relish the task. He felt that he had no standing, and did not see how he, a slave, could interrogate with any kind of authority those whom he might wish to question. It had been different when he had been employed as an investigator by the Emperor; he had then possessed powers. But now he was nothing more than a slave lent by his own master to the household of the lady Valeria.

He found the house of the murdered man in the occupation of soldiers from one of the Urban Cohorts, with the City Prefect there in person, for Sempronius had been an important man.

It was a lucky chance that one of the soldiers at the door recognized him and knew of his reputation as a solver of mysteries. This soldier, who was named Gratianus, stepped forward and barred his entrance.

"This slave attends me," said Valeria haughtily.

"I am not forbidding him entrance, lady," answered the soldier. "I wish, with your leave, but a word with him."

"Come to me as soon as you are allowed," said Valeria, turning to Sollius and ignoring the other. "A domestic shall be in wait for you."

She passed in through the portico, a hard-eyed, silent Fury. Gratianus made a grimace, and then caught Sollius by the arm.

"Why are you here?" he whispered. "Is she employing you . . . to save young Quintus? I doubt if he is innocent. The evidence against him is very strong."

"My master has lent me to the lady Valeria," replied Sollius, shrugging his shoulders, "and I must do what I can. I must do even nothing – if nothing, as you hint, is all I can do! – with the proper diligence and energy."

He smiled disarmingly and took a step towards the portico, but the other still had a hand on his arm, and restrained him.

"Listen," said Gratianus in a low tone. "The Prefect in yonder is not too happy. Young Quintus is his son's friend. He would be glad if a flaw could be found in the evidence, and who would find it – if a flaw there is – better than you? Shall I tell him you are here? He will know of you, for did you not give evidence about those treasury thefts before him in the secret enquiry about it? I was there on duty, and heard you."

"I remember," answered Sollius, and rubbed his chin, and then he said: "I should be most grateful, Gratianus, if you would tell the Prefect of the City why I am here."

The soldier released him, clapped him on the back, and motioned him to go forward. Sollius entered the house with a feeling of relief. He would be able to ask his questions after all. But apparently it was no light task that had been forced upon him, and a touch of uneasy despair in his thoughts made his limp more than usually noticeable. A domestic, as had been promised, was waiting for him in the atrium, and led him at once into a lofty, ornate chamber where the lady Valeria was seated on a Greek couch, with a youngish man standing before her. Believing that this was her accused son, Sollius took good note of him. He saw a tall, rather hard-bitten man, who seemed older in experience than in years; he was dark, with a long face, a predatory nose, and thin, decisive lips, and he was clean-shaven. He stood, thought Sollius, like a soldier.

"This is my stepson," announced Valeria, "my husband's son. It is a sad beginning to his leave from the frontier."

"I arrived," said Platorius, "to find my father – murdered. I have not been home for over six years, and now it hardly seems a home-coming at all."

Sollius murmured his sympathy, and looked from one to the other in turn.

"I have told my stepson about your cleverness in solving mysterious happenings," said Valeria, "and that you have been lent to us by Titius Sabinus to help clear my son from the ridiculous accusation against him."

Sollius bowed, and looked at Platorius.

"My name," said the latter, "is Gaius Sempronius Platorius, and I am my father's true son; Quintus was not only his stepson, but his adopted son. It is as well to get these family relationships clear," he added with a smile.

"The more I am told at first," replied Sollius, deceptively meek in manner, "the better I can measure what I may learn afterwards. But I cannot do anything until you tell me the circumstances of the murder."

"I myself can tell you nothing," said Platorius. "All, alas, had happened before I arrived home. Had I been here," he added, a fierce note entering his voice, "I would have marked the villain with his own blood, by the gods!"

"Do you mean you would have marked the lord Quintus? Do you suspect the lord Quintus yourself?" asked Sollius.

Taken aback at the slave's uncompromising directness, Platorius answered that he had meant the murderer, whoever he was.

"I know nothing at all," he continued. "I have no evidence to give, and therefore can have no suspicions of anyone – and certainly I do not suspect Quintus. The accusation can only be some official blunder: it is entirely unbelievable!"

"What points to him?" asked Sollius, turning to Valeria.

"My husband, who was ever a poor sleeper," she narrated, "always rose very early, often before dawn, and would go either into his library, when he might summon a slave to read to him, or, if it was warm weather, into the garden. Last night – but it would have been to-day, and before sunrise," she interjected mournfully – "he left his bed as usual, but since I was myself still asleep I did not hear him go. I was only awakened, indeed, by the clamour when he was found. I was then fetched by Cleander, my husband's Greek reading-slave, and he told me . . ."

Sollius had no compunction about interrupting her.

"Could I speak with this Cleander?" he asked. "Evidence at second hand, lady, is less valuable than a man's own remembrance of what he saw and heard."

"My stepmother can be trusted to tell the truth," burst out Platorius.

"To tell the truth about what she herself witnessed," said Sollius quietly. "But Cleander may have deceived her as to what *he* witnessed. He may even have reported – in quite good faith – mistakenly. I can only judge his reliability by hearing him tell his own tale himself. Will you, lady, send for him?"

"What, slave, you would give orders here?" cried Platorius.

"Peace, Gaius," said his stepmother. "He is more here than just a slave. The Emperor himself has employed him to unravel such things. I will send for Cleander. Dorica!" she called.

A female slave ran swiftly and quietly in.

"Send Cleander hither!" commanded her mistress, speaking in Greek, and the slave-girl, who was little more than a child, ran out again as swiftly and quietly as she had entered.

("A little Ægean dove . . ." thought Sollius to himself.)

"Is your son under arrest?" he asked aloud.

"He is still being questioned," answered Valeria. "The Prefect of the City now has come himself: the first questioning was by a subordinate, and he accused my son to his face. But here is Cleander . . ."

The Greek's story was that his master had aroused him and bidden him come to the library to read aloud to him. As soon as he was dressed, he had gone to the library as instructed. That chamber opened on to a small pillared portico which led directly into the garden. Not finding his master seated in the usual place, he had crossed to this portico to see if he had stepped out into the garden, and in the dim light, for only a small lamp was burning in the chamber, he had stumbled over his master's body, lying across the two or three shallow marble steps that led down to a statued terrace. Over the body, drawing a legionary's short stabbing-sword from a deep wound in the side, was leaning the young lord Quintus, and not only was he drawing the sword from the gash, but he was also smeared with blood on the front of his tunic. He seemed overcome with horror, and Cleander, unable to obtain a coherent statement from him, had at once aroused the household. He knew no more.

Sollius put no questions, and Cleander was dismissed.

"Did your son, lady, give you an explanation of his being found in such suspicious circumstances?" the slave detective then asked.

"Only that he had himself found his father stabbed with the sword, and at the point of death."

"And the sword?" asked Sollius. "Was it your husband's sword, or your son's – or the weapon of some unknown person?"

"It was my son's own sword," murmured Valeria, white to the lips, but with her head high, nevertheless.

Before Sollius could answer her, one of the apparitors attending the Prefect of the City entered without ceremony and addressed himself to the slave:

"His Excellency wishes to see you," he said, "and has sent me for you."

Sollius bowed to the lady Valeria, and followed the apparitor to another part of the house and into the dead man's library. Three men stood there on the threshold of the portico leading into the air: the Prefect himself in full, gleaming military garb; a subordinate, also in soldier's uniform, and a young man, pale, distraught, whose fashionable attire was disordered and streaked with dried blood. The Prefect came forward at once to speak in low tones to Sollius.

"I cannot tell you," he said, "how relieved I am at this good fortune. I know your skill, slave, and never was it more needed to save the innocent. I have no other course than to arrest the young man, for everything points to his guilt – I say, points to it, but there is no proof, and I cannot believe that he did it. But unless it is proved that he did *not* do it, I must give him to the law and condemn him myself. By the godhead of Cæsar, it is horrible!"

"You have questioned the young man?" asked Sollius.

"Examined and cross-examined him, statement by statement, three times over. It is always the same tale – a damning tale unless we can see it in some other light, and so be led to another culprit, at present only too well hidden. Will you question him yourself?"

"I was hoping to be allowed to do so, Excellency."

The Prefect smiled briefly, and led the way back to the two whom he had left.

"Tell your tale again," he commanded, addressing the young man whom Sollius took to be the accused.

"It is no tale, Prefect!" replied Quintus, but his tone was weary and sullen rather than defiant.

"Your Excellency's pardon," put in Sollius, "but might I question him instead of listening to what will now, true or not, be already a set story?"

"As you will," answered the Prefect, a puzzled note in his voice, though whether from his being so curtly overruled, or from a genuine sense of surprise in the procedure, none of them there could tell.

The young man stared at the slave, and the slave at the young man.

"Who is this?" demanded Quintus.

"Your questioner," snapped the Prefect, re-establishing his personal authority over Quintus and Sollius alike.

Quintus turned haggard and bloodshot eyes upon the slave, and with a sigh of exasperated acquiescence, signed to him to begin.

"You were the first, lord, to find your stepfather's body?"

"I was."

"You had come from your chamber? So early?"

"I was entering the house – from outside."

"Through this portico?"

"I have entered the house this way many times. It was quite usual."

"Had you been out all night?"

Quintus hesitated a moment before replying, and then his reply was simply a curt nod.

"A love-affair?" asked Sollius.

He liked the young man, who was handsome, upstanding, and with crisply curling chestnut hair, and had smiled at him as he spoke.

"I am not a boy," cried Quintus, flushing angrily. "And what has my being out at night to do with my stepfather's murder?"

"It might be," suggested Sollius, "that your stepfather had caught you on your return, that a quarrel had arisen, and that in the heat of it you had struck him down."

"It was not so," replied Quintus hotly. "I found him already dying. He died, in fact, as I drew the sword from the wound," he added, and his face puckered with grief, and he turned away his head to conceal a sudden gush of tears.

Sollius could not logically have explained why he went on with his questioning more hopefully:

"I am told that it was your own sword which had been used. Can you account for that?"

"Yesterday," answered Quintus, "I was on duty at a parade before the Augustus, and on my return home my stepfather asked me to work with him over some accounts. He was impatient to begin at once. I flung my sword, my helmet and my cloak in the corner yonder: the cloak and helmet – see! – are there still. The sword was taken – and used . . . Perhaps my stepfather, disturbing a thief, caught it up, was disarmed – and slain by the very weapon which he had taken for his defence."

"You could still have used the same weapon – and in precisely that way – yourself," put in the Prefect.

Quintus sighed deeply, and spread out his hands.

"Excellency, I did not!" he reaffirmed, and his tone was deep and earnest, and again Sollius felt that he believed him.

"The killer," said Sollius, "could have gone but a short time before you arrived. Did you catch no glimpse of him – of one fleeing? Or hear any sound?"

Quintus shook his head.

"Has anything been stolen?"

"Nothing," answered the Prefect, "or so I am informed."

"It is true," said Quintus.

"Your innocence being, for the moment, assumed," went on Sollius, "have you any suspicion as to the murderer?"

"I am wholly bewildered," replied Quintus. "I know of no one who was his enemy. If it was some thief, he escaped. It is incredible that anyone of the household could be such a villain."

"Except yourself," commented Sollius dryly.

"I know myself better than my accusers do!" flung back Quintus. "Were I told that I had done it in sleepwalking, I should not believe it: even my unconscious spirit is incapable of injuring a single hair of his head! I loved him."

Sollius gave him a long look, and then intimated to the Prefect that he had no further questions to put.

"Take the prisoner away!" commanded the Prefect.

III

"You see," began the Prefect when he and Sollius were alone, "everything – except his own character – points to his guilt, and there is no alternative suspicion. And yet I believe him innocent."

"Let us have open minds," said Sollius. "Let us attack the problem, not from the angle of our wishes – for I, too, I confess it, would like to see the young man cleared – but from that of how the murder was committed. With a sword, certainly; and with the young man's sword: he admits it. Let us suppose that it was as he said, and that the sword, as yonder still the military cloak and the helmet, lay in the room ready for the attacker. That argues one thing at least: that the murder was improvised, that the attacker had not come armed for the purpose, but took the first weapon that he found to his hand."

"Go on," encouraged the Prefect.

"The killing, then, would be after a quarrel, a killing in haste and on the spur of the moment."

"That is how I myself had argued," said the Prefect, "and it points once again to the young man: for who else, coming home late, and so dubiously, was more likely to be the recipient of angry reproaches?"

Sollius suddenly beat his hands against his brow.

"Dolt, dolt that I am!" he cried. "Of course, there was no quarrel: there was no time for a quarrel. Cleander would have interrupted it before there was time for it to blaze so high. No, no; there was no quarrel: the killer came to kill, and killed at first sight."

"If that were so," argued the Prefect, "why did he not come provided with his own sword?"

"Perhaps he did," breathed Sollius, "but seeing the other to his hand, preferred to use it – and to leave it as evidence against – the lord Quintus?"

The Prefect began pacing slowly about.

"It was no thief," he murmured, "unless Cleander disturbed him."

"Who has a grudge against the lord Quintus?" asked Sollius.

"Nobody, I should think," replied the Prefect. "He is the pleasantest young man you could meet. My son is devoted to him, a Damon to his Pytheas."

Sollius coughed.

"Are the two stepbrothers a Damon and a Pytheas?" he asked quietly.

The Prefect halted abruptly in his pacing about, and swung round.

"Do you know the position here between the two: the son by nature and the son by adoption?"

"My master explained it to me before I came," replied Sollius, and the two looked at one another.

"Gaius Platorius was not here," said the Prefect. "He arrived well after the discovery of the murder."

He began pacing about again.

"Sir, could his itinerary be checked?" whispered Sollius.

"It will have to be checked," the Prefect answered with a sigh. "You can leave that to me. When it is done, I will send for you. In the meantime," he added, laying a hand on the slave's shoulder, "learn what you can from the lady Valeria and from Cleander. I recommend the interrogation of Cleander particularly to you! You have authority to come and go and question as you will. I am grateful for your help: we must clear the lord Quintus if we can. Meanwhile I shall confine him to his own chamber with a strong guard. Farewell!"

IV

Sollius returned to the apartment where the lady Valeria had received him, and found her still there with her stepson.

"What did the Prefect have to say to you?" she asked eagerly. "Is my son released?"

"The lord Quintus, lady, is under guard in his own chamber."

"Can I see him?"

"No, lady."

"Why not? What did the Prefect say?"

"He let me question the lord Quintus in his presence. At the moment, lady, there is nothing to do but to await the result of an enquiry to be made by the Prefect – an enquiry, lady, which should be in favour of your son."

"What enquiry is that?" asked Platorius in the tone of a Roman officer speaking to a Gallic or Pannonian auxiliary.

"Only the Prefect, sir, can answer you that," said Sollius.

"How, slave! You dispute my command?"

"Peace, Gaius," murmured Valeria.

"It is an impertinence!" cried Platorius. "How dare a slave speak to me like that?"

"This slave is different, Gaius," said Valeria. "I told you so."

"A slave is a slave!" answered Platorius, and disgustedly turned away; nevertheless, Sollius noticed, he seemed to listen with a fully attentive ear to what followed.

"Can you give me any hope?" asked Valeria. "I am in despair, Sollius: justice in Rome is so hard a procedure."

Sollius carefully considered his reply, and when finally he uttered it, he spoke in a voice that would in no way strain the hearing of the listening tribune from the Army of the Danube.

"I have certain ideas, lady, that I must ponder and test before committing to words, even to you. Yet I think," he added with a touch of solemnity which it amused him to assume deliberately, "a more likely murderer than the lord Quintus might be postulated without unreason. But," he hastened to continue, before her maternal anxiety could interrupt his statement, "I cannot name him – even to myself. The Prefect is permitting me to follow my own line in the investigation, and I must not say more until I have compared my activities with his official action. But be of good hope, lady: for what it is worth, I think your son is innocent."

"Oh, praised be the gods!" she cried, and the tears streamed down her face. "Do what you will in this house: I have already given orders that you are to be obeyed in anything you may demand."

To the mutter of a contemptuous oath from the tribune, he turned, and withdrew in search of Cleander, but half-way down the passage leading to the atrium he purposely slackened step. He knew that Platorius would follow him, and was not surprised at being overtaken.

"Slave, did you mean what you said?" demanded the tribune.

"That I believe the lord Quintus to be innocent? Yes, lord."

"I believe it, too," exclaimed the other, looking carefully round as he spoke, and then he murmured underbreath: "I like not eavesdroppers. I trust, by the gods," he went on in a clearer voice, "that you can prove it."

"I hope so, lord."

"You have found evidence pointing to another?" pursued Platorius, catching him by the arm.

"No, lord, nothing. There is no true evidence anywhere, only oblique evidence, and even that may be falsely laid – or even false in itself. Yet suspicions are not always based on evidence."

"And you have suspicions?" whispered Platorius, and his grip tightened.

Sollius hesitated. A trickle of icy dewdrops seemed to moisten his spine. How should he answer?

"I will not call them suspicions, lord," he said quietly. "But – I have a guess. Ah, here is Cleander, and it is Cleander whom I am seeking."

He blessed the unexpected appearance of the murdered Senator's reading-slave, and was able to break off his present conversation easily and without subterfuge.

V

"I want to speak with you, Cleander. Where can we talk alone?"

Cleander considered for a moment, and then led the way to a small courtyard which contained a fountain.

"Well?" he asked.

Sollius did not feel that the other was antagonistic: but certainly he felt that he was cautious.

"Did you see anyone inside the house just before you went to join your master in his library? Think well before you answer."

"I saw nobody."

"Did you hear any unusual sound? Any sound of voices, for instance?"

"None."

"Not even your master's fall when stabbed?"

"I heard nothing," said Cleander, and his eyes, widely open, were honest.

"How long have you been a slave here?" asked Sollius, abruptly changing the attack. "Have you been in the household long enough to remember the quarrel between your master and his son, the lord Gaius?"

"It was only six years ago," said Cleander. "I remember it very well. But it was more a disagreement than a quarrel. I mean, there was no violence of words: only a cold silence, which ended in the lord Gaius leaving home for the wars on the frontier. It is true that he was disinherited."

"Then the disagreement," commented Sollius, "must have been very serious."

"It was. It was over the wild life which the young man led. My master was of the old school, always quoting Cato as the only proper example to all Romans, and the young man could not stomach it."

"I understand," murmured Sollius. "Has the lord Gaius been home since – on leave, for instance – or is this his first return after the break with his father?"

"The very first," replied Cleander, "and a terrible homecoming it is. His bowels will be filled with remorse. Why else did he come home without warning –?"

"Without warning?" interjected Sollius.

"We had no idea of his coming. He would not have come like that if he had not found that time and experience had developed in him his better, rather than his worse, qualities. His tragedy is double: he has lost both a father and the satisfaction of repentance. We all pity him."

Sollius remained silent for a moment. Then he asked:

"How long after the discovery of the murder did he arrive?"

"Many hours," replied Cleander. "The murder was discovered when it was barely light; the lord Gaius arrived after midday."

Sollius nodded.

"I saw him weep," pursued Cleander.

Sollius nodded again.

"And the lord Quintus?" he asked abruptly. "Did you see *him* weep?"

"He seemed too frozen and stunned for tears. All he did was to cry for vengeance."

"Of course," said Sollius with grave irony, "he was only the adopted son. Nature would not speak in him, but only gratitude."

VI

It was four days before the Prefect summoned Sollius by the same Gratianus whom the slave already knew, and the meeting took place in the austere headquarters of the Urban Cohorts which had jurisdiction over the domestic peace of Rome.

"Platorius, at least, is guiltless," the Prefect announced as soon as the slave detective was admitted into his presence.

"Oh!" exclaimed Sollius blankly.

"You are disappointed, I can see," said the Prefect. "But there is no doubt about it: he was asleep at an inn too far off for him to be here in Rome at the time of his father's murder. That has been tested by my officers."

"If Platorius is cleared," replied Sollius, plucking at his underlip, "there is only the lord Quintus left – unless your Excellency," he added, looking up hopefully, "has been able to unearth another suspect."

The Prefect sighed, and shook his head.

"It must lie between the two of them. Both had, doubtless, motive, but only one of them opportunity."

"It cannot be accidentally," Sollius mused aloud, "that the lord Quintus has been made to appear guilty: to use his sword, if a ruse of the moment, was deliberate – a swift decision, certainly. That swiftness of decision," he went on, looking fixedly at the Prefect, "is the sign of a soldier."

"So you are not convinced of a certain soldier's innocence," said the Prefect with a wry smile, "in spite of my assurance that he lacked opportunity?"

Sollius flushed.

"Forgive me, Excellency. I was disrespectful. I should have remembered to whom I was speaking . . ."

"Sollius," broke in the Prefect seriously, "you are no ordinary man, and I am not treating you as a slave. The Emperor spoke to me about you last night. He is concerned over this case, and is pleased that I am using you as an assistant. You have full leave to make any investigation which you consider may help justice – and justice, by its own nature, will acquit young Quintus of this parricide. If, therefore, you need powers to pursue your course, take them. I grant them freely."

"May I first hear, Excellency," begged Sollius, "the steps that were taken to prove that Platorius was asleep at an inn too far away for him to be in Rome when his father was murdered?"

The Prefect frowned, and then, commanding himself, laughed.

"You are an obstinate fellow," he said, "but it is an obstinacy for a good purpose. Gratianus shall tell you: it was he who conducted the investigation. I can find no flaw in his conclusions. But he is your friend, and both as a friend and an official will speak easily and openly about it. You may even wish to go over the same ground. You have leave to do so."

Sollius thanked him, and was dismissed.

"What is this all about?" asked Gratianus as soon as they were alone together. "Do you think I have had no experience in these matters? I have tracked the movements of hundreds of men. I am trained to do it."

"I know, I know, Gratianus," said Sollius placatingly. "I am not doubting your skill. I am only wondering whether this Platorius has not deceived you with a peculiar cunning."

"It will have been a very peculiar cunning," muttered Gratianus, still unappeased.

"Well, let us go over it together. Two heads are always better than one, even if only to confirm what the first head came to think."

"Answer *me* this question yourself," said Gratianus earnestly. "Why do you suspect Platorius so strongly?"

"He has two motives," replied Sollius, "revenge and cupidity; then the manner of the murder had a soldier's touch; finally, I . . . *sensed* his uneasiness. It was a very curious feeling, a kind of feeling which I have had before – and have always found reliable. Indeed," he added seriously, "I have never disregarded it without being sorry afterwards."

"You talk like a woman, Sollius," derisively answered Gratianus. "I think otherwise, because I know otherwise. Will *this* satisfy you? Platorius spent the night – the innkeeper and other witnesses prove it – at an inn . . . He even hired a girl to be his companion, and I can produce the girl – and, besides, no horse could have borne him hither from that inn, back again to the inn, and then hither again, and be in the condition it was on his arrival to find his father already murdered. No, Sollius, it is quite impossible."

VII

Leaving the headquarters of the Urban Cohorts, Sollius walked back through the narrow, crowded and eternally noisy Roman streets towards the house of Titius Sabinus, his master. Absorbed in his cogitations, he made way from time to time for wayfarers in a hurry, chariots and litters with their huge, running bearers, in a kind of dream, acting automatically for his own safety, yet completely unaware the while of the identity of any for whom he stepped aside.

But one of such, at least, recognized *him*, and a curt order brought a pair of litter-bearers to a jolting halt.

"Here, you! You there, slave!" cried out a deep, insolent voice which roused Sollius at once from his thoughts. "Come hither, slave!"

"Lord?" enquired Sollius, going to the litter and looking in upon two men lolling together on the cushions.

"I was told you were good at solving mysteries," went on the same deep, insolent voice. "My stepmother thinks so, or says she does. But what have you done about my father's murder? Nothing, I'll be bound! Slave, you are a fraud! I have seen many a sly face like yours. Haven't you, Torquatus, too? Sly with the pretence of a cleverness not possessed! I know your kind! Don't you, Torquatus, too?"

His friend laughed. Both men, thought Sollius, seemed very pleased with life. Clearly Platorius was anticipating the uses of the inheritance which he could expect to receive after the execution of Quintus, and his friend was sharing in the good fortune.

"Lord," replied Sollius with great outward respect, "I have but just now left his Excellency the City Prefect, and can report that the case of your father's murder is . . . nearing its close."

He knew that he had claimed more than he should, but Platorius's manner had nettled him, and he had not guarded his tongue. But when he saw the swift look which Torquatus flashed upon his friend, and the twin, smouldering, half-ruined stars which were the eyes of that friend himself, he no longer regretted his unwary boasting, but followed it up with a remark which now was deliberate in its lack of caution.

"It is all a question," he said, trying to appear as foolish and fatuous as he could, "of disproving what the murderer said he did."

He had partially closed his eyes while speaking, and now he opened them full, and stared upon Torquatus. But it was Platorius who answered:

"What, slave, you know the murderer? Then why is he not under arrest?"

"He will be arrested," replied Sollius turning to him, "as soon as I have proved one piece of evidence . . . concerning his whereabouts at a certain time."

"By the gods," exclaimed Torquatus, "you will be a clever fellow if you can prove that a man is here, or there, when he says the contrary."

Sollius again turned his gaze upon Platorius's companion. He saw a thick-necked, burly man with a rounded, jovial face and a very large nose, a man almost the exact opposite to his friend, who was lean, long-faced and sardonic.

"Is the Prefect making this enquiry himself?" demanded Platorius.

"The Prefect," answered Sollius deliberately, "does not know what *I* know. I shall take him the knowledge with the proof. That is my way," he added, appearing still more fatuous in his affectation of self-esteem.

"Get on, you lazy cattle!" cried Platorius to his bearers sharply, and he flung himself back on the cushions as the litter lurched forward and went on.

VIII

Sollius was no horseman, and a two-horsed chariot had been provided for him, which Gratianus drove. Two mounted men of the Urban Cohort rode with them.

"How far is it to this inn?" Sollius asked when they were well on their way.

Gratianus told him.

"It is the first posting-inn out of Rome northwards," he added, a trifle surlily, for he had not welcomed the slave's suggestion that the investigation of the movements of Platorius should be done again, but the Prefect had agreed and ordered it, and Gratianus did not conceal that the fact rankled.

The day was dry and hot even when they set out in the early light, and by the time they reached the inn for which they were making the sky was brazen with noon. It was a busy and well-conducted place: Sollius could see that with the first glance; but his interest was not in the inn as an inn, nor even in the questions which his companion put to the innkeeper. The answers only confirmed what had already been elicited: that Platorius, an army officer on leave who gave that name, had stayed at the inn on the night in question. That being so, his presence in Rome at the time of the murder of Sempronius was impossible.

"Do you wish to interrogate the girl whom he hired?" asked Gratianus maliciously.

"That is a very good idea," gravely answered Sollius. "Will you send for her?"

Gratianus stared. He had not expected his jesting offer to be taken seriously.

The girl, when brought to them, was pretty enough, and too young to need as much paint as she thought it proper and needful to put on; but she was already hard in eye, and tiredly wary of the offers and promises of men. She came suspiciously, determined to give as good as she might get.

But with his first question Sollius disarmed her by the virtue of surprise. Gratianus, too, was jolted out of his surliness and momentary malice.

"Is your memory good?" Sollius had asked.

The girl tossed her head.

"I remember any man with money!" had been her answer.

"The man about whom I am asking," said Sollius, "had money to spend on you, and spent it."

"I have been asked about him before," replied the girl. "I remember that, at least. It was you who asked about him," she went on, turning to Gratianus. "I remember you, too. I can swear that he was here, and that his name was Gaius Sempronius Platorius. He told me that that was his name over and over again in his cups. He was quite drunk in the end, thank the gods!" she concluded reminiscently.

"Yes, yes," said Sollius with some irritation. "It was to impress that name upon your memory. But that is not what I want to know if you remember, but something else. And I hope, I do hope, that your memory is good. Verily, a young man's life hangs upon it."

She grew interested at that, and became more natural.

"What is that 'something else'?" she asked in a lower and less brittle tone.

"Do you," pursued Sollius in his gentlest voice, "remember what Gaius Sempronius Platorius was like?"

"I remember that very well," she answered with a laugh. "We girls have to take the fat with the thin – and he was one of the fat, with his red moon-face and his large nose."

Gratianus gasped.

"The truth," said Sollius, "lies there. You may go, girl!"

IX

"There were two in it," stated Sollius as they drove away from the posting-inn, "Platorius and a friend. I have seen the friend, but do not know his name."

"I know *that*," answered a meeker Gratianus. "It is Torquatus."

"Torquatus, at least," went on Sollius, partly musing aloud, "was not the murderer. He was here – under the name of Platorius – and fortunately for himself he can prove it, or we can prove it for him, which is unfortunate for the other. I begin now to see the whole plot in orderly shape."

"Plot?" exclaimed Gratianus.

"It was a plot, and most cunningly undertaken," asserted Sollius. "I see it like this: Platorius was determined to win back his lost inheritance, and could do that by only two means, a reconcilation with his father, or his father's death. He must have had no hope of the former, or he would not have laid his plot."

"But to kill his father," expostulated Gratianus, "would only make the lord Quintus inherit, not himself."

"An executed man cannot inherit anything," said Sollius grimly.

"But it was only by chance that the lord Quintus's sword was there to be used," Gratianus obstinately pointed out.

"I know that. It was the soldier in Platorius which evolved a new tactical stroke on the instant. I have no doubt that he had some plan for fixing the murder upon Quintus. But he saw Chance, as he considered, favouring him, and followed his luck as a clever general does at the crisis of a battle."

"I begin to see," muttered Gratianus. "You are as sharp as they say, after all!"

"We now have to work out the itineraries of *both* of them," pursued Sollius, and his tone took on a new energy.

"How do we begin?" asked Gratianus.

"We need not trouble about Torquatus. You have already proved that he stayed the night here and left at a certain hour on the morning after. The only difference is that you thought it was Platorius. When Torquatus reached Rome does not matter in the least. He dropped out of events as soon as he had provided Platorius with a named personality at a particular place during certain hours. But what, during those same hours, was Platorius himself doing?"

"It is easy to ask!" muttered Gratianus.

"Let us begin to think," said Sollius. "Draw in the horses under that group of elms yonder."

They descended from the chariot and sat down in the only highway shade, as it seemed, for miles, for the dusty landscape was but sparsely furnished with trees of any kind. The two mounted men of the Urban Cohort took their rest, too, near at hand in the same shade, allowing their horses to graze disappointedly on the scanty wayside herbage.

"It seems clear," pursued Sollius, "that Platorius would have ridden beyond his friend Torquatus, and have reached Rome in the night, or towards dawn. He would remember his father's habit of early rising, and had determined to profit by circumstances. Probably he found his father stepping out of the portico into the garden and returned into the house with him. Then he noticed the sword, used it instead of his own, and immediately slipped away – perhaps on hearing the lord Quintus's approach, a stroke, as he would have thought it, of additional luck. His horse would have been tethered near by, and he would have ridden out of Rome, to return in the middle of the day as though arriving directly from his long journey. It is that ride out of Rome, Gratianus, which we must seek to follow. He would have had some place in which to linger out the time. If we can discover that . . ."

"No loiterer, certainly no horseman, was seen leaving the garden of Sempronius," said Gratianus. "I had every enquiry possible made as to that, hoping to find another suspect, but . . . well, it was barely dawn, and a cloudy morning at that, and nobody was about."

"Luck alone could have given us such evidence!" sighed Sollius gloomily.

The two were sunk in their thoughts for some while, savouring, as it were, both silence and shade. Then Sollius said:

"There will be – there *must* be – some inn, probably of low character and perhaps sequestered a little from the direct highway, somewhere between the posting-inn which we have just visited and the outskirts of the city. Torquatus, as Platorius, put up at the posting-inn, and rode on at his leisure the next morning; Platorius would not have halted at the posting-inn. He must have ridden considerably farther on, and have put up at some other inn from which he could reach Rome, and get back to the inn, quickly and with ease. He would have pretended to stay the night there, but have slipped away, murdered his father, returned to the inn as secretly as he had left it, and then, after lying late, have continued his open journey in time to arrive at his father's house by midday. But we can only prove all this by finding that second inn."

"It is all guesswork," complained Gratianus. "But the Prefect will only back you up, so we had better set to work to discover this inn – if it exists at all! We will search the whole district, in width as well as in depth, between here and Rome, and if your deductions, Sollius, have misled us, I'll souse you in Father Tiber myself!"

X

But Sollius was in no danger of an immersion in the yellow Tiber, for they found the ramshackle inn where Platorius had stabled his horse on the fatal night. The innkeeper, fearing worse discoveries, met their questions grovelling. Yes, a traveller on horseback certainly had put up at his inn on that night, and had ridden away the next morning. He scratched his head over the suggestion that the traveller might have left the inn during the night: he had not seen him leave, nor yet seen him return. His horse? But his horse next morning had been perfectly fresh. No, they were mistaken to think otherwise. He had seen the condition of the horse himself. Suddenly his eyes gleamed, his mouth opened, and he guffawed aloud.

"What are you remembering, rogue?" snapped Gratianus.

"But there was another horse. I had a good bargain with that other horse!" replied the innkeeper, rubbing his hands together with greedy satisfaction.

"What other horse?" asked Sollius eagerly.

"I will tell you," replied the innkeeper with a leer of ingratiation. "A traveller came and left a horse in my stable the day before, paid for its stalling and keep for a day, saying he was on a visit in the neighbourhood. I took it to be a visit of love," he explained, winking grotesquely. "I cared not, for I could sell the horse if he never came back – which he never did. And I did sell the horse," he added, "and for a good price. But I can tell you this, sirs," he went on in a lower tone, as if an eavesdropper might be about, "*that* horse had been out during the night. It was still in sweat when I saw it in the morning."

"Two horses," murmured Sollius, "one planted by Torquatus, and then ridden into Rome and back by Platorius in the night; and two men, a false and a true Platorius, one at the posting-inn and the other committing murder. They could afford to throw away a horse! Do you see it, my friend?"

"I see it now," growled Gratianus, flushing with annoyance that he had not seen it himself before. "But can we prove it?"

"We have good witnesses in two innkeepers and a girl," said Sollius, "and we could trace, no doubt, that second horse."

A sudden cry from outside broke into their talk, a cry that was followed by the clash of steel. Gratianus hurried out, while Sollius stared after him from the doorway. But dusk had already fallen, and all he could see was a lurid shadow cast from a flaring torch, itself out of sight, and the twigs and bushes near the gate a-drip with the same lurid glow. Whatever was happening was round the angle of the building. The innkeeper behind him began moaning and wringing his hands.

And now Gratianus, with a bleeding gash in his left arm, ran back indoors, and his own drawn sword was bloody down all its keen length.

"Bar the door, innkeeper!" he cried breathlessly, and sprang to help the other lift the great wooden bar and thrust it through the iron sockets of the doorposts.

"What is happening?" asked Sollius.

"Platorius and Torquatus, with some armed ruffians, have followed us. With both of us slain, and the innkeeper here either slain, too, or well bribed, they will be safe from detection for ever."

"Where are the two soldiers?"

"One is dead, stabbed in the back. I shouted to the other – who was still in the saddle as the villains crept through the gate – to ride for help, but we shall have our work cut out to keep them off until it comes."

"I am no fighting man," said Sollius dismally.

Gratianus clicked impatiently with his tongue.

"This door will not last long," he muttered.

"Is there no way out at the back?" suggested Sollius. "There is still the chariot . . ."

"A way out – and as good a way in," snapped Gratianus, "and they have taken the horses from the chariot. We are here till relieved!"

"How many are there?" asked Sollius, more out of curiosity than fear.

"Some three now, as well as Platorius and the other, for I killed one. Too many for us, I can tell you! But we must hold them off for over an hour. It is a fair distance to Rome and back."

"Platorius rode it," said Sollius grimly.

"Twice in a long night," growled Gratianus. "*We* have to abide a danger that never touched *him*. I can already smell burning!"

Loud cries of terror from the innkeeper's wife and serving-girl now came to them from the inn's back quarters.

The two women and an old stableman came running in.

"Curses on you!" cried the innkeeper furiously. "The whole back o' the house is ablaze!"

"You there – stableman – and you, innkeeper, unbar the door," commanded Gratianus with a fine show of calm, Roman efficiency. "Then take the bar, and use it as a ram. Sollius, take the one end of it, and keep it level and straight. When you are ready, I'll open. Rush out at once, ramming your way. You two women, follow close behind. I'll protect the rear with my sword. We should reach that old dovecot beside the gate. I saw it as I came in. They can't burn brick – though they can try to smoke us out. But it will give us a measure of time, and time is our sole riches!"

With their desperation to infect them with strength, they found the sufficient courage to do his will. Smoke and the fierce crackle of fire insistent behind them, they hauled out the heavy wooden bar, swung it round to project before them like a battering-ram, and stood ready to burst forth; and then Gratianus, sword in hand, tore open the door.

In the glare of a raised, flame-dripping torch Platorius, Torquatus and three others stood awaiting them in a ring. Gratianus swore.

"I thought they'd be dispersed round about!" he muttered, and swore again.

"It is no use," laughed Platorius. "We are too many. And you look for help? With what hope? Your man broke his neck when his horse fell! This road won't take a gallop – as I know from experience, you pestilent slave!" he added, his face working. "Are you coming out? 'Tis all one to me: either we kill you here, or you stay where you are, and burn. By Jupiter, slave, but you, at least, are too clever to live!"

The innkeeper's wife shrieked, and fell in a swoon into her man's arms. The heavy bar dropped with a crash. The serving-girl sank to her knees, wailing, and calling upon what gods she could remember, and the stableman made a blind dash outside, turning off towards the stables, only to be checked and cut down by one of Platorius's hired ruffians. Gratianus lowered the point of his sword, and stood rigid: he had no further invention for the situation as it now was. Laughing again, Platorius turned down his thumbs.

"Mithras, Saviour of the World, accept my breath!" murmured Gratianus, staring in front of him.

Sollius, who had a certain predilection towards the worship of Isis, prayed to that goddess silently; but, on a sudden, as he prayed, began wondering if there might not be a better efficacy in the deity of the Christians: he had heard good things of the Christians' God. Then he shrugged his shoulders, and again prayed to Isis.

"Are you coming?" impatiently called out Platorius, "or must we come in ourselves and sweep you backward into the flames?"

"Is there nothing we can do?" besought Sollius.

"I, armed, can at least die fighting!" muttered Gratianus.

"The altar is ready, the knives are sharpened, victims!" cried Platorius in a jesting tone, and then they heard it: the tramp, tramp, tramp, tramp of feet in the unison of a march, and the gathering roar of a soldiers' chorus:

> *"We do not fear the Dorians,*
> *The Britons or Isaurians,*
> *Nor yet the Hyperboreans,*
> *For we are the Prætorians,*
> *Disposers of the State!*

War is where we tramp;
Peace is where we camp;
And what we do is Fate:
For we are the Prætorians,
The greatest of the great!"

Nearer and nearer they came, the tramping and the singing: a cohort of Prætorian Guards on a route-march. They would surely investigate the burning inn on their way!

"Are we saved, think you?" whispered Sollius.

"Unless these fellows rush us in revengeful desperation," answered Gratianus. "But one of 'em – perhaps two! – will die before I do, I promise you that," he added grimly.

The Prætorian cohort was swinging into view.

"Halt!" rang out a voice of command. "What goes on here?"

"Decius! Oh, Decius!" cried Sollius, half sobbing in his relief.

"Who calls me?" answered the voice. "Castor and Pollux, *you*, slave?"

And Decius the centurion, who once, at the Emperor's command, had acted as Sollius's bodyguard, ran up to the inn. At the same instant, Platorius, in the high Roman fashion – as befitted a tribune of the Danubian army – drove his sword into his own heart.

A MITHRAIC MYSTERY
Mary Reed and Eric Mayer

In the last volume I introduced the character of John the Eunuch, who served as Lord Chamberlain to Justinian, the last of the great Roman emperors who ruled from Byzantium in the sixth century. Once again Eric Mayer's ideas and Mary Reed's writing have combined to bring us another mystery to solve, this one even more dangerous than the first. Mary has had several mystery stories published in Ellery Queen's Mystery Magazine, but the bulk of her writing has been non-fiction, including a book about fruits and nuts of which its spiritual ancestor finds its way into the following story. Eric has also been a frequent writer of non-fiction for such diverse publications as Baby Talk, Festivals, and Running Times. For the latter he went on a half marathon to write about his experiences, but he admits that collaborating on this story was considerably less painful.

Although he spoke four languages fluently, John the Eunuch swore in Egyptian, at least on those public occasions when it was merited. Privately, however, was a different matter, and the Lord Chamberlain's language upon hearing the news brought to him by the Emperor's secretary Anatolius would have horrified most of the Byzantine Court, less for the quality of the profanity than for its theological basis.

"By Mithra's Seven Runged Ladder! By the great Bull! I can hardly believe it!" John's staccato oaths matched his angry strides up and down the long sitting room. The day had just begun. The sun, rising over the Bosphorus, sent shafts of light through the octagonal panes of the room's single, tall window, lying in bright fringes across the mosaic hunting scene beneath John's feet.

Anatolius nodded miserably. "I had it from the captain of the excubitors."

John paced furiously, treading upon garishly costumed hunters and fantastic prey alike. "I must see the body before it's moved. In the mithraeum itself, of all places!"

When John strode from the room, Anatolius followed without a word. As an Occult, he was awed not by John's lofty public position but rather by the fact that the sunburnt Greek, a fellow Mithran, had achieved the sixth rank, Runner of the Sun, and was thus only a step away from advancement to Father, the seventh and highest rung on the Mithraic ladder. The irony of this did not escape Anatolius, though he did not engage in coarse jests at John's expense as did some of the Palace drudges, devotees of the fleshpots of Venus and Ashtoreth.

The two men crossed the cobbled street outside John's residence. Gulls, gathered to feed on the refuse that accumulated even within the grounds of the Great Palace, scattered and screamed their displeasure like Green and Blue partisans at the Circus. The men passed the Daphne Palace, the Pantheon – the Empress's official residence – and the Church of St Stephen. An unobtrusive doorway, in the dim recesses of an armory behind a barracks, led to a series of damp, slippery stairs and subterranean corridors and, finally, hidden away at the back, the mithraeum.

Usually these musty catacombs were deserted, but this morning spear-wielding excubitors stood guard at each turn. They looked glum. John recognized most as followers of Mithra.

Otto, the captain of the excubitors, met John and Anatolius outside the entrance to the mithraeum.

"Mithra forgive me, I was ordered to secure the mithraeum by the Master of Offices himself," said Otto, naming John's immediate superior in the Palace administration.

"Who discovered the body?" asked John.

"The Master didn't say. An informer, like as not."

John entered the holy place. The sacred flame, burning as always on the altar at the end of the sunken nave, illuminated the marble bas relief of Mithra wrestling the Great Bull behind it, and, on the steps before the altar, the body of a man, naked except for a Phrygian cap, the same type of head covering worn by the God Himself.

John went down seven steps into the lower level without hesitation but Anatolius hung back. Occults were not privileged to partake in the Mysteries, but only observed, faces obscured by black veils, from the wooden benches overlooking the area.

The body felt cold beneath John's thin hand. It was a young man, slight but muscular, barely twenty. His eyes had been bandaged, his hands bound with chicken entrails, in the manner of a Mithraic initiation mystery; in this case the ritual murder had not been simulated. There was a bloody wound in his side and on the otherwise unmarked marble floor, next to the body, was written in blood "Thus perish all who hate the Lord of Light".

John's summons to the Empress Theodora's private residence came unexpectedly. Theodora, a bear-keeper's daughter, former whore and worse – if the rumors were to be believed – greeted him warmly. Dressed in gold-embroidered robes, her hair tied in coils at the sides of her head, thin lips abundantly rouged to contrast with the pallor of her face, she was a beautiful and desirable woman. Or so John had been told. When he reflected upon the number and frequency of Theodora's affairs, and her lovers' habit of leaving for Malaga or Philae or some other far corner of the Empire when they fell from favor, he was glad that Fate had seen fit to spin his life as She had.

"How good to see you, Lord Chamberlain," said the Empress, taking his arm as her slaves withdrew, closing the heavily gilded door softly behind them.

She was much shorter than John, himself a man of average height.

"I must congratulate you again on the arrangements for the Egyptian Envoy's banquet," she said. "A most satisfying event."

John recalled the Empress had drunk too much wine and spent most of the banquet trying to convince an exceptionally muscular Egyptian scion to take dwarf olives from her pursed lips. Afterwards, emboldened by the Empress's advances, the man had actually tried to bribe him. "It is my privilege to serve the Imperial family," John replied.

"Come and sit with me." She led John towards one of the many low couches scattered amidst carved teak tables, the seat scarcely visible beneath a riot of rainbow-hued cushions. The room was furnished with an eye toward luxury, if not ostentation, from purple silk wall hangings to rosy plum and azure blue Indian carpets. A man of austere tastes, John found the room both overwhelming and vulgar, rather like Theodora herself.

"You must come and talk more often," said the Empress, leaning forward so that John could feel her warm breath on his neck and smell her musky perfume. "I have so little opportunity to talk to men in an intelligent manner. They are all such beasts. But you and I might discuss epigrams or even theology."

"Surely you haven't asked me here to discuss theology."

"No, I haven't. Such a pity." The Empress drew a forefinger down John's cheek. "I like a smooth face," she confided.

John found himself looking into her eyes. They were, from a distance, narrow eyes. But up close he could see that her pupils were tiny pinpoints. It gave her a knowing, almost oracular look, as if her gaze were focused on some perfect, distant truth. John almost wished he might experience the madness that had led so many men to throw away their lives for the pleasures those eyes promised. Then he recalled that her fashionably contracted pupils were merely the result of applications of deadly belladonna, and his momentary curiosity evaporated.

The Empress apparently noticed. She drew away slightly. "I am afraid I have asked you here about an unpleasant matter," she said. There was disappointment in her voice, and perhaps a touch of anger as she continued. "One of the Emperor's bodyguards, and therefore a man under your own command, Lord Chamberlain, has been found brutally murdered. Apparently this was the result of some hellish secret rite."

She stared at him with those poisonous eyes. John was careful to suppress his surprise. Although they were technically under his jurisdiction, John did not directly command the Silentiaries who guarded the Emperor, at least ceremonially, and would be unlikely to have known the victim.

"Where did this information come from?" he asked.

"The Master of Offices. He tells me the victim was named Alexander, a low born Thracian, new to the city just last year."

"And the hellish rites?"

"Mithrans," said Theodora. "It has been rumored that they engage in human sacrifice, although, until now, they have managed to keep their abominations secret. Here, what do you think of these figs?" She gestured toward a filigreed silver bowl of fruit on a nearby table.

John took one of the figs, bit into it and chewed slowly while his mind raced. As an initiate in the Mysteries, he knew that contrary to common wisdom such rites had not been carried out for hundreds of years, if ever. But he could hardly reveal his knowledge to the Empress. Though Mithraism, like some other pagan religions, was tolerated, a high official in the Christian Byzantine court would hardly dare reveal allegiance to an officially outlawed cult.

"But why have you summoned me about this matter?" he asked at last.

"The victim was under your command, as the murderer might be. It has been said that the Emperor's bodyguard has become a breeding ground for these vipers. I want you to investigate – discreetly."

"And what of the Emperor?"

"Justinian will be conducting his own investigation. So you need not report to him."

"And what if he finds out about . . . me?"

Theodora gave a brief, guttural laugh. "He will have no suspicions where you are concerned."

"I understand," said John. His face remained an expressionless mask. "I will look into the matter, but I can promise nothing." He rose from the couch. "The figs, by the way, are excellent."

"I'm glad you find them so, Lord Chamberlain. I will be sure to have more, when you return to talk to me."

She stood. Gold flashed from the threads of her robe, the tied coils of her hair, the rings on her fingers, her earrings.

"They are grown on a special tree," she said. "Not far from Trebizond." Theodora's thin, scarlet lips curved into a scythe of a smile. "It is said the peasants must use a seven-runged ladder to harvest the choicest fruits."

Mithraism was a soldier's religion, exclusively male, valuing above all the military virtues of discipline, self sacrifice and chastity. Perhaps because chastity came too easily to John, the Lord Chamberlain was zealous in practicing the other virtues. So it was, when he went to the Baths of Zeuxippus, as he always did immediately upon leaving the Empress, he inevitably confined himself to the cold pool.

The shock of icy water against his naked skin dissipated the sickly fog that had seemed to follow him away from the Empress's rooms. He scrubbed his wiry arms and splashed his face until he had washed away the last traces of her musk.

Emerging from the circular pool onto the slick marble, he was pleased to find Anatolius. It was no surprise, since it was not uncommon for the higher classes to attend the baths two or even three times daily. Judging from his flushed face, and the way his black hair lay in ringlets against the side of his head, John's friend had just come from the steam bath.

"I have just been to see Theodora," said John, seating himself at the pool's edge. The pool, and the surrounding cubicles were deserted, so though his voice echoed off the friezes overhead, there was no one to overhear.

Anatolius tested the water with his foot and grimaced. "So your morning has been doubly distasteful," he observed.

"She wants me to investigate the murder. Secretly. The victim was apparently a Silentiary."

"His name was Alexander," said Anatolius. "He was a fellow Occult."

John allowed his face to register surprise.

Anatolius said, "After leaving the mithraeum I spoke to one of the excubitors on guard, another man of my own rank. He had seen the body and recognized it."

"This may be even more difficult than I thought," said John. "Theodora seems to think the murder was committed by Mithrans."

"We aren't murderers." Anatolius seated himself beside John. Now that the effects of the steam bath were wearing off, his skin appeared pale, in contrast to John's deep brown coloring. "Besides," he added, "only Lions are allowed to take the part of the sufferer. Alexander was two steps removed from that rank."

"But I can hardly explain that to the Empress."

"No, not in your position."

"And she referred to the seven-runged ladder. Do you suppose she suspects me?"

"Theodora has always had an unhealthy interest in the forbidden," replied Anatolius, "including proscribed religions. A young scribe I knew told me a story he had from a servant girl in the Empress's service. According to the girl, Theodora actually accompanied her to one of the rituals of an Ashtoreth cult. The reality of it disappointed her. No less than the servant girl disappointed my friend, I may say." He smiled.

"But why would she care, suddenly, to persecute Mithrans?" continued John.

"Maybe she doesn't want to persecute Mithrans. Maybe she simply wants to clear them out of the Emperor's bodyguard."

"Or undermine the guard," said John. "Introduce her own men."

"Your mind is almost as devious as hers," commented Anatolius. "No doubt she has multiple aims, every one unwholesome and ruinous. Isn't it common knowledge among a certain class that she and Justinian are twin demons sent to plague humanity? Hardly a week passes that some wretch doesn't flee the Palace, convinced he's seen faceless devils stalking the halls at night. Last week, in fact, two fled. If you don't stop thinking so hard you'll convince yourself to follow them."

"Maybe that is her aim," John mused.

Anatolius rose and waded out into the pool. In truth, the Empress's words and actions troubled him, but he saw no point in revealing this. Even under the best of circumstances John was given to brooding like the hero of a Greek Tragedy.

John remained by the side of the pool. The air against his skin felt pleasingly cool. There had been a time when it had shamed him to reveal himself in the public baths. Although he had long since mastered those feelings, he still appreciated that Anatolius did not make a point of too politely averting his gaze.

Watching him wash his slim, muscular limbs, John was reminded of elegant sculptures of Greek antiquity, but more so of a woman he had known once. Was that why he had befriended Anatolius?

"Anatolius," John called. "Could you look into a few things for me?"

The fetid odor of streets and harbor filled John's small kitchen. In a few months, when winter's cold would force him to close its one small window, and his cook lit the charcoal brazier, the room would smell of roast lamb and boiled duck. On this hot August afternoon, however, John endured the ripe stench of decay because the alternative seemed to be suffocation.

He had emptied the contents of a leather pouch out onto the scarred wooden table. Sitting hunched over the table, he examined the objects he had found on the floor of the mithraeum. It had been a laborious search, in the guttering light of the altar flame, and he was not certain he had found everything there might be to find, or that what he had found bore any relationship to the crime.

There was a pearl clasp from a cloak. A shrivelled apple core, discarded recently enough, he decided, that the rats had not yet chewed it. A delicate gold chain. A gold solidus, drastically clipped, showing on its obverse – ironically John thought – the crucifixion of the Christian's gentle god. And, finally, a lopsided die, which may have been ivory. All were objects men might have carried on their persons for one reason or another and small enough not to be missed if dropped during the rituals.

John wiped sweat from his gaunt cheeks. Outside children yelled and he heard the clackety-clack of a hoop being rolled along cobbles. The murderer certainly knew where the mithraeum was now, but had he known before the killing? Was he actually a Mithran, or had he followed the victim? But then, why should a killing occur in the mithraeum at all?

Even in his own kitchen John could feel the poisoned eyes of the Empress upon him. Although it was Alexander who was dead, John felt that it was he himself who was the prey.

In his state of mind, footsteps on the wooden stairs leading up from the courtyard startled him more than they should, but it was only Anatolius, returning from his inquiries.

"I don't think I'll invite myself for dinner tonight," said his friend, glancing at the objects on the table. "Still looking for plots?"

John smiled tiredly. "Anatolius, I owe my position in court to mere survival, and I owe my survival mostly to my ability not just to feel the eyes on my back but to sense who they belong to. What did you find out?"

As Secretary to the Emperor, Anatolius had free access to the Imperial residence, and indeed, more than once he had assisted John. The Lord Chamberlain was a friend, after all – not to mention one of the more influential officials in the Palace. "I found very little," said Anatolius. "The Master of Offices claims he never ordered Captain Otto to the mithraeum, that he heard of the murder first from the Captain."

John frowned and began to speak but Anatolius cut him off.

"That may mean nothing," he cautioned. "I also learned that the Master was so drunk last night that he didn't know what day it was when he woke up this morning. He admitted it himself. Begged me not to tell the Emperor."

"He also conveniently wouldn't remember who informed him about the body, if he really was drunk," observed John.

"He looked hungover to me," said Anatolius. "He was green as a month-old leg of mutton."

"I see. What else?"

"The usual gossip in the Empress's residence. Her favorite stallion has gone lame. The large Egyptian who has been hanging around the court lately is, on the other hand, rumored to be in fine mettle. Some wall hangings weren't dyed correctly. A new servant – a country bumpkin named Michael – fled last week. Needless to say this is believed connected with a silver rouge pot once owned by Pulcheria. The Imperial life is difficult."

"Indeed," said John. "And apparently dull and unfulfilling as well. Do you know, the Empress wants to talk to me about epigrams and theology."

"If I were you, I would be at the library," said Anatolius.

As John approached Captain Otto's office he heard a crash and was nearly knocked down by a huge Egyptian who burst through the doorway like a fury.

John stepped aside nimbly. "Dioscurus," he said, remembering the man who had tried to bribe him after the envoy's banquet. It was the man's size, rather than the bribe, which were common enough, which was memorable. Many tried to curry favor with the Master of Offices through the Lord Chamberlain.

"Lord Chamberlain," said Dioscurus in perfect Greek. His heavy lips curled. "I apologize for offending you the other night. I imagined I was observing the custom of your great city."

"Never mind," said John, "I'm sure you must find our civilization confusing."

"Next time I will know to offer more," Dioscurus replied curtly.

Watching the young Egyptian on his way out, John realized that he must be Theodora's new consort – the one Anatolius had mentioned. And to think that a few weeks ago he had aspired only to gaining the Master of Office's wrinkled old ear, and failed at that. What was he doing in Captain Otto's office, John wondered?

He found the Captain hunched grimly over his ivory-inlaid desk. Beside his chair, and scattered across the floor, were the remains of a porphyry vase.

"Otto," said John, feigning more friendliness than he felt, for Otto was commander of the excubitors, a militia stationed inside the Palace, and they had at times been at odds since John was head of the Emperor's largely ceremonial bodyguard, the Silentiaries. Still, they were both Mithrans, the German having attained the rank, appropriately, of Soldier.

Otto replied with a grunt.

"Did the Empress send her young man to ensure you're pursuing the murder investigation?" asked John.

"No. He came about – another matter."

"He seems to have been rather clumsy."

"I shouldn't have had the vase so near the corner of the desk." John noticed that the Captain, usually a blunt and straightforward man, refused to meet his eyes.

A knot of cold formed in the pit of John's stomach. Perhaps Theodora had sent her Egyptian on account of John. Was it really John she was pursuing, and not Mithrans? Or was he just too ready to see plots and counterplots, as Anatolius said?

"What is it you want, Lord Chamberlain?" asked Otto. Though he had been in Constantinople for a decade his accent remained barbaric.

"I am not here, strictly, as the Lord Chamberlain," said John. "I am here more as a follower."

"So, then. What is it?" The rugged face which had turned unflinchingly toward foes more threatening than the thin eunuch, if not more formidable, remained averted.

"You said you had been ordered to the mithraeum by the Master of Offices. I believe this is not true. I am told he was dead drunk last night."

Now Otto did look at John, his chin pushed forward. His face reddened. "I am not known as a liar."

"As another who is climbing the ladder, I will tell you that some highly placed persons may use this murder as a weapon against all of us. Or have you learned that from the Egyptian, already?"

"As I said, I was ordered by the Master to secure the mithraeum."

"I am not inquiring as your Lord Chamberlain but as one who will very soon hold the rank of Father," John said bluntly.

Otto shrugged his broad shoulders. "I can't say more. I am a military man. I obey my superiors."

John had a sudden thought. "How are the chariot races treating you?"

"My bets have been blessed lately," said Otto. "What does that have to do with this?"

"I'm not sure," replied John. "Nothing, perhaps."

John slept poorly that night. The heat and stench of the city lay against his face like a stifling shroud. In the least of his nightmares, of those he remembered clearly upon wakening, he ran through dark catacombs, pursued by roaring demons. In his darker dreams, unimaginable horrors gnawed at the underside of reality, as quietly as rats.

The miasma of nightmare still lingered in his mind, even after he had risen and washed. Now he stood looking out over the deceptively calm Bosphorus from the window of his sitting room. The lower classes, those who swore the Emperor was a demon, also whispered that Theodora practiced the black arts. Had she disturbed his sleep, plucking at his mind with talons of mist? Surely Mithra would protect him from the darkness. But the Lord of Light had not seen fit to protect Alexander. Why had the young excubitor been killed? Had he died merely because he was a Mithran?

And what of the murderer? Had he too been a Mithran? How else could he have discovered the mithraeum?

John wondered also about Otto? Had he lied about the Master ordering him to the well-hidden holy place? And if he had, why?

It was late afternoon by the time John left through the gate of the Palace grounds, making his way across the Augustaeum and past the Hippodrome. He had dressed simply, but the length of his brown tunic, his soft leather shoes and his bearing distinguished him from town people. Sellers of perfumes and melons and jewelry singled him out, calling raucously from their stalls, and passersby did not jostle him as they did each other but stepped politely aside to let him pass.

He waited for Anatolius at a bookseller's stall. Under the blank gaze of the antique statues in front of the Baths of Zeuxippus, he examined the seller's collection of ancient papyrus scrolls and more recent parchments.

He was admiring one of the new, bound, codexes – a life of the Saints – when his friend arrived. "Look at these illuminations," John said. "If only our artists could match these Christians. Certainly our subject matter is far more glorious and dramatic."

"The Christians do have an advantage, not having to work in secret," remarked Anatolius. "Here, this new collection of love epigrams by Agathias may be more interesting to you."

"Don't worry, I haven't forgotten about the Empress's desire to discuss literature. What about Alexander?" John had asked Anatolius to inquire about him, fearing that the dead man's fellow Silentiaries might not speak so truthfully to their ultimate commander.

"Apparently, he was nothing more than what he seemed," said Anatolius. "A young, rough fellow from Thrace who came to Constantinople to make his way at court. It's a common enough story."

"What about dangerous vices? Did he have a taste for gambling, or wine or quarrels? Was he a womanizer? Which faction did he support at the circus?"

"He was young. I suppose he indulged in all the common vices. But, from what I gathered, he was a good Mithran. He would probably have traded his Occult's veil for a Soldier's helmet before I did."

Anatolius was sorting through abandoned geometries and Latin grammars. As he spoke, he picked up a large parchment. "Fruit and Nuts in Symbolism and Celebration," he read. "This might serve you well in your official duties, John."

"Yes. But can't you tell me anything more?"

Anatolius sighed. "I'm afraid he was an exemplary young man. A friend of his told me that in June, when a contingent of the guard accompanied the Imperial family to their summer retreat in Asia Minor, most returned with stories that would make an actress blush. But Alexander refused to say a word. Said it wasn't his place to speak against his rulers. Some of the guards considered him a stick-in-the-mud. But I doubt that's grounds for murder."

John nodded. "And Michael, the servant who ran away? Could you find out anything about him?"

"I obtained the address of his lodgings," was the reply. "But I would suggest you take a guard, or let me accompany you."

"I won't come to any harm." John hoped he sounded more confident than he felt.

"Michael? You won't find him here. You can't hurt him any more. He's dead." The young woman clutched the wooden cross that hung from a chain around her neck, glaring defiantly at John. She looked haggard and old beyond her years. The points of her skinny shoulders showed through her dirty, poorly mended tunic.

"I'm sorry," said John. "I didn't intend to harm him."

"You're from the Palace, aren't you? I can smell it." The woman backed away slightly. In truth there was little space to back away in the bare box of a room. Michael had, before entering service at the Palace, occupied this cramped, bare space on the fourth floor of a wooden tenement. Through the open window John could hear the sound of hammering as workmen toiled on Justinian's newest project, the Church of the Holy Wisdom.

"How did it happen?"

"As if you don't know. His poor neck was slashed. It was the work of a beast. Or a devil. Some unnatural thing. Like you." The woman's eyes glittered in their dark sockets.

"Please help me," said John. "Another man has also been murdered, and it might be the doing of the same person."

"No person. Devils."

"Why do you say that?" asked John, uneasily. His nightmares had left behind a residue of irrational dread.

"Because that was what he found in the Palace. Devils. We came from the country. We had a good life, working the fields. But he wanted more. The City tempted him, like Satan tempted Christ. We'd have a house, he said. I could tie my hair back with gold chains and wear silk robes like the ladies of the court. And instead, he found devils."

She bowed her head, clasping the cruxifix in both hands as if she were praying. A tear ran down along the shadowed concavity of her cheek.

"What do you mean, he found devils?" asked John.

The woman blinked back her tears. "It was the Emperor himself, the very King of the Demons. That's what he told me when he got here, running all the way from the Palace. His heart was practically bursting. He said . . . he said he wouldn't stay another night in that hellish place. He'd seen it before, a figure – stalking the halls. There's always someone around the halls at night. Up to no good, I'll wager. And they say the Emperor barely sleeps. But one night he saw a figure making its way toward the Empress's bedchamber. He came upon it accidentally, surprised the thing . . . the Emperor. It turned and looked right at him in the candle light. And it had no face! Where a head should be was only darkness."

When John left the tenement, the sun had fallen behind the city's seven hills (how appropriate it was, he often mused). Constantinople's soaring columns were barely visible against a sky whose faint lavender glow was deeping to Imperial purple. As he walked briskly through the darkening streets he thought he heard a movement behind him. He stopped, looked back. There was no one. He looked up. He was standing at the base of the modest pillar of a stylite.

He could barely make out the shadowy form of the Christian Holy Man who sat atop the pillar, night and day, exposed to the elements, mortifying his flesh. John couldn't help wrinkling his nose at the stench drifting down to the street. He couldn't understand a God who would welcome such a gross insult to a body He had created in His own image.

Had the noise been the stylite shifting his weight? John listened but heard nothing. Nor could he detect any motion atop the pillar.

Something moved again, and quick as a shadow dodging a swinging torch, John stepped to one side. There was the ring of a metal blade hitting the base of the stylite's pillar.

Now he got a glimpse of his attacker. He was a huge man, wearing an excubitor's helmet. He saw the glint of the raised sword and threw himself onto the cobbles, rolling sideways. Again the blade cracked against the pillar.

The stylite shrieked.

It was a choked, monstrous shriek. The sound the Great Bull must have made when Mithra dragged him to the cave and slit his throat.

John heard voices. People came running towards him.

The excubitor fled into the darkness, and John, too, slipped away, from the wondering crowd which had gathered below the man who had remained publicly silent for so many years.

As the Mithran made his way carefully, and uneventfully back to his dwelling, he wondered if he now owed his life to the inscrutable Christian God.

Though he expected more fearful dreams, John slept soundly enough until he was awakened by a pounding on his door. It was an obviously agitated Anatolius.

"John, have you heard? Captain Otto is dead. He threw himself from the Column of Arcadius sometime during the night."

"I was attacked by someone wearing an excubitor's helmet last night," said John.

"Could it be that – do you think – the captain was the murderer? Although, Mithra knows why he would desecrate the holy place. And you'd just been to see him, too. No doubt he feared for his safety." He paused, pondering the puzzle. "Nobody actually reported the murder

to him – they wouldn't have had to . . . if he was the murderer."
Enlightenment spread over his face.

"I don't believe that," said John. "He was a follower."

"But why would he take his own life?"

"A good question. Do you know, there are 233 stairs leading to
the platform under the statue of Arcadius. I know because of a
commemorative ceremony we staged there long ago. Think about
that. 233 steps to the top. 233 chances to turn back, lose resolve,
rethink one's imminent death. What could be so terrible that a man
would decide to die 233 times?"

"I don't know," said Anatolius. "I would have thought death itself
was the most terrible thing – forgetting of course that we shall all be
reborn in Mithra."

John smiled wanly. "Anatolius, I consider you a friend. There is a
loose brick just to the right of my kitchen hearth. There are important
papers behind that brick. If it becomes necessary I would appreciate
you taking charge of those papers. Please excuse me now, I must
dress. I am going to see the Empress."

The Empress saw him immediately. "I am told the Mithran murderer
has taken his own life," she said, without preamble, glaring at John
through the black pinpoints of her poison-contracted pupils. "It is
said he was the one who murdered Alexander. Do they think they
can escape justice by offering yet another bloody sacrifice? I intend
to enforce the law. These pagan monsters will all be sent directly to
that hell at which they scoff."

She was dressed in a purple robe glittering with precious stones and
gold thread, a gem-studded tiara atop her coiled hair. She did, indeed,
look more an Empress than a bear-keeper's daughter, John thought
ruefully. Unfortunately, he had no choice but to oppose her.

"The murder was not committed by a Mithran," he said. "Nor
was it part of a Mithraic ceremony."

"And how does the Emperor's Lord Chamberlain come to know
the secrets of Mithra?"

Controlling the quaver that threatened to creep into his voice,
John replied, "I know about them because I have attended them,
just as you have."

"You condemn yourself doubly, by your own admission and by
your scurrilous slander."

"Do you really think not one man there recognized you, in your
flimsy disguise?"

"Of whom do you speak?"

Ignoring her question, John pulled a delicate golden chain from

A MITHRAIC MYSTERY 117

inside his cloak. "Do you recognize this chain? It is the sort of thing a woman uses to fasten her hair. And yet Mithraism is a man's religion. The mithraeum is forbidden to women."

"A man's religion?" Theodora laughed. A coarse, raucous sound, like the cry of a hungry gull. "I would have more right to attend than you! But why would I?"

"Curiosity. Haven't you attended the rites of Ashtoreth, among others? Besides, you had taken a Mithran lover."

John hoped the pitch of his voice was not being taken by the Empress as a sign of the fear he was trying to conceal. She could have him killed, instantly, if she wished, before he had a chance to explain what such an act might cost. She glared as he continued.

"You must have singled out young Alexander when he accompanied the excubitor guard that you took to your summer retreat earlier this year. He became your intimate. He entered your residence at night, his face obscured by the Occult's veil he wore during ceremonies, apparently, thinking nothing of the blasphemy of it. I suppose you thought it funny that your superstitious servants mistook him for the rumored King of the Demons.

"And when one of the servants who was frightened by the charade fled, you had him killed, just in case he talked too much."

Theodora's sharp stare seemed to bite into his soul. He continued, his words more measured. "You killed Otto too. Of course he couldn't tell me who had alerted him to the murder because it was you, and you'd commanded his silence. He could neither betray you nor his God. A quick death was preferable."

"But only after he failed to kill you last night."

"You have already heard of that? Do you think I would have survived an attack by a trained excubitor? Hardly. It was a large man. Your newest lover, the Egyptian Dioscurus."

For the first time the Empress looked surprised.

"A hot-headed young man," said John. "He lost his temper when he discovered you and Alexander together, in this house. So inconvenient, a murder in your own bed chamber. So you had Dioscurus carry the body to the mithraeum. It was nearby. You had been there. There was no blood under the body, in front of the altar. That was how I knew he was not killed there"

"I think your infirmity has finally driven you mad, Lord Chamberlain." Theodora moved toward John until he could smell her musk. "I won't have you killed," she said, a smile working at the corners of her red lips. "As a kindness I shall have your eyes put out, so you will not be tortured by more hallucinations, and have your tongue cut off, so you cannot disturb others with your insane delusions, and then

I shall have you transported to a rock in the Mediterranean where you may enjoy the rest of your existence. I understand persons of your type live a long time."

"And then all that I have related will become public knowledge."

Theodora laughed. "Do you think the Emperor imagines me to be some poor virginal creature? Does every person in the Palace not tremble at my approach, knowing I have murdered and will murder again?"

"Justinian may not feel the need to excuse the fact that his wife is a whore, but what about the fact that she has blasphemously worshipped in the temple of a forbidden God? How will he explain that to the Patriarch or to his political supporters?"

"Who will testify I was there? Some dirty soldiers and stinking peasants? Who will take their word against mine?"

"No one would. But what about the word of a great landowner, senators, one of the Empire's most respected generals? Did you recognize those powerful men behind their veils and masks, Empress?"

"Why would they reveal themselves now?"

"Because they are Mithrans and you have shaken your fist at our God."

"I don't believe that. They would have more to lose than I would."

"Is it worth the chance? Can you be certain how the Emperor will choose to calculate costs? Besides, you may be sure your Egyptian will tell his story. He is too important a man to be detained because of some religious misstep."

For a second John expected Theodora to spring at him, like a street girl. But she controlled herself. "Leave my sight," she said, in a husky whisper. "And never forget, Lord Chamberlain, that the wife of the Emperor wishes you to burn in hell."

"I suspect she enjoyed it, binding the hands of the corpse with entrails, covering its eyes, writing out the message in blood in front of the altar. The perversity would have appealed to her. And, after all, she was an actress once."

John paused, pouring more wine into his cup. He and Anatolius were seated at a table, in a cafe, not far from the Augustaeum. A cool breeze carried the salty smell of the Sea of Marmora to them.

"I still don't understand it all," his friend confessed.

"She did it on a whim. It was the first thing that came to her mind. And not a bad idea, really. The military is largely Mithran. By persecuting Mithraism she might have been able to fill its high posts with men under her power."

"But why ask you to investigate?"

"Sheer perversity, perhaps. Or because her lover had a grudge against me." John bit into the fig he had taken from the wooden bowl on the table. It tasted much better than the figs in Theodora's chambers. "Or maybe it was more a . . . contest. I must have seemed an interesting challenge to her, since so many of her usual weapons are rendered useless by my infallible self-control." A wry smile creased his thin face.

"Still," said Anatolius. "She did get away with murder, or at least with assisting in one."

"Well, this is the Empire. She is the Empress. We take what justice we can get."

"And what kind of justice do you suppose the Empress has in store for you?"

"You forget, Anatolius. The Grand Chamberlain is the Emperor's personal servant. I am one of his closest confidants. Even before they became advisors and officers of state, Grand Chamberlains wielded influence because they had the Emperor's ear every day, in a society where most citizens are lucky to catch a glimpse of his face during their lifetimes. I think I can depend on his protection – as much as anyone can."

"Which still leaves the real murderer, Dioscurus, free to return to Egypt."

"You mean you didn't hear?" John put down his cup.

Anatolius looked at him blankly.

"And you are usually the one bringing the news to me," said John. "Dioscurus is dead. It happened at a small dinner party in the Empress's residence last evening. Officially it is a heart attack, or maybe some bad shellfish." John took a long draught of wine. "The Palace physician, who is a follower, told me that in reality he was poisoned – with belladonna."

And with that, John the Eunuch, follower of Mithra, realizing he had made a bitter enemy in Theodora, set off for home.

ABBEY SINISTER
Peter Tremayne

*Since the publication of "The High King's Sword" in the previ-
ous volume, Peter Tremayne's stories featuring Sister Fidelma have
been going from strength to strength. In addition to at least half-
a-dozen short stories (probably more by the time this sees print),
there have been two novels,* Absolution by Murder *(1994) and*
Shroud for an Archbishop *(1995). She is an advocate of the
Irish Brehon Court, and has been called a "Dark Age Perry Mason".
Peter Tremayne (b. 1943) is an expert on Celtic history and the
author of over fifty books, including many novels of fantasy and
horror fiction. His knowledge of Dark Age Britain means he can
throw some light on that mysterious past and show that, contrary
to what we might have believed, there was still law and order in
those days.*

The black guillemot, with its distinctive orange legs and mournful, warning cry, swooped and darted above the currach. It was an isolated traveller among a crowd of more hardy, sooty, white-rumped storm petrels and large, dark coloured cormorants, wheeling, diving and flitting against the soft blue May sky.

Sister Fidelma sat relaxed in the stern of the boat and let the tangy odour of the salt water spray gently caress her senses as the two oarsmen, seated facing her, bent their backs to their task. Their oars, dipping in unison, caused the light craft to dance over the waves of the great bay which seemed so deceptively calm. The clawing waters of the hungry Atlantic were not usually so good natured as now and often the islands, through which the currach was weaving, could be cut off for weeks or months at a time.

They had left the mainland, with its rocky terrain and scrawny vegetation, to cross the waters of the large estuary known as Roaring Water Bay, off the south-west coast of Ireland. Here the fabled Cairbre's "hundred islands" had been randomly tossed like lumps of earth and rock into the sea as if by some giant's hand. At the moment the day was soft, the waters passive and the sun producing some warmth, making the scene one of tranquil beauty.

As the oarsmen stroked the vessel through the numerous islands, the heads of inquisitive seals popped out of the water to stare briefly at them, surprised at their aquatic intrusion, before darting away.

Sister Fidelma was accompanied by a young novitiate, a frightened young girl, who huddled beside her in the stern seat of the currach. Fidelma had felt obliged to take the girl under her protection on the journey to the abbey of St Ciaran of Saigher, which stood on the island of Chléire, the farthest island of this extensive group. But the escort of the novitiate was purely incidental for Fidelma's main purpose was to carry letters from Ultan, the archbishop of Armagh, to the abbot at Chléire and also to the abbot of Inis Chloichreán, a tiny religious house on one of the remoter rocky islands within the group.

The lead rower, a man made old before his time by a lifetime exposed to the coastal weather, eased his oar. He smiled, a disjointed, gap-toothed smile at Fidelma. His sea-coloured eyes, set deep in his leather-brown face, gazed appreciatively at the tall young woman with the rebellious strands of red hair escaping from her head dress. He had seen few religieuses who had such feminine poise as this one; few who seemed to be so effortlessly in command.

"There's Inis Cloichreán to our right, sister." He thrust out a gnarled hand to indicate the direction, realizing that, as he was facing the religieuse, the island actually lay to her left. "We are twenty minutes from it. Do you wish to land there first or go on to Chléire?"

"I have no need to be long on Chloichreán," Fidelma replied after a moment of thought. "We'll land there first as it is on our way."

The rower grunted in acknowledgement and nodded to the second rower. As if at a signal, they dipped their oars together and the currach sped swiftly over the waves towards the island.

It was a hilly, rocky island. From the sea, it appeared that its shores were nothing more than steep, inaccessible cliffs whose grey granite was broken into coloured relief by sea pinks and honeysuckle chambers which filled the rocky outcrops.

Lorcán, the chief rower, expertly directed the currach through offshore jagged peaks of rock, thrusting from the sea. The boat danced this way and that in the foam waters that hissed and gurgled around the jagged points of granite, creating tiny but dangerous whirlpools. He carefully manoeuvred a zig-zag path into a small, sheltered cove where a natural harbour awaited them.

Fidelma was amazed at his skill.

"None but a person with knowledge could land in such a place," she observed.

Lorcán grinned appreciatively.

"I am one of the few who know exactly where to land on this island, sister."

"But the members of the abbey, surely they must have some seamanship among them to be here?"

"Abbey is a grandiose name for Selbach's settlement," grunted the second oarsman, speaking for the first time since they had left the mainland.

"Maenach is right," confirmed Lorcán. "Abbot Selbach came here two years ago with about twelve brothers; he called them his apostles. But they are no more than young boys, the youngest fourteen and the eldest scarcely nineteen. They chose this island because it was inaccessible and few knew how to land on it. It is true that they have a currach but they never use it. It is only for emergencies. Four or five times a year I land here with any supplies that they might want from the mainland."

"Ah, so it is a hermitage," Fidelma said. There were many of the religious in Ireland who had become solitary hermits or, taking a few followers, had found some out of the way place to set up a community where they could live together in isolated contemplation of the faith. Fidelma did not really trusts hermits, or isolated communities. It was not, in her estimation, the way to serve God by shutting oneself off from His greatest Creation – the society of men and women.

"A hermitage, indeed," agreed Maenach mournfully.

Fidelma gazed around curiously.

"It is not a large island. Surely one of the brothers must have seen our landing yet no one has come to greet us."

Lorcán had secured the currach to a rock by a rope and now bent forward to assist Fidelma out of the craft while Maenach used his balance to steady it.

"We'd better all get out," Fidelma said, more for the attention of the frightened young novitiate, Sister Sárnat, than Maenach. The young girl, no more than sixteen, dutifully scrambled after Fidelma, keeping close like a chick to a mother hen.

Maenach followed, pausing to stretch languidly once he stood on dry land.

Lorcán was pointing up some steps carved in the granite slope which led from the small cove up to the top of the cliff.

"If you take those steps, sister, you'll come to Selbach's community," he said. "We'll await you here."

Fidelma nodded, turning to Sister Sárnat.

"Will you wait here or do you want to come with me?"

The young sister shivered as if touched by a cold wind and looked unhappy.

"I'll come with you, sister," she sniffed anxiously.

Fidelma sighed softly. The girl was long past "the age of choice" yet she was more like a ten-year-old, frightened with life and clutching at the nearest adult to protect her from potential lurking terrors. The girl intrigued Fidelma. She wondered what had possessed her to join a religious house while so young, without experience of life or people.

"Very well, follow me then," she instructed.

Lorcán called softly after her.

"I'd advise you not to be long, sister." He pointed to the western sky. "There's a backing wind coming and we'll have a storm before nightfall. The sooner we reach Chléire, the sooner we shall be in shelter."

"I'll not be long," Fidelma assured him and began to lead the way up the steps with Sárnat following quickly behind.

"How can he know that there'll be a storm," the young novitiate demanded breathlessly as she stumbled to keep up with Fidelma. "It's such a lovely day."

Fidelma grimaced.

"A seaman will know these things, Sárnat. The signs are there to be read in the sky. Did you observe the moon last night?"

Sárnat looked puzzled.

"The moon was bright," she conceded.

"But if you had truly examined it then you would have seen a red glow to it. The air was still and comparatively dry. It is almost a guarantee of stormy winds from the west."

Fidelma suddenly paused and pointed to some plants growing along the edge of the pathway.

"Here's another sign. See the trefoil? Look at the way its stem is swollen. And those dandelions nearby, their petals are contracting and closing. Both those signs mean it will be raining soon."

"How do you know these things?" asked the girl wonderingly.

"By observation and listening to the old ones, those who are wise in the ancient knowledge."

They had climbed above the rocky cliffs and stood overlooking a sheltered depression in the centre of the island where a few gaunt, bent trees grew amidst several stone, beehive-shaped huts and a small oratory.

"So this is Abbot Selbach's community?" Fidelma mused. She stood frowning at the collection of buildings. She could see no movement nor signs of life. She raised her voice. "Hello there!"

The only answer that came back was an angry chorus of disturbed seabirds; of newly arrived auks seeking their summer nesting places who suddenly rose, black and white or dark brown with brilliantly coloured bills and webbed feet. The black guillemots, gulls and storm petrels followed, swirling around the island in an angry, chiding crowd.

Fidelma was puzzled. Someone must have heard her yet there was no response.

She made her way slowly down the grassy path into the shallow depression in which the collection of stone buildings stood. Sárnat trotted dutifully at her side.

Fidelma paused before the buildings and called again. And again there was no reply.

She moved on through the complex of buildings, turning round a corner into a quadrangle. The shriek came from Sister Sárnat.

There was a tree in the centre of the quadrangle; a small tree no more than twelve feet high, bent before the cold Atlantic winds, gaunt and gnarled. To the thin trunk of this tree, secured by the wrists with leather thongs, which prevented it from slumping to the ground, the body of a man was tied. Although the body was secured with its face towards the tree trunk, there was no need to ask if the man was dead.

Sister Sárnat stood shaking in terror at her side.

Fidelma ignored her and moved forward a pace to examine the body. It was clad in bloodstained robes, clearly the robes of a religious. The head was shaven at the front, back to a line stretching from ear to ear. At the back of his head, the hair was worn long. It was the tonsure of the Irish church, the *airbacc giunnae* which had been an inheritance from the Druids. The dead man was in his sixties; a thin, sharp featured individual with sallow skin and a pinched mouth. She noticed that, hanging from a thong round his neck, he wore a crucifix of some value; a carefully worked silver cross. The bloodstains covered the back of the robe which actually hung in ribbons from the body.

Fidelma saw that the shoulders of the robe were torn and bloodied and beneath it was lacerated flesh. There were several small stab wounds in the back but the numerous ripping wounds showed that the man had clearly been scourged by a whip before he had met his death.

Fidelma's eyes widened in surprise as she noticed a piece of wood fixed to the tree. There was some writing on it. It was in Greek; "As the whirlwind passes, so is the wicked no more . . ." She tried to remember why it sounded so familiar. Then she realized that it was out of the "Book of Proverbs".

It was obvious to her eye that the man had been beaten and killed while tied to the tree.

She became distracted by the moaning of the girl and turned, suppressing her annoyance.

"Sárnat, go back to the cove and fetch Lorcán here." And when the girl hesitated, she snapped "Now!"

Sárnat turned and scurried away.

Fidelma took another step towards the hanged religious and let her eyes wander over the body, seeking more information. She could gather nothing further other than that the man was elderly and a religious of rank, if the wealth of the crucifix was anything to go by. Then she stepped back and gazed around her. There was a small oratory, no larger than to accommodate half-a-dozen people at most behind its dry stone walls. It was placed in the centre of the six stone cells which served as accommodation for the community.

Fidelma crossed to the oratory and peered inside.

She thought, at first in the gloom, that it was a bundle of rags lying on the small altar. Then, as her eyes grew accustomed to the dim light, she saw that it was the body of a young religious. It was a boy not even reached manhood. She noticed that his robes were dank and sodden. The fair brown hair dried flat against his temples. The features were not calm in death's repose but contorted in an odd manner, as if the boy had died in pain. She was about to move forward to make a closer investigation, when she nearly tripped over what seemed to be another bundle.

Another religious lay stretched face downwards, arms outstretched, almost like a supplicant praying towards the altar. His hair was dark. He was clad in the robes of a brother. This religious was older than the youth.

She moved forward and knelt down, seeking a pulse in his neck with her two fingers. It was faint but it was there right enough but the body was unnaturally cold. She bent further to examine the face. The man was about forty. Even unconscious the features were placid and quite handsome. A pleasant face, Fidelma conceded. But dried blood caked one side of the broad forehead where it had congealed around a wound.

She shook the man by the shoulder but he was deeply unconscious.

Checking her exhalation of breath, Fidelma stood up and, moving swiftly, she went from stone cell to stone cell but each one told the same story. There was no one hiding from her within the buildings. The cells of the community were deserted.

Lorcán came running along the path from the cove.

"I left the girl behind with Maenach," he grunted as he came up to Fidelma. "She was upset. She says that someone is dead and . . ."

He paused and stared around him. From this position, the tree with its gruesome corpse was hidden to him.

"Where is everyone?"

"There is a man still alive here," Fidelma said, ignoring the question. "He needs our immediate attention."

She led the way to the small oratory, stooping down to enter and then standing to one side so that Lorcán could follow.

Lorcán gasped and genuflected as he saw the young boy.

"I know this boy. His name is Sacán from Inis Beag. Why, I brought him here to join the community only six months ago."

Fidelma pointed to the figure of the dark-haired man on the floor which Lorcán had not observed.

"Do you recognize that brother?" she asked.

"The saints defend us!" exclaimed the boatman as he bent down. "This is Brother Spelán."

Fidelma pursed her lips.

"Brother Spelán?" she repeated unnecessarily.

Lorcán nodded unhappily.

"He served as Abbot Selbach's *dominus*, the administrator of this community. Who did this deed? Where is everyone?"

"Questions can be answered later. We need to take him to a more comfortable place and restore him to consciousness. The boy – Sacán, you called him? – well, he is certainly beyond our help."

"Sister," replied Lorcán, "my friend Maenach knows a little of the physician's art. Let me summon him so that he might assist us with Spelán."

"It will take too long."

"It will take but a moment," Lorcán assured her, taking a conch shell from a rough leather pouch at his side. He went to the door and blew on it long and loudly. It was echoed by a tremendous chorus of frightened birds. Lorcán paused a moment before turning with a smile to Fidelma. "I see Maenach on the cliff top with the young sister. They are coming this way."

"Then help me carry this brother to one of the nearby cells so that we may put him on a better bed than this rough floor," instructed Fidelma.

As she knelt down to help lift the man she suddenly noticed a small wooden cup lying nearby. She reached forward and placed it in her *marsupium*, her large purse-like bag, slung from her waist. There would be time to examine it later.

Between them, they carried Brother Spelán, who was quite heavy, to the nearest cell and laid him on one of two wooden cots which were within.

Maenach came hurrying in with Sister Sárnat almost clutching at his sleeve. Lorcán pointed to the unconscious religious.

"Can you revive him?" he asked.

Maenach bent over the man, raising the unconscious man's eyelids and then testing his pulse.

"He is in a deep coma. Almost as if he is asleep." He examined the wound. "It is curious that he has been rendered so deeply unconscious from the blow that made this wound. The wound seems superficial enough. The brother's breathing is regular and untroubled. I am sure he will regain consciousness after a while."

"Then do what you can, Maenach," Fidelma said. "Sister Sárnat, you will help him," she instructed the pale, shivering young girl who still hovered uncertainly at the door of the cell.

She then took the boatman, Lorcán, by the arm and led him from the cell, turning him towards the quadrangle, and pointing silently to the figure bound to the tree.

Lorcán took a step forward and then let out a startled exhalation of breath. It was the first time he had observed the body.

"God look down upon us!" he said slowly as he genuflected. "Now there are two deaths among the religious of Selbach!"

"Do you know this person?" Fidelma asked.

"Know him?" Lorcán sounded startled at the question. "Of course. It is the Abbot Selbach!"

"Abbot Selbach?"

Fidelma pursed her lips with astonishment as she reexamined the body of the dead abbot. Then she gazed around her towards the empty landscape.

"And did you not say that Selbach had a community of twelve brothers here with him?"

Lorcán followed her gaze uncertainly.

"Yes. Yet the island seems deserted," he muttered. "What terrible mystery is here?"

"That is something we must discover," Fidelma replied confidently.

"We must leave for the mainland at once," Lorcán advised. "We must get back to Dún na Séad and inform The Ó hEidersceoil."

The Ó hEidersceoil was the chieftain of the territory.

Fidelma raised a hand to stay the man even as he was turning back to the cell where they had left Brother Spelán.

"Wait, Lorcán. I am a *dálaigh*, an advocate of the Law of the *Fenechus*, holding the degree of *anruth*. It is my task to stay and

discover how Abbot Selbach and little Sacán met their deaths and
why Brother Spelán was wounded. Also we must discover where the
rest of the community has disappeared to."

Lorcán gazed at the young religieuse in surprise.

"That same danger may yet attend us," he protested. "What
manner of magic is it that makes a community disappear and
leaves their abbot dead like a common criminal bound to a tree,
the boy dead and their *dominus* assaulted and unconscious?"

"Human magic, if magic you want to call it," Fidelma replied
irritably. "As an advocate of the law courts of the five kingdoms
of Ireland, I call upon you for assistance. I have this right by the
laws of the *Fenechus*, under the authority of the Chief Brehon. Do you
deny my right?"

Lorcán gazed at the religieuse a moment in surprise and then
slowly shook his head.

"You have that right, sister. But, look, Abbot Selbach is not long
dead. What if his killers are hiding nearby?"

Fidelma ignored his question and turned back to regard the
hanging body, her head to one side in reflection.

"What makes you say that he is not long dead, Lorcán?"

The sailor shrugged impatiently.

"The body is cold but not very stiff. Also it is untouched by the
scavengers . . ."

He gestured towards the wheeling birds. She followed his gaze and
could see among the seabirds, the large forms of black-backed gulls,
one of the most vicious of coastal scavengers. And here and there
she saw the jet black of carrion crows. It was the season when the
eggs of these harsh-voiced predators would be hatching along the
cliff top nests and the young birds would be demanding to be fed by
the omnivorous parents, feeding off eggs of other birds, even small
mammals and often rotting carcasses. She realized that the wheeling
gulls and crows would sooner or later descend on a corpse but there
was no sign that they had done so already.

"Excellently observed, Lorcán," she commented. "And presumably Brother Spelán could not have been unconscious long. But do
you observe any other peculiar thing about the abbot's body?"

The boatman frowned at her and glanced at the slumped corpse.
He stared a moment and shook his head.

"Selbach was flogged and then stabbed three times in the back. I
would imagine that the thrust of the knife was upwards, between the
ribs, so that he died instantly. What strange ritual would so punish
a man before killing him?"

Lorcán stared more closely and sighed deeply.

"I don't understand."

"Just observe for the moment," Fidelma replied. "I may need you later to be a witness to these facts. I think we may cut down the body and place it out of reach of the birds within the oratory."

Lorcán took his sharp sailor's knife and quickly severed the ropes. Then he dragged the body into the oratory at Fidelma's direction.

Fidelma now had time to make a more careful examination of the young boy's body.

"He has clearly been immersed for a while in the sea. Not very long but several hours at least," she observed. "There are no immediate causes of death. He has not been stabbed nor has he been hit by any blunt instrument."

She turned the body and gave a quick sudden intake of breath.

"But he has been scourged. See, Lorcán?"

The boatman saw that the upper part of the boy's robe had been torn revealing that his back was covered in old and new welts and scars made by a whip.

"I knew the boy's family well on Inis Beag," he whispered. "He was a happy, dutiful boy. His body was without blemish when I brought him here."

Fidelma made a search of the boy's sodden clothing, the salt water drying out was already making white lines and patches on it. Her eyes narrowed as she examined the prayer cord which fastened the habit. A small metal hook was hanging from it on which a tiny leather sheath was fastened containing a small knife, a knife typical of those used by some rural orders to cut their meat or help them in their daily tasks. Caught on the projecting metal hook was a torn piece of woollen cloth. Carefully, Fidelma removed it and held it up.

"What is it, sister?" asked Lorcán.

"I don't know. A piece of cloth caught on the hook." She made a quick examination. "It is not from the boy's clothing." She placed it in her *marsupium*, along with the wooden cup. Then she cast one final look at the youthful body before covering it. "Come, let us see what else we can find."

"But what, sister?" Lorcán asked. "What can we do? There is a storm coming soon and if it catches us here then here we shall have to remain until it passes."

"I am aware of the coming storm," she replied imperturbably. "But first we must be sure of one thing. You say there were twelve brothers here as well as Selbach? Then we have accounted for only two of them, Spelán and Sacán. Our next step is clear – we must search the island to assure ourselves that they are not hidden from us."

Lorcán bit his lip nervously.

"What if it were pirates who did this deed? I have heard tales of Saxon raiders with their longboats, devastating villages further along the coast."

"A possibility," agreed Fidelma. "But it is not a likely one."

"Why so?" demanded Lorcán. "The Saxons have raided along the coasts of Gaul, Britain and Ireland for many years, looting and killing . . ."

"Just so," Fidelma smiled grimly. "Looting and burning communities; driving off livestock and taking the people to be slaves."

She gestured to the deserted but tranquil buildings.

Lorcán suddenly realized what she was driving at. There was no sign of any destruction nor of any looting or violence enacted against the property. On the slope behind the oratory, three or four goats munched at the heather while a fat sow snorted and grunted among her piglets. And if that were not enough, he recalled that the silver crucifix still hung around the neck of the dead abbot. There had been no theft here. Clearly, then, there had been no pirate raid on the defenceless community. Lorcán was even more puzzled.

"Come with me, Lorcán, and we will examine the cells of the brothers," instructed Fidelma.

The stone cell next to the one in which they had left Spelán had words inscribed on the lintel.

Ora et labora. Work and pray. A laudable exhortation thought Fidelma and she passed underneath. The cell was almost bare and its few items of furniture were simple. On a beaten earthen floor, covered with rushes strewn as a mat, there were two wooden cots, a cupboard, a few leather *tiag leabhair* or book satchels, hung from hooks, containing several small gosepl books. A large ornately carved wooden cross hung on a wall.

There was another maxim inscribed on a wall to one side of this cell.

> *Animi indices sunt oculi.*
> The eyes are the betrayer of the mind.

Fidelma found it a curious adage to exhort a Christian community to faith. Then her eyes fell on a piece of written vellum by the side of one of the cots. She picked it up. It was a verse from one of the Psalms. "Break thou the arm of the wicked and the evil man; seek out his wickedness till thou find none . . ." She shivered slightly for this was not a dictum of a God of love.

Her eyes fell on a box at the foot of the bed. On the top of the box was an inscription in Greek.

Pathémata mathémata. Sufferings are lessons.

She bent forward and opened the box. Her eyes rounded in astonishment. Contained in the box were a set of scourges, of whips and canes. There were some words carved on the underside of the lid. They were in plain Irish.

> God give me a wall of tears
> my sins to hide;
> for I remain, while no tears fall,
> unsanctified.

She looked across to Lorcán in surprise.

"Do you know whose cell this was?" she demanded.

"Assuredly," came the prompt reply. "Selbach shared this cell with his *dominus* – Spelán. The cell we placed Spelán in, the one nearest the oratory, belongs to two other members of the community."

"Do you know what sort of man Selbach was? Was he a man who was authoritarian, who liked to inflict punishment? Was the Rule of his community a harsh one?"

Lorcán shrugged.

"That I would not know. I did not know the community that well."

"There is evidence of pain and punishment in this place," Fidelma sensed a cold tingle against her spine. "I do not understand it."

She paused, noticing a shelf on which stood several jars and bottles. She moved to them and began to examine the contents of each jar, sniffing its odours or wetting the tip of her finger from the concoctions before cautiously tasting it. Then she reached into her *marsupium* and took the wooden cup she had retrieved from the floor of the oratory. It had recently been used for the wood still showed the dampness of its contents. She sniffed at it. A curious mixture of pungent odours came to her nostrils. Then she turned back to the shelf and examined the jars and bottles of herbs again. She could identify the dried heads of red clover, dried horse-chestnut leaves and mullein among the jars of herbs.

Lorcán stood watching her impatiently.

"Spelán uses this as the community's apothecary," he said. "On one of my trips here I cut my hand and it was Spelán who gave me a poultice of herbs to heal it."

Fidelma sighed a little as she gave a final look around.

Finally she left the cell, followed by an unhappy Lorcán, and began to examine the other cells again but this time more carefully. There was evidence in one or two of them that some personal items and articles of clothing had been hurriedly removed but not enough to support the idea of the community being attacked and robbed by an outside force.

Fidelma emerged into the quadrangle feeling confused.

Lorcán, at her side, was gazing up at the sky, a worried expression on his face.

Fidelma knew that he was still concerned about the approaching weather but it was no time to retreat from this mystery. Someone had killed the abbot of the community and a young brother, knocked the *dominus* unconscious and made ten further members of the brotherhood disappear.

"Didn't you say that the community had their own boat?" she asked abruptly.

Lorcán nodded unhappily.

"It was not in the cove when we landed," Fidelma pointed out.

"No, it wouldn't be," replied the boatman. "They kept their boat further along the shore in a sheltered spot. There is a small shingled strand around the headland where a boat can be beached."

"Show me," Fidelma instructed. "There is nothing else to do until Spelán recovers consciousness and we may learn his story."

Somewhat reluctantly, with another glance at the western sky, Lorcán led the way along the pathway towards the cove but then broke away along another path which led down on the other side of a great rocky outcrop which served as a headland separating them from the cove in which they had landed.

Fidelma knew something was wrong when they reached a knoll before the path twisted and turned through granite pillars towards the distant pounding sea. Her eyes caught the flash of black in the sky circling over something on the shore below.

They were black-backed gulls. Of all gulls, these were birds to be respected. They frequently nested on rocky islands such as Inis Chloichreán. It was a carrion eater, a fierce predator given to taking mammals even as large as cats. They had obviously found something down on the beach. Fidelma could see that even the crows could not compete with their larger brethren. There were several pairs of crows above the mêlée, circling and waiting their chance.

Fidelma compressed her lips firmly.

Lorcán continued to lead the way down between the rocks. The area was full of nesting birds. May was a month in which the black-backed gulls, along with many another species, laid their eggs. The rocky cliffs of the island were ideal sites for birds. The females screamed furiously as they entered the area but Lorcán ignored their threatening displays. Fidelma did not pretend that she was unconcerned.

"The brothers kept their boat just here . . ." began Lorcán, reaching a large platform of rocky land about twelve feet above a short pebbly beach. He halted and stared.

Fidelma saw the wooden trestles, on which the boat had apparently been set. There was no vessel resting on them now.

"They used to store the boat here," explained Lorcán, "placed upside down to protect it against the weather."

It was the gathering further down on the pebbly strand, an area of beach no more than three yards in width and perhaps ten yards long, that caused Fidelma to exclaim sharply. She realized what the confusion of birds was about. A dozen or more large gulls were gathered, screaming and fighting each other, while forming an outer circle were several other birds who seemed to be interested spectators to the affair. Here and there a jet black carrion crow perched, black eyes watching intently for its chance, while others circled overhead. They were clustering around something which lay on the pebbles. Fidelma suspected what it was.

"Come on!" she cried, and climbed hastily down to the pebbly strand. Then she halted and picked up several large pebbles and began to hurl them at the host of carrion eaters. The scavengers let forth screaming cries of anger and flapped their great wings. Lorcán joined her, picking up stones and throwing them with all his strength.

It was not long before the wheeling mass of birds had dispersed from the object over which they had been fighting. But Fidelma saw that they had not retreated far. They swirled high in the air above them or strutted nearby, beady eyes watching and waiting.

Nonetheless, she strode purposefully across the shingle.

The religious had been young, very young with fair hair.

He lay on his back, his robes in an unseemly mess of torn and frayed wool covered in blood.

Fidelma swallowed hard. The gulls had been allowed an hour or so of uninterrupted work. The face was pitted and bloody, an eye was missing. Part of the skull had been smashed, a pulpy mess of blood and bone. It was obvious that no bird had perpetrated that damage.

"Can you tell who this was, Lorcán?" Fidelma asked softly.

The boatman came over, one wary eye on the gulls. They were standing well back but with their eyes malignantly on the humans who had dared drive them from their unholy feasting. Lorcán glanced down. He pulled a face at the sight.

"I have seen him here in the community, sister. Alas, I do not know his name. Sister, I am fearful. This is the third dead member of the community."

Fidelma did not reply but steeled herself to bend beside the corpse. The leather *crumena* or purse was still fastened at his belt. She forced herself to avoid the lacerated features of the youth and his one remaining bright, accusing eye, and put her hand into the purse. It was empty.

She drew back and shook her head.

Then a thought occurred to her.

"Help me push the body over face down," she instructed.

Keeping his curiosity to himself, Lorcán did so.

The robe was almost torn from the youth's back by the ravages of the birds. Fidelma did not have to remove the material further to see a patch of scars, some old, some new, some which showed signs of recent bleeding, criss-cross over his back.

"What do you make of that, Lorcán?" Fidelma invited.

The boatman thrust out his lower lip and raised one shoulder before letting it fall in an exaggerated shrug.

"Only that the boy has been whipped. Not once either but many times over a long period."

Fidelma nodded in agreement.

"That's another fact I want you to witness, Lorcán."

She stood up, picking up a few stones as she did so and shying them at two or three large gulls who were slowly closing the distance between them. They screamed in annoyance but removed themselves to a safer position.

"How big was the community's currach?" she asked abruptly.

Lorcán understood what she meant.

"It was big enough to carry the rest of the brethren," he replied. "They must be long gone, by now. They could be anywhere on the islands or have even reached the mainland." He paused and looked at her. "But did they go willingly or were they forced to go? Who could have done this?"

Fidelma did not reply. She motioned Lorcán to help her return the body to its original position and stared at the crushed skull.

"That was done with a heavy and deliberate blow," she observed. "This young religious was murdered and left here on the strand."

Lorcán shook his head in utter bewilderment.

"There is much evil here, sister."

"With that I can agree," Fidelma replied. "Come, let us build a cairn over his body with stones so that the gulls do not feast further on him – whoever he was. We cannot carry him back to the settlement."

"Isn't it best to leave him here?"

"No. The evidence might be needed later."

When they arrived back at the community, having completed their task, Maenach greeted them in the quadrangle with a look of relief.

"Brother Spelán is coming round. The young sister is nursing him."

Fidelma answered with a grim smile.

"Now perhaps we may learn some answers to this mystery."

Inside the cell, the brother was lying against a pillow. He looked very drowsy and blinked several times as his dark, black eyes tried to focus on Fidelma.

She motioned Sister Sárnat to move aside and sat on the edge of the cot by Spelán.

"I have given him water only, sister," the girl said eagerly, as if expecting her approval. "The boatman," she gestured towards Maenach, who stood at the doorway with Lorcán, "bathed and dressed the wound."

Fidelma smiled encouragingly at the brother.

"Are you Brother Spelán?"

The man closed his eyes for a moment, his voice sounded weak.

"I am Spelán. Who are you and what are you doing here?"

"I am Fidelma of Kildare. I am come here to bring the Abbot Selbach a letter from Ultan of Armagh."

Spelán stared at her.

"A letter from Ultan?" He sounded confused.

"Yes. That is why we landed on the island. What has happened here? Who hit you on the head?"

Spelán groaned and raised a hand to his forehead.

"I recall." His voice grew strong and commanding. "The abbot is dead, sister. Return to Dún na Séad and ask that a Brehon be sent here for there has been a great crime committed."

"I will take charge of the matter, Spelán," Fidelma said confidently.

"You?" Spelán stared at her in bewilderment. "You don't understand. It is a Brehon that is needed."

"I am a dálaigh of the court qualified to the level of anruth."

Spelán's eyes widened a fraction for he realized that the qualification of anruth allowed the young religieuse to sit in judgement with kings and even with the High King himself.

"Tell me what took place here?" Fidelma prompted.

Spelán's dark eyes found Sister Sárnat and motioned for her to hand him the cup of water from which he took several swallows.

"There was evil here, sister. An evil which grew unnoticed by me until it burst forth and enveloped us all in its maw."

Fidelma waited without saying anything.

Spelán seemed to gather his thoughts for a moment or two.

"I will start from the beginning."

"Always a good place for starting a tale," Fidelma affirmed solemnly.

"Two years ago I met Selbach who persuaded me to join him here in order to build a community which would be dedicated to isolation and meditative contemplation of the works of the Creator. I was the apothecary at an abbey on the mainland which was a sinful place – pride, gluttony and other vices were freely practised there. In Selbach I believed that I had found a kindred spirit who shared my own views. We searched together for a while and eventually came across eleven young souls who wanted to devote themselves to our purpose."

"Why so young?" demanded Fidelma.

Spelán blinked.

"We needed youth to help our community flourish for in youth lies strength against the hardships of this place."

"Go on," pressed Fidelma when the man paused.

"With the blessing of Ultan of Armagh and the permission of the local chieftain, The Ó hEidersceoil, we came to this isolated place."

He paused to take another sip of water.

"And what of this evil that grew in your midst?" encouraged Fidelma.

"I am coming to that. There is a philosophy among some of the ascetics of the faith that physical pain, even as the Son of the Living God had to endure, pain such as the tortures of the flesh, is the way to man's redemption, a way to salvation. Mortification and suffering are seen as the paths to spiritual salvation."

Fidelma sniffed in disapproval.

"I have heard that there are such misguided fools among us."

Spelán blinked.

"Not fools, sister, not fools," he corrected softly. "Many of our blessed saints believed in the efficacy of mortification. They held genuine belief that they must emulate the pain of Christ if they, too, would seek eternal paradise. There are many who will still wear crowns of thorns, who flagellate themselves, drive nails into their hands or pierce their sides so that they might share the suffering of Christ. No, you are too harsh, sister. They are not fools; visionaries – yes; and, perhaps, misguided in their path."

"Very well. We will not argue the matter at this stage, Spelán. What is this to do with what has happened here."

"Do not mistake my meaning, sister," replied Selbach contritely. "I am not an advocate for the *gortaigid*, those who seek the infliction of such pain. I, too, condemn them as you do. But I accept that their desire to experience pain is a genuine desire to share the pain of the Messiah through which he sought man's redemption. I would not call them fools. However, let me continue. For a while we were a happy community. It did not cross my mind that one among us felt that pain was his path to salvation."

"There was a *gortaigid* among you?"

The *dominus* nodded.

"I will spare the events that led to it but will simply reveal that it was none other than the venerable Abbot Selbach himself. But Selbach was not of those who simply inflicted pain and punishment upon himself. He persuaded the youthful brothers we had gathered here to submit to scourgings and whippings in order to satiate his desire to inflict pain and injury so that, he argued, they might approach a sharing of Christ's great suffering. He practised these abominations in secret and swore others to keep that secret on pain of their immortal souls."

"When was this discovered?" demanded Fidelma, slightly horrified.

Spelán bit his lip a moment.

"For certain? Only this morning. I knew nothing. I swear it. It was early this morning that the body of our youngest neophyte, Sacán, was found. He was fourteen years old. The brothers found him and it was known that Selbach had taken him to a special place at the far end of the island last night to ritually scourge the boy. So fierce did he lash the youth that he died of shock and pain."

The *dominus* genuflected.

Fidelma's mouth tightened.

"Go on. How were you, the *dominus* of this community, unaware of the abbot's actions before this morning?"

"He was cunning," replied Spelán immediately. "He made the young brothers take oath each time not to reveal the ritual scourgings to anyone else. He took one young brother at a time to the far end of the island. A shroud of silence enveloped the community. I dwelt in blissful ignorance."

"Go on."

"Selbach had tried to hide his guilt by throwing the poor boy's body over the cliffs last night but the tide washed the body along the rocky barrier that is our shore. It washed ashore early this morning at a point where two of our brethren were fishing for our daily meal."

He paused and sought another sip of water.

Behind her Lorcán said quietly: "Indeed, the tide from the headland would wash the body along to the pebble beach."

"I was asleep when I heard the noise. When I left my cell the brothers' anger had erupted and they had seized Selbach and lashed

him to the quadrangle tree. One of the brothers was flogging him
with his own whip, tearing at his flesh . . ."

The *dominus* paused again before continuing.

"And did you attempt to stop them?" inquired Fidelma.

"Of course I tried to stop them," Spelán replied indignantly. "I
tried to remonstrate, as did another young brother, Snagaide, who
told them they could not take the law into their own hands nor
punish Selbach. They must take their complaint to Dún na
Séad and place it before the Brehon of The Ó hEidersceoil. But the
young brothers were so enraged that they would not listen. Instead,
they seized Snagaide and myself and held us, ignoring our pleas, while
they flogged Selbach. Their rage was great. And then, before I knew
it, someone had thrust his knife into the back of Selbach. I did not
see who it was.

"I cried to them that not only a crime had been done but now
great sacrilege. I demanded that they surrender themselves to me
and to Brother Snagaide. I promised that I would take them to Dún
na Séad where they must answer for their deed but I would speak
on their behalf."

Spelán paused and touched the wound on the side of his head once
more with a grimace of pain.

"They argued among themselves then but, God forgive them, they
found a determined spokesman in a brother named Fogach who said
that they should not be punished for doing what was right and just
in the eyes of God. An eye for an eye, a tooth for a tooth, they argued.
It was right for Selbach to have met his death in compensation for the
death of young Brother Sacán. He demanded that I should swear an
oath not to betray the events on the island, recording the deaths as
accidents. If I protested then they would take the currach and seek
a place where they could live in peace and freedom, leaving me and
Snagaide on the island until visited by Lorcán or some other boatman
from the mainland."

"Then what happened?" urged Fidelma after the *dominus* paused.

"Then? As you might expect, I could not make such an oath. Their
anger spilt over while I remonstrated with them. More for the fear
of the consequences than anger, I would say. One of their number
knocked me on the head. I knew nothing else until I came to with
the young sister and the boatman bending over me."

Fidelma was quiet for a while.

"Tell me, Spelán, what happened to your companion, Brother
Snagaide?"

Spelán frowned, looking around as if he expected to find the brother
in a corner of the cell.

"Snagaide? I do not know, sister. There was a great deal of shouting and arguing. Then everything went black for me."

"Was Brother Snagaide young?"

"Most of the brethren, apart from myself and Selbach, were but youths."

"Did he have fair hair?"

Spelán shook his head to her surprise. Then it was not Snagaide who lay dead on the strand.

"No," Spelán repeated. "He had black hair."

"One thing that still puzzles me, Spelán. This is a small island, with a small community. For two years you have lived here in close confines. Yet you say that you did not know about the sadistic tendencies of Abbot Selbach; that each night he took young members of the community to some remote part of the island and inflicted pain on them, yet you did not know? I find this strange."

Spelán grimaced dourly.

"Strange though it is, sister, it is the truth. The rest of the community were young. Selbach dominated them. They thought that pain brought them nearer salvation. Being sworn by the Holy Cross never to speak of the whipping given them by the abbot, they remained in silence. Probably they thought that I approved of the whippings. Ah, those poor boys, they suffered in silence until the death of gentle, little Sacán . . . poor boy, poor boy."

Tears welled in the *dominus'* eyes.

Sister Sárnat reached forward and handed him the cup of water.

Fidelma rose silently and left the cell.

Lorcán followed after her as she went to the quadrangle and stood for a moment in silent reflection.

"A terrible tale, and no mistake," he commented, his eyes raised absently to the sky. "The brother is better now, however, and we can leave as soon as you like."

Fidelma ignored him. Her hands were clasped before her and she was gazing at the ground without focusing on it.

"Sister?" prompted Lorcán.

Fidelma raised her head, suddenly becoming aware of him.

"Sorry, you were saying something?"

The boatman shrugged.

"Only that we should be on our way soon. The poor brother needs to be taken to Chléire as soon as we can do so."

Fidelma breathed out slowly.

"I think that the poor brother . . ." she paused and grimaced. "I think there is still a mystery here which needs to be resolved."

Lorcán stared at her.

"But the explanation of Brother Spelán . . .?"

Fidelma returned his gaze calmly.

"I will walk awhile in contemplation."

The boatman spread his hands in despair.

"But, sister, the coming weather . . ."

"If the storm comes then we will remain here until it passes." And, as Lorcán opened his mouth to protest, she added: "I state this as a *dálaigh* of the court and you will observe that authority."

Lorcán's mouth drooped and, with a shrug of resignation, he turned away.

Fidelma began to follow the path behind the community, among the rocks to the more remote area of the island. She realized that this would have been the path which, according to Spelán, Abbot Selbach took his victims. She felt a revulsion at what had been revealed by Spelán, although she had expected some such explanation from the evidence of the lacerated backs of the two young brothers she had seen. She felt loathing at the ascetics who called themselves *gortaigid*, those who sought salvation by bestowing pain on themselves and others. Abbots and bishops condemned them and they were usually driven out into isolated communities.

Here, it seemed, that one evil man had exerted his will on a bunch of youths scarcely out of boyhood who had sought the religious life and knew no better than submit to his will until one of their number died. Now those youths had fled the island, frightened, demoralized and probably lost to the truth of Christ's message of love and peace.

In spite of general condemnation she knew that in many abbeys and monasteries some abbots and abbesses ordered strict rules of intolerable numbers of genuflections, prostrations and fasts. She knew that Erc, the bishop of Slane, who had been patron of the blessed Brendan of Clonfert, would take his acolytes to cold mountain streams, summer and winter, to immerse themselves in the icy waters four times a day to say their prayers and psalms. There was the ascetic, Mac Tulchan, who bred fleas on his body and, so that his pain might be the greater, he never scratched himself. Didn't Finnian of Clonard purposely set out to catch a virulent disease from a dying child that he might obtain salvation through suffering?

Mortification and suffering. Ultan of Armagh was one of the school preaching moderation to those who were becoming indulgently masochistic, ascetics who were becoming fanatical torturers of the body, wrenching salvation through unnatural wants, strain or physical suffering.

She paused in her striding and sat down on a rock, her hands demurely folded in front of her, as she let her mind dwell on the evidence. It certainly appeared that everything fitted in with Spelán's explanation. Why did she feel that there was something wrong? She opened her *marsupium* and drew out the piece of cloth she had found ensnared on the belt hook of the youthful Sacán. It had obviously been torn away from something and not from the boy's habit. And there was the wooden cup, which had dried out now, which she had found on the floor of the oratory. It had obviously been used for an infusion of herbs.

She suddenly saw a movement out of the corner of her eye, among the rocks. She swung round very fast. For a moment her eyes locked into the dark eyes of a startled youth, the cowl of his habit drawn over his head. Then the youth darted away among the rocks.

"Stop!" Fidelma came to her feet, thrusting the cup and cloth into her *marsupium*. "Stop brother, I mean you no harm."

But the youth was gone, bounding away through the rocky terrain.

With an exasperated sigh, Fidelma began to follow, when the sound of her name being called halted her.

Sister Sárnat came panting along the path.

"I have been sent by Brother Spelán and Lorcán," she said. "Lorcán entreats you to have a care of the approaching storm, sister."

Fidelma was about to say something sarcastic about Lorcán's concern but Sárnat continued.

"Brother Spelán agrees we should leave the island immediately and report the events here to the abbot of Chléire. The brother is fully recovered now and he is taking charge of things. He says that he recalls your purpose here was to bring a letter from Ultan to the Abbot Selbach. Since Selbach is dead and he is *dominus* he asks that you give him the letter in case anything requires to be done about it before we leave the island."

Fidelma forgot about the youth she was about to pursue.

She stared hard at Sister Sárnat.

The young novitiate waited nervously, wondering what Fidelma was staring at.

"Sister . . ." she began nervously.

Fidelma sat down on the nearest rock abruptly.

"I have been a fool," she muttered, reaching into her *marsupium* and bringing out the letters she was carrying. She thrust back the letter addressed to the abbot of Chléire and tore open Ultan's letter to Selbach, to the astonished gaze of Sister Sárnat. Her eyes rapidly read the letter and her features broke into a grim smile.

"Go, sister," she said, arising and thrusting the letter back into the *marsupium.* "Return to Brother Spelán. Tell him and Lorcán that I will be along in a moment. I think we will be able to leave here before the storm develops."

Sárnat stared at her uncertainly.

"Very well, sister. But why not return with me?"

Fidelma smiled.

"I have to talk to someone first."

A short while later Fidelma strode into the cell where Spelán was sitting on the cot, with Lorcán and Maenach lounging nearby. Sister Sárnat was seated on a wooden bench by one wall. As Fidelma entered, Lorcán looked up in relief.

"Are you ready now, sister? We do not have long."

"A moment or two, if you please, Lorcán," she said, smiling gently.

Spelán was rising.

"I think we should leave immediately, sister. I have much to report to the abbot of Chléire. Also . . ."

"How did you come to tear your robe, Spelán?"

Fidelma asked the question with an innocent expression. Beneath that expression, her mind was racing for she had made her opening arrow-shot into the darkness. Spelán stared at her and then stared at his clothing. It was clear that he did not know whether his clothing was torn or not. But his eyes lighted upon a jagged tear in his right sleeve. He shrugged.

"I did not notice," he replied.

Fidelma took the piece of torn cloth from her *marsupium* and laid it on the table.

"Would you say that this cloth fitted the tear, Lorcán."

The boatman, frowning, picked it up and took it to place against Spelán's sleeve.

"It does, sister," he said quietly.

"Do you recall where I found it?"

"I do. It was snagged on the hook of the belt of the young boy, Sacán."

The colour drained from Spelán's face.

"It must have been caught there when I carried the body from the strand . . ." he began.

"*You* carried the body from the strand?" asked Fidelma with emphasis. "You told us that some of the young brothers fishing there saw it and brought it back and all this happened before you were awakened after they had tied Selbach to the tree and killed him."

Spelán's mouth worked for a moment without words coming.

"I will tell you what happened on this island," Fidelma said. "Indeed, you did have a *gortaigid* here. One who dedicated his life to the enjoyment of mortification and suffering but not from any pious ideal of religious attainment . . . merely from personal perversion. Where better to practise his disgusting sadism than a hermitage of youths whom he could dominate and devise tortures for by persuading them that only by that pain could they obtain true spirituality?"

Spelán was staring malignantly at her.

"In several essentials, your story was correct, Spelán. There was a conspiracy of secrecy among the youths. Their tormentor would take them one at a time, the youngest and most vulnerable, to a remote part of the island and inflict his punishment, assuring the boy it was the route to eternal glory. Then one day one of the youths, poor little Sacán, was beaten so severely that he died. In a panic the tormentor tried to dispose of his evil deed by throwing the body over the cliffs. As he did so, the hook on the boy's belt tore a piece of cloth from the man's robe. Then the next morning the body washed ashore."

"Utter nonsense. It was Selbach who . . ."

"It was Selbach who began to suspect that he had a *gortaigid* in his community."

Spelán frowned.

"All this is supposition," he sneered but there was a fear lurking in his dark eyes.

"Not quite," Fidelma replied without emotion. "You are a very clever man, Spelán. When Sacán's body was discovered, the youths who found him gathered on the shore around it. They did not realize that their abbot, Selbach, was really a kindly man who had only recently realized what was going on in his community and certainly did not condone it. As you said yourself, the conspiracy of silence was such that the youthful brothers thought that you were acting with Selbach's approval. They thought that mortification was a silent rule of the community. They decided to flee from the island there and then. Eight of them launched the currach and rowed away, escaping from what had become for them an accursed place . . ."

Lorcán, who had been following Fidelma's explanation with some astonishment, whistled softly.

"Where would they have gone, sister?"

"It depends. If they had sense they would have gone to report the matter to Chléire or even to Dún na Séad. But, perhaps, they thought their word would be of no weight against the abbot and *dominus* of this house. Perhaps these innocents still think that mortification is an accepted rule of the Faith."

"May I remind you that I was knocked unconscious by these same innocents?" sneered Spelán.

Maenach nodded emphatically.

"Indeed, sister, that is so. How do you explain that?"

"I will come to that in a moment. Let me tell you firstly what happened here. The eight young brothers left the island because they believed everyone else supported the rule of mortification. It was then that Brother Fogach came across the body and carried it to the oratory and alerted you, Spelán."

"Why would he do that?"

"Because Brother Fogach was not your enemy, nor was Brother Snagaide. They were your chosen acolytes who had actually helped you carry out your acts of sadism in the past. They were young and gullible enough to believe your instructions were the orders of the Faith and the Word of God. But inflicting punishment on their fellows was one thing, murder was another."

"You'll have a job to prove this," sneered Spelán.

"Perhaps," replied Fidelma. "At this stage Fogach and Snagaide were willing to help you. You realized that your time was running out. If those brothers reported matters then an official of the church, a *dálaigh*, would be sent to the island. You had to prepare your defence. An evil scheme came into your mind. It was still early. Selbach was still asleep. You persuaded Snagaide and Fogach that Selbach was responsible in the same way that you had persuaded their fellows that Selbach approved of this mortification. You told them that Selbach had flogged Sacán that night – not you – and now he must be ritually scourged in turn. Together you awoke Selbach and took him and tied him to that tree. You knew exactly what you were going to do but first you whipped that venerable old man.

"In his pain, the old man cried out and told your companions the truth. They listened, horrified at how they had been misled. Seeing this, you stabbed the abbot to stop him speaking. But the abbot's life would have been forfeit anyway. It was all part of your plan to hide all the evidence against you, to show that you were simply the dupe of Selbach.

"Snagaide and Fogach ran off. You now had to silence them. You caught up with Fogach and killed him, smashing his skull with a stone. But when you turned in search of Snagaide you suddenly observed a currach approaching. It was Lorcán's currach. But you thought it was coming in answer to the report of the eight brothers.

"You admitted that you were a trained apothecary. You hurried to your cell and mixed a potion of herbs, a powerful sleeping draught which would render you unconscious within a short time. First you picked up a stone and smote your temple hard enough to cause a nasty-looking wound. But Maenach, who knows something of a physician's art, told us that he would not have expected you to be unconscious from it. In fact, after you had delivered that blow, you drank your portion and stretched yourself in the oratory where I found you. You were not unconscious from the blow but merely in a deep sleep from your potion. You had already worked out the story that you would tell us. It would be your word against the poor, pitiful and confused youths."

Fidelma slowly took out the cup and placed it on the table.

"That was the cup I found lying near you in the oratory. It still smells of the herbs, like mullein and red clover tops, which would make up the powerful sleeping draught. You have jars of such ingredients in your cell."

"You still can't prove this absurd story," replied Spelán.

"I think I can. You see, not only did Abbot Selbach begin to suspect that there was a *gortaigid* at work within his community but he wrote to Ultan of Armagh outlining his suspicions."

She took out the letter from Ultan of Armagh.

Spelán's eyes narrowed. She noticed that tiny beads of sweat had begun to gather on his brow for the first time since she had begun to call his bluff. She held the letter tantalizingly in front of her.

"You see, Spelán, when you showed yourself anxious to get your hands on this letter, I realized that it was the piece of evidence I was looking for; indeed, that I was overlooking. The letter is remarkably informative, a reply to all Selbach's concerns about you."

Spelán's face was white. He stared aghast at the letter as she placed it on the table.

"Selbach named me to Ultan?"

Fidelma pointed to the letter.

"You may see for yourself."

With a cry of rage that stunned everyone into immobility, Spelán suddenly launched himself across the room towards Fidelma with his hands outstretched.

He had gone but a few paces when he was abruptly halted as if by a gigantic hand against his chest. He stood for a moment, his eyes bulging in astonishment, and then he slid to the ground without another word.

It was only then that they saw the hilt of the knife buried in Spelán's heart and the blood staining his robes.

There was a movement at the door. A young, dark-haired youth in the robes of a religious took a hesitant step in. Lorcán, the first to recover his senses, knelt by the side of Spelán and reached for a pulse. Then he raised his eyes and shook his head.

Fidelma turned to the trembling youth who had thrown the knife. She reached out a hand and laid it on his shaking arm.

"I had to do it," muttered the youth. "I had to."

"I know," she pacified.

"I do not care. I am ready to be punished." The youth drew himself up.

"In your suffering of mind, you have already punished yourself enough, Brother Snagaide. These here," she gestured towards Lorcán, Maenach and Sárnat, "are witnesses to Spelán's action which admitted of his guilt. Your case will be heard before the Brehon in Chléire and I shall be your advocate. Does not the ancient law say every person who places themselves beyond the law is without the protection of the law? You slew a violator of the law and therefore this killing is justified under the Law of the *Fenechus*."

She drew the youth outside. He was scarcely the age of credulous and unworldly Sister Sárnat. Fidelma sighed deeply. If she could one day present a law to the council of judges of Ireland she would make it a law that no one under the age of twenty-five could be thrust into the life of the religious. Youth needed to grow to adulthood and savour life and understand something of the world before they isolated themselves on islands or in cloisters away from it. Only in such sequestered states of innocence and fear of authority could evil men like Spelán thrive. She placed a comforting arm around the youth's shoulder as he fell to heart-retching sobbing.

"Come, Lorcán," Fidelma called across her shoulder. "Let's get down to the currach and reach Inis Chléire before your storm arrives."

Sister Sárnat emerged from the cell, holding the letter which Fidelma had laid on the table.

"Sister . . ." She seemed to find difficulty in speaking. "This letter from Ultan to Selbach . . . it does not refer to Spelán. Selbach didn't suspect Spelán at all. He thought that mortification was just a fashion among the youthful brothers."

Fidelma's face remained unchanged.

"Selbach could not bring himself to suspect his companion. It was a lucky thing that Spelán didn't realize that, wasn't it?"

THE TWO BEGGARS
Robert van Gulik

Robert van Gulik (1910–67) was a Dutch ambassador to Japan. He became intrigued by the traditional Chinese stories about the seventh-century magistrate Judge Dee, and he translated these into English as Dee Goong An *in 1949. Thereafter he continued the series with a long run of novels and stories which vividly recreated this fascinating character. The following story is set in the year 668 and takes place shortly after the events described in* The Chinese Bell Murders (1958) *and just before those in* The Red Pavilion *(1964).*

W hen the last visitor had left, Judge Dee leaned back in his chair with a sigh of relief. With tired eyes he looked out over his back garden where in the gathering dusk his three small sons were playing among the shrubbery. They were suspending lighted lanterns on the branches, painted with the images of the Eight Genii.

It was the fifteenth day of the first month, the Feast of Lanterns. People were hanging gaily painted lanterns of all shapes and sizes in and outside their houses, transforming the entire city into a riot of garish colours. From the other side of the garden wall the judge heard the laughter of people strolling in the park.

All through the afternoon the notables of Poo-yang, the prosperous district where Judge Dee had now been serving one year as magistrate, had been coming to his residence at the back of the tribunal compound to offer him their congratulations on this auspicious day. He pushed his winged judge's cap back from his forehead and passed his hand over his face. He was not accustomed to drinking so much wine in the daytime; he felt slightly sick. Leaning forward, he took a large white rose from the bowl on the tea-table, for its scent is supposed to counteract the effects of alcohol. Inhaling deeply the flower's fresh fragrance, the judge reflected that his last visitor, Ling, the master of the goldsmiths' guild, had really overstayed his welcome, had seemed glued to his chair. And Judge Dee had to change and refresh himself before going to his women's quarters, where his three wives were now supervising the preparations for the festive family dinner.

Excited children's voices rang out from the garden. The judge looked round and saw that his two eldest boys were struggling to get hold of a large coloured lantern.

"Better come inside now and have your bath!" Judge Dee called out over to them.

"Ah-kuei wants that nice lantern made by Big Sister and me all for himself!" his eldest son shouted indignantly.

The judge was going to repeat his command, but out of the corner of his eye he saw the door in the back of the hall open. Sergeant Hoong, his confidential adviser, came shuffling inside. Noticing how wan and tired the old man looked, Judge Dee said quickly, "Take a seat and have a cup of tea, Hoong! I am sorry I had to leave all the routine business of the tribunal to you today. I had to go over to the chancery and do some work after my guests had left, but Master Ling was more talkative than ever. He took his leave only a few moments ago."

"There was nothing of special importance, Your Honour," Sergeant Hoong said, as he poured the judge and himself a cup of tea. "My only difficulty was to keep the clerks with their noses to the grindstone. Today's festive spirit had got hold of them!"

Hoong sat down and sipped his tea, carefully holding up his ragged grey moustache with his left thumb.

"Well, the Feast of Lanterns is on," the judge said, putting the white rose back on the table. "As long as no urgent cases are reported, we can afford to be a little less strict for once."

Sergeant Hoong nodded. "The warden of the north quarter came to the chancery just before noon and reported an accident, sir. An old beggar fell into a deep drain, in a back street not far from Master Ling's residence. His head hit a sharp stone at the bottom, and he died. Our coroner performed the autopsy and signed the certificate of accidental death. The poor wretch was clad only in a tattered gown, he hadn't even a cap on his head, and his greying hair was hanging loose. He was a cripple. He must have stumbled into the drain going out at dawn for his morning rounds. Sheng Pa, the head of the beggars, couldn't identify him. Poor fellow must have come to the city from up-country expecting good earnings here during the feast. If nobody comes to claim the corpse, we'll have it burned tomorrow."

Judge Dee looked round at his eldest son, who was moving an armchair among the pillars that lined the open front of the hall. The judge snapped: "Stop fiddling around with that chair, and do as I told you! All three of you!"

"Yes, sir!" the three boys shouted in chorus.

While they were rushing away, Judge Dee said to Hoong: "Tell the warden to have the drain covered up properly, and give him a good talking to! Those fellows are supposed to see to it that the streets in their quarter are kept in good repair. By the way, we expect you to join our small family dinner tonight, Hoong!"

The old man bowed with a gratified smile.

"I'll go now to the chancery and lock up, sir! I'll present myself at Your Honour's residence again in half an hour."

After the sergeant had left, Judge Dee reflected that he ought to go too and change from his ceremonial robe of stiff green brocade into a comfortable house-gown. But he felt loath to leave the quiet atmosphere of the now empty hall, and thought he might as well have one more cup of tea. In the park outside it had grown quiet too; people had gone home for the evening rice. Later they would swarm out into the street again, to admire the display of lanterns and have drinking bouts in the roadside wine-houses. Putting his cup down, Judge Dee reflected that perhaps he shouldn't have given Ma Joong and his two other lieutenants the night off, for later in the evening there might be brawls in the brothel district. He must remember to tell the headman of the constables to double the night watch.

He stretched his hand out again for his teacup. Suddenly he checked himself. He stared fixedly at the shadows at the back of the hall. A tall old man had come in. He seemed to be clad in a tattered robe, his head with the long flowing hair was bare. Silently he limped across the hall, supporting himself on a crooked staff. He didn't seem to notice the judge, but went straight past with bent head.

Judge Dee was going to shout and ask what he meant by coming in unannounced, but the words were never spoken. The judge froze in sudden horror. The old man seemed to flit right through the large cupboard, then stepped down noiselessly into the garden.

The judge jumped up and ran to the garden steps. "Come back, you!" he shouted angrily.

There was no answer.

Judge Dee stepped down into the moonlit garden. Nobody was there. He quickly searched the low shrubbery along the wall, but found nothing. And the small garden gate to the park outside was securely locked and barred as usual.

The judge remained standing there. Shivering involuntarily, he pulled his robe closer to his body. He had seen the ghost of the dead beggar.

After a while he took hold of himself. He turned round abruptly, went back up to the hall and entered the dim corridor leading to the front of his private residence. He returned absent-mindedly the respectful greeting of his doorman, who was lighting two brightly coloured lanterns at the gate, then crossed the central courtyard of the tribunal compound and walked straight to the chancery.

The clerks had gone home already; only Sergeant Hoong was there, sorting out a pile of papers on his desk by the light of a single candle. He looked up astonished as he saw the judge come in.

"I thought that I might as well have a look at that dead beggar after all," Judge Dee said casually.

Hoong quickly lit a new candle. He led the judge through the dark, deserted corridors to the jail at the back of the courtroom. In the side hall a thin form was lying on a deal table, covered by a reed mat.

Judge Dee took the candle from Hoong, and motioned him to remove the mat. Raising the candle, the judge stared at the lifeless, haggard face. It was deeply lined, and the cheeks were hollow, but it lacked the coarse features one would expect in a beggar. He seemed about fifty; his long, tousled hair was streaked with grey. The thin lips under the short moustache were distorted in a repulsive death grimace. He wore no beard.

The judge pulled open the lower part of the tattered, patched gown. Pointing at the misshapen left leg, he remarked, "He must have broken his knee once, and it was badly set. He must have walked with a pronounced limp."

Sergeant Hoong picked up a long crooked staff standing in the corner and said, "Since he was quite tall, he supported himself on this crutch. It was found by his side, at the bottom of the drain."

Judge Dee nodded. He tried to raise the left arm of the corpse, but it was quite stiff. Stooping, he scrutinized the hand, then righting himself, he said, "Look at this, Hoong! These soft hands without any callouses, the long, well-tended fingernails! Turn the body over!"

When the sergeant had rolled the stiff corpse over on its face Judge Dee studied the gaping wound at the back of the skull. After a while he handed the candle to Hoong, and taking a paper handkerchief from his sleeve, he used it to carefully brush aside the matted grey hair, which was clotted with dried blood. He then examined the handkerchief under the candle. Showing it to Hoong, he said curtly: "Do you see this fine sand and white grit? You wouldn't expect to find that at the bottom of a drain, would you?"

Sergeant Hoong shook his head perplexedly. He replied slowly, "No, sir. Slime and mud rather, I'd say."

Judge Dee walked over to the other end of the table and looked at the bare feet. They were white, and the soles were soft. Turning to the sergeant, he said gravely, "I fear that our coroner's thoughts were on tonight's feast rather than on his duties when he performed the post-mortem. This man wasn't a beggar, and he didn't fall accidentally into the drain. He was thrown into it when he was dead already. By the person who murdered him."

Sergeant Hoong nodded, ruefully pulling at his short grey beard. "Yes, the murderer must have stripped him, and put him in that beggar's gown. It should have struck me at once that the man was naked under that tattered robe. Even a poor beggar would have been wearing something underneath; the evenings are still rather chilly." Looking again at the gaping wound, he asked: "Do you think the head was bashed in with a heavy club, sir?"

"Perhaps," Judge Dee replied. He smoothed down his long, black beard. "Has any person been reported missing recently?"

"Yes, Your Honour! Guildmaster Ling sent a note yesterday stating that Mr Wang, the private tutor of his children, had failed to come back from his weekly holiday two days ago."

"Strange that Ling didn't mention that when he came to visit me just now!" Judge Dee muttered. "Tell the headman to have my palankeen ready! And let my house steward inform my First Lady not to wait for me with dinner!"

After Hoong had left, the judge remained standing there, looking down at the dead man whose ghost he had seen passing through the hall.

The old guildmaster came rushing out into his front courtyard when the bearers deposited Judge Dee's large official palankeen. While assisting the judge to descend, Ling inquired boisterously, "Well, well, to what fortunate occurrence am I indebted for this unexpected honour?"

Evidently Ling had just left a festive family dinner, for he reeked of wine and his words were slightly slurred.

"Hardly fortunate, I fear," Judge Dee remarked, as Ling led him and Sergeant Hoong to the reception hall. "Could you give me a description of your house tutor, the one who has disappeared?"

"Heavens, I do hope the fellow didn't get himself into trouble! Well, he wasn't anything special to look at. A tall thin man, with a short moustache, no beard. Walked with a limp, left leg was badly deformed."

"He has met with a fatal accident," Judge Dee said evenly.

Ling gave him a quick look, then motioned his guest to sit in the place of honour at the central table under the huge lantern of coloured silk hung there for the feast. He himself sat down opposite the judge. Hoong remained standing behind his master's chair. While the steward was pouring the tea, Guildmaster Ling said slowly, "So that's why Wang didn't turn up two days ago, after his weekly day off!" The sudden news seemed to have sobered him up considerably.

"Where did he go to?" Judge Dee asked.

"Heaven knows! I am not a man who pries into the private affairs of his household staff. Wang had every Thursday off; he would leave here Wednesday night before dinner, and return Thursday evening, also at dinner time. That's all I know, and all I need to know, if I may say so, sir!"

"How long had he been with you?"

"About one year. Came from the capital with an introduction from a well-known goldsmith there. Since I needed a tutor to teach my grandsons, I engaged him. Found him a quiet, decent fellow. Quite competent too."

"Do you know why he chose to leave the capital and seek employment here in Poo-yang? Did he have any family here?"

"I don't know," Ling replied crossly. "It was not my habit to discuss with him anything except the progress of my grandchildren."

"Call your house steward!"

The guildmaster turned round in his chair and beckoned the steward who was hovering about in the back of the spacious hall.

When he had come up to the table and made his obeisance, Judge Dee said to him, "Mr Wang has met with an accident and the tribunal must inform the next of kin. You know the address of his relatives here, I suppose?"

The steward cast an uneasy glance at his master. He stammered, "He . . . as far as I know Mr Wang didn't have any relatives living here in Poo-yang, Your Honour."

"Where did he go then for his weekly holidays?"

"He never told me, sir. I suppose he went to see a friend or something." Seeing Judge Dee's sceptical expression, he quickly went on, "Mr Wang was a taciturn man, Your Honour, and he always evaded questions about his private affairs. He liked to be alone. He spent his spare hours in the small room he has in the back yard of this residence. His only recreation was brief walks in our garden."

"Didn't he receive or send any letters?"

"Not that I know of, sir." The steward hesitated a moment. "From some chance remarks of his about his former life in the capital I gathered that his wife had left him. It seemed that she was of a very jealous disposition." He gave his employer an anxious glance. As he saw that Ling was staring ahead and didn't seem to be listening, he went on with more self-assurance: "Mr Wang had no private means at all, sir, and he was very parsimonious. He hardly spent one cent of his salary, never even took a sedan chair when he went out on his day off. But he must have been a wealthy man once, I could tell that from some small mannerisms of his. I think that he was even an official once, for sometimes when caught off guard he would address me in rather an authoritative tone. I understand he lost everything, his money and his official position. Didn't seem to mind, though. Once he said to me: 'Money is of no use if you don't enjoy life spending it; and when your money is spent, official life has lost its glamour.' Rather a frivolous remark coming from such a learned gentleman, I thought, sir – if I may make so bold, sir."

Ling glared at him and said with a sneer, "You seem to find time hanging heavily on your hands in this household! Gossiping instead of supervising the servants!"

"Let the man speak!" the judge snapped at Ling. And to the steward: "Was there absolutely no clue as to where Mr Wang used to go on his days off? You must know; you saw him go in and out, didn't you?"

The steward frowned. Then he replied, "Well, it did strike me that Mr Wang always seemed happy when he went, but when he came back he was usually rather depressed. He had melancholy moods at times. Never interfered with his teaching, though, sir. He was always ready to answer difficult questions, the young miss said the other day."

"You stated that Wang only taught your grandchildren," the judge said sharply to Ling. "Now it appears that he also taught your daughter!"

The guildmaster gave his steward a furious look. He moistened his lips, then replied curtly, "He did. Until she was married, two months ago."

"I see." Judge Dee rose from his chair and told the steward: "Show me Mr Wang's room!" He motioned to Sergeant Hoong to follow him. As Ling made a move to join them, the judge said: "Your presence is not required."

The steward led the judge and Hoong through a maze of corridors to the back yard of the extensive compound. He unlocked a narrow door, lifted the candle and showed them a small, poorly furnished room. There was only a bamboo couch, a simple writing-desk with a straight-backed chair, a bamboo rack with a few books and a black-leather clothes-box. The walls were covered with long strips of paper, bearing ink-sketches of orchids, done with considerable skill. Following Judge Dee's glance, the steward said:

"That was Mr Wang's only hobby, sir. He loved orchids, knew everything about tending them."

"Didn't he have a few potted orchids about?" the judge asked.

"No, sir. I don't think he could afford to buy them – they are quite expensive, sir!"

Judge Dee nodded. He picked up a few of the dog-eared volumes from the book rack and glanced through them. It was romantic poetry, in cheap editions. Then he opened the clothes-box. It was stuffed with men's garments, worn threadbare, but of good quality. The cash box at the bottom of the box contained only some small change. The judge turned to the desk. The drawer had no lock. Inside were the usual writing materials, but no money and not a scrap of inscribed paper, not even a receipted bill. He slammed the drawer shut and angrily asked the steward, "Who has rifled this room during Mr Wang's absence?"

"Nobody has been here, Your Honour!" the frightened steward stammered. "Mr Wang always locked the door when he went out, and I have the only spare key."

"You yourself told me that Wang didn't spend a cent, didn't you? What has happened to his savings over the past year? There's only some small change here!"

The steward shook his head in bewilderment. "I really couldn't say, Your Honour! I am sure nobody came in here. And all the servants have been with us for years. There has never been any pilfering, I can assure you, sir!"

Judge Dee remained standing for a while by the desk. He stared at the paintings, slowly tugging at his moustache. Then he turned round and said: "Take us back to the hall!"

While the steward was conducting them again through the winding corridors, Judge Dee remarked casually, "This residence is situated in a nice, quiet neighbourhood."

"Oh yes, indeed, sir, very quiet and respectable!"

"It's exactly in such a nice, respectable neighbourhood that one finds the better houses of assignation," the judge remarked dryly. "Are there any near here?"

The steward seemed taken aback by this unexpected question. He cleared his throat and replied diffidently, "Only one, sir, two streets away. It's kept by a Mrs Kwang – very high class, visited by the best people only, sir. Never any brawls or other trouble there, sir."

"I am glad to hear that," Judge Dee said.

Back in the reception hall he told the guildmaster that he would have to accompany him to the tribunal to make the formal identification of the dead man. While they were being carried out there in Judge Dee's palankeen, the guildmaster observed a surly silence.

After Ling had stated that the dead body was indeed that of his house tutor and filled out the necessary documents, Judge Dee let him go. Then he said to Sergeant Hoong, "I'll now change into a more comfortable robe. In the meantime you tell our headman to stand by in the courtyard with two constables."

Sergeant Hoong found the judge in his private office. He had changed into a simple robe of dark-grey cotton with a broad black sash, and he had placed a small black skull-cap on his head.

Hoong wanted to ask him where they were going, but seeing Judge Dee's preoccupied mien, he thought better of it and silently followed him out into the courtyard.

The headman and two constables sprang to attention when they saw the judge.

"Do you know the address of a house of assignation in the north quarter, close by Guildmaster Ling's residence?" Judge Dee asked.

"Certainly, Your Honour!" the headman answered officiously. "That's Mrs Kwang's establishment. Properly licensed, and very high class, sir, only the best . . ."

"I know, I know!" the judge cut him short impatiently. "We'll walk out there. You lead the way with your men!"

Now the streets were crowded again with people. They were milling around under the garlands of coloured lanterns that spanned the streets and decorated the fronts of all the shops and restaurants. The headman and the two constables unceremoniously elbowed people aside, making way for the judge and Sergeant Hoong.

Even in the back street where Mrs Kwang lived there were many people about. When the headman had knocked and told the gatekeeper that the magistrate had arrived, the frightened old man quickly conducted the judge and Hoong to a luxuriously appointed waiting-room in the front court.

An elderly, sedately dressed maidservant placed a tea-set of exquisite antique porcelain on the table. Then a tall, handsome woman of about thirty came in, made a low bow and introduced herself as Mrs Kwang, a widow. She wore a straight, long-sleeved robe, simple in style but made of costly, dark-violet damask. She herself poured the tea for the judge, elegantly holding up with her left hand the trailing sleeve of the right. She remained standing in front of the judge, respectfully waiting for him to address her. Sergeant Hoong stood behind Judge Dee's chair, his arms folded in his wide sleeves.

Leisurely tasting the fragrant tea, Judge Dee noticed how quiet it was; all noise was kept out by the embroidered curtains and wall-hangings of heavy brocade. The faint scent of rare and very expensive incense floated in the air. All very high class indeed. He set down his cup and began, "I disapprove of your trade, Mrs Kwang. I recognize, however, that it is a necessary evil. As long as you keep everything orderly and treat the girls well, I won't make any trouble for you. Tell me, how many girls have you working here?"

"Eight, Your Honour. All purchased in the regular manner, of course, mostly directly from their parents. Every three months the ledgers with their earnings are sent to the tribunal, for the assessment of my taxes. I trust that . . ."

"No, I have no complaints about that. But I am informed that one of the girls was bought out recently by a wealthy patron. Who is the fortunate girl?"

Mrs Kwang looked politely astonished. "There must be some misunderstanding, Your Honour. All my girls here are still very young – the eldest is just nineteen – and haven't yet completed their training in music and dancing. They try hard to please, of course, but none of them has yet succeeded in captivating the favour of a wealthy patron so as to establish an ah . . . more permanent relationship." She paused, then added primly, "Although such a transaction means, of course, a very substantial monetary gain for me, I don't encourage it until a courtesan is well into her twenties, and in every respect worthy of attaining the crowning success of her career."

"I see," Judge Dee said. He thought ruefully that this information disposed effectively of his attractive theory. Now that his hunch had proved wrong, this case would necessitate a long investigation, beginning with the goldsmith in the capital who had introduced Wang to Guildmaster Ling. Suddenly another possibility flashed through his mind. Yes, he thought he could take the chance. Giving Mrs Kwang a stern look he said coldly:

"Don't prevaricate, Mrs Kwang! Besides the eight girls who are living here, you have established another in a house of her own. That's a serious offence, for your licence covers this house only."

Mrs Kwang put a lock straight in her elaborate coiffure. The gesture made her long sleeve slip back, revealing her white, rounded forearm. Then she replied calmly:

"That information is only partly correct, Your Honour. I suppose it refers to Miss Liang, who lives in the next street. She is an accomplished courtesan from the capital, about thirty years old – her professional name is Rosedew. Since she was very popular in elegant circles in the capital, she saved a great deal of money and bought herself free, without, however, handing in her licence. She wanted to settle down, and came here to Poo-yang for a period of rest, and to have a leisurely look around for a suitable marriage partner. She's a very intelligent woman, sir; she knows that all those elegant, flighty young men in the capital don't go for permanent arrangements, so she wanted a steady, elderly man of some means and position. Only occasionally did she receive such selected clients here in my house. Your Honour will find the pertaining entries in a separate ledger, also duly submitted regularly for inspection. Since Miss Liang has kept her licence, and since the taxes on her earnings are paid . . ."

She let her voice trail off. Judge Dee was secretly very pleased, for he knew now that he had been on the right track after all. But he assumed an angry mien, hit his fist on the table and barked, "So the man who is buying Rosedew out to marry her is being meanly deceived! For there is no redemption fee to be paid! Not one copper, neither to you nor to her former owner in the capital! Speak up! Weren't you and she going to share that fee, obtained from the unsuspecting patron under false pretences?"

At this Mrs Kwang lost her composure at last. She knelt down in front of Judge Dee's chair and repeatedly knocked her forehead on the floor. Looking up, she wailed, "Please forgive this ignorant person, Excellency! The money has not yet been handed over. Her patron is an exalted person, Excellency, a colleague of Your Excellency, in fact, the magistrate of a district in this same region. If he should hear about this, he . . ."

She burst into tears.

Judge Dee turned round and gave Sergeant Hoong a significant look. That could be no one else but his amorous colleague of Chin-hwa, Magistrate Lo! He barked at Mrs Kwang: "It was indeed Magistrate Lo who asked me to investigate. Tell me where Miss Liang lives; I shall interrogate her personally about this disgraceful affair!"

A short walk brought the judge and his men to the address in the next street that the tearful Mrs Kwang had given him.

Before knocking on the gate, the headman quickly looked up and down the street, then said, "If I am not greatly mistaken, sir, the drain that beggar fell into is located right at the back of this house."

"Good!" Judge Dee exclaimed. "Here, I'll knock myself. You and your two men keep close to the wall while I go inside with the sergeant. Wait here till I call you!"

After repeated knocking the peephole grate in the gate opened and a woman's voice asked, "Who is there?"

"I have a message from Magistrate Lo, for a Miss Rosedew," Judge Dee said politely.

The door opened at once. A small woman dressed in a thin

houserobe of white silk asked the two men to enter. As she preceded them to the open hall in the front court, the judge noticed that despite her frail build she had an excellent figure.

When they were inside she gave her two visitors a curious look, then bade them seat themselves on the couch of carved rosewood. She said somewhat diffidently: "I am indeed Rosedew. Who do I have the honour of . . ."

"We shan't take much of your time, Miss Liang," the judge interrupted quickly. He looked her over. She had a finely chiselled, mobile face, with expressive, almond-shaped eyes and a delicate small mouth – a woman of considerable intelligence and charm. Yet something didn't fit with his theory.

He surveyed the elegantly furnished hall. His eye fell on a high rack of polished bamboo in front of the side window. Each of its three superimposed shelves bore a row of orchid plants, potted in beautiful porcelain bowls. Their delicate fragrance pervaded the air. Pointing at the rack, he said: "Magistrate Lo told me about your fine collection of orchids, Miss Liang. I am a great lover of them myself. Look, what a pity! The second one on the top shelf has wilted, it needs special treatment, I think. Could you get it down and show it to me?"

She gave him a doubtful look, but apparently decided that it was better to humour this queer friend of Magistrate Lo. She took a bamboo step-ladder from the corner, placed it in front of the rack, and nimbly climbed up, modestly gathering the thin robe round her shapely legs. When she was about to take the pot, Judge Dee suddenly stepped up close to the ladder and remarked casually:

"Mr Wang used to call you Orchid, didn't he, Miss Liang? So much more apposite than Rosedew, surely!" When Miss Liang stood motionless, looking down at the judge with eyes that were suddenly wide with fear, he added sharply: "Mr Wang was standing exactly where I am standing now when you smashed the flower pot down on his head, wasn't he?"

She started to sway. Uttering a cry, she wildly groped for support. Judge Dee quickly steadied the ladder. Reaching up, he caught her round her waist and set her down on the floor. She clasped her hands to her heaving bosom and gasped: "I don't . . . Who are you?"

"I am the magistrate of Poo-yang," the judge replied coldly. "After you murdered Wang, you replaced the broken flower pot by a new one, and transplanted the orchid. That's why it's wilted, isn't it?"

"It's a lie!" she cried out. "Wicked slander. I shall . . ."

"I have proof!" Judge Dee cut her short. "A servant of the neighbours saw you dragging the dead body to the drain behind your house here. And I found in Wang's room a note of his, stating that he feared you would harm him, now that you had a wealthy patron who wanted to marry you."

"The treacherous dog!" she shouted. "He swore he didn't keep one scrap of paper relating to . . ." She suddenly stopped and angrily bit her red lips.

"I know everything," the judge said evenly. "Wang wanted more than his weekly visits. Thus he endangered your affair with Magistrate Lo, an affair that would not only bring in a lump sum of money for you and Mrs Kwang, but also set you up for life. Therefore you had to kill your lover."

"Lover?" she screamed. "Do you think I allowed that disgusting cripple ever to touch me here? It was bad enough to have to submit to his odious embraces before, when we were still in the capital!"

"Yet you allowed him to share your bed here," Judge Dee remarked with disdain.

"You know where he slept? In the kitchen! I wouldn't have allowed him to come at all, but he made himself useful by answering my love letters for me, and he paid for and tended those orchids there, so that I would have flowers to wear in my hair. He also acted as doorman and brought tea and refreshments when one of my lovers was here. What else do you think I allowed him to come here for?"

"Since he had spent his entire fortune on you I thought perhaps . . ." Judge Dee said dryly.

"The damnable fool!" she burst out again. "Even after I had told him that I was through with him, he kept on running after me, saying he couldn't live without seeing my face now and then – the cringing beggar! His ridiculous devotion spoilt my reputation. It was because of him that I had to leave the capital and bury myself in this dreary place. And I, fool that I was, trusted that simpering wretch! Leaving a note accusing me! He's ruined me, the dirty traitor!"

Her beautiful face had changed into an evil mask. She stamped her small foot on the floor in impotent rage.

"No," Judge Dee said in a tired voice, "Wang didn't accuse you. What I said just now about that note wasn't true. Beyond a few paintings of orchids which he did when thinking of you, there wasn't one clue to you in his room. The poor, misguided man remained loyal to you, to his very end!" He clapped his hands. When the headman and the two constables had come rushing inside, he ordered: "Put this woman in chains and lock her up in jail. She has confessed to a foul murder." As the two constables grabbed her arms and the headman started to chain her, the judge said: "Since there is not a single reason for clemency, you shall be beheaded on the execution ground."

He turned round and left, followed by Sergeant Hoong. The woman's frantic cries were drowned by the loud shouts and laughter of a happy group of youngsters who came surging through the street, waving brightly coloured lanterns.

When they were back in the tribunal, Judge Dee took Hoong straight to his own residence. While walking with him to the back hall, he said, "Let's just have one cup of tea before we go and join the dinner in my women's quarters."

The two men sat down at the round table. The large lantern hanging from the eaves, and those among the shrubs in the garden had been extinguished. But the full moon lit up the hall with its eerie light.

Judge Dee quickly emptied his cup, then he sat back in his chair and began without further preliminaries:

"Before we went to see Guildmaster Ling, I knew only that the beggar was no beggar, and that he had been murdered elsewhere by having the back of his skull bashed in, probably with a flower pot – as suggested by the fine sand and white grit. Then, during our interview with Ling, I suspected for a moment that the guildmaster was involved in this crime. He hadn't said a word about Wang's disappearance when he came to visit me, and I thought it strange that later he didn't inquire what exactly had happened to Wang. But I soon realized that Ling is that unpleasant kind of person who doesn't take the slightest interest in his personnel, and that he was cross because I had interrupted his family party. What the steward told me about Wang brought to light a fairly clear pattern. The steward said that Wang's family life had been broken up because he squandered his wealth, and his mentioning Mrs Wang's jealousy pointed to another woman being involved. Thus I deducted that Wang had become deeply infatuated with a famous courtesan."

"Why not with some decent girl or woman, or even with a common prostitute?" the sergeant objected.

"If it had been a decent woman, Wang would not have needed to spend his fortune on her; he could have divorced his wife and married his lady-love. And if she had been a common prostitute, he could have bought her out at a moderate price, and set her up in a small house of her own – all without sacrificing his wealth and his official position. No, I was certain that Wang's mistress must have been a famous courtesan in the capital, who could afford to squeeze a lover dry, then discard him and go on to the next. But I assumed that Wang refused to let himself be thrown away like a chewed-out piece of sugar cane, and that he made a nuisance of himself. That she fled from the capital and came to Poo-yang in order to start her game all over again. For it's well known that many wealthy merchants are living here in this district. I assumed that Wang had traced her here and had forced her to let him visit her regularly, threatening to expose her callous racket if she refused. Finally, that after she had caught my foolish colleague Lo, Wang began to blackmail her, and that therefore she had killed him." He sighed, then added: "We now know that it was quite different. Wang sacrificed everything he had for her, and even the pittance he received as tutor he spent on orchids for her. He was quite content to be allowed to see and talk to her every week, frustrating and humiliating as those few hours were. Sometimes, Hoong, a man's folly is engendered by such a deep and reckless passion that it lends him a kind of pathetic grandeur."

Sergeant Hoong pensively pulled at his ragged grey moustache. After a while he asked, "There are a great many courtesans here in Poo-yang. How did Your Honour know that Wang's mistress must belong to the house of Mrs Kwang? And why did it have to be his mistress who murdered him and not, for instance, another jealous lover?"

"Wang used to go there on foot. Since he was a cripple, this proved that she must live near to the guildmaster's house, and that led us to Mrs Kwang's establishment. I asked Mrs Kwang what courtesan had been recently bought out, because such an occurrence supplied the most plausible motive for the murder, namely that the courtesan had to get rid of an embarrassing former lover. Well, we know that Wang was indeed embarrassing her, but not by threatening to blackmail her or by any other wicked scheme. It was just his dog-like devotion that made her hate and despise him. As to the other possibilities you just mentioned, I had of course also reckoned with those. But if the murderer had been a man, he would have carried the body away to some distant spot, and he would also have been more thorough in his attempts at concealing his victim's identity. The fact that the attempt was confined to dressing the victim in a tattered beggar's gown, loosening his top-knot and mussing up his hair, pointed to a woman having done the deed. Women know that a different dress and hair-do can completely alter their own appearance. Miss Liang applied this method to a man – and that was a bad mistake."

Judge Dee took a sip from the cup the sergeant had refilled for him, then resumed, "As a matter of course it could also have been an elaborate scheme to inculpate Miss Liang. But I considered that a remote possibility. Miss Liang herself was our best chance. When the headman informed me that the dead beggar had been found at the back of her house, I knew that my theory must be correct.

However, when we had gone inside I saw that she was a rather small and frail woman, who could never have bashed in the head of her tall victim. Therefore I at once looked around for some death-trap, and found it in the potted orchids on the high shelf, where the wilted plant supplied the final clue. She must have climbed up the ladder, probably asking Wang to steady it for her. Then she made some remark or other that made him turn his head, and smashed the pot down on his skull. These and other details we'll learn tomorrow when I question Miss Liang in the tribunal. Now as regards the role played by Mrs Kwang, I don't think she did more than help Miss Liang to concoct the scheme of getting the fictitious redemption fee out of Lo. Our charming hostess draws the line at murder; hers is a high-class establishment, remember!"

Sergeant Hoong nodded. "Your Honour has not only uncovered a cruel murder, but at the same time saved Magistrate Lo from an alliance with a determined and evil woman!"

Judge Dee smiled faintly. "Next time I meet Lo," he said, "I'll tell him about this case – without mentioning, of course, that I know it was he who patronized Miss Liang. My gay friend must have been visiting my district incognito! This case will teach him a lesson – I hope!"

Hoong discreetly refrained from commenting further on one of his master's colleagues. He remarked with a satisfied smile: "So now all the points of this curious case have been cleared up!"

Judge Dee took a long draught from his tea. As he set the cup down he shook his head and said unhappily: "No, Hoong. Not all the points."

He thought he might as well tell the sergeant now about the ghostly apparition of the dead beggar, without which this murder would have been dismissed as an ordinary accident. But just as he was about to speak, his eldest son came rushing inside. Seeing his father's angry look, the boy said with a quick bow: "Mother said we might take that nice lantern to our bedroom, sir!"

As his father nodded, the small fellow pushed an armchair up to one of the pillars. He climbed on the high backrest, reached up and unhooked the large lantern of painted silk hanging down from the eaves. He jumped down, lit the candle inside with his tinderbox, and held up the lantern for his father to see.

"It took Big Sister and me two days to make this, sir!" he said proudly. "Therefore we didn't want Ah-kuei to spoil it. We like the Immortal Lee, he is such a pathetic, ugly old fellow!"

Pointing at the figure the children had painted on the lantern, the judge asked: "Do you know his story?" When the boy shook his head, his father continued: "Many, many years ago Lee was a very handsome young alchemist who had read all books and mastered all magic arts. He could detach his soul from his body and then float at will in the clouds, leaving his empty body behind, to resume it when he came down to earth again. One day, however, when Lee had carelessly left his body lying in a field, some farmers came upon it. They thought it was an abandoned corpse, and burned it. So when Lee came down, he found his own beautiful body gone. In despair he had to enter the corpse of a poor old crippled beggar which happened to be lying by the roadside, and Lee had to keep that ugly shape for ever. Although later he found the Elixir of Life, he could never undo that one mistake, and it was in that form that he entered the ranks of the Eight Immortals: Lee with the Crutch, the Immortal Beggar."

The boy put the lantern down. "I don't like him anymore!" he said with disdain. "I'll tell Big Sister that Lee was a fool who only got what he deserved!"

He knelt down, wished his father and Hoong good night, and scurried away.

Judge Dee looked after him with an indulgent smile. He took up the lantern to blow out the candle inside. But suddenly he checked himself. He stared at the tall figure of the Immortal Beggar projected on the plaster wall. Then he tentatively turned the lantern round, as it would turn in the draught. He saw the ghostly shadow of the crippled old man move slowly along the wall, then disappear into the garden.

With a deep sigh the judge blew the candle out and put the lantern back on the floor. He said gravely to Sergeant Hoong, "You were right after all, Hoong! All our doubts are solved — at least those about the mortal beggar. He was a fool. As to the Immortal Beggar — I am not too sure." He rose and added with a wan smile, "If we measure our knowledge not by what we know but by what we don't, we are just ignorant fools, Hoong, all of us! Let's go now and join my ladies."

PART II
The Middle Ages

THE INVESTIGATION OF THINGS
Charles Ardai

We stay in ancient China for the next story, though we move on four hundred years. Charles Ardai (b. 1969) is a New York writer and editor who, in addition to his stories in Ellery Queen's Mystery Magazine *and* Alfred Hitchcock's Mystery Magazine, *has edited several anthologies, including* Great Tales of Madness and the Macabre *(1990) and* Great Tales of Crime & Detection *(1991). He has also been the story consultant for several television series, including* The Hidden Room *and* The Hitchhiker. *It was while he was studying and lecturing on British Romantic Poetry at Columbia University that he began to research eleventh-century Chinese history. That was when he discovered the real-life characters of Ch'eng I and Ch'eng Hao who feature in this story. He also discovered the Judge Dee stories at that time. "The characters cried out to have a mystery written around them," Ardai told me, "and the van Gulik novels inspired me to experiment with a more mannered style than I normally employ." Here's the result. My thanks to writer Lawrence Schimel for alerting me to this story.*

"The extension of knowledge lies in the investigation of things. For only when things are investigated is knowledge extended . . ."

Ta Hsueh, The Great Learning

Ch'eng I sat in the Grove of the Ninth Bamboo studying tea. He had twenty-four varieties on a great wooden palette, spread out before him like a portrait artist's paints. Each was labeled in meticulous calligraphy and kept in place with a bit of paste. Ch'eng I noted the subtle variations in the contours and textures of the leaves, labeling salient points directly on the wood with a fine-point brush.

Next to him, his brother, Ch'eng Hao, sipped from a teacup and watched in silence.

Ch'eng I selected a pouch from among the twenty-four at his feet. He pulled out a pinch of tea and spread it on his palette, separating the leaves with the end of his brush. "You see, brother," he said without looking up from his task, "the lung-ching is flat, like the edge of a fine sword, and slick, like wet hair."

"It tastes excellent," Ch'eng Hao said, tossing back the last of his tea, "not at all like wet hair. Beyond that I know nothing. What else matters about tea? How it tastes, whether it pleases one, that is all. You are not a tea farmer, to worry about the plant. You are not Lu Yu, to write another *Ch'a Ch'ing*. You ruin your eyes peering at tea when you should be drinking it."

Ch'eng I pulled a pinch from another pouch and spread it on his board. "Pi lo-chun dries in a spiral. It is the smallest of all the teas I have examined." He scratched a few more notes onto the wood, then laid the brush aside and looked up at his brother. "Please try not to be so selfish. Tea is not merely a flavor in your mouth. Tea exists even if your mouth does not. You must not understand tea in terms of yourself. You must understand yourself in terms of tea."

Ch'eng Hao shook his head. "You do not understand yourself. You do not understand tea. You spend your days picking things apart, but there will always be more things than there are days. Your tea, your pouch, your brush, your tunic — these are all tools. You shouldn't study them. You should use them: drink your tea, write with your brush, wear your tunic. When you sit down to think, you should think about *this*." Ch'eng Hao tapped a finger against his forehead.

Ch'eng I gathered his materials, wrapping the palette in its silk case and stringing the pouches along his belt. "No, brother, you are mistaken." He tapped his head. "This is the tool. You should use it to think about this — " He swept his free hand around him in an open gesture. "About this — " He lifted one of the pouches and let it fall to his side again. "And this — " He ran his hand along the trunk of a tree. "Grow until your mind is the size of the world. Do not try to compress the world to make it fit inside your mind."

"But there is more in the world than you can ever hope to know," Ch'eng Hao said.

"So you would argue that I shouldn't try to know anything?"

"I say only, as Chuang Tzu says, that 'To pursue that which is unlimited with that which is limited is to know sorrow.' The world is huge; we are small and have short lives."

"When did you become a Taoist," Ch'eng I said, "that you quote Chuang Tzu?"

"Not a Taoist, I, a realist." Ch'eng Hao tried to wave the whole discussion away. "You will have to learn this for yourself. It is at least possible for one to fully understand oneself. That is a finite task. Through this understanding, one can understand everything else in the world."

"No, brother. The *Great Learning* says that self-perfection must come from the Investigation of Things, not the Investigation of Self."

"All things can be found in the self," Ch'eng Hao said.

"Now," said Ch'eng I, "you sound like a Buddhist."

"If you weren't my brother," Ch'eng Hao said, "I would demand an apology."

"If I weren't your brother," Ch'eng I said, "I might give you one."

Ch'eng Hao was about to answer when a scuffle of footsteps arose and a messenger burst into the grove. The messenger bowed deeply. The two brothers returned the courtesy, their argument temporarily set aside.

"Forgive me, please, for intruding," the messenger said, "but you are the brothers Ch'eng, are you not? Hao and I?"

Ch'eng I nodded. "We are."

"Then you must come. The Seventh Patriarch has requested your presence."

The brothers exchanged surprised glances. The Seventh Patriarch was the leader of the district's Ch'an Buddhist temple, and rarely one to invite outsiders into his sanctuary. Especially Confucian outsiders.

"He wants to see us?" Ch'eng Hao said. "Why?"

The messenger tried to look Ch'eng Hao in the eye and failed. His eyes fell on the ground and remained there, his chin pressed against his chest.

"What is it, man?"

The messenger spoke quietly: "There has been a murder."

The Temple of the Seventh Patriarch rose out of the flat land it was built on like a needle piercing upwards through a piece of fabric. It was a tower five times the height of a man, roughly pointed at the top, with walls of packed earth supported by wooden beams. The structure looked unstable and precarious, yet Ch'eng Hao knew that it was older than he was.

The messenger, who had identified himself as Wu Han-Fei, led them to the entrance and then stepped aside. "I may not enter," he said, in answer to the unasked question.

Ch'eng Hao and Ch'eng I stepped inside cautiously.

A body lay on the ground, its feet toward them. It was clearly that of a Buddhist monk – there was no mistaking the coarse robe or the waxy pallor of the skin, so deathlike in life, how much more so in death! Ch'eng I knelt beside the corpse to examine it more closely while Ch'eng Hao looked around the inside of the room.

The neck of the monk's robe was soaked with a liquid Ch'eng I knew to be blood – indeed, the entire front of the robe was. When he opened the robe, Ch'eng I discovered a ragged hole in the man's throat. He lifted the head and pulled off the hood. The monk's head was neatly shaved, as Ch'eng I had known it would be. The wound in his throat penetrated cleanly, ending in a round, puckered hole on the other side. The ground beneath the body was coated with blood, by now nearly dry, and the beams in the far wall were spattered with brown spots. Ch'eng I laid the man's head back down and replaced the hood.

Ch'eng Hao paced around the room's perimeter. It was not a large room, though it took on a sense of space because of the high roof. Other than the body and themselves, the room was completely empty and devoid of decoration. There was no more mistaking a Ch'an meditation room than there was a Ch'an monk. Only prisons were this spare in the outside world . . . and graves.

Ch'eng I left the monk's body and walked over to the far wall, where the spray of blood had struck. He examined it closely, inching his way down from eye level until he stopped about two feet above the floor. He pulled his drawing brush from his belt and knelt to his work, using the handle to pry something out from a tiny hole in the wall. Ch'eng I had to be careful not to break the brush, but he worked as quickly as he dared. Ch'eng Hao stood behind him, watching.

"What have you found?" Ch'eng Hao asked.

"I do not know yet. I will have to investigate."

Ch'eng I scraped around the edges of the hole, coaxing out the object that was lodged inside. Finally, it fell to the ground and Ch'eng I picked it up. He tested it with a fingernail. "It is a piece of soft metal," he said, holding it out on his palm for his brother to see. It was a dark, flattened lump slightly larger than a cashew. Then he held up his thumbnail. "Coated with blood, as you can see. This little ball seems to have killed the unfortunate man at our feet."

"This ball?" Ch'eng Hao was incredulous. "How can that be?"

Ch'eng I stepped over to the open entryway. "Through here. It came in, struck the monk in the throat, and killed him."

"But that is impossible!" Ch'eng Hao said. "Think of the force required! Think how hard it would have had to have been thrown in order to pierce the man's neck!"

Ch'eng I shook his head. "It is worse than that. The metal was thrown with enough force to pierce the monk's neck and then continue its flight to the opposite wall, where it lodged itself three finger-widths deep. But you are wrong to say it is impossible. The evidence of our senses demonstrates that it has happened."

Ch'eng Hao looked at the bloody metal and at the corpse and said nothing.

Wu Han-Fei reappeared at the entrance. "The Seventh Patriarch will see you now," he said.

"Will he?" Ch'eng I took the murder weapon back from his brother and found an empty pouch for it on his belt. "How good of him." He left the temple. Ch'eng Hao followed.

Ch'eng I scanned the landscape more carefully than he had before. The temple was the only building in sight, surrounded at a distance of ten yards by a dense forest; it stood like an obelisk in the center of a flat and empty meadow. "Where will we find the Seventh Patriarch?" he asked.

"You will follow me," Wu Han-Fei said. He started off for the forest.

"Hold on," Ch'eng I shouted. Wu Han-Fei stopped and turned around. "I realize that we will follow you. What I asked is *where* we will find him, not *how* we will."

Wu Han-Fei was confused. "There." He pointed in the direction he had started to walk.

"In the forest?"

He shook his head. "In a clearing. Like this."

"How far?"

He shrugged uncomfortably. "Not far. You will see."

"Yes, I imagine I will see. But first – "

"Never mind," Ch'eng Hao interrupted. "There will be plenty of time for your questions later." Then to Wu Han-Fei: "You will have to forgive my brother. He wants to know everything there is to know."

This explanation apparently satisfied the messenger, who turned around again and continued into the forest.

"I will not interfere with your investigation," Ch'eng I said as they followed their guide, "and I will ask you kindly not to interfere with mine."

"Brother," Ch'eng Hao said, "if I hadn't interfered, you would still be badgering this poor man with your questions. You'd have kept at it until we all died of old age out there."

"Perhaps," Ch'eng I said. "Perhaps I would have found the truth sooner than that."

"The truth? You were asking him how far it was to where we are going! Of what possible consequence – "

"You think truth is limited to thought and reason and motive,"

Ch'eng I said calmly, "and that is a mistake. Truth is also distance, and size, and weight, and force. You can seek truth in your way. I will seek it in mine."

"Sirs," Wu Han-Fei interrupted. "We are here."

They had passed through about forty feet of dense forest and were now in another clearing. A dozen small buildings were clustered in the center. The messenger pointed to one of them. "You will find the Patriarch there."

"And you?" Ch'eng I looked closely at the man for the first time. This was no Buddhist – he had a fine head of long, black hair and a dark, earthy complexion; and if his robe was coarse it was due to poverty, not piety. Most telling, a respect for the public authority Ch'eng I and Ch'eng Hao represented was clear in the way he never met their eyes for more than a second; a devoted Buddhist would stare down the Emperor himself, even if it meant death. It was indeed as Hui-Yuan had written: "A monk does not bow down before a king."

"I will go no further," Wu Han-Fei said.

"What are you doing here?" Ch'eng Hao asked, suddenly curious. "You are not one of them."

"No," Wu Han-Fei said. "I am their link with the secular world."

"I thought they did not need one," Ch'eng Hao said.

"They thought so, too." Wu Han-Fei spread his hands before him. "Murder changes such things."

"Tell me again," Ch'eng Hao said, "exactly how you found Kung." He paced as he spoke and did not turn to face the Patriarch when the old man answered.

"Kung was meditating," the Patriarch said. He had a voice that rumbled softly like a running stream. Ch'eng Hao was not insensible to beauty; he appreciated the sound of a wise and serene voice. But he listened with a suspicious ear to hear the silences, the words that remained unspoken. "Kung had grave matters on his conscience. Very grave."

"What were these grave matters?" Ch'eng Hao asked.

"Kung would not say." The Patriarch looked genuinely saddened by his monk's death, but Hao was aware that such apparent sadness might be no more than a mask. Men conceal, as he had often told his brother, in a way that nature does not. Honesty is a path only infrequently followed, and even then not without straying.

"Why would he not?"

The Patriarch caught Hao's eye and held it. "Ssu-ma Ch'ien was offered suicide but chose castration. He felt an honorable death would impair his mission on earth. So he sacrificed personal honor for the greater good."

"And . . .?"

The Patriarch said nothing more.

"I want none of your *koans*," Ch'eng Hao said sharply. "Speak plainly or not at all."

"Silence is the sound of a man speaking plainly," the Patriarch said. And silence fell.

After the strained quiet had stretched out for a minute, Ch'eng I spoke. "It would be helpful if you would describe the circumstances under which Kung's body was discovered."

The Patriarch nodded. "Kung left for the temple early in the morning. Before an hour had passed, Lin-Yu came to see me. He told me that he had gone to the temple and found Kung's body, in the condition that you observed."

"Who might have killed him?" Ch'eng Hao asked.

"Any one of us," the Patriarch said, "myself included."

"Did you?"

The Patriarch favored Ch'eng Hao with a condescending smile. "I do not think so . . . do you?"

Hao shook his head. "No. Had you killed him you could easily have arranged to rid yourself of the body without any attention. The outside world is unaware of what goes on here – even apathetic. If I had an illustrious ancestor for every time someone has said to me, 'Let the monks starve to death, we do not care,' I would be the most favored man under heaven. You would have had no reason to ask us to investigate, for that could only call punishment down on your head. No, you did not kill Kung. But," and here Ch'eng Hao paused for a bit to let his words have their full effect, "I would be very surprised if you did not know why he was killed."

The old man shook his head. "Then I will have the pleasure of surprising you, Ch'eng Hao. For I know nothing of this matter beyond the fact that I was unfortunate enough not to be able to prevent it. One of my men killed another: a son has murdered a brother. I want to know who and I want to know why."

"And how." This from Ch'eng I.

The Patriarch nodded slowly. "'How' and 'why' are such similar questions, so fundamentally intertwined. You will not find one answer without the other."

"Then the investigation commences," Ch'eng I said. He stepped out of the room abruptly and headed toward the forest.

"If I might speak with the monks," Ch'eng Hao said, "all of them at once, it might give me the perspective necessary to understand the murderous act."

The Patriarch stood. "It shall be so."

Ch'eng I measured the distance from the edge of the forest to the temple using his own footsteps for a standard. Forty paces brought him from the nearest trees to the entrance.

It was extraordinary, he thought, that such a thing was possible. For surely the attacker had concealed himself in the forest – Kung had been facing his attacker when he had been hit in the throat after all, and he would not have stood still had he seen that an attack was imminent. But for a pellet of metal, even a small one, to be propelled forty paces through the air, then through a man's neck, then for this pellet to penetrate three finger-widths deep into a solid earthen wall . . . It was extraordinary indeed.

But more extraordinary things had happened in history. Had not the Yellow Emperor fought off an army single-handedly? Had not the Duke of Chou braved the fury of heaven and lived? A metal ball had been propelled with great force? So be it. It remained only to determine how it had been accomplished.

No arm could be strong enough, Ch'eng I decided quickly, or at least no *human* arm could. An inhuman arm was a possibility he did not care to contemplate. But murder, he knew, was not a tool of the spirits. Murder was an act of man against man.

This knowledge reassured Ch'eng I. If a man had done it, a man *could* do it, as impossible as it appeared to be. And if a man could do it, then Ch'eng I could figure out how. It was that simple.

The monks under the Seventh Patriarch's tutelage drew together in their largest building, one they normally used for the preparation and service of meals. Ch'eng Hao stood next to the Patriarch, who instructed the monks to answer all of the investigator's questions.

There appeared to be no resistance to this order; Ch'eng Hao had feared there might be. But then resistance, he knew, like dishonesty, does not always appear on a man's face when it burns in his heart. It remained to be seen whether the monks actually *would* answer his questions, or whether they would dance around him with elaborate riddles and pointless anecdotes as their Master had done.

"A man has been murdered," Ch'eng Hao said to the assembled monks. It was best to get the basic information out of the way immediately. "As most of you know, it was your fellow monk, Kung." It galled Ch'eng Hao to refer to the dead man only by his chosen name; the man had once had two names like everyone else, and neither had been "Kung." But Kung was the name he had taken when he had severed his ties with his earthly family, and Kung was the name by which his fellows knew him. Ch'eng Hao swallowed his contempt and went on. "Kung was killed in a most unusual manner. My esteemed brother, Ch'eng I, is investigating this aspect of his death. I am concerned with only one question. That question is, *Who killed Kung?*" Knowing the positive effect of a weighty pause, Ch'eng Hao paused.

"It was almost certainly someone in this room."

No one moved. It was unnerving, Ch'eng Hao thought, the stoicism with which they received this accusation. Any other roomful of people would have been fidgeting with anxiety and outrage. Not these men. They would not fidget if their own parents accused them of murdering their children. Of course, for that they would have had to have children, as most – shamefully enough – did not.

"I will speak with each of you in turn," Ch'eng Hao said. "If any of you know anything about Kung's death, I strongly suggest you divulge it without hesitation." Still no response. "You," he said, picking a fellow out of the front row at random. "You will be first."

Ch'eng I bent over the corpse and inhaled deeply. It was not only death he smelled, though that scent was powerful; there was an acrid edge to the still air in the temple, a smell of fire and ashes. Incense was Ch'eng I's first thought, but he found no sign that an incense burner had been in the temple: the ground was unbroken and the walls showed no smoke stains. Then, too, the smell lacked the pungent sweetness of incense. But something, he was convinced, had been burning.

He put that thought aside and began a meticulous study of Kung's body. Ch'eng I searched it inch by inch, making mental notes as he went. The monk had been relatively healthy, he saw – somewhat undernourished, perhaps, but then who these days was not?

The first curious observation Ch'eng I made was when he came to Kung's right hand. The fleshy pads of his fingers were singed – not so severely burned as to destroy the flesh, but burned all the same, as though Kung had taken hold of something burning and had not let go. This corroborated Ch'eng I's earlier suspicion, but beyond corroboration it offered little other than puzzlement.

The second curious observation was this: Kung's head was scarred in two places, at the base of his skull and under his chin. The scarring had evidently occurred many years before, appearing now only as raised, white scar tissue against the dark tan of the rest of Kung's head. But the scarring was clearly not the result of an accident, since the two scars were identical – the shape was that of the character *wang*, three short horizontal lines intersected by a vertical.

Ch'eng I considered this for some time, deciding eventually that it was most likely the result of early childhood scarification, a common enough practice among the families of the plains. Kung's father would have placed the mark on his son, as his father's father must have done before him, and his great-grandfather before that. Ch'eng I could not help but wonder if this brutal tradition had influenced the young Kung in his decision to abandon his family for the monastery.

This thought, too, Ch'eng I set aside for further consideration at another time. Soon the body would start to decompose in earnest and at that point no further study would be possible. Ch'eng I focused his attention on the wound. It was at this point that he made his third curious observation: the neck of Kung's robe had no hole in it.

"Would you say that Kung was a well-liked man?" Ch'eng Hao asked.

"I would say that Kung was a man." A heavyset monk named Tso sat across from Ch'eng Hao, looking and acting like a stone wall.

"Had Kung no enemies?"

"Is one who bears you ill will an enemy?"

"I would say so."

"Then evidently he had at least one enemy," Tso said.

"But you have no idea who that might be."

Tso said nothing. He was well trained, Ch'eng Hao thought. Half the art of Buddhism is appearing to have all the answers and the other half is being sure never to give them. Even the Patriarch had been more helpful than this.

"You may go," Ch'eng Hao said. Tso was difficult on purpose, but then so were all the other monks he had interviewed. He had no reason to believe that Tso knew anything about Kung's death.

On his way out, Tso sent the next man in.

Bo-Tze was the oldest of the monks, by at least ten years. If he was not quite as old as the Patriarch, it was only because *no one* else was that old. The Patriarch was four hundred and three, rumor said; and even if rumor exaggerated, the Patriarch had certainly seen the tail end of ninety and was moving up on the century mark. Bo-Tze, Ch'eng Hao guessed, was about sixty.

His face had the texture of a hide left too long out in the sun and his robe was more worn than the others Ch'eng Hao had seen. He looked well weathered, a point Ch'eng Hao knew Bo-Tze would have prided himself on if monks permitted themselves pride. Unlike the other monks Ch'eng Hao had spoken to, Bo-Tze sat in front of him without even a trace of nervousness.

"Mister Ch'eng," Bo-Tze said, stressing the family name with disdain, "Kung was an undisciplined man. This was quite a serious problem. Do you know anything about Ch'an Buddhism, Mister Ch'eng? Ch'an is not what people in the world outside the monasteries think it is. Ch'an means 'meditation,' and meditation is our practice. Silent meditation: internal quiet, external harmony." The old monk took a raspy breath. Ch'eng Hao waited for him to continue.

"Kung was a dreamer and a visionary. We do *not* have visions, Mister Ch'eng. We are not the navel-staring mystics you think we are."

"I think no such thing," Ch'eng Hao said. Then: "Kung had visions?"

"Irrepressible visions," Bo-Tze said. "Or *irrepressed*, in any event. All men pray, in their fashion; Kung thought that his prayers were answered. When he meditated, he saw visions. He turned these visions into art – into art and into artifice. Then Heaven saw fit to strike him down. Surely this tells us something."

"What does it tell us?"

"That Kung's visions were not favored by . . ." Bo-Tze seemed to be groping for a concept.

"By . . .?" Ch'eng Hao prodded.

"By a force powerful enough to do to him what was done to him."

"Which was?"

"I do not know, Mister Ch'eng." Bo-Tze kept up his placid facade, but Ch'eng Hao sensed a vein of anger in his voice. "But it killed him. I regret his death, of course – " of course, Ch'eng Hao thought "– but only because he died unenlightened. He will return to plague this world again and again until he achieves Nirvana, which he never will if he keeps on like this. *Visions!*" Bo-Tze spat the word out like a plum pit.

Vituperation aside, this was the most information Ch'eng Hao had gotten about the dead man from anyone. Kung had had visions? At last, a line of inquiry to pursue.

"Where is this 'art' you referred to," Ch'eng Hao asked, "in which Kung recorded his visions?"

Bo-Tze waved the question away. "In his cell, I am sure. But you do not understand. Kung was doing things he should not have been doing. This is why he died."

"You mean it is why you killed him," Ch'eng Hao ventured.

Bo-Tze absorbed the remark with a slow blink of his eyelids. "I did not kill Kung," he said. "A monk does not kill."

Monks *do* kill, Ch'eng Hao wanted to say, or at least one monk did, since a monk is now dead and it does not look as though suicide is a plausible explanation. But he said none of this. "You may go."

Bo-Tze rose calmly and exited. Only Lin-Yu remained for Ch'eng Hao to see.

A grotesque figure, Lin-Yu moved painfully and with great difficulty. His legs were withered almost to the point of uselessness, but somehow they just managed to keep his great bulk from collapsing. One sleeve of his robe flapped empty at his side and he was missing an eye. The empty socket stared at Ch'eng Hao. He looked aside.

"Bo-Tze tells me that Kung had visions," Ch'eng Hao said. "Do you know anything about this?"

"Bo-Tze is an old man. He talks too much and thinks too little." Lin-Yu's voice was soft, almost feminine. "Kung was a fortunate man, possessed of life's most generous curse: a creative soul. He created in a night's sleep works of greater ingenuity than most men create in a lifetime of waking hours. Kung was the best man here."

"What were the visions visions *of*?" Ch'eng Hao asked.

"Everything." Ch'eng Hao had expected this: a typically obscure Ch'an answer. But Lin-Yu explained, "Sometimes, merely images. Mandalas, with a thousand buddhas in the eye of the thousand-and-first. You can see some of these – the Patriarch keeps them in his cell. He appreciated Kung's talent."

"But surely there was more to it than mandalas – "

"Oh, of course!" Excitement lit Lin-Yu's face. "He dreamt machines and tools – why do you think we are able to farm on such poor land as we have? Kung created tools for us. The universal buddha nature spoke through him, gave him knowledge of the unknown . . . For instance – "

Lin-Yu stood and lifted the skirts of his robe. His withered legs were bound in metal-and-leather braces with fabric joints at the knees. "Kung made these for me. Mister Ch'eng, please understand, Kung was a genius and a compassionate soul. This is a very rare and special combination."

Ch'eng Hao noticed that when Lin-Yu said, "Mister Ch'eng" the words carried no tone of disapproval.

"I believe you," Ch'eng Hao said. "I only wish the others had been as open with me as you are."

"The others are performing for you, Mister Ch'eng," Lin-Yu said. "How often do they have the pleasure of an outsider's presence? They want to show each other how good they can be at the game. They have much to learn. But then, don't we all?"

Much to learn. Yes, Ch'eng Hao thought, we have much to learn.

I, for instance, have to learn who killed this compassionate, visionary monk – so far I have made little progress. "Thank you," Ch'eng Hao said. He hoped he sounded more appreciative than he knew he usually did. "You may go."

"One moment please!" Ch'eng I dashed into the room through the parted tapestry that hung over the entrance. He put a hand on Lin-Yu's shoulder. "There are questions *I* must ask, brother." Ch'eng Hao nodded his assent.

"What can I tell you?" Lin-Yu asked.

Ch'eng I helped Lin-Yu once more to a seated position. "Please describe for me the condition in which you found Kung's body."

"Kung was dead," Lin-Yu said. The words came haltingly and tears formed in Lin-Yu's single eye. "He had a wound in his throat. There was blood all over the ground."

"You say 'throat,'" Ch'eng I said. "Do you not mean 'neck'?"

Lin-Yu considered this. "I suppose 'neck' is as good. I said 'throat' because he was on his back."

"He was on his back," Ch'eng I repeated. "Fascinating. And he was not wearing his hood?"

"No," Lin-Yu said, "he was. His hood was on."

"Brother," Ch'eng Hao said, "have you gone mad? You know all this. This is how he was when *we* saw the body."

Ch'eng I turned to his brother. "You must be less cavalier with your accusations, Hao. I am not mad, merely curious. You see," here he turned back to Lin-Yu, "when we saw him, Kung *was* as you describe. But this is not how he was when he was killed."

Lin-Yu arched an eyebrow; it was the one above the empty socket and Ch'eng Hao had to look away again.

"I have spent a good deal of time examining Kung's body," Ch'eng I said. "He was hit with this." He pulled the lump of metal from its pouch and showed it to Lin-Yu. "But he was not hit in the throat. He was hit in the back of the neck. He did not fall backward; he fell forward. And he was not wearing his hood at the time."

"How do you know all this?" Ch'eng Hao asked, caught between admiration and disbelief.

"Simple." Ch'eng I ticked off points on his fingers. "The pellet penetrated Kung's neck and continued to the opposite wall. Yet there was no hole in Kung's hood. How can this be? Kung was not wearing his hood.

"Next: the front of Kung's robe was soaked with blood as well as the back. If the force of the attack had knocked him backwards, the front of his robe would have received very little blood. If, on the other hand, he fell forward, into his pooling blood, it

would account for the condition of his robe. Therefore, he fell
forward.

"Finally: the wound on the back of his neck was smaller and more
contained than the wound in his throat. This suggests that the latter
was the exit wound, not the entry wound. Therefore, he was hit in
the back of the neck."

"Very well," Ch'eng Hao said. "I accept your analysis. But why
then was Kung not on his chest with his hood off when Lin-Yu
found him?"

"Someone changed the position of Kung's body," Ch'eng I said.
"Turned him over and covered his head." Also, he said to himself,
took away whatever had been burning in the temple and erased all
signs of his presence. "Why someone would do this is a mystery.
However, we do know now that there was someone with Kung when
he died."

"Yes, the murderer," Ch'eng Hao said. "We already knew that."

"No," said Ch'eng I, "a third man. Because the murderer was
at the edge of the forest directly across from the temple entrance
– where I searched and found this." He undid the strings of the
largest pouch on his belt and poured two objects out onto the floor:
a small metal mallet and a flattened metal capsule not much larger
than the murder weapon.

"What is this?" Lin-Yu asked. He picked up the mallet and turned
it over in his hands. The head was remarkably heavy for a tool
so small.

"It is part of the murderer's device," Ch'eng I said. "I am still
trying to piece together just how the device operated. It would help
if I had it in its entirety. However, these pieces give us a starting
point. Smell the capsule."

Ch'eng Hao picked up the dented metal packet. "You mean this?"
Ch'eng I nodded. Ch'eng Hao sniffed at it. "It smells like . . ." He
hesitated. "I cannot place it. But I know I have smelled it before."
He handed the capsule to Lin-Yu.

"Black powder," Lin-Yu said as soon as he put the piece to his
nose. "We use it from time to time for certain ceremonies. In explosive
pyrotechnics."

Ch'eng I nodded enthusiastically; his suspicions had been confirmed. "A bamboo tube," he recited, "packed with black powder.
One end open, the other closed except for a tiny hole. A fuse is
attached to the latter. An explosive projectile is placed in the tube
above the powder. The fuse is lit. The ignition of the powder
ejects the projectile, which in turn explodes in mid-air. Am I
correct?"

"That is how the fireworks work, yes," Lin-Yu said, "although I cannot imagine how you found out. It is a secret among monks – "

"I have experimented on my own," Ch'eng I said abruptly. "The principles are readily apparent. What is not so clear is how they were adapted to destructive ends." He thought the problem through aloud. "A narrower tube to suit the smaller projectile, I imagine . . . and, of course, the tube would be aimed at a target rather than at the sky . . . and in place of a fuse, this capsule . . . the capsule containing a small amount of black powder, which when compressed by a blow from the mallet explodes, igniting the main load of powder in the tube . . . and finally, a tripod to steady the apparatus, to account for the three circular indentations in the soil where I found the mallet and the capsule." Ch'eng I folded his arms and waited for his brother's reaction.

"Fireworks as a weapon," Ch'eng Hao whispered. "Ingenious." Then he realized what he had said and he shot a glance at Lin-Yu, whose expression betrayed that he had had the same thought. Ch'eng Hao voiced it for both of them. "One of Kung's inventions."

"No one else could have invented it," Lin-Yu said.

Ch'eng I was taken back. "You think Kung invented the weapon that killed him? I find that unlikely – "

Ch'eng Hao silenced him. "I will tell you what I have learned while you were away," he said. "In the meantime, we should see Kung's cell. I will fill you in on the way."

The cells they passed on the way to Kung's were as bare as the temple. Wooden cots with no matting were the only furniture the brothers saw and the walls were unadorned. But Kung's cell was different. He, too, had the painful looking cot but every inch of his walls was covered with ink drawings and elaborate calligraphy.

As Lin-Yu had said, much of the art was religious. One entire wall, for instance, was devoted to images of the Buddha and his boddhisatvas in intricate interrelations. The painting was flat and monochromatic, but somehow deeply hypnotic.

It was the other walls that revealed Kung's true genius, however, for it was there that he had composed dozens of sketches for tools and devices of mind-boggling complexity. Lin-Yu's braces were on the wall, along with drawings of the special plows and wells Kung had designed for the monks – as well as plenty of drawings of objects at whose function the brothers could only guess. The one drawing that was conspicuously absent from the wall was that of the murder weapon. None of the sketches looked similar to the machine Ch'eng I had described.

"All of these," Lin-Yu said when Ch'eng Hao asked, "are devices that Kung actually finished and gave to us. Perhaps the weapon was not perfected yet."

"It certainly worked well enough," Ch'eng Hao said.

"We do *not* know that for certain," Ch'eng I corrected his brother. "We do not yet know what happened."

"If these are Kung's finished inventions," Ch'eng Hao asked Lin-Yu, "where did he sketch ideas for new projects?"

"On the floor," Lin-Yu said. He indicated a sharp stick leaning against the cot and then a particularly scarred portion of the dirt floor. It did look as though Kung had used the space for this purpose – Ch'eng I was able to make out a character here and there – but trying to "read" it would have been futile.

"Had he no more permanent record?" Ch'eng I asked.

Lin-Yu knelt in front of the cot and reached under it. After groping for a few seconds he pulled out a flat metal board. "He used this from time to time. When he wanted to show an idea to the Patriarch, for instance. He would stretch a piece of fabric over it and then draw on it." Lin-Yu pointed to four hook-shaped protrusions at the corners of the board. "He designed this, too."

"So there may be a fabric sketch of the weapon somewhere . . ." Ch'eng Hao began – but Ch'eng I was already out of the room.

Ch'eng Hao ran after him. Lin-Yu followed as quickly as he could. They caught up with him outside Bo-Tze's cell. Ch'eng I burst in before they could restrain him.

Bo-Tze was seated in the lotus position on his cot, his legs crossed tightly over one another, his hands outstretched on his knees. As Ch'eng I entered, Bo-Tze opened his eyes with a start and dropped his hands to his sides.

"You were contemptuous of your fellow monk," Ch'eng I said without preamble. Then, in answer to the confusion in the old man's eyes, "My brother told me what you said about Kung. That he had 'visions' – and that you hated him for it. That you feel the world looks down on *you* because of men like him. That on some level you were obsessively jealous of him."

"I was never jealous of that man," Bo-Tze snarled. In the heat of confrontation, he did not even try to hide his anger. "He was a disgrace to us."

"Why?" Lin-Yu asked. There was pain and loss in his voice. "Because of his imagination?"

"Yes," Bo-Tze said, "if you want to call it that. But that is not all. He was dealing with the outside world!"

Lin-Yu shook his head. "That is ludicrous."

"I agree," Bo-Tze said. "It is ludicrous. It is also a fact. Kung was not just creating things for our use. He was also selling his creations in the secular world. He was not a monk – he was a merchant!"

"No," Lin-Yu insisted. "You know he never left the grounds. How could he – "

"Are you *completely* blind now?" Bo-Tze shouted. "*Wu* sold Kung's goods for him."

"Wu Han-Fei?" Ch'eng Hao asked. "The messenger?"

"Our 'link to the secular world,'" Bo-Tze said sarcastically. "It was a mistake to employ him, as I predicted it would be. But who talked the Patriarch into it? Kung did! Do you not see? *Do none of you see?*"

"It is clear that you want desperately to prove yourself right," Ch'eng I said. "Is that why you went to the temple this morning when you knew Kung was there?"

Bo-Tze's guard went up at last. "I was nowhere near the temple," he said.

Ch'eng I reached out and grabbed Bo-Tze's right hand. Bo-Tze resisted but Ch'eng I was by far the stronger man. Slowly, Ch'eng I turned the monk's hand palm upwards. The pads of Bo-Tze's fingers were seared red. "Note the singed fingers," Ch'eng I said. "Compare them to the seared fingers of Kung's body. Identical."

Bo-Tze pulled his hand away. "Yes," he said, breaking down at last, "yes, I was there! I was there because it was my last chance to expose Kung to the lot of you!" Ch'eng Hao was surprised – it was hard to believe that this was the same man he had interrogated unsuccessfully so recently. Corner a lion in the field and it attacks, he reminded himself, but corner one in its den and it falls at your feet.

"I cornered Wu outside the dining hall," Bo-Tze said furiously. "He is a coward! I threatened to expose him, and he turned on Kung like this." Bo-Tze snapped his trembling fingers. "Wu said that Kung had gone to the temple to burn all the evidence of their dealings. I went there to get this evidence for myself. Sure enough, Kung was there. There was a sheet of cloth stretched out on that metal board of his and he had already set it on fire. I grabbed it; he grabbed it, too. We struggled over it – then, all of a sudden, there was a loud explosion and Kung fell forward with blood spurting all over his face and I ran out of there as quickly as I could . . ." Bo-Tze was crying and out of breath; his chest heaved and his head sank forward until it almost touched his ankles.

Ch'eng Hao pulled his brother and Lin-Yu out of the room. Bo-Tze was not the murderer they sought, Ch'eng Hao knew; and at an exposed moment like this even a Buddhist deserved his privacy.

The Patriarch's cell was no larger than any of the others. He slept on the same cot. But like Kung's, his walls were not bare. Also like Kung's, his walls were covered with Kung's art: complex ink drawings, passionate attempts to render the transcendent universe accessible to the human eye – Ch'eng Hao would have found it all very moving if he had been a Buddhist. As it was, he could only marvel at the artist's skill.

"We all have our failings," the Patriarch said. He was staring at Kung's largest image and his voice betrayed the rapture he felt. "Kung was an artist at heart, I a connoisseur. Neither is appropriate for a monk: a monk must lose all attachments to the things of this world, because such things, in their impermanence, can only produce suffering. The more beautiful a thing is, the more pain it will bring by its inevitable absence." The Patriarch sighed. "Yet if life is suffering, can we not take from it what little pleasure there is to be had? How could I tell Kung not to paint? That would have increased his suffering – surely our purpose is not *that*."

"There is more to this matter than the art," Ch'eng Hao said.

"Yes," the Patriarch said. "The tools. I should let my men starve rather than use the tools Kung devised? This is Bo-Tze's position, but he is a fool. If we cannot use Kung's tools, from the same argument we should not use any tools at all. We should dig in the dirt with our hands as our ancestors did. Perhaps we should not farm at all, since our oldest ancestors did not. Innovation is not evil; new tools are not worse than old. And heaven knows it is easier to meditate with a full belly than an empty one. Gautama himself said so – the Buddha himself! Starvation is not for Buddhists any more than decadence is."

"I understand," Ch'eng Hao said, "and I agree. But there remains the question of Kung's trade with the outside world."

For a long time, the Patriarch was silent.

"Bo-Tze says – "

"He is correct," the Patriarch whispered. "I looked the other way."

"You knew – "

"Ch'eng Hao, how could I not know?" At this moment the Patriarch looked very old and helpless. "I simply chose to tolerate it. Kung was too special a man, and too valuable to our lives, for me to risk losing him over such a minor point. So he sent his creations to people like yourself? There are graver sins. Perhaps it even made some Confucians think twice before cursing us. Surely it did no harm."

"No harm," Ch'eng Hao said, "but now Kung is dead."

"Yes," the Patriarch said. "That is so. And this is what comes of forming attachments to things of this world – now that we have lost him, we suffer."

Ch'eng Hao considered for a moment. "When we first spoke, you indicated that Kung had grave matters on his conscience. But if he knew that you tolerated his dealings with the outside world, surely he was not anxious about that?" The Patriarch shook his head. "What then?"

"I repeat what I told you before: I do not know."

Ch'eng Hao let this pass. "Just one more question," he said. "When Kung traded his goods through Wu Han-Fei, what did he get in return? Not money, obviously; he had no use for that."

The Patriarch shrugged. "It is a question I never considered." Ch'eng Hao could see from the Patriarch's face that he really *hadn't* considered it. "Perhaps he simply received the satisfaction of knowing his creations were being put to good use."

To good use. The phrase resonated for Ch'eng Hao. Yes, he thought, good use. But surely that was not all?

Lin-Yu directed Ch'eng I to a small building on the outskirts of the monastery complex. It was no more than a hut, really, but a solid and well-constructed one as huts went. Lin-Yu stood guard outside the door while Ch'eng I went inside.

A few minutes later, Ch'eng I emerged carrying a scorched square of fabric and a bamboo tube.

Ch'eng I steadied the tripod he had brought by pressing it down in the damp soil at the edge of the forest. The bamboo tube was clamped in place, the repaired capsule inserted in the tube's smaller hole. Lin-Yu had procured the necessary black powder and, what was equally important, the spare monk's robe that knelt, stuffed to overflowing with straw and twigs, just inside the temple entrance. Ch'eng Hao held back the small crowd of onlookers he had gathered: the Patriarch, Bo-Tze, Tso, and a handful of other monks. Wu Han-Fei was not among the group.

"I am ready," Ch'eng I announced.

Lin-Yu moved to join the others. They all turned to face the dummy Ch'eng I had erected.

Ch'eng I aimed the bamboo tube carefully, sighting along its length. Then he inserted the small white stone he had selected as a projectile and took several test swings with the mallet. He steadied himself with two deep breaths.

"Proceed," Ch'eng Hao said.

Ch'eng I swung the mallet again. This time it connected with a sharp crack, squeezing the capsule flat. This tiny explosion was followed by a much larger one, one that startled all the spectators. Even Bo-Tze, who knew what to expect, started at the noise.

But the dummy did not fall. After the cloud of smoke around him cleared, Ch'eng I inspected the tube. The projectile *had* been ejected. He ran to the temple and made a quick search of the far wall. The white stone he had chosen expressly for this reason stood out clearly against the brown of the packed earth in which it was now embedded.

"Come here," he said. The others crowded into the temple, pushing the dummy aside. They stared at the stone in the wall as though it was a religious relic and worthy of their rapt attention. Ch'eng I pushed his way back through the crowd until he was able to join his brother outside the temple.

"You missed," Ch'eng Hao said.

"Indeed. It was the strike of the mallet that ruined my aim. I had not taken it into account."

"Never mind," Ch'eng Hao said. "It is of no consequence. You will never need to use that cursed instrument again."

"I do not doubt that you are right," Ch'eng I said, "but I disagree that it is of no consequence. You see – "

But at that moment Bo-Tze and the Patriarch exited the temple and intruded on the brothers' conversation.

"So that is how the murder was accomplished," the Patriarch said, clapping a hand to the small of Ch'eng I's back.

"Wu used Kung's own machine against him when he thought Kung might expose him," Bo-Tze said, his voice once again thick with disdain. "In a thief's camp, no man sleeps with both eyes closed. Kung should have known Wu would silence him if it ever proved necessary."

"How and why the murder was committed," Ch'eng Hao agreed. "You now have your answers. And we must give full credit to Ch'eng I for the greater part of this investigation – his methods proved most fruitful."

"Esteemed brother," Ch'eng I said, holding up his hand for silence, "I do not deserve your praise, or indeed any man's, if I allow the investigation to end here."

"What do you mean?" the Patriarch said. "We have seen proof – or do you, of all people, think that this was not the murder weapon?" He gestured toward the distant tripod.

"It was the murder weapon," Ch'eng I agreed.

"And did you not find the weapon, together with other incriminating evidence, in the hut of Wu Han-Fei?" Bo-Tze added.

"I did," Ch'eng I said.

Even Ch'eng Hao was confused. "And did you not put Wu Han-Fei in restraints? Surely you would not have done that unless you were as convinced as we are that he is the murderer."

"I did and I am," Ch'eng I said, "but that is only the beginning of an answer to what went on here this morning. You wrongly indict a man if you credit him with motives he did not hold."

Ch'eng Hao put a hand on Ch'eng I's shoulder. "Brother, I bow to your expertise in matters scientific, but do me the courtesy of acknowledging my insight into human character. It has to be as I explained it to you.

"Kung distributed his creations as widely as he could out of sheer good will. Lin-Yu testifies to this. Wu Han-Fei, on the other hand, had a more concrete motive for getting involved with Kung: he sold Kung's inventions for personal profit." The word "profit" always wore a sneer the way Ch'eng Hao said it, and this time was no exception.

"Recently," Ch'eng Hao continued, "Kung dreamt up the extraordinary weapon you just demonstrated. In his initial enthusiasm he gave a working model to Wu. But Kung was a compassionate man, dedicated to the easing of life's sufferings – consider his other inventions: implements to improve farming, Lin-Yu's leg braces, and so forth. Now, for the first time, he had created a weapon. This horrible realization, combined with the fact that he had placed it in the hands of an unscrupulous man, preyed mightily on his conscience. This is why he went to the temple: to destroy the plans for this device. The murderer stole the plans from the scene of Kung's death – and are they not the very same half-burned plans you found in Wu Han-Fei's hut?

"There is nothing more to know about this murder."

"Nothing?" Ch'eng I directed this remark at all three men, but his next was reserved for his brother. "I am disappointed in you, Hao. If Wu Han-Fei planned Kung's murder, why did he send Bo-Tze to the temple to witness it? You might argue that Bo-Tze *forced* Wu Han-Fei to tell him where Kung was – but if this was the case, why didn't Wu delay the murder until a more propitious time? And how do you explain the change in the position of Kung's body after his death?"

Ch'eng Hao said nothing.

"There can be only one answer," Ch'eng I said. "Wu Han-Fei knew Bo-Tze wanted to expose Kung's dealings with him, so he lured Bo-Tze to the temple with a story about Kung's 'destroying evidence.' Then he hid in the forest, intending to use Kung's weapon to silence Bo-Tze." Bo-Tze drew a sharp breath. "Kung was not Wu Han-Fei's intended target. Bo-Tze was."

"I bow to your superior perception," Ch'eng Hao said, grasping Ch'eng I's reasoning. "So you would argue that Wu Han-Fei wanted to kill Bo-Tze – but that from a distance of forty paces, two men in brown robes looked too similar to tell apart and as a result he killed the wrong man."

"No," Ch'eng I said. "Trust your own eyes. Do you not see that Bo-Tze's robe is considerably more worn than Kung's and that his skin looks visibly older? You will recall that at least one man was not wearing his hood."

"Very likely neither man was," Ch'eng Hao said. "But one bald head looks much like another – "

Ch'eng I shook his head. "They look entirely different."

"But from a distance of forty paces – "

"Entirely different," Ch'eng I said firmly. "It is not only that Bo-Tze's head looked older – Kung's bore a highly visible mark. A prominent scar at the top of his neck. Am I correct?" This question was directed to the Patriarch.

"You are," the Patriarch said.

"A scar?" Ch'eng Hao asked.

"Not just any scar," Ch'eng I said, "a family brand. Clearly visible at forty paces, particularly if one is looking for it. As I believe Wu Han-Fei was. Consider this: suppose you were right that Wu Han-Fei could not tell the two men apart – do you think under those circumstances that he would have used the weapon?"

After a moment, Ch'eng Hao slowly shook his head. "Then how do you account for what happened?"

"The device was not perfected," Ch'eng I said gravely. "Wu Han-Fei knew which man he wanted to hit. *He simply missed.*"

They stood outside Wu Han-Fei's hut, Ch'eng I and Ch'eng Hao, Bo-Tze and the Seventh Patriarch. They stood outside because none of them wanted to enter.

"If what you have said is true," Bo-Tze said, "then we have been victims of an even greater deception than I feared."

"It cannot be," the Patriarch said.

"There is only one demonstration that will convince you," said Ch'eng I. He stepped into the hut.

The other men followed. Inside, Wu Han-Fei was in a seated position, his wrists and ankles bound behind him. The room was furnished better than the monks' cells: there were small windows with mullioned glass panes and swing shutters controlled from the inside; a mattress padded with layers of reed matting; and a stool whose top opened to reveal a bowl and a set of utensils. Ch'eng I pointed all this out while Wu Han-Fei watched in silence.

"This is the extent of Wu Han-Fei's personal profit," Ch'eng I said. "Things Kung created especially for him. If he did sell Kung's goods for money, he kept none of it. Perhaps it was all sent back to . . . his family."

Ch'eng I walked behind Wu Han-Fei and put his hand on the kneeling man's head. "A fine head of hair. He is not a Buddhist, so he can keep his hair – and can live here at a distance from the monks. A neat arrangement. When they need something from the outside world – such as men to investigate a murder – he brings it. Otherwise, he is left to himself.

"But why would a man who is not a Buddhist attach himself to a monastery in this way? It is the worst of lives, surely, caught with one leg in each of two worlds that despise one another. One must have a compelling reason to choose such a life. Why," Ch'eng I asked Wu Han-Fei, "did you?"

Wu Han-Fei said nothing.

"This was one of the questions that bothered me." Ch'eng I said. "Why would he live here? And: why would he kill to protect a monk? What was the worst the monks could do to him if his activities were exposed – send him away? Hardly a severe punishment for a man who has no ties to the monastic life anyway. No, the man they could punish was Kung – but why would a mercenary secularist care?

"A fine head of hair," Ch'eng I said again, running his fingers through Wu Han-Fei's black locks. "A lifetime of growth concealing a scalp that hasn't seen the sun in thirty years." He turned to Ch'eng Hao. "You know, when we first met Wu, I thought he lowered his eyes out of respect for us, or perhaps fear. But then I realized it was neither – it was for want of a beard."

He bent forward over Wu's shoulder. "Look up," he commanded. Wu Han-Fei shot a sullen glance at the ceiling.

"No," Ch'eng I said, "turn your head up." Wu Han-Fei did not respond. "Your *head*, Mister Wu . . ." – Ch'eng I took a tight grip on the young man's hair and pulled his head back – ". . . or should I say Mister *Wang*?"

Bo-Tze stared at the character carved in white relief on the underside of Wu Han-Fei's chin. The Patriarch sat on the edge of the mattress and put his head in his hands. Ch'eng I released Wu Han-Fei's head. "What was Kung's real name," he asked, "his birth name?"

"Wang," the Patriarch said, nodding, his voice rumbling like the largest and saddest of gongs. "Wang Deng-Mo."

"Wang Deng-Mo," Ch'eng I repeated. "And this, we can assume, is *Wang*, not Wu, Han-Fei."

"I do not understand," the Patriarch said. "Why . . .?"

"Why?" Ch'eng I said. "Because family is a more powerful bond than you give it credit for being. Kung took on a new identity when he joined your monastery – and so did his . . . brother?"

Wang Han-Fei let a single word escape through his clenched teeth. "Yes."

"His brother," Ch'eng I said. "As I thought. To maintain the family tie despite all else; to send resources back home, to help the rest of the family survive; to live and die and kill for a brother *because* he is a brother – *this* is 'why.' "

"But brother," Ch'eng Hao said, his face red with chagrin, "how could you possibly have known? What started you thinking in this direction?"

"The question that was at once the simplest and the most complex," Ch'eng I said. "Why had Kung's body been moved? Bo-Tze would not have done it, not when it would have meant returning to the scene of the murder. Lin-Yu might have done it but he would not have concealed it from us if he had. This meant it had to have been the murderer who had done it. But why would the murderer have moved Kung's body? I asked myself this question again and again.

"Then all at once I understood. Kung's body had not merely been moved. You will recall that Bo-Tze said Kung's blood spurted all over his face when he was hit – yet when we found the body, Kung's face was clean; his hood was neatly arranged; and he was lying on his back in a dignified position. It is no way for a man to be found, lying face down in his own blood – but that a killer recognizes this is most unusual. That is how I knew that the killer had compassion for his victim. More than compassion, even – love, and more than love, a sense of duty."

Ch'eng Hao had more questions to ask, and he asked them; Ch'eng I answered them in more detail than was absolutely necessary; Bo-Tze and the Patriarch left as quickly as they could; and no one noticed when off in his corner, his head hung low, Wang Han-Fei began to weep.

Ch'eng Hao sipped from a cup of bone-stock soup that Ch'eng I had prepared. Was that the faint flavor of tea he tasted, whispering under the rich marrow? Perhaps it was. Ch'eng Hao knew his brother was wont to experiment in the oddest directions. He set the cup down. "I would not have released him," he said.

Ch'eng I paused at the fire then went on stirring. "Why, brother? Because he was a killer and killers should not go unpunished?"

"No," Ch'eng Hao said. "He killed his brother. That was punishment enough for both of them."

"Why, then?"

"Because you should have known he would kill himself."

Ch'eng I tipped the stock pot forward to fill his cup. The thick soup steamed and he held his hands in the steam to warm them. "Forcing him to live would have been the most cruel of punishments. He could not have escaped the voice of censure no matter where he fled under heaven. A man's greatest freedom," Ch'eng I said, "is the freedom to hoard or spend his life as he chooses."

Ch'eng Hao could not disagree. "The tragedy of it is that a man such as Kung had to lie to live as he chose, that his brother had to lie to be near him, and that these lies accumulated until a killing became inevitable. A pointless killing . . ." He turned to other thoughts, less troubling for being more abstract. "I still do not understand, brother, how you knew to investigate Wu – Wang – in the first place. Even granting that you suspected that the killer was a family member – why him?"

"You were investigating the monks and making no progress," Ch'eng I said. "I trusted that had there been progress to be made, you would have made it. So I operated on the assumption that you were looking in the wrong direction entirely. As you were."

"But my approach was the logical one – "

"Yes, it was," Ch'eng I said, "but not the correct one. Therein lies one of life's great mysteries."

Ch'eng Hao bent once more to his soup. November winds were beginning to roar on the plains and the small warmth was welcome. The chill in his soul was not to be so easily dispelled. "I," he said, "If it came to that, would you kill to defend me?"

Ch'eng I looked up from his task. "I am your brother," he said. He brought the cup to his lips. "Heaven grant me good aim."

THE MIDWIFE'S TALE
Margaret Frazer

In the previous volume I introduced the first short story featuring Sister Frevisse, a nun at the abbey of St Frideswide in fifteenth-century Oxfordshire. The character has appeared in four novels, The Novice's Tale *(1992),* The Servant's Tale *(1993), which was nominated for an Edgar award,* The Outlaw's Tale *(1994), and* The Bishop's Tale *(1994). The next in the series,* The Boy's Tale *should be published by the time this book appears.*

> O cursed synne of alle cursedness!
> O traytours homycide, O wikkednesse!
>
> *The Pardoner's Tale*

The light from the yet unrisen sun flowed softly gold and rose between the long blue shadows of the village houses and across the fields and hedgerows full of birdsong. Ada Bychurch, standing in the doorway of Martyn Fisher's low-eaved house, shivered a little in the morning's coolness and huddled her cloak around her, hoping for more warmth from its worn gray wool.

She wished she could as readily huddle away from the sorrow in the house behind her. She was village midwife and had done what she could but it had not been enough and now there was nothing left but the hope that after Father Clement's ministrations, Cisily's soul would go safe to whatever blessings she had earned in her short life. But despite her faith Ada could not help the feeling Cisily's mortal life had been too short. Far too short for the motherless newborn daughter and the grieving husband she was leaving behind her, however fortunate Cisily was to be soon free of the world's troubles.

Martyn Fisher's house was at the nunnery end of the village, just before the lane curved and the houses ended and the road ran on a quarter mile or so between fields to the nunnery gates. Cisily had often said how she loved the fact that there were no houses across the way from her, that she could see through a field gate to the countryside from her front doorstep. And she had been pleased,

too, that just leftward not so very far was the village green and all
the village busyness.

Priors Byfield was a fair-sized village, with all a village's interests
and pleasures. Ada looked toward the green where the last drift of
smoke from last night's Midsummer bonfire was a fading smudge
across the sunrise. The revelling had gone on nearly to dawn as
usual, and she doubted anyone would be out to the early plowing
and knew for certain that the bailiff would be hard put to bring folk
to the haying by late morning or maybe even afternoon despite the
fact it looked to be a second fine, fair day after a week of damp and
drizzle. It had been taken as a sign of God's favor when yesterday
had early cleared for the young folk to be off to the woods and ways
to gather Midsummer greenery and the older folk to build up the
bonfire for the evening's dancing and sport.

Father Clement had given his usual sharp sermon last Sunday
against what he felt were such unchristian ways, but the Midsummer
bonfire and other such revelling through the year were like the bone
in the village's body: no one could imagine doing without them. And
Ada doubted that even Father Clement would have grudged Cisily
Fisher her midsummer revels this year, if it could have replaced her
slow bleeding to death in childbed. Hardly a year married and now
this, and her husband still so in love with her he had dared, when
it was clear there was nothing else Ada as midwife could do, to go
to the nunnery and beg for their infirmarian's help. He must have
pleaded most pitiably because the infirmarian had not merely sent
some mix of medicines but come herself and was still here, though
there was no more hope for Cisily's life, only for a painless death and
nothing left for anyone to do except give comfort.

"I pray you, pardon me," someone said softly behind Ada's
shoulder. She looked around, then moved out of the doorway and
aside on the broad, flat stone that served as step beyond the low
doorsill, out of the way for the nun who had accompanied Dame
Claire, the infirmarian, from the priory.

With an acknowledging bow of her head, she stepped out, raised her
face to the lightening sky and drew a deep breath. Her face was almost
as pale as the white wimple that encircled it inside the black frame
of her veil, and Ada guessed that, like her, she had been unable to.
endure the stifling, blood-tainted air inside the house any longer.

Ada thought she remembered her name and hazarded, "Dame
Frevisse, aren't you?"

The nun inclined her head again, politely, but said nothing. And
that was only right, Ada supposed. In cloister or out they were
supposed to be as silent as might be; and of course, being a

nun, she was far better born than Ada, was at least of gentle
and maybe even noble blood. She was tall for a woman, with a
strong-boned face and beautifully kept, long-fingered hands. Her
gown was plain Benedictine black, just as it should be, but amply
made from fine-woven wool, its color all even despite black being
notoriously hard to dye, and there were uncountable small black
buttons from wrist to nearly elbow of the black undergown's tight
sleeves. Probably more buttons than any ten women of the village
had all together, Ada guessed. But except for the gold ring on her
left wedding finger and her belt-hung rosary of richly polished wood,
she had no finery such as Ada had heard tell was all too common
among some nuns. Nor did she seem arrogant, only tired and sad,
and Ada liked her the better for it.

They stood silently side by side while the daylight broadened
around them and birdsong rose from hedgerows as if joy were newly
discovered in the world, until in the house, where there had been
deep stillness for this while and a while past, people began to move,
to talk low among themselves, some of them trying to comfort a man
weeping. The wait was over and the task of dealing with the dead
was come. It was a task that every village woman knew, and all did
their best at it, knowing it was something that sooner or later would
have to be done for each of them, when her time came.

The baby made a mewling cry and was quieted. She seemed healthy
enough, was already baptized, and Johane living just down the way
had already said she would suckle it with her own, she having milk
enough for a calf, as she put it, so that was all right.

Ada knew she should go back in now, was bracing herself for it
when someone came up behind her in the doorway. She and Dame
Frevisse both shifted further aside to make way, Ada supposing it was
Dame Claire, leaving now there was nothing more the nuns could do,
but it was Elyn Browster, Cisily's neighbor from two houses farther
along, right at the village's very end. Though barren herself, Elyn
was at almost every child birthing and always took a loss like this
to heart; and this one even more to heart than usual, it looked like.
Normally a vigorous, wide-gesturing woman, she was gray-faced with
weariness and grief and she would have gone between Ada and the
nun without speaking except Ada said, "It's a sorry thing. Martyn
is taking it hard, seems."

"There'll be those who'll comfort him," Elyn said and went on
without pause or a look up from where her feet were trudging. It
was the way she showed pain, Ada knew. She had feelings that cut
deep, did Elyn, but kept them to herself as much as might be.

"Jenkyn to see to?" Ada asked at her back.

"Aye," Elyn said and went on, a swag-hipped woman on tired feet, along the verge of the lane still muddy from the past few days of rain.

"She's a good woman, is Elyn Browster," Ada said, not because she thought Dame Frevisse needed to know but simply to have something in her own mind besides thought of Cisily lying dead now. "Her husband Jenkyn, he's not much and would be less if it weren't for her. She's had to take the man's part around their holding more often than not because he won't. It's not what she wanted when she married him, I'd guess, but she's never faltered. She – "

Ada broke off as she found Dame Frevisse's gaze fixed on her with a disconcerting directness that made her realize she had been gossiping to someone who not only had no interest in such things, but should not be hearing them at all.

She was saved from deciding what to say next by Dame Claire, the infirmarian, coming out. She was a small woman and seemed smaller for being beside Dame Frevisse. She looked as sad and tired as Elyn Browster had and her surprisingly deep voice grated with weariness as she said, "I think maybe you should go in, Mistress Bychurch. Father Clement is beginning to comfort Martyn Fisher."

Knowing exactly what that meant, Ada dropped a deep curtsy to them both and hurried back into the house. Father Clement might be a good priest, but he was rigid and had no gift for solace. What Martyn needed was real comforting, a shoulder to cry on and someone saying how sorry they were, not a lecture on how priceless was the saved soul gone to God.

Just as Frevisse had, Dame Claire lifted her face to the clear, bright sky and drew a deep breath. The early light had thickened to a flow of molten gold now; the thick dew on the grass was sheened to silver.

"The baby looks likely to live," Dame Claire said.

"And the woman who's taking her to nurse seems clean and healthy." Frevisse offered that comfort as gently as she could. St Frideswide's Priory was small, with only eleven nuns, and set lonely in the Oxfordshire countryside, so that all of them had to have as many skills as they could. To that end, Frevisse had been set this past half year to assist Dame Claire in her duties as infirmarian and learn from her. Though not so apt as Dame Claire at herbs and healing, she had done well enough, able to do what she was told and to grasp Dame Claire's admonition, "You have to try to understand what's happening inwardly as well as outwardly to a body, and you have to think about what it means or you can never well tend to anyone's hurts or illness, only pretend to."

What Frevisse understood now was that Dame Claire was grieving for the woman she had not known until a few hours ago and had not been able to save. Unable to say anything to mend or comfort that – assuredly nothing so useless as "You did what you could" – she held silent, both of them gazing out at the morning, until in a while Dame Claire sighed deeply, said, "Come then. We'd best be going," and stepped away from the door, bound for the nunnery.

Side by side as much as they could while keeping to what there was of a grassy verge along the muddy road, they passed the last few houses of the village, walking quickly, partly to warm themselves against the morning's chill, partly in hope that though they were surely late for the office of Prime and its dawn prayers, they might be in time for breakfast and Mass.

They were beyond the last house, with only the dawn-bright road and hedges ahead of them, their shoes and the hems of their black gowns already soaked through with dew, when a woman behind them called out, "Sisters! Pray you, come back, please!" desperate and frightened enough that they swung around together.

Elyn Browster was standing in the muddy road outside the doorway of the village's last house, her hands wrung in her skirt as she went on saying, "Come, please. Hurry!" even as they came. "He's hurt. He's . . ." The words she needed were not there. "He's . . ." She pointed at her open doorway. "There. I can't . . . he won't . . . Oh, please, my ladies!" Her finger shifted its vague, stunned pointing into the house to the grassy patch beside the stone doorstep. There were muddy footprints on the stone, but Elyn was asking them to wipe their feet clean. Frevisse knew how one could cling to the familiar to keep the frightening at bay, so she followed Dame Claire's lead and wiped her soft-soled shoes on the grass before following Dame Claire inside, Elyn behind them.

The shutters had been slid down from the windows, letting in the morning light, but even so the room was dark to her eyes after the brilliant outdoors. She and Dame Claire both paused, waiting to see better, only gradually able to tell more about where they were. Like most village houses, the front door was near the middle of one long side. To their left was the living area, with hearth and a large, heavy wooden table, two benches, a scattering of stools, a bed along the farthest wall, a large chest at its foot. Rightward then should be where the animals were kept but there was no smell of them, and she realized that instead of stalls there was a board wall making a second room of the house's other end.

"He's here," Elyn said at their backs. "Just over here. Come."

But she went no nearer herself, stayed where she was beside them, pointing to the floor left of the door. No, not at the floor. Frevisse's eyes had adjusted and now she could see the man lying in the shadows there, stretched stiffly out, flat on his back, arms rigid at his sides. Except that he was dressed for going out to work, even to the cloth coif closely covering his head, tied neatly under his chin, he was like a corpse laid out for burial.

But he was alive; even as she and Dame Claire crossed themselves, supposing the worst, he drew a hoarse, snoring breath.

"Oh, merciful God," Dame Claire said and went quickly forward to kneel beside him.

"He's drunk?" Frevisse asked.

"He never drinks that much!" Elyn said. "And there's naught in the house for him to be that drunk on."

"Did you lay him out like this?" Dame Claire asked. Her hands were briskly going over the man, feeling for what might be broken and for a pulse at throat and wrists.

"He was like that when I found him. Just like that." Elyn wrung her hands more tightly into her skirt. "He's a considerate man, is Jenkyn. Thoughtful. He . . . he's . . ." Her voice caught on a rising note of desperation. Without looking around from Jenkyn, Dame Claire said, "Take her outside."

Grasping the woman by one arm above the elbow, Frevisse guided her out the door. Elyn was nearly her height and as well-muscled as her life demanded of her but she came outside and sank weakly down on her doorstep and bent over as if in pain, her skirt huddled up to hide her face, muffling her voice as she said, "He's dying, isn't he?"

"Dame Claire will know soon." That was all the comfort Frevisse dared offer and saw with relief one of the women who had been at the Fishers' coming along the road to her own house next door.

But even as Frevisse raised a hand to beckon her, the woman saw something was amiss, turned her head to call to someone out of sight around the lane's curve, and then came on briskly past her own door to Elyn and Frevisse, asking as she came, "Elyn, what's toward with you? What is it?"

Her face still hidden as if her tears were something of which to be ashamed, Elyn said, "It's Jenkyn. He's hurt himself somehow."

"And it's bad?"

"I don't know. He's breathing all odd, and he won't wake up."

Two other women came hurrying to join them, one of them the firm-handed, kind-spoken midwife Frevisse remembered from the Fishers'.

"There now," Ada said when she understood how matters stood, her arm around Elyn's shoulders. "Dame Claire's with him and she'll do all that can be done. She's a good hand at this manner of thing."

The other women murmured agreement and reassurance, one of them patting Elyn on the knee comfortingly the while.

Frevisse had drawn back, knowing they would do more for Elyn than she could, and now turned toward the doorway with relief as Dame Claire appeared. Her relief faded as she saw the infirmarian's face was set in the particular way she had when calmness was an enforced choice. "I need you to come back in, please, Dame."

Elyn lifted her head and started to rise. Dame Claire gestured for her to stay. "Not yet. Soon." To the other women she said, even more quietly, "One of you had best run for Father Clement."

A cry escaped Elyn. The midwife's arm tightened around her, her head close to Elyn's as she murmured comforts.

Frevisse followed Dame Claire inside where nothing was changed except that the man's breathing was, if anything, louder and less steady. Standing over him, Dame Claire said bluntly, "His skull is broken."

"Badly?"

"I can feel the skull bone give at the back of his head. Smashed. And I'd guess that's where he hit it." She pointed to the wall above where he lay. A common enough wall of wattle and daub – clay over interlaced withies, a rough coat of white plaster over the clay. At about eye level a hand's breadth of the plastered clay was caved irregularly inward, and it looked lately done.

Frevisse looked around the neatly kept room and asked, "What could he have fallen over?" None of the sparse furnishings was near enough, not even one of the joint stools. "Was he drunk, do you think, despite what his wife says?"

"There's no smell of ale on him. It might have been a seizure maybe, but I don't know what kind it would be, to fling him so hard against the wall . . ."

Dame Claire trailed off, not going on to the next possibility. Frevisse, not wanting to either, said after a moment too full of Jenkyn's ugly breathing, "How long ago did it happen?"

"I can't tell. With something like this you can die on the instant or linger an hour or even a day. He can't have been lying here long, he's dressed to go out to work, and it's only just sunrise."

"But he won't live?"

"It would be a miracle if he did. When the skull is smashed like this . . ."

Frevisse heard a man's voice outside encouraging Elyn to be brave in the face of God's will and then Father Clement entered. He paused for the moment his eyes needed to adjust to the house's dimness, started forward toward Jenkyn, and pulled up short, startled at sight of him stretched out so rigidly on the rushes, with blue lips, nostrils flared, his breathing strange.

"God have mercy!" Father Clement turned his exclamation into blessing by drawing a hasty cross in the air over Jenkyn.

Frevisse and Dame Claire crossed themselves in echo, and Dame Claire said, "He needs to be shriven."

Elyn had followed Father Clement into the house. Now her despairing cry startled Father Clement out of his shock. Brisk with officious importance because what needed to be done only he could do, he said, "Then best you let me see to it. Ada, take Elyn over there. You others go with her too. Pray. A pater, an ave, a creed. And Dame Claire, Dame Frevisse, if you'll help me here."

The women urged Elyn to the far side of her hearth, sat her on a stool, and clustered around her with soothing sounds. She was crying almost silently, tears gleaming on her face as she looked past the women to the priest as he put down and opened his box of priestly things, brought with him from the Fishers', and took out the candles, the chrism, all the things needed to see Jenkyn's soul safe from his body into heaven. With the nuns' assistance, the matter was quickly seen to. And to clear effect, because as Father Clement folded his stole and put it away, Jenkyn drew a long, gargling breath and let it out in a forced gasp that brought the eyes of everyone in the room around to him.

He drew another, not quite so long but driven out of him with all the force of the first. And another after that, long and gargling and let out in a rush.

"What is it?" one of the women whispered.

Dame Claire opened her mouth to answer, but Father Clement said, "He's forcing the devils out of him that would have taken his soul to hell."

Another breath drove from Jenkyn's unconscious body. Elyn groaned and, shuddering, covered her ears. Everyone, Father Clement included, crossed themselves.

Ada Bychurch would not have thought there was that much evil in Jenkyn Browster to be driven out. He had always seemed a quiet, goodly man. But who but God could judge a man's heart?

Because it would be easier on everyone to be doing something, she said, "Can't he be moved now he's shriven? Won't it be better if he dies in his own bed?"

Dame Claire said, "He's past being harmed. Do it."

Ada could see Father Clement was annoyed at the nun for giving permission instead of leaving it to him in his greater authority. He had long since settled into complacency with himself and his place in

the village, and in return the village was used to him. He always had
the right words if never quite the right sympathy, and never cared to
be crossed in anything.

Now he looked around and demanded, "Where's Pers?" with the
clear thought that two men were better than one in lifting poor
Jenkyn even though Jenkyn by any description was nowhere near
a big man.

For the first time Ada wondered too where Pers was. He was
Jenkyn's nephew and heir and had come to live with his uncle and
aunt two years ago when his older brother had taken a new wife and
wanted that the house he and Pers had shared to himself and her. Pers
had taken it in good part, and the Browsters had welcomed him, a well
grown, happily disposed young man willing to ~~~ himself to whatever
work was to hand. And it had been the more col   nient because a few
years before then Jenkyn, at Elyn's prompting, ha l asked the priory's
steward for the holding next to theirs when it fell vacant with no heir
to claim it. He had been given it, and Elyn had seen to turning its
house into a byre so there had been no longer need to keep their cow,
the sheep, and chickens in their own house, and she had had Jenkyn
build a wall to make that end of their house a separate room, used
for storage but given over to Pers when he came to live with them.

So where was he now when his uncle needed him for this final
kindness?

"He's not . . . here," Elyn choked out between sobs.

"Then where – ?" Father Clement began, but paused, maybe with
the same thought Ada had.

Yesternight had been Midsummer Eve, and Pers had likely been
out with all the other village young folk, gone to the woods for greenery
and dancing at the bonfire so, "Likely he's at Pollard's," Ada said.
"He's been working there of days when he wasn't needed here and
has his eye on Pollard's Kate."

"And she on him," Mary Cedd, one of the other women, put in.
"Aye, likely he's there. I'll go for him."

She left. Father Clement with Ada to help him lifted Jenkyn and
carried him to his bed along the far wall, Dame Claire steadying his
head. His breathing was shorter now, a gasping in and a gasping out.
The straw-stuffed mattress crackled under his slight weight as they
settled him onto it, and Dame Claire eased his head down onto the
pillow as gently as if maybe he would feel it.

With a final gasp, his breathing stopped.

Stillness filled the room, no one moving, staring at him, waiting
for it to begin again, longer and longer, until the waiting broke and
they realized it was over.

But then he drew a long, gargling suck of air deep into his lungs and drove it explosively out. And drew another after it. And another.

In too calm a voice, Dame Claire said, "I've seen a man die of a broken skull this way before. The breathing stops and then comes back, with the breaths shorter and shorter each time, until it finally stops altogether."

Elyn moaned and hid her face in her hands. Ada murmured something between a prayer and protective spell, crossing herself as she did, then with her arm around Elyn again said, "Come sit by him now."

Face still covered, Elyn shook her head, refusing.

Ada had seen this before – the idea that by not doing what was expected of you, you could keep the inevitable at bay. Before she could urge Elyn again to what would bring her greater comfort in the long run despite what she thought now, Father Clement said, "You have to trust in God's mercy, Elyn. For him and for yourself. And let us all see the lesson in it. That anyone can be taken to God's judgement on the instant and all unprepared. 'You do not know the day or the hour.' It comes by God's will and – "

"This may not be God's will," the taller of the two nuns said. Dame Frevisse. She had been so silent this while that Ada had thought she was deep in prayer for Jenkyn's soul, but now she was looking at the wall where Jenkyn had struck it.

Father Clement, not used to being interrupted, snapped, "What do you mean?"

Apparently not noticing his tone, she answered, "Look at the wall here. Jenkyn's not a tall man. Shorter than I am." That was true; Jenkyn was shorter than his wife, and she was a head shorter than Dame Frevisse. "But see where he hit." She pointed at the dent. "It's almost as high as where I would have struck, if I'd fallen against the wall. And if I'd fallen hard enough, over something or however, to break the wall like that, I'd have been falling very hard indeed and would have hit the wall much farther down, much lower than my head level, because I'd be falling. The dent in the wall should be *lower* than Jenkyn's head, not higher the way it is. He didn't fall against the wall."

"He didn't fall?" Father Clement repeated her ridiculous statement. "Then how did he hit the wall?"

"He might have been standing on something and fallen off it," Ada said promptly.

Too promptly, because she realized the problem with that even as Dame Frevisse asked, "Off what? Nothing is near the wall. Unless, Elyn, did you move anything when you first came in?"

Elyn was staring at her. "No," she said uncertainly. She thought a moment. "I came in and called to Jenkyn and when he didn't answer I thought he was gone to his work and went about opening the shutters for some light and didn't see him until I came to open the one beside where he was. I didn't move anything." She steadied to certainty. "No, not a thing."

"Then he didn't fall against the wall," Dame Frevisse said.

"But of course he did," said Father Clement. He was beginning to be overtly indignant. "There's the place where he hit it. That break wasn't there when I was here yesterday. How else could it have happened?"

"He could have been thrown."

The response to that was startled silence, until Father Clement declared, "Nonsense!"

But, "How else?" Dame Frevisse asked back.

"But there was no one here," Elyn protested. "He doesn't hold with Midsummer wandering. We stayed home and he was already to bed when I was called to Cisily."

"He's dressed now and with his coif on for going out," Dame Frevisse pointed out.

"Midsummer's come. He meant to be out early to cut the thistles in the far field."

Since thistles cut before Midsummer Day grew back threefold, sensible men waited until then to deal with them.

"But Jenkyn has been cut down instead of them," Father Clement said. "God's hand – "

"– did not throw him against the wall," interrupted Dame Frevisse. Father Clement's face darkened with displeasure. Ignoring that, she said, "There were a man's muddy footprints on the doorstep when we came in, side by side as if he had stood there and knocked."

"They could be Jenkyn's footprints," Father Clement shot back. "He could have stepped out to see how the morning did."

Even if he had, he'd not have been so dull as to muddy his shoes and Elyn's doorstep, Ada thought tartly, while Dame Frevisse met the priest's challenge with, "There's no mud on his shoes."

Elyn, rousing to something she understood, put in, "Those are his house shoes. He'd never muddy them. His outdoor shoes are kept by the back door always."

Ada looked toward the door that led into the garden behind the house. "They aren't there now."

Elyn pulled away from the women around her and took a few uncertain steps toward the door, staring at the place where Jenkyn always set his shoes. "Where are they?" she asked, bewildered.

"They're always there." Her expression opened with a thought and she exclaimed, "They've been taken! Someone's stolen them!"

Ada went to take hold of her again, less comforting now than trying to steady her. "They're only misplaced, likely. You know men. As like to put a shovel in the turnip bin as hang it where it's supposed to be. We'll look for them. They're here somewhere. Come you, sit down by Jenkyn now and say farewell to him."

But Elyn stayed standing where she was, insisting, "He wouldn't put them somewhere else. Where else would he put them? He always put them there. They're gone and I'm telling you so! Someone was here and took them!" Her face harshened with alarm. "Our money!" She ran to the hearth, knelt down heavily, and with knowing fingers pried up one of the stones around it.

Why do we think that's a clever place to hide things? wondered Ada. Everyone she knew did it, including herself, when they had any that didn't need to be spent at once. It was nobody's secret.

"No," Elyn said with naked relief, her hand on the bag that lay in the hole she had opened. "All's here still." She began to refit the stone, stopped, and said in a different voice, "But the stone's the wrong way around. Look, you can see!"

"Jenkyn, likely," Ada said.

"He'd never. He knew better." Elyn rose clumsily to her feet, looking desperately around the room. "There's been a thief here! He's taken Jenkyn's shoes and was after our money!"

"But he didn't take it," Father Clement said. "You have to calm yourself. No one's been here. A thief wouldn't have left the money."

Elyn turned wide, frightened eyes toward him. "I frightened him away ere he could take it! He'd hurt Jenkyn but when he heard me coming he ran away! He was here when I came home!"

"Of course!" exclaimed Ada, suddenly grasping what Elyn was saying. "And he went out the back way! When he heard you at the front, he went out the back!"

She started for the back door, the women and Father Clement with her, but Dame Frevisse was suddenly before them, stopping them with her arm across the doorway, saying, "Whatever happened, he's long gone by now and you'll trample over any tracks he's left if you all go out. I'll see what he's left."

What indignation Ada might have felt was lost at sight of Father Clement's face, surprise going to red-tinged indignation on it at realization that a woman – and a nun at that – had told him what he should do and she would do; and by the time he had his mouth working to object, Dame Frevisse was already gone. Ada pushed past

him to crane her head out the door to see what she was about. On his
dignity, Father Clement turned back to go on uncomforting Elyn.

Frevisse, with no compunction at all for thwarting Father Clement
and careless of what the women thought, stood on the rear doorstep
and overlooked the garden that ran from almost the back door to the
woven withy fence that closed it off from the byre yard to one side, the
neighboring garden to the other, and the field path and bean field to
the back. It was long and narrow, like the house, and its only gate led
into the byre yard. The path that ran from the back door to there
between beds rich with the late June growth of peas and beans and
greens was narrow and neatly surfaced with small, round river stones,
showing no trace of footprints, muddy or otherwise. Frevisse walked it
with her eyes down, hoping something had been dropped or a careless
footprint somehow left, but she found nothing.

At its end, the gate was a new one, hung on leather thongs, with
another thong to latch it closed and a flat stone laid under it to keep the
way from wearing hollow. It was a little open, enough that someone
turned sideways could have easily slid through. A narrow someone,
for a spider's elaborate orb web was silver laced and sparkled with
diamond dew across it now.

From the byre – it looked to have been a house not too long ago –
a cow was lowing in complaint over her unmilked udder and chickens
were softly cawing to be uncooped so they could be at their morning
scratching. Frevisse stayed where she was inside the gate, studying
the muddy yard before turning to go back into the house.

The two village women made no pretense they had not been
watching her. They backed hastily inside as she approached, and
she followed them in, to say to everyone – priest and the wife and
Dame Claire, too, "There's nothing in the garden, but beyond the
gate into the byre yard, there's a line of footprints – a man's by the
size of them – through the mud, overlaying all the others and going
straight across to the outer gate. The garden gate and that one are
both open," she added with an inquiring look at Elyn, who promptly
said, "We never leave those open. They're always closed. Always."

"Then surely he's gone that way!" the midwife declared. "Along
the field path and probably toward the woods! We have to raise the
hue and cry!"

If it could be shown a village had not pursued and done their best
to seize a felon by hue and cry fresh after a crime, the village was
liable to heavy fine for the failure. Because of that, and for the plain
joy of hunting down a legal quarry, a hue and cry was rarely hard to
raise. But this was early morning after Midsummer's Eve and there
was surely more interest among the village men in being in their

beds for as long as they could manage rather than haring across the countryside.

Frevisse was darkly amused to see that counted for nothing with the women or Father Clement. They had been up all the night and not at merrymaking for most of it. He and one of the women after quick talk and a nod from the midwife hasted out the door and shortly could be heard calling the hue and cry around the village green.

The midwife had turned back to Elyn by then, left standing alone by her hearth, and gone to put an arm around her. "At least come pray beside your man," Ada said. "There at the foot of the bed."

Head bowed, shoulders hunched, arms wrapped around herself, Elyn sank down on the nearest stool. "He's going to die," she muttered brokenly, "And Father Clement has done what can be done. There's no use in my prayers then, is there?"

Ada had no answer to that that Elyn would find reasonable. Even the nuns held silent, pity on their faces, and the only sound in the room was Jenkyn's noisy, snoring breathing. After a moment Elyn closed her eyes and began to rock back and forth in silence, leaving Ada nothing to do but stand beside her, ready to give more comfort if it were wanted.

Dame Frevisse went to Dame Claire. Their heads close and voices low, they spoke together briefly, then Dame Frevisse went aside, to the room's other end, and beckoned for Ada to come to her. Since Elyn seemed to be noticing nothing beyond herself, Ada went, curious and a little wary as to why she was wanted.

But it was only for a bit of gossip, it seemed, which went to show nuns were not so different after all, because Dame Frevisse said low-voiced beyond Elyn's hearing, "Everything looks to have been going so well for them, it's a pity it's come to this. Were they happy together?"

Ada thought about that. Happy or unhappy did not much matter after a marriage had gone on long enough, just so the pair rubbed along as best they might. And Elyn and Jenkyn had done that well enough, she supposed. "Aye, they did well together," she said. With the desire to think of something other than Jenkyn's unnerving breathing, she went on, "And that's been mostly Elyn's doing. Jenkyn is – was – is – " The wording was so difficult, things being as they were. "– so easy-going a man he'd likely never have brought himself around to marrying at all except she took a liking to him fifteen years – " She paused to think about that. "Nay, closer to twelve maybe. Or thirteen."

"A while," Dame Frevisse suggested. "It was a while ago."

"Yes, it was surely that," Ada agreed. "Elyn took a liking to him, despite her father had doubts and her mother thought she could do better, but she knew what she wanted and managed him to the church door, just as she meant to. And they've done well. Mostly because of her, I'll have to say and so would anyone else who knows them, but Jenkyn's been a good husband to her." She was keeping an eye on Elyn, still sitting with her eyes closed and arms wrapped around herself. Ada lowered her voice even farther. "Except they've had no children and that's a pity, for Elyn sorely wanted them. It was when she still had hope of having them that she pushed Jenkyn into asking for the tumble-down holding next door when it came vacant, so she could keep the animals over there and have a better house with more room here. But the children never came, and she gave herself over to managing Jenkyn in their stead. He'd be content to have no better than a barn to sleep in and do naught more than he had to to eat, only she stirs him up, and they've both lived the better because of it. Though mind you, it's helped that Pers has come to live with them these past two years. There's only so much Elyn can do with a man who's not – was not – " This was annoyingly difficult. "– a big man or strong. Nor so young as he once was."

"Pers is the nephew, who's missing now?" Dame Frevisse asked.

"He's not missing, only at Pollard's courting their Kate." Ada smiled fondly over the thought. "That will be a match before long, and a good one, that's certain."

"But Pers won't inherit when Jenkyn dies, will he?" Dame Frevisse asked.

"No. All this goes to Elyn for her lifetime. Though likely Pers will stay on here to help at least until he marries. But since he's like to marry Pollard's Kate, he'll do well enough, she being Pollard's only child and everything to come to her eventually."

"But Pers has no inheritance of his own?"

"Not while Elyn lives, and she's a healthy woman, God bless her. Though we're all in his hands," she added conscientiously, seeing over Dame Frevisse's shoulder that Father Clement was giving them both a hard stare. She was gossiping, Ada had to admit, but felt no guilt at it. And closed up in that nunnery, the nun must have little enough of it in her life.

But before she could go on, the front door was pushed hard open and five men rushed in. Elyn, lost in her grieving until then, rose to her feet with a startled cry. Ada went hastily to hold her, saying angrily, "Will! Nab! The rest of you! There's a man dying here. Where's your sense?"

Abashed, the men crowded to a halt. Will muttered, "Sorry. We're right sorry. Only we were told to come, and – "

"Aye, aye," Dickon agreed. "It's hue and cry, my woman said, so which way do we go?"

"Out the back. There. Go on." Ada pointed them out the back door. "There's footprints through the byre yard. That's your trail."

"I'll bring the others round," Nab said and went back out the front where voices in the road told other men were coming. Will and the other three hastily crossed themselves as they went on past Jenkyn on his bed, their faces showing their dismay at the look and sound of him.

Father Clement followed them out to bless their mission. The room was left to Jenkyn's harsh breathing and the muffled tangle of men's voices, in the byre yard now, until a single hard rap at the front door brought in two more men, a barrel-chested older one and a youth tall enough he had to duck below the lintel as he entered.

"You're nigh too late, Tom Pollard," Ada said. "Haste out back, or they'll be gone."

"No need to push, Ada," Pollard rumbled. "My regrets, Elyn," he added to the widow-to-be; but his gaze swung around the room, speculative and assessing, and that was Tom Pollard to the core, Ada knew. A hand to the plow and plans for the harvest all at once. "You'd best stay here, Pers," he said. "For your uncle and to help your aunt. There's enough of the rest of us to see to what needs doing."

Pers' broad, pleasant face under its thatch of tow hair betrayed how much he did not want to stay, and Ada did not blame him. He was hardly seventeen yet, for all that he was so well grown. Too young yet to be easy around someone's dying. But he stayed and Pollard left, as outside the men's voices rose in a flurry, Father Clement's blessing done and the hue and cry begun in angry earnest.

Hesitantly, Pers looked around the room, then went uncertainly to his uncle's side.

"He's beyond us now," Dame Claire said kindly. "I doubt he's feeling anything."

Pers nodded without looking at her, his gaze fixed on his uncle, his expression grading from wariness to increasing horror as the dying man's breathing sank through its pattern, each indrawn breath shorter than the one before, each breath rasping harshly out . . . Dame Claire began to explain that the breathing was something that went with a broken skull, but Father Clement entered then and, seeing Pers, went to him to lay a hand on his arm and cut off what she was saying to offer his sympathy and add, "The men are off now. They'll do all that can be done to right this wrong."

Pers nodded dumbly, still watching his uncle. The breathing

stopped and they all waited, frozen in the silence, until Jenkyn's chest heaved upwards again, drawing in another hideous breath, and the pattern went on, perhaps more shallow now, more slow.

Elyn on her stool crouched more in on herself. Pers pulled out of Father Clement's hold and said in a strangling voice, "I'd best see to the animals. Clover needs milking sure by now. I'll be back."

Without waiting for any answer, he escaped out the back door. Frevisse waited until Father Clement had bowed his head to pray over Jenkyn, then drifted quietly after Pers.

The sun was above the hedgerows now, bold in a cloudless sky, the day perfect for haying but so early yet that dew still silvered wherever shadows lay. For all his haste to be away, Pers had gone no farther than the garden's end and stood there now, holding to the top of the gate, staring out. Moving slowly, careful to let him hear her coming, Frevisse joined him. He acknowledged her with a look and a low bow of his head, but when she did not speak, neither did he and they stood together looking out for a few moments, Frevisse noticing that the hue and cry had trampled out the earlier footprints with the myriad of their own, and left the outer gate wide open behind them. Someone had bothered to shove the garden gate almost closed, though, and the spider had begun to spin her web again. So far only a single strand across the gap, but she was already dropping another down from it. Watching her, Frevisse said, "I'm sorry about your uncle, that there was nothing we could do to help him."

"It's as she said, then? There's no hope?"

"None, I'm afraid."

Pers drew a deep, uneven breath and let it out in a ragged sigh. "He's always been good to me. He's a kind man."

"He's likely glad then you'll be here for your aunt, and have the holding after her, when the time comes."

"Oh, aye," Pers said as if the thought were new to him.

"But your aunt will have the rule here while she lives, no doubt of that."

"Aye, she will!" Pers was very clear on that.

"But you'll stay on to help her."

"Surely. That's the right way of it." His mind was still only half on her questions and his answers, and he showed where his thoughts more strongly were by saying suddenly, "I should have gone with the hunt despite what Pollard said. I want my hands on the cur who did this!"

"They'll bring him back here if he's taken."

"Aye, *if* he's taken. But it's none so far to the forest and if he's right away to there, they'll likely never have him then.

Some ditch-living bastard, clean away and my uncle dead!"
Remembering too late to whom he was talking, he added, "Beg
pardon, my lady."

Unoffended, Frevisse asked, "You think that's how it was? A
passing stranger taking a chance at theft and murder?"

He looked at her. "How else could it have been? There's no one
here would harm my uncle. He never quarreled with anyone nor
anyone with him."

"Not even his wife?"

"Aunt Elyn?" Pers scorned the notion. "She might quarrel with a
neighbor, but not him. He never gave her cause, always did what
she asked of him."

"And will you when you're living with her? Do what you're
told?"

A blush brightened under his tan. "For a while," he said uncomfortably. "But I'm marrying at Lammastide." Despite his effort to hold it
back, a shy but broadening smile tugged at his mouth. "We agreed on
it last night, Kate and me." He added hastily, as if worried that Frevisse
might be off to spread the word on the instant, "Only don't say so to
anyone! No one knows yet. We were going to tell her Da today. Well,
ask him if we could but he'll say yes to it and be glad, we know."

His happiness shone on him, burning for the moment even stronger
than his anger and grief. For him, just now, Death was a thing that
happened to other people, not something that should come near him
or his Kate. The thought crossed Frevisse's mind that a year ago it
must have seemed just so to Martyn Fisher, grieving now for his
dead young wife.

"I'll tell no one," she said and let her questioning fall aside for
a while.

But she did not leave him, only contented herself with watching
the spider at her web-weaving between the gate and gatepost. A
lovely spider, mottled light brown and gold, almost as big as her
thumbnail. The creature had nearly finished her web's frame. Then
would come the spiral outward from its center, and she was precise
but quick about her business because there was food to be caught
and no telling when forces beyond her spidery comprehension would
bring her work to naught again.

The cow lowed earnestly from the byre, and Pers reached to open
the gate, to go through. Frevisse put out her hand, stopping him.
"Go around," she said. "Or over the fence." He stared at her as if
in doubt of her senses, and she added, "I'm watching the spider."

Pers drew back. "Oh, aye," he agreed but plainly seeing no sense to
it. "But I have to see to the animals and this is the way through."

"Go over the fence."

"It's too high to jump, please you, my lady, and it'll crack if I climb it," he replied, carefully, as if beginning to think she were simple. But what he said was true enough. The fence was too high to jump and its withies would not hold much weight beyond a very small child's.

Patiently, Frevisse said, "Then go back through the house, out the front door and around. I'm watching the spider."

Pers louted her a bow and went, taking his perplexity with him, because after all half the village was owned by the nunnery, maybe even the Browster's considerable holding, and that gave Frevisse authority to tell him what to do, woman though she was. Authority like no woman in the village had over any man, unless she came to it the way Elyn Browster had, simply by being the stronger in her marriage, and even that was not so very much power in the long run.

But Elyn would have a prosperous widowhood; and maybe after her first grief eased, she would even enjoy it. Or would she, without someone over whom to wield her authority? Jenkyn would be gone and Pers would shortly go, and though she could likely find another husband if she chose, was she likely to find another as amenable to her will as Jenkyn had been?

Patiently – could it be called patience and a virtue when done simply out of a creature's blind nature? – the spider crept on around her strands, beginning her webbed spiral in the morning sunlight.

Ada would not have thought that Jenkyn could have gone on breathing for so long. The huge gasping lasted less long between the nerve-jerking silences but always it came back again. Father Clement stood at the foot of the bed, praying of course, but his hands clenched together as if holding himself there by force of will. More quietly, Dame Claire stood at Jenkyn's head. Neither Pers nor Dame Frevisse had returned; and Elyn still sat on the stool by the hearth, elbows on her knees, head in her hands, eyes fixed on her lap. Half a dozen other women had come after the men had gone, roused to Elyn's need, but she had taken no comfort from them. Though occasionally one or another patted her shoulder, whispered something kind to her, she seemed beyond noticing them.

It was a relief to hear the men's voices coming along the road out front. Though by the sound of them the hue and cry had had no luck, at least it was a change from their own miserable waiting. As Ada went quickly to open the front door to them, Dame Frevisse returned through the back. She went to stand beside Dame Claire. Pers came in almost immediately behind her, his feet unwiped from the byre so that he stopped just inside the back door as Ada opened the front.

Most of the men there were standing away, in the road, some of them already trailing on toward their homes. It was Pollard who came to the door and started, "We're back then but – "

"Come in with it, man," Father Clement called. "We all want to hear."

Pollard looked back at his fellows. They waved him on, willing to leave it to him, so he came in, glanced at the bed and immediately away, looked at Elyn for some notice he was there and when she gave none, went on with, "It wasn't any use. There was no trail to follow once we were out of the yard. And we were tired to start with and it's growing hot – " He was half-apologizing as well as explaining. "– and the bailiff expects us to the haying soon. We did what we could but there was no use to it, truly."

Father Clement said, "You did what you could. That will be enough for the sheriff and crowner." Enough to save the village a fine, anyway. "But we'd best send someone around to the near villages to warn them there's a murdering thief at large."

"There's no need for that," Dame Frevisse said quietly. "Whoever did this didn't run away."

Father Clement frowned at her. "We know that he did, dame."

"Ran out the back when he heard Elyn coming in," Pollard said. "Through the byre yard. We all saw his prints. They show clear what he did."

Dame Frevisse shook her head. "The footprints in the yard mud are a lie. No one went out that way at dawn today."

Sternly, letting his disapproval of her show, Father Clement said, "That's a foolish thought, dame. Leave this to those who know."

Ada listened amazed to such talk between nun and priest. Nuns were more bold than she had thought. Or at least this one was. And even now, faced with Father Clement's reproof, Dame Frevisse said, "There's more to know than that, I think." She turned from him to Dame Claire and asked, "May I lift Jenkyn's head? Will it cause him any harm?"

"Dame, this is hardly – " Father Clement began to protest.

Ignoring him, Dame Claire answered, "He's past more harm. May I help? What do you want?"

"To take off his coif."

Dame Claire carefully lifted Jenkyn's head and held it while Dame Frevisse carefully untied and took off his coif, laid it aside, and then felt at the back of his head with her long fingers.

"Yes," she murmured to herself. And to Father Clement, "Come here, if it please you, Father. And you." She included Ada; and Ada, more eagerly than the priest, went to her. As gently as if Jenkyn might feel it, Dame Frevisse took hold of his head from Dame Claire and turned it sideways so they could see the back of it. "You see there's blood here, matted in his hair."

Father Clement, managing not to look too closely at skull or blood, snapped, "As well there might be." Elyn moaned and covered her ears with her hands.

"But no blood on the coif," Dame Frevisse said. She set Jenkyn's head down on the pillow again and picked up the cloth hat. "See. There's blood in plenty dried into his hair but none on his coif."

"And there should be," said Ada, grasping what she meant.

"There should be," Dame Frevisse agreed. "Elyn, when did you leave your husband last night?"

"Last night?" Elyn repeated, lifting her head. She made an effort to gather her wits. "We went to the bonfire on the green and watched the dancing. He wouldn't dance, he hasn't for years, but we watched. And then we came home and he went to bed." The effort to think seemed to be steadying her; she became more certain. "He went to bed but I stayed up a little and was about to cover the fire when Ada came because of Cisily and I left him sleeping and went out with her."

Ada nodded readily. "That's right. I came for her when it began to look bad for Cisily and I didn't come in because Elyn feared I'd wake Jenkyn."

"But you didn't see him?"

"Well, no. Not from outside, would I?"

A little more roused, Elyn said, "He was sleeping when I left. He meant to be out at dawn to cut those thistles. He was in bed and when I came home at dawn I found him like that." Her eyes flinched toward the bed and away again. "On the floor and all dressed but like that." Her voice quavered toward tears.

Ada and the other women closed around her, Ada murmuring, "It's all right, love. It's all right."

It was Pollard who said indignantly, "A thief came in while he was readying to go out this morning, killed him, and then ran out the back way when he heard Elyn coming. That's plain."

"It isn't plain," Dame Frevisse snapped. "If it happened that way, there should be blood on the coif and there isn't. And when I first went into the garden, before anyone else did, there was a spider's web across the open garden gateway. An unbroken spider's web all hung with dew. No one went through that gateway this dawn."

"Then he went over the fence," Pollard said impatiently.

With a glance at Dame Frevisse and the air of someone accurately repeating a lesson, Pers put in, "The fence is too high to be jumped and too weak to be climbed." Then flushed as Pollard looked angrily at him.

"And aside from that," Dame Frevisse said, "the footprints show he went through the gateway, not over the fence."

"You just said he didn't go through the gateway!" Pollard quickly pointed out.

"Not at dawn," Dame Frevisse answered back. "Whoever did this to Jenkyn didn't run through that gate at dawn. He would have broken the spider's web, and it wasn't broken. This was done last night." To Father Clement she said, "Among the men Jenkyn knew, who had reason to want him dead? Or will have the most from his death?"

With a shock, Ada found that she had looked without thinking at Pers. And that so had everyone else in the room. He gaped back at them, speechless, but Elyn exclaimed, "No! He'd not harm a hair of Jenkyn's head! There'd be no point. Everything comes to me. Everyone knows that."

"But he'd be the man here," Dame Frevisse said. "Just you and he to run things and no Jenkyn in the way."

Elyn flushed a dark, shamed red at what was implied behind the words. Furiously indignant for both of them, Father Clement cut in. "Here now! No one's ever thought of any such thing!"

"There's nothing between us," Elyn whispered. "There's nothing and never has been."

More loudly and more definitely, Pers declared, "That's right!"

Pollard, more outraged than either of them, said, "He's to marry my girl!"

Ignoring their combined indignation, Dame Frevisse asked Pers, "Did you dance with Pollard's Kate at the bonfire last night?"

"Aye. Of course." Defiantly.

"And spent the night with her?"

Angrily Pollard put in, with an uneasy glance at Father Clement – fathers had to pay fines for girls who were wayward before their marriage – "That he did, but in my house with all the rest of us. So we know where he was all last night and he had no chance of doing anything to his uncle."

Dame Frevisse turned to Ada, and Ada found her direct, demanding gaze disconcerting even before she asked, "Did Elyn come out with you right away when you came last night? Or did you have to wait a while?"

"She said she had to cover the fire and I should go back to Cisily," Ada answered, trying to see why it mattered. This was all going too quickly for her. "She said she'd be there just after me and she was."

"A little after? Or longer?"

Beginning to understand but unwilling to, Ada answered slowly, "I was busy with Cisily. I don't know. A little while. Not much."

"Enough while that she could have put on Jenkyn's shoes and made those footprints on the doorstep and across the byre yard?"

Ada wanted to say, No, there hadn't been enough time for Elyn to have done all that; but as she started to, she looked at Elyn's white, frozen face and held silent.

From beside the bed Dame Frevisse said, "The footprints were like those of a child wearing shoes too big for him, deep in the heels and nothing in the toes. You've little feet, Elyn, for your size, and Jenkyn has a man's. Where did you hide the shoes so you could claim someone had stolen them?"

Elyn, staring at something in front of her that was not there for anyone else to see, did not answer. It was Pers, his voice raw with disbelief and hurt, who asked, "But why?"

Elyn did not answer nor her expression change. Surprisingly gently, Dame Frevisse said, "Why, Elyn? What was the reason?"

Where there had been nothing, feeling shimmered at last in Elyn's eyes. "Because I couldn't bear him. Not anymore."

"Jenkyn?" Ada asked, her disbelief an echo of Pers'. "You couldn't bear Jenkyn?"

Still staring in front of her, Elyn nodded and finally said, in a low voice, "He was so nothing. No matter what I did, he was nothing. And last night, at the bonfire, I was watching Pers." Her gaze slid up to him and then away to the floor in front of her feet. "I watched him dancing with his Kate. Both of them so beautiful. And happy. And then I had to come home with Jenkyn, because he wouldn't dance. It was too much trouble, he said. Nor he didn't like staying up at night nor Midsummer wandering. He didn't much like anything that cost him any effort."

Bitterness and scorn and the anger that must have been in her for a long time before last night tightened her voice. "I tried to talk with him when we were home, trying to make him see how things could be different, better between us. But everything was too much trouble for him. I always had to talk a week to make him do a day's work. He was forever dragging back on everything I asked him. He wouldn't . . ." Her hands, knotted in her lap, clenched and unclenched. "I suddenly couldn't bear him any longer. He stood up, saying he was going to bed, and I . . . I took him and threw him . . . he weighs hardly more than my big iron kettle . . . backwards against the wall. I'd wanted to do that to him . . . do something to him . . . hurt him . . . for so very long. I didn't know, I didn't mean . . ." She stopped, then said dully, "Or maybe I did. Maybe I did mean it to kill him. I don't know."

Gently but with the same remorseless searching, Dame Frevisse said, "So he was lying there, and you were trying to decide what to do when Ada came to say you were needed, and you thought maybe there was a way out of what you had done after all."

Elyn nodded into her hands. "The idea came to me all at once and I knew what I could do. Make it look like a thief came in, a stranger, and killed him. I made the footprints, just as you said. The shoes are in the midden by the byre. Then I went to Cisily. I thought he'd be dead when I came home. He wasn't and that was awful. And there was the blood but he wasn't bleeding anymore so I shifted the rushes, buried the bloody ones under clean ones, meaning to be rid of them later and no one the wiser, and put his coif on him to cover what was in his hair. I'd be the one to ready him for burial and no one would have to see and likely no one would have thought about it anyway." She raised sad, accusing eyes to the nun. "But you did. I should have waited until you'd gone before I came out crying about him. Then it would have been all right."

Stirred at last out of the silence holding them all, Father Clement said, "You've sinned, Elyn. And sinned worse in meaning to let him die unshriven, his soul likely bound straight for hell."

Ada shivered and was not the only one to cross herself at that. But Elyn only said bitterly, "He never sinned enough to go to hell. And purgatory wouldn't hurt him any worse than he's hurt me these years. Only – " Now she wrapped her arms around herself and looked toward the bed resentfully. "– only I hadn't thought he'd go on alive so long. And with that breathing. Isn't he ever going to stop it?"

He did, a little later. One last, faint rasping out of breath and, this time, nothing after it. The silence drawing out and out, until they knew he would not breathe again.

And afterwards, freed at last to go on home, matching her long stride to Dame Claire's shorter one as they walked again along the lane's grassy verge toward the priory, Frevisse tried to find a prayer that would answer, for her at least, some of the pain the past hours had held. And Dame Claire's mind, too, was behind them rather than ahead, because out of the quiet between them she suddenly asked, "Would you have paid so much heed to the footprints if it hadn't been for the spider's web?"

"No. I doubt it. I'd probably not have thought about them at all. Or wondered about the blood."

"So it wasn't the footprints or the blood that trapped her."

"No. Only the spider's web." And the fact that Frevisse had chosen to think about it.

A spider's web and a moment's thought. So small a pair of things to be so deadly.

As small as the break in a woman's heart between enduring and despair.

THE DUCHESS AND THE DOLL
Edith Pargeter
(*Ellis Peters*)

There is no doubt that it is the success of the Brother Cadfael novels by Ellis Peters that has made the historical detective story so popular. Ellis Peters has written only three short stories about the wily monk, all of which are included in the book A Rare Benedictine (1988). It seemed unnecessary to reprint another when they are so widely available. The success of these stories has, ironically, over-shadowed Ellis Peters's earlier work, particularly her early short stories, mostly written under her own name of Edith Pargeter. One of these, "The Duchess and the Doll", has remained unreprinted since 1950; it is not so much a detective story as a fascinating retelling of a genuine case of witchcraft and heresy in the reign of Henry VI.

On Sunday, 23 July 1441, at Paul's Cross, at sermon-time of the morning, this history begins.

A crowd had gathered about a high stage, reared to draw in all eyes to a fellow-creature's penance. If an example be not as public as the mind can devise, who will profit by the warning? And though the sermon against witchcraft was eloquent as lengthy, and touched a dark world every man knew to be close at his heels even in broad daylight, yet words go by very lightly without some picture to stamp home the lesson.

It was not at the priest they gazed, but at the penitent. He was a man of middle age, wrapped in robes signed with mysterious and terrifying signs, and seated in a chair from the corners of which projected four swords, with small copper images impaled upon their points. In his right hand was propped a sword, and in his left a sceptre that wavered and recovered as he wearied in the July heat. His face was fixed as a mask, and had the calm of a mask, but no less the suggestion of incalculable terrors behind. As yet he had only been questioned and brought to confession, and to this public abjuration of his art; trial was yet to come, verdict and sentence yet to break on him. He had but begun to draw upon the length of his endurance.

The instruments of his art, by which he had attempted to know and perhaps to alter the future, were disposed about him upon the scaffold, as terrible and mysterious as the signs upon his clothing; and among them, alone of instant significance to the layman's eye, stood a small image of wax, a roughly shaped doll. Those behind craned to see it better; those before passed back information concerning it. It was clearly made to represent a human being, they said; it was male, it had features, but who could say it resembled this man or that?

Likeness was not held to be necessary where not every practitioner had an artist at his elbow. Baptism could bestow the doubled personality more surely than any resemblance, and they whispered that if this mannikin wore no crown its name might none the less be Henry Plantagenet. This once said, the rest came rushing upon its heels. To what exact use had the doll been put? Had it been set to the fire? For the King had not ailed more gravely than at any other time. Yet the process might have been no more than begun when the information was laid which brought Roger Bolingbroke to Paul's Cross and penance.

The thing must be done slowly, a wasting away so gradual that the victim may be past help before he knows he needs the physicians. Perhaps the heat had never got beyond a glaze and a glisten on the little naked waxen body before the wizard and his accomplices had been taken into hold. His stars and all his instruments, and all the devils he could raise by their means, had never been long-sighted enough to show him the gallows, the bench or the block, but he surely saw them now clear enough before him without the aid of ink or glass.

Latecomers pressing in upon the skirts of the crowd asked eager questions.

"Who is he? What has he done?"

"Roger Bolingbroke, one of Duke Humphrey's chaplains, so they say. He knows astrology, and other arts beside. He has conjured; he confesses it."

"Has he renounced his art? What did he say?"

"He says he was seduced to it against his conscience."

"By whom?"

The answer was whispered, "By the Lady of Gloucester."

They would never give her her title if they could help it, but always used this name for her. Let her be what she might, the King's aunt by marriage, the first lady of England, yet they hated her. She knew it, and understood the reasons for it. They hated her because she was no better born than many a merchant's wife of London, and yet had made a capture of the great Duke of Gloucester, a prince and a Plantagenet, and had taken him from a princess, too, by right of conquest; and no less because she had been his mistress before she was his wife; but most of all because she had never stirred herself to court them from their bad opinion of her, and their most daring affronts had drawn from her only flashes of contempt. Now was come, it seemed, the time when this haughty lady should learn how far the high have to fall.

"Does he say she made the image?"

"He says it was she who would have it made."

"Then this is high treason she stands accused of?"

"The highest."

"Duke Humphrey was not enough for her, it seems!"

"Not enough as he stands. She would have him the taller by the height of a crown."

This and all the other white-hot gossip of the town came back in due course to Her Grace the Duchess of Gloucester, that handsome, imperious and unpopular woman. She heard all in silence, and a whole day bore her knowledge without sign. It was none of it new, for she had been hearing some such tidings in nightmares ever since the chaplain had vanished from his place; only it had drawn perceptibly nearer to her liberty and her life. Nor was the lance levelled only against her own breast. Man and wife are one flesh. The steel would lodge where they meant it should who were already behind the opportune thrust, in the heart of Humphrey Plantagenet, Duke of Gloucester. Not Cardinal Beaufort, not Suffolk, not Stafford, not the greatest nor the least of his enemies had forged the weapon to destroy Humphrey. They had recognized it, they would know how to use it, but it was she who had made it and put it into their hands.

And was that all she had done for him in the end? In more than ten years of marriage, and longer of love, was that all she had given him for a keepsake? No heir, no new lustre to his name, no land, no wealth, nothing but her body for a season of passion and this deathblow at the end of it. All her ambitions, all her pride, dropped to earth here, and her life after them. Much may be ventured against a duchess whose death will loose no war of vengeance against the land, whose fortune left behind will cause no factions to form about it across the grain of those far too many factions already in being.

For Jacqueline, graced and glittering with her regalia of half the

Netherlands, Hainault, Holland and Zeeland, swords might be drawn
and armies take the field, but for Eleanor Cobham of Sterborough,
dubious daughter of a minor English nobleman, there would never
be even a brush of men-at-arms in a London street. Let her be the
first woman of England while the sun shone on her, at the fall of the
first shadow she would be stripped naked to the cold of justice and
not a hand raised for her.

It was a long time since she had thought of Jacqueline, but now,
going restlessly about her house with her ears stretched for the
first strange hoofbeat upon the walk and her heart in her bosom
shrinking hard with fear, she remembered her very clearly. A fine
woman at her coming to England twenty years ago. Some had found
her person beautiful, some her three counties in the Low Countries
more beautiful yet, while some had sighed their hearts out for her
romantic wrongs, and her courage and fire in maintaining her cause
against all odds. Which aspect of her had first caught Humphrey
Plantagenet's eye he best knew, but with his bold breadth of vision
he had certainly missed none of the three in the end. Beauty and
estate were much to his mind, yet to do him right the challenge of
her exiled condition would have called him to her side as surely, if
not for chivalry's sake for pride's. For consider her story.

Widowed from her first weakly husband, the Dauphin John, she
had entered into all her father's lands just in time to marry them
innocently to a second as feeble, the Duke John of Brabant, the
cousin and pawn of Philip of Burgundy, and in less than two years
had suffered the humiliation of seeing this lord of hers separate her
from certain of her lands to Philip's profit.

She had foreseen in this first mild lopping the final loss of all, and
with indignation had taken her person out of the keeping of such a
husband to find asylum in England, where the Council had made her
godmother to the infant King, and given her a pension to keep her in
some shadow of her accustomed state. Humphrey's hand had been
in the matter even thus early, no doubt, for he took his hazards as fast
as they came, and more often than not leaped to meet them; for the
following year the Spanish anti-Pope, Benedict XIII, had declared
her Brabant marriage annulled, and by the autumn she had taken a
third husband. Doubtless in this Plantagenet, Lord Protector of the
realm of England and second in line of succession to the crown, she
had grasped at a powerful, willing and ambitious ally. Doubtless,
too, she had looked upon this man, thirty years of age, handsome
for all his excesses, lettered, learned, a patron of scholars, courtly of
manner, brilliant of bearing, and loved him.

Well, they had gone far to undo England's interests in France by the match. Burgundy was necessary to Bedford's designs there, and Burgundy was rudely estranged now by Gloucester's alliance with Brabant's dubiously-divorced wife and her titles. One bone between two dogs, snapped at fiercely by both, the Netherlands bade fair to cast English arms out of Europe.

And here began the ludicrous expedition which first threw Eleanor Cobham in the Duke's way. The French had seized eagerly upon the quarrel, and by means of forged letters had sought to prove that even Bedford himself, the regent of England in France, was joined with his impulsive brother in a plot against Burgundy's life. Bedford had made hurried efforts to mediate, calling Pope Martin V into the arena as peace-maker; and Humphrey had stopped his mouth as sharply by taking his wife and all her train of ladies, and leading an army into Hainault. There had been no resistance; he had been received submissively as Count. None the less, Jacqueline had lost all her hopes there upon a bloodless field.

Her ladies! There had been one among them who was handsomer than the rest, and readier to seize the passing chance of his notice when his wife grew tedious and her cause harassing. A woman of unobtrusive birth, questionably legitimate, but magnificently grasping when opportunity leaned to her. His match in arrogance and audacity, her high temper pleasing to him, her hot nature satisfying beyond Jacqueline's royal reach. Eleanor, daughter of Lord Cobham of Sterborough; her reputation as dubious as her birth, her aim as lofty as her looks. Remembering the first of it, when his eyes as yet barely lit and lingered upon her, she could still smile for a moment. Poor Jacqueline!

Where do they go, these passionate attachments, these banners and trumpets and laurels of love, when they suddenly and silently fold up their glories and pass from us? He, who had set out to win a kingdom for his bride, and thrown England into the scale to weigh it low enough for his hand, by what enchantment did he fall into this new sickness of indifference before the fanfares were well out of his ears?

Too confident of his royal privilege to assume a grace where he had lost it, Humphrey had not dissembled his weariness with his wife, and at the most had covered the nakedness of his new amour with no more than the cynical pretence of decency. Burgundy had helped him there, with his grandiloquent offer of single combat to settle the dispute; and gravely he had confided to Jacqueline that he must set England's affairs in order, no less than his own, before he took his life to the issue. He was well assured that Bedford would never suffer the duel to take place, but the pretext was good, and impotently she watched him go from her. Nor did he sail for England alone; his wife's household was the less by one lady-in-waiting that night. Within the month Jacqueline was a prisoner of Burgundy.

But who would have thought the new love would last longer than the old? The victor herself, had she gambled upon gaining more than a short summertime of favour? She remembered vividly that April voyage home, the insolent entry into London, the bewildered people almost too startled to shout for their "good Duke Humphrey" because the lady by his side was not the right lady. She remembered old Beaufort's thunderous face, and the way the words stuck in his throat as he welcomed his nephew home. Oh, they had hated her then and they hated her now, the noble and the simple alike. Yet none of them had ever dreamed how high she would rise. Even when the Pope had declared Humphrey's marriage with Jacqueline null and void they had not supposed he would dare to make his mistress royal, nor she to accept the honour and the challenge.

Those righteous London housewives who accosted the Lords on her account in 1428, protesting at the Lord Protector's abandonment of his wife to her distresses while he amused himself with a harlot like Eleanor – their very words, God damn them! – had they imagined she dared be so splendidly avenged? Even Jacqueline in Holland, surrendering at last her citadel of defiance, taking Philip for heir and co-regent of her lands and acquiescing bitterly in the annulment of that brief English marriage, had she foreseen that the harlot dared so superbly put on the duchess before the whole world? Yet he had married her. More, she had kept him. Double the years of Jacqueline's marriage she had kept him, a faithful lord no less for innumerable infidelities. She had him still, his heart and his mind. After weariness of all other women he came to her breast still.

Was it the philtres? She had never quite dared to suppose she had no more need of them, and ever and again he had drunk magic in his wine through those ten years. How if this must come to light now? Her heart raged at the thought of the smiles which would flash from lip to lip through London when it was known that after all no charms of hers had drawn him to her, but spells bought with money. Yet the philtres had been no more than a beginning. There was high treason now to answer, and more than mockery to fear. Bolingbroke had abjured his art, and named her for the instigator of his traitorous blasphemies; Margery Jourdemayne was taken, Hume taken, Southwell taken, all in prison but Eleanor Cobham, the patroness, the procuress of witchcraft.

What a fool she had been to go on beyond the philtres! Yet it had begun innocently and simply. The Duke of Bedford was six years dead in France, and the King in his teens a sickly, bookish boy not yet married. Surely it was right and meet that the wife of one now heir to the throne should spend some pains to make herself fit for her destiny? She had only sought to know her own future, that she might be ready to make faithful delivery of all that should be required of her. Was it treasonable that she should ask by divination: "Am I to be called to this last duty? Is this my fortune?"

But she knew, only too well, in what other and most sinister light they would regard it. "Shall I rise yet higher?" is a dangerous question from one already close to a throne; it may be only a step from the thought to the deed. And beyond the instruments of divination, beyond the Mass which had been said over them, there was the wax doll.

What had Bolingbroke said of it? If she but knew what tale he had told to account for it she might yet come off safely. Does a man under the question think fast and clearly? Had he had the wit to bestow another identity upon that miserable mannikin of wax? Surely, even to stave off torture, he had not fallen in with all they wished him to say, and agreed with them to call the thing King Henry VI of England? But if he had! How richly Jacqueline was avenged if he had!

Southwell had been their mistake, the chink by which discovery had come in to them. Bolingbroke would have a priest to say Mass over his tools, that the divination might be true and trenchant, and therefore they had taken to them the Canon of St Stephen's, an old, subtle and reverend man, but one with a houseful of servants long-eared and ready at keyholes. Who could say for sure if the Mass in Hornsey Park had not been spied on? At least they knew of it now, and Southwell was in the Tower, and never likely to come forth again but for sentence and the traitor's double death. There had been too many of them. First Southwell, then, because of her knowledge of the ingredients of low magic and the use of wax, Margery had been called from her philtres to a more dangerous service. Too many by far for so perilous a secret.

As one had already cast the burden upon her, so would they all. How better be rid of it? This hated woman, this upstart duchess, she shall carry all the guilt, for by this means at least we may get what countenance the favour of the commons can give us. There will be a hope at least, some shadow of a hope of pity and pardon for whoever throws Eleanor Cobham to the dogs. So they would reason, and rightly.

Bolingbroke had already shown the way, and Margery would not be slow to follow, for she had little title to leniency unless by this means. Once already, ten years ago now, but the memory of the law

is as long as its arm, she had been taken up for a suspected witch and
borne away from her prosperous little business of herbs and charms
in the manor of Eye, to face a charge of sorcery at Windsor. Clerks
were ever her natural companions. Friar Ashewell and John Virley
then, Roger Bolingbroke and Canon Southwell now, she had but
moved a step or two up in the world. But then for lack of hanging
evidence they were all loosed, and went cautiously back to their old
practices, and that was a thing which would not happen a second
time. Certainly they would wish to take her with them to hell, or
wherever else they were bent.

What, then, was to be done? She could do no more than hold fast
her good sense, and go about as if no circumstance threatened her;
and his name, his power, might still avail to frown them off from
touching her.

She bore it until nightfall on Tuesday, and then could bear it no
more. Panic fell on her with the darkness. Sick with waiting, she
roused herself and fled into sanctuary at Westminster, and after her
as at the snapping of a leash swooped all the haggards of fear. It had
needed only this one false step to make her enemies content.

So it began. She was summoned forth to deliver herself from
formal charges of necromancy, witchcraft, heresy and treason. You
cannot for ever stay in sanctuary, nor can you ever hope to leave it
unobserved; it is the last place where the wise take refuge. She knew
these things too late, but she did what could be done to recover the
ground she had thrown away. She had flown to hiding like a runaway
servant, but she came forth like a duchess, and submitted herself with
a stony calm to her first examination.

It was in St Stephen's Chapel at Westminster that she was called
to appear, before two who hated her as well as any. The Cardinal
Bishop of Winchester, who had fought a long battle for dominance
with Humphrey and must now be seeing clearly his way to winning
it at last, and his fellow, Archbishop Ayscough, like all of his cloth
as loyal a Beaufortite as Beaufort himself: two such as these could
hardly be expected to show any sorrow for an event which gave their
faction the absolute power in England.

Yet they were grave, courteous and fatherly with her, as befitted the
custodians of her soul. The old man, himself a Plantagenet by-blow of
the house of John of Gaunt, had as much ambition in his venerable
head as Humphrey could lay claim to, though his bend sinister had
made him turn left-handed to the Church for his kingdom; the main
difference was that he had lived longer and more warily, and grown
more practised in seeming other than he was. He knew how to lean
his head on his hand and look upon her with the sorrowing love of a

father as he questioned her of heresies and treasons, hoping to have her heart out of her to hold before Humphrey's eyes when next they crossed. He, whose bullies had ruffled it in London streets with the Gloucester men-at-arms not long since, and fetched the harassed Bedford over from France to make peace between them! He, who felt cunningly in every move for a thumbhold over young Henry's manhood faster than any Humphrey had kept over his infancy! Well, it was not with that poor little half-monk, half-student he had to deal here, and so he should find.

Two grasping churchmen, one the King's great-uncle, the other the King's confessor: how could they justly judge? Was it possible they could empty their heads of the conviction that the waxen doll was certainly an image of Henry, named for him and designed to be his death? Yet Eleanor knew by then what path she must follow, and though it would mean careful walking she was prepared to accept the risk.

Some degree of confidence in the name of Gloucester had returned to her. Deny all at first, but in such general terms that you may admit later those items which must be admitted, without too abject an about-face. The doll cannot well be denied, for they have seen it and handled it; it can only be translated into something harmless. There may be other things as absolute, and these too may be painted in milder colours but not utterly painted out. So proceed, she thought; an inch at a time, and let them go before.

But old Henry Beaufort could be as subtle and delicate as any woman when he would, and had the advantage of her in this, that he was not afraid. The chill feel of death laid hold on her before she was out of his presence, though she kept her head and her resolve. She owned that she had been indiscreet, and had perhaps induced others to actions which could be misinterpreted. She had shown interest in astrology and other obscure arts, which were diabolical only to the ignorant, since God Himself had set the stars in their significant order and made herbs to grow upon the earth; but malice or treason she firmly denied.

Had she caused spirits to be raised to answer her questions? No. Had she procured that Mass should be said over the instruments of divination? It was the part of every devout enquirer, surely, to attempt nothing upon which God's blessing dared not be invoked.

No deed of hers had been or needed to be so hidden. The paper of figures with which some play had been made against Bolingbroke was no more than it seemed to be, a table of calculations concerned with the casting of her horoscope. The church had not forbidden this study. And the chaplain's confession? She kept fast hold of her

courage here, for she did not know exactly what he had confessed.
She said only that she had committed no treason, nor intended any.
What a man in fear of his life will say to serve himself was not for her
to guess, nor could she go aside from truth to confirm or combat it.
She had never knowingly seduced him to do for her anything which
was unlawful. She had desired to know her own future, but not to
any other creature's detriment.

And the doll of wax? Was that also a part of her future? She
answered yes, it was her dearest hope. She had been ten years
married, and was still childless. The doll was a charm to represent
the heir she most ardently desired to give to the Duke before her life
was too far spent. It was designed to procure her a son, and for no
other end. No fire had ever warmed it, but only her hands and her
body while she kept it constantly about her. A desperate remedy for
an ill she began to find desperate; perhaps an error of judgement
and feeling; certainly no crime against any body or soul but her own.
With what name then, they asked her, had the figure been baptized?
She said firmly that it never had, for the child could have no name
until it should be born.

To this she held, seeing no hope of a better front to put on. It was
not deliverance, it might not be even life, but she could do no more.
This was but the beginning; they would be in no haste to bring her
to a trial which must either acquit or destroy her, when by delay
and doubt they could drive Humphrey in harness whichever way
they wished him to go. A long wait, Eleanor. She wondered where
it would be spent.

It was to Leeds Castle in Kent they committed her, on the 11th day
of August, there to remain until October, and longer, perhaps, if
Humphrey had not gone about the raising of her case with all the
energy left in him. Such word as reached her from him in this period
was brief always, and devious often, for the ears of the Beauforts were
everywhere.

It seemed to her that he had receded from her not merely by the
inconsiderable miles separating her prison from London, but by the
width of worlds. Often for days together she never thought of him,
and ever oftener as time lengthened away from their last meeting she
could spare no thought for anyone but herself.

But ever and again his image came back to her, not as he was, but
as her fearful and lonely mind desired him to be; not an intelligent,
dissolute and cynical man of fifty suddenly smitten into premature age
by the shock of his wife's disgrace, but young Humphrey Plantagenet
at his height, the great Duke, the Protector of England, levelling

his truncheon in anger against his enemies and hers. Almost she persuaded herself he was about the business of raising forces to come and snatch her out of captivity; almost she believed he would indeed come, and listened for the first alarm of trumpets at the gate. That Italianate spirit of his, insatiable in curiosity, ambition and arrogance, should have manifested itself now in arms; his will should have flashed sword-like across the processes of law, and shaken after it echoings of swords.

But at this point he was as English as any of them. He did not come. He sent her no word but the measured and temperate counsel of his love, that she should keep a good heart, speak her defence moderately, and abide the movement of justice as he for his part must abide it.

His mind, which she had believed as lawless as her own, was at bottom a pattern of order. He had committed crimes against it, perhaps, but he had never denied it. Whatever he had done in that long and audacious pursuit of his princely interests, he had never quite lost his reverence for the law of the land, that image he had helped to maintain after his fashion even while he transgressed against it. He had kept the faith of the State as forcibly as he had kept the faith of the Church. He had burned heretics; the Lollards had withered before his fires. How then should he lift his voice for a relapsed witch, two heretical priests and their employer, though she was the very stuff of his own being?

Eleanor fell from this into sick rages, cursed him for a coward and a renegade because he had left her to the mercy of her enemies, wept passionately for her own griefs until she could not see his. Between waiting for him and despairing of him she divided her days most miserably. Jacqueline in Holland, watching in vain for the money and troops he had promised her, and seeing Philip's Burgundians close in upon her at leisure, must have suffered the same anguished alternations of hope and desperation. Jacqueline in the end must have let fall the last of hope out of her hands, and said farewell to the image of him as to a dead man. So at last did Eleanor. A part of that debt for old treason was paid. Her circumstances were comfortable enough, her state maintained; so had been Jacqueline's. She was, none the less, a close prisoner and abandoned by her lord; so had Jacqueline been imprisoned, so forsaken. There might have been less bitterness left in that old wound now, could she have known how exquisitely she was avenged.

By early October they were ready to proceed, the readier because they were assured by then that no armed attack would be made to release her. A special commission had been set up to examine the case against all the accused, and before this panel they were at last indicted of treason, Bolingbroke and Southwell as principals, Eleanor Cobham and Margery Jourdemayne as accessories.

Now at length the Duchess saw her creatures again, and wondered if she herself was so greatly changed. Southwell from old was grown very old in a few short weeks, whitened like a worm that lives underground, dim and peering of vision. A breath of wind must have swayed him, and a gust broken him. His face was so fallen dull with senility that it was not easy to know if he followed what passed with dread or indifference, or indeed if he followed it at all. She thought they would have to make haste if they wanted to hang him. Bolingbroke was not so. He had been a man of vigour and intellect, and without the means to exercise either had grown gaunt and wild and pining as an unflighted hawk. His face was a horn lantern of terror, hard and fixed without, flame within. She did not forget that it was he who had most surely betrayed her. Let him die, as hideously as they could devise, if she could but separate herself from him.

As for the wise woman of Eye, she had wept herself away to a swollen, blowsy distress from which Eleanor turned her eyes in loathing. She was growing old, was Margery, and had hoped to die in her bed; but even after the warning of Windsor she could not let herbs and philtres alone. It was powerful in the blood, this love of being more knowing than the neighbours; and even at some risk, a woman must live.

Their very looks, thought the Duchess, condemn them; but are they to be allowed to damn me also? Or is it possible that I bear myself as wretchedly and seem as guilty as they? I have wept a great deal; I am pale from confinement; but is my face so signed with fear as theirs? She looked about her wonderingly, meeting the eyes of many who had eaten at her table; they regarded her as if she had indeed changed out of recognition, warily, curiously, with an expectation in which she believed she saw pleasure.

The sun had passed from the Duchess of Gloucester now; it was not worth while to smile upon her. None of them had ever courted her for any other reason but to be in the sun, and they made haste to scamper away now she was in shadow, to a place from which they could enjoy her eclipse. Hers she thought it, until she turned her head to see where their sidelong glances travelled from her, and saw her husband seated apart.

Then she understood fully at last their satisfaction in her fall. It was not even for her own sake they most hated her, and delighted deepest to see her disgraced. She was no longer a woman in her own right, innocent or guilty; she was a knife to be slipped in his back and twisted until he died of it, first in reputation, then in very body.

And he was only fifty years old! Seeing him now for the first time in two months, she felt her heart turn in her at his ageing face. Was this her signature? He had lived, it was true, wildly and at the wind's speed since he was made knight at eight years old, and innumerable women before her had contributed their mite to undo him body and mind; yet she had never before remarked this dullness of eye in him, nor seen his forehead so seamed with the shadows of old age and great weariness. He had burned out with too much loving and hating the half of his more than ordinary energy, but she had put flame to the other half before the hour was ripe. He had spent sixty years' value of action and thought in much less of time, but the remaining riches of his life she had poured out for a wizard's fee and left him bankrupt. She looked upon him with anguish, for after her fashion, with all the tenacity and more than the greed of other women, she had loved him.

He went sumptuously, as ever, and bore himself proudly, for pride had been the habit of his body lifelong, and needed no motion of his mind or will to keep it in being. What remained of his beauty now was but colourless and cold, a shell of withered comeliness through which looked out at the eyes an old, sick, sad man prisoned in loneliness and silence from all his fellow-men. This she had made of him.

For a moment she lost her fear for herself and all her resentment of his quiescence in a passion of sorrow which was wholly for him. For a moment only. For this was her life; and happiness, his or hers, was but a secondary prize. Yet her eyes went back to him again and again even while the lords of the Commission questioned her, so that sometimes she answered astray, and had to be prompted a second time. And always she drew back her mind from this groping pursuit of him in renewed dread, almost in anger that he should still be able to trouble her when he no longer could or would help her. It was not in her experience that she should continue to love what had ceased to be profitable to her.

The Commission presented a very comprehensive array of the enemies of Gloucester, apart from a few of the judges, put there, she supposed, to lend credit to the enquiry. There was Huntingdon, there was Stafford, there was William de la Pole, Earl of Suffolk, looking grave and grim and satisfied like a cat sodden and sleepy with cream.

Not even a Beaufort could have hated Humphrey more than he did. What hope had she against such examiners as these? What hope was she meant to have? And there was the whole wretched story to be dragged through and through again and again, to weariness, to sickness, the first innocent enquiries after her horoscope, the deeper questionings after, the Mass in Hornsey Park by night over the instruments of divination, the wax doll. She must remember to deny that the mannikin had ever been christened; had it been so it must have represented either the King or some other living person for harm, since unborn children bear no Christian names.

Whatever these others might swear against her, she must be positive in this. If Southwell in extremity said he had baptized the thing, she would contend they had already driven the old man past the incalculable point where truth loses its meaning, after which he would pour out confession after confession upon every crime they thrust into his consciousness, from a conviction that only by so doing could he hope ever to be left alone.

If Bolingbroke said it, he lied from malice against her, believing her the source of his sufferings, and desiring to make her suffer no less terribly. If Margery – But Margery was now so abject, so miserable a creature that there was little to fear from her if the others could be silenced. At the worst she must hold by her story though they all combined against her. It was at least better to be Eleanor Cobham than Margery Jourdemayne in this one thing, that they dared not use the instruments to bring a duchess to confession.

She told over the same story, the credible story of her longing to give Gloucester an heir. The future she had wished to know was her future as the mother of a son. But when she looked again at Humphrey she saw that he had leaned his head by the temple upon his hand in order that his face might be in shadow even from her. Rings upon his long fingers took the light. In his curled hair she saw wastes of grey encroaching. He remained quiet; even the movement to hide himself had been made with an unobtrusive grace. Of what use was it to continue thus in dignity at all cost, when the dullest there must know he was broken with grief past mending? Again she thought, "Is this all I have done for him in the end?"

Once – she remembered it well – he had not been able to ride through London without a crowd running at his stirrups, cheering and shouting for their "good Duke Humphrey". He had every grace the Cardinal Bishop of Winchester lacked, and could flourish the people's adoration in the old man's face whenever he pleased, merely by showing his own upon the streets. She remembered the rash pageant of the embarkation for Flanders, when she had ridden in Jacqueline's train admiring the casual grace of his back as he saluted his people king-like along the way, tossing his smiles left and right for largesse, the very pattern of his brother Harry, and adored for it by his brother Harry's citizens. The puny little King had been nothing then, for here in the Protector's person rode royalty itself. He had laughed at the title they gave him, knowing himself no closer acquainted than most men with goodness, nor willing for expediency's sake to draw any nearer to so unprofitable a virtue; but he had kept the legend alive without an effort, and always that shouting had gone before him through the town.

All his life until then he had gone surrounded by clouds of witness. When had the tide begun to ebb? It was far out now, and would not turn again. When she had thought thus far she could not well keep out of her mind those London housewives, women of good repute and fair standing, who had felt so bitterly about her that they had gone to the Lords to protest against the Duke's abandonment of his wife to her distresses for the sake of a harlot. Was not this clear enough? For them the harlot had remained a harlot even after she had supplanted the wife, and never again could Humphrey's gracious manners make them forget or forgive the irregularities of his private life. He was to blame in this, that he had made that life a matter of public interest; but it was she who had made it a public scandal.

What had followed? The turbulent period of the quarrels with the Cardinal had helped to make London perhaps a little weary of both Beaufort and Plantagenet. The Council had so detested his rule that they had caused the King to be crowned in 1429, at eight years of age, and declared the protectorate to be at an end, the better to be rid of the stranglehold of Gloucester, and for all he had been supreme again while Henry was being crowned in France, Archbishop Kemp and others of Beaufort's party had seen to it that his power was narrower than before.

The commons had liked his strict dealings with heresy among the Lollards, and his championship of British rights in France, never observing that it was he himself who had made them impossible of maintenance; yet the reins had somehow slipped from his hands since he took her to wife. Of late no more public appointments, less shouting for him in the streets; and now at last the shadow of treason drawing so near him that his face was blackened. There he sat shading his eyes with his hand, an old man, with the ruins of all his titles, past and present, lying in invisible shards about him; Humphrey Plantagenet, Duke of Gloucester, Earl of Pembroke, veteran of Harfleur and Agincourt, Lord of the March of Llanstephan near Carmarthen, Warden of the Cinque Ports, Constable of Dover, Lord of the Isle of Wight and of Carisbrooke, and of God knew what lands beside. He had been a whole man until his wife had broken his life in pieces.

For her tears she scarcely saw the faces of her examiners as they

gave judgement, and for the thunder of the outgoing tide of his fortune
in her ears scarcely heard or understood what was said of herself.
Afterwards they told her that she was committed to the ecclesiastical
court with Margery Jourdemayne, but Southwell and Bolingbroke
were in the hands of the secular justices. Nor was the waiting long.
Of this she could be glad even in the stupor of her despair, as men
under torture are glad to draw nearer to death.

She was now so exhausted with emotion that she sat her days
through in a dead calm, which was never broken but for those rare
moments when some word or message carried the memory of her
husband again into her heart. No other news did more than ripple
her indifference. When they told her that Canon Southwell was dead
in the Tower she seemed only to grudge him his happiness. And
again more gently she wished that Margery too might die before
sentence, for she had dealt honestly in the matter of the philtres,
and even purchased so his faithfulness had been no little nor light
possession.

On the 21 October she came again to St Stephen's Chapel before
a new Commission of bishops, and heard the full indictment against
her, in all twenty-eight articles of treason, conspiracy, witchcraft and
heresy. Once again she firmly denied every count of treason or heresy,
but thought well to admit her unwisdom in certain minor counts.

It was now so familiar as to be wearisome, and her lips stiffened
against the long stupidity and sorrow of speaking it again. Still they
questioned, and still she must reply. It was not for her to collapse
in incoherent weeping, half imbecile with terror, like poor Margery.
Whatever witnesses were brought to testify against her she must
keep her countenance and her calm. So much at least she owed
to Humphrey. But if Southwell's damned servants had been more
strictly watched, all this coil need never have begun. She dared not
think of that now. It was enough to remember and repeat, in spite
of her fatigue and disgust, the story of her design to gain a child by
sympathetic means. That was the mainspring. She could do no more,
and if this did not avail she would remain erect, at least, and utter no
appeal. Having repeated in face of the testimony of witnesses her firm
denials, she said only that she submitted herself to the correction of
the bishops in the matter of her lesser errors; and so was silent.

They were found to be guilty both, as in her heart she had known
they must be.

Sentence was not pronounced until her last appearance before
the Commission, upon the 13th day of November. Margery, as a
relapsed witch, was condemned to the fire at Smithfield, and for
Eleanor there waited three days of public penance, and thereafter

perpetual imprisonment. Sir Thomas Stanley was named as the warden of her captivity, and for her maintenance, because she was the consort of a prince, the sum of one hundred marks a year was set aside. Nevertheless this was a death, and the price the price of a funeral.

When she was again removed to her solitude she asked what was become of Bolingbroke, and learned that he was to suffer the traitor's death. Hume, long since pardoned, for what services she could well guess, would think himself happily delivered of this dolorous company. Perhaps he would be in the streets tomorrow when the crier belled for her, and the candle was set in her hand. She dared not think of Humphrey now. Let him forget for three days at least that he had ever taken a second wife. She now for the first time would have her own progress through London streets, shouting enough about her ears, and crowds to run beside her. This time they would be content with their duchess at last.

She performed her penance. For three days she was paraded through London upon a triple penitential pilgrimage, wrapped in the loose white garment of the returned sinner, bareheaded, barefooted, bearing a two-pound candle in her hand. Such a show was always worth seeing, whoever the victim might be; but for Eleanor Cobham they made full holiday.

Such things are not forgotten, because the mind receives from them not merely an impression, as though a hand had pressed deeply into a cushion, but a patterned corrosion which time may weather a little but never efface until the material itself perishes. Her penitent's sheet was no whiter than her face as she went upon her barefoot triumph.

She looked like an image of snow, or like her own waxen mannikin. Unborn child or recluse King, what did it matter now? If it had been meant to kill it had not failed of its effect, for three deaths had already been brought about by it, and who knew how many more might not follow? If it had been meant to bring to birth the ritual had somewhere gone terribly awry, for all it had engendered was pain, ruin and despair. Let it rest now. It was enough, surely, that she walked thus steadily with filed eyes and marble mouth, looking neither to left nor right for all the faces that crowded upon her, and all the voices that shrilled in her ears. It was enough that her soiled feet trod tenderly and slow, leaving smears of blood along the cobbles, and her outstretched hand wavered under the candle's weight, and her heart in her breast felt to her like a white-hot stone.

Three days in indignity and exhaustion she made her enforced devotions, setting her candle upon the altar out of a hand that shook violently at the relief from its weight, staring mutely into its flame as it settled into a steady burning, and turning from it upon her return journey without a look aside for fear she should somewhere see among the many faces the one face she dreaded most to see. And having so far discharged under guard the worst of her punishment, she lay all night sleepless, regarding her blank and bitter despair.

Before she was taken away to her prison at Chester Castle her husband was permitted to see her. They looked upon each other for what it seemed must be the last time.

There was little to say, now that they were given time and opportunity; it was too late by far for reproaches or for hopes. The case at law was dead ground, and her presumption and folly as far past as his abandonment of her to justice. There was little left to be said. Strange silences came down between them, during which they looked fixedly upon each other, as though the eyes had a more articulate language left them than had the tongue.

"I shall not cease," he said, "to intercede for you with the King until I obtain your pardon."

"The King will not let you into his presence," she replied. "You stand too close to me to be safe company for kings."

"I have stood in my time close to him also, and it has been to his profit. We are of the same blood; he will not forget that."

"And we are one flesh," she said, "and he will not forget that, either. Save yourself, for I am damned."

"What avails, then, my salvation, since we are one flesh? Yet do not doubt, my lady, that I shall reach him by one means or another. If I live, your cause shall be constantly before him until he relents towards you. This is all I can promise, and this I vow to you from my heart."

"Do not entertain any hope," she said, "for death has been let loose between us, and I doubt I shall never get by him to join hands with you honestly again." And suddenly she shook for the rising thoughts of Margery shrieking in the fire, and Bolingbroke's head shrivelling upon London Bridge and his dismembered body scattered among the cities of England.

At the end, when he was about to leave her, she looked up at him suddenly and said, "You do not call me innocent, nor ask me anything of what I have done."

"To what end?" he said. "Whether the answer be well or ill, I am yours no less. We have known each other too well to live upon virtue or faith. Birth, death – it is all one in the end."

"But you do not believe me guilty?" she said.

"Nor innocent either. My mind is quite gone by it."

It was in this fashion they parted. Long afterwards a woman who waited upon her asked in strictest confidence the question he had forborne to ask, "Madam, tell me truly, was the wax image indeed of the child you lacked, or was it to stand for the King?" And she smiled, for by then in a sombre fashion she could smile; but she made no answer.

She had been wise after her kind, for the summer of Gloucester was over. From that time the King, nervous of the very name, denied him his presence. It was safe for any man to lift the threat of impeachment against him, to allege this misconduct or that in the years of his protectorate, to hint at calling him to account for old sins. She in her solitude, at Chester first and then at Kenilworth, heard rumours of his usage, and knew at whose door it lay. Between them they had done infamous things; no worse, perhaps, than most creatures do into whose hands fortune drops the corruption of power, yet infamous things. But all came home in the end.

By the year 1447, when the last requital fell due, she was in Peel Castle in the Isle of Man, there to remain until her death; and there they brought her word of his.

Parliament met at Bury that year on 10 February, and certain of his enemies made great play with the fact that Humphrey was not there to the day. He was in Wales, they said, raising an armed revolt against the King; and they so worked upon the poor wretch – what could not his new spitfire of a wife do with him, all the more surely with William de la Pole to back her arguments? – that he sent out to meet the Duke at his late coming before he could enter the town, and ordered him directly to his lodging in the North Spital of St Saviour's, on the Thetford Road. There after dinner on the same night Buckingham and Beaumont and others came to him and put him under arrest at the King's orders, and after him most of his followers were also placed under guard. After that who could say what had happened? He was lost to sight of all but his keepers. They said he fell ill; it might well be true. On 23 February he died, so much was certain. Death is a very positive thing, however shy and irresolute its causes may be. He was dead, and they had buried him, on the north side of the shrine at St Albans, where he had once spent Christmas with Jacqueline of Hainault, and with her been admitted to the fraternity of the abbey. All comes home in the end. If her body was not laid with his, no doubt but she had left a morsel of her heart there to wait for him.

"Is it true," said Eleanor, pondering, "that he went to Bury under arms?"

"It is true, madam, that he had some force with him, but not a great force."

Enough, however, she thought, to intimidate Henry at a pinch. For he had sent her word he was determined to use this Parliament to get the King's ear, and give him no peace until he had granted her pardon. No peace, but perhaps a sword. His best special pleading had always been done with the sword. How could she know if his death was murder, or his deed treason? And did it matter that she must never know? It might well be that his arrogant heart, worn out with long misuse and vehement grief, had burst at this last indignity. But there were other possibilities. A pillow over the face in sleep! A little draught in the wine of a guarded man! These things have been known.

Whether so cold a wind had blown on it or whether it had guttered out of itself, the flame was extinguished now. Why should she question if he had not questioned? Every man, every woman, is alone at last with secrets. Let it rest, and let him rest. As for her, now that he was gone her function was ended, and no-one would trouble about her any more. She would not even die, but only dwindle away inchmeal from every mind which had known her, and in the end be forgotten of man, disappearing into the obscurity from which she had come. She was dead while she still lived.

So in his new grave on the north side of the shrine at St Albans, on the 4th day of March, 1447, his history and hers end together.

ORDEAL BY FIRE
Mary Monica Pulver

We have already encountered Mary Pulver as one half of the writing team whose nom de plume is Margaret Frazer. Mary Pulver is an accomplished author in her own right, with a series of novels about mid-west police detective Peter Brichter. But she has also written a short series about Father Hugh, a fifteenth-century priest, who has some rather unorthodox methods of rooting out sin and solving crimes. The following is a new story, specially written for this anthology.

Father Hugh, mass priest of St Osburga's Abbey, invited his three visitors in and seated them in the main room of his little house outside the cloister wall. It was between Vespers and Compline, and the early evening air was further darkened by a light fog, but he had said it would be a brief meeting on a matter of some importance.

Because of the fog the air was chill, though it was May. Father Hugh offered each visitor a cup of mulled wine from a pot he was keeping warm before the fire. He sat on his little stool in front of the hearth, and the three men sat down to drink their wine.

"Robin, I want to thank you for braving the flames when Annie Bridges' house burnt three nights ago," Father Hugh began conversationally. "It was a blessing you happened by." He was a small man, barely more than child-sized, though his tonsure was less an artifice each year. "If you hadn't, poor Annie might have been burnt in her bed."

Robin Fitzralph bent his fair head and blushed to the tips of his ears. He was sitting on the room's second stool in the middle of the floor, unable to decide whether to sprawl and be comfortable, or keep his knees drawn up and so take up less space. "I wished I'd known about the piglets," he murmured. "I could've carried out two small piglets along with her, easy." He was seventeen, tall and very strong, the second son of a prosperous franklin, but for all that as shy as a girl.

"Nae the less, she's the better for the fire, now, be'nt she?"

demanded Pers Hawkins from his place on the bench against the wall. He thumped a work-marred hand on the table in front of him, an unconscious gesture of frustration. Pers was a prosperous villein, working hard to earn the money that would purchase his freedom. He had been elected reeve this year by his fellow villager, and was resentful of the burden this office laid on him. A gaunt man, he had a long, narrow face with a nose that stuck out like the blade of a hatchet.

"God works in mysterious ways," remarked the man sharing the bench. Father Clement, rector of St Mary's in the nearby village, was tall, with a square, strong face. He was not clever, and was made nervous by people trying to rise above themselves, a too-common ambition in this year of our Lord's grace, 1451.

Since her husband had died two years ago, Annie had often been at her wits' end to keep body and soul together. She had somewhere gotten two sickly piglets, and had hoped to save them by keeping them warm by her hearth. Though in the end Father Clement had comforted her as she stood weeping in the ashes of what had been her house, first he rebuked her for not properly banking her fire.

"'Tis greed for more than God wants you to have that brought you to this," he had said. "You were trying to keep those piglets alive, and let your fire burn after you went to bed instead of covering it. And see what happened? Sparks from it rose up and set your thatch alight."

Annie had denied it, of course; some folk, even caught redhanded in sin, were brought to contrition only with difficulty. It hadn't helped that the whole village rallied around to build her a new cottage that was sounder of roof and wall than her old one. Worse, it was like a slap to his rebuke when Robin brought her a fine young gelt to replace the sick piglets.

To her credit, Annie had said she didn't deserve a new pig. That set off a quarrel so loud half the village came to see what the noise was about. Mortified with shyness and embarrassment, Robin had explained that he'd failed to save her piglets, so this was not a gift but his way of setting things right. The onlookers found this backwards argument – he insisting she take a valuable pig, she trying to refuse it – amusing. It had become a joke for miles around. Both for saving her life and giving her the pig, the still foolish but now also brave Robin had become a kind of folk hero, which left him in a more or less permanent blush. And Annie, instead of suffering for her sin of greed, was rarely in want of friends or help any more.

"Yes, she's not in danger of losing her holding, is she?" said Father Hugh now, in reply to Pers' angry question. Annie Bridges had in right of her late husband only a single strip in each of the three great fields that sprawled around the village; and one, of course, must lie fallow each year. But the strips had produced just enough grain and peas to keep her going.

Then her old ox had died this past winter, so she could not add to the village plow team. Nor was she strong enough to help in some other way and so maintain her right to sow and reap in the fields. Pers' several strips lay alongside hers, as his big house sat beside her cottage in the village; and with three strong sons and four oxen, well able to add to his holding. It had seemed inevitable that he would be granted hers, and that she would become another of the beggars that came daily to the abbey gates seeking the meager remains of the nuns' dinners.

That would have been a harsh end for Annie, Pers agreed, but he felt he needed that holding. The King, pushed by his voracious wife, had overspent himself and Commons, in its supine way, had voted a rise in taxes to help him meet his needs. The tax collectors had been unusually thorough, and Pers' lord had passed along the pain, asking more of his peasants. Meanwhile the country was being overrun by government officials eager to sniff out treason. Last year, Pers' oldest son had sympathized with the Jack Cade rebellion, and Pers feared he might have to find the bribes it would take to deaden the official noses. He needed to expand in order just to stay even.

But it now appeared he couldn't volunteer to take on Annie's holding until she died, since the village was willing to exert itself to keep Annie, and the pig joke, going.

The rise in the village's good will and charity was so marvelous that Father Clement was ready to believe it was another of God's mysterious workings – if he could only be convinced the root cause of the whole event wasn't Annie's greed.

"Your horse must have eyes like a cat," said Father Hugh to Robin as he refilled his cup. "I hear you like to ride at night."

"No, he's just a plain old horse," replied Robin. "But in the dark he just barely lifts his feet off the ground, and so he doesn't stumble. It makes for a smoother ride than in daylight."

"I hope you give your horse a chance to rest during the day, to make up for your working him at night," said Father Hugh, who had a soft spot in his heart for animals.

"Er-hem," said Father Clement diffidently, but seeing the meek eyes of the young man turned to him, dared to ask, "What does your father say about your going out when good Christians are in bed?"

"Oh, nothing much." But as if replying to his father's "nothing much," the boy continued defensively, "I've nothing better to do, anyhow. My brother is the heir, he's the one who needs to rest from his labors. Besides, it was my going out that saved poor Annie's life, and that was a deed worth doing."

"Amen," said Father Hugh.

"I have a horse that would fall into a hole the size of a church in broad daylight," said Pers, partly in order to boast that he had a riding horse himself. "When I have to go out at night, I go on foot."

"Were you also out and about the night Annie's cottage burned?" asked Father Hugh.

Pers blinked at him. "No," he said.

"Someone set fire to Annie's cottage, you know," said Father Hugh.

"Here now, you don't mean it!" said Father Clement.

Robin rose from the low stool he had set in the center of the room. "Of course he doesn't," he said with a too-big gesture. "We all know the abbey priest is fond of jests. This one has come up lame, Father," he said, turning to the monk. "And so now perhaps you will tell us why you asked us here. You said you had a purpose."

"I do. I wish to discover who set Annie's house on fire." Father Hugh peered upward nearsightedly at Robin, who was gaping foolishly at him. The monk was gentle in mien and normally soft-spoken, but he was ruthlessly honest and he hated sin, in himself as much as others. With his common manners and his racy sermons, no one was quite sure how he had come to be mass priest for an abbey of gentle nuns, but few were surprised when he took a more than passing interest in the worldly affairs of the neighborhood.

Robin recovered enough to blush and sit down again. Robin's father had recently consulted Father Hugh about sending the boy to Oxford and making a priest of him. Though he had not put it so strongly, Father Hugh felt Master Fitzralph could sooner make a silk purse of a pig's ear. Robin was no scholar, and a boy of his size and strength would be welcome to take livery and maintenance in almost any lord's household. Father Hugh was sorry Robin's father had not taken his advice; becoming a liveried retainer might have knocked some of the foolishness out of the young man, and his parents would have been well rid of a hearty eater who had nothing better to do than teach his horse to ramble in the dark.

Pers asked in his gruffest voice, "What makes you think the fire was set?"

Father Hugh sipped his wine and said, "For one thing, it began on the outside of the cottage. Several people who came running to Robin's shout told me the whole thatch was alight when Robin staggered out with Annie in his arms. If it had begun inside and spread to the roof, Robin could not have gone in and lived."

"But a spark from an uncovered fire will go through the smoke hole –" began Father Clement.

"Annie's fire was banked," interrupted Father Hugh.

"So she says, but those piglets she somehow acquired – "

"– were not in front of the fire but in her bed with her."

"She never told me – "

"She was ashamed of it, of course. Sleeping with pigs, very like the prodigal son before he repented. But she was trying hard to save the creatures, as hard as if they'd been the children God never blessed her with, to her sorrow and shame."

There was a little silence. Children were an essential blessing. They grew up and cared for their parents as they had been cared for, even as they expected to be cared for by their own children in turn. It was the way of the world, and a good and proper way. Unless, like Annie, one had no children.

"Nab's barn fire started on the outside," said Pers. "Are you saying it was set as well? Perhaps you think all fires hereabouts lately were set!" With houses routinely thatched with reeds and straw, and every one of them containing an open fire, accidents were not uncommon. It was a wonder more people were not burnt in their beds.

"I believe at least three of them were. Nab's barn, Annie Bridges' cottage, and Robin's father's house."

"No, no," protested Robin, rising again to gesture largely. "'Twas the cook, leaving the pot of grease too near the fire while he went out to the jakes. It spilled and ran into the fire and the whole kitchen went up." Robin's eyes grew round with the memory. "I was coming to see how long before dinner, and I heard our servant Jennie screaming and I just ran in and pulled her out. Lost my eyebrows and burnt my hand." He rubbed the back of it reflectively. "She said she was scrubbing parsnips and didn't go near the fire nor the grease pot."

"Going in for her, that was very bravely done, Robin," said Father Clement warmly.

"Yes, people think very well of you for your courage, Robin," agreed Father Hugh.

"I ain't afraid of a bit o' fire," Robin murmured dismissively, but he grinned at the praise.

"Even a bonfire scares me," said Pers with a shudder. "Them sparks flying in every direction. I'd sooner die of cold or starvation than be burnt."

"'Man is born to trouble, as the sparks fly upward,' " said Father Hugh, not exactly pertinently. He was regarding Pers closely.

Robin said to Pers, "I don't like being burnt, either, but I happened to be near, and I couldn't just watch, could I? There's little to fear if you move quick. I wish I could be at every fire, to save people."

"God save your stout heart!" said Father Clement, raising a hand in blessing.

Robin tried to hide the return of his shy grin by turning away, but ran into Father Hugh's regard, which made him blush even deeper. But he lifted his chin and said, "As for someone setting the fires, I never saw anyone running away from my father's kitchen nor Annie's house."

"Were you looking for someone running away?"

"Well . . . no, I guess not." Made restless by Father Hugh's piercing look, Robin began a circuit of the room, seeking a new topic. But the small room was bare of anything more than a table and bench, two books on a shelf, and a pair of stools. "Here, what's this?" he said, pointing with his foot at a narrow length of black iron beside the hearth. It was rough surfaced, as if it had been long neglected until someone had rubbed the rust off.

"It's the ordeal iron from St Frideswide's in Oxford," said Father Hugh. "They were going to give it to the smith to make into horseshoes, but I wouldn't let them. It was famous in its time."

"Famous for what?"

"Back in the days when men trusted to the judgement of God," replied Father Hugh in a voice that suddenly held echoes of his high-pitched sermon cry, "if a man was suspected of a crime, they would accuse him before the altar, and if he still denied his guilt, they would lift that iron out of a brazier with pincers. Red hot, it was, and the accused had to take hold of it in his naked hand and walk ten paces before he dropped it. They would say a Mass and pray God would judge the case, and wrap the hand in a clean cloth and leave it three days. If it was healing clean when they unwrapped it, he was innocent. But if the burn mortified, he was guilty."

"Pah, that's but superstition," said Pers, who was something of a freethinker.

"I think God wants us to use our wits and our hearts when we seek the truth of evil doing," agreed Father Clement, but mildly, because he was willing to see the hand of God in everything. "I was taught that because our Lord Jesu said, 'Thou shalt not tempt the Lord thy God,' we don't do the ordeal any longer."

"What, am I the only man present who believes in miracles?" said Father Hugh.

"Nay, nay," said Robin, "God can do anything, we all know that. Why, Father Hugh, you know yourself my Aunt Elizabeth had a growth in her throat that melted away when she prayed that St John might ask our Lord Jesu to help her. She went on pilgrimage to Compostella in thanksgiving. You have said many a time that God watches over each of us."

"And so He does," said Father Clement.

"Why then the iron shouldn't burn the hand of the innocent at all, should it?" asked Pers, boldly arguing theology in the face of two priests. "God should put His own hand between the hot iron and the innocent flesh of the man being tested, leaving it whole."

"Pers, if I should heat this iron red hot in the forge in your village and ask you to walk ten paces with it, would you expect God to protect your hand?" asked Father Hugh.

Pers hesitated. "That's not fair," he said at last. "I am innocent of fire-setting, but I believe my hand would be burnt, same as any man's would be, even your own."

"But you did say when Annie's cottage burnt down that you should acquire her holding."

Pers was suddenly aware of the danger he was in. "But I didn't think it beforehand! I didn't ever say, *if* Annie's cottage should burn down, I would ask for her holding. It only come to me after that it should."

"That sounds like an honest reply. Still – Hand me the iron, Robin."

The young man stooped eagerly to pick it up. And immediately screamed and dropped it again, making everyone else start to his feet.

"Here, what's the matter?" asked Father Clement, coming to take Robin by the arm.

"My hand, it burnt my hand!" gasped the young man, gripping himself at the wrist. Father Clement turned it over to show the palm red and blistered.

"Well, why did you reach into the fire for it, then?" asked Pers.

"It wasn't in the fire." The boy was staring first at the iron, then his injured palm.

Father Hugh stooped and picked up the bar, ignoring a warning cry from Robin. "It doesn't feel warm to me." He tested its weight in his hand before dropping it with a loud clang. Father Clement gaped at him, but the little monk only came to peer at Robin's hand. "Oh yes, what an ugly blister! Come along, you need to have that seen to. Dame Agnes, our infirmarian, has a salve that soothes burns. Get the door, Pers."

But Pers was gaping, too, his eyes moving from Father Hugh to Robin and back again. "What nonsense is this?" he demanded.

"Does this look like nonsense?" cried Robin, holding out his hand. "See how it burnt me but not Father Hugh? We don't need any salve, there's no salve that will keep this hand from mortifying. This was the hand that set Nab's barn alight, and spilled the grease onto the kitchen hearth! This was the hand that kindled the thatch of Annie Bridges' cottage; God saw it and God has judged me!"

Pers crossed himself and Father Hugh said, "Speak ye true, Robert Fitzralph?" calling the young man by his Christian name.

"Aye, by my head, I do."

"This is God's doing!" proclaimed Father Clement. "How else to explain cold iron burning a guilty man's hand?"

"But – why?" asked Pers. "Did you have a quarrel with Annie Bridges?"

"Yes, tell us," said Father Hugh in a high-pitched voice. "Why did you burn the barn, and your father's kitchen, and Annie's cottage?"

"I have no quarrel with any man," said Robin. "It began as a prank. I was out riding at night, and saw the barn all alone in the field, no one around, and set it alight with my lantern. I had no reason, it was just for fun, and I hid behind a tree and watched it burn. But two servants ran in and saved some of the wool that was stored in it, and folks made heroes of them. I knew I could be as brave as any servant, if I had the chance. So then I spilled the grease into the fire, and when Jennie began screaming, I ran in and dragged her out. 'Twasn't much of a fire, but I never had such a round of shoulder clapping and praise before. My heart swelled in me, and I liked that. So I set Annie's house on fire, shouted so people would come to watch, then ran in and saved her. That was harder, but I did it. And everywhere I went, I was not pointed out as a fool like before but the man I truly am."

"Yes, we see now the kind of man you are," said Father Hugh in a strained voice. "But enough, come along. Take hold of him, Father Clement. Get the door, Pers. After we put something on that hand, Robin, we'll have to find a safe place to keep you until the crowner comes. Excuse me, I will go ahead to the cloister gate and ring the bell for our infirmarian to come at once."

Robin was treated and then locked in an empty larder. Father Clement rode off on Robin's horse to notify his family. The bell for Compline not yet having rung, Father Hugh was granted an audience with the abbess.

"I first suspected Pers, because he had a strong motive, and thinks his need is even greater than it is. Then I suspected Robin because he was seen riding out after dark, and is a great foolish gawp who too clearly enjoyed being a hero. And he too readily agreed to give Annie a pig after I talked with him."

"So you were sure Robin was the guilty one before he came to your house," guessed Abbess Margaret.

"No, not until I talked to both of them in my house. It was as we talked I became certain that Robin was guilty of all three fires. I was already reasonably sure he set the kitchen fire, for no one else was there besides Jennie, and she would not start a fire that would trap her in the kitchen with it. Pers had a better motive for Annie's house, but he's afraid of fire; he is the sort who would not dare stand under a thatch and light it lest its flames reach out and burn him to a crisp. And Robin's sudden fondness for riding at night bespeaks a man doing what he does not wish anyone to see. His description of his horse's stepping carefully fits that of a horse walking without the aid of a lantern."

Abbess Margaret asked shrewdly, "If God's truth disagreed with your reasoning and Robin's hand was not burnt, would you have handed the ordeal iron to Pers?"

"The ordeal iron would have burnt the hand of any man who grasped it, Domina."

"So it wasn't a miracle," said the abbess.

"No, I heated the iron all afternoon in my fireplace, and then let the talk go on until I could barely feel the heat from it with my foot before I asked the guilty man to pick it up. I wouldn't have minded letting a fire-setter's hand burn to the bone, but I knew to make him confess I would have to pick it up after him." Domina Margaret's eyebrows lifted and he hastened to explain, "A man cannot be a priest without working fingers, and I wasn't about to risk that. And never fear the false rumor of a miracle; I made sure Father Clement and Pers both saw Dame Agnes put her salve on my hand as well." When the bandage on his right hand was changed three days later, the burn was healing clean.

THE CHAPMAN AND
THE TREE OF DOOM
Kate Sedley

I only encountered the Roger the Chapman novels by Kate Sedley after I had finalized The Mammoth Book of Historical Whodunnits. *The series has so far run to four novels, the first of which was* Death and the Chapman *(1991). The year is 1471, and we encounter Roger, a nineteen-year-old lapsed Benedictine novice who, having discovered that he is not suited to the monastic life, has set out on the road as a chapman, or pedlar. He soon finds himself trying to solve the mystery of not one but two disappearances. His adventures have followed in* The Plymouth Cloak *(1992),* The Hanged Man *(1993) and* The Holy Innocents *(1994), by which time we have only reached 1475, so there is clearly much more to tell of Roger's long and active life. The following is the first short story about Roger's travels and investigations and was written specially for this anthology.*

Kate Sedley is the pen name of Brenda Clarke (b. 1926), the author of a dozen romantic novels and, under her maiden name of Brenda Honeyman, the author of a further sixteen historical novels, starting with Richard by Grace of God *(1968). She is a native of Bristol, the setting of several of Roger the Chapman's adventures, and took to writing after a period in the Civil Service and a stint with the British Red Cross during the latter part of the war.*

Although the wind tasted salt in my mouth, the sea was not yet in sight. I was walking through a clinging September mist, and in the distance, I could hear the gentle sobbing of the waves.

My chapman's pack weighed heavily, for I had been on the move since early morning, with only a single halt at an alehouse, now some miles behind me. The landlord had done his best to dissuade me from travelling further.

"You could lose yer way easy in this weather, chapman," he advised, in his thick Devonshire burr. "And few enough people in those fishing hamlets to make it worth your while when you get there."

I shrugged. "There are women, I suppose, who need needles and thread and pins. And I've never met a female yet, however isolated her existence, who won't spend the odd coin on a ribbon or a piece of lace. I've walked the South Hams before, although not this particular stretch of them."

My host shrugged and left the matter there. I might have followed his advice and turned back inland, but for a temporary lightening of the sky which determined me to press on and reach my goal. I had only walked a few miles, however, when a mist descended, hampering my progress.

Now, however, it lifted abruptly, as it is apt to do in those parts, and in something less than the length of half a furrow, I had stepped from a grey pall into clear, if pallid sunshine. Ahead, I could see the edge of a line of cliffs, and in a few moments more, was looking down at the shining stretch of sand below me.

I was standing on a headland, a promontory which separated two bays, each with its own cluster of slate-roofed cottages. Fishing nets were laid outside to dry. A line of redshanks waded in the shallows, their black bills pecking hungrily at bits of flotsam, whilst a flock of gulls wheeled and screamed overhead, their bellies and underwings gleaming in the sunlight, turning them into the firebirds of ancient myth. Thin grasses crested the dunes, affording protection for upturned boats, and the rocks were veined with yellow seaweed.

But what really drew my attention was an island, some two or three hundred yards offshore, connected to the mainland by a causeway of hard-packed sand; a causeway plainly submerged at high tide, pitted and rutted as it was by the constant washing of the tide. On the summit of this rocky mound stood a chapel, part of the monastic building closer to the water's edge. Sheep grazed on the rising ground and the man who tended them wore the white habit of the Cistercians, indicating that this was a cell of either Buckfast or Buckland Abbey. There was also a small stone cottage like those of the fishermen, enclosed in a wattle paling. It was a peaceful scene.

I became aware of someone standing beside me, and glanced down to see a thin, barefoot girl, holding a basket of mushrooms.

"Want to buy some?" she asked. "They're fresh. I just picked 'em."

"It's forbidden to sell field mushrooms by law," I answered. "They resemble the death cap mushroom too closely."

The child snorted. "City law don't run 'ere, maister. We makes our own." She pointed to a solitary, wind-bitten tree which grew some few feet back from the edge of the cliff, sinister somehow in its isolation. "That's what we call the Tree of Doom, that is." She turned a sharp little face up to mine, the pale eyes glittering with a morbid excitement. "There'll be goings on there, this morning. They're goin' to 'ang the stranger and Colin Cantilupe from that tree. And then they'll burn Rowena." A nervous tongue shot out to lick the pretty lips. "That's what they do to women 'oo murder their 'usbands."

I turned the girl round to face me and I could feel the fragile bones beneath the skin.

"What do you mean?" I demanded suspiciously. "Who are 'they'? And what authority do they have to put people to death without trial?"

"Lemme go!" She wriggled furiously in an effort to free herself. "The elders, that's 'oo 'they' are. An' if you don' believe me, look down there!"

She pointed triumphantly at the shore below us, and I saw that the tranquillity of a few moments earlier had been banished by a procession which was now wending its way across the causeway from the island. Two men and a woman, frantically protesting, their arms tightly pinioned, were being dragged by a score or so of others towards the mainland. One of their captors carried a stout hempen rope coiled around his shoulder, while one of the white-robed monks trotted alongside, flapping ineffectual hands and making a half-hearted attempt to halt the procession's progress. The remaining Brothers watched from the safety and distance of the monastic enclosure.

I released the girl so suddenly that she toppled over, and her invective pursued me as I ran down the stony track which led from the cliff top to the sands. My pack thumped against my back, but I scarcely noticed it, so intent was I on preventing what was about to happen. I raced towards the grim procession, shouting, and the leaders gradually slowed to a halt, their mouths sagging open with surprise. I stopped in front of them, my arms widespread, and after a moment, a tall, grey-haired man with a weather-beaten face stepped out of the ruck and fixed me with a pair of piercing blue eyes.

"Who are you," he asked, "and what is your business here?"

I nodded at the prisoners. "Whatever crime you accuse these people of committing, you cannot execute them out of hand. The sheriff's officers must be sent for from Plymouth. They must be given a fair and proper hearing."

There was an angry murmur and several of the men made

threatening movements in my direction, but the older man raised
an arm and at once there was silence.

"I ask again, who are you? And how dare you interfere in our
affairs?"

I returned his gaze steadily, but was suddenly afraid. There was
an air of menace about the little crowd, heightened by the loneliness
of the spot and the grey, tossing, restless waves.

"I'm just a chapman," I answered, "come to see if your womenfolk
have need of my wares. But I can't stand by and watch you take the
lives of three people who haven't received the full benefit of law."
I appealed to the monk, who stood miserably kneading his hands
together. "Brother, you and the other members of your cell cannot
possibly give your blessing to such proceedings."

"My son," he replied, "we have to live among these people and
our protests are not heeded. It is wild and remote here, and they have
their own ways of dealing with offenders. We are peaceful men."

And scared men, too, I thought. Too scared to inform your Abbot
of what goes on in these parts for fear of what may happen to you.
I knew that there were many communities like these fishermen, cut
off from the life of the towns, subject to no laws but those of their
own devising. Their retribution was usually harsh and swift.

I glanced at the three accused; at the extreme terror on the face
of the half-fainting woman, at the wild-eyed ferocity of the younger
man, and at the older's expression of mingled fear and resignation. I
swung up my cudgel, grasping it in both hands and weighing it with
slow deliberation.

"I am willing to offer myself as these people's champion," I
said. "You may kill them without trial, but you will have to kill
me first."

My heart beat even faster as I waited for someone to call my
bluff. Would I really have laid down my life for three strangers,
who, for all I knew at the time, might well have been guilty of
the crime of which they were charged? I have often wondered,
for I am a coward at heart, like most men. I was relying, as I
had done so often in the past, on my height and girth to impress
my audience. I raised my heels slightly so that I towered above
them, even their leader, who was himself only a little short of six
feet tall.

Taking advantage of their momentary hesitation, I continued, "At
least tell me what your prisoners are accused of."

It was the woman captive who, gathering her scattered wits and
buoyed up by a sudden, unexpected gleam of hope, answered my
question.

"They say Colin and I paid this man here to kill my husband!" Her voice rose hysterically. "But we didn't! We didn't!"

"Before God, we did not!" the younger man echoed. "Michael Cantilupe was a good man and my uncle. I would never have had him done to death."

A feminine voice shrilled, "But you didn't mind cuckoldin' 'im, did you?"

There was a mutter of agreement from the rest of the crowd, and once again the mood became threatening. The grey-haired man said, "We are wasting time! Take the men to the cliff top and hang them! Then gather wood for the fire."

The woman let out a howl of animal terror, and this time fainted clean away. I swung my cudgel and stood my ground.

"Listen to me!" I shouted. "If you have no respect for man's law, have respect for God's! Think of the peril to your immortal souls if even one of these three is innocent of the charge laid against them. Brother! Tell them that everyone here will be guilty of murder should that prove to be so."

The Cistercian nodded vigorously, made bolder by the presence of an ally. The group fell back a little, seized by doubt and looked towards the older man for guidance. He, however, was not so easily intimidated.

"Michael Cantilupe was my friend. I'll not see his murderers go free." His eyes blazed defiance at me.

"Then send to Plymouth for the sheriff."

His lips curled angrily.

"We've no need of city justice! For generations, we've known how to deal with our own." He turned to the others. "Take them up!"

"Wait!" I pleaded desperately. "First listen to what I have to say. Your prisoners may be guilty, but for the sake of Our Blessed Lady, let us be certain. I have had some small success in solving mysteries and ferreting out the truth of such things. It's a talent that the Good Lord, in His wisdom, has bestowed upon me. Give me until noon tomorrow to talk to people, to ask questions. If, at the end of that time, I have nothing more to add to what you already know, I will go on my way and make no trouble for you or yours. On that you have my solemn promise."

The grey-haired man eyed me with hostility.

"You don't understand, chapman." He indicated the eldest of the prisoners. "This man, who calls himself Baldwin Zouche, was caught by Brother Anselm in the act of withdrawing his knife from Michael's back, and he has since confessed that Rowena and Colin Cantilupe paid him to do the deed. The money, six gold angels, was found upon his person."

"It's a lie!" Colin Cantilupe shrilled. "We didn't hire him to kill anyone. Where would I lay my hands on so much money?"

"Did I say that the coins were yours?" the older man asked grimly. "But Michael was a thrifty man who worked hard all his life and saved his money. Who would know better where he kept it than his wife?"

Mistress Cantilupe, who had recovered consciousness in time to hear this accusation, spat viciously.

"He never told me where he kept his precious hoard!"

I saw that she was not a woman who would win much sympathy. She had once been very pretty, but discontent had carved deep lines about her eyes and mouth. It was, like the younger man's, a weak face, and I judged that here were two unhappy people drawn together by a mutual bond of misery and dissatisfaction.

I switched my gaze to Baldwin Zouche, the only one of the three who had confessed to the murder. But why should he accuse the other two if they were innocent? I studied him carefully and noted that in spite of fear for his approaching end, there was a look of secret satisfaction in the slight smile that lifted the corners of his mouth. I had met people of his stamp before; people who gloried in making mischief. Even standing on the brink of eternity, they could derive a malignant pleasure from the thought of doing further evil.

And it was in that moment that I became convinced of Colin and Rowena Cantilupe's innocence. But who was Baldwin Zouche protecting by his lies? I turned again to the fishermen's leader.

"A day," I begged. "That's all I ask to try to discover the truth of this matter. A short enough time, I should have thought, to ensure the health of your immortal souls."

A little sigh ran through the assembled company, and there was a sudden slackening of intent. I could feel it and so could the grey-haired man. He hesitated a moment longer, but knew that he was being willed to agree. Grudgingly, he gave his assent.

"A day then, that's all. This time tomorrow, unless you can show us any reason to the contrary, the fire will be lit and the Tree of Doom receive its fruit." He turned once again to his followers and indicated the prisoners. "Take them back to Michael's cottage and lock them in, then set a guard about the place. No one but the chapman is to be allowed in or out, except one goodwife who will take them food." He swung back to me. "Very well, you have had your way. I am Jude Bonifant, the Chief Elder of this community." His hawk-like features relaxed a little. "Are you hungry?" And when I nodded, he added,

"In that case, you'd better come with me. My Goody will feed us, and while she does so, I'll tell you of Michael Cantilupe and what happened on the island last night."

While we drank a good fish soup and ate bread fresh from Goody Bonifant's oven, her husband told me the history of the murdered man.

"Michael Cantilupe was born here and christened for the Archangel Michael, patron saint of mariners, whose chapel you may see atop the island. Cantilupes, Shapwicks and Bonifants've lived along this shore and on the other side of the headland for as long as men can remember. Most of us stay here and are content to do so, but Michael, when he was a young man, got restless and vanished for a while. When he returned, some three or four summers later, he said he'd been soldiering in France." Jude Bonifant took a swig of ale. "Didn't talk much about it, though I recall him saying once that he'd fought under the Earl of Shrewsbury."

"Knew 'e'd made a mistake by going away," Goody Bonifant put in. "But 'e saw sense while 'e were still young and came back 'ome. 'E married Jane Shapwick, a lass as lovely to look at as 'e was 'andsome. They made as pretty a young couple as you'd see in many a long day."

Jude Bonifant ignored the interruption and continued, "Michael Cantilupe was a good man, a loyal friend, a skilled fisherman and a generous neighbour. You'll find no one on either side the headland who'll have a bad word to say of him. When he got older – and he'd seen more'n forty summers – "

"More like fifty," his wife amended.

"– he was appointed by the lord Abbot to aid the monks on the island. He was given the cottage next to the enclosure and it was his job to light the lamp in the chapel tower on stormy nights. He helped, too, with the sheep and tended the vegetables. His woman did the cooking for the Brothers."

"Until she died," Goody Bonifant snorted. "This one – " she spoke with venom "– this Rowena, she can't cook! Found 'er in Plymouth, 'e did, on one of 'is trips. Ensnared 'im, I reckon, in 'er witch's toils."

I thought of the tired, strained face of the woman I had seen and asked, "How long ago were she and Michael Cantilupe married?"

"Eight year or more. A summer and a winter after poor Jane died." Jude rubbed his chin, looking perplexed. "When that happened, we expected Michael would take another wife. A man can't live alone with no woman to care for him, but we thought he'd wed a cousin of mine, Anne Bonifant, a decent, sober body whose own man had been drowned the previous spring. She'd've had him, too, and pleased to do so, but no! He clapped eyes on Rowena during one of his visits to Plymouth and nothing would do but he must have her. It was the only time Michael and I fell out. 'No fool like an old fool,' I told him, but he was set on her, and there was no getting him to change his mind."

"Did Master Cantilupe go away often?"

"Now and then. He'd feel the need to be off, but only for a while, and he never again went further than Plymouth."

"Had he been there of late?"

Goody Bonifant felt that she had been silent long enough and cut in before her husband could reply.

"A week nor more 'e went last an' was away two nights. Told me 'e'd offered to take Rowena with 'im, but she wouldn't go." The Goody spat. "O' course she wouldn't go! Good chance, wasn't it, fer 'er to cuckold 'im with 'is nephew!"

"She and Colin Cantilupe, had they been lovers long?"

"A year, maybe more." Jude Bonifant wiped the last of his soup from the bowl and licked his fingers. "Several of us'd tried to warn Michael what was going on, but he wouldn't believe us. There'd been others afore Colin, I reckon. She was always a restless, discontented piece."

"It must have been lonely here for a young girl bred up in the town," I suggested, but I could see by their faces that such a thought was beyond their understanding. This life was all they knew, this wild, windswept shore their only horizon. I went on quickly, "Tell me about the events of last night."

Jude Bonifant shrugged. "There's little enough to tell. Just before dinnertime, when the sun was westering, I saw Michael walking across the causeway towards the island. Colin was with him and Michael had his arm about Colin's shoulders, for he'd never believe any ill of him, no more than he would of Rowena. It's my belief Colin had invited himself to dinner, knowing what was going to happen. The tide was rising. It comes from both directions until it meets in the middle of the causeway and cuts off the island from the shore. Because of the cross-currents, trying to return by boat, especially in the dark, would have been hazardous, even for the most skilled of oarsmen."

"So Colin would have had to stay the night?"

"He would that. And then, a bit later, when I went to haul in my nets, I saw the stranger walking across the causeway. By then it was almost flooded, but there was just enough sand left for a man to keep his feet dry if he were careful."

"How could you tell it was a stranger?"

Jude looked at me with mild astonishment.

"I know every man, woman and child in this community. I can recognize their shape and the way they walk at a greater distance than I was from that man yesterevening. Anyhow, I weren't the only one to remark him."

Goody Bonifant was quick with her support.

"I saw 'im, too, chapman. Jude called me outside. 'A stranger goin' to the island this time o' day,' he said. 'Now what can 'e want?'"

"And what did you decide?" I asked.

"That he were a messenger from the Abbot of Buckfast to the Brothers." Jude sucked the last remnants of fish from a broken tooth. "They come every now and again, and some of 'em are laymen."

"And then?" I prompted, as my host fell silent.

"A sudden squall o' wind blew up, about an hour later. We were thinking of going to bed, for the nights draw in early this time of year. We'd noticed the wind rising, but thought nothing of it until we heard shouting. We went outside and saw folk running to and fro along the sands. Then I saw that a boat out at sea was in trouble. Someone said it was Stephen Shapwick and his daughter, Marianne, rowing home round the headland after visiting his brother. The squall had blown 'em off course and they were in danger of being smashed against the rocks of the island."

"I saw one o' the Brothers run down to the water's edge," Goody Bonifant added as Jude paused for breath. "Then 'e ran back quick to Michael's cottage, shoutin' and flappin' 'is arms. After a few moments, Michael came out. You couldn't mistake 'im in that white frieze cloak 'e always wore. Never seen 'im wear anything else. Said 'e took it off a Frenchman. Said it'd last 'is lifetime." Tears welled up in her rheumy eyes. "'E never said a truer word."

"There, there, my girl." Her husband patted her hand. "He's gone straight to Heaven. You can be sure of that." His lips thinned to a vengeful line. "But we'll hang his killers and burn that murderess, never fear." He suddenly recollected my presence. "If they're guilty," he added. But it was easy to see that he had no doubts on that score.

"What happened after that?" I urged. "How was Master Cantilupe murdered?"

Jude waved his wife to silence and resumed the story.

"By that time, thanks to his own skill and the fact that the wind had dropped as suddenly as it had risen, Stephen Shapwick had brought his boat safely into the lee of the island and managed to make it fast. There's a stake driven hard into the sand between two rocks, and half of it stands clear of the water, even at high tide. Michael was scrambling down towards the boat, to help Stephen and his daughter climb ashore, when a figure comes rushing out of the darkness and stabs him in the back, clean through the heart. Brother Anselm and two of the other monks who had come out to give aid and succour were witness to everything."

The tide was at its lowest ebb and the causeway therefore at its widest. My boots left clear impressions in the firm, wet sand.

There were three or four stalwart fishermen standing guard outside Michael Cantilupe's cottage, and they eyed me with hostility as I climbed the short, steep path which led to its door. I did not immediately demand entrance, however. Instead, I turned aside to enter the monks' enclosure. One of the Brothers I could see up on the hill, tending the sheep, but the others were within, including Brother Anselm. Jude Bonifant had described him to me – "short and stout with at least three chins" – and I had no difficulty in recognizing my man. I requested some of his time and this he willingly granted as Vespers was some while off.

We went outside to talk, sitting on an outcrop of rock, staring over the water to the distant bays and inlets of the shore.

"A terrible business! A terrible business!" Brother Anselm declared, his chins quivering with horror. "What the lord Abbot would say, should he ever hear of it, I dare not think. A murder on church land is bad enough, but for the community to take punishment of the malefactors into its own hands is even worse."

"Can't you or one of the other Brothers dissuade the villagers from this course?" I asked.

The little monk shook his head sadly.

"What can we do? So few against so many. And it has always been their way in these parts. The Sheriff and his officers know full well what goes on, but prefer to feign ignorance. It saves the expense of a trial and transporting witnesses to Totnes or to Plymouth. They wouldn't thank anyone who drew the matter to their attention."

"We are too late to prevent the first murder," I said, "but let us try to avoid at least two more. Will you tell me what you know of this business?" And I recounted quickly what I had already learned from Jude Bonifant.

Brother Anselm spread small, plump hands. "Then you know almost as much as I do. After the other Brothers and I had wrestled this man to the ground, we dragged him into the cottage and bound him with a rope Michael had been carrying. Indeed, the villain offered little resistance and seemed resigned to his fate."

"And where were Mistress Cantilupe and the dead man's nephew while this was happening?"

"Colin Cantilupe assisted us in our endeavours. Mistress Cantilupe, when she realized what was toward, ran screaming out of doors, looking for her husband, and Brother Jerome followed to fetch her back, afraid that she might do herself a mischief. He's a strong lad, which is just as well, as he was forced to carry her. Master Cantilupe then went to comfort her, after which she sat on a stool in the corner, sobbing."

"Not the sort of behaviour you would expect of either if they had arranged the murder?" I suggested.

Brother Anselm regarded me with small, shrewd eyes, embedded in rolls of fat.

"Or precisely the sort of behaviour you would expect if they wished to avert suspicion."

I smiled acknowledgement of this thrust, but was ready with my parry.

"Doesn't it seem to you, Brother, a very clumsy way to murder an unwanted husband? With the sea so close at hand, a drowning 'accident' would have been much simpler. And where and when did either Rowena or Colin Cantilupe meet this Baldwin Zouche? When did they hand over the money which was found upon his person? And why would he agree to kill Michael Cantilupe for them?"

"My reply to your first question is that people are not always clever about these things. As for your second and third, I do not know the answers. And in response to your final query I would only say that, sadly, some men will do anything for money."

"But Baldwin Zouche was almost certain to be caught," I argued. "There was no chance that I can see for him to escape."

"As matters fell out, no," Brother Anselm agreed. "But the sudden storm was unexpected, as was the appearance of Stephen Shapwick."

I shook my head. "There is something in all this that makes no sense. But tell me about events before the murder. Was it you who first espied the boat?"

"It was indeed. I had gone out to satisfy myself that the sheep pen was safely fastened. The catch of the gate is broken, and I was afraid it might swing open in the wind. It was then I saw the boat and heard the cries of Stephen and his daughter. They were nearly on the rocks and I ran to Master Cantilupe's cottage."

"And what were he and his wife and nephew doing when you burst in upon them?"

Brother Anselm blinked. "I'm not sure. Just sitting, I think, and talking."

"And when you gave your news?"

"Michael grabbed his cloak and a length of rope and ran outside.

"Immediately?"

"Yes, of . . . course." The monk's voice had a dying fall, however, and I glanced at him sharply. He continued thoughtfully, "Well, now you ask, there was a momentary hesitation because I remember urging him to hurry. 'Master Shapwick and Marianne will be drowned!' I said. 'Come quickly!'"

"And then?"

"Oh, he leapt up at once and threw on his cloak. The rope he took from several coils lying in a corner."

"Did his nephew follow?"

"Not immediately. A minute or two later, perhaps. At the time I thought nothing of it, but now I suppose it was because he didn't want to witness his uncle's murder."

"Michael Cantilupe was dead then when Colin made his appearance?"

"He was struck down before he had time to reach the water's edge. I was a few paces behind, calling Brother Jerome and Brother Mark who had come out to see what had delayed me, when suddenly a shadow rushed out of the darkness and fell upon poor Michael. He went down with a great cry, sprawled across the rocks, and the man we now know to be Baldwin Zouche knelt beside him to withdraw his dagger.

"After that, all was confusion. The Brothers and I threw ourselves upon the attacker, and meanwhile, Master Shapwick had managed to make fast his boat to the mooring post and clamber ashore with Marianne. Colin had arrived by then, and he helped Brother Jerome to drag the assailant indoors, where we bound him with the rope Michael had been carrying. But I have told you this already. Brother Mark, who had remained with Michael, came briefly to the cottage door to say that he was dead, and it was then that Mistress Cantilupe ran out screaming."

"And what of Master Shapwick and his daughter?"

"They, naturally enough, were at first too shaken by their own brush with death to take in what had happened. Brother Mark conducted them indoors and assisted Jerome to make up the fire. Later, Mark and Jerome went to carry Michael's body up to the chapel."

"And what of Baldwin Zouche all this while?"

"He just sat silent in the corner where we had put him, watching us with those strangely colourless eyes of his. Once, he asked to be allowed to relieve himself and we unbound his legs so that he could walk outside. Jerome and Mark went with him, although with his arms pinioned and the tide still in, there was little chance, as you pointed out just now, that he could have run away. But that was all. There was nothing that any of us could do until the causeway was once more passable."

"Baldwin did not immediately accuse Rowena and Colin Cantilupe of hiring him to murder her husband?"

"No. It was not until the villagers were all assembled on the island the following morning, and the elders were questioning him, that he made his accusation."

"And they believed him?"

Brother Anselm rose stiffly from his rocky perch, rubbing his buttocks tenderly. I also rose, glad to stretch my limbs.

"His word was accepted without question, partly, I suppose, because it was what everyone wanted to believe. Michael Cantilupe was a revered and well-liked man, who had recently been appointed to the ranks of the village elders. It had been long suspected that Rowena was betraying him with his nephew, and it was only Michael's refusal to allow one word to be said against either of them that had prevented an open accusation of adultery. So their protestations of innocence fell on deaf ears. They were condemned out of hand along with Baldwin Zouche, and were being dragged to their deaths when, by the grace of God, you intervened."

"Do you think them guilty?"

"I should prefer them to stand trial," was the careful answer, but further than that, Brother Anselm refused to be drawn.

Michael Cantilupe's dwelling was guarded by a ring of stout fishermen, all armed with staves and cudgels, and the three prisoners were held within. I needed to see each one separately, however, so I asked for Colin and Rowena Cantilupe and Baldwin Zouche to be brought to me outside, one at a time.

But first, I walked around the cottage, mounting the higher ground to the back of it, where the island sloped gently towards its summit. At the cliff edge, I could see something snared on one of the rocks below; a cloak, judging by its clasp, turned now to a black sodden mess by the flying spume and last night's rain. I thought it likely that it belonged to Stephen Shapwick.

I returned to the cottage and requested one of the fishermen to have Baldwin Zouche brought out to the rock which I had shared earlier with Brother Anselm. There was some reluctance on the part of the two young men who accompanied the prisoner to leave him with me, until I pointed out that they could stand within sight of their charge, but out of earshot. Also, his arms were bound.

Baldwin Zouche was, I judged, well into his latter years, maybe between forty-five and fifty summers. He had a livid scar which ran from his left temple down to his chin, puckering the lined and weather-beaten skin of his cheek. His eyes were as Brother Anselm had described them, so pale a grey that they appeared almost devoid of colour. His clothes, which had seen better days, were roughly patched and there was a hole in the toe of one of his boots. His manner was civil, but cold, even sneering, and he glanced frequently towards the distant shore and the Tree of Doom perched high on its cliff top. He knew that he could not escape his grisly end, and had the courage to look upon death without flinching.

He confessed that he had been hired to kill Michael Cantilupe, but insisted that it was Colin who had done the hiring. The little, secret smile which accompanied this admission again persuaded me that he was lying, but to most of my other questions he remained mute, refusing to say where he had met Colin, or when and how they had struck their murderous bargain. On the subject of his past life he was equally reticent, except for a single unguarded reference to having recently been discharged from the ranks of the Duke of Brittany's mercenaries.

"After you reached the island," I persisted, "where did you conceal yourself?"

Again, he did not answer directly, but, with a jerk of his head, indicated a nearby outcropping of rock and a stunted tree.

I thought this improbable, but did not, for the moment, contest it.

"How were you sure, in all the rain and darkness, that it was Michael Cantilupe who had come out of the cottage?"

Zouche bared his teeth in a death's head grin.

"The white frieze cloak that he always wore had been described to me."

"But why did you choose to kill him then, when three of the Brothers were present as witnesses?"

"I didn't see them."

"You must have seen Brother Anselm enter the cottage, or at least heard him calling for help. By such a public knifing, you made escape for yourself impossible."

But Baldwin Zouche had said his last word, lowering his chin upon his breast and closing his eyes against a world which would soon have done with him forever. I signalled to the fishermen to remove him, but as they hustled him roughly away, I called out, "Master Zouche! Were you ever at Castillon, in southern France?"

He glanced back, startled, but again did not answer. All the same, I felt certain that the bow I had drawn at a venture had hit its mark.

I asked for Colin Cantilupe to be brought to me next. His guards had loosed him from his bonds, evidently fearing nothing from him. Indeed it was impossible to conceive of him making a bid for freedom, trembling as he was with terror and abject self-pity. It was several minutes before I could coax any sensible answers from him, but eventually I was able to persuade him to talk.

"You must . . . understand," he said, haltingly at first, then the words coming out in a rush, "that . . . Rowena and I have never betrayed my uncle. We love one another, yes, but we have never betrayed him! Never!" Tears sprang to his eyes and he raised a hand to dash them away. "I cannot believe that God will let us be punished for what was only in our hearts!"

I felt I could not answer for God, so I urged him gently, "Tell me about yesterday evening."

He sniffed and wiped his nose with his fingers.

"My uncle came to my cottage about three o'clock of the afternoon and asked me to dine with him and Rowena. He knew I had been sick these past few days and unable to go out fishing. My parents are both dead," Colin added by way of explanation, "and Michael is – was – closest to me in blood in the community."

"And you went with him."

"And glad to, and not just because it meant that I could see and be near Rowena. I respected my uncle and was thankful for some company other than my own for an hour or so. I had intended returning home after the meal."

"Why didn't you?"

"Dinner was delayed for one reason and another – at one point my uncle had to put on his cloak and go out to light the lamp in the church tower, because the wind was rising – and by the time we had finished eating, the sea had covered the causeway. Uncle wouldn't hear of me rowing myself home, for the cross-currents are very dangerous."

"So Master Bonifant told me. Go on! What happened later?"

"The three of us were sitting, talking, by the fire when Brother Anselm burst in, shouting that a boat was in trouble. My uncle seized his cloak and some rope and went rushing out of the cottage."

"He didn't hesitate?"

Colin looked vaguely surprised. "Well . . . only momentarily, perhaps, as a man may do when events catch him unawares."

"And you followed him?"

"Yes. I was delayed a moment or two because I couldn't find my cloak, and in the end I was forced to run out without it." Colin's voice caught in his throat. "But . . . by that time it . . . had happened. My uncle had been murdered. The man was there, kneeling beside his body, and then the three Brothers bore him to the ground."

The rest of Colin's story was much the same as Brother Anselm's, and when he had concluded, he again denied all responsibility for his uncle's death.

"I never saw this Baldwin Zouche in my life before," he whimpered.

Once more I made a sign to the two young fishermen who were watching intently from a distance, but before they reached us, I asked, "What is your cloak like? Of what material?"

Colin stared at me for a second, puzzled, before answering, "Of dark brown byrrhus."

"And have you found it?"

"No. But I haven't had another chance to look for it." His voice rose and he gave a high-pitched laugh which cracked in the middle. "It isn't important now, I suppose. I'm not going to need it."

His gaolers escorted him back to the cottage and brought out Rowena.

I could detect the remnants of beauty in a face that was now heavily lined and pitted by the merciless weather. There had probably been a time when that leathery skin was as soft and delicate as that of a peach. I did not question her concerning the events of the previous evening. Instead, I asked her how she had come to meet Michael Cantilupe.

"I lived in Plymouth with my father. Michael first saw me during one of his visits. His wife, he told us, was a dying woman and he was looking for another. My father was anxious to get rid of me and forced me into the marriage as soon as Michael's first wife had died. I had no mother to intervene on my behalf."

"I'm sorry," I murmured. "You didn't love your husband?"

Rowena grimaced. "He was too old. And demanding!" she added, suddenly vicious. "But then, who am I to complain? He had a husband's rights."

"A beautiful girl such as you must surely have had other suitors. Why did your father favour Master Cantilupe?"

Her tone was bitter.

"Because Michael offered him more gold for me than any of the others."

"Do you know how your husband came by this money?"

"He said he ransomed a prisoner when he was soldiering in France." Her lips curled. "Maybe. Or maybe he stole it from some wretched Frenchman. He thought I didn't know where he kept his precious hoard, but I did. It was buried under a stone in a corner of the chapel."

"This is the money which was found on Baldwin Zouche's person?"

"Yes." Realizing what she had said, Rowena turned large, scared eyes upon me. "But I didn't give it to him! I never touched it!"

I patted her hand. "No, I don't think you did. How did Master Cantilupe treat you?"

"Well enough to begin with. For the first few years he was kind and considerate, but for a long time now he's ignored me, except to demand his rights as a husband. I'm not pretty any more, as you can see."

"And are you and Colin Cantilupe lovers?"

"No!" Her tone was fierce. "He's a kind, gentle soul and we love one another, but he wouldn't betray his uncle."

It was the same answer that Colin had given me.

I had two more things to do before giving the village elders the benefit of my reasoning in the morning. I obtained from one of the fishermen on guard the location of Stephen Shapwick's cottage, then walked across the causeway, which was rapidly disappearing beneath the incoming tide. I knocked on the Shapwicks' door and waited for someone to open it.

My luck was in, for the person who answered could be none other than Stephen Shapwick's daughter. The girl's eyelids were red with weeping and her general appearance unkempt, but nothing could mar her youthful prettiness. She was about fifteen years of age with huge, dark eyes, softly curving, cherry-red lips and a mane of black curls which hung about her shoulders.

A voice from within called, "Who is it, Marianne?" and an older woman appeared in the open doorway. "And what might you want?" the goodwife demanded truculently. Without, however, giving me time to reply, she added briskly, "Be off with you! We want no strangers here. This is a house of mourning."

I did not argue. I had found out what I needed to know, and made my way along the cliffside path to the Bonifants' dwelling. Goody Bonifant was preparing their evening meal, and once again I was invited to share it. I was also offered a bed for the night, and gratefully accepted both food and lodging. I had not been looking forward to sharing the austerity of the Brothers' enclosure on the island.

"Well, what progress have you made, chapman?" Jude Bonifant inquired as I rid myself of my cloak and pack and propped my cudgel in a corner.

I drew up a stool and sat down with him at the table.

"Enough, I trust, to convince you and the rest of your community tomorrow morning that Colin and Rowena Cantilupe are innocent of this conspiracy." My host raised his eyebrows at that and I nodded. "Oh yes, I'm sure there was a conspiracy, but not of their making."

"Do you have proof?" he demanded bluntly.

"I hope to persuade Baldwin Zouche to confess the truth, and I hope too that I shall be given a fair hearing."

Master Bonifant regarded me with hard, bright eyes. "As long as Michael's murderer is brought to justice, we shall be satisfied. Is there anything more that I can tell you?"

"Yes, which is the reason why I'm here." I propped my elbows on the board and cupped my chin in my hands. "I need honest answers to two questions."

Jude Bonifant looked suddenly wary, but after a moment he answered reluctantly, "Very well. I'll do my best to help you."

We were all assembled, the prisoners, the Brothers, myself and every inhabitant from both sides of the headland. The wet foreshore, where we stood, gleamed corpse-like in the early morning light, while above us, on the cliff-top, the Tree of Doom spread its wind-bitten branches. Someone had already placed a rope around one of them and Baldwin Zouche passed his tongue over dry, cracked lips.

Jude Bonifant and his fellow elders stood gravely in a semi-circle, facing the rest of us. No boats had as yet put to sea, for everyone wanted to be present when Michael Cantilupe's murderers paid the penalty for their heinous crime. There was a hungry, predatory look on all their faces, one which I had seen huntsmen wear just before the chase. There was a general hum of anticipation.

Jude Bonifant held up his hand and the noise ceased immediately. He nodded in my direction.

"Chapman, you may begin."

I cleared my throat.

"My friends," I said, "you may not like what I am about to tell you, but I beg, in God's name and the cause of justice, that you will hear me out. I am not here to speak in defence of Baldwin Zouche. He killed Michael Cantilupe, of that there can be no possible doubt, but he killed the wrong man. He was meant to murder Colin. And his fellow conspirator was Michael himself."

There was a growl of disbelief and Mistress Shapwick, who had a comforting arm about her daughter's waist, shrilled, "That's a lie! Seize him! He's as bad as the others!"

I glanced at Master Bonifant who, though eyeing me askance, stepped forward and once again commanded silence.

"We will hear the pedlar out. Then we will judge him and his story. Continue, chapman."

I went on bravely, "Michael Cantilupe had a weakness, as I see it, for young and beautiful wives, but when they got older and began to lose their looks he no longer wanted them. His first, Jane Shapwick, so Elder Bonifant and his good lady informed me, was a very lovely girl, about the same age as her kinswoman is now, when Michael first married her. But Mistress Jane grew plainer with the passing years, as happens to us all.

"Now, Michael Cantilupe used to go twice a year to Plymouth, and it was on one of these visits that he saw Rowena, who at that time was as young and pretty as her predecessor had once been. Would anyone deny that? When he married her after the death of his first wife and brought this lady here, was she not beautiful?"

No one spoke. Indeed there was no sound at all except for the hushing of the sea as the little waves broke upon the sands. But I could almost feel their resistance to my argument, so strong was their desire to believe no ill of Michael Cantilupe, who had always been so revered amongst them. I lifted my chin defiantly.

"Now, however, Rowena has lost much of those youthful charms. It's a hard life you lead here, at the mercy of storm and wind. But Marianne Shapwick is not yet old enough to be touched by the inclemency of the weather. She is young and lovely, just blossoming into womanhood. Sooner or later, she was bound to catch Michael Cantilupe's eye." I raised my voice. "And before any of you attempt to deny it, Elder Bonifant himself told me last night that Michael has spent much time of late at the Shapwicks' cottage, certainly more than he used to do in days gone by."

Heads turned in the direction of Jude Bonifant who was looking a little shaken. But to his credit, he did not deny my words.

"Friends, kinsmen, it is true. I admit that until now I saw no deeper motive in the visits than an increased friendship on Michael's part with Stephen. But proceed, chapman. We've promised you a hearing."

I thanked him and continued with growing confidence.

"Elder Bonifant also told me last night that Jane Cantilupe's death was not a lingering one, as Michael had pretended to Rowena and her father. Instead, she died swiftly, through eating a poisonous mushroom. A simple enough accident, I grant you, and that is why the law condemns the picking of field mushrooms, which can so easily be mistaken for the white-gilled death cap; a law which, like so many others, you seem to ignore in these parts. And for that very reason no one queried Jane Cantilupe's death. You all thought it a tragic mistake. Suppose, however, that it wasn't. Suppose the death cap was given to her deliberately by her husband because he wanted her out of the way, so that he could marry his new love, Rowena?"

There was an outcry then, and Jude Bonifant demanded sternly, "Can you prove this?"

It was the question I had been dreading. I had to gamble everything now on Baldwin Zouche telling the truth. I turned towards him.

"Well?" I asked. "Didn't your old comrade-in-arms open his heart when he hired you to murder his nephew?"

"Comrade-in-arms?" another of the elders asked sharply. "Do you mean to say that this evil rogue was a friend of Michael?"

I forced myself to speak with authority, in order to convince my listeners that my guesses were in truth facts.

"They were soldiers together. Michael Cantilupe, again according to Elder Bonifant, fought in France, under the banner of the Earl of Shrewsbury. When I asked this man if he had ever been to Castillon, in southern France, he did not deny it. Shrewsbury met his death there. Moreover, Zouche has, on his own admission, recently been in the pay of the Duke of Brittany. Returning to England, where would he be most likely to disembark? Why, at Plymouth, where, a week or so ago, Michael Cantilupe met up with him again quite by chance. But that meeting suggested to him a way of disposing of both his wife and his nephew, without besmirching his own spotless reputation."

Elder Bonifant would have intervened at that moment, but I begged him to let me finish what I had to say before he questioned his prisoner.

"Several things," I went on, "puzzled me about the happenings of the night before last, as they were recounted to me. Firstly, according to Colin, his uncle went out during the evening to light the warning lamp in the chapel tower. He wore his white frieze cloak, which Baldwin Zouche claims had been described to him. So why did he not kill his quarry then, when no one else was about to witness the crime, and throw the body into the sea? Secondly, when news was brought of a boat being in trouble, Master Cantilupe did not immediately bestir himself. Is that not what you told me, Brother Anselm?"

"That . . . That is so, yes," the little monk conceded.

"But when you told him that it was Stephen Shapwick and his daughter in the boat, he ran out immediately?"

"Yes, yes. But what does that prove?"

"To me, Brother, it suggests that Master Cantilupe was loath to leave the cottage until he heard that Marianne Shapwick was in danger, when all other considerations were wiped from his mind. And the reason for his reluctance was that he knew Baldwin Zouche to be lying in wait for a man in a white frieze cloak."

Jude Bonifant took a hasty step forward. "What nonsense is this?" he demanded. "How could he possibly have known?"

I stood my ground.

"Because he was the one who had brought Baldwin to the island. Wait! Let me finish! Brother Anselm, when Colin ran out of the cottage, was he wearing a cloak?"

The monk thought for a moment, then he slowly shook his head.

"No. No, he wasn't."

"That was because he couldn't find it. Nor has he discovered its whereabouts since. But I know where it may be found. It is trapped on the rocks below the far side of the cottage. But who threw it there, and why? Only Michael went out of doors after his nephew's arrival; that nephew he had persuaded to stay for the night. He could easily have taken it without being noticed, while the other two were talking, and tossed it, as he thought, into the sea."

"But why?" The words were startled out of Colin Cantilupe himself.

I looked at him. "I am certain that you were to be persuaded, under some pretext or another, to leave the cottage later on that night, when the tide had begun to turn and the causeway was becoming passable. And when your cloak could not easily be found, your uncle would have offered you his. You would then have been despatched with a dagger between the shoulder-blades, and Baldwin Zouche sent on his way with his money."

Jude Bonifant spoke for all when he said, "I still do not understand."

"Baldwin had made no secret of his presence on the island. He had crossed the causeway while it was still light, not caring who might see him. It was part of the plan that he was known to be there. Michael Cantilupe's story would be that his wife and nephew had hired someone to murder him, but that the plot had miscarried because Colin was wearing his cloak. In fact the opposite of what actually happened. With the greatest show of reluctance and profoundest sorrow, he would have been forced to accept his wife's complicity in the conspiracy. There would have been nothing he could have done to save her from the rest of you when, as always, you took it upon yourselves to mete out punishment."

There was a moment's silence. Then Jude Bonifant exclaimed, "It's a farrago of nonsense! I don't believe a word of it. Chapman, you're out of your wits."

"Ask this man," I said, turning to Baldwin Zouche. "Baldwin, remember that you hold two innocent lives in your hands. Within the hour, you will go to meet your Maker. Think of your immortal soul! Admit the truth."

He did not answer at once and my heart sank, but suddenly he glanced up and shrugged.

"Very well . . . All you've said is as it happened. I met Michael in Plymouth a week or more ago and we recognized each other at once, even though we hadn't met for many years. Yes, we fought in France together." He sneered. "From our very first encounter, I'd known him to be a kindred spirit. The only difference between us was that while I didn't care who knew I was a villain, Michael always liked to keep his vices secret. Except with me. He knew I couldn't be fooled. During that meeting in Plymouth, at the sign of the Turk's Head, he told me everything; how he had murdered his first wife and no one any the wiser. And how he now wanted to be rid of his second, but dared not again use the death cap mushroom. So we devised the plot between us and fixed a day when high tide was early in the evening and his nephew could be persuaded to stop the night."

"But why," I asked, "did you kill the wrong man? You must have realized that it was much earlier than the time arranged for the murder and that there were other people about. And, more importantly, you must have recognized that the man in the white frieze cloak was Michael himself and not his nephew, Colin."

"I lost my temper. It's always been my downfall, and Michael had tried to cheat me over the money when he came to the chapel where I was hiding. I got to remembering all the times he had cheated me in the past; the girls he had lured away from me with lies and false promises, the punishments I'd received for misdeeds which were really his. And that cloak! It was mine. He must have stolen it the very day we parted company in France. It had been my father's and his father's before him. It was my talisman, and I've not had a day's good fortune since I lost it. I didn't know, until I met him in Plymouth, that he was the one who took it. But I should have guessed."

"And so you succumbed to a momentary desire for revenge and thereby encompassed your own doom. But why did you pretend that it was Rowena and Colin Cantilupe who had hired you?"

Once again, Baldwin gave his death's head grin.

"It amused me. I had no doubt that I was going straight to hell, so I might as well be hanged for a sheep as for a lamb. But now I swear to you, by Our Saviour's death upon the Cross, that they are as innocent of plotting Michael Cantilupe's death as he was guilty of planning theirs. And that is all I have to say."

I had saved the lives of Rowena and Colin Cantilupe, but there was nothing more that I could do for Baldwin Zouche. He would forfeit his life for his misdeeds, just as his desperate need for revenge, the need that now and then God stirs in all of us, had ensured that his co-conspirator and fellow murderer had paid the penalty with his.

I left him to his fate and went my way, glad to be free of that wild and desolate place. But as I reached the summit of the rising ground and glanced back over my shoulder, I saw that the Tree of Doom already bore its grisly fruit.

PART III
The Age of Discovery

THE MURDER
OF INNOCENCE
P. C. Doherty

Paul Doherty is currently the most prolific writer of historical detective novels with around twenty novels to his credit under both his own name and several pseudonyms. As Doherty, his best known character is Hugh Corbett, the thirteenth-century clerk to the King's Bench, who becomes a detective and spy for King Edward I. His adventures began in Satan in St Mary's *(1986) and have continued through* Crown in Darkness *(1988),* Spy in Chancery *(1988),* The Angel of Death *(1989),* The Prince of Darkness *(1992),* Murder Wears a Cowl *(1992),* The Assassin in the Greenwood *(1993) and* The Song of a Dark Angel *(1994). Writing as Paul Harding he has created Brother Athelstan, a parish priest in fourteenth-century Southwark, who is assistant to the City of London coroner, Sir John Cranston. His adventures have appeared in* The Nightingale Gallery *(1991),* The House of the Red Slayer *(1992),* Murder Most Holy *(1992),* The Anger of God *(1993) and* By Murder's Bright Light *(1994). As Michael Clynes he has produced a series about Sir Roger Shallot, a rather Falstaffian rogue in the reign of Henry VII, whose investigations have been recorded in* The White Rose Murders *(1991),* The Poisoned Chalice *(1992),* The Grail Murders *(1993) and* A Brood of Vipers *(1994). Meanwhile, as C. L. Grace, he has created a new series featuring Kathryn Swinbrooke, a physician and chemist in fifteenth-century Canterbury. So far there has appeared* A Shrine of Murders *(1993) and* The Eye of God *(1994). And this is not all of Doherty's output!*

When I asked Paul whether he would be able to contribute a story to this anthology he decided to create a new character, set in a slightly later period, in the early years of the reign of Elizabeth I. So, may I unveil the first extract from the true memoirs of Mary Frith ("Moll Flanders"), set early in her life, long before her tumultuous career in the Elizabethan Secret Service: the Office of the Night.

Yesterday I hanged three men. As High Sheriffess of the county, I travelled by carriage to the crossroads where the scaffold stands. The prisoners, three Moon men, wanderers, had ambushed two bawdy baskets on a lonely, windswept trackway out on the moors. Having cruelly ravished and then killed the women, these reprobates buried their bodies in a ditch. Of course, as High Sheriffess, all I did was sit in my carriage and watch the three prisoners being pushed up the scaffold. When the ladder was turned, I glanced away. I felt no pity: evil men, they deserved their fate. Afterwards, as I journeyed back, the bright green fields became overcast: clouds swept in from the north, low, black and threatening. My escort begged me not to continue and so we stopped in a small village and I took chambers at the *Kestrel*; a pleasant hostelry where the chamber was swept, the bed was narrow but the sheets were clean and free of fleas.

One of my servants built up the fire; I sat as I often do, thinking about the past. Taverns bring back so many memories: when you sleep in your own bed, between your own sheets you are safe, like a baby nestling in a cot. You think your usual thoughts, your feet are set on the path you intend to tread. But a new bed turns the mind to fanciful matters and, when you are old, there is nothing new under the sun, so you journey back in time. The *Kestrel* reminded me of another tavern, the *Bishop's Mitre* in Smithfield where I and my Worshipful Guardian, Parson Snodgrass, Vicar of St Botolph's in Islip, Kent, stayed. Every year Parson Snodgrass travelled to London to meet the Dean of the Arches near St Paul's: he always stayed at the *Bishop's Mitre* in Smithfield. In that particular year, the time of the great sweating sickness when Elizabeth had been only two years on the throne, Parson Snodgrass took me with him. I, poor Molly Frith, foundling of the Parish who had been taken into the Parson's much trumpeted loving care.

Now Smithfield is a large open space between the great abbey church of St Bartholomew and the fleshing market of London. The houses round that great open expanse are crammed together, divided by dark, furtive alleyways. In my time a filthy, fetid place: chamber pots were emptied out of the windows and offal from the butchers' stalls oozed and slipped across the execution ground where men were hanged or women burnt to death, tied to a thick, blackened beam. Even the trees stank of death: the kites, busy after tearing at freshly severed heads, would build their nests amongst the branches with rags and pieces of offal. The *Bishop's Mitre* fronted all this, a spacious tavern with its own garden, yards and even a balcony: here, visitors could stand on execution day and have a good view of some hapless felon being choked to death in his hempen noose. We were on the second floor. Worshipful Guardian had a chamber, I and a tavern maid shared a narrow closet alongside. I forget the girl's name. She was rosy-cheeked and fresh-eyed and whispered stories about lusty grooms and their constant invitation to join them in the tavern hay loft.

Now, on the second morning of our stay there, Worshipful Guardian and I had gone down to break our fast on strips of roast duck and a basket of freshly cut bread. There were other guests present but Parson Snodgrass, strict in his ways, kept to himself and bade me do the same.

"You are too sharp, Moll," he would comment. "And your tongue clacks as fast as your wits." Then he would stroke my face with his thumb, the only time he ever touched or showed me any sign of affection.

I would force a smile and Worshipful Guardian's eyes would take on a wistful, dreamy look. He was a clever, subtle man with a deep knowledge of herbs and potions and always hoped for a grander living with a stately house and spacious gardens where he could dabble to his heart's content. Anyway, on that bright summer's day with the sunshine pouring through the open doorway, Murder announced itself. There was a shouting and clashing on the stairs and a young man, handsome faced, his blond hair curled, his beard neatly clipped, burst into the morning room shouting for the landlord.

"What is it, sir?" Worshipful Guardian rose, knocking over the goblet he had been sipping.

The young man, his face pale, eyes starting, scratched at his tufty beard then played with the buckle of the belt he carried. He had apparently not finished his dressing, he had one shoe on, the points of his breeches were not fully tied whilst the collar of his doublet was all awry.

"It's Uncle!" the young man cried.

He looked down at his stockinged foot and blushed with embarrassment. The landlord came bustling in; fresh from gibbeting some chicken, he wiped bloody fingers on his stained apron.

"Lackaday, lackaday, sir, what is the matter?" he cried.

"It's my uncle. Sir Nicholas Hopton."

I vaguely remembered the evening before. The young man was more serene then, sitting in a corner of the tavern at the table specially screened off by a wooden partition. His companion had been an older man, plump, red-faced with popping eyes and silver-white hair combed back to cover a bald patch, his voice deep and plummy. The young man had left and, when Worshipful Guardian and I were obliged to help the older man up to his chamber, he struck me as one who had drunk deeply of the wine of life and savoured every drop.

"I am a Parson," Worshipful Guardian intervened. "Though I am not of these parts." He grasped the young man by the shoulders. "What is wrong with your uncle?"

"I cannot wake him," the young man replied. "I hammered on his door but there was no reply."

"Master Charles," the taverner interrupted. "Your uncle, as ever, drank deep last night."

"Nonsense!" Charles Hopton replied, pleading with Worshipful Guardian. "Uncle was no toper and there's blood seeping out from under the door."

The landlord hurried off, quick as a whippet up the stairs, the fumbling young man trailing after him. Worshipful Guardian followed and, of course, so did I. The Hoptons had the chambers on the first gallery overlooking the sweet-smelling garden well away from the dirt and foul odours of Smithfield. The door of the young man's chamber was open. I noticed how the door was of thick, blackened oak reinforced with strips of metal and rows of iron studs. The second door was of similar quality, a pool of blood oozed out from beneath the rim forming a dark, accusing puddle on the polished wooden floor. Parson Snodgrass and the landlord pounded on the door but, of course, the dead cannot answer. Charles Hopton danced from foot to foot then hurried back to his chamber, so he told me, to find his other shoe.

"It's futile," Worshipful Guardian exclaimed, at mine host's pounding on the door.

The landlord, a sly cozen, fluttered his bloodied fingers and wailed disconsolately. Now many people regard me as a wild devil, a Winchester goose who made her fortune filching white money or spending my time at a vaulting house down on Southwark side. However, that was all in the future. I had not yet fallen into ruin and acted upon the stage or dressed in male swagger, or gone to the Tower to meet Lord Cecil and the other spies and dagger boys of the Office of the Night. To be sure, in my youth, I was a rumskuckle, a tomboy, but I had sharp eyes and keen wits and, watching that landlord flail his podgy hands and pick at his hairy nose, I smelt villainy.

"Take the door off!" Parson Snodgrass exclaimed.

"Impossible!" Hopton came back out to the gallery and the landlord chorused what he said. "For the Lord's sake, the doors are solid oak, the hinges are steel not leather!"

"True, true!" the landlord wailed. He crouched down and peered through the key-hole. "And the key's still in the lock, I cannot open it!"

"The chamber overlooks the garden?" Parson Snodgrass asked. "Then come, sirs."

We went downstairs out along the pebbled path, around the tavern and into a sweet-smelling fragrant garden. Beyond were the stable yards and, at my Worshipful Guardian's insistence, the landlord scurried off, bringing back a ladder. He placed this carefully against the wall.

"See." The landlord pointed up to a casement window, the mullion glass gleaming in the sunlight. "That's Sir Nicholas's chamber."

Young Hopton put one foot on the rung of the ladder, but Parson Snodgrass waved him away. He pointed down to his long leather boots.

"I'd be safer." He smiled and tousled my black, curly hair. "As young Mary will tell you, I am used to scaling the ladders of my belfry or mending my roof."

I nodded solemnly. Indeed, he was: Parson Snodgrass could climb as nimble as a squirrel.

"I'll go up," he declared gravely and waved away the ostlers and grooms who had now begun to gather.

"You'll need a chisel," the landlord shouted and sent a tapster to fetch one.

Worshipful Guardian grasped this then scampered up the ladder as skilfully as a monkey up a pole. At the top he pressed his face against the window.

"What can you see?" the landlord shouted.

"Nothing," Worshipful Guardian replied. "The shutters within are closed."

He drew back the chisel, told us to stand away and shattered one of the small panes of glass. He put his hand carefully inside and lifted the latch. Next we heard the sound of breaking wood as Worshipful Guardian battered against the inside shutters. These flew open and in he climbed. We waited for a while then Worshipful Guardian poked his head out of the window, his face all pallid.

"Your uncle . . .!" It was more of a strangled sob than a cry.

"Take the ladder away!" he urged. "Come round. I shall open the door!"

The landlord obeyed and we hurried back into the tavern and up the stairs. Just after we arrived, we heard the bolts drawn, the key turned and the door swung open. Inside was a scene the playwright Middleton or that roaring boy Dekker would have been proud of:

chaos, blood and gore! Despite the open window and flung back shutters the place smelt foul. There was a close stool in the corner over which fat, black flies buzzed like imps from hell. The sheets on the four-poster bed were crumpled and disarrayed. A chest had been knocked over but Sir Nicholas's corpse drew all eyes. He lay sprawled on the rushes, his throat slashed from ear to ear. The blood had poured out like that of a gutted pig, seeping amongst the rushes, finding its way along the paving stones and under the door.

"God have mercy on us!" Worshipful Guardian breathed.

I stared at old Hopton's face, so surprised by death: the white bristling moustache and beard, the sunken cheeks, the tongue curling out like that of a snake: the eyes were terrifying: popping as if Sir Nicholas had seen a vision of hell and all its fury before he died. The floor was sticky underfoot and I had to seize my mouth, close my eyes and pray that my stomach would not betray me. Young Charles, all a-trembling, sat down on a stool.

"I came through the window," Worshipful Guardian explained. "Sir Nicholas was just lying there." He smiled wanly. "I'm sorry for any delay but," he glanced round fearfully, "I thought the assassin was still here." He pointed to the door. "The key was still in the lock and the windows all shuttered . . ."

"So how did it happen?" young Charles bleated.

The commotion began again and a search was made: the cup Sir Nicholas had brought up from the taproom lay on the floor, the wine all gone but the water in the bowl and jug on the great wooden lavarium was still pure and unused. While they all babbled and scampered about, I went across to the bed. I was always fascinated by the way people had slept: how they lay and what did they do when darkness fell. I ran my hand across the grimy sheet. The bed was cold but then I espied it, a woman's stocking, blue and decorated with yellow clocks. I pulled this out and held it up to admire it.

"Your uncle's?" I asked.

Hopton whirled round, his jaw fell: behind him the landlord's hand went to his mouth.

"It seems my uncle was not alone last night. Here fellow," Hopton turned back to the landlord. "Sir Nicholas was no dog. Help me lift him onto the bed."

The landlord obeyed like some mute bereft of speech. Whilst Hopton picked up his uncle's body under the armpits, the landlord lifted the feet but his eyes never left that stocking still in my hand.

"He's so cold," Young Hopton whispered. "He must have been dead for hours."

Worshipful Guardian came over and snatched the stocking out

of my hand and stared round the room: Sir Nicholas's own clothes hung on a peg on the wall, his boots beneath it.

"Is there anything missing?" Worshipful Guardian asked.

"Oh, Lord save us!" Hopton wailed.

He drew the sheet over his uncle's face then, like some Abraham man devoid of wit, he scampered round the room muttering to himself. Coffers and chests were flung open, clothes rummaged through. A pair of leather panniers unbuckled, their contents spilled onto the floor.

"What is it?" Worshipful Guardian asked.

"The money belt!" Hopton cried, running a hand through his hair. "Twice a year, two days after Lady's Day and then again after the feast of St Michael and All Angels, Uncle brought his gold to the merchants in Cheapside. He was to bank it today but now it's gone!"

The landlord, his face turning yellow like a lump of doughy paste, edged out of the room and disappeared down the gallery. Hopton slumped down on a stool at the foot of the bed.

"My uncle was murdered!" he exclaimed. "Someone came into his chamber last night." He pointed to the stocking. "Some whore took my uncle's money belt and slit his throat."

Worshipful Guardian, all christian concern, went over and patted him gently on the shoulder.

"You are sure of this?" he asked.

"Of course!" Hopton cried. "Uncle was fit and happy when I left him."

"And did you visit him again?"

The young man looked up sheepishly. "I went out," he stammered. "The pleasures of the town, sir. London is a far cry from the fields and woods of Sussex."

"And your uncle?"

"He was a ladies' man," Hopton confessed. "He was well known to the women of the town."

Oh, aye, I thought, a precious pair these two, uncle and nephew, full of the good things of life. They came up to town in their richly garbed clothes, bellies full of wine and pippin pie, then out to the nearest brothel to bestride some callet or fresh young pullet. Young Charles had to find his own, but a man like Sir Nicholas would demand such soft flesh be brought to him.

"Where's the landlord?" Hopton suddenly asked, rising to his feet. "Where is that jackanapes?"

He ran out of the room and down the gallery. Worshipful Guardian followed but I stayed. Even though of the gentler sex, I had a hard heart and a curious nose. The chamber was now deserted. I looked at the blood which had congealed upon the rushes thick and crusting: the overturned chests and coffers: the broken window and shattered shutters, the key in the lock. I tiptoed over to the bed and pulled back the sheet. Sir Nicholas lay, eyes open, beaky nose up in the air. I wondered idly where his soul was: to die after taking a whore, the imps might surely have it! I stared curiously at the cheeks, noticing the little veins streaked there, silent testimony to Sir Nicholas's love of claret and deep bowls of canary. Then, pushing my nose closer, I sniffed and caught the cheap perfume which still lingered on the straggling grey temples of hair and bloodstained night shirt.

"Mary!" Worshipful Guardian shouted over an ever-growing hubbub of noise. "Mary, where are you? Come down now!"

Of course, I disobeyed, lingering a few more minutes for this was the first time I'd been in a death chamber. I recalled the old stories of how the ghost loved to linger. Heigh nonny no, fifteen years of age, I was already wilful and set in my ways. Worshipful Guardian called again so I hurried down: the taproom seemed full of people, shouting and gesturing at each other. At the far end the landlord sat slumped on a stool. Now and again he would lift his head and howl like a dog before hiding his face in his hands; beside him stood the high constable, a brave burly boy with his staff of office and broad-brimmed hat: a man of importance who made sure everyone was fully aware that he was an officer of the law, the Queen's own man. On the other side of the landlord was a strapping lass with golden curls, the bodice of her bottle-green dress cut so low her breasts, ripe young pears, jutted out ready for the touch. However, her face was red with anger, her eyes flashing as she raved like some Bess o' Bedlam.

"Worshipful Guardian." I pulled my face into the most pious grimace. "What is happening?"

"Master Hopton and the Constable are questioning the maid." Parson Snodgrass bent down. "Apparently the stocking belonged to her."

"What's your name?" the Constable asked, his face only a few inches away from the girl's.

"Sarah," the girl replied all a-quiver: despite her defiance, Sarah had to clench the edge of the beer barrel to stop herself fainting.

"Sarah what?"

"Bartholomew. I was a foundling."

"What's this then?"

A young man came through the back door: he had greasy red hair and a dirt-smeared face. He took one look at quivering Sarah and

would have launched himself on the Constable if the landlord had
not intervened and pulled him back.

"Who's he?" Hopton stepped back, frightened of this angry young
man with his snarling, gap-toothed mouth and flailing hands.

"He's my only son," the landlord wailed. "Simkin."

"And sweet on Sarah," I whispered to Worshipful Guardian.

The whole scene would have ended in fisticuffs and violence if
Parson Snodgrass hadn't intervened. He plucked the Constable by
his cloak and whispered in his ear, the fellow nodded portentously.

"No good will come of this," the Constable trumpeted. He waved
to one of the tables. "I have to make my enquiries." He continued,
"I can make them here or in the gatehouse at Newgate."

The prospect of a visit to that foul, pestilential place sent everyone
hurrying round the table, Worshipful Guardian included, whilst I
stood behind his chair and watched, open-mouthed. Nothing in
my short but very boring life could equal that scene. Neither the
mummers who visited our village nor even Widow Grayport's noisy
tirade against Goodwoman Cuthbertson outside the parish church
could rival the awful hangman drama in that tavern taproom so
many years ago. The Constable, for all his pomposity, was a sharp
man, and the sight of his cudgel on the table, which he raised now
and again for silence, kept good order. Sarah, flustered, wept and,
glancing fearfully at Simkin, blubberingly confessed.

"I was with the old gentleman," she wailed. "He offered me a
silver piece."

"To do what?" the Constable asked.

I would have sniggered but I kept as still as a statue lest Worshipful
Guardian should remember I was present.

"To accommodate him," Sarah muttered.

This was too much for Simkin who rocked backwards and forwards
on a stool. I thought he was a fool. If Sarah with her dangling tits
was his idea of chastity then never did a man so richly deserve a
cuckold's horns.

"He gave me a coin," Sarah continued. "I slipped into the
old man's chamber to, to . . ." she stammered. "To frolic for a
while."

"And?" the Constable barked.

"The old man was fuddled, in his cups. I left him."

"Did he lock the door when you went?"

"Oh, yes, he did!"

Sarah leaned forward on the table, the Constable licked his lips
before he remembered who he was and tried not to stare down into
her bodice.

"Stay here!" the officer declared and, taking the landlord by the arm, dragged him away from the table.

There was a whispered conversation and the landlord led him off up the stairs, walking like a felon on his way up to meet Jack Ketch at Tyburn.

For a while we sat in silence. Sarah trembled, Simkin slouched, head in his hands, Hopton nervously drummed his fingers on the table. Worshipful Guardian looked over his shoulder and smiled at me.

"Master Charles," I gabbled, hoping to divert the Parson's attention. "How long do you intend to stay in the city?"

"Oh, another day," he replied off-handedly. "I was to stay here whilst Uncle went to Cheapside."

I was about to ask him where he had gone the previous evening when there was a crashing on the stairs. The Constable swept into the kitchen holding a blood-stained dagger triumphantly before him.

"I found it." He pointed at the quivering Sarah. "In your closet behind some clothes."

"And the money?" Young Hopton sprang to his feet.

The Constable shook his head. "No sign." He marched across and laid a hand on Sarah's shoulder. "Sarah Bartholomew," he intoned, "I arrest you in the name of the Queen for the horrible crimes of murder and robbery."

He dragged the young woman to her feet even as he blew on his whistle. Two bailiffs came in from outside, loathsome men with greasy spiked hair, beer-sodden faces and bleary eyes. One of them lashed the young girl's hands together behind her back even as the other took liberties with her body, grasping her around the breasts, chuckling to himself. The Constable raised his stick threateningly.

"She's the Queen's prisoner, not a sack of goods!" he warned.

And, without further ado, the Constable swept out of the tavern, the two bailiffs almost carrying the sobbing Sarah between them. I quickly looked round: the landlord for all his fear had a calculating look, and what I thought was a smirk. Simkin did not seem too contrite whilst Parson Snodgrass, my Worshipful Guardian, leaned his elbows on the arms of the chair, steepling his fingers as if in prayer.

"Truly," he muttered, "the love of riches is the root of all evil."

Hopton moved his stool across and stared at Worshipful Guardian. He narrowed his eyes. "Sir, I have seen you before?"

"Possibly," Parson Snodgrass replied. "I had a curacy in Sussex. Perhaps it was there."

Hopton blinked, muttering under his breath.

"And what will you do now, sir?" my Worshipful Guardian

asked, as the landlord and son shuffled to their feet, mumbling about work to be done. They scuttled into the kitchen to whisper amongst themselves. Hopton watched them go.

"I shall stay here for a while," he replied slowly. "Uncle's corpse has got to be dressed, embalmed and carted back to Tidmarsh before the weather becomes too warm."

"And the money?" I asked, slipping onto a stool beside my guardian.

"Oh, yes, the money. That, too, has to be found."

Parson Snodgrass shook his head mournfully. "The wench has hidden it away."

"I think she's innocent," I blurted out.

"Why, Mary, dearest," Parson Snodgrass looked at me in surprise. "Whatever makes you say that?"

"She's big and brawny," I replied. "But poor Sarah does not have the wit to carry out such a crime. Your uncle was a healthy man?"

Hopton nodded, watching us carefully.

"He was an old ram," I continued, ignoring my Worshipful Guardian's gasp of surprise. "Not a man to bare his throat to the slayer. There was no struggle, no sound was heard, yet we are to believe that she cut your uncle's throat, took the money belt and heigh-ho off to her own chamber. She was apparently bright enough to hide the money but not the dagger which will send her to the gallows." I paused. "Nor has anyone explained how she could have locked the door from inside."

"True," Worshipful Guardian added, "but she may have an accomplice."

Hopton pulled his stool closer. "What are you saying?"

I pointed to the scullery. "I think it's best if you had words with mine host and his son, Simkin."

My Worshipful Guardian, steepling his fingers before his mouth, stared at me for a while.

"Out of the mouths of babes and infants," he intoned. "Stay awhile, Master Hopton."

And, striding into the scullery, Parson Snodgrass shouted for mine host and Simkin and led them back into the deserted taproom. All the other drinkers and diners had long fled: even the drovers and butchers from Smithfield Market, like ancient priests of old, had divined the signs. A murder had been done at the *Bishop's Mitre*, a bloody corpse had been found and the Constable had arrived. Those who were close to such a death might be implicated in it. In a place like Smithfield I suppose everyone has something to hide.

The taverner and his son sat down at one end of the grease-covered table, Parson Snodgrass, Hopton and myself on the other. I had to stifle a smile; we looked like three justices on circuit whilst the landlord and his son, with their greasy faces and sly-eyed looks, would not have been out of place in any hanging cart.

"Do you think Sarah is guilty?" Parson Snodgrass began. "She is in your service."

"A mere foundling," mine host replied callously.

Oh, my heart went out to her. Nevertheless, I smiled beatifically, tossing back my ringlets; silently, I cursed this dirty tub of lard who would allow a girl to swing from the scaffold just because she was a foundling.

"And you, Simkin?" Hopton asked. "You were sweet on the girl?"

The young man opened his mouth in a fine display of yellow, rotting teeth.

"We had a tryst," he stammered. "I met her at St Bartholomew's Fair three years ago. My father gave her employment."

Aye, to warm your beds, I thought, but I kept my mouth shut.

"Last night," Parson Snodgrass continued, "what happened at the tavern?"

The landlord waved his dirty hands, his nails were thickly caked with muck. I quietly vowed I'd eat no more in this tavern.

"Sir, you know as much as we do," he replied. "Sir Nicholas and his nephew dined on lamb stew. You and your – "

"My ward," Worshipful Guardian supplied.

"Yes, yes, you saw them here."

"And then what happened?"

"Well, I left for the city," Hopton replied.

"And your uncle stayed down here for a while," the landlord said. "You remember him, sir?" he said, pointing at Worshipful Guardian.

"Aye, we had a few words with him," Parson Snodgrass replied. "But he was well in his cups."

"Parson Snodgrass and I helped him up to his chamber," I added.

"And young Sarah?" Worshipful Guardian asked.

Again the landlord stretched those filthy hands. "When the day is done," he replied, "and all duties are finished, who am I to say who goes where or does what?"

"Was Sarah in the habit of entertaining old men?" Hopton asked harshly.

"Old men, young men," mine host replied. "What does it matter? The girl had an eye for a silver piece."

"Did you send her to him?" I asked.

The landlord threw me a look of contempt whilst his son Simkin pulled a face.

"Well, did you?" Hopton asked. "Surely you must have missed her in the scullery or taproom?"

"What are you implying?" mine host demanded.

"We are implying nothing," Parson Snodgrass intervened smoothly. "We simply find it difficult to believe that Sarah had the strength to kill a man like Sir Nicholas. We also wondered at her foolishness in managing to hide away the money belt and yet not conceal the dagger. And where would she get such a knife, eh?"

"I was going to ask the same questions."

We spun round, the Constable stood in the doorway. He walked leisurely across and placed a leather sack on the table, opened the cord at the neck and let the long-bladed knife fall out. We all stared at it.

"Do you recognize it, sir?" the Constable asked, turning to the landlord.

"Of course," mine host stammered. He picked it up by the battered wooden handle: it winked in the light, blood still stained its evil-looking point. "It's one of our fleshing knives," the landlord declared. "There are at least a score of these in the kitchen. It would be easy for anyone to pick it up and smuggle it out."

The Constable's leathery face broke into a smile. "Truly spoken!" His grin widened as he sat down. "I see there's a Court of Inquiry in session here and I would like to join it. Poor Sarah's in Newgate. But that does not mean she's guilty." His words hung like a noose in the air. "As I walked up Giltspur Street," the Constable continued, "and watched poor Sarah being carried like a sack in the hands of those bailiffs, I wondered how such a girl could kill a wily old man like Sir Nicholas with so much stealth and silence." His smile faded. "And I am no fool. Why should I find the knife and not the money? So," he loosened his cloak and let it fall around him, "in the porter's lodge at Newgate I made Sarah an offer. Tell me where the money was and she'd have a pardon." He tapped his hand on the table like a man beating a drum. "Now any man or woman faced with a stay in a condemned hole, followed by a ride in the hell-cart to Tyburn, would seize such an offer with both hands." He paused his tapping. "She claimed to be innocent of any crime. Moreover," he continued, "there's a problem with the key, isn't there? It was in the lock: the old man must have turned it but he couldn't do that if his throat was slashed." He bowed mockingly at Worshipful Guardian. "Parson Snodgrass, you bravely broke into the room, how did you find it?"

"The shutters were closed," my Worshipful Guardian replied. "As was the window casement itself." He pulled a face. "The door was both bolted and locked, the key turned. Poor Sir Nicholas was lying on the floor, his throat all gutted."

"And the body was cold?" the Constable asked.

"Like ice," young Hopton replied. "It was ten o'clock in the morning when we burst in. Uncle must have been dead at least eight hours."

The Constable studied him closely. "And you, sir, were his beloved nephew and now his heir?"

"Yes," Hopton replied. He straightened his shoulders, puffing his chest out. "According to my uncle's will, I am heir to his manor and his estates. Why, sir?"

"Honi soit qui mal y pense," the Constable replied drily. "Evil to them who evil think."

"I left the *Bishop's Mitre* last night," Hopton snapped, looking flushed. "My uncle was here, in the tap room, slightly drunk but very much alive. I went up Giltspur Street to a molly house in Cock Lane. Ask the mistress there, Nan Twitchett."

"I know her very well," the Constable interrupted with a half-smile.

"I played a game of dice." Hopton bit his lip and closed his eyes. "Hazard. Then a young lady with hair as black as night and a face like a gipsy entertained me into the early hours. I came downstairs and broke my fast on light ale, bread, butter and some lovely jam."

"Quite so, quite so." The Constable grinned at me. "Mistress Twitchett's sweetmeats are well known. And when you came back, sir?"

"I went upstairs to my own room, washed and bathed. I then went to wake uncle and saw the blood. The rest you know."

"And you, sir?" The Constable turned to Worshipful Guardian.

"As I have told you," Parson Snodgrass replied, calm and serene as ever; at that moment my Worshipful Guardian had the face of a saint, like a Solomon come to judgement, his grey hair, neatly parted down the middle, falling down to his snow-white collar above his black gown. "Little Mary here and myself dined in the taproom. Sir Nicholas was much in his cups and we helped him up the stairs. Isn't that right, girl?"

I nodded.

"Sir Nicholas was in good spirits, a wine cup in one hand, full of mine host's claret. We steered him into his room. I never saw him again."

"Which leaves mine host," the Constable declared.

"We live and work here," the fellow replied. "And neither my son nor myself went anywhere near Sir Nicholas's chamber. Even if we did, how could we get in? The door was locked and bolted from the inside, the key in place, the windows were shuttered and, before you ask, there are no secret tunnels or passageways inside. You can search the room yourself," mine host sighed. "It was as you saw it, with one window and a door."

The Constable breathed out noisily. "So, we have Sir Nicholas who leaves the taproom. By the way, where was the money belt?"

"As always, strapped round his waist," Hopton replied. "He even went to bed with it. My uncle was not the most generous of men and most untrusting to human kind, which explains why the windows were closed and shuttered."

"So," the Constable replied. "He goes into his bedroom and changes. Earlier in the day he'd made an assignation with young Sarah who now comes tripping along to service him. She says he was much the worse for drink. There was a tussle on the bed which achieved very little. Out she went and he locks the door behind her. Now, Sir Nicholas may have had another visitor who cut his throat and took his money belt but, how could that happen, if the door remained bolted, the key turned in the lock and the window shuttered?" The Constable got to his feet. He threw his cloak over one arm and grasped his cane. "So, there's nothing for it but to visit young Sarah again."

"We should all go!" I exclaimed.

Worshipful Guardian turned, his eyes rounded in amazement.

"Child, child," he intoned. "The horrors of Newgate are not for you."

"She's a foundling," I replied. "And so am I. She's been wrongly accused and must be terrified." My wits grew sharper. "Surely, sir, we should go. Did not the good Lord tell us to visit those in prison?"

Parson Snodgrass smiled benignly. "I have business, child."

"I could take her," the Constable offered kindly.

I smiled back, feeling guilty at the hasty judgement I'd first made about him.

"But that's improper," Parson Snodgrass blustered.

"I'll go too," Hopton volunteered.

Worshipful Guardian steepled his fingers as if in prayer.

"Very well," he declared. "But be not too long. Give the poor girl all the comfort you can." He glanced at Hopton. "Surely you should look after your uncle's cadaver?"

"There is very little I can do now," the young man replied. "But

I can call in to see the vicar at St Sepulchre's and pay a fee to have it taken to the death house there."

Worshipful Guardian agreed. The Constable and I left the tavern. We stood outside the gate, just near the butchers' stalls whilst young Hopton went back to his room to prepare himself for the city. The Constable held my hand, leaning on his staff of office. He looked down at me and winked. I blushed with embarrassment and turned away. A butcher's apprentice came from behind a stall. He grasped the head of a sheep bleating in terror and, with one slash of his knife, cut the poor creature's throat: its legs buckled and it fell into its own pool of splashing hot blood. The gore burst out like water from a fountain. The Constable caught my gaze.

"It's a cruel world, child," he commented. "And you'll come to worse sights by and by." He patted me on my black mop of hair. "The poor creature's well gone: this is a wicked world and the devil tramples on every side. Ah well, here comes our rich, young heir."

Hopton came swaggering out, he had changed into a blue tabard jacket with a peascod belly and multi-coloured hose. He now wore his swordbelt and carried a silver-topped cane, walking with all the hauteur of a rich, young courtier.

"Quite the man about town," the Constable whispered out of the corner of his mouth. "And hardly the grieving nephew."

Hopton gave us a mocking bow and we all crossed Smithfield market. We pushed our way through the throng, past the stocks, the neck, the hand, the feet and the finger, all full to overflowing with the naps and foists. As the Constable passed, he was greeted by a raucous cheer from these miscreants whilst he lifted his hat in a sardonic salute.

At the entrance to Giltspur Street we had to pause for a while as two cat's-meat men, poles slung over their shoulders with pieces of offal hanging from them, fought over who should lead the motley collection of cats which now thronged hungrily about them.

"Why are they doing that?" I whispered.

"Whoever gets the cats," the Constable replied gruffly, "gets their skins."

"People wear catskin!" I exclaimed.

"Of course," the Constable replied. "Some people swear by it, especially when it rains."

We went up the street. I gazed round-eyed at all the sights: courtiers in their silks and taffetas strutting like peacocks; bare-arsed children begging for coins. An Abraham Man, naked except for a piece of cloth round his private parts, did a curious dance outside St Bartholomew's Hospital. Two whores, lashed back to back, their skirts raised to expose grimy thighs and knees, were dragged down to the stocks by a sweaty-faced bailiff. A doctor with a mask covering his face wandered by, a staff in his hand. The mask was like something out of a nightmare: his face and neck were fully covered, the eyelets of the hood covered by pieces of glass and it had a strange bird-like beak which, the Constable explained, was stuffed with perfumes to keep away the contagious air. At last the great, dark mass of Newgate, stone towers soaring above its iron-clad gates, came into view. I thought we would go there but the Constable stopped at the entrance to a narrow, dark street. On the corner was the *Ship* tavern and outside this stood a pretty young woman standing over a plate of charcoal, her skirts hoist. Hopton saw this and smirked.

"What is she doing?" I whispered.

"She's a whore. She's fumigating herself against the pox," the Constable replied. "Now you, my dear, just stay here with this gentleman."

The Constable bowed mockingly at Hopton. "This is Cock Lane, sir, and it won't take me long to see if Mistress Twitchett corroborates your story."

The Constable walked down the alleyway, swinging his staff of office, impervious to the shouts and catcalls which came out from the doors and windows as he passed. Hopton watched him go with a narrow-eyed look.

"A strange fellow," he drawled. He glanced sullenly down at me. "What are you looking at, cat eyes?"

"I don't know," I replied tartly. "The label's fallen off!"

He took a step threateningly towards me.

"I'll scream!" I warned.

Hopton's lips curled. "Well stay there, waiting for your Constable." He pointed to the spires of St Sepulchre's. "I cannot tarry here to wait for that base-born rogue to tell me I've been speaking the truth."

And, swinging his cane, he sauntered off. I wasn't afraid. My stomach tingled and, beneath the serge dress I always wore, my legs trembled but that's because I was free. No Worshipful Guardian, no ladies of the parish telling me how fortunate I was, none of their children sweeping past me, noses in the air. I, Mary Frith, or Moll as I liked to be called, was, for a short while, truly alone in a strange place.

I stood, open-mouthed, drinking in the sights. A journeyman wandered by, a tray slung round his neck. He winked at me as he shouted, "Elixirs, cures, come buy my plague water!" He tried to stop a young fop swaggering along with his codpiece out like a standard before him. "Have some unicorn's horn, rampant as a boar it will make you! Or you, my lady." He tried to grasp the sleeve of a woman passing by, a hood across her hair, a mask over her face. "Frogs' legs!" he called. "Give it to your husband and you'll have no need for a lover!"

He went on by. A young boy ran up, a small cage in his hand. He held it up before me. I looked at the sorry little linnet perched on a rod and turned away. Parson Snodgrass never gave me any coins. I felt a hand on my shoulder: an old man, his blue eyes watery and bleary, his face flushed, his breath heavy with ale, looked down at me. He ran his wet tongue round his lips.

"A pert little piece," he lisped. "A tumble for a shilling?"

His hand came down to squeeze one of my breasts. I could not move, but suddenly the Constable's cane blurred past my eyes and struck the fellow harshly on the back of his hand. The old man yelped like a dog and leapt back. The Constable pushed him further away, prodding his chest with the pointed end of his staff.

"Be gone you toper and leave the child alone!"

The old man stumbled against a whore coming out of Cock Lane, the woman a veritable harridan, turned screeching like a cat. The Constable, his hand still on my shoulder, led me off.

"Where's Hopton?" he growled.

I caught my breath. The Constable squeezed my shoulder gently.

"Don't worry about the old poltroon," he declared. "There are some who think everything in the city is for sale and," he added cautiously, "they might be right."

"Hopton's gone to St Sepulchre's," I replied.

"He shouldn't have left you!" The Constable took me into the sweet-smelling darkness of a baker's shop and bought me a slab of gingerbread.

"Mistress Twitchett?" I asked between mouthfuls.

"He was where he said he was," the Constable replied. He took me round to the front of St Sepulchre's and, lifting his staff, pointed to the door. "That's where she'll go," he explained. "Poor Sarah, after she has been condemned, will be taken across there and made to sit on her coffin whilst a parson lectures her before she's put into the death cart and heigh-ho to Tyburn."

"Do you think she'll hang?"

"Aye. A man has been killed and she has the knife."

He led me across the busy thoroughfare, dodging between carts and pack horses, and pulled at the bell-rope of Newgate prison. A side door swung open and the Constable led me, like Virgil did Dante, into a veritable hell-hole. Passageways and corridors where the stone walls were moist and dripping green with mossy slime. Dark as night it was, except for the tallow candles, their flames low and sullen as if oppressed by the stinking, fetid air. The Constable grasped my hand as I stumbled across the sour rushes, trying not to start or scream as dark furry bodies came darting out of every crevice and corner, eyes bright as beams, the rats of Newgate were foraging for food.

We passed cells from which a raucous din emerged: screams, shouted obscenities, the chanting of the deranged and sometimes the sheer howling of the forgotten and the desolate. The turnkey went before us, head pushed back into his shoulders. He was like some gruesome waddling toad; now and again he'd bang at the iron-grilled doors with his keys. At last he stopped before one cell, inserted a key in the lock and ushered us into the stinking pit of Newgate's condemned cell, a narrow room about eight foot high and three foot across. Sarah sat on a pile of wet rushes in the corner manacled at the wrists and ankles by metal gyves. All her prettiness was gone. She seemed to have aged in a matter of hours: her cheeks were hollow, shadows ringed her eyes. She looked fearfully at the Constable and tried to smile at me. I pushed the remaining gingerbread into her mouth. She chewed it greedily.

"If I could have some water?" she muttered.

"I'll arrange for it as I leave," the Constable replied. "We have come to ask you some questions."

"What's the use?" the girl replied. "I'll hang." She blinked and stared around. "I've done nothing wrong," she muttered. She lurched forward but her chains dragged her back. "I'm a good girl, sir. I . . ." She leaned back against the wall, tears streaming down her face. "I didn't kill the old man," she sobbed. "Nor rob his silver."

"Tell me," the Constable said, "last night when you were with Sir Nicholas, did he have the money belt round his waist?"

Sarah closed her eyes. "Yes, yes, he did. I remember it because it hurt me."

"And did you copulate?" the Constable asked bluntly.

"Oh no," she replied. "Though Sir Nicholas could be vigorous."

"Could be?" the Constable asked.

"Oh yes, he stayed at the *Bishop's Mitre* twice a year on the same dates.' She forced a laugh. "It wasn't the first time I'd visited him in his room. Always the same pattern. He in his cups. His young nephew off to savour the pleasures of the town. I and Sir Nicholas would bounce on the bed." She shrugged in a rattle of chains. "But that night was different. He was tired so I left. He locked the door behind me and I went back to my own chamber, a small garret at the top of that tavern."

"And in the morning?" the Constable asked.

"I was up early, going about my business." She wiped her dirty face and stared hard at the Constable. "You know that." She whispered hoarsely. "You drink many a tankard there."

"The landlord and Simkin will miss you," I added slyly.

Sarah flounced her head. "No, they won't. They are glad I'm gone."

"Why?"

"I told them I was pregnant," Sarah replied. "But I am not. I hoped Simkin would marry me." She put her face in her hands and began to sob. "I wish I was," she blurted out. "I wish I was, then I wouldn't hang." She raised her dirty, tear-streaked face. "The parson," she whispered, "Vicar Snodgrass, ask him to come and see me. He knows I am a good girl."

I leaned over and patted her hands. "Of course I will."

We left shortly afterwards. The Constable stopped to order a pannikin of fresh water and some victuals for poor Sarah. Then he took me back to the *Bishop's Mitre*, chucking me under the chin and telling me to be a good girl.

I wandered into the taproom. It was deserted, the sour rushes had been cleaned, the floor swept and mopped, giving it a fresh soapy smell. Simkin came staggering in, a pail of water in each hand. I asked if Worshipful Guardian had returned but he morosely shook his head. I went out and sat in the garden. It was one of those beautiful, sun-filled English afternoons: the air was fragrant with a flowery perfume, bees buzzed lazily, hunting for nectar and crickets sang in the long grass. It reminded me of the graveyard at Parson Snodgrass's church. I'd always gone there to hide from him and his sharp-tongued wife. Lord save me, I have seen more christianity in a toad than in that puffed-up bag of wind. No wonder Worshipful Guardian liked to visit London to see the Dean of the Arches. I stared at the herbs. Parson Snodgrass loved herbs and was skilled in making poultices and potions. I sat, my back against a wall, half-dozing, dreaming about what had happened: Parson Snodgrass climbing the ladder; Sarah desperate in prison; the Constable tall and protective; the sheep having its throat cut in Smithfield Market; the blood bubbling out; old Hopton's face. How had he been murdered? How could anyone enter that room with the key still in the lock?

"Mary?"

I turned. Worshipful Guardian was standing in the doorway. He was dressed in his best gown and fine Spanish leather shoes with their high-wedged heels.

"Mary, are you well?"

"Yes, Worshipful Guardian," I replied.

He smiled benignly and went back in. I remembered the blood splashing from that sheep's throat – that's what was wrong! I felt a tingle of excitement in my belly. I waited a while, re-entered the tavern and crept up the stairs to old Hopton's room. The door was unlocked, I creaked it open. It smelt sour and fetid. The grisly corpse still lay in the bed under a dirty sheet. I stepped inside the door and examined the blood on the floor, recalling where Sir Nicholas had lain. With the toe of my shoe I brushed the rushes aside. I then studied the blood stain which had seeped under the door now dried to a rusty red. I stood thinking, my heart stopped hammering. I left the chamber and returned to Parson Snodgrass: the room was empty so I grasped his boots and felt very carefully inside. My hand touched the sticky wetness, I could have screamed with relief. I was washing my hands in the bowl, watching the water turn a dullish red when I heard the footfall behind me.

"Why, child, what are you doing?"

Worshipful Guardian stood in the doorway.

"I know who murdered Sir Nicholas," I smiled, folding the napkin carefully, hoping he wouldn't notice it.

Parson Snodgrass walked towards me. I backed away so he sat on the bed, his face framed by lank, grey hair. He was all sanctimonious and serene with that benign smile which never reached those watchful, dark eyes. He sat, hands clasped in his lap, legs crossed at the ankles like some Brownist ready to declaim the Lord's praises.

"Young Sarah killed Sir Nicholas," he explained, slowly as if I was devoid of wit and understanding.

"Worshipful Guardian," I replied. "How could she? How could a young girl murder a man like Sir Nicholas and meet no resistance? She tumbled with him on the bed so where could she hide the knife she'd brought to kill him? And, if she cut his throat, why did he so obligingly get up to lock and bolt the door behind her?"

"What are you saying, dearest child?"

"You come to London quite often," I replied. "You stay here at the *Bishop's Mitre*. Young Hopton recalled you but couldn't place the time and whereabouts. You knew about Sir Nicholas and his heavy belt of gold. You knew his routine, his love of the deep-bowled cup and those lusts of the flesh which you always lecture us about every Sunday."

The smile faded from Parson Snodgrass's lips.

"You planned his murder," I continued defiantly. "You brought me here to be your catspaw. Who would ever suspect the saintly Snodgrass? The pious parson who, from the kindness of his heart, had taken a young girl into his care?"

"But you were there!" Worshipful Guardian exclaimed, head on one side as if I were the dimmest child in his Sunday School class. "You saw the blood seeping from under the doorway. You saw the key in the lock and how I climbed up and prised open the shutter. Are you a Bess of Bedlam, Moll? Has the visit to Newgate numbed your wits?"

"Last night we stayed in the taproom," I replied. "You and I helped Sir Nicholas up to bed during which you slipped some powder or potions into his bowl of claret. What was it, Worshipful Guardian? Some henbane, some hemlock or a little nightshade? Sir Nicholas becomes weak. Little Sarah trots along but she is then dismissed. Sir Nicholas locks the door behind her and, shortly afterwards, falls into a deep swoon and so into death."

"And?" Parson Snodgrass eased himself back on the bed.

I could tell from the paleness of his face and the sneer round those thin, prim lips that I'd hit my mark.

"Early this morning," I continued, "you brought up a small pouch of blood, bought in the market outside, and pushed it under the door. Once it was in place, you pierced it with a pin and the blood seeped out. You then hurried along up to little Sarah's garret: the fleshing knife, which you'd filched from the tavern and smeared with cattle blood the previous day, you hid in her closet. And the stage was set."

"For what?"

"Master Charles coming back and glimpsing the blood trickling underneath his Uncle's door. He raised the alarm, you made sure that we are in the taproom ready to intervene. I thought it was strange that you put your riding boots on. Why should a parson dressed in his best, ready to go down to St Paul's, put on his riding boots? Unless, of course, you were preparing to climb a ladder? Everyone would accept that: a man of God is 'used to climbing the ladders in his church steeple'," I smiled. "You'd prepared well: you knew how thick and heavy the doors of this tavern are. The only way to break into a chamber is through an outside window. And you were ready to do that. The landlord gives you a chisel and up you go. You force both the shutter and the window and climb in. Sir Nicholas is sprawled on the floor. You do three things whilst the rest of us are waiting. You slit Sir Nicholas's throat with the knife concealed in your boot. You take off the money belt and slip it round your waist and you pick up the remains of the small pouch of blood and push it into the stinking close stool where no one will think of looking. The poisoned wine you drain into the rushes. You clean your hands from the water jug, draw back the bolts, then unlock the door. Who would suspect? Everyone thought Sir Nicholas had his throat cut before you ever climbed that ladder. And, of course, because your potion had done its deadly work, his body is cold."

"But, dearest child, how could I possibly do all this, you were all outside?"

"You were prepared," I answered. "The knife in your boot, you climb into the room, Hopton's throat is slashed, the knife slipped back, the tattered, bloody pouch thrown into the close-stool, the cup drained, fingers washed, the water splashed on to the rushes, who'd notice? And, finally, Hopton's money pouch wrapped round your waist, carefully hidden beneath your jerkin and priestly gown."

"But it would take so long!"

"Nonsense!" I scoffed. "Worshipful Guardian, if I counted slowly to sixty, you could do all that I've described. Remember, how we waited for a while in the yard below before you came back to the window? How we had to come round and climb the stairs and then wait again? Oh, you had time enough!"

"And what further proof do you have, dear child?" Parson Snodgrass's lips were curled like a mastiff ready to attack.

"Oh, I went back to Sir Nicholas's room. I noticed how the blood from the old man's throat had trickled through the rushes on to the floor, but there's a gap, at least five to six inches, between that blood and the stain which seeped under the door. Now, why should that be, eh? Secondly, I was puzzled by you wearing your boots so I came up here and felt inside. There's a bloodstain still there where you hid the knife." I gazed round the chamber. "Somewhere here is Sir Nicholas's money belt, not to mention the stockings you later changed, before you left to meet the Dean of the Arches."

"Sharp, dear child!"

"Thank you, Worshipful Guardian."

"You have been thinking deeply, my child."

"As did you, Worshipful Guardian. Sir Nicholas was a creature of habit, mean, miserly and a toper. You studied him closely: how he drank deeply and entertained his doxy for a while. He'd always keep his window shut and, to keep his money belt safe, he made sure the visiting trollop did not stay the night. The potion you gave him would take hours to work: Sir Nicholas, however, could get little help from his dear nephew, who'd be off to Cock Lane as fast as a whippet after a bone."

"I was risking a great deal!" he snarled.

"No, Worshipful Guardian, you were not: the doors in this tavern are of solid oak and cannot be forced. All you had to risk was being the one to climb that ladder. Even if that opportunity slipped, you were stil protected. Who'd suspect? Once you were in the room, you were alone, to do what you wanted. And in the hubbub afterwards, who'd suspect you?"

Parson Snodgrass rose to his feet.

"If you come any closer," I whispered, smiling beatifically, "I shall scream." I picked up the bowl of water from the lavarium. "And throw this with such force through the window that everyone in Smithfield will know something is wrong."

Parson Snodgrass sat down. "So, what do you want, dear child?"

I stared at him even as my mind raced. I remembered the freedom I had enjoyed earlier in the day, the Constable's warm hand, the delightful sights and smells of the city compared to my grim days at the Parsonage.

"Some of the gold," I lisped.

"And?"

I pointed to the door. "I shall walk out of here and you'll never see me again."

"Stay in London all by yourself? That's dangerous!"

"Not as perilous," I replied, "as staying with a Parson who commits murder and robbery and who plans, in the near future, to leave his boring little parish and his sharp-tongued wife for pastures new."

Parson Snodgrass rose to his feet. "Those who ask shall receive," he intoned piously and, shifting the bed, he lifted a loose floor board and drew out Sir Nicholas's money belt, its fat purses bulging along the edge. "How much?" he asked.

"Three of the purses," I replied. "Place the money on the table," I demanded. "And, remember, I can still scream."

Parson Snodgrass obeyed. I made him go back and sit on the bed whilst I placed the coins in a napkin and tied my little bundle up. I glanced at Worshipful Guardian's face and saw the hatred blazing in his eyes.

"And what about poor Sarah?"

"Oh, she can hang!" I replied flippantly. "Now, Worshipful Guardian, please lie down on the bed."

Still clutching the money belt, he obeyed. I raced like a greyhound for the door. I took the key from the lock, slammed the door shut, locked it, ignoring Worshipful Guardian's cries, I skipped downstairs, the bundle in my hand, eager to get into the market place and seek the Constable's help.

CASSANDRA'S CASTLE; or, The Devious Disappearances
J. F. Peirce

Elizabethan and Stuart England is a ripe setting for stories of international intrigue and mystery. Back in 1964, J. F. Peirce wrote a satire on Shakespearean scholarship called "The Great Shakespeare Mystery" (Ellery Queen's Mystery Magazine, May 1964), *which revealed his extensive knowledge of the Great Bard, so it is not too surprising that a few years later he returned to Shakespeare as the central character in a series of detective stories. The series began with* "The Double Death of Nell Quigley" *(EQMM, December 1973), and he wrote four others of which* "Cassandra's Castle" *(EQMM, May 1975) was the last. Peirce (b. 1918) is emeritus professor of English at Texas A&M University where he taught for over thirty-seven years.*

"The reason I summoned you," Lord Burleigh said, addressing the young actor-playwright, Will Shakespeare, "is far different from the last, when I sought your assistance with respect to the increasing number of rogues and vagabonds in the city. This time the matter is of little consequence. It has to do with a scandal at Court – a conundrum that plagues our curiosity."

He paused and gestured to the three men seated with them in a conversational circle – William Davison, Queen Elizabeth's Scottish secretary; Sir Francis Walsingham, Her Majesty's Secretary of State; and Henry Herbert, the Earl of Pembroke and President of Wales.

"Frankly," the Lord High Treasurer continued, "I have bet these gentlemen a considerable sum that you can undo the tangled skeins of events that comprise this puzzle. If you do, half my winnings will be yours. But win or lose, I will pay all expenses."

"His Lordship has bragged mightily on you," Walsingham said. "We've been anxious to make your acquaintance."

Both Davison and the Earl nodded.

"First, let me give you the facts as we know them," Lord Burleigh said, pulling at his beard. "No doubt you've heard of the Countess of Chommondley, who is famous for her height, which is o'er six feet, and for her constant companion, an ugly little man, no larger than a child, who's called The Monkey."

Shakespeare nodded.

"He was a magician when they first met. In fact, he still entertains at the Countess's parties. Women are attracted rather than repulsed by his appearance – perhaps because he makes the ugliest of women *seem* attractive by comparison."

"Not that the Countess has any need for such comparison," the Earl said. "She's a damned attractive woman with a willowy figure." He coughed, then added, "That is, those who've seen her in *other* than a farthingale report so."

Lord Burleigh smiled and curled the ends of his moustache with the backs of his index fingers. "It's the curse of our age that women conceal their nether halves in such floor-length garments."

"I confess I agree, Your Lordship," Shakespeare said.

"Though The Monkey's had numerous chances to betray the Countess with younger, more attractive women," Burleigh continued, "he remained faithful to her till recently. Then a few months ago he met the courtesan, Cassandra – "

"The one they call The Giantess, Your Lordship?"

Burleigh nodded. "She's o'er six and a half feet tall, and by piling her hair high and wearing those damnable Italian *chopines*, she adds another half-foot or so to her height. You do know what *chopines* are?"

"Aye. Shoes with thick, cork platform-soles," the playwright said. "Boy actors who play women's parts wear them to increase their stature." He paused, then asked, "How came The Monkey to meet Cassandra, Your Lordship? I thought she ran a brothel in Southwark?"

"She does," Burleigh said, "and a most successful one." He frowned, then went on: "The Court attracts all kinds. Some, bored with their lives and their own kind, surround themselves with such courtesans and criminals to add zest to their existence. One such fool introduced Cassandra to the Court. And as she towers o'er the Countess and is statuesque, whereas the Countess is slender, The Monkey fell madly in love with her – and she with him. Since then he's spent most of his time with her to the dismay and displeasure of the Countess."

"Why does he not leave the Countess altogether, Your Lordship?"

"Because she's a woman of great wealth and his tastes are many and expensive."

"I should think that Mistress Cassandra would be equally wealthy, running as she does such a notorious brothel."

"Nay. Her wealth is as poverty compared with that of the Countess."

"Have you seen her brothel? – Cassandra's Castle, as 'tis called," Walsingham asked.

"Only from a distance, Sir Francis."

"Let me describe it for you, then. In effect it's an island, as 'tis surrounded by a moat. And it can be entered from but one side – by a drawbridge, which is guarded by a pander dressed in full armour and carrying a halberd. And its three-storey house has a studded door containing an espial wicket."

He paused, then continued. "I don't know about Lord Burleigh, but the rest of us have all been there for one reason or t'other. It's the fashionable place to go – to see and be seen. The island has a large formal garden for amorous strolling and an arbour for *al fresco* entertainment. One can obtain the finest of food and drink there, be entertained with music and the reading of plays and poetry, and see elaborate displays of fireworks at night."

"Fortunately it's located outside the city," Davison interjected. "Otherwise, our Puritan friend, the Lord Mayor, would have ordered it closed."

Lord Burleigh coughed, and Walsingham and Davison allowed the Lord High Treasurer to pursue his tale.

"As time passed," Burleigh said, "the Countess became increasingly distraught. And each time The Monkey went out, she set lackeys to following him. Last week, after a rather disagreeable argument between them, she decided to bring the matter to a head. She had twenty of her lackeys in disguise follow him. At first, he appeared unaware that he was being followed, for he made straight for Southwark.

"But once he had crossed London Bridge, he evidently realized that men were dogging his heels, for he tried to elude them – but without success. When he entered the castle, the men surrounded it as if laying siege. And a short time later the Countess arrived at the gallop in her carriage, like a general about to direct the course of battle."

Lord Burleigh paused and pushed up the ends of his moustache with the backs of his index fingers. "Seeing the Countess," he went

on, "the guard notified Cassandra, who set about entertaining her
'guests' royally to take their minds off the fact that they were, in
a sense, imprisoned. Food and wine were brought from the cellars.
Strolling musicians played for their entertainment. There was much
merriment and carousal. But amidst all this activity, no one caught
even the briefest glimpse of The Monkey.

"The Countess, for her part, made arrangements for a house to
be available to her nearby. She sent for food and water and more
lackeys. And when they arrived, she stationed them about the moat
with the others to watch the castle. At most no two of them were
more than six yards apart.

"Darkness approached. The Countess ordered torches, and each
sentry was given enough to last out the night. On the island, lanterns
and flambeaux were lighted. There was dancing, and there were water
displays and fireworks. Rockets spangled the night with coloured
stars. A fire-drake winged its way across the sky. Reflected light
danced upon the water."

The Lord High Treasurer paused again. "The revelry lasted
throughout the night, and the Countess and her men maintained their
ceaseless vigil. Then, with the first light of dawn, the drawbridge was
lowered, and Cassandra in a red velvet farthingale swept majestically
across it, like Drake's *Golden Hinde* under full sail swept before the
wind. She was closely followed by her guard, walking stiff-legged in
full armour.

"'What do you want?' Cassandra demanded rudely when she at
last stood before the Countess.

"'My Monkey! My precious Monkey!' the haggard Countess
replied.

"'Go home!' Cassandra commanded. 'You'll find him there.'

"'You lie, for he lies with you in the castle!'

"'Nay. I swear he's not under my roof, though he's under my
protection. Go home! You'll find him there. He's at home where he
is.'

"'Let me enter the castle and see for myself!' the Countess
demanded.

"'Very well,' the courtesan replied and gestured towards the open
doorway.

"Leaving half her men still surrounding the island, the Countess
led the others across the drawbridge. They searched the house from
cellar to rooftop and the garden and the arbour as well. But The
Monkey had disappeared as the night with the coming day.

"At last convinced that he was not there, the Countess retreated
in defeat across the bridge without looking at or speaking to the

courtesan, who had remained with her guard on shore. Leaving some of her men still to watch the castle, the Countess returned home to discover The Monkey asleep in his room, a smile of satisfaction o'erspreading his features.

"At the sight of him, the Countess broke down and wept. And when her weeping awakened him, she begged his forgiveness, and while the rogue had her thus at his mercy, he made her agree to a villainous bargain – to allow him to divide his time between herself and Cassandra."

"Now our question is," the Earl said, leaning forwards, "how did The Monkey escape from the island?"

Shakespeare frowned. "Is there no chance that he escaped before the guards were posted, My Lord?"

"None. The men saw him enter the castle, and they had the island surrounded before he could escape."

"Did anyone leave the castle *after* he entered, My Lord?"

"No one. A short time after The Monkey entered, a boy entered with a sack o'er his shoulder, crossed the bridge *to* the castle, and once he was across, the drawbridge was raised."

Shakespeare frowned. "What would a boy be doing on the island, My Lord?"

"There are two boys who work there. They care for the garden, run errands for the girls, and do such-like."

"I see. Could any of the lackeys have been bribed to look elsewhere, My Lord, while The Monkey escaped?"

"I doubt it. Too many others would have seen him."

Shakespeare bent his brow in concentration, and the others waited in silence for him to speak.

"There are three ways of escape from the island," Shakespeare said at last. "By air, o'er the water, and across the bridge. Four if, by chance, there's a tunnel under the moat."

Lord Burleigh shook his head. "We've anticipated you on that score," he said. "The man who built the castle still lives, and he assures us there is no tunnel."

Shakespeare slitted his hooded eyelids and ran his thin fingers through his swept-back auburn hair. "I assume we can rule out that he flew through the air like the fire-drake. Can he swim? Perhaps he swam the moat and escaped when one of the lackeys had his attention momentarily distracted."

"He's an excellent swimmer," Burleigh said. "He's strong and wiry and has defeated much larger men in hand-to-hand combat who have made slighting remarks about his appearance and size. But the moat is guarded by two crocodiles, ten feet in length or longer. They're rumoured to be well fed, but I doubt he would care to test that rumour."

"Surely they aren't in the moat constantly, My Lord."

"No. There *are* ramps that they can climb and walkways on both sides of the moat for them to crawl about on and sun themselves. The walkways are guarded by spiked-iron fences, high enough so that the crocs cannot escape into the street or the garden. On occasion the beasts are pinned down with forked sticks and chained to one of the fences so that the girls and their guests can swim in the moat. But they weren't chained that night. Several of the guards reported seeing them floating in the water."

"Then he must have escaped across the drawbridge, Your Lordship."

"But how? It was kept raised till morning." He pulled at his beard thoughtfully. "Well, do you think you can solve this puzzle?"

"I can try, Your Lordship. How long do I have?"

"A week," Burleigh said, glancing at the others, who nodded.

"Could Cassandra be persuaded to let me put on a performance duplicating The Monkey's escape?" Shakespeare asked.

Lord Burleigh turned to the Earl.

"I think it can be arranged," the Earl said. "My secretary, Peregrine, is a frequent visitor to the castle. Cassandra's quite fond of him."

After learning the whereabouts of the Earl's secretary, Shakespeare rose and said, "Then I'll meet Your Lordship and these gentlemen at the castle at this time next week." And bowing, he departed.

The next morning, accompanied by Dick Burbage, the talented actor-artist, and Peregrine, the Earl's hawk-like secretary, Shakespeare went to Cassandra's Castle. The island was as it had been described. Two crocodiles floated lazily in the water. One opened its great mouth, revealing its sharp white teeth, and the playwright shuddered.

Overhead, a thin wire stretched from a triple window on the third floor of the castle to a double window on the second floor of a building on shore. The wire canted downwards at a 15-degree angle. It was obviously not strong enough, Shakespeare observed, to support the weight of a boy, not even of a small one.

A fire-drake, or fiery dragon, rode above the wire. The winged dragon, as the playwright knew from having helped make one as a boy, was constructed of thin strips of wood, bent and tied to form the shape of the dragon. This framework had been covered with paper scales and the scales had been painted.

Metal canisters containing a slow-burning gunpowder were located in the dragon's mouth and tail, so that when they were lighted, the dragon would appear to belch fire. A larger canister of gunpowder hung below the wire, counterbalancing the dragon and supplying its motive power. Neither the dragon nor the canister, Shakespeare noted, was large enough to conceal The Monkey, thus eliminating the dragon as a means of escape.

The pander on guard was dressed in armour made of thick, heavy leather, and as they approached, he raised his visor and smiled. Peregrine spoke to him familiarly, and they were permitted to cross the bridge and enter the brothel. Inside they were greeted by Cassandra, who towered over them. Shakespeare was both attracted to and repulsed by her.

After gaining her permission, Peregrine conducted the actor and the playwright on a tour of the castle. In Cassandra's quarters, while searching her wardrobe for a possible hidden passage, Shakespeare discovered two of The Monkey's suits, both bright orange, concealed amongst the courtesan's clothing, and he could not help smiling at the disparity in their sizes.

Later in the garden, Peregrine introduced Shakespeare and Burbage to Cassandra's girls. The courtesans were of different colours, shapes, and sizes, and Shakespeare was amazed at the variety.

Once the tour was completed, the playwright instructed his companions as to what he expected of each of them.

"That's too much to accomplish in but a week!" Burbage protested. "I doubt it's possible."

"Get Cuthbert and others to help you. Money's no problem — you'll be well rewarded."

"If you insist," the actor grumbled. "I'll try."

"Good lad! I know you can do it," the playwright said.

Burbage and Peregrine left the castle shortly thereafter, but Shakespeare remained a while longer to get the feel of the island and observe its life.

Later that morning Shakespeare appeared at the manor house of the Countess of Chommondley. A few pieces of silver to the cook gave him entrance to the kitchen and the answers to a number of questions. A few pieces more enabled him to search The Monkey's bedroom and wardrobe. At the sight of so many pastel-coloured suits, the playwright gave an involuntary whistle. He whistled again when The Monkey's manservant pointed out the suit The Monkey had worn the day he disappeared. The suit was bright orange and of a distinctive design.

After obtaining the name of The Monkey's tailor, Shakespeare sought out one of the lackeys the Countess had had follow the little man that day. And for a few pieces of silver, the lackey led the playwright along the path The Monkey had taken.

He had made straight for Southwark; then, realizing that he was being followed, he had taken a twisting-turning route down alleys and sidestreets. But the last hundred yards were in the open. It would have been impossible in daylight for his pursuers to have mistaken or overlooked either the colour of his costume or its distinctive design.

Later that day at The Monkey's tailor, Shakespeare was not surprised to learn that The Monkey was in the habit of ordering several suits at a time. And as the tailor kept patterns for all of them, he readily agreed to make six copies of The Monkey's bright orange suit and at once set his apprentices to work on them.

The following week, as stipulated, Shakespeare met Lord Burleigh and the others at the drawbridge of Cassandra's Castle. Accompanying the playwright were four boy actors whom Peregrine had recruited for him from the Children of The Royal Chapel at Blackfriars. Each of the boys wore a floppy orange hat, a bright orange suit, and a monkey's tail and mask that Dick Burbage had made. The youngsters were capricious and unruly, and Shakespeare had to reprimand them often.

The group was joined moments later by the actor, Will Kemp, who approached them from across the bridge. He was wearing Cassandra's red velvet farthingale, and its skirt had been hastily pinned up to keep it from dragging on the ground. For though Kemp was a big man, he was half-a-foot shorter than the giant courtesan.

The four "monkeys" scampered about him, leaping and jumping. They moved hunched over, their knuckles touching the ground, and they chattered: "Chi! Chi! Chi!" in their high-pitched voices till Shakespeare silenced them.

Once all was ready, Shakespeare sent Kemp back across the bridge to the island and then had one of the boys remove his mask and tail, so that he could be readily identified. The boy had a large strawberry birthmark on his right cheek, and Shakespeare had Burleigh and the others inspect it, so that they would know that it was real and not make-up.

Then with Burleigh, Davison, Walsingham, the four monkeys, and forty lackeys following him, Shakespeare led the way to the spot where The Monkey had realized that he was being followed. At this point, Shakespeare sent the boy with the strawberry birthmark on ahead to play The Monkey's part, and the boy set off along the path The

Monkey had taken, followed closely by the rest. He was out of sight for brief moments when he turned corners suddenly, but at last he was in the open with no place to hide, and he made his way quickly across the drawbridge and into the castle.

Shakespeare then asked Walsingham to play the part of the Countess, and Walsingham gave the lackeys careful instructions, stationing them around the moat.

Shortly thereafter, a boy carrying a sack over his shoulder crossed the drawbridge and entered the castle. Shakespeare, followed by the three remaining monkeys, crossed the bridge also, and the bridge was at once raised.

Immediately a party began in the garden. But though Kemp, dressed as Cassandra, and Shakespeare were much in evidence, nothing was seen of the four orange-suited boy actors or the boy with the sack. Shakespeare appeared briefly at the third-floor window to check the fire-drake for the evening's performance, and later he was seen in the garden, drinking and flirting with some of the girls. Later still he was noticed walking about the edge of the moat, as if checking on the positions of the crocodiles.

The day wore on. Afternoon became evening. The watchers grew impatient. Burleigh sent for food and drink and a supply of torches. Though the liquid refreshments were plentiful and varied, the men did not drink heavily, wishing to keep their heads clear and their eyesight sharp.

Night fell. Rockets sent rainbows arching across the sky or burst in showers of falling stars. The fiery dragon winged its way over the moat in search of St George or a beautiful damsel. A water fountain became a liquid vase of fluid flowers. Those on the island caroused into the night, their revelry continuing till sunrise.

Then the drawbridge was lowered, and Kemp, dressed as Cassandra, clomped across the bridge, followed by the playwright and the stiff-legged guard in full armour. Kemp stumbled once and almost fell when he tripped on the hem of the farthingale, but Shakespeare fortunately caught him.

The big actor seemed to have grown in his part, for when he and Walsingham repeated the angry exchange between the Countess and Cassandra, his gestures were properly mincing and his voice convincingly falsetto.

Once the exchange between them was completed, Walsingham called twenty of his men to follow him and led them across the bridge. As before, the castle was searched from cellar to rooftop, and the garden and the arbour as well, but none of the four boy actors was found. And the boy who had carried the sack across the bridge was also missing. At last admitting defeat, Walsingham gathered together his men and returned to the shore.

"Well, are you satisfied, gentlemen?" Burleigh asked.

"Damn me, no!" the Earl exclaimed. "And I'll not be till I receive an explanation of their disappearance." He turned to the playwright. "My compliments, young man. I'm sure we all agree that his Lordship has most definitely understated your talents."

"I confess that I, too, am anxiously awaiting your explanation," Burleigh added.

"Instead, allow me to give you a demonstration if you will," Shakespeare said. He whistled and the four boy actors minus the floppy orange hats they had worn and the boy with the sack appeared out of a house nearby, and followed by Kemp and the visored guard, they scampered across the drawbridge, which was once again raised.

"You'll recall," Shakespeare said, "that I explained that there were three ways to escape from the island – by air, by water, and across the bridge. Four if there was a tunnel, which was eliminated on the builder's evidence and my own examination of the castle and island. Now let me demonstrate, first, how The Monkey *could* have escaped by air."

The playwright pointed to the third-floor window of the castle where one of the boys was attaching a fire-drake to the wire stretching from the island to the shore.

"Now," Shakespeare said, "see what happened under cover of darkness, while your attention was centred on the lewd carousal taking place in the garden before the fireworks began."

The playwright whistled, and the boy was joined at the window by Peregrine and Dick Burbage, who removed the fire-drake and began pulling on the wire, which was loosened by Cuthbert Burbage, who stood in the second-floor window of the house on shore.

To the end of the wire, as it issued from the house window, Cuthbert attached two ropes – one heavy, the other light. And once the heavy rope was secured inside the castle, Peregrine started pulling on the lighter rope, drawing a larger, sturdier fire-drake out of the window of the house on shore. When it reached the castle, its hinged top was thrown open, and the boy entered. The gunpowder was lighted, and the dragon flew down the rope and was caught by Cuthbert Burbage, who helped the boy out of its bowels.

"Marvellous!" Lord Burleigh exclaimed.

"It's like a *deus ex machina*, a machine in which the gods come down to earth to settle the affairs of mortals, as used in the masques at Court," Davison said.

Shakespeare nodded. "Now imagine that the aerial fireworks cease. The watchers' eyes are drawn by a sudden burst of activity to the people in the garden. But keep *your* eyes on the castle window and see what *could* have happened under the cover of night."

Shakespeare whistled. A second boy climbed out the window. Grasping the thick rope, he swung hand-over-hand down it, to disappear into the house on shore as the watchers applauded.

Immediately the rope was pulled back into the window, and the wire installed in its place.

"Now consider the possibility of escape by water. Pray look at the crocodile in the water," Shakespeare said. "Remember that it is night with only flick'ring torches to light it and shimm'ring reflections to confuse the eye."

The playwright whistled, and on cue the crocodile swam across the moat and crawled up the ramp to the walkway along the shore.

"Keep *your* eyes on the crocodile," Shakespeare said, "but imagine, if you will, a tremendous burst of rockets that would draw the eye of e'en the most dedicated watcher skyward."

Again the playwright whistled, and the crocodile reared upwards, revealing a shell-like framework that had concealed a third boy dressed in dark clothing, his face and hands blackened with burnt cork. Quickly the boy slid the crocodile shell into the water, then slipped over the fence and, keeping low, ran towards the house on shore.

"Where did he come from?" Burleigh demanded.

"He donned the shell and slid quietly into the water while you were engrossed in watching the fire-drake wing its way across the sky. Like the fire-drake, Your Lordship, the crocodile was designed by Dick Burbage and built under his direction. The real crocodiles are chained at the back of the garden."

Again he whistled. "It's daybreak," he said.

As he spoke, the drawbridge was lowered, and Kemp, followed by the stiff-legged guard, strode across it towards them. Reaching the shore, Kemp acted overly coquettish till Shakespeare frowned, causing him to assume a more decorous demeanour.

"Now let us examine the possibility of escape across the draw-bridge," Shakespeare said. "Imagine, if you will, the dialogue behind Cassandra and the Countess. Visualize her men moving across the bridge towards the castle. *Look!* Look at the open doorway!"

Though Burleigh and the others looked as directed, nothing happened – no one appeared. Then, turning back to the playwright, they gasped. For a fourth boy stood by his side.

"God's blood!" Burleigh exclaimed. "How did you perform *this* miracle?"

Stepping over to Kemp, Shakespeare lifted the skirt of his red velvet farthingale, revealing the *chopines* that added half-a-foot to his height. And at a nod, the boy actor slipped between Kemp's legs, and Shakespeare dropped the skirt as he would a curtain.

"So *this* is how The Monkey escaped the island!" Burleigh exclaimed. "Apollo gave the Trojan Cassandra the gift of prophecy, then placed a curse upon her when she would not lie with him, so that none would believe her. Like her namesake, Mistress Cassandra spoke the truth *and* the Countess did not believe her. 'He's not under my roof,' she said, 'though he's under my protection . . . He's at home where he is.' He *was* under her 'protection' – for he was under her dress which protected them both. And surely he *was* 'at home' between her legs."

"God's wound!" Walsingham exclaimed. "What a delightful way to disappear!"

"But *where* is the fifth boy?" Davison demanded.

Shakespeare turned to the guard, who lifted his visor, revealing himself to be the fifth boy.

"He's wearing short stilts 'neath his armour," Shakespeare said. "And his gauntlets are designed with false hands to make his arms appear longer."

"But where is the orange suit of the boy in black face?" Pembroke asked. "They all appeared white and were dressed alike when they returned to the island after their escape."

Shakespeare pointed to a sack beside him. "The boy who escaped betwixt Kemp's legs carried the orange suit," he said.

Burleigh frowned. "But by which of these means *did* The Monkey escape?" he demanded.

Shakespeare smiled and said, "By none of them, Your Lordship." He whistled, and the boy with the strawberry birthmark came out of the castle. "I sent him across the bridge to the castle with the others since, as you recall, the lad dressed as the guard did not remove his disguise during the first escape."

The viewers appeared dumbstruck.

"Your Lordship was right," Shakespeare continued, "in saying that, like her namesake, Cassandra spoke the literal truth. But you were mistaken in your interpretation. The Monkey *was* at home – at the Countess's manor. He both supped and slept there whilst the Countess spent a drear day and a sleepless night watching the castle."

"God's blood!" Burleigh said. "Keep us not in suspense! How did he manage it? How do you know?"

"I *know*," Shakespeare said, "because I questioned the Countess's cook and The Monkey's manservant – something no one else bothered to do. They told me that The Monkey provoked a quarrel with the Countess on the morning he 'disappeared,' that he goaded her into sending men to follow him by saying that if she caught him on the island, he would give up Cassandra, but that if she tried and failed, he'd give up *her*."

"Monstrous!" Burleigh said.

"Earlier I'd discovered two orange suits belonging to The Monkey hidden amongst Cassandra's clothing. Later I discovered a third orange suit in The Monkey's wardrobe. This, plus the fact that on his way to the castle he'd have been out of the view of his pursuers each time he turned a corner and could have escaped at these times, yet apparently he made no effort to – which aroused my suspicions."

Burleigh nodded.

"Then I remembered the lad with the sack o'er his shoulder and the strange fact that once he crossed o'er the bridge, it was raised as if on cue. 'What,' I asked myself, 'if The Monkey had hired the two boys who work at the castle to hide in doorways along his route dressed in identical floppy hats and suits of orange clothing – could he not have slipped into a doorway on turning a corner where one of the lads was hidden, and that lad then took The Monkey's place in the chase?"

"But why *two* boys?" Pembroke asked.

"To make doubly sure of his escape, My Lord, because of the high stakes for which he was playing. If his pursuers were following too close when he reached the first lad's hiding place, he could increase his lead and change places with the second. Then, whichever lad was passed by could remove his orange suit, having his own clothes under it, put the suit in the sack, the sack o'er his shoulder, and return to the castle."

"But why would The Monkey concoct such a scheme?" Davison asked.

"To trick the Countess into agreeing to his dividing his time betwixt herself and Cassandra. In that way he would have the best of both of his worlds – love *and* money!"

Burleigh frowned. "What I cannot understand," he said, "is *why*, knowing The Monkey did not escape from the island, you still put on such an elaborate performance?"

"For two reasons, Your Lordship. For one, since you had such a sizeable bet with these gentlemen, I wished to give them the most for their money."

"And the other?"

"To be perfectly honest, Your Lordship, I wished to determine how *I* would have escaped had *I* been trapped on the island."

Walsingham laughed. "And which method would you have used?" he asked.

"Can there be any doubt in your mind as to that, Sir Francis?" the playwright countered.

Lord Burleigh smiled, and the others applauded.

MAN'S INHERITED DEATH
Keith Heller

One of the earliest letters of comment I received on The Mammoth
Book of Historical Whodunnits *was from Martin Edwards, who
drew my attention to the works of Keith Heller. One of the real pleasures
of producing books and hearing from readers is in making such new
discoveries. Heller (b. 1949) has written a series of novels about George
Man, a London parish watchman. The first book,* Man's Illegal Life
*(1984), was set in the year 1722, and brings London life at that time
vividly into focus. It also portrays Man, who was then aged 45, as
an honest, shrewd, conscientious and extremely painstaking watchman.
Two other novels appeared.* Man's Storm *(1985) is set in 1703, and*
Man's Loving Family *(1986) in 1727. I was delighted to discover
there had been two short stories featuring Man, and the first of them is
reprinted here.*

*Heller has also written two stories under the alias Allan Lloyd which
feature the Chinese magistrate Ti Jen-Chieh on whom Robert van Gulik
based Judge Dee, and more recently he has created a new series of
detective stories around that eighteenth-century painter and visionary,
William Blake.*

I n the deeper half of January, 1729, in the short darkness of York
Street, one of the dingiest Covent Garden tributaries London had
to offer, George Man – fifty, hoarse, and wearied, a professional
watchman for most of his adult life – stood stiff and winded, with
his staff and lanthorn in his hands, and decided it was time for him
to quit.

He should not have come out at all tonight, should have stayed
snug and drinking in the watch-house with the other men. No one
needed him tonight, no one else had been foolish enough to brave
tonight's weather, not even the usual hard and screaming revelers
who nightly circulated about Covent Garden like clods in sludge. It

was two o'clock – he had just called it out to the deaf and inanimate street – and he had met no more than a handful of people all night. Like him, they had been too busy struggling for breath to bother thinking of trouble, too intent upon finding or reaching some door that they could close against the cold. And once inside, they probably wanted nothing more than to fall into the kind of wrapping sleep a January snowstorm can give.

Man was jealous of them, of their secured windows and their mounded, heating blankets. He had fought long enough tonight against the crazing wind and cutting snow. He had kneed his way through enough cold and solid drifts for one night, grappled with plenty of dizzying gusts; and now his boots were cracking, his nose was pinched, and his eyelids were shriveled almost shut. He must be a fool. Nothing could be happening tonight.

It was a wonder that he heard the window opening at all, what with the storm and his wet ears. A crashing somewhere in the darkness above him sounded across his shoulders and a sharp voice came down to him, brittle and shrunken with the wind.

"Here, man! Help me! Here!"

The watchman hoisted his lanthorn higher and saw only whipped snow. "The watch, the watch is here! Name yourself!" Man thought his voice was too weak to rise, the wind was taking it too far away.

"Wait," the man called. "I see your light. I'll be down, sir. To the door, the door of the shop."

Reaching forward with his light, Man saw the barred door of a shuttered house. The beaten signboard above it could be barely read: *Edmund Cowley, Jeweller*. An etched depiction of a lion holding a huge ring in his mouth, a rough border of loose stones. The sign hung dangerously from a bending rod.

A bank of swept snow drifted up toward the door. Man saw a single, vague set of bootprints, now all but filled, there was heard an inward noise of bolts and latches, and then another lanthorn mirroring his own. A shaking hand reached out.

"Will you come up, sir?" Man heard a normally strong voice quaver. "It's my father. Upstairs. He is dead, I think."

The watchman was led through an unaired shop toward an invisible flight of back stairs. He had doused his own candle and now followed the host light through a succession of skimming visions – murky shelves and cabinets, a forbidding counter crowned with more than one pair of scales, low doors suggesting rarely unlocked storerooms – all the trademarks of the shrewd and careful jeweller. It was the kind of shop that, in a newer house and in a higher neighborhood, might well invite some of the best society of London. Man sensed a stark economy surrounding him, but no poverty. It was rather as though all had been drawn in and tightened, sealed off from the outside, as if to make ready for the storms of avarice and envy that would always threaten.

The light showed the watchman a little of the man ahead of him. A man of about forty years, fastidiously dressed in a serviceable coat and inexpensive wig, a lean man, almost gaunt and hungry but with the enduring leanness of a cautiously whittled switch. His wrung face looked whiter than the yellowing candle alone should have made it. Man noticed in his movements a tension that could have been mere force of character, personal determination; yet right now it seemed more like painfully restrained excitement. Halfway up the steps and still climbing, his host was already upstairs, talking even faster than he had climbed.

"I came in late tonight, due to the heat of the storm. I thought I might not get back at all, such piles of snow turning me right out of the Strand. This day and night have made a most dreadful havoc among the trades."

They had reached the upstairs landing and come to a stop in a short hallway with three doors, all closed. The air about them was stale and very cold.

"I came up here to wish my father a good night before going to my own bed. There was no light, but I know he sleeps very little. And – he wanted to see me." The watchman listened to the man's voice, hearing the terror or joy or madness hidden in it. "I found him at his table – sleeping, I thought – but when I touched him – " The lanthorn shook the frail light. "I cannot quite believe it yet."

Man frowned at him, set down staff and lanthorn, and brushed past him into the unlocked room.

The room was small, a cramped marriage of business and rest. A low, curtained bed took up most of one wall. It was old and breaking, and it had not been slept in tonight. An unmatched pair of elbow-chairs stood with their backs to it, facing a ponderous walnut desk that was symmetrically bordered with piled ledgers and bound papers. A sloping stand for books rested on top, next to a bowed figure that looked as if it had been crumpled and twisted and thrown hurriedly aside. Man noticed first, ridiculously, the breathing rise and fall of white neck hairs in a secret draft. Then the quill pen discarded near one hand and the bare space on the desktop.

"Was he writing?"

The watchman's question distracted the other's examination of the business ledgers shelved on the wall behind the desk. He looked blankly at the still pen.

"What? Writing?"

Man glanced about him. "You have moved nothing? Removed nothing?"

"I assure you, sir, I have not."

Bending over the dead man, the watchman observed the uncomfortable grey nightgown, the old wrenched throat, the sparrow's face hardened first by life, then by death. The cheek was cold as new paper.

"This is your father, then?"

"It was, sir." The inflection stood alone in the dulled room. "He was Edmund Cowley, the jeweller. I am his son, Harold Cowley. His first son."

The watchman reached beneath his greatcoat for his pipe, to warm himself. He could hear the storm outside, jostling thickly the tired house.

He found a twist of straw in his pocket and with it lit his pipe from the lanthorn.

"You have a brother?"

"Christopher, yes."

"But he does not live here in his father's house?"

Harold Cowley was fingering some papers almost at his father's elbow. Man's question straightened him, stiffening.

"My brother is married, sir. He has his own family. In Rood Lane, next the shop where he works as a journeyman joiner. He has been there I should say almost ten years now. Living with his wife and son." A distant satisfaction. "Very poorly, I am afraid."

Man was smoking, slowly stalking the room. "Does no one else live here?"

"No one, sir."

"No servants, then?"

"My father could never abide them, nor their demands." He paused, added proudly: "I have always done for him myself, sir."

The watchman came to a stop behind the inert father. Very carefully, he took the pipe out of his mouth, read the dome of fine ash in the bowl, and stuffed it burning back into his pocket. He spoke gravely, officially, staring at nothing somewhere off to the younger man's left.

"Your father, sir, has had his life choked out of him this night, that much is clear. Now I am nothing beyond a simple watchman myself. I can do no more, say no more. We have no way of saying who has done this act: I have no felon here that I can lay hold of and carry to the nearest watch-house, which is all my work." He looked, explaining, directly at Harold Cowley, then away again. "You understand, sir, that we cannot alone take your father through the streets in this dark storm. Enough for us to find a way for ourselves through the high snow without."

"I must go with you, then?" The jeweller's first son sounded as if he wanted never to move again, though he obviously was not tired. "Where must we go?"

Man considered it.

"Constable Marlowe's house is hard by us here – in White Hart Yard, as I remember. We should be able to reach there in half an hour or less. Quicker than the watch-house in the Strand, at any rate. And he's a man of lively parts, never one to mind his being taken from his sleep. His dreams, he tells me, only weary him more than his waking."

Facet by facet, the watchman smoothly studied the room a last time. Then he delicately drifted the jeweller's son toward the door. "If the storm dies some, the coroner will want to sit here tomorrow to question the death formally," he said, opening the door. "Do you have a key?"

"Of course," Cowley assured him. "For this and for the other rooms. And the street."

Just as they were leaving the quiet of the room, Man had another thought.

"Is anything missing, do you think?"

The other's eyes searched, wondered, could not decide. "I've been looking all this while. I think not. But – " He strained for perfect honesty. "There's really not so very much here, you see, and I know it all so well. There's nothing taken, I think, nothing that should be here and is not. I'm certain. And yet – from the first tonight I've thought the room was different in some way. Some way changed. Everything is in its place, but there is something altered somewhere. I don't know." Harold Cowley faltered. "Perhaps it is only his death that has made the room seem new to me."

"Yes," Man agreed quietly. "Death can do that."

The next day – cold, but still and clear – found George Man sharing more than one cup of warmed wine in the house of Constable Marlowe. The watchman slept through most of most mornings, but today his wife, Sarah, had thrown him out with the corner dust. They were in the process of moving – no, Sarah was in the process of moving them – from their long-lived apartments in Ironmonger Row off Old Street north of the City to others somewhat smaller and less dear in Bow Street. Now was the worst season of the year, and the worst weather of the season, to move: how many times had Man told her? But once set in motion, Sarah could not be stalled. So now she was hectoring and frazzled, hip-deep in opened trunks and roped boxes. The few possessions they meant to keep had interbred overnight, hiding most of the floor. Man could have gone anywhere, but he was curious about last night's death, and he was always ready to trade cups and news with Constable Marlowe.

Humphry Marlowe was a bony, yellowish man, a drooping and dour cutler and razor-maker. His was not a happy face. The indentation in his upper lip had formed from a lifetime spent refining daily miseries, the dent in his forehead from a dread of contentment as deep-seated as most men's fear of paralysis. Marlowe distrusted joy, especially his own – he could never feel at ease with it. Now he had the unpaid and compulsory position of parish constable to add to his own continuing trade, to take him hourly away from his rightful work, to introduce him to the purest trouble the streets had to show. He hadn't felt this good in years.

The watchman was sitting with him at a scored table midway between a healthy fire and a window sparkling with cold sunlight. The granular falsetto of a grindstone reached between them from a back room, but the constable had learned long since to modulate his voice in harmony with it.

"Aye, George," he said, "Coroner Dicey is even now sitting in the jeweller's house in York Street, doubtless casting his legal dust about him and blinding every eye. He's a very complete man is that one!" Constable Marlowe made a rude noise in his tapered nose. "Have the fellow stripped and on his knee by this hour, say I."

"Was it not your business to attend?"

The constable looked even more hurt than usual.

"My business is here, sir, and it is failing me even as we speak. And I don't love Mr Dicey so much, I'll own it to any who will hear. Our coroner and I have found us a conflict between us, you see. Of minds," he added dryly. "I have one."

"What will be the upshot of it, do you know?" Man spoke with some care, knowing his own powerlessness in the parish and the constable's dissatisfied pride in not excelling in a job he did not want. "Will Mr Dicey determine it a killing theft?"

The thin cutler mulled a mouthful of wine and thoughtfully lifted his overgrown pipe off the table.

"Bring us a piece of fire, will you, George?"

Man stepped over to the fireplace and carried back a flaming straw. In a minute the two men were clouding the air over their heads blue and dimming at the window the light and silence of White Hart Yard.

"Well, there's little question of the end of last night's work, is there?" Constable Marlowe asked. "I know myself a small something of that shop in York Street and of the man that made it. Edmund Cowley was widowed with the two sons as quick as the second pulled his feet out of the mother. She was glad to go, I'd wager, before her man could think of some way to make her pay him for her passage to heaven. Aye, that was a pinching penny-father, was that one. One that would make the boys chew the same lump of bread twice, my thought. I heard it said that he never so much as slept the night for fear he might forget the day's count. Loved it, they say, as a right-minded man loves his smoke. And he taught his first son the same song, until he could sing it even better than his father."

"The business thrived, then?"

"Few better in this side of the town. The father made and sold stones to those whose names he'd never dare write out. He gave that work mainly to Harold – best said Harold took it for himself. That's where the boy was supposed last night, out carrying a pocketful of rings to a dame in Golden Square. Took him a long hour or more to fight his way home – if you believe his word."

Man squinted through his smoke at the constable's sour look.

"You think otherwise, Mr Marlowe?"

"I do. As does Coroner Dicey and most other men. 'Tis no great puzzler, is it?" Marlowe asked the watchman lightly. "Look you, the first son's a chip of the same block with the father, truth? He knows the trade even better, loves it more, the height of coin it can get him. He's the very image of him, a second Edmund. And for too long now he's been naught but the running link-boy of the shop, carrying the scraps from Westminster to Wapping, waiting for the sire to kick up long past his time. There's a turn, friend, will weary a man in a time. First-born and working day by day for the old man's shop, and then comes the last will and testament as the final and meanest cast to – "

"What will is this you speak of?" Man interrupted.

The cutler allowed himself to show a thin triumph.

"Well, the same the jeweller himself writ out this same week!"

"It has been found, then."

"Eh? Why, no, not quite now. But there's a lawman over in Gray's Inns who promises that Father Cowley made it. And – " Constable Marlowe breathed slyly "– he says the paper, every word on it, saves the shop and every stone and every penny for the second son – this Christopher that lives only to hammer his master's chairs and tables together. As if he wanted it, as if he knew what to do with it if he had it!"

"Nothing for the older brother? Nothing?"

"Not a shadow to sell a blind man!"

The watchman was surprised. "But why?"

The constable paused to stare disconsolately into his pipe bowl, then he rapped out the dead ash onto the floor. The distant grindstone slowed down, ground to a stop.

"As well as I can know it, the old man never loved the young woodworkman over-well, and never forgave him the running out from the family, the trade. I can see that – a man wants what he leaves behind him to be his still. And the boy's been as much help as a pair of Mahometan whiskers on a new bride's lip, carrying himself off to another street, showing his back to what his father made for him." He shook his head at such unmercantile ingratitude. "Still, seems the boy did, at hazard, at last gift the old fellow with what he'd all the time wanted more than anything – more even than his shop and all."

Man nodded.

"A grandson," he murmured.

His sudden insight keenly disappointed Constable Marlowe.

"As you say. A boy to keep the name living even longer than the trade – something the other son could most like never manage. And so the old man makes his plans to give all he's got to him that don't want it, until – " the voice crackled significantly "– until the son that's earned it learns who it's going to and spirits away father and paper at one single swoop. He knows it's his as first-born, so he picks a stormy night to murder the jeweller and – "

"And runs to the window to call me in as witness and invite himself at once to the gallow-tree at Tyburn. Yes, that is wise."

Suspicious and unhappy, the constable regarded Man with a long, unwinking stare and started to scrape his chair backward. "Wise enough at leastways to gull a simple watchman, eh? But not sharp enough to hoodwink the rest of them that know!"

Humphry Marlowe walked him to the door, but Man thought it closed a little more roughly than usual. Yet it could have been the cold, or even the fitful wind that was growing in the brisk street. There could be many explanations.

The fact was, the Mans had a favorite chair that needed mending badly. It had never sat level or well; and what better time to have it fixed than en route to Bow Street? Rood Lane lay out of his way, but the joiner's shop in it was said to do good work.

If the streets had been clear of snow, Man could have borrowed a wheelbarrow; by the time he got there, he had had enough of carrying it and his arms ached with cramp. As he tapped on the front door of the shop, his first thought was to wonder if the proprietor might not happen to own some kind of a cart, lying idle for the day.

The master joiner was nowhere to be found, but Man did not trouble himself greatly to look. A dusted workman led him and his chair into a long, low-ceilinged room that was a concentrate of hot sawdust, aromatic shavings, the grunting and noisiness of six or seven working men. There was nothing crowded or chaotic about the shop: each man seemed satisfied with his place and work, the floor was comfortably carpeted with fresh litter, the air was that of an open wood. It was the kind of place that Man had always liked best – a place of simple accomplishment and simple rest – and as he lowered his chair he felt that he was in no real hurry to question the young man coming forward gladly to greet him.

Christopher Cowley was a solid and healthy man of thirty or so, robust as apples, who looked as though he could never be unsettled or rushed. He wore a leather apron hung with dully glinting tools, a cloth of limpid green roped around his neck, and a tight cap; and the watchman thought he had two of the firmest hands to be seen anywhere in London.

The journeyman joiner greeted the chair first.

"She's standing a bit poorly, ain't she?"

Man explained the circumstances of his wife's preference for the chair and of their moving.

"Let's carry her over to the corner here so we can see after her quiet-like," the joiner said, cradling it.

In the corner, the watchman bent over Christopher Cowley, admiring his work. "May I say, sir," he said in a low voice, "that I can feel your present sorrow."

The joiner looked up, his clear face shadowed.

"You are Mr Christopher Cowley?"

"Kit, sir."

"Kit. I am George Man. I – know something of your family and its new – reverses."

He saw the joiner tense slightly, the working of his hands intensify.

The watchman, interested in both the man and his craft, crouched down beside him.

"It's a hard chance, Kit, that makes a man lose both father and brother at the one throw – the father murdered, the brother accused. I say nothing of shame, trust me," Man hurriedly reassured him. "No, this runs far deeper."

Kit Cowley hesitated, then turned to him.

"My brother, sir, cannot be guilty of this."

"Your forgiveness. Yet even now he lies chained in Newgate Prison. Few men are ever Newgated for nothing."

"He is innocent."

"Perhaps. Yet I fear – " Man began.

"That small hammer there, sir, if you please."

The joiner busied himself with what he knew best. The shop became a detached wash of energy around the two kneeling men, around their gentle probing of one another. Kit Cowley was shy, anxious, defensive; the watchman was caring and insistent. He shifted his weight, coming closer, and tried again.

"I may tell you," he lied softly, "that the Justice of Peace and I are close. It may be that a word to him – "

"You would do that for him, sir?"

"Do you wish your brother freed from this once and away?"

"Of course, of course." Troubled, the joiner seemed to distance himself from his work, trusting his hands to their mechanical experience. "My brother and I have never agreed – we might have been born and grown in different streets – yet he is my brother, and older, and I have always loved him as one. When I left our father's house ten years ago or more, he had a mouthful of hard words for me – harder even than my father's, and his were hard enough. Neither of them understood me, could know me deeply enough to understand. The business has ever been as nothing to me, no more than a sinking burden attached to the Cowley name. And the stones are cold, dead – only things to please the eye alone." The young man stroked a leg of the chair, felt its grain, followed a warm curve with his blunt fingers. "I found a craft for myself that I could follow with care and pride, making the wood grow and change as I willed it. It lives, it can be used to make another man's life easier and happier. And even before I turned away from the house, I had found another to share it with."

"Your wife?"

Cowley nodded. "They would not love her, they would not believe that she wanted to love them. My brother could never see her as more than one who was bent upon injuring the family. Perhaps it is his remembering our mother too well, too sorrowfully. He knew her."

Man gave him a moment, then asked him, "You have prospered?"

"I think I have, sir," he answered, smiling contentedly. "My good wife has given me one tall son and is now big with another child. I am blessed with greater treasures than most men, I think."

"I meant," Man corrected him gently, "in your trade."

The young man tugged uncomfortably at a joint in the chair.

"I think I do as well as I can. I have modest enough talents for the work; at times I find each one of my fingers turned a thumb."

What might have sounded false from another man became an honest complaint from Kit Cowley, the uneasiness of a man who can never trust himself to succeed.

Man watched him coaxing the chair back into shape and marveled at the precise efficiency of his gestures.

"No, Kit, I should call you as able a man as any other, perhaps more. I wonder that you do not make a shop of your own someday and become master of yourself."

The journeyman squatted back and dropped his voice. He spoke directly at his work, losing the watchman.

"A master? To lay me down at night with waking fears of the morrow and start the day in dread of losing all? To work with the ghost of failure and disgrace always at my side? To lower all my loved family into shadow so that they will not distract me from my love of gain?" He paused, seeming to contract himself into a smaller space. "No, sir. I have seen too much of the cold and misery that come with a fuller purse. They can kill a man against his will – his wife, his children, his life's happiness."

Man looked away, thinking he understood him now. He felt the active shop wrapping itself more snugly about them.

The chair stood firm and true now. Both men rose to their feet, clumsily avoiding each other's eyes. The wooden smells of the room were so clean and piercing that the watchman felt a moment's dizziness. He knew what he had to say.

"A man makes his own happiness, Kit. And a purse may be worn as easy heavily as no. You will have to learn that yourself, when the will is found."

The young man stumbled without moving.

"What will?"

"Your father's, of course. You knew of it." It was a statement, not a question. "Even more of it than your brother, am I right?"

"What? Harold? But he knew nothing of it!"

"Are you certain of this?" Man asked him closely.

"Yes – yes, I am. I learned of it only two or three days before our father's death, when I carried back the reading-desk I had mended. He meant to tell my brother sometime later."

The joiner ended weakly, adrift, but Man believed him. The old jeweller would have wanted his first-born son to wait this time.

"Can you save my brother?" Kit asked, grieving.

Man turned to him sharply. "I hope to do so. I do not wish his death. Neither of us does. Remember this, Kit," he insisted. "If he hangs, there is no way you can stop the shop from coming to you."

The young face blanched – it was seeing something the first time. Kit was a wild bird in a dark and narrowing cave.

"But what can be done?" he begged to know.

The shop was beginning to coast into its mid-day halt. A few workmen had already unwrapped their bread and cheese, uncorked their thick bottles of ale. A dusty quiet settled into the room, the elementary peacefulness of unthinking rest. One man, old and pitted with scars, was cutting his food into mouthfuls with his working saw. The master joiner had never appeared.

The watchman took it all in at once: the unchanging rhythm of the shop, the rooted steadiness of laboring men, the security, the anonymity, the worry and irresolution of the young journeyman joiner. Everything here, Man could now see, formed an enduring whole.

He set down his chair with a grateful sigh and bent slightly forward.

"I think you have nothing for it, Kit, but to own to be guilty of the murdering yourself."

The Mans were finally settled into their new rooms in Bow Street, and George Man at least approved. Their old home in Ironmonger Row had been somewhat bigger, certainly less stuffy, and constantly perfumed with the rising odors of the bake-shop downstairs; but the street, so far to the north and near to the fields, lay so much apart from the current of the city's life. Bow Street had more to offer, more shouting and trading by day and more arguing and fighting by night. Every class of people met and passed through Bow Street, not always peaceably, and that civic heartbeat was enough to make Man feel right at home.

Sarah Man felt the same, though she would never admit it. She grumbled about the want of space, the noise and danger outside, the little light. She missed the friendliness of the bake-shop and she was sure one of their new neighbors lived with a mistress. Yet the liveliness of the street had already worked on her almost as much as on her husband, and she sometimes spent as much time as he did leaning and nodding out the flung-open window.

Today Man was sitting near the window in his mended chair, appreciating its new and comforting sturdiness. He was enjoying, too, the sight of Sarah hovering over their tiny oven, baking the kind of home-raised bread he had missed when she used to depend upon the bake-shop.

The afternoon in the street outside was mild and grey, the sky low, and the air soft with random flakes. Sarah had just laid the bread out to cool, brown and crisp, when the knock Man had been expecting all day rattled the door.

Harold Cowley was a different man, profoundly altered, aged and overshadowed even since the last time Man had seen him. That had been only two days before, a heartbreakingly frozen day when they had both watched the shivering body of Christopher Cowley, narrowing and twisting slowly from the gallows at Tyburn. The faces of the brothers then had never looked more alike.

Now the jeweller sat across from Man at the window and accepted a cup of his brandy. The watchman wondered if he would ever lose the fine shaking in his hands.

"Constable Marlowe told me, Mr Man, that I have you to thank for my life." Cowley bowed his shoulders formally. "I thank you, sir."

Man accepted his gratitude with a grim nod.

"But I do not understand the deaths of my father, my brother – "

A shadow marred the window: a clod of snow falling from the roof.

"Your father was dying?" Man asked suddenly.

The jeweller had not expected this.

"He was, sir. He knew it. The doctors promised he would never finish the year. I had thought he was making himself ready to go."

"And he did. An old man who has worked and excelled all his days, with little thought of his end, finds much to hurry him as it finally comes nearer. He sees most things newly, he finds new losses he had never noticed before, he easily forgets old promises, spoken or not." Man looked kindly at the merchant across from him. "If your father thought to leave his work to your brother, it was no insult to your long help. It was only that he feared leaving nothing behind him but coins and stones. An old man pains sometimes for something more."

Sarah Man helped enclose the room with her homely bustling, the way she lovingly swaddled the bread in a clean cloth.

Harold Cowley began saying something about his father's illness, but Man was only half listening. He was remembering leading Kit Cowley out of the shop in Rood Lane. The young joiner had turned for a final look at the energetic room. He had seemed to be trying to memorize it all – the yellow air, the wooden clatter, the manual persistence of the workmen. He had left his apron and tools in a far corner, and at the door he had gazed back at them with a yearning that could be seen in his entire body. His last words to a fellow workman had been barely audible:

"Tell Mr Singleton, would you, that I'll not be needing my place tomorrow?"

Man poured another cup for Harold Cowley, politely avoiding the desperate questioning in his look.

"And so you knew nothing of your father's wish to write his will."

"I promise you, I did not. I knew he had been ailing especially of late – worse, the afternoon of that day – but I knew nothing of what he meant to do." The jeweller frowned uncertainly at a brown scar in the floor. "He must have felt very bad to call my brother out on such a night. And I was not with him."

Man gave him a long moment to recover, then explained: "He was afraid, I think, that he had waited too long, that he might not have enough time to write it out and give it, with his reasons, to your brother. So he sent for him, storm or no, to come to him at once. You should feel no pain, sir, for your actions that night. You were about your father's business."

"If I had only known that Kit had been there with him."

"You sensed it, in a fashion. Remember? Your feelings that something in that room had been changed or moved? It was your father's lectern, the reading-desk he used for his ledgers. A small enough matter, I grant you, but significant."

"But it was there on the desk that night when I took you in, sir – I remember!"

"Of course it was," Man said with some excitement. "But it should not have been there. Remember? Your brother had taken it to Rood Lane to mend. Do you recall his carrying it back?"

Cowley considered for a time. "I do not," he said finally.

"Because he brought it back on the night of your father's death. He must have done so. The truth is, you had grown so familiar with the sight of it in its place that you could not remark that it should still have been at the workshop. Nothing was missing from the room, but something had been added that night – by your brother."

"It must have been as you say. But how did you know it?"

"I did not," Man admitted grimly. "I supposed it. And then, sometime later in Rood Lane, I recognized Kit's workmanship." Unconsciously, he dropped his hand to stroke a jointure in the mended chair beneath him.

Mostly to himself, the other man groaned: "But how could our Kit have murdered him? It should have been myself, I think."

In his voice, Man heard the same brittle echo of private agony, hollow as regret, that he had heard in Kit Cowley's, locked in the solid dark of Newgate Prison and helpless to explain the knotted reasons for the murder.

"Many thought you did," Man said, willfully misunderstanding him. "But you, sir, are altogether too much your father; and what man in his right senses ever chooses to murder himself? Your brother, now, was someone else. He early left his family and home to make his own, he left riches for meanness, he found his happiness in being no one – in being one of a thousand common workmen in a thousand common streets, each of them content to live unknown, unremarked, invisible to all the world. He was never a man who could show himself, not even to raise himself higher in his chosen work, though he was able. Mr Singleton, the master joiner in Rood Lane, tells me that Kit could have many times made his own shop – more than one had promised him money to start. But he was afraid – do you understand? – he was afraid to be seen, or afraid that he might succeed too well and become his father."

Man looked into the clouded, distant eyes in front of him. "It must have made him mad that night to hear his father's plan to burden him with a life he could not live, to see him begin to write it out. I'm certain it was only accident that made him push his father back so hard from the paper. He told me his hands had ever been stronger than he knew. He remembered almost nothing."

Harold Cowley turned painfully away, breathing, "And I thank God for that."

Man walked the jeweller down to the street, comforting him with empty talk of the weather that had now begun to settle into blanketing flurries. It was not until he learned that Harold Cowley was going to visit for the first time his brother's family in Rood Lane that the watchman knew this work was done.

Death is never easy for any man, he reflected, as he stood rooted deep in the Bow Street drifts. For Kit Cowley, it must have been doubly bitter, dying as he had done before the hundreds of straining eyes in Tyburn's habitually craning crowd. There, and during the ride up Holborn in an open cart, his life's worst nightmare had kept him awake. For those few hours, he had been the most famous man in all London.

The watchman made his way back upstairs, looking nowhere. He was trying not to remember the young joiner's last moments, how he had finally turned away from the crowd's ogling to approach the gallows, how one broad hand had been stretched out to the scaffold as if for support. But then, trembling, the hand had moved in one slow and sensitive touch, the workman admiring the wood, the craftsman approving of the enduring workmanship.

Man only hoped it had helped.

THE CURSE OF THE CONNECTICUT CLOCK
S. S. Rafferty

In the first volume I reprinted "The Christmas Masque", one of Rafferty's stories featuring administrator Captain Jeremy Cork who travels throughout colonial America solving his "social puzzles". The following is set eight years after "The Christmas Masque" and features one of my favourite ploys – the cryptogram.

T he fact that Captain Jeremy Cork, my employer, avoids profit-able endeavors in favor of dabbling in the solution of social puzzles is my cross to bear, and I accept it and persevere in spite of him. However, the pawky methods he uses to resist my making him the richest man in the American colonies are downright frustrating, although admittedly ingenious.

No better example of his cleverness at resisting industry, while thoroughly enjoying a crime, exists than in the autumn of 1762, when we returned to the Oar and Eagle on the Connecticut coast. Cork considers this his home port, although we pass no more time there than anywhere else. The only reason for giving this snug inn *dominium* status is that it contains the only bed in the Americas that will accommodate his six-foot-six frame. That massive sleeping couch is part of the private rooms, fitted as a ship's cabin, that he rents on an annual basis. His apartment is on the ground floor, off the public rooms. Mine is above stairs, although I work at an accounts dais in his chambers during the daylight hours and take my meals there.

It was in the forenoon of a crisp October day when I decided to broach the subject of manufacturing his Apple Knock and shipping it about the colonies. It is a potent potable which has gained great favor with his friends, and it occurred to me that a good profit could be turned from the venture.

"I believe we would gain more if we barrel it by the percheon or pipe rather than by hogshead," I said, bringing a rather brilliant analysis to a close. "That would mean lower cost per gallon shipped and . . ."

"You would involve me in barter and score?" he roared. "*Sell* liquor? By Jerusalem, Wellman Oaks, you are without soul. TEDDERHORN!"

Bertram Tedderhorn is the innkeeper of the Oar and Eagle who believes Cork is the next best thing to the Divinity. Considering the rent and the lavish meals the Captain pays for, he may be right. He burst into the chamber within seconds of Cork's shout.

"Yes, Captain?" He was breathless because his corpulence is not given to quick movements.

"After this moment, we are now to use the winter formulation for the Knock." Cork took up a quill. Tedderhorn looked confused.

"But sir, it is only October 30. The solstice is weeks away."

"True, Tedderhorn," Cork said as he wrote on a piece of paper, "but we are victims of habit, and be wary that habit becomes ritual, and ritual breeds dogma, and that is not healthy for the mind *or* body. The receipt is as before with the addition of one new ingredient which I have written here and will be known only to you and me."

As he handed the innkeeper the paper, Tedderhorn gave me a sheepish look. As well he should, for I am Cork's confidential yeoman, and usually nothing is privy from me. Yet I held my tongue and bore no ill will for the innkeeper. He was merely a pawn in my employer's playful game.

It was what you can expect from Captain Jeremy Cork. All he had to say was "no" to the venture, but that wouldn't have been dramatic enough. A simple negative response would have robbed him of a chance to jape me.

Tedderhorn was leaving the room when he suddenly turned. "'Pon my word, I forgot, Captain. There's a man to see you. I was coming in to tell you when you called."

"Show him in, by all means." Cork went back to his book with a self-satisfied look on his face.

I am not a man to waste energy in hurt feelings. "I assure you I have no intention of skulduggering around to learn the new receipt," I told him. "It was only a suggestion."

"Your suggestions, Oaks, have a way of becoming burdensome realities. People who sell liquor are in the same class as people who sell love, and they share a common name. One may traffic with whores without becoming one. Hello, sir, come in, I think we have met before."

This last statement was to the man who had entered the room. My heart sank, for now, on the heels of my idea having been scuttled, was a person obviously distraught and in need of help. Before he even spoke, I knew it, for I have come to recognize the characteristics of a new puzzle looming into view.

"Yes, Captain, we met several years ago at the Widow Chandler's in Fairfield. My name is Gerret Hull."

"Of course. What can I do for you, Mr Hull?" Cork indicated a chair and Hull sat. He was a shortish man, clean shaven and dressed in a plain suit and obviously fresh linen for his visit.

"I have had a great tragedy in my life recently, and until today, I was convinced it was God's will, and humbly accepted it. Now . . ." he drew something from his coat which turned out to be a copybook. ". . . well, now I'm not sure that my fourteen-year-old son's death was accidentally caused by a schoolboy prank."

Cork requested details, and I sat there and listened to the father tell his sad story with but mild interest.

Gerret Hull went on. "I am not a wealthy man, gentlemen. Just a small farm and a fair sized cooperage. But if life had limited my horizons, I was bound that it would not be so for my oldest boy, Chad. It was hard on my purse, but I enrolled him at the Fenway School above New Haven in the hope that he would go on to Yale and then to a profession. He was not happy at Fenway during his first year, for he was a poor boy among the sons of wealthy families, which is not always an easy road. But Chad stuck to his books and returned to Fenway this September with high hopes. Then, last week, the awful news came. Chad had been killed while performing the foolish prank of scaling a belltower in the middle of the night. It is not uncommon for a boy to try to place a chamberpot or underdrawer on the spire for all to see in the morning."

"He fell?" I asked.

The father closed his eyes as if in the grip of some horrible mental picture. "No, Mr Oaks, he was stabbed to death by a jacamart."

For an instant I shared Hull's horrible picture. A jacamart is a life-sized statue, usually a knight in armor, that moves across the face of a tower clock to strike the hour bell with a sword or lance.

"The school officials told me that Chad must have reached the clockface platform at precisely one o'clock, and was impaled on the jacamart's sword as he stood there preparing to scale higher."

"How ghastly," I said, "and unfortunate that the poor boy was there just at the stroke of one."

"Precisely as I felt, Mr Oaks. I saw it as fate. Although Chad was not a wild boy, I assumed he wanted to be one of the fellows, and fell victim to the accursed clock."

"But now you have reason to question the accidental aspects of the affair? What is the source of your suspicion?" Cork wanted to know.

"Suspicion is a strong word, Captain, for I wouldn't want to cast any shadows over Fenway's reputation. It's more a feeling that I do not have the whole story." He opened the copybook and withdrew a piece of notepaper. "I received this letter from Chad earlier this week. On the face of it, it is a dutiful son informing his father that he is trying his best." He handed the letter to Cork, who read it through and passed it to me. It was in a neat hand without the scholarly flourishes so common to academicians.

> Fenway School
> Derby, Connecticut
> 21 October 1762
>
> Father:
> All is much the same here, but I persevere. But take heart, for I have come onto something which may take the burden of my education from your shoulders. Be of good spirit, sir, and wish me well. My best to all.
>
> Your son,
> Chad
>
> P.S. I shall try my best to put my mind to the task.

"You see, gentlemen, Chad had previously mentioned that there was the possibility of receiving emoluments for good scholarship, and I assumed he was in competition for one. A student grant would obviously ease my financial load."

"That is certainly a reasonable interpretation," I said, giving him back the letter.

"I agree, Mr Oaks, but yesterday, I finally overcame my grief enough to go through the clothes and things I brought back home with Chad's remains. In this copybook, I came across some queer notations which puzzle me. I have heard of your reasoning powers, Captain Cork, and wondered if you could make something of it."

Cork took the book, and I leaned over his shoulder as he leafed through it. It appeared to be a typical lesson book, with each page containing daily lessons.

"The Fenway curricula seems to be well rounded," Cork remarked as he perused page after page of Latin translation, Ancient History, Mathematics, and Physics.

"To be sure, Captain, the school is the finest of its kind. The notations to which I refer are in the back of the copybook, where the boys are allowed to make their own scribblings and work out problems."

Cork turned to the back pages and finally found one bearing a very peculiar inscription. It read:

Blandersfield Program

Sept 19
        EF/FG/GA/AB/BC/CD/DE/EF?
Oct 10
        78−34=44=GB?
        78−32=46=GA?
Oct 20
        VI=EF!

The Captain furrowed his brows and studied the symbols for some minutes. "It's quite cryptic, of course," he said at last, "but schoolboys are often given to secret writings as a pastime, Mr Hull. What makes this suspicious in connection with your son's death?"

"The 'Blandersfield Program' overline, Captain. Blandersfield is what the boys at Fenway call the jacamart, 'Sir Jack Blandersfield'."

Rarely have I ever seen Cork shift from mild interest to intense occupation so rapidly. "Most interesting indeed. Tell me, on what date did Chad meet his death?"

"So you've noticed it then. October 21, the evening after the last notation, or really the morning of the 22nd, since he died at one o'clock in the morning. All I can make of it is that Chad had an interest in the jacamart beyond a prank."

"Yes, that seems patent," Cork agreed. "If he were merely trying to put a chamberpot atop a spire, why all the hocus-pocus with codes?"

"Perhaps he was trying to compute the proper time for the jacamart's movements," I put in.

Cork looked up at me with that smirk-a-mouth of his. "Hardly, Oaks. That could be done by a child of no education. These notations are a thought progression. The first, on September 19, obviously did not give him an answer since he ends it with an interrogation mark. Then, on the 10th of October, he has refined his thinking, but still we have an interrogation mark. But on the 20th of October, Chad discovered something in the VI=EF equation, for he ends it with an exclamative. And then he died in the process of putting his theory to a test."

"But what does the last entry mean, Captain?" Hull asked.

"Several notions present themselves, but to speak now would be to conjecture, based on a paucity of facts. It looks as if we shall be going to school again, Oaks."

"Then you believe there is foul play involved, Captain?" Hull was obviously agitated.

"No, sir, I venture no such idea, for the minds of young boys are labyrinths, full of twists and turns which can be confounding to the adult who ventures in there. This I *will* say, Mr Hull. Initially, it struck me as odd that Chad was on the clock face platform at the exact stroke of one. Now this Blandersfield enigma adds more to the mystery. Mind you, my inquiries may produce aspects of your son that you might not care to know. Will you chance it?"

Hull bowed his head as if in prayer; his voice was low as he piously intoned, "I swear by his soul that Chad was a good boy."

"To be sure. Tell me, sir, was the boy a musician of any kind?"

The father smiled, recalling an old thought. "No, sir, no ear for it at all. My wife has taught the children to sing, but poor Chad had a voice like a strangled bird."

"I see. Then it is done. Go about your business, sir, and try to balm your grief. I should have something for you in a few days."

When the farmer-cooper had left, I went back to my place at the accounts dais. Tedderhorn came in bearing a tray with two tankards on it and set them down, one before each of us. I sipped the Knock and said, "Do you think it could be murder?"

Cork shrugged and took a deep draft. "What I said about the minds of boys still holds. They can be a pack of scoundrels at times. Chad could have been put up to it by his school chums, but his letter to his father indicates that he expected to be in funds very soon."

"The emolument, of course."

"I think not. His lesson book shows an average mind, and certainly not one of high scholarship. No, if he was to soon be in funds to alleviate his father's burden, it had to come from another source."

"Blackmail, possibly?"

"Very perceptive, Oaks. It's a possibility. Boys have eyes and ears, and they sometimes use them effectively."

"But whom would he blackmail?"

"A schoolmaster? A classmate? The students are all wealthy."

"But the Blandersfield notations. They confuse it."

"No, Oaks, they put more raisins in the bun. These alphabetical notations are some sort of progression. Note the September 19 notation. The first two are EF, the second set repeats the last of the first and adds a new letter, becoming FG. In the third, the

'G' has become the initial letter, and 'A' is added. Actually, he is only dealing with the letters E,F,G,A,B,C, and D in a repeating pattern."

"Perhaps the letters, properly arranged, spell out a word."

"I think not, at least not a meaningful word. And that does not seem to have been Chad's thinking either, for, on October 10, he tries a completely different trick, using two sets of subtractions. But where did he get the numerals? No matter, for the moment. It is obvious that he took the two remainders, 44 and 46, and went back to his September 19 progression to count the fourth and eighth letters to arrive at 44=GB and 46=GA."

"And you feel that Chad wasn't a bright student, Captain? This certainly seems to indicate an inquring mind of some subtlety at work."

"An embrangled mind, Oaks. One that has mired itself in a complex approach to a solution. It is not limited to schoolboys. Too many times, seemingly intelligent people cannot find an answer when it lies in front of them. Obviously, Chad woke up to his error on October 20, for a new element, 'VI,' has jumped into his mind. The first two notations on September 19 and October 10 are mere exercises in garbled logic. I am sure the October 20 thought was a stroke of luck. He even matches it with an exclamative to prove the point, like someone stepping back and saying, 'My, my, there it is!' No, the boy was no genius, and indeed, may have been a fool. How is the Knock?"

I smacked my lips. "It tastes the same to me."

"That's the subtlety of it. Well, we shall be off for Fenway at dawn with a short stop off in New Haven."

"For lunch?"

"No, my old son, I think it is time we had your watch cleaned."

The trade of Jared Elliot was proclaimed by a wooden sign displaying a clockface fixed forever at twenty minutes after eight o'clock. The shop itself was a small bow-windowed establishment tucked into a commercial alley just off High Street. Its owner was a gnome-like, white-thatched man with thick spectacles and a scratchy voice. The interior of the place was filled with timepieces of all description, lantern clocks of brass and long case instruments of beautiful floral marquetry. One unique item was an elephant clock with the dial and bell in the howdah and the beast's eyes moving with every tick of each minute. Cork's attention was on the watchmaker as he opened the case of my pocketwatch and peered into the works through an optical glass.

"I see you travel a bit, Mr Oaks, for many a watchmaker has put his hand to this piece."

I was fascinated by the elephant's eye movements and merely agreed with a nod. Cork, on the other hand, showed great interest in Jared Elliot's work, and enjoined him in conversation. As he put questions to the old man, I could see the reason for our visit.

"You seem to be a master at watches, sir, and house clocks. Do you have any knowledge of tower clocks?"

"Great Clocks is the proper name," Elliot grumped. "I don't build them. Too old."

"I hear there is one of great interest out at the Fenway School. Well worth seeing."

"That old monstrosity! Ha, it's something out of the fourteenth century, son."

"That old? It must have been brought over from the old country."

"It's only a score and some. Twenty-five's the more like it. Built by an old faker named deJoonge."

"Didn't know his business, I take it?"

"That's a mild way to put it, son. That clock has a foliot for a time controller, mind you, as if the man never heard of the pendulum. It's only been around since old Christian Huygen invented it in 1656."

"I'm sorry, but I've just gotten interested in clocks. What is a foliot?"

"The old makers used to employ them centuries ago. It's a swing bar that has an unpredictable period of swing or vibration. It's the pendulum that makes present day clocks accurate. Old deJoonge had some gall, passing himself off as an 'orologier,' he did. That monster has stone weights," he started to chuckle and shake his head to emphasize his incredulousness. "Never saw the like of it."

Cork continued to coax information from him. "I'm told the clock has an ingenious jacamart."

"Ingenious! Now that's a bold face concoction. It's not a true jacamart at all because it doesn't really strike the chimes. They are in the spire above the clock. All the jacamart does is come out of a guardhouse on the hour and cross the face of the clock where its sword fits into a slot in the far buttress. It's a fake, like deJoonge himself."

"Did this deJoonge move on after the Great Clock was built?"

"No, son, he stayed right out there at Fenway. Still there, six feet under. He died just after the clock was finished." Elliot closed the inner dome of my pocketwatch and snapped the outer silver back with a snap. "Just a bit of dust was all. Hardly worth the charge."

"Perhaps we can remunerate you in another way. Would you rent me those books back there on your shelf?"

The old watchmaker turned his head and looked at the two volumes. "You must surely be interested in clocks and watches, sir. *The Horologium* by Huygens is in Latin, and makes rough reading. The other, *A Compendium of Watchmaking*, is easier going."

"Two pence for each, per day," Cork suggested.

"To be sure. But don't waste your time on that Fenway clock. You'll learn nothing from it."

"Probably not." Cork gave him some coins. "I am told there was some sort of misfortune out there recently."

"Could have been. I keep to myself and my clocks. They are more reliable than people. What was the misfortune?"

"Some poor lad was accidentally killed by the jacamart," I said.

His wizened old face grew dark and his eyes behind the spectacles popped wide. "Killed by the jacamart! My Lord, that's just the way old deJoonge died. Yes sir, the day after the clock was completed. He was making an adjustment on the face when the jacamart broke loose and ran him through." He gazed off in space for a moment and then turned to us. "Maybe the stories are true that the clock is cursed. My, my. But they do have a heart of their own, you know, and their own logic. My, my."

Captain Cork has many skills, and one of them is the uncanny ability to read while riding a horse. I tried it the once and got a headache for my efforts. All the way to Fenway, he had his nose buried in the books he had rented from the old clockmaker.

It was drawing near to four in the afternoon when we turned off the King's Highway at a rude sign that indicated the school lay to the northwest. All afternoon, during our silent ride, I had been thinking about this mystery the Captain had created. It could be nutmeg, or possibly cinnamon, but I was damned if I could taste it. Now if he had changed the formulation for the summer Knock, the new ingredient would have been more easily discernible, since the summer version does not have a slab of butter and a fist of sugar to mask any subtle additives.

"You amaze me, Oaks," I heard his voice say as we turned off to the northwest. "Here we are, heading into what might be a most tantalizing confrontation, and you waste your time toying with the new Knock receipt."

I looked at him with some amazement. "You have learned to read minds from these new books of yours?"

"No, but you have been moving your lips and tongue in a manner to suggest you were trying to remember the taste of something. When you are trying to discover a hidden substance or meaning, it is better to rely on facts, and not vague memory. Ho, there is our nemesis hoving into view in that vale."

We had come over a small rise, and there below in a gentle dip in the earth was a large quadrangle of field by a belltower that rose out of the main structure some forty feet into free air. The clock, I assumed, faced the inner courtyard, for the towerside in our view was solid stone; an ominous grey finger becoming hazy in the descending autumnal dusk. We were about to start into the vale when we heard the grim tolling of four o'clock from the tower top.

"Do you confirm it?" Cork asked me and I checked my newly cleaned timepiece.

"No, I show five minutes after the hour."

Cork smiled and put spurs to his horse. "Come, old son," he said as he galloped away, "I want to see this jacamart at work."

We clattered through the gate at Fenway seconds later in time to see the clock sentinel still poised at the far side of the clockface. Jack Blandersfield was garbed as a fourteenth-century knight with a coat of mail covering the upper torso and jambs and sollerets at the cuffs and feet. A two-edged sword held upright in the right gauntlet withdrew from a slot in the far buttress as the deadly knight moved slowly backward to its guardhouse. We were both looking up at this instrument of death when an elderly gatekeeper raced up to us, shouting, "Here, here, you men. What's this racing in here like a thunderstorm? You'll have Headmaster to answer to, my fine swift fellows."

He had been dealing with schoolboys for so long that he obviously treated everyone as a child. Cork slid from his saddle and his immense height seemed to prove he was no adolescent. The man was undismayed, however. "Fine thing, fine doings. You'll catch a switching for this, mind you, and I hope Mr Crisp lays it on, for he's the best at it."

"Mr Crisp is the headmaster then?" Cork asked.

"None of your devilment. All knows who the headmaster be. Now come away with me, you scuds, the Reverend will do for you."

The Reverend Obadiah Travistock, the headmaster of Fenway School, looked like a willow tree in winter. His limbs and trunk were thin and grey, but you detected a certain resilience in his very marrow, which is uncommon among men of the cloth in New England. Stern, to be sure, dedicated, no doubt, but long years of teaching boys to be men had mellowed him to a point of amused acceptance. His chambers were an admixture of religious simplicity and scholarly messiness. There were piles of paper everywhere.

"You will have to excuse Amos, gentlemen. He has been at his gate duties so long he has lost track of time. When I took over here from my late father, over fifteen years ago, it took him a long time to accept me. Well, you have an interest in old Great Clocks, you say."

"Yes," Cork said it with aplomb and without the hesitation of a man about to lie to a man of God. "I was considering doing a treatise on clocks in the colonies. Mr Oaks is aiding in the preparation."

"Admirable undertaking, Captain, but I must be honest and ask you to be judicious when writing about the Fenway clock."

Cork feigned a puzzled look and the headmaster smiled. "You see, the clock has a rather sordid history, and a more recent notoriety that could foul the school's reputation if broadcast about like seed. In fact, I had a mind to tear the cursed thing down, but the undermasters have dissuaded me. Perhaps they are right. Accidents will happen."

"Accidents?" Cork asked. "With the clock? Pray, Reverend Travistock, anything you tell me will be held in confidence."

The headmaster then related all that we already knew, with the addition of another student who had fallen from the tower twelve years ago when engaged in a midnight attempt to affix a pair of ladies' undergarments to the weathervane atop the spire.

"What was this latest boy . . . er, Hull, I think you said . . . what was the object he attempted to use in his prank?"

The headmaster looked a bit embarrassed. "A chamberpot, I'm sorry to say. It was found on the clockface platform where he dropped it when the jacamart struck."

"Tell me," Cork leaned forward in his chair. "Is there no way to get to the upper tower other than by scaling it?"

"Of course. There is a ladderway on the inside that leads up to the clockworks and a door opening onto the clockface, but the tower is locked at night, so the only way up is to scale the outside."

"And what of deJoonge? Did you know him?"

"I was just a child when he built the tower and the clock. A Dutchman who wandered by one day and offered to do the work for my father at cost and room and board. Then, just when it was done, he was killed. I'm still not sure the tower shouldn't be torn down." He looked up at a woman who had just entered the room carrying a tea service. "Ah, Manites, how good of you. Gentlemen, my sister, Manites Travistock."

Miss Travistock was a familial copy of her older brother, but her eyes were blacker and her bearing more erect. She nodded when we bowed and we all resumed our seats. I watched her as she poured and handed the cups to us. There was a flintiness in her speech that indicated a taciturn nature, and the darting movements of her black eyes could be taken for suspicion.

"I hope, Obadiah dear, that you have not been boring our guests with that talk about the clock," she said. "You must forgive my brother, good sirs, but there are times when he prattles on like one of his own students."

"Not at all, Miss Travistock," Cork sipped the tea without making a face. "How many boys do you have here at Fenway?"

"Forty-four, Captain," she said. "In four forms. All from the finest families, I might add."

"Now, Manites," the headmaster wagged a finger at her, "there is no such thing as quality in heaven, so let's not have it here on earth."

"I am merely stating that it is our duty to provide for those who know their station. These upstarts who have their souls above buttons have no place here. Next we'll have farriers' sons among us."

The headmaster was about to chastise her when the room was filled with the ringing of a loud gong. Miss Travistock reached for the watch attached to the chatelaine belt around her waist. She checked the time and muttered, "Seven minutes late now. Such a watch."

Confused, I took my own timepiece from my pocket. It was quarter past five, and yet the tower clock had rung only once.

"I see you are a bit dismayed by our queer clock, Mr Oaks," the headmaster chuckled. "Old deJoonge was a frugal Dutchman, and used a Roman strike in the tower clock instead of the conventional system."

"Roman strike?" I asked.

Cork nodded his head. "Of course, most ingenious, and very rare, Reverend. A Roman strike, Oaks, uses two bells, one low toned and another of a higher pitch. The low bell stands for five, and when struck twice, it means it is ten o'clock."

"Quite correct, Captain," Travistock beamed. "Thus, Mr Oaks, the hours one through four are struck on the high bell, one for each hour. Five o'clock is sounded just as you heard, once on the low bell."

"Ah," I said, "and eleven o'clock would be two low and one high bells."

"Let me see," Cork did a quick mental calculation. "Yes, frugal indeed. Instead of the regular seventy-eight strikes required to sound out individual hours, this Roman system needs only thirty-four blows to run through the hours."

The Reverend chuckled. "Oh, that's not correct, I'm afraid. You see, the clock doesn't strike at six o'clock at all, so there are only thirty-two blows in the Fenway run of hours, since six o'clock would be one low and one high bell."

"Was it always so?" Cork asked.

"Yes. It was one of those things left unfinished by de Joonge's death. And we are all quite used to it."

Cork turned to Miss Travistock. "But you said your watch was wrong, m'am."

"Always is, sir." She corrected the watch hands with the stem. "I will never understand how de Joonge could have made a tower clock that is always right, and a watch that is always wrong."

"Do tell. May I see it, please?"

She freed the timepiece from the chain and handed it to him. It was an elaborate thing in a beautifully tooled case that hung from a metal fob to which the winding key was attached.

"It is a lovely thing," the Captain handed it back, "but it is not strange that it is inferior, for clockmakers rarely make good watch mechanisitions. Do you have a music master on faculty, Reverend?"

"Music! Heavens no. It is difficult enough getting Latin and Greek and history and mathematics into their heads. However, my sister has taught the boys their scales for choir practice. Why do you ask? Are you interested in music, too, Captain?"

"Only of late. I take it that forty-four boys require a large staff."

"Oh, that it were possible." The headmaster looked rueful. "There is just myself, Mr Crisp for mathematics, Mr Goselow for languages, and young Biggard for everything else. Quite proud of Biggard we are. One of our own boys who went up to Yale from here and came back to his alma mater to teach. Always hoped he would be drawn to the ministry. Well, I see that darkness is upon us, and the boys will be at supper in a few minutes. We will take supper when they are finished. Of course, you won't be able to examine the tower clock now in the dark, so I offer you our humble hospitality for the evening. In the meantime, I have my evening meditations to attend to, and my sister must oversee the dining hall. Perhaps you would care to spend some time in our common room. The faculty uses it for lesson preparations and social talk. Come, I'll introduce you around."

The common room was a roomy hall with exposed beams. At its center was a long mahogany table where the staff obviously took their meals. In each of the four corners was an alcove with a writing table and chairs, which we learned was the working area for the undermasters and Miss Travistock. The walls of each alcove were lined with books, as was most of the main room. A fire blazed in the north wall fireplace, but its cheeriness did little to warm the greeting of the room's two inhabitants. Tom Biggard, we were told, was on proctor duty at the boys' mess in the far wing. Mr Moses Crisp and Mr Alonzo Goselow were hard at work on the boys' copybooks.

"Dolts, pure and simple," Mr Crisp said, handing a pile of the copybooks to his colleague. "I hope they did better with declensions than they have with my fluctions today, Goselow." Crisp was a heavy florid man of forty-odd years who had been at Fenway for the past six. Alonzo Goselow was decidedly Crisp's junior in age, but not in pedanticism.

"I haven't the heart to read them tonight," he said, "but I have a duty to the ancients. You are here to see the clock, Captain?"

"And just in time. I understand the Reverend is thinking of tearing it down since the unfortunate episode recently."

"The headmaster has become a bit over-excited," Goselow said with a prissy grin. He was no more than thirty, and thin and pale as a flounder's belly. "It's ludicrous, isn't it? Tear down a perfectly good clock because some jackanapes decides to play a prank and gets himself killed. Hull was a common boy – a mere farmer, and what he was doing here, I'll never . . ."

"For an education, Mr Goselow, which is not an exclusive preserve."

The speaker was a young blond fellow who had just entered the room.

"Ah," Goselow said, turning toward the new arrival, "enter the schoolboys' hero, our own Mr Biggard. Have your darlings been fed and bedded?"

Tom Biggard ignored Goselow and strode across the room toward us.

"You must be Captain Cork and Mr Oaks," he said, shaking our hands. "You'll have to forgive my colleagues, gentlemen. The dust of antiquity clouds their humanity."

"Schoolboys have no humanity," Crisp said, yawning. "When do we eat?"

There was a knock at the door and it opened without anyone having answered. Amos, the gatekeeper, shuffled in carrying a large keyring. "All's secured, Tommy," he said. "Tower, dorm, and main gate." He hung the ring on a hook to the left of the door. "Nighty to you, Tommy and all," he mumbled over his shoulder as he left.

"Why you allow that ignorant old fool to call you by your Christian name, I'll never know," Crisp said. "It's disgraceful."

"Amos knew me when I was here as a lad, Mr Crisp. I take no offense."

"Do I understand that the main gate is locked?" Cork got to his feet. "You see, Oaks and I must be leaving."

"I understood you were to spend the night here. Reverend Travistock just told me so."

"He offered, Mr Biggard, but I must apologize that we cannot accept. We have business to the north and will stop to see the clock on our way back. Tomorrow, or the next day at the latest. You will give our regards to the headmaster and his sister. No, don't bother, gentlemen, I see your supper has arrived. Just give me the key and I will give it to Amos to return to you when we have passed through."

"But it's after dark," Mr Crisp warned us.

"Things are more interesting by moonlight at times. Here, Oaks, we'll take some of these hot biscuits to tide us over on the ride."

I thought it quite rude of him when he took several rolls from the basket that a serving girl had placed on the table. He then took the keyring, and we were off like a gust of wind. Amos was locking the gate behind us when Cork steadied his mount and said, "Tell me, good fellow, is there a farrier in the neighborhood? Our horses are still summer shod, and there seems to be a heavy frost up."

"A mile north, ya night birds, ya. Don't go for unlocking and locking and unlocking all night, so you're out to stay and that's the end of it. Horseshoes at night. Bah. Look for the sign of the Inn of the Hanging Dog and you're there."

The moon was at the full when we reached the Inn of the Hanging Dog. It was a rude one-storied structure quite unlike the accommodations we were used to. The host was a morose fellow named Jobbot who was not happy to have tired and hungry guests at his doorsill. A few coins from Cork's purse rekindled any hospitality the scoundrel ever had. He told us that he had but one sleeping room, for the place was more a country tavern than a hostelry, and he sent his wife to prepare it.

The Captain and I took a table in the deserted public rooms where we were promised cold pork and beans. Sly dog that he is, Cork ordered straight rum lest he have to divulge his precious Knock's secret ingredient in front of me.

"Is there a blacksmith in these parts, innkeeper?" Cork asked when the plates were put down before us.

"Aye, Lemuel Stroud has a forge nearby."

When he had left us to our meal, I asked, "A smith? I thought you wanted a farrier to shoe the mounts, and while I'm at it, have we convinced ourselves that Chad Hull's death was an accident?"

"Our needing a blacksmith should answer your question." He

reached into his pocket and brought forth one of the biscuits he had taken from the table. He had torn it in two, and a curious imprint was sunk into the soft bread.

"The key, you made an impression of the key when we were on our way to the gate. But why? And if Chad was played foul, shouldn't we have stayed to see it through?"

"Best to allay any suspicions. I believe the boy was done in, but I do not yet know why. The rest is all in place, but the reason eludes me, damn it."

"The whole affair eludes me. How are you so sure he was killed . . . ouch . . ." he had poked me soundly in the ribs, and I dropped my mug of rum. "What the devil . . .?"

"Precisely the point, my old son. If you had a chamberpot in your hand, you would certainly have dropped it when a jacamart's sword pierced your back, and it would have been smashed to a million pieces. Chad would have dropped the pot off the platform and yet it was found laying next to his body."

"Possibly, but it could have happened."

"Also consider that the tower was locked, so he had to scale the outside of the edifice carrying the item. It's an impossible task, I feel."

"But if not out to make a prank, then why climb the tower in the first place?"

"Good Lord, man, use your memory. The boy sends a letter home implying that money will soon be his. His copybook contains a cryptic progression of thought that now makes sense."

He suddenly looked up at the innkeeper who was just leaving the tap with a tray of mugs. "So there we have it. I should have guessed."

"Guessed what, the meaning of the notations?"

"No, the reason why an innkeeper would be drawing four mugs of cider for the third time in an hour."

"It is an inn, is it not?"

"An empty inn, Oaks, and a one-storey inn at that. And yet, while we sit here talking, you can hear shuffling up in the eaves."

"Squirrels, no doubt."

"Well, a nest, at least. Come, Oaks, quickly."

I followed him out of the public room and stopped behind him in the shadows of the passageway. Suddenly the passage ceiling seemed to lower itself, and by the gods, it was a hidden ladderway that lowered on ropes. The innkeeper was descending, and we let him pass in the half light, and then Cork raced to stop the stairway from ascending to the ceiling again. We slowly made our way up the stairs; voices could be heard somewhere above. A chill went up my back as we listened to the voices chanting in unison:

"Find my measure
Find my treasure
Know no pleasure
Death, death, death"

"Now!" Cork cried, and we rushed up the last two steps and into one of the most bizarre rooms I have ever seen in my life.

The candlelight from atop a circular table cast eerie shadows about the walls and danced upon a life-sized painting. I gave a gasp, for the image was that of Blandersfield, the jacamart. The four figures around the table jumped up in startlement at our bounding in on them.

"Please be seated, gentlemen," Cork commanded. "I believe I have the pleasure of addressing the leading members of the Fenway School Fourth Form, do I not?"

What then ensued was a jumble of tumbled chairs, frightened faces, and much calming by the Captain. When he had convinced the lads that he meant them no harm, the students took their seats and introduced themselves and explained the ritual. As Cork surmised, they were all fourth form members: Lemfent Pieterse, Pardee Davis, Edmund Edwards, and Jonathan Lott. Pieterse was the eldest at sixteen, Lott the youngest at fourteen.

"We are doing no harm, Captain Cork," Pieterse said. "Blandersfield's Ba . . ." he stopped and looked at his cohorts.

"You are among men, Master Pieterse," Cork chuckled.

"Blandersfield's Bastards has been a school club for years. All our fathers belonged to it. It's just a spot of fun, sir."

"And what of the incantation?"

"Well, Captain," Pardee Davis spoke up, "it's just an old tale that's as old as the school."

The boy went on to tell the same story that had been handed down from member to member over the years. Hector deJoonge, so the legend went, was a Dutch pirate who used the Fenway School to hide from his fellow cutthroats from whom he had stolen a sack of jewels. Having been trained as a clockmaker in his youth, he posed as a benevolent man wanting to make a contribution to the school, and built the Great Clock. He had hidden his treasure somewhere in or near the tower and set Jack Blandersfield to guard it.

"All these years, no one has ever found it, but the club goes on just for fun," Pardee Davis concluded.

"Was Chad Hull a member?" Cork asked.

"Hull!" Jonathan Lott said. "That clod?"

"He was all right, Johno," Pieterse corrected him. "Just a bit awkward."

"But he could have known about the legend?"

"Oh, to be sure, Captain," Pieterse answered for all. "Most of the young 'uns have heard about it, but no one seriously believes about the treasure."

"I have a feeling that Chad Hull did, and it cost him his life, lads. How would you like to help me snare a killer?"

Their eyes went wide in wonder and the answer was a resounding yes.

"Good, now which is the best sneak here? No modesty, please, my lads."

"Johno, to be sure," Pieterse said with admiration, and all eyes turned to young Lott.

"The envy of your peers is a compliment indeed, Johno. Do you think you can slip into the common room tomorrow night and take the keyring?"

The boy's smile showed that the task was not a maiden voyage for him.

Cork returned the grin. "Excellent, now, tell me, are your copybooks turned in at the end of each day?"

"At three on the dot," Johno assured him.

"You have pen and paper there on the table. May I please? Tomorrow, Johno, you will copy what I write here exactly into the back of your book and turn it in as usual. Then, at night, just after the clock strikes ten o'clock, you will borrow the key from the common room and let yourself into the clock tower and climb to the clockface platform."

"Whatever for, Captain?"

"To meet Mr Oaks, who will be there waiting for you. Now this notation is done, and take care to copy it exactly."

I looked on as the boys read it:

BLANDERSFIELD PROGRAM 10/31

```
                              DO
                        TI
                     LA
                  SO
               FA
            ME
         RE
      DO
      V        I!
```

"Makes little sense to me," I said after the boys had left and we were in our room. "And how am I to get to the top of the tower . . . oh yes, I see, the key impression in the bread and your need for a blacksmith. And where might you be, may I ask?"

"Tripping my snare."

"One thing hasn't gotten past me. You asked at the school if the boys studied music, and tonight you wrote out the do-re-me's for Johno (what an appalling hypocorism) to copy. So we now know that Chad was after this mythical treasure and someone stopped him."

"Who said it was mythical?"

"But Captain, the boys implied that it was only an old tale perpetuated by a secret club."

"People are seldom murdered over myths, Oaks. Over the years, these true stories take on the trappings of myth, but some are true all the same." He took out his rented books and began to read again.

"And you think the treasure is hidden in the clock?"

"I *know* where the treasure is. I don't need a snare for that. Now why don't you get some sleep? You'll need it."

"Yes, of course. One thing, though. If the students are locked in every night, how the deuce did these four get out?"

He gave me that smirk-a-mouth again. "Wellman Oaks, I am now convinced that you came into this world a fully grown man with a ledger book under each arm. Man has dictated many a rule and many a circumscription, but these do not apply to boys, for boyhood is the epitome of cleverness. At least not on this night, man. The date, man, think. It is All Hallow's Eve."

I closed my eyes thinking there had been one extra boy at the meeting of the Blandersfield Bastards this night.

I woke the next morning to the chagrin that I had overslept, and to my surprise, Cork was gone. A note and a large iron key were at my bedside table:

Oaks:
Herewith your means of entry to gate and tower. Stay here till nine tonight and thence to Fenway. Enter the tower after the stroke of ten and await Johno on the clockface platform. I am about other business, but shall be there when needed. Mind, lock the tower and gate behind you.

Godspeed,
Cork

It was ten-ten by my timepiece as I stood huddled against the clockface. The wind had turned from west to nor'west, and the fingers of coming winter played upon me. The moon was slipping behind high clouds, leaving me with alternate light and sudden dark. To be sure, I was truly shaken. Here I had climbed a perilously long ladder inside the tower and fumbled in the darkness to find the opening to the outer platform. That was wearing enough, but now I stood on a platform of very small width looking down at the quad, which seemed miles away. On the right side of the clock platform was the ominous jacamart's guardhouse, its shadow standing in deadly stillness in the intermittent moonlight.

A fissure of panic started to crease my brain. If for some reason young Lott could not get the key, and perchance I miscalculated the time, I could well meet the same fate as Chad Hull. Suddenly, my ears harked. I could hear a muggled noise down below, and, minutes later, the creak of the ladder within the tower. My heart was a'bump and the creak came closer and closer.

"Mr Oaks," a voice whispered. "It's Johno, Mr Oaks."

"Out here, lad," I said. "Take care the edge now."

"Where is the Captain?" the boy asked when he reached me. "I thought he would be here too." His voice sounded more than disappointed. More excited or nervous. My Lord, the thought struck me, could this stripling be the murderer? Had Cork used me as the lure for his snare, and if so, where was he? "Don't stand too close, my boy," I told him gingerly, "this is a small platform indeed."

"I know, sir, I've been up here before."

"When?"

"Last . . . what's that? Someone's coming up the ladderway!"

Thank God, I told myself, Cork hadn't failed me. The two of us could handle this young murderer.

"Johno," a voice whispered, "you out there, lad?"

"Yes, who is it?"

"Where in the dome, Johno, my boy? Where is it? We could split the treasure, laddie."

"Split it!" my voice got away from me.

"Who's with you out there?" the man asked as he stepped out onto the platform. At that moment the moon slipped from behind a cloud, bathing the figure of Tom Biggard, a sword in his hand. He started out for us, his weapon held treacherously in front of him.

"So you're back, Mr Oaks. Well, that makes it all the better. It will be a simple case of you two killing each other over the loot."

He started for us and I grabbed the Lott boy and put him on the other side of me to protect him from the first thrust of the blade. He was at the center of the platform now, and ready to strike, when I saw it move. The jacamart came rushing forward and ran Biggard through with its steel.

"Well, don't stand there, Oaks," the jacamart said to me. "Hold this fiend up. I don't want him splattered all over the Reverend's quad."

Tom Biggard was badly wounded but alive when the Justice of the Peace came and had his men take him away. We were all in the common room, where Cork was holding forth with gusto in front of a slateboard.

"Oh, the shame of it," Reverend Travistock was saying. "One of our own graduates."

"And who else, sir? He had been a student here, he well knew the legend, and was probably once a member of a secret club which shall remain mercifully nameless."

"But I don't understand all this nonsense about Lott putting that do-re-me gibberish in his copybook," Crisp was yawning, but not bored.

"To fully appreciate the affair, let me say you were all suspects when I arrived here, and then the pieces began to fall in place. Let me put Chad Hull's September 19 notation on the slate." He wrote:

EF/FG/GA/AB/BC/CD/DE/EF?

"As a mathematics teacher, does that suggest anything to you, Mr Crisp?"

"It's a progression. The second letter of the first set becomes the first letter of the next set, and so on. But it doesn't make any sense to me."

"As well it shouldn't, unless you knew that Chad was attempting to find the jacamart's treasure. The letters in progression are the notes of the musical scale. I believe Chad felt the uniqueness of the Roman strike, and tried to find some clue in the notes of the scale, since he runs from E, a low note, to F, a high note. But he gets nowhere with it. He is truly embrangled. It is almost the same on October 10, but he starts to get closer to the mark in a small way.

"He shifts from the musical scale to the frugality of the Roman strike system." Cork wrote the October 10 notation on the board:

$78-34=44=GB?$
$78-32=46=GA?$

"Now, this is nothing more than finding the stroke differences between the regular strike system and the Roman strike system, and transferring the numbers into his progression scale of notes. Pure rot. But the second line of the notation shows us that a glimmer of light has come through, for Chad now calculates the difference between the regular strike and deJoonge's Roman system minus two strokes for the missing six o'clock sounding. Chad is still at sea, but at least he is thinking like old deJoonge. If a man were hiding a treasure, he would not mark a path for a confederate with such complexities. He would make it decidedly simple. I have reason to believe Chad had no real ear for music."

He knew very well, for so Chad's father had informed us. Miss Travistock, however, confirmed it again, thus protecting our previous association with the Hull family.

"Hark," Cork said, "the clock is striking eleven."

We all listened to the two low gongs and the one high. "What notes in the scale would you say those bell sounds are?"

She smiled. "I have known that since I was a girl. They are E and G, the first and third letters of the scale."

"And since the Reverend has told us that there are only two bells in the system, the scale notes are always the same in one E or G combination or another. So the missing six o'clock strike, VI, or one low and one high, would be EG. Of course, Chad Hull's tin ear at first saw it as EF, the first and second notes in the scale. But that would make the low and high rings almost indiscernible, and deJoonge widened the bell tone scale to EG, and thus told us where the treasure is by leaving six o'clock silent."

"I can't see where EG gets us," Crisp, the mathematics teacher, said.

"No, not as EG, but suppose they were sung in the so-fa syllables such as children do."

"Do and mi," Miss Travistock said.

"Or do and *me*, as it is often expressed in the tonic scale, so-fa."

"Do . . . me, dome," I said. "The dome of the clock is where the treasure is hidden. That's why you had young Lott put the do-re-me's into his notebook."

"Since all the instructors would see it and believe that Chad's work had been decoded, his killer would watch Lott like a hawk, and he did."

The Reverend looked dumbly at the slate. "You mean there really is a treasure up there in the tower? When I was a child, I remember some tough fellows showed up just after deJoonge died, looking for him. It was the only lie my father ever told. He informed them that the Dutchman had gone south to the Carolinas, and they left in pursuit.

My father never talked about it again, although I heard talk during my student days."

"A headmaster's son is hardly a schoolboy's confidant, Reverend."

I was overcome with glee. After all, if Cork had solved the riddle, then the treasure was rightly his. "Well, shall we start a thorough search of the dome?" I suggested.

"I'm afraid you would search in vain, Oaks."

"Then there is no treasure?"

"Oh yes, my old friend. I believe there is. But think, the tower does not have a dome. It has a spire. No, deJoonge was a sly old fox, but he gave himself away. You'll remember that our watchmaker in New Haven told us of the crudity of the Fenway clock. It doesn't even keep proper time. And yet, the same man constructs the beautiful piece of precision hanging now from Miss Travistock's chatelaine."

"This old thing?" she said holding it up. "I always correct it to match the tower clock."

"And thus fall for the Dutchman's deception. May I have it again, please? I'm afraid you weren't paying much attention, Oaks, when the New Haven man was cleaning your watch. He told you that your timepiece had been worked on by several people over the years. Do you know how he knew that? No, because you, like most people, are hesitant to open a precision instrument that you might harm." He put his thumbnail along the back of the catch and flipped the cover open.

"Do you see this inner cover? It's called a dome, is it not, and if we open that we find . . . ah yes, an inscription in the same place watchmakers carve their initials or mark when they work on a timepiece. Does 'the foot of the westward oak' mean anything to you, Reverend? I think you will find your treasure buried there."

Mr Goselow, the professor of Greek and Latin, looked at Cork with unabashed admiration. "How perfectly Socratic, sir. My compliments."

"My compliments" indeed, for that's all our reward was to be. We were back at the Oar and Eagle the next evening, and I sat at the accounts dais glaring at him. "At least we could have claimed half of the jewels," I said. "Poor boys' scholarship, indeed."

"And why not? Old deJoonge's evil has done some good at last. Besides, possibly one of the indigent lads who will benefit from an education will become a doctor or lawyer and save you from sickness or me from the gallows. Come in, Tedderhorn. Good, you've brought the Knock. I've missed it."

I half-heartedly took my mug and sipped.

"Well, Oaks, have you figured it out yet?" Cork chaffed.

"Cloves," I said. "I'm sure of it."

"Good. Tedderhorn, hand the paper I gave you the other day to Oaks."

I read it and fumed:

Tedderhorn:
Add nothing to the Knock, but don't tell Oaks.

Cork

"This is . . . ah . . . dishonesty, foul play," I cried.

"Nonsense, my old son, it is deception, no more."

"And do you not consider deception dishonest?"

"Not when all the facts are in front of you. You had your sense of taste. I just misdirected you. Come, man, as Shakespeare says, 'would you pluck out the heart of my mystery?'"

I persevere.

THE SCENT
OF MURDER
Theodore Mathieson

From Captain Cork to Captain Cook. In 1960, Theodore Mathieson (b. 1913) published a volume called The Great "Detectives" *which featured ten historical mysteries solved by famous characters from history starting with Alexander the Great and ending with Florence Nightingale. The stories are ingeniously researched selecting a theme wholly relevant to the character and creating a mystery that could so easily have happened. The following story was the first of them to be written. The series so fascinated Frederick Dannay (one-half of the Ellery Queen writing team) that he called it "one of the most ambitious literary projects ever envisioned."*

On the night of June 11, 1770, fourteen months after His Majesty's ship *Endeavour* had left England, and while she explored the waters three hundred miles off the coast of "New Holland," Captain James Cook was suddenly faced with a problem that he could not solve by quadrant or caliper.

It was two bells, most of the crew were below, and the captain slowly paced the afterdeck. He reached the starboard side, grasped the taffrail, and looked aloft to where the three masts of the sturdy sailing ship rose black against the tropical moonlight, when he heard a cry from the ladder.

"Captain, sir," a voice said shakily from the shadows.

"Come up, Blore," Cook said, recognizing the voice of the quartermaster of the watch.

"It's Prout, sir, the bosun's mate. He's dead. I just found him midship, hanging over the rail. There's a knife in his back. I haven't touched him, sir."

Cook hesitated a moment, looking down at the deep, concealing shadows on the main deck. This could be a trick. The men had been giving trouble, wanting to turn back after New Zealand, saying he'd gotten what the Admiralty had sent him for – the transit of Venus. It was true. On Tahiti three months ago he'd made the observation which, when combined with measurements made by scientists at other points on the globe, would determine for the first time in history the distance from the earth to the sun.

But now the men were homesick. The captain had been forced, after the outbreak of a drunken, resentful riot in the forecastle, to cut the ration of grog to a fourth. The men were in a sullen, threatening mood.

"Prout has been drinking, sir," Blore said, clucking his tongue. "Smells like he's been wallowing in the hogshead."

Cook made his decision. "Bring him here," he said sharply. "Get Hicks the cook to give you a hand. I see the light in his galley."

"Yes, sir, but – " Blore half turned away.

"But what?"

"I think it might be Hicks that did it, sir, after what happened between them this morning."

"Get Hicks to help you," Cook repeated.

Ship's surgeon Monkhouse, a mountain of a man, stood beside his stubborn-lipped captain as Blore and the cook, Hicks, lowered the body gently to the deck. It was still flexible and warm, although the bearded face of the bosun's mate had had time to smooth out, so that he looked peaceful and unconcerned over his sudden and violent end. Probably he'd not even caught sight of his assailant before he died, although it was doubtful if he'd been able to recognize him if he had.

"Grog must be coming out of his pores, sir," Monkhouse said. "Smell that."

"Ain't it something terrible?" Hicks, the wiry, whey-faced little cook said fervently. Fresh from the galley, his white apron gleamed in the moonlight.

At the captain's order Monkhouse leaned over and removed the knife from the dead man's back. He had a little difficulty, at which Blore made a choking sound and ran for the rail.

"An ordinary butcher's knife," the captain said. "Like one you use, Hicks, isn't it?"

"I wondered where it'd got to," the cook said, wetting his lips. "It's been gorn since last night."

The captain studied the little Cockney briefly, while the rigging creaked in the sway from the ocean swell.

"Come into the cabin, all of you," he said.

Inside the captain's cabin it was warm and close. Through the stern windows the moonlight could be seen coruscating upon the waves. The captain, a gaunt six-footer, lean of cheek and long of nose, stood for a moment in the stern alcove, seeming to tower over his men. Then he sat down at his writing desk and the others gathered round him, their faces white and tense in the light of the lantern swinging in brass gimbals over the desk. The captain's cat, Orleans, jumped on his master's lap and settled down undisturbed.

"You may sit down," the captain said, and as Blore entered belatedly, looking a sickly green, he admonished as an afterthought, "And *you* had better stay near the door." The captain swung around to the cook.

"What happened between you and Prout this morning?"

The unexpectedness of the question caused Hicks to gasp. Then his little black eyes narrowed and he slid them murderously toward Blore.

"I – don't quite know what you're gettin' at, Cap'n," Hicks said with a yellow-toothed smile. "Prout and I wasn't friends exactly, but – "

"I want to know what happened this morning."

"We had a little argument, that's all," Hicks mumbled.

"Perhaps I can tell you," Monkhouse the surgeon spoke up. "I went down to call on a patient during the noonday mess. Prout is – was – something of a bully. I think most of the men can tell you that. He was always making Hicks here take back his food and get him something else."

"Couldn't please 'im anyhow!" Hicks said venomously.

"It's gone on for six months, now, sir," Blore spoke up from the door. "Today Prout became pretty violent and sent food back twice. Said Cooky was the worst slob of a cook that'd ever sailed in His Majesty's service. Cooky got mad and swung the iron frying pan at Prout's head. Would have killed him if Prout hadn't jerked away. The frying pan made a gash in the table you could put your hand into."

"But I didn't kill him, did I?" Hicks protested in a shrill voice.

"You tried to," the captain said quietly. "And as for being a bad cook, I've had occasion to send certain dishes back myself, if you recall."

"I do me level best," Hicks whined. "That's all a bloke can do, beggin' your pardon, Cap'n."

"There's only one reason that makes me think you didn't do it," the captain said, looking at Hicks as one might look at a cockroach sitting on a tablecloth. "You hated Prout all right – that's clear to all of us. But I think you'd like to have had him suffer a little for bullying you these six months. The knife would have been too quick for you, I think."

The cook nodded quickly. "That it would," he said.

"Especially since if you had merely reported Prout, who has obviously broached the hogshead, he would have been strapped to the bowsprit and you could have seen him die slowly of hunger and exposure. That was the fate I ordered, as you all know, for anyone found tampering with the grog."

"Aye, 'e's 'ad it too easy, I'd say!" Cooky said, sniffing.

The surgeon stirred his heavy body and started to rise, then sat back again.

"There's still another one who might have done this," he said. "Although I – "

"No changing course now," the captain warned.

"It's young William Backus. First trip, has learned the ropes quickly. A likely lad . . . I hate to mention it, but in all fairness to Cooky here . . ."

"Backus wouldn't do it," Blore said quickly. "He's too nice a lad. Reads his Bible regular."

"But you think I did it!" Hicks cried shrilly, and the captain silenced him with a gesture. He turned back to the surgeon.

"But the lad had a grudge against Prout?"

"I'm afraid he did. The boy has his hammock next to Prout's. He'd try to sleep at night and Prout would push his foot against the lad's hammock. Prout didn't sleep well, so Will didn't get much sleep either. He tried to move away but Prout wouldn't let him. Finally the boy came to me, but I told him to fight it out for himself. He did fight it out, but Prout beat him almost to a pulp, and then went right on keeping him awake."

Blore said suddenly, "Prout was just asking to be killed, Captain! None of the men could get on with him."

"Except you," the surgeon said blandly. "I saw you and Prout together now and then. Very friendly, you seemed."

"I always try to see the other man's side of it," Blore said with a quiet dignity. "Besides, I recognized Prout for the bully he was, and never took anything from him. First week out from Plymouth I fought him, and laid him out flat on the deck. We got on together fine after that, but I didn't seek out his company."

The captain sighed. He knew it would not do to let the murder go unpunished among a crew whose temper was reaching a lawless pitch. He would have to sift and question, to find the murderer and make an example of him.

"Bring me Backus," he said to Blore.

Blore went out with a show of reluctance, and the captain had barely time to turn to Hicks, whom he was on the point of dismissing, when the quartermaster of the watch was back in the cabin, with his mouth hanging open, breathing heavily.

"Well, what is it?" the captain demanded.

"It's Prout, sir. We left him on the deck out there, but there's no trace of him. The body's gone, sir."

At the captain's order Monkhouse and Blore set about searching the ship unobtrusively for the corpse. From the heavy sprit to the boxy stern they looked, above and below deck, into the hollow cores of coils of hempen line, among the piles of uncut canvas, and between pyramids of oaken casks. They stumbled as noiselessly as they could manage over spars and blocks and pulleys and belaying pins. Breathing fetid air, they crawled on hands and knees in the forecastle beneath the hammocks of sleeping men. And at the end of two hours they concluded that the obvious solution had been the correct one: the body of the bosun's mate had been thrown over the side.

During the search Blore checked the spigot of the hogshead and found it still sealed, but another spigot, concealed by a bulkhead, had been thrust into the back of the cask. Prout had doubtless drunk his grog on the spot, not daring to carry it away in containers, for there was a quarter-filled mug in the shadow of a cask block. But for all his precautions the bosun's mate had overestimated his capacity, and if the murderer hadn't doomed him, his obvious condition would have.

Captain Cook found himself liking the boy Will Backus at once. He was tall, muscular and blond, about nineteen, red-cheeked and clear-eyed, although there were telltale dark circles under his eyes. He entered the captain's cabin with evident anxiety, but was self-possessed.

"Sit down, Backus," the captain said curtly. "I suppose Blore has told you what happened to Prout."

"Yes, sir."

"I understand you and he were not the best of friends."

The boy lowered his eyes and his lip trembled. "No, we were not, sir."

"Do you mind telling me why?"

Backus explained the trouble between him and the bosun's mate much as Monkhouse had done. When he had finished, the boy put his hand petitioningly on the captain's desk.

"Would you please believe me, sir," he said, "that although I had every reason to hate Mr Prout, I made every effort not to feel that way toward him."

"So I understand. You're a great reader of the Bible, Mr Blore tells me."

"Yes, sir. I promised my father I would read it and follow its precepts faithfully. I try to hate no man."

"But you'll agree that Prout made himself decidedly hateful to most of the men. And besides yourself, to the cook Hicks, particularly?"

"The Bible does not say that one should fail to recognize evil when he meets it. I believe Mr Prout was evil."

"And deserved to be murdered?"

"That would be God's decision, sir."

"And you would not think of being His instrument?"

The boy looked at the captain, paled, but did not answer.

"Answer my question."

"I believe, Captain Cook, that God often chooses His instruments to do – certain acts – on earth. But I swear to you, sir, that I did not kill Mr Prout."

Captain Cook reached for his pipe, filled it, and when he had it going well, he asked, "Did you know that Prout was soddenly drunk when he was killed?"

"Mr Blore did mention that, sir."

"And if you stepped up behind him to do him harm, and found him intoxicated, would you have reported him to your superior officer and have the ship's discipline punish him?"

"I cannot answer that, sir. I do not know."

"You do not know if it would satisfy God's justice to see Prout on the bowsprit, suffering day after day the pangs of starvation and thirst?"

"No, no!" the boy cried suddenly. "I could not want that. Nor would God want it."

Captain Cook pointed at the door of the cabin with the stem of his pipe.

"That will be all just now, Backus," he said.

The next morning the captain sat down wearily at his desk and took his journal from the drawer. With the sun warming his back, and the quill poised over the page, he sat staring at Orleans, curled upon his bunk.

There was so much more to be done, if the men could only understand. There were islands in these South Seas still unclaimed by Spain, Portugal, France or Holland. There were unknown waters to chart, and most important of all, there was the possibility of discovering a new continent for the glory of Britain.

He sighed and began writing: "After staying up half the night interrogating the men and officers, I have come to only one conclusion. Only two men have *suffered* sufficiently at Prout's hands to have murdered him – Backus and Hicks. The others have been able to handle Prout, and one of them, Blore, seemed even to be friendly with him. Blore is a problem. Although he has no apparent reason for murder, and got on well with Prout, still he was the only one of those who first knew of Prout's murder (Monkhouse, Hicks and myself) who was outside of the cabin long enough to have accomplished the removal of the body. Was he actually sick when the surgeon withdrew the knife, or was he pretending? The more I think about this, the more confusing it becomes. I shall keep Blore in mind, and for the moment add him to my list of possible criminals.

"As I see it, the answer to Prout's murder lies in how each one of these three men – Hicks, Backus, and Blore – would *actually* react if they knew that by merely reporting Prout's dereliction the bosun's mate would be condemned to a slow death. It is certain, I think, that men often are of two kinds – pain-givers and pain-savers. Prout was killed suddenly, quickly, while deeply intoxicated. Without question all three men knew of the penalty for broaching the hogshead. That means that whoever murdered Prout, although he knew he might have had much more satisfaction out of seeing Prout languish on the bow-sprit, preferred to kill him quickly and save him pain. The murderer, then, was a pain-saver. Now of these three men, who are the pain-savers and who are the pain-givers? Young Backus says that he is a pain-saver. Hicks is obviously a pain-giver. Blore, with his quiet ways and queasy stomach, would seem to be a pain-saver. Yet, how often does a man really know himself well enough to give an accurate description of his tendencies? *I cannot depend upon what these men say about themselves, or what they seem to me to be.*

"The only answer is to devise some sort of test and catch their reactions unexpectedly . . ."

The idea of the test came soon – as Cook watched his tabby, Orleans, playing with a pen that had fallen to the deck. The captain made his preparations, and on the evening following the murder he called Hicks into his cabin.

The cook had taken off his apron and slicked his hair in deference to the occasion. He stood smiling ingratiatingly in the doorway.

"Come in," the captain said affably. "I want you to feel at ease, Hicks. I'm not making any accusations. I just want to find out more about what happened last night, and I'd appreciate your help. Have a drink of brandy?"

Hicks lost his smile in bewilderment at this egalitarian treatment, but recovered sufficiently to bob his head at the invitation to imbibe.

As the captain carefully poured two brandies, a scratching from a wooden box set on the captain's desk attracted Hicks's attention.

"Orleans loves to play with a baby mouse now and then," Cook said casually. "And I enjoy watching the sport. You may look in."

Hicks nodded and peered down eagerly. Orleans held his young enemy lightly under his right paw.

"Of course, I believe in being fair about it," the captain said. "If the mouse manages to stay alive for the time it takes this hourglass to pour five minutes of its sand – to this mark – I let the mouse go."

"To plague the ship, Cap'n?"

"If he runs into you, of course, that's his misfortune. But he has earned his reprieve from me."

Hicks nodded noncommittally and continued avidly to watch Orleans and his prize. The captain sat down and began asking questions about the night before – perfunctory questions which had already been asked, but Hicks, with his attention divided, didn't seem to notice. Once or twice Orleans chased the little mouse from corner to corner with a commotion that threatened to upset the box, but the captain paid no attention, and continued his questioning. Hicks grew more and more excited.

"There, that makes it time," the captain said finally, turning the hourglass over.

"Oh, not yet, Cap'n!" Hicks said, pleading. "The cat hasn't begun to play proper yet."

"But the time is up."

"Please, Cap'n," Hicks said, his eyes on the box.

The captain waited deliberately, and a few seconds later Orleans pounced once more and a mortal squeal from the mouse told the story.

"There! 'e's damaged now, all right!" Hicks cried triumphantly.

"We waited too long," the captain sighed, and put the box upon the deck.

"Hicks is exactly what he appeared to be – a pain-giver," the captain wrote in his journal late that night. "And Backus didn't like the cat and mouse idea right from the start. He wouldn't even look, and I am convinced he was not shamming. He, too, was right about himself. Blore was the only one of the three who seemed to detect what I was about, and let me know it by his manner. He is an intelligent man, and I cannot be sure about his reactions. He looked on with little show of emotion, and when the time was up quietly agreed that I should terminate the struggle.

"I do not like what this leads me to surmise. It puts the boy Backus first in my suspicions, with Blore in the middle, and Hicks last. Unless

I can think of another plan of investigation, I'm afraid we shall not uncover the truth about Prout's murder . . ."

The captain solved it the very next morning.

He sat at breakfast, looking through the stern windows at a huge island looming up on the horizon like a great cloud. He could hear the leadsman's chant as he sounded from the chains. "The existing maps do not show an island here," the captain was thinking. "We must investigate." Then his thought broke off like a thread. In the middle of a bite he crashed his cup of tea into the saucer, rose, and strode to the door of his cabin.

"Monkhouse!" he thundered at the surgeon who stood at the rail outside. "Get those three up here – Backus, Hicks, and Blore. Right away!"

Too startled for words, the surgeon nodded and made for the ladder to the main deck. The captain withdrew to his cabin again, poured three small drinks, and placed them in a row on the table.

Blore was the first to arrive, wiping his hands on a cloth; he had been helping the botanists rearrange the specimens in their cabin.

"You called, Captain?" Blore asked mildly.

"All three of you, yes," the captain said grimly. "I think I have discovered a way of revealing the criminal."

"Will he give up that easily, sir?"

"Two of you will help me hold him should he become violent," the captain said, smiling.

Backus arrived, his hands still soapy from washing the companionway to the forecastle. His hair was tousled and his eyes wide with excitement.

"I came right away, sir," he said eagerly.

"Yes. Give him your cloth, Blore, and let him wipe his hands free of soap."

"Thank you, sir," Backus said, busy with the cloth.

And then Hicks came, not having bothered to remove his apron this time, nor slick back his hair.

"At your service, Cap'n," he said easily, presuming on the friendliness the captain had shown him the night before.

The captain closed the door, then stood up before the three of them.

"I wish you to drink with me – a little toast to the island we see ahead. It is uncharted, and possibly uninhabited."

The captain handed the three glasses to the men.

"Do not drink until I give the word," he said sharply, and then more slowly, "In a minute or two I think we shall find the criminal who murdered Prout. And when we do, he will have the choice of swinging from the yardarm or of being marooned on that island."

"You know who it is?" It was Backus, his voice sounding high and young.

"Yes, I think I do, Backus. All I need now is proof."

"How do you propose to get it, Captain?" Blore asked.

Hicks said nothing; his look was almost uncomprehending.

"I shall answer your question after you drink my toast," said the captain. "But first, I should be considerably hurt if you do not consider the bouquet of this fine brandy." The captain raised the glass to his nose and sniffed, and the others did likewise.

"Now drink," he said, and swallowed the contents of his own glass quickly. When he looked at the others, two of them stood gazing at him wonderingly, their glasses still full in their hands. The third was spluttering, his eyes watering, his glass empty.

"Don't you like vinegar, Hicks?" the captain asked quietly. "*If you had been able to smell it when you sniffed, perhaps you wouldn't have drunk it.* The others didn't. You murdered Prout, didn't you? You would have let the ship's punishment take care of him the long and painful way if you could have smelled his drunkenness the other night; but since you couldn't, you killed him the quick, merciful way, which was quite unlike you."

"You don't know what you're talkin' abaht, Cap'n," Hicks said, his cheeks wet with tears drawn by the vinegar. "I was inside the cabin with you when the body was moved. The murderer did that, so I ain't the murderer."

"Yes, you are, Hicks," Backus said quietly. "I saw you do it. But because you'd been bullied the way I'd been bullied, I threw Prout overboard so you wouldn't be blamed for it. I thought I was justified, but it's been a terrible weight on my conscience. Now that God has let Captain Cook see the truth, I cannot hide it any longer."

"You little rat!" Hicks shrieked and rushed frantically toward Backus. Blore seized the little man by the collar and held him firmly, cuffing him until his protestations ceased.

"You burnt my breakfast once too often," the captain said. "Anyone who burns food as often as you, Hicks, must have a defective sense of smell. So you gave yourself away, you see."

Later, when Blore and Backus were gone and Hicks was safely locked in the hold, the captain said to the surgeon:

"We exchange one mystery for another, Monkhouse."

"How do you mean?" the surgeon asked.

"Where in the devil are we going to find another cook?"

THE INN OF
THE BLACK CROW
William Hope Hodgson

During the sixties and seventies the rediscovery of the works of William Hope Hodgson (1877–1918) raised him to almost cult status in the field of weird fiction. He was one of the most visionary writers of fantastic fiction in the first decades of this century in both the novel and short story forms. Indeed, his magnum opus, The Night Land *(1912), set on a dying Earth millions of years in the future, is like nothing else ever written. All of his novels, especially* The House on the Borderland *(1908), are worth reading, as are many of his short stories, most of which reflect the horror of the sea that he knew so well. Although he is also known for his psychic detective stories collected in* Carnacki the Ghost-Finder *(1913), Hodgson's name is not immediately linked with detective fiction. But as he sought to make a living full-time writing in the years before the First World War, Hodgson began to churn out fiction in all genres, some of it highly original and some of it transparently imitative. I will give no prizes for the author Hodgson was copying here, but it is a creditable story nonetheless. This story has not been reprinted since its first appearance in* The Red Magazine *for October 1, 1915, and I am grateful to Jack Adrian for securing me a copy.*

June 27th I cannot say that I care for the look of mine host. If he tippled more and talked more I should like him better; but he drinks not, neither does he speak sufficiently for ordinary civility.

I could think that he has no wish for my custom. Yet, if so, how does he expect to make a living, for I am paying two honest guineas a week for board and bed no better than the Yellow Swan at Dunnage does me for a guinea and a half. Yet that he knows me or suspects me of being more than I appear I cannot think, seeing that I have never been within a hundred miles of this desolated village of Erskine, where there is not even the sweet breath of the sea to blow the silence away, but everywhere the grey moors, slit by the lonesome mud-beset creeks, that I have few doubts see some strange doings at nights, and could, maybe, explain the strange crushed body of poor James Naynes, the exciseman, who had been found dead upon the moors six weeks gone; and concerning which I am here to discover secretly whether it was foul murder or not.

June 30th That I was right in my belief that Jalbrok, the landlord, is a rascal, I have now very good proof, and would shift my quarters, were it not that there is no other hostel this side of Bethansop, and that is fifteen weary miles by the road.

I cannot take a room in any of the hovels round here; for there could be no privacy for me, and I should not have the freedom of unquestioned movement that one pays for at all inns, along with one's bed and board. And here, having given out on arriving that I am from London town for my health, having a shortness of breath, and that I fish with a rod, like my old friend Walton – of whom no man hereabouts has ever heard – I have been let go my way as I pleased, with never a one of these grim Cornishmen to give me so much as a passing nod of the head; for to them I am a "foreigner," deserving, because of this stigma, a rock on my head, rather than a friendly word on my heart. However, in the little Dowe-Fleet river there are trout to make a man forget lonesomeness.

But though I am forced to stay here in the inn until my work is done, and my report prepared for the authorities, yet I am taking such care as I can in this way and that, and never do I venture a yard outside the inn without a brace of great flintlocks hidden under my coat.

Now, I have said I proved Jalbrok, the landlord of this inn of the Black Crow, a rascal. And so have I in two things; for this morning I caught him and his tapman netting the little Dowe-Fleet, and a great haul he had of fish, some that were three pounds weight and a hundred that were not more than fingerlings, and should never have left water.

I was so angry to see this spoiling of good, honest sport that I loosed out at Jalbrok with my tongue, as any fisherman might; but he told me to shut my mouth, and this I had to do, though with difficulty, and only by remembering that a man that suffers from a shortness of wind has no excuse to fight. So I made a virtue of the matter, and sat down suddenly on the bank, and panted pretty hard and spit a bit, and then lay on my side, as if I had a seizure. And a very good acting I made of it, I flattered myself, and glad that I had held my temper in, and so made them all see that I was a truly sick man.

Now, there the landlord left me, lying on my side, when he went away with all that great haul of good trout. And this was the second thing to prove the man a rascal, and liefer to be rid of me than to keep me, else he had not left me there, a sick man as he supposed. And I say and maintain that any man that will net a stream that may be fished with a feathered hook, and will also leave a sick man to recover or to die alone, all as may be, is a true rascal – and so I shall prove him yet.

July 2nd (Night) I have thought that the landlord has something new on his mind lately, and the thing concerns me; for twice and again yesterday evening I caught him staring at me in a very queer fashion, so that I have taken more care than ever to be sure that no one can come at me during the night.

After dinner this evening I went down and sat a bit in the empty taproom, where I smoked my pipe and warmed my feet at the big log fire. The night had been coldish, in spite of the time of the year, for there is a desolate wind blowing over the great moorlands, and I could hear the big Erskine creek lapping on the taproom side of the house, for the inn is built quite near to the creek.

While I was smoking and staring into the fire, a big creekman came into the taproom and shouted for Jalbrok, the landlord, who came out of the back room in his slow, surly way.

"I'm clean out o' guzzle," the creekman said, in a dialect that was no more Cornish than mine. "I'll swop a good yaller angel for some o' that yaller sperrit o' yourn, Jal. An' that are a bad exchange wi'out robb'ry. He, he! Us that likes good likker likes it fresh from the sea, like a young cod. He, he!"

There is one of those farm-kitchen wind-screens, with a settle along it, that comes on one side the fireplace in the taproom, and neither Jalbrok nor the big creekman could see me where I sat, because the oak screen hid me, though I could look round it with the trouble of bending my neck.

Their talk interested me greatly, as may be thought, for it was plain that the man, whoever he might be, had punned on the gold angel, which is worth near half a guinea of honest English money; and what should a creekman be doing with such a coin, or to treat it so lightly, as if it were no more than a common groat? And afterwards to speak of liking the good liquor that comes fresh from the sea! It was plain enough what he meant.

I heard Jalbrok, the landlord, ringing the coin on the counter. And then I heard him saying it was thin gold; and that set the creekman angry.

"Gglag you for a scrape-bone!" he roared out, using a strange expression that was new to me. "Gglag you! You would sweat the oil off a topmast, you would! If you ain't easy, there's more nor one as ha' a knife into you ower your scrape-bone ways; and, maybe, us shall make you pay a good tune for French brandy one o' these days, gglag you!"

"Stow that!" said the landlord's voice. "That's no talk for this place wi' strangers round. I – "

He stopped, and there followed, maybe, thirty seconds of absolute silence. Then I heard someone tiptoeing a few steps over the floor, and I closed my eyes and let my pipe droop in my mouth, as if I were dosing. I heard the steps cease, and there was a sudden little letting out of a man's breath, and I knew that the landlord had found I was in the taproom with them.

The next thing I knew he had me by the shoulder, and shook me, so that my pipe dropped out of my mouth on to the stone floor.

"Here!" he roared out. "Wot you doin' in here!"

"Let go of my shoulder, confound your insolence," I said; and ripped my shoulder free from his fist with perhaps a little more strength than I should have shown him, seeing that I am a sick man to all in this part.

"Confound you!" I said again, for I was angry; but now I had my wits more about me. "Confound your putting your dirty hands on me. First you net the river and spoil my trout fishing, and now you must spoil the best nap I have had for three months."

As I made an end of this, I was aware that the big creekman was also staring round the oak wind-screen at me. And therewith it seemed a good thing to me to fall a-coughing and "howking," as we say in the North; and a better country I never want!

"Let un be, Jal. Let un be!" I heard the big creekman saying. "He ain't but a broken-winded man. There's none that need ha' fear o' that sort. He'll be growin' good grass before the winter. Come you, gglag you, an' gi'e me some guzzle, an' let me be goin'."

The landlord looked at me for nearly a minute without a word; then he turned and followed the creekman to the drinking counter. I heard a little further grumbled talk and argument about the angel being thin gold, but evidently they arranged it between them, for Jalbrok measured out some liquor, that was good French brandy by the smell of it, if ever I've smelt French brandy, and a little later the creekman left.

July 5th Maybe I have kissed the inn wench a little heartily on occasions, but she made no sound objections, and it pleased me,

I fear, a little to hear Llan, the lanky, knock-kneed tapman and general help, rousting at the wench for allowing it. The lout has opinions of himself, I do venture to swear; for a more ungainly, water-eyed, shambling rascal never helped his master net a good trout stream before or since. And as on that occasion he showed a great pleasure, and roared in his high pitched crow at the way I lay on the bank and groaned and coughed, I take an equal great pleasure to kiss the maid, which I could think she is, whenever I chance to see him near.

And to see the oaf glare at me, and yet fear to attack even a sick man, makes me laugh to burst my buttons; but I make no error, for it is that kind of a bloodless animal that will put a knife between a man's shoulders when the chance offers.

July 7th   Now a good kiss, once in a way, may be a good thing all round, and this I discovered it to be, for the wench has taken a fancy to better my food, for which I am thankful; also, last night, she went further, for she whispered in my ear, as she served me my dinner, to keep my bedroom door barred o' nights; but when I would know why, she smiled, putting her finger to her lip, and gave me an old countryside proverb to the effect that a barred door let no corn out and no rats in. Which was a good enough hint for any man, and I repaid the wench in a way that seemed to please her well, nor did she say no to a half-guinea piece which I slipped into her broad fist.

Now, the room I sleep in is large, being about thirty feet long and, maybe, twenty wide, and has a good deal of old and bulky furniture in it, that makes it over-full of shadows at night for my liking.

The door of my room is of oak, very heavy and substantial, and without panels. There is a wooden snick-latch on it to enter by, and the door is made fast with a wooden bolt set in oak sockets, and pretty strong. There are two windows to the room, but these are barred, for which I have been glad many a time.

There are in the bedroom two great, heavy, oaken clothes-cupboards, two settees, a big table, two great wood beds, three lumbersome old chairs, and three linen-presses of ancient and blackened oak, in which the wench keeps not linen, but such various oddments as the autumn pickings of good hazel nuts, charcoal for the upstairs brazier, and in the third an oddment of spare feather pillows and some good down in a sack; and besides these, two gallon puggs – as they name the small kegs here – of French brandy, which I doubt not she has "nigged" from the cellars of mine host, and intends for a very welcome gift to some favoured swain, or, indeed, for all I know, to her own father, if she have one.

And simple she must be some ways, for she has never bothered to lock the press.

Well do I know all these matters by now, for I have a bothersome pilgrimage each night, first to open the great cupboards and look in, and then to shut and snick the big brass locks. And after that I look in the linen-chests, and smile at the two puggs of brandy, for the wench has found something of a warm place in my heart because of her honest friendliness to me. Then I peer under the two settees and the two beds; and so I am sure at last that the room holds nothing that might trouble me in my sleep.

The beds are simple, rustic, heavy-made affairs, cloddish and without canopies or even posts for the same, which makes them seem very rude and ugly to the eye. However, they please me well, for I have read in my time and once I saw the like – of bedsteads that had the canopy very great and solid and made to let down, like a press, upon the sleeper, to smother him in his sleep; and a devilish contrivance is such in those of our inns that are on the by-roads; and many a lone traveller has met a dreadful death, as I have proved in my business of a secret agent for the king. But there are few such tricks that I cannot discover in a moment, because of my training in all matters that deal with the ways of law-breakers, of which I am a loyal and sworn enemy.

But for me, at the Inn of the Black Crow, I have no great fear of any odd contrivance of death; nor of poison or drugging if I should be discovered, for there is a skill needed in such matters, and, moreover, the wench prepares my food and is my good friend; for it is always my way to have the women folk upon my side, and a good half of the battles of life are won if a man does this always. But what I have good cause to fear is lest the landlord, or any of the brute oafs of this lonesome moor, should wish to come at me in my sleep, and, maybe, hide in one of the great presses or the great cupboards to this end; and there you have my reasons for my nightly search of the room.

On this last night I paid a greater attention to all my precautions, and searched the big room very carefully, even to testing the wall behind the pictures, but found it of good moorland stone, like the four walls of the room.

The door, however, I made more secure by pushing one of the three linen-presses up against it, and so I feel pretty safe for the night.

Now, I had certainly a strong feeling that something might be in the wind, as the sailormen say, against me; and a vague uneasiness kept me from undressing for a time, so that, after I had finished making all secure for the night, I sat a good while in one of the chairs by the table and wrote up my report.

After a time I had a curious feeling that someone was looking in at me through the barred window to my left, and at last I got up and loosed the heavy curtains down over both it and the far one, for it was quite possible for anyone to have placed one of the short farm-ladders against the wall and come up to have a look in at me. Yet in my heart I did not really think this was so, and I tell of my action merely because it shows the way that I felt.

At last I said to myself that I had grown to fancying things because of the friendly warning that the wench had given me over my dinner; but even as I said it, and glanced about the heavy, shadowy room, I could not shake free from my feelings. I took my candle and slipped off my shoes, so that my steps should not be heard below; then I went again through my pilgrimage of the room. I opened the cupboards and presses, each in turn, and finally once more I looked under the beds and even under the table, but there was nothing, nor could there have been to my common-sense reasoning.

I determined to undress and go to bed, assuring myself that a good sleep would soon cure me, but at first I went to my trunk and unlocked it. I took from it my brace of pistols and my big knife, also my lantern, which had a cunning little cap over the face and a metal cowl above the chimney, so that, by means of the cap and the cowl, I can make the lantern dark and yet have a good light burning within ready for an instant use.

Then I drew out the wads from my pistols, and screwed out the bullets and the second wads, and poured out the powder. I tried the flints, and found them spark very bright and clean, and afterwards I reloaded the pistols with fresh powder, using a heavier charge, and putting into each twelve large buckshot as big as peas, and a wad on the top to hold them in.

When I had primed the two pistols, I reached down into my boot and drew out a small weapon that I am never without; and a finely made pistol it is, by Chamel, the gunsmith, near the Tower. I paid him six guineas for that one weapon, and well it has repaid me, for I have killed eleven men with it in four years that would otherwise have sent me early out of this life; and a better pistol no man ever had, nor, for the length of the barrel, a truer. I reloaded this likewise, but with a single bullet in the place of the buckshot slugs I had put into my heavier pistols.

I carried a chair close to the bedside, and on this chair I laid my three pistols and my knife. Then I lit my lantern, and shut the cap over the glass; after which I stood it with my weapons on the seat of the chair.

I took a good while to undress, what with the way I kept looking round me into the shadows, and wishing I had a dozen great candles, and again stopping to listen to the horrid moan of the moor wind blowing in through the crannies of the windows, and odd times the dismal sounding lap, lap of the big Erskine creek below.

When at last I climbed up into the great clumsy-made bed, I left the candle burning on the table, and lay a good while harking to the wind, that at one moment would cease, and leave the big, dark room silent and chill-seeming, and the next would whine and moan again in through the window crannies.

I fell asleep in the end, and had a pretty sound slumber. Then, suddenly, I was lying there awake in the bed, listening. The candle had burned itself out and the room was very, very dark, owing to my having drawn the curtains, which I never did before.

I lay quiet, trying to think why I had waked so sharply; and in the back of my brain I had a feeling that I had been wakened by some sound. Yet the room was most oppressive quiet, and not even was there the odd whine or moan of the wind through the window crannies, for now the wind had dropped away entirely.

Yet there were sounds below me in the big taproom, and I supposed that a company of the rough creek and moor men were drinking and jollying together beneath me, for as I lay and listened there came now and then the line of a rude song, or a shouted oath, or an indefinite babel of rough talk and argument, all as the mood served. And once, by the noise, there must have been something of a free fight, and a bench or two smashed, by the crash I heard of broken woodwork.

After a while there was a sudden quietness, in which the silence of the big chamber grew on me with a vague discomfort. Abruptly I heard a woman's voice raised in a clatter of words, and then there was a great shouting of hoarse voices, and a beating of mugs upon the benches, by the sounds.

I leaned up on my elbow in the bed and listened, for there was such a to-do, as we say, that I could not tell what to think.

As I leaned there and hearkened I heard the woman begin to scream, and she screamed, maybe, a dozen times, but whether in fear or anger or both I could not at once decide, only now I drew myself to the edge of the bed, meaning to open my lantern and have some light in the room. As I rolled on to the edge of the bed, and reached out my hand, the screaming died away, and there came instead, as I stiffened and harked, the sound of a woman crying somewhere in the house. And suddenly I comprehended, in some strange fashion of the spirit, that it was because of me – that some harm was to be done me, perhaps was even then coming.

I stretched out my hand swiftly and groped for the lantern; but my hand touched nothing, and I had a quick sickening and dreadful feeling that something was in the room with me, and had taken the chair away from the side of my bed, with all my weapons.

In the same moment that this thought flashed a dreadful and particular horror across my brain, I realized, with a sweet revulsion towards security, that I was reaching out upon the wrong side of the bed, for the room was so utter dark with the heavy curtains being across the windows.

I jumped to my feet upon the bed, and as I did so there sounded two sharp blows somewhere beneath me. I turned to stride quickly across, and as I did so the whole bed seemed to drop from under me, as I was in the very act of my stride. Something hugely great caught me savagely and brutally by my feet and ankles, and in the same instant there was a monstrous crash upon the floor of the bedroom that seemed to shake the inn. I pitched backwards, and struck my shoulder against the heavy timbers, but the dreadful grip upon my feet never ceased. I rose upright, using the muscles of my thighs and stomach to lift me; and when I was stood upright in the utter darkness I squatted quickly and felt at the thing which had me so horribly by the feet.

My feet seemed to be held between two edges that were padded, yet pressed so tight together that I could not force even my fist between them.

I stood up again and wrenched, very fierce and mad, to free my feet, but I could not manage it, and only seemed to twist and strain my ankles with the fight I made and the way I troubled to keep my balance.

I stopped a moment where I stood in the darkness on my trapped feet, and listened very intently. Yet there seemed everywhere a dreadful silence, and no sound in all the house, and I could not be sure whether I was still in the bedroom or fallen into some secret trap along with the bed when it fell from under me.

I reached up my hands over my head to see if I could touch anything above me, but I found nothing. Then I spread my arms out sideways to see whether I could touch any wall, but there was nothing within my reach.

All this time, while I was doing this, I said to myself that I *must* be still in the bedroom, for the taproom lay just below me; also, though the bed had fallen from under me, and I also had seemed to go down, yet I had not felt to have dropped far.

And then, in the midst of my fears and doubts and horrid bewilderment, I saw a faint little ray of light, no greater than the edge of a small knife, below me.

I squatted again upon my trapped feet, and reached out towards where I had seen the faint light; but now I could no longer see it. I moved my hands up and down, and from side to side, and suddenly I touched a beam of wood, seeming on a level with the thing which held my feet.

I gripped the beam and pulled and pushed at it, but it never moved; and therewith I put my weight on it and leaned more forward still; and so in an instant I touched a second beam.

I tried whether this second beam would hold me, and found it as firm and solid as the first. I put my weight on to it, using my left hand, and reached out my right hand, carrying myself forward, until suddenly I saw the light again, and had a slight feeling of heat not far below my face.

I put my hand towards the faint light and touched something. It was my own dark lantern. I could have cried out aloud with the joy of my discovery. I fumbled open the hinged cap that was shut over the glass, and instantly there was light upon everything near me.

A new amazement came to me as I discovered that I was yet in the bedroom, and the lamp was still upon the chair with my pistols, and that my feet had been trapped by the bed itself; for the two beams that I had felt were the supporting skeleton of one side of the heavy-made bedstead, and the mattress had shut up like a monstrous book; and what had been its middle part was now rested upon the floor of the bedroom, between the beams of its upholding framework, whilst the top edges had closed firmly upon my feet and ankles, so that I was held like a trapped rat. And a cunning and brutal machine of death the great bedstead was, and would have crushed the breath and the life out of my body in a moment had I been lying flat upon the mattress as a man does in sleep.

Now, as I regarded all this, with a fiercer and ever fiercer growing anger, I heard again the low sound of a woman weeping somewhere in the house, as if a door had been suddenly opened and let the sound come plain. Then it ceased, as if the door had been closed again.

Now, I saw that I must do two things. The one was to make no noise to show that I still lived, and the second was to free myself as speedily as I could. But first I snatched up my lamp and flashed it all round the big bedroom, and upon the door; but it was plain to me that there was no one gotten into the room, yet there might be a secret way in I now conceived, for how else should they come in to remove the dead if the door of the room were locked, just as I, indeed, had locked it before I made to sleep?

However, the first thing I shaped to do was to get free, and I caught up my knife from the chair and began to cut into the great box-mattress where the padding was nailed down solid with broad-headed clouts.

But all the time that I worked I harked very keen for any sound in the room that might show whether they were coming yet for my body. And I worked quick but quiet, so that I should make no noise, yet I smiled grim to myself to think how strange a corpse they should have to welcome them, and how lively a welcome!

And suddenly, as I worked, there came a faint creaking of wood from the far side of the big, dark room where stood one of the great clothes-cupboards. I stabbed my big knife into one of the edges of the closed mattress where it would be ready to my hand in the dark, and instantly closed the cover over my dark lantern and stood it by the knife. Then, in the darkness, I reached for my pistols from the chair seat, and the small one I stood by the knife, pushing the end of the barrel down between the mattress edges, so that its butt stood up handily for me to grip in the dark.

I caught up my two great pistols in my fists, and stared round me as I squatted, harking with a bitter eagerness, for it was sure enough that I must fight for my life, and, maybe, I should be found in the morning far out on the moor, like poor James Naynes was found. But of one thing I was determined, there should go two or three that night to heaven or to hell, and the choice I left with them, for it was no part of my business, but only to see that the earth was soundly rid of them.

Now there was a space of absolute silence, and then again I heard the creaking sound from the far end of the room. I stared hard that way, and then took a quick look round me, through the dark, to be sure that my ears had told me truly the direction of the sounds.

When I looked back again, there was a light inside the great cupboard, for I could see the glow of it around the edges of the door.

I knew now that there must be a hidden way into the bedroom, coming in through the back of the cupboard, which must be made to open; but I smiled a little to remember that I had locked the door, which had a very good and stout brass lock.

Yet I learned quickly enough that this was not likely to bother the men, for after I had heard them press upon the door, there was a low muttering of voices from within the cupboard, and then a sound of fumbling against the woodwork, and immediately there was a squeak of wood, and one end of the cupboard swung out like a door, and all that end of the bedroom was full of light from the lamp they had inside the cupboard.

In the moment when the end of the cupboard swung out there

came to me the sudden knowledge that I must not be seen until the murderers were all come into the room, otherwise they would immediately give back into the cupboard before I could kill them. And I should indeed be in a poor case if they fetched up a fowling-piece to shoot at me; for they could riddle me with swan-shot, or the like, by no more than firing round the edge of the great oak cupboard; and I tethered there by the feet and helpless as a sheep the moment I had fired off my pistols!

Now, all this reasoning went through my brain like a blaze of lightning for speed, and in the same moment I had glanced round me, for the light from the cupboard was sufficient to show those things that were near me. I saw that there was half of a coverlid draped out from between the two edges of the great trap, and I snatched at it, and had it over me in a trice, and was immediately crouched there silent upon the edge of the mattress, as if I were simply a heap of the bed-clothing that had not been caught in the trap.

I had no more than covered myself and crouched still, when I heard the men stepping into the room.

"It's sure got un proper!" I heard the voice of the knock-kneed Llan say.

And he crowed out one of his shrill, foolish laughs.

"There'll be less of these king's agents an' the like after this!" I heard Jalbrok's voice growl.

"Gglag the swine!" came a familiar voice. "I'll put my knife into un, to make sure. Why, blow me if he don't know enough to gaol us all."

"There'll be no need o' knives," said Jalbrok; "an if there is, it's me that does it. He's my lodger!"

"Share plunder alike! Share plunder alike!" said another voice from the cupboard, by the sound of it.

And then there was the noise of heavy feet approaching, and the sound of scuffling in the big cupboard, as if a number of the brutish crew were fighting to get their clumsy bodies into the room, all in a great haste to see how the death trap had worked.

In that instant, and when the men were no farther from the bed than five or six paces, I hove the covering clean off me, and stood up on my trapped feet, but keeping my two great pistols behind my back, for I had them all now at my mercy.

I think they thought in that first moment that I was a ghost by the howl of terror that some of them sent up to heaven. Such a brutish crew no man need have paused to shoot down; yet I did, for I wished to see what they would do now that I had discovered myself to them.

They had, all of them, their belt-knives in their hands, as if they had meant to thrust them into my dead body rather than let no blood. The landlord carried a lantern in one hand and a pig-sticker's knife, maybe two feet long from haft to point, in the other, and his eyes shone foully with the blood-lust such as you will see once in a lifetime in the red eyes of a mad swine.

So they had all of them stopped as I rose, and some had howled out, as I have told, in their sudden fear, thinking I was dead, and had risen in vengeance, as was seemly enough to their ignorant minds.

But now Jalbrok, the landlord, held his lantern higher, and drew the flat of his knife across his great thigh.

"Good-morning, mine host and kind friends all," I said gently. "Wherefore this rollicking visit? Am I invited to join you in jollying the small hours, or does Master Gglag, you with the open mouth there, desire my help in the landing of good liquor from the sea?"

"Slit him!" suddenly roared Jalbrok, with something like a pig's squeal in the note of his voice. "Slit him!"

And therewith he rushed straight at me with the pig-sticker, and the rest of that vile crew of murdering brutes after him. But I whipped my two great pistols from behind my back, and thrust them almost into their faces; and blood-hungry though they were, like wild beasts, they gave back like dogs from a whip, and the landlord with them.

"In the name of James Naynes, whom ye destroyed in this same room," I said quietly.

And I fired my right hand pistol at Jalbrok, and saw his face crumble, and he fell, carrying the lamp, and a man further back in the room tumbled headlong. The lamp had gone out when the landlord fell, and the room was full of a sound like the howling of frightened animals. There was a mad rush in the darkness for the great oak cupboard, and I loosed off again with my left-hand pistol into the midst of the noise; and immediately there were several screams, and a deeper pandemonium. I heard furniture thrown about madly, and some of the men seemed to have lost their bearings, for I heard the crash of broken glass as they blundered into the far window.

Then I had my lamp in my hands, and my third pistol. I opened the shutter, and shone the light upon the blundering louts; and as they got their bearings in the light there was a madder scramble than before to escape through the cupboard.

I did not shoot again, but let them escape, for I judged they had seen sufficient of me to suit their needs for that one night. And to prove that I was right, I heard them go tumbling away out of the front doorway at a run. And after that there was a great quietness throughout the inn.

I threw the light upon the men on the floor. Jalbrok and his murdering helpman appeared both to be dead, but there were three others who groaned, but were not greatly hurt, for when I called out to them to go before I shot them truly dead, they were all of them to their knees in a moment, and crept along the floor into the cupboard, and so out of my sight.

I had my feet free of the trap in less than the half of an hour, and went over to the men upon the floor, who were both as dead as they deserved to be.

Then I loaded my pistols, and, with one in each hand, I entered the cupboard, and found, as I had supposed, a ladder reared up within a big press that stands in the taproom from floor to ceiling, and the top of which is the floor of the cupboard in the bedroom. So that I was wrong when I thought, maybe, that there had been a false back to it.

I found the wench locked in a small pantry place where she slept, and when she saw me alive she first screamed, and then kissed me so heartily that I gave her a good honest guinea piece to cease; also because I was grateful to the lass for her regard for my safety.

Regarding the great machine in the bedroom, I made a close examination of this, and found that the hinged centre of the monstrously heavy mattress was supported upon a strut which went down into the taproom through the great central beam that held the ceiling up, and was kept in place by an oak peg, which passed through the beam and the supporting strut. It was when they went to knock the peg out that the wench screamed, and the two blows I heard beneath the bed were the blows of the hammer on the peg.

And so I have discovered, as I set out to do, the way in which poor James Naynes met his death, and my hands have been chosen to deal out a portion of the lawful vengeance which his murderers had earned.

But I have not yet finished with this district – not until I have rooted out, neck and crop, the ruthless and bloodthirsty band that do their lawless work in this lonesome part of the king's domain.

THE SPIRIT OF THE '76
Lillian de la Torre

Within only a few days of the publication of The Mammoth Book of Historical Whodunnits, *I was very saddened to learn of the death of Lillian de la Torre in September 1993 at the remarkable age of 91. For fifty years she had painstakingly (and all too infrequently) produced a series of clever stories in which Samuel Johnson resolved crimes and mysteries of his day, his investigations faithfully recorded by his equivalent of Dr Watson, James Boswell. The stories, all originally published in* Ellery Queen's Mystery Magazine, *have been collected in four volumes:* Dr Sam: Johnson, Detector (1946), The Detections of Dr Sam: Johnson *(1960),* The Return of Dr Sam: Johnson *(1985) and* The Exploits of Dr Sam: Johnson *(1987), with two subsequent stories remaining uncollected. Although spread over nearly fifty years the series totals only thirty-three stories, and now there will be no more.*

Occasionally, Miss de la Torre would take liberties with history. Sam Johnson and Benjamin Franklin never met, but this story seeks to explore what might have happened had they done so. Apparently Franklin was rather bitter toward Johnson because of an anti-American pamphlet he had written, Taxation No Tyranny, *in 1775. In December 1776, Franklin was at sea on his way to France, and it would not have taken much to have blown him off course to England. Here is a little of history revisited.*

"Free and equal!" growled Dr Sam: Johnson in high dudgeon. "All men, forsooth, created equal! What is to become of the proper order and subordination of society, if such frantick levelling doctrines are to prevail? Free and equal! Signed, John Hancock! Mark my words, sir, we shall yet see this fellow's head spiked above Temple Bar!"

"Is he sole authour of this independent declaration?" I wondered, for secretly I admired it.

"No, sir. This treasonous manifesto comes, I am told, from the pen of a planter named Jefferson, aided and abetted by Benjamin Franklin."

"Dr Franklin!" said I. "Now there's a head that would ill become Temple Bar. I dined in his company once, sir, some years since, and found him an agreeable companion, and moreover an ingenious contriver of devices to improve the lot of man, as his Pennsylvania fire place, his lightning rod, *et caetera*."

"I, too, Bozzy, have encountered the fellow. He was presiding at a meeting of benevolent gentlemen associated to provide education for the unfortunate Negroes of the New World. He then appeared to be a sincere friend to humanity, not at all addicted to republican phrenzy. Yet more's the pity, sir, he's a traitor to his King, and belongs on the scaffold with the rest of them!"

"Would you put him there?"

"Aye would I, and twenty such, let me but come in sight of them!"

"Which you are not like to do," I remarked. "They are safe on the other side of the water. Why should any of them put his head in the lion's mouth?"

"There you are out, sir, that same Franklin is now, they warn us, on the high seas, making for France – "

I doubted it not. Dr Johnson had recently made his pen useful to the Ministry, and his sources of information were many.

"– so that we may hope that a tempest will drive him upon our shores, or a man-o'-war catch him and bring him hither."

I hoped not; but I said no more. As to the dispute with our fellow subjects across the sea, Dr Johnson and I differed widely. Now that, with the Declaration of Independence, the breach had come, my friend was vehemently wishing success to our arms in putting down the insurgents; while, despite all, I wished them well, and desired they might all escape Jack Ketch.

This conversation took place in December of the year '76, in my philosophical friend's commodious dwelling in Bolt Court, Fleet Street. Tall, broad and bulky, in his full-skirted grey coat and broad stuff breeches, his little brown scratch-wig perched above his wide brow, he stood in the many-paned sash-window, looking down on the court. I felt once more a strong satisfaction that I, James Boswell, an advocate of North Britain thirty years his junior, was so often privileged to observe his proceedings as *detector* of crime and chicane. At that moment no problem engaged his massive intellect, unless the treason of America's rabid revolutionaries; but that situation was about to change.

As I stood at his shoulder looking down, a coach drew up with a jingle, and a lone woman descended, muffled in a dun-coloured capuchin. Another moment, and black Francis ushered her in to us. She burst into speech at once:

"Forgive my lack of ceremony, Dr Johnson. Your goodness is known so widely, I make bold to beg you – the child is stolen away, Dr Johnson! He's only seven, what am I to do?"

She choked back a sob. Dr Johnson took her slender hand and gently led her to the armed chair by the fire.

She was a small creature of a certain age, her soft face gently wrinkled, her grey hair pulled up in a plain pompadour above direct blue eyes now stained with tears.

"Be comforted, ma'am, we'll find him," said Dr Johnson reassuringly; "but you must tell me all you know of the matter."

"I will try. I am Mrs Stevenson – Margaret is my name. I dwell in Craven Street, Strand, and thence Benny has been spirited away."

"Your grandson, madam?"

"No, sir, but committed to my charge, and dearly loved."

"Perhaps he has wandered away?" I hazarded.

"No, sir, Benny was whipping his top before the door, when two men came by and carried him off. A servant saw from the window."

"Why did he not follow?"

"The wench is a she, and not over-bright. She formed the opinion that Benny was arrested by bailiffs, and knew not what was proper to do. I was from home, and only learned of the matter upon my return. What can they want of the boy? I have no money to buy him back."

"If he's to be bought back," remarked Dr Sam: Johnson, "we shall soon hear. Meanwhile, let us look over the ground in Craven Street."

In the modest dwelling in Craven Street, the wench Katty was stubborn, being what Dr Johnson is wont to denominate a "mule fool." She set her long jaw and stood to it. Master Benny was in the hands of the law. Time was wasted on her, before she remembered to say to her mistress:

"And, ma'am, there's a billet handed in for the gentleman – "

Mrs Stevenson seized it, scanned it, and extended it to my friend. At a sign, I moved to his elbow to share it with him.

Dear Doctor:
    As you regard Benny, see that you present yourself at the Cat & Fiddle in Bow Street, this Day at five of the

clock, & you shall hear further. Come alone. Fail us not, at
Benny's Peril.

> I am, Sir,
> As you shall deal in this,
> Your Friend

Dr Johnson turned the missive in his strong, well-shaped fingers.

"Hm – paper of the best quality – a fair copying hand – this was
never writ by a parcel of bum-bailiffs. Well, well, Mrs Stevenson, I'll
present myself as directed, to hear further as they promise. There is
not long to wait."

"O sir, you'll never go alone!"

"I must, at Benny's peril. But Boswell shall be handy, in case of
trickery."

Thus it was that before five of the clock I was approaching the Cat
& Fiddle, alert to detect the miscreants we had come to meet. As I
neared the lighted doorway in the foggy darkness, my eye fell on a
tall, burly figure in the shadow. At first I thought it was Dr Sam:
Johnson himself in outlandish disguise, for the fellow was his replica
in height and breadth. His powerful figure was enveloped in a vast
coat of bull's hide, and a large fur cap was pulled down over his
straggling grey locks. He wore a pair of cracked spectacles set in
wire, and carried a porter's coil of rope. As I approached, he moved
off, and I entered the Cat & Fiddle.

I was established on the fireside settle with a pint, when the door
squeaked open, and a couple of rough-looking fellows made their
appearance. Katty perhaps had not been so foolish, for sure enough
they looked very like bum-bailiffs. Like bailiffs they took up their
station on either side of the door. The potboy gave them a look, and
discreetly vanished.

Another squeak, and Dr Sam: Johnson stood in the doorway. He
was wrapped in his large dark grey greatcoat, and his cocked hat
was firmly tied down by a knitted scarf.

From left and right the two fellows closed in and seized him.

"We arrest you," cried the smaller of the two triumphantly, "in
the King's name!"

"Arrest me, ye boobies!" cried Dr Johnson. "What call have you
to arrest me? Everyone knows me: I am Dr Johnson."

"O aye, Dr Johnson, Dr Brown, Dr Robinson, 'tis all one.
We know you, Doctor, right enough, you must come along with
us."

"I'll come with you to the magistrate in Bow Street, and no further,"
growled Dr Johnson.

"You're wanted elsewhere."

"What's the charge?"

The big one with the stupid face swelled up to proclaim it, but the
ferret-nosed little one plucked his sleeve.

"Stubble your whids, Ned, 'ware rescue, we are not alone (jerking
a gesture in my direction). There's a great price on this fellow's head.
Do you want to share it?"

"Carry me before Sir John Fielding," insisted Dr Johnson. "We'll
see if there's a price on my head!"

They hustled him off. I set down my pot and followed. It was but
a step along Bow Street to the Publick Office. Beside the doorway a
lighted lanthorn flickered. As we approached, the catchpolls began
to edge their captive away from the light, when Dr Johnson with a
powerful motion jerked suddenly from their grasp. Simultaniously the
big pandour was pulled off his feet by the loop of a porter's rope.

Dr Johnson collared the ferrety one and dragged him inside,
leaving Ned *hors de combat* on the pavement, and the doughty old
porter vanished. Another moment, and the three of us stood in the
publick room before the magistrate.

Sir John Fielding, the famous Blind Beak of Bow Street, sat quietly
in the magistrate's chair, a large, handsome personage with venerable
white locks and a fold of black silk over his sightless eyes. He turned
his ear as we entered, and spoke in an edged voice:

"What, is it you, Greentree? There's no missing that effuvium of
dirty linen and gin. What miscreants have you brought me?"

"I've taken up a traitor, sir, is wanted at the Ministry."

"Sir John," said Dr Johnson calmly, "the foolish fellow mistakes
me for another."

Sir John, an old friend, knew the voice at once.

"Dr Johnson, your servant! And where is Mr Boswell? Not far
away, I'll wager."

"Right here, Sir John, at your service."

Waiving courtesies, Dr Johnson at once adverted to the matter
in hand.

"This Greentree," he said urgently, "baited me hither by stealing
a child and sending this billet."

He began to read it out.

"I know nothing of your billet," muttered Greentree. "'Twas writ
at the Ministry. I had only to nap the kid, which I did – arrest the
Doctor when he broke cover, which I did – and fetch him to the
Minister."

"What Doctor?"

"My Lord did not say."

"He gave you a warrant?"

"Well, no, sir, 'twas to be done in secret."

"Illegality upon illegality!" remarked Sir John. "Where is the child? Discover him, or you shall be the worse for it."

"In Water Lane," uttered the fellow grudgingly.

Instanter a posse of constables, with Greentree pinioned in their midst, conducted us to Water Lane. Our captive led us to a miserable hovel at the water's edge, where a slatternly harpy whined:

"Which I kept him secure as you bade me. He's locked in the loft that looks on the river. This way, gentlemen, you shall see he's safe enough."

The rusty key screeched in the lock, the door grated open. Dr Johnson started forward; but save for a small pair of buckled shoes, the room was empty. The cracked casement swung on one hinge. We looked out in dismay on the brown waters of Thames. Had the child been done away with in this lair?

Sir John's men took up the cursing woman, and bore her with Greentree off to the roundhouse, there to be sifted further. We were left to make our way back to Craven Street with news of our failure.

With heavy hearts we mounted the slope. I liked the neighbourhood ill. Fleet Ditch stank. Ragamuffins prowled or slept in doorways. Trulls loitered, and bullies swaggered. Once I thought I glimpsed the burly old porter with his rope, but then he was gone again in the darkness.

As the street rose, out of the foggy dark one more ragamuffin appeared. This one approached us confidently, a sandy-haired, solid-built little boy, shoeless and dripping wet. As we paused, he recited in a clear voice:

"Please, sir, my name is Benjamin Franklin Bache, I dwell at Craven Street in the Strand. My new Granny is Mrs Stevenson. Will you take me to her?"

"What, boy, did you say Benjamin Franklin?"

"He is my grandfather."

"Well, well, Bozzy, it appears there is more in this than meets the eye. Where is your grandfather, boy?"

"In Craven Street, sir."

"Then," said Dr Johnson, "in the King's name, on to Craven Street!"

We wrapped the shivering child in my waistcoat, and set a brisk pace. As he trotted along between us, he readily told what had befallen him.

"The men, they said they were officers of police, and I must come along. I didn't like them. I misliked the old witch too. I waited and waited for my grandfather to come. I was hungry and cold, and I went away from there."

"Went away! How?"

"Through the window, sir."

"In the *water*?" I ejaculated, dumfounded, since I cannot swim a stroak. "What, little boy, can you swim?"

"My grandfather," said the child with pride, "is the greatest swimmer in the world, and he taught me. 'Twas but a few stroaks to the nearest water stair."

"I can swim further than that," the small voice chattered on. "When the sloop was like to founder in the storm, my grandfather bade me fear nothing, we could swim for it. But the *Reprisal* made her way to shore at Hoy Cove, and as soon as the Westcombe men have put her to rights, we'll away to France."

"Will you so, my boy?" said Dr Johnson drily.

"Yes, indeed, sir. – I'm sleepy," he added with a prodigious yawn, and fell silent.

We arrived at Craven Street without further parley. Mrs Stevenson fell on the child with transport, but Dr Johnson held him fast.

"I claim the privilege," he said, "of restoring Dr Franklin's grandson to his arms myself."

Mrs Stevenson looked affrighted, but could not gainsay him. She ushered us to the two-pair-of-stairs parlour.

"Benny!" The sturdy old gentleman by the fire held out his arms, and the boy flew into them.

I stared. Gone were the bull's-hide coat and the porter's rope; but the fur cap and the spectacles remained to tell us that the old fellow who had dogged us on our errand was none other than Dr Franklin himself. I scanned the cheerful lined face. It was a face that had mellowed with the years, not handsome, but winning with its look of pleased surprise, as if perpetually astonished and gratified by the spectacle of the world in its infinite variety. The hazel eyes sparkled with a penetrating intelligence. Over the boy's tawny curls, the brilliant gaze turned to us.

"Dr Johnson, I believe?"

"Your servant, Dr Franklin."

"I am your debtor, sir," said Franklin stiffly, "little as I desire it. I regret that Margaret was so impulsive as to call upon your aid."

"Ben!" cried Mrs Stevenson softly, "we are much in Dr Johnson's debt for his efforts!"

"Dr Franklin knows," observed Dr Johnson, "for he trusted me so little. He dogged my every move in guise of a street porter."

"Trust?" exclaimed Franklin. "Why would I trust a man who wrote against us and counselled the Ministry to set upon us the Red Men and the Blacks?"

"You misread me, sir," said Johnson calmly. "True, I would give the Blacks their freedom, with means of sustenance and defence; from which, if memory serves, you yourself are not averse. And as to the raids of the Red Men, what else can you expect, if you renounce the protection of British arms?"

"The protection of British arms!" echoed Franklin bitterly. "It was British arms that shot down innocent people in the Boston Massacre!"

"We all deplore it, sir," conceded Johnson.

Franklin set down the boy from his lap.

"Make your bow, Benny, and go now with Granny."

The mannerly boy inclined solemnly to each of us, and left us. As Dr Franklin turned to us with an air of dismissal, a newcomer erupted into the room. From the tall form, the long dark face, the Satanick quirk of the black eyebrows, I recognized him with mixed emotions. It was Sir Francis Flashwood, he who raised the Devil in the caves under Hoy Head, whose witching daughter I had once thought to woo, whose Coven we had quelled at Westcombe in the '68 (all which I have set forth at large in my account of "The Westcombe Witch").

We had heard of that gentleman's doings since then, how with his close friend Benjamin Franklin he had "reformed" the Prayer Book – Satan rebuking sin? – how as Lord LeSpenser he had gone into politicks, acting as Postmaster General to such effect that he was now respectable, and the Westcombe Blacks were heard of no more.

Now he paid us not the slightest heed, but rushed to Franklin crying:

"Up, Ben, there's not a minute to waste! There's a plot against you at the Ministry. I have it on the surest advices. Since you are too elusive to be caught, they will lay hands on Benny, and so force you to come in, to who knows what fate – "

"Why, Francis," said Franklin calmly, "I thank you, but your warning is belated – "

"What, they have him?"

"No, no, dear friend, the attempt has been made, but it has been frustrated by Dr Johnson here."

For the first time my Lord's eyes focused upon us where we stood by the fire.

"Dr Johnson," he said wryly. "Yes, a notable frustrater. And Mr Boswell too. How do you, Sir Brimstone of Tophet?"

"Well, I thank you, sir," said I, grandly ignoring this allusion to my diabolical misadventures in the caves at Westcombe, "and how does your lovely daughter, Miss Fan?"

"Fan is wed to her cousin Talley. She lives in the West Country and raises a numerous progeny. But there's no time for gossip. Dr Franklin is in the gravest danger. O Ben, Ben, you might have been safe at Westcombe, why would you insist on coming up to London?"

"Money, business, and love," smiled Franklin, "what other human motives are there? To fetch the gold intended for the cause, to recover my papers, and to see once more my dear Mistress Margaret."

"Let us hope your recklessness will not cost you all three, and life besides. We must depart for Westcombe with all speed. My travelling coach stands waiting at the door, and the men of the Westcombe Blacks are a-horse and ready to escort us."

"A desperate set of men," remarked Dr Johnson. "I had thought them won over to the side of the law."

"Well, sir," Sir Francis smiled thinly, "not entirely, when my friend's life is at stake. For him they'll do their utmost. And you, Dr Johnson, what will you do for us? The issue now is greater than a few French bales. Will you keep silence?"

Johnson said nothing, and I struck in:

"You have *my* parole, sir. I wish the Americans only good."

"Then you may go, Mr Boswell."

"Not if Dr Johnson remains."

"He remains," said Sir Francis emphatically. "We cannot have him running to Lord North behind our backs."

"Tut, sir, I told you once, I am no catchpoll."

"And I believe you, Dr Johnson," said Franklin quietly.

"No, Ben, we cannot risk it. He shall go with us to Westcombe."

I started forward to protest, but Dr Johnson shook his head at me. I shrugged, and composed myself for the journey.

Now all was bustle. Papers were bagged, portmanteaus slammed shut, hampers filled with viands. Benny, dried off and warmly cloathed anew, was swathed in shawls and tucked in a corner of the travelling carriage, where he promptly fell asleep. In the hurly-burly, we might easily enough have slipped away, but Dr Johnson unaccountably sat on in smiling calm.

Soon we stood at the door bidding adieu. Franklin took little Margaret Stevenson warmly in his arms, and embraced her tenderly.

"Farewell once more, my dear, and once more, thanks for years together of sunshine without cloud. Let us be grateful to the storm which blew me hither and allowed us to meet for one more time; and if we never meet again, remember me."

We left her weeping in the doorway as we rolled off into the night. The dark-clad figures of the Westcombe Blacks closed in about us with silent hooves, and so we trotted briskly out of town and took the road towards the sea. No spies dogged us. The misadventure of Benny had clearly put the Ministry forces in disarray. If we could only get clear before they rallied!

It was a long way to go, to the harbour at Westcombe, where lay the *Reprisal*, refitted now and ready to slip her cable for France. The Westcombe Blacks had smoothed our way. Fresh horses awaited us at posting-houses, where we could refresh while the ostlers bustled, and the Westcombe men waited upon us – and watched us – attentively.

At first we rode together in stiff silence, which merged into sleep as exhausted nature claimed her due.

The day dawned sunny. We explored the contents of the hampers, and then sat back invigorated. The coach was new and commodious, smelling of leather and horseflesh and creaking lightly on easy springs. I regarded my companions. Sir Francis, clad in a bottle-green cloak with multiple capes, lounged in his corner, his watchful dark eyes fixed on Dr Johnson; who, for his part, sat complaisantly smiling with the pleasure he always derived from the swift motion of a carriage.

Dr Franklin in his snuff-coloured greatcoat wore neither wig nor hat, but that same fur cap, like a brown bee-hive, pulled down almost to his spectacles; through the round panes of which, he drank in the passing prospect. Next him sat small Benny, emerged from his cocoon. In the smiling quirk of his small upper lip and the brilliance of his eyes, the resemblance to his grandfather was strong.

It was impossible we should continue in sullen silence. My companions were men of wit and ingenuity, and had much to say to one another if it could but be brought out. And who should bring it out better than your humble servant, James Boswell? If I had been able to reconcile my stern friend to that devil Jack Wilkes – as I recently had done – it would go hard but I would bring Johnson and Franklin together.

Warmed by my breakfast glass, I first undertook to kindle the atmosphere with one of my own songs. I considered the bawdy strophes of "Gunter's Chain": Sir Francis would certainly relish it, and Dr Franklin with his almost-smiling mouth looked receptive. But I glanced at the lofty countenance of my moral mentor, and instead trolled out a stave of my ditty celebrating "Currant Jelly."

Franklin then reciprocated with a convivial drinking song of his own composition, writ, he said, some thirty years since, in praise of friendship and wine. His voice was husky, but true.

> "Then toss off your glasses and scorn the dull asses
> Who missing the kernel still gnaw the shell.
> What's love, rule, or riches? Wise Solomon teaches
> They're vanity, vanity, vanity still,
>   For honest souls know
>   Friend and a bottle still bear the bell."

"On this we can all agree," I exclaimed, "for Dr Johnson is wont to bid us, 'Keep your friendships in repair'."

"And in my country," replied Dr Franklin, "the Red Indians have a saying, 'Keep the chain of friendship bright'."

"What, has Benny no song to sing?" prompted Flashwood, smiling at the bright-eyed little boy.

At this Benny shrilled out a jolly jig tune entitled "Yankee Doodle."

> "Father and I went down to camp
>   Along with Cap'n Good'in,
> And there we saw the men and boys
>   As thick as hasty puddin'.
>   Yankee Doodle, keep it up,
>   Yankee Doodle Dandy,
>   Mind the musick and the step
>   And with the girls be handy!"

"With the girls!" repeated Dr Johnson, unable to repress a smile. "A precocious Yankee Dandy, Benny, indeed!"

Encouraged by my friend's smiling regard, Benny prattled on in his small high tones:

"I shall go to school in France," he told Dr Johnson proudly, "and when we have won the war – "

"Won, my boy?"

"Yes, sir, of course we shall win." The clear voice rang out. "We'll fight the redcoats on the beaches, in the streets, if need be in the wilderness: and thereto we have pledged our lives, our fortunes, and our sacred honour!"

"Why," said Dr Johnson, still smiling, "what an eloquent young rebel it is!"

"An eloquent young parrot," observed my Lord. "That last flourish, if memory serves, was writ by Thomas Jefferson of Virginia."

"With the assistance," added the American, "of Benjamin Franklin of Pennsylvania."

"And such," concluded Flashwood, "is the spirit of the '76!"

"Cant!" muttered Johnson, and I hastily turned the subject.

"Pray, Dr Franklin, what projects have you to the fore for the good of mankind?"

The smile that touched his lip deepened, and for a moment I thought he would say "Freedom!" Instead he replied civilly:

"Why, sir, I have newly made observations on the Gulf Stream, on the Aurora Borealis, and on further improvements in opticks."

"There, sir, I heartily wish you success," said Dr Johnson, "for my eyes serve me ill, and I have found no spectacles by which I can both read and view the world about me. I have wondered whether one might not be able to combine the two functions by joining two pieces of glass into one pane, the lower for reading, the upper for looking afar."

"Why, sir," replied Franklin, smiling, "not only can it be done, I have done it: as you may see by the spectacles I wear."

He took them off and handed them over. Johnson brought them up close to his near-sighted eyes and examined them attentively. I saw now that what I had hastily, in the half light of Bow Street, taken for cracks, were really the lines where two half circles joined.

"Ingenious!" said Dr Johnson, and put them to his eyes. After a moment he handed them back, shaking his head regretfully.

"They will not serve my turn."

"Of course not," said Franklin, "each double pane must be suited to the eye that wears it. Well, sir, when I come to France – if I am so fortunate – I purpose to set the lens-makers to work. If all goes well, you shall hear of this further."

Chatting thus of matters scientifick, we passed the rest of the morning in amity.

"You were right, Bozzy," said my friend in my ear at the next posting-house, "that's too well-furnished a head to let the Ministry have it to adorn Temple Bar!"

The sun was well past the meridian when with a sense of relief we rolled in to the village of Westcombe. There we turned in at the Admiral's Head, that our voyagers might recruit before going aboard the *Reprisal*. The master shipwright awaited us with the welcome news that she rode well and was ready for sea. His men at once carried off the baggage while we took a glass.

A sound of hooves thudding our way in hot haste broke our complacency, and a breathless youth flung into our presence.

"The redcoats, my Lord!" he cried. "We have been betrayed! Some one has given the word at Carnock Castle, and the troopers are riding this way to apprehend us. They cannot be ten minutes behind me!"

"Keep watch, Gannett!" commanded Sir Francis. "Up, Ben, we'll go by the caves. That way it is but two minutes to safety!"

I remembered the caves of Westcombe with their secret passage to the harbour, and took heart. But almost at once Gannett was back in the room, crying:

"They're coming, my Lord, they are at the top of the street. We are all trapped!"

Dr Sam: Johnson rose resolutely to his feet.

"Not yet. Give me a horse, and I'll draw them off."

"*You*, Dr Johnson," exclaimed Franklin, "you'll do so much for America?"

"Let us say I'll do it for Benny. Quickly, Doctor, here's a wig in exchange for your fur hat, and a grey coat for your brown one – "

The exchange was made, and most convincing it appeared, for the two tall, burly old men, tho' unlike in face, were of an age, and much alike in figure and bearing.

With the briefest of farewells we took horse in the inn yard; the gates were opened; we set spur and dashed into the street. Not a hundred yards away we perceived the redcoats trotting our way with a measured jingle of harness. Johnson wheeled his horse with a roar, and with incredulity I heard the words that he roared:

"Long live the United States of America!"

"Hold your fire!" cried the officer in the lead. "After him, for he's to be taken alive!"

In this coil it was well that in the '68 we had learned to know the ways of Westcombe. By a byway we left the town, and galloped away over the down.

Dr Johnson always said he rode harder at a fox-chace than anybody, and he rode harder now. Had I not been mounted on as swift a horse, and riding lighter in the saddle, I could not have kept pace with him. As it was, too soon our mounts were blown, and the soldiers cornered us in a fold of the hills.

"Benjamin Franklin," cried the lanky young officer, "I arrest you on a charge of high treason! And your accomplice too," he added with a jerk of his head towards me.

"Whither do you carry us?" I demanded.

"To London, sir, with all speed."

Johnson said nothing. The less he said, in his Litchfield accent, the less would our captors suspect trickery; and the longer we went unsuspected, the better the *Reprisal*'s chances of making good her escape to France. The soldiers closed in, and so we began the weary way back to London.

As we crossed the brow of the hill, we glimpsed the blue of the bay, and the schooner with all sails set standing out to sea for France. I sent a wordless wish after it: Success to your mission!

The return journey seemed interminable; but at last we entered London Town. Whither would our captors lead us now? Bow Street, Newgate Prison, the Tower? Had we seen the last of the sun?

Instead, the young lieutenant set our course for the fashionable end of the town, and drew rein before a handsome house in Grosvenor Square. Stiffly we dismounted and followed our guide within. Knocking, he flung wide a door, and announced with a flourish:

"My Lord, I have the honour to present – Dr Benjamin Franklin!"

A man with a star on his coat rose smiling from a marquetry writing table. By his florid face and prominent eyes, for one thunderstruck moment I thought him the King. Then I knew him for Lord North, the King's first Minister, about whose resemblance to his King courtiers talked behind their hands.

"My Lord!" Dr Johnson, who always prided himself on paying a nobleman the ceremony due him, removed the fur bee-hive and executed a stately bow. My Lord started, and peered close. The smile dissolved in a frown.

"What nonsense is this, Leftenant? This man is not Dr Franklin, but Dr Sam: Johnson, to whom I am indebted for political pamphleteering. By G-d, I am ill served by clodpates! Leave us, fellow! (The crestfallen soldier withdrew.) And you, Dr Johnson? What do you here in a rebel's coat? Have you turned your coat in earnest?"

Dr Johnson glowered. Tho' he upheld my Lord's politicks, he despised his person.

"I am no turncoat, my Lord," he replied sturdily. "I reprehend rebellion as much as ever I did. Yet when a man is to be secretly trepanned – and that man a benefactor of mankind – without colour of law, at the expense of a child, and for what clandestine purpose? Secret assassination, perhaps?"

"Not so!" cried North, stung, but Johnson swept on:

"Then I shall do what I can to save my country from such infamy.

If my company can protect, no matter how, my company shall be afforded."

"That explains," I cried, enlightened, "why you submitted – "

Johnson gave me a look which silenced me, and continued coolly:

"The Leftenant's mistake has given me much fatigue, my Lord; I beg leave to withdraw."

Would leave be granted? In a swift vision I again saw the Tower and the scaffold before me. Then my Lord smiled coldly.

"As you perceive, Dr Johnson, this transaction, were it known, would make my Ministry a byword and a laughing-stock. You have leave to depart; and see that you both hold your tongues."

"Yours to command, my Lord. But give me leave to tell you, after hours spent in company with the American and his grandson, I can prophesy the end. For determination, bravery and ingenuity, the Americans have never seen their match, and I fear your Lordship will find it difficult to prevail against the spirit of the '76!"

PART IV
Regency and Gaslight

DEADLY WILL
AND TESTAMENT
Ron Burns

*Just as I was putting the final touches to the last volume,
I came across a copy of* Roman Shadows *by Ron Burns, set
in the Rome of 43 BC. I learned Burns had written another such
novel,* Roman Nights, *set at the end of the second century AD,
after the death of Marcus Aurelius, though I've still not been able
to obtain a copy of that. Soon after, he surfaced with a new character
and a new series.* The Mysterious Death of Meriwether Lewis
(1993) and Enslaved *(1994) feature Harrison Hull, a confidant of
Thomas Jefferson. When I contacted Ron Burns to see if he might
contribute to this anthology he readily agreed and produced a new
Harrison Hull story. Like the two novels, this story is based on actual
events that happened in Richmond, Virginia, in the early years of the
nineteenth century.*

I am crouching in the dark in a tiny upstairs closet of a little house
in Richmond, Virginia. There are two loaded pistols on the floor
beside me and a dagger in my belt.

It is my fourth night of this . . . waiting. And there is a growing
shrillness to my thoughts – if thoughts can be shrill: I am the one
who found the arsenic. I pointed the finger of guilt. So why do *I*
have to hunker down in hiding? Indeed, I wonder morosely, why
am I here at all?

An unexpected sound! Vague, off in the distance. Even so, my heart
pounds and I listen, breathless. I wait until . . . Nothing. Nothing
more. It is, I decide, only the breeze that's come up, or maybe just
the house itself. I wipe the back of my hand across my forehead. It
is hot in this closet, hot all over Richmond in fact – as always in the
summer.

Richmond! That's where this nightmare started back in . . . God,
is it nearly two months already? I'd planned to be here just a few days

to attend a cousin's wedding. And it could have been that brief – I admit it. My family matters finished quickly, and it could be argued that what kept me was, strictly speaking, none of my business. But I've never been much for doing the predictable, especially when a friend was involved, or even a friend of a friend. In this case, a man named George Wythe was at the center of a series of events that would engulf us all.

Wythe had once been law tutor to President Jefferson and was one of the hallowed signers back in '76. There was even a little reception for him (the day before my relative's nuptials) to mark the thirtieth anniversary of the event, and I dropped by his house, which was just down the street, to pay my respects. Before that I'd met him only twice, but his rare blend of worldly wit and avuncular demeanor made him easy to admire and impossible to forget. So when trouble came I could hardly shrug it off. Indeed, taking a hand in the matter seemed unavoidable. Even inevitable.

What's that! I jump at another distant noise, probably a creaking step or floorboard. I reach for one of the pistols, but realize it is only Duval in his nightshirt heading for the water closet. As a precaution against even the chance of being overheard, I have ordered him not to talk to me after dark. But tonight, walking past, he hears my agitated breathing and stops just outside the closet door.

"You all right, Harry?" he asks very, very softly.

I tell him I am, and he shuffles away. And I cannot help smiling at the small irony of his unflappable obedience. For this is Duval's house, after all, his closet in which I hide these nights, waiting. It is also his work that has made this possible. For William Duval is a famous calligrapher and, incidentally, the designer of Jefferson's famous polygraph copying machines, as well as several of his writing desks.

Yes, I'm all right, I tell him. But I realize more and more that my nerves are feeling the strain, and once again my mind wanders to the troubles. They began when the Wythe household was stricken right after supper on the seventh of July, two days after the wedding. At first they thought it was cholera – what a joke! – though they'd set it right soon enough. The doctors voiced their doubts and the lawyer opened the will and then old Wythe regained consciousness and told us everything. And then it had seemed so simple – open and shut, as the lawyers like to say. Yet somehow it had all gone terribly wrong.

Besides Wythe, two others were afflicted: Wythe's Negro housekeeper, Lydia Broadnax, and a light-skinned Negro boy of fifteen, Michael Brown. Brown died within a few hours, while Wythe and

Broadnax remained unconscious for days, barely alive. The news swept the city – as I say, the rumor was cholera – and I walked over to Wythe's next morning to have a look. I met the doctors, who after a few tongue-tied moments conceded that there were "questions" even then about the diagnosis. I also met Duval who helped me in the search.

The houses – Wythe's and my cousin's – were on stately Kingman Avenue, a tree-lined street of handsome Virginia-style brickfronts, cultivated southern voices, chirping birds and the occasional clink of crystal in the soft summer breezes. It seemed, in other words, to be a place as far removed from mayhem and murder as any place could be.

Wythe's house in particular was filled with the mementos of a lifetime: scrolls from William and Mary College celebrating his legal abilities, a framed letter of thanks from Jefferson, a plaque from the governor of Virginia, and countless trophies, letters, awards from one town or another, merchants' groups, farmers' associations. Silhouettes of his late wife dotted each room and hallway, and assorted trinkets and bric-a-brac were everywhere. Finally, there was a portrait of Wythe himself in the front parlor that hardly did him justice. It captured well enough his imposing gray mutton chops, but turned his lively bright eyes flat and dull and replaced his engaging smile with pursed lips and a hard, taciturn jaw.

I searched through all this, with Duval beside me, finally uncovering the small bottle on the floor of an upstairs hall closet (not unlike the one I am in now, it suddenly occurs to me) tucked behind a formidable pile of old clothes, obscure papers and assorted other junk. I was certain what it was almost at once because though the container was well-corked traces had spilled down the sides and the aroma was unmistakeable. Duval knew, as well.

"Arsenic," he gasped, his skin suddenly snow-white.

We also found a sealed packet of documents in Wythe's study that were almost certainly his last will and testament. With the old man clinging to life just down the hall, Duval refused even to discuss tearing it open. I said little – I was hardly about to press for so radical a breach of custom (radical, even in my view). Still, Duval kept arguing, more with himself, I realized, than me – until finally at his most adamant he seemed to find a way around his dilemma.

"That's it, I'll get the lawyer," he said excitedly. "If these must be opened, he must be present."

And off he dashed to the offices of Wythe's attorney, Edmund Randolph, a mile or so away.

As I waited, still casually looking around, someone else came to the house, someone I'd never met before but whose name I'd already heard many times that day.

"Do I know you, sir?" George Sweney said. He'd walked in on me in Wythe's parlor and stared for an uncertain minute or two. I stared back at the look of pure spoiled brat snobbery on his face: eyes narrowed mischievously, mouth turned up just at the corners. It was a look I'd seen and dealt with all my life. Truth be told, I'd used it myself now and then. So I rather enjoyed it now, from Sweney, and my apparent amusement seemed to sap a little of the smugness from his face – even though I was the interloper, after all. For Sweney was Wythe's nephew and lived in this house.

"Yes, Harrison Hull, we met briefly the other day," I lied. "At your uncle's reception. A happier circumstance."

I put out my hand in greeting, but he just looked me up and down a while longer, too long really, then finally said, "O-o-o-o-h, yes," stretching that out too long, as well. Right from the start, it was Sweney's trouble: He was always overdoing things a bit. At last he shook my hand with nicely contrived reluctance, and it was all I could do to keep from laughing out loud.

Now *that* is a dangerous sound, I think with another jump. Like a window, probably downstairs someplace, being forced open. This time I really grab one of the pistols and snap to my feet. I listen but hear only my own pulse, breath. Whoever he is he's taking his time, moving carefully, that's for certain. But what else should I have expected? There's a lot at stake, after all, and he's worked a long time, come a long way to get this far. So he's in no hurry; he won't get clumsy or careless now. I listen and wait, but still the silence closes in. Is there a solitary prison cell somewhere this quiet? I wonder. Or perhaps the tomb of an ancient Pharaoh? Yet even now I cannot clear my mind of events leading to this moment.

"I heard of the illness here, I came to inquire after your uncle," I told George Sweney with as grim a face as I could manage. I said it partly to be polite, but also as a distraction to keep from laughing. "Terrible thing," I added.

"Terrible, yes," he said. The posturing manner was suddenly gone and his face wore a truly forlorn expression, and I recalled the story: that the childless Wythe had taken in the orphaned Sweney and raised him as his own; that the two were more like devoted father and son than mere uncle and nephew.

"I suppose you can be thankful you weren't stricken with the others," I said.

Sweney, who had turned away to fondle some trinket on the fireplace mantle, abruptly faced me. And just for an instant I caught a wildly angry flash in his eyes. I suppose that was thoughtless – what I said, I decided.

"Pardon me, my apologies, I meant nothing by it," I added hastily. I even bowed my head slightly, and just as quickly Sweney's anger vanished.

Just then Wythe's front door burst open and in came Duval, a bit breathless, with Edmund Randolph right behind.

"George? You all right? How are they? Any change? How's your uncle? Miz Lydia?" The lawyer's questions boomed like so many cannon shots, reducing poor Sweney to a kind of stuttering befuddlement.

"I . . . I don't know. The doctors aren't – "

Again, the door burst open, this time admitting the doctors, who now had with them an entourage of stretcher bearers and attendants. Through the window I could see an ambulance waiting in the street.

"What . . . what is this?" Sweney said. His eyes suddenly sparkled with anger again and his mouth curled up indignantly.

"We're here to check on our patients, of course," one of the doctors said. His voice was so sweetly soothing I felt a flush of embarrassment. Is he another who tends to overdo? I wondered. Or is it me, after all? Have I been schooled so well for so long in the subtleties, the so-called nuances, of human deportment that any demonstrable tone or expression leaves me fairly overcome with feelings of derision?

"Yes, yes, I know," Sweney began, "but what's all – "

"The nurse will stay behind. To care for – "

"I see, that's fine, but – "

"And the bearers are here for Michael Brown's body."

"Oh no, no, no," Sweney shouted at once. "That stays here, for proper burial out back."

The doctor shook his head implacably. "I have an order from the judge," he said, pulling a paper from his inside coat pocket. As he showed it to Sweney, I glimpsed the other doctor already leading the bearers upstairs.

Sweney stared at the paper, then passed it to Randolph who cleared his throat and nodded. "It's all legal, George," he said.

"We want to examine his remains, George," the doctor added.

Sweney seemed on the verge of another protest, but stopped short when Randolph put a calming hand on his shoulder. In a few minutes the physicians were gone and the ambulance rumbled off down Kingman Avenue.

"Why wasn't this on file in my office, George?" the lawyer suddenly demanded, waving yet another set of papers in Sweney's face.

The nephew opened and closed his mouth. Clearly, this wasn't one of his better days. "I don't . . . What . . . what is it?"

"It's your uncle's will, and it's not something that should be left lying around the house," Randolph grumbled.

The lawyer scratched his chin, while Sweney breathed heavily, seemed about to speak once or twice, but finally said nothing at all. All the while, Duval hadn't said a word – and for that matter neither had I.

"And who are you again?" Randolph said. Suddenly I was the dubious object of his attention, and – I couldn't help it – I actually gulped with nervous anticipation. "Oh yes, Duval told me. Hull, is it?"

"Harrison Hull, yes sir," I said.

"And just what brings you here, Mr Hull?"

I looked into his dark, dour eyes and a frown that bordered on the ferocious. He was an imposing man, even intimidating, who obviously knew he was and enjoyed the effect. So I would have feigned a stammer just to please him – even if I really hadn't been a little overwhelmed and quite honestly at a rare loss for words.

"It's . . . Actually, it's, uh, Captain Hull, Mr Randolph."

"State militia?"

"United States Army, Mr Randolph. In the past I've done some special assignments for my friend, Meriwether Lewis. And for the President, as well."

Randolph nodded slowly, and I swear I detected a microscopic flicker of a smile on his lips.

"Lewis? The explorer? Not back from the wilds yet, is he?"

"No, not yet, sir. Everyone's expecting word any time now." I paused, but he just widened his eyes and cocked his head. "In any case, when Mr Jefferson heard I was coming to Richmond he asked me to look in on Mr Wythe if I could. Naturally, when I learned he was ill . . ."

I let my words trail off with a gesture of upturned palms, and Randolph simply stared and rubbed his chin.

"Well, yes," he finally said, half under his breath. "As to this – " He seemed to study the will a moment. "Quite out of the question to open it now, of course, with Wythe still alive." He wheezed and muttered some more, then pulled out a cigar and lit up. "Still, certain . . . questions arise . . ." He mumbled and drew several long puffs. Then, abruptly, in a commanding tone: "Be at my office. All three of you. Ten o'clock tomorrow morning."

And with that he wheeled around and left the house at once.

It's mild to say the meeting was full of surprises. "First, let me tell you that I've spoken with the doctors and they say cholera definitely was *not* the cause of Michael Brown's death," Randolph said with quiet dignity.

"What then?" Sweney asked. But Randolph simply waved him off, then, with more of a flourish in his voice, fairly intoned: "What I am about to do is both extraordinary in itself and, for this very reason, entirely off the record." After a brief pause – obviously (to me) for dramatic effect, he unsealed Wythe's will and read the principal provisions. Quite simply, they named the housekeeper, Lydia Broadnax, heir to Wythe's house and substantial other properties, and Michael Brown heir to half of Wythe's bank stock. Sweney would inherit the other half.

The big shock was what wasn't said – what didn't need to be said. For the will in effect affirmed the long-standing secret, the secret that was never to be spoken of except in hushed tones in darkened corners. Now, upon Wythe's death, it would become public; it would be – that hated word – official: that Broadnax was Wythe's mistress, and had been for many years, and that Michael Brown was their illegitimate mulatto son. As if to add to the jolt, to invite even greater scandal, the will named no less than the President of the United States, Thomas Jefferson, executor in charge of young Brown's "maintenance, education and other benefit."

I'd known the secret, or known of it, but never gave it much thought, only half believed it. Now, taken aback by the inevitable publicity to come, my jaw fell and I gasped. But no one joined me: Duval's usually flat, open features revealed a tinge of smugness, as if to say that naturally he'd known it all along. Sweney, always a tad disdainful, even sneering, could not hide the anger, the rage, he felt.

"Goddam!" I heard Sweney mutter, but there was no time to discuss the point. Right then, one of Wythe's houseboys burst in: "Massa Wythe" had regained consciousness, he told us, and wanted to see us at once. As there were no horses or carriage at the ready, we madly dashed the mile and a half to Wythe's house – Randolph, Duval and I all moving as quickly as we could, arriving quite out of breath. It was only as we climbed the little front stoop and opened the door that I realized Sweney was lagging far behind.

Aging though still vigorous a few days before, Wythe now lay withered and trembling as he spoke in halting tones. "Poisoned," he whispered the moment we entered the room. "Arsenic." He stopped, apparently exhausted by the effort. Or was he just overcome? With anger, perhaps? Or remorse? "Like my own son," he said.

Just then, Sweney came in and that seemed to oddly invigorate him. "Sweney did it," he said, his voice suddenly firm and clear and unmistakeable. It was a condemnation of rare power, carrying, I believed, the clear sense of justice to come.

"He found out he had to share the estate," Wythe went on. "He's been so angry, making threats. I tried to calm him. I thought he'd let it go. But I guess he couldn't."

Another servant had gone for the doctors, and just then they came into the crowded bedroom. "Arsenic killed Michael Brown," one of them announced at once.

"Yes," Wythe answered, his voice weak again, but, it seemed to me, filled with relief – his accusations confirmed. "After supper. In the strawberries and coffee."

The doctors nodded. "Very likely," one said.

Then, for a moment it was as if a gloomy cloud had filled the room. Wythe lay back exhausted and the rest of us stood around, speechless. Helpless.

"How are the others?" Wythe finally asked. It was the question we'd been dreading.

Randolph looked at me and I looked at Duval, who finally stepped to the edge of the bed. "Lydia's still unconscious, George," he said, then paused. "Young Michael is dead."

A curious, animal-like noise rumbled from Wythe's throat – a noise, it seemed to me, of anger and resignation and inestimable sadness. "New will, Edmund," he said, very feebly, and Randolph swiftly pulled out pen and paper.

As Wythe dictated and the lawyer wrote, Duval and I hung back among the shadowy corners of the room. Almost unnoticed, Sweney had slipped out. Predictably, Wythe removed his nephew as his heir, leaving everything instead to Lydia Broadnax, should she survive.

Later, as we sat around the downstairs parlor together, it occurred to me that something was missing from the general flow of conversation. Something perhaps about Sweney's fate. Something about calling in the town marshals. After all, hadn't a boy been murdered? And wouldn't it be usual to have brought in the authorities by now? So why hasn't that been done? Could the niddling trace of a suspicion in the darkest recess of my mind be anywhere close to the truth? It made me sick even to consider the possibility; little did I know it was only a pale prelude.

The next morning, George Wythe, distinguished legal scholar, mentor to Thomas Jefferson and signer of the Declaration of Independence – thirty years before almost to the day, died of poisoning by arsenic at the hand of his nephew. Now the marshals were summoned at once, the formal charges made, and George Sweney was arrested for murder. Remarkably enough, within a few hours Lydia Broadnax seemed to rally from her coma. By early evening she regained consciousness, and the doctors pronounced her recovered. The next day, when she was strong enough, she confirmed Wythe's account of Sweney's actions, and the road to justice seemed swift, sure and undeniable.

The first inkling otherwise was not even that, but what seemed at the time to be a figment, a specter, looming only in my always-energetic imagination. It was what I took as, possibly, an unfriendly glance from one of Wythe's neighbors standing on her front porch across the street. Perhaps my eyesight is beginning to fail, I thought, for surely this amiable woman cannot be grimacing so nastily in my direction. But then when I said good afternoon to the neighbors right next door, that woman said, "Hmmph!" and the man shook his head dismally.

By then the newspapers had been trumpeting the story for days, and when I began reading them more closely I realized that the initial shock over Sweney's mere murders was quickly giving way to horror and outrage at the scandal of Wythe's miscegenation. Even so, I still felt that my imagination must be getting the best of me. After all, what could possibly outweigh these ghastly attacks by a beloved nephew on the very hand that had fed him for so long?

The day the trial opened Edmund Randolph unleashed his thunderbolt. At least for me that's what it was, though naturally nobody else in Richmond seemed to think much about it: that in Virginia Negroes could not testify against whites, so Lydia Broadnax would *not* be called to give her version of the events leading to the murders. What's more, Randolph said, the judge was considering a defense motion to deny admission of our versions of Wythe's deathbed denunciations on grounds that they were hearsay.

So it finally sank in. And over numerous brandies that evening I found myself asking just where had I been all these weeks? In what dream world had I been dwelling? Duval joined my commiserations at a local tavern, where talk predictably turned to the forthcoming trial. "Old Wythe been sticking it where it shouldn't be stuck, eh?" one man offered up. His companion snickered in reply, adding, "Too big an insult to let pass; poor Sweney did what he had to."

I started to turn toward them; I felt like killing them both. But Duval implored me otherwise and hurried me out. We finished our drinks in the solitary parlor of his little bachelor's bungalow.

"You know where I stand, Harrison," he said, and I did at that. He'd told me plainly enough, even showed me a copy of his letter to

Jefferson. "I share what must be your sorrow and grief over these terrible events," Duval had written, "and I will personally do all in my power to see that George Sweney is met with the full measure and power of the law."

"Harry to my friends," I told him over yet another round of drinks.

In the next few days, as the trial wore on, I scoured the neighborhood looking for any clue, any witness that might give credence to the truth. I even advertised, but all I got for my trouble was a rock through my cousin's front window and three letters telling me, variously, to "Leave town," "Drop dead," or "Prepare to die."

By the time I took the stand nine days later, the newspapers were in a virtual frenzy. "George Wythe's scandalous and utterly irrational behavior poses a grave insult to all freedom-loving Virginians," opined one editorial. "And while we cannot excuse murder in rebut, George Sweney's actions clearly bring to mind the label 'justifiable homicide.'"

My testimony was limited to a description of events leading up to my discovery of the container of arsenic. With the help of an unsuspecting prosecutor's laborious questions, I went through it all in meticulous detail. Then, with the court bored and half asleep, I shouted in defiance of the judge's earlier ruling: "Mr Wythe denounced his nephew on his deathbed. George Sweney murdered his uncle by poison."

It woke everybody up – that was certain. Otherwise, my efforts won me nothing save two days in jail for contempt. By the time I got out the all-white jury was ready to come back. It had taken them less than an hour to decide: George Sweney was not guilty.

And there was further insult to come. Two days later the charge of murdering Michael Brown was quashed without a trial, and the following week the courts even set aside Wythe's new will. Now Sweney was not only free but rich, for the judge awarded him Michael Brown's share of the estate as well as his own.

For a while, I seriously considered murdering Sweney. After all, I thought, in a place where justice is so unjust what else can one do save administer justice. And isn't that the way of the world? I could murder George Sweney, make good my escape, and chances are find that justice back in my home outside Philadelphia would adjudge me savior and hero. But if history is any guide it is only the very wicked (and now and then the very, very good) who can bring themselves to so single-mindedly and single-handedly impose justice upon the world. Clearly, I am neither sort of person.

So after a few more nights of rather morose drinking sessions with

Duval, and some with Edmund Randolph, I snapped out of it and understandably dispensed with outright murder as a possible course of action.

And then, exhausted, out of ideas, beaten down at last by such peculiar notions of right and wrong, I elaborately told my relatives goodbye, said my farewells to Duval and Randolph, made certain that a newspaper editor or two learned of my departure and left Richmond for good.

Or so it seemed.

In my hiding place in William Duval's closet I hear from somewhere downstairs the faint sound of a glass trinket tinkling; somewhere, another floorboard creaks. Down the hall Duval rustles edgily in his bedroom; obviously, he is no more asleep than I. Quiet down, William, I say to myself; stay calm. And mercifully he does; the noises from his room subside.

So, you ask, what am I doing here crouched in this closet? Did I leave Richmond or not? And if not, why not?

Well, it's simple enough, really: I left and then came back — snuck back, I should say, late that same night. And I've been back ever since, sleeping by day, keeping shy of the windows by night, eating sparingly, talking only when necessary, not talking at all after dark.

All the while Duval has kept me informed of certain events of importance. It seems that a few days after my return a messenger delivered a mysterious new set of documents to Edmund Randolph, and after checking up a bit the lawyer summoned Sweney and Duval to his office. He also called in a civil court judge of his acquaintance, one Phillip Lewiston, who had known George Wythe for many years. Randolph then explained to the three that from the markings on the outer envelope he had traced the documents back to a small transcription service.

"I personally spoke with the director of the service," Randolph said, "and he confirmed that an employee of his witnessed George Wythe writing these words at approximately seven o'clock on the morning of his death — actually about three hours before he died." The director, Randolph said, told him that this particular employee had since resigned his position and left Richmond. But he said the scribe had given him absolute assurances that Wythe himself had written the document. He said the employee later transcribed it into official form.

Randolph then unsealed the papers and showed them around, and all agreed the writing was Wythe's. Randolph also produced the professional transcription and read the essential parts: It was, as they had all suspected, a new will in which Wythe named "my old and trusted friend, William Duval, heir to all my property, my house, my bank stock, all my worldly possessions" – though with the provision that in the event of Duval's death, everything once again would revert to Sweney.

Sweney (Duval told me) sat through this literally open-mouthed, his eyes red with anger. "No," he kept saying, all the while shaking his head. But in the end Randolph declared the will genuine, and Judge Lewiston agreed.

"It's clearly his handwriting," the judge said, "and all the evidence shows plainly enough when it was written." Then, pausing to pick up the document, he declared, "There is no doubt that this is George Wythe's last will and testament."

Sweney stormed out and, from what Duval learned later, went straight to his own lawyer, who, after consulting Randolph, told his irate client that nothing could be done. Over the next ten days or so, Sweney was seen in half the saloons in Richmond, each time more drunk and angry. Neighbors reported him rampaging through his uncle's house late into the night, shouting curses and smashing up the place.

"Old fool," they heard him say more than once. "Nigger-loving, bastard-loving fool."

Then, a few nights ago, he grew quiet, and that was when I became alarmed. And now, loaded pistol in hand, I wait in Duval's upstairs hall closet.

And now, having waited so many nights, tonight I hear it plainly – the first creak at the bottom of the staircase. Then another. Then one more. Now I cannot hear my own breathing or the beat of my heart. Now I hear nothing in the world except this man on the stairs in the dark coming closer.

What drives men to such acts? I wonder. I have baited this silly trap, but he suspects nothing. He is blinded by his greed. And his hatred. He feels . . . victimized. I'm sure of it – that in his mind he's the one who's been put upon, swindled, deprived.

The groans on the stairs are much closer now, and then I hear him mount the last step and turn down the hall. The closet door is ajar, as it has been all along, and I see him walk past with graceful silence toward Duval's bedroom.

I stand up and slowly, quietly cock the pistol. But I wait till he is fully in the bedroom before I step into the hallway a few feet behind. The location of the doorway as he stands at the foot of Duval's bed keeps him fully in my line of fire, and I watch, his back to me, as he raises a knife above his head, ready to plunge it downward with all possible strength.

At last, my pistol aimed straight for him, I shout in a commanding tone, "Stop, thief!" as if I believe he is a burglar. But it is only to complete the ruse in case some lonely, late-night passerby should overhear us. "Stop," I say again, and for an instant he does stop, but he does not drop the knife. Still holding it above his head, he turns toward me, or starts to, but I do not let him turn entirely around. I do not wait; the waiting is over. I fire one round, and he drops instantly to the floor. I walk over to him with Duval behind me, kneel down and take a close look. It is George Sweney, all right, and I have killed him with one shot to the right temple.

Duval is trembling and ghostly pale, but I press the pistol into his hand. "Don't forget your promise, William," I say. I mean it as a joke, but he misunderstands.

"Yes, give you a few minutes before sounding the alarm," he says.

"Uh, yes, that, too," I answer with a feeble laugh. "But I mean about the money." It is my reminder, quite needless – as I say, a joke – to give all his "inheritance" to Lydia Broadnax.

He glares at me a moment, not sure what to make of it, then smiles thinly. He has relaxed a little, which is what I had intended. "Of course, Harry," he says. "I couldn't keep Wythe's money, you know that. So what choice do I have? It's either give it to Lydia, or . . . what? Maybe admit that I forged that last 'will' of George's? Maybe explain about you being here and about my brother-in-law owning that transcription service?"

I shake my head and laugh softly. "No, no," I say, and he laughs, too.

Then without another word, I slip out of the house, saddle a fast horse and leave Richmond.

And this time it is real. And for good.

THE GOD OF
THE HILLS
Melville Davisson Post

I must confess I have a passion for the Uncle Abner stories of Melville Davisson Post (1869–1930). Although they seem curiously dated and idiosyncratically American, they conjure up vivid images of a god-fearing but dangerously lawless rural landscape in early nineteenth-century Virginia. The original stories were published as Uncle Abner, Master of Mysteries *in 1918. Ten years later Post returned to Uncle Abner and produced four more stories. These are much darker works. By then Post was in an increasing state of depression following the death of his wife and then of his father, to whom he was very close, and on whom Abner was probably based. These later stories, of which "The God of the Hills" was one, were not collected into book form until 1974 when the Aspen Press issued them as* The Methods of Uncle Abner. *To my knowledge these final stories have never been published in Britain.*

Abner used to say that one riding on a journey was in God's hand.

He never knew what lay before him; death standing in the road, invisible, as before the prophet; or a kingdom as in the case of Saul. One set out with his little intention, and found himself a factor in some large affair.

It is certain that my uncle had no idea of what he would come into when he rode on this early summer morning to Judge Bensen's house. It was some distance through the hills and he traveled early, with the dawn. He wished an hour with Bensen before the judge rode in to the county seat; for it was in the court term, and Bensen was the circuit judge.

It was a custom remaining in Virginia after the dominion of King George had passed.

The circuit judges were persons of property and distinction. They traveled on their circuits, holding their courts here and there about the country. There would be a group of counties in a circuit. And the county seat would take its name, not infrequently, from the fact that it was the domicile of these circuit courts. One finds the name remaining – Culpepper Court House, and the like.

Land was the evidence and insignia of distinction in Virginia.

One's importance was measured by his acres.

Every man who would command the attention of his fellows stood on an estate in lands. Judge Bensen lived some miles from the county seat. He had got a thousand acres from his father, and added to it. He had never married. He lived alone, with Negro servants, in their white-washed quarters, at some distance from his ancient house. His earnings and his salary from the state went to the purchase of new lands.

He had introduced the Hereford, and turning aside from the customs of the men about him, he bred young cattle, instead of fattening the beef bullock for the market. It happened then that Bensen's young cattle were not easily to be equaled. If one bought from him one got a drove of bullocks of one type, with no mongrel to be sold off to the little trader. Bensen had 200 young cattle – stockers, as they were called – for sale. And my uncle went, early, on this summer morning to see the drove: and to buy the cattle if he could, before Bensen set out for his court – on his horse with his legal papers in his saddle bags.

It was scarcely daylight when Abner descended into the long valley that extended north to the county seat, and in which lay the Bensen lands. At the foot of the hill where the road entered the valley he came on a man sitting his horse in the road. It was early, an hour before the sun, and there was a vague mist in this lowland.

The man and the horse looked gigantic.

Beyond them through an avenue of trees was the heavy outline of a house, still dark, from which the life within it had not yet awakened to the new day.

The whole earth was dry and the road bedded down with dust. My uncle was almost on the man before he knew him. It was Adam Bird, a traveling preacher of the hills, on his gray mare. The big old man was sitting motionless in his saddle looking up through the avenue of maples toward the shadowy house. He did not hear my uncle's horse in the soft dust until it was nearly on him. His hands lay on the pommel of his saddle and his face was lifted like one in some deep reflection.

He called out when he saw my uncle.

"Abner," he said, "do you see that house."

He did not pause for a reply from Abner nor for any formality of salutation. He went on, and directly, as though he merely uttered now aloud the thing that was passing in his mind.

"Caleb Greyhouse lived there until the devil took him. He married Virginia Lewis – for a woman when she is young will be a fool. She is long dead but she left a daughter that is a Lewis too. Not a Greyhouse, by the mercy of God! And now Abner," and he brought one of his big hands, clenched, down on the pommel of the saddle, "these accursed judges are going to dispossess her of her inheritance!"

My uncle knew what the man meant. It was common knowledge. Caleb Greyhouse had left a will written some years before, when the girl was young, leaving his estate, houses and lands, to his daughter, with a bequest to his brother who was to be the guardian and administrator of it. It had been written by Coleman Northcote, one of the best lawyers in Virginia, and so remained, until the girl had grown up. Then, when she had fallen in love, and wished to marry the son of a neighbor with whom Greyhouse had quarreled over a few acres of ridge land, the irascible old man had added a codicil to the will giving the whole estate to his brother, and no dollar and no acre to the girl.

The case was before the circuit court, now sitting, for the girl had got a sort of lawyer, and brought a suit.

But she had no money and no case.

Northcote had written the will only too accurately, with precise care for every technical detail. The codicil added by Greyhouse followed the form in Mayo's Guide. It was written and signed by the testator and contained no legal flaw. There seemed nothing that any court could do. Nevertheless, Bensen had called in a judge from a neighboring circuit to sit with him and decide the case. The case was before the judges. And it was the act of these judges and the case before them that moved the traveling preacher of the hills.

"Did Bensen decide the case?" replied my uncle.

"He did not," said Bird, "but the judge with him clamored to decide it and have it done, for he wished to go back to his circuit. Bensen delayed a little for he had a plan of his own about this thing. He said he would write an opinion and they would decide today. But it was an abominable pretension, Abner. They will dispossess the girl . . . unless the Lord God Almighty moves somewhere in this thing."

Again his big hand descended on the pommel of his saddle, as though he pounded the timber of a pulpit.

"And He will move in it! It is so written in The Book. If the widow and the orphan cry to me I will surely hear their cry."

He brought his big hand up and over his face and his voice descended into a lower note.

"She came to me and said, 'Uncle Adam, will you pray for me to win my case.' And I said I will not pray; for I will not supplicate the Lord God Almighty to do justice. I will call His attention to this wrong . . . And I stood up and cried to Him! And the word of the Lord came to me. And I saddled my horse, and rode down here and called Bensen out. He came shuffling with his little lawyer talk. It was the law. He had no discretion. He could not help the wrong of it. And besides I was in contempt of his court to talk with him about the case.

"In contempt of his court, Abner!"

And again the old man made his powerful dramatic gesture.

"I, the servant of God, in contempt of his court when I protested against a wrong! . . . I told Bensen that he was in contempt of God's court, and that if he went forward with this injustice Jehovah would include him in the damnation that followed after it."

He paused and looked my uncle in the face.

"For Bensen, Abner, is not guiltless in this thing. He will profit by it. He has coveted these lands as we all know and tried to purchase them. Old Caleb Greyhouse would not sell. But this brother will sell. And Bensen will get the lands he covets."

And again the old man returned to his dramatic vigor.

"And he shall not escape the damnation that followed Ahab the King of Samaria; because he takes the land he covets through the act of another.

"The writing of clerks and seals of courts shall not bring it to him guiltless, even as the writing of Jezebel and the sealing thereof did not bring the lands that he coveted to Ahab guiltless . . . I go now, Abner, as Elijah went to the King of Samaria! And if he say like that other, 'Hast thou found me, O mine enemy?' I will answer, I have found thee!"

He made a great sweeping gesture and turned his horse north in the valley. He rode as though he rode alone in the vague mist that lifted from the lowland and hung above the fields; a thin gray smoke screen spreading like a blanket.

The old man had not asked whither my uncle rode nor to what end.

He went like one on some tremendous mission, alone.

Abner followed. The circuit rider had brought a new element into this affair. A gain to Bensen at the end of it that my uncle had not considered. But now that the point was touched on he remembered. It was common knowledge that it was a covetous intent with Bensen to extend his lands; to add a field. He had endeavored to buy the Greyhouse tract. And it was the truth that while Caleb Greyhouse would not sell, this brother who took the estate under the written codicil would sell it to the last acre. He had sold all that he had received from his father as an inheritance except a few acres and a house on the highway near the Bensen residence.

There was a dissolute, a reckless strain in the man that was not in Caleb Greyhouse.

He wished to be a factor in political affairs, and lacking the confidence of the people he attached his fortunes to other men; and so he had got to be a sort of deputy about the courthouse, and a chimney-corner lawyer, with knowledge enough to thumb through the deed books searching for some defect in a title upon which he could bring a suit, or extort a blackmail.

He had a marked pride in this pretension.

In the suit before the judges, on the will, he appeared with much visible ostentation for himself. There was, as it happened, little peril to his case, for the girl, with no money to hire a competent attorney, had only a chimney-corner lawyer like himself. And so the case was one for judges to decide as it appeared, on its face, before them . . . Bensen would get the land. This Barnes Greyhouse, in funds, would try for the Assembly of Virginia. And with money he might win. There was here, as in every land, an element of the electorate that could be persuaded by a demagogue and a little money in the hand.

My uncle rode on after the old preacher, his big chestnut horse moving noiselessly in the deep dust.

But his heart was troubled.

The girl came up sharply outlined in his memory: fair-haired and slender, with the hope and the charm of the immortal morning. There was no reason why she should not go, in joy, to the youth that she loved.

He was of a better family and a better blood than Greyhouse.

Because that irascible old man had quarreled with the boy's father about some acres of stony land along a ridge line, everyone of the blood was damned. All were enemies, and endowed by that enmity with every vice.

Old Greyhouse would have no marriage with his enemy.

He fell into a fury of wild talk at the mere mention of it. And on a certain night, heated in that fury, he had written out the codicil that divested his daughter of his estate. It was not certain that at the bottom of the man he, in fact, wished to make that alienation.

In anger, affection is sometimes overridden.

Perhaps if he had had time, in illness, for reflection, he would have canceled it. Blood, as the old adage said, was thicker than water when death approached and one came to pass on the material things that one had gathered together in one's life.

But he had no such time.

Death came on him in the fields.

He had fallen, in harvest, at a stroke of sun. The farm hands carried him in. But he was already out of life. He lay for some hours in a coma, in his daughter's arms. Once, as the field hands told, he tried to stroke her hair and make known to her something that moved vaguely in his mind.

But he had had his hour, and he was granted no extension.

What he had written, he had written.

Death would not release his hand to cancel it.

It was the old eternal story.

Men acted in their anger to do wrong, as though they had a privilege of life; as though at their wish or need, in extremity, they would be granted a stay of execution until they could set their affairs in order and adjust any wrong they had accomplished.

The day was breaking.

The fog, extended through the valley, was lifting and parting into long streamers of white mist. The hills in the distance were sharp and clear in the morning light. In a short time the sun would appear. Already in the fields the cattle were at pasture.

My uncle had come up with the circuit rider.

And at once when the big chestnut emerged from the mist by his gray mare, the old man began to talk. He began, as before, with no introductory sentence.

"Abner," he said, "your father lived long in this land, and he did good in the sight of the Lord and not evil. And I can name a hundred men like him who have stood for righteousness. But in that company there is no Greyhouse. Old Caleb was the best. He was hard and mean but he was not a liar nor a thief. But this other, this Barnes Greyhouse, is the worst of an evil generation. His hands are full of evil. Did not little Benny Wilmoth, in despair, shoot himself in his house because this creature searching through the deed books found a defect in his title and brought a suit to dispossess him of his farm. It was a sort of murder, Abner!"

He thrust his clenched hand out.

"There was no law to hale Barnes Greyhouse into the court and hang him. But was he any less guilty for that lack? The hand of Virginia could not reach him. But, Abner, is he beyond God's hand? By little twists and turns a nimble man may slip away from the law. But he will not slip away from the vengeance of God."

His clenched hand made a great sweeping curve, as though it cleared a swathe before him.

"Abner," he said, "I will not be silent before this outrage. I will call Bensen to his door and warn him. I have seen it in a dream. He is a party to this wrong, and the Lord will make his house like the house of Jeroboam, the son of Nebat . . . and this Barnes Greyhouse!" He spread out the fingers of his extended arm as in the pronouncement of a curse. "As the dogs licked up the blood of Ahab in the pool of Samaria, shall the dogs lick up his blood! . . . for in shame, and in blackness, and in violence shall he go out of life!"

My uncle did not reply. This old man of the hills who stood for righteousness, like all who give themselves wholly to some principle of honor, had the dignity of the thing behind him. And he was not afraid. Neither courts nor judges could overawe him.

My uncle was in a deep reflection. He knew of this matter what was current gossip in the hills. But he did not know, until this morning, the sweeping terms in which Caleb Greyhouse, in his anger, had written out the codicil to this will. It would be, he had imagined, a sort of guardianship in the brother over the girl's estate until she came to a legal age, or some manner of trust. With such a writing there would be hope. But with a direct bequest in terms there would be no hope.

He was in a great perplexity and his mind turned from the mission on which he came.

It was broad day now with the sun beginning to appear.

They drew near to Bensen's house.

In the pasture by the road strolling down to water at the brook were the drove of young Hereford cattle. They were unequaled; as like in form and coloring as though they were all born of one mother, by some miracle of maternity on the same day of the year, and so reared and suckled. No cattleman of the hills could have passed that drove and not pulled up his horse to look it over, for in his mind's eye, after that, he would have carried the model for all other young cattle in the world.

And yet my uncle did not pull up his horse.

The two men passed in silence and, making a sharp turn in the road beside some oak trees, came to Bensen's house. They stopped in wonder. The house was open; the Negroes were hovering about as in a panic. Randolph's gig was before the door. He came out when they appeared.

"Abner," he said, "you are come, and I was about to send a Negro for you. Bensen is dead!

"You arrive also, Adam," he said, "as at a direction of God. It is the house of death that you have come to, and it is one of the duties of the preacher of the Gospels to minister to the dead. Come in."

"I will not come in," replied the old man. "But I will get down and sit before the door, for I did not come in peace."

But my uncle cried out astonished.

"Dead!" he echoed. "Bensen dead! What killed him?"

"Now, that," replied Randolph, "is the mystery that I was about sending after you to solve. Bensen was killed in the night as he sat here in his library at work among his books."

On the way in with Abner, Randolph explained the details of what had happened.

The circuit court was sitting.

The case over the will of Caleb Greyhouse was on the docket.

For some reason Bensen wished another judge to sit with him to decide the case and so had called in West from a neighboring circuit. There was no reason for this, Randolph said, for there was no ground on which to contest the will. Coleman Northcote had written it some years before. Northcote was the best chancery lawyer in Virginia, and he made no errors in a legal paper. The will was correctly drawn, signed by the testator, and witnessed as the law required.

Later, Caleb Greyhouse had added a codicil in his own hand-writing, on the blank sheet of the will. The codicil followed the form in Mayo's Guide and was signed, dated, and sealed in every feature, also as the law required.

Of course this attack on the will broke down at once.

There was no technical error in it.

The codicil added below the will on the same sheet of foolscap was also unassailable. It followed the legal form, was written by the testator in his own hand and signed by him.

It became thus, under the law of Virginia, a holograph will and required no witnesses.

West wanted to decide the case at once from the bench, so he could get back to his circuit. But Bensen said they would take it under advisement until morning.

That night all the Negroes about the place went to a frolic at the county seat.

They left the judge at work in his library, when they went out at dark.

In court time it was the custom of the judge to work late over his legal papers and so they had put new candles in the sticks on his table and lighted them before they left the house. They had been delayed in setting out, and as they left the house the judge had come to the door and directed them to stop on the way and ask Barnes Greyhouse to come and see him.

The man lived not farther than a quarter of a mile along the road.

They gave the message and saw him take his hat and cane and set out.

The frolic ran late. It was well toward dawn when the servants returned.

There was no light in Bensen's library or about the house and they naturally assumed that the judge had put out the lights and gone to bed.

In the morning when they came into the house they found the tragedy, and in terror sent for Randolph.

He found the library as the assassin had left it, for the Negroes had not gone in.

The judge had been killed as he sat before his table. He had been struck down from behind, apparently without warning. The assassin had used the poker from the fireplace. It was a terrific blow for it had crushed in the skull. The man had fallen sidewise under the table, for a second blow aimed at him had struck the table itself, leaving an indentation in the walnut wood.

The iron fire-poker lay on the floor behind the chair in which the judge had been sitting.

The deed had been done late, for the candles had burned down almost to the cup of the sticks before they had been extinguished. They had been snuffed out.

Randolph pointed out the iron poker, the mark on the walnut table, and the blood smear on the hardwood floor where the judge had fallen. Abner looked carefully about the room. And while he thus studied the situs of the crime, Randolph gave his opinion.

"This, Abner," he said, "will be the work of some vindictive convict. Our circuit judges are always in peril from these creatures when they come back from the penitentiary. I have seen them, when they were sentenced, scowl hard at the judges and mutter what they would do in revenge, when they should at length go free.

"This will be the work of such a creature. Bensen, in the counties of his circuit, will have sentenced all sorts of men for all sorts of felonies.

"But it is a peril of honor, Abner. And the one who dies from it dies in the service of his country, as though he died in battle before her enemies."

My uncle did not reply.

But there came a voice through the open door in answer.

The voice of the old circuit rider sitting in the sun.

"He did not die in honor, Randolph. Bensen died as a dog dieth!"

Randolph made a gesture as of one who dismisses the extravagances of a child with whom he will not contend. He got out some sheets of paper and sat down at a corner of the table to make a note of the details of the tragedy, accurately as he had found them on this morning.

Abner remained standing by the table, his big hand gathered about his chin, looking at the two tall candlesticks, with their bits of candles burned down to the cups.

New tallow candles had been put in on this night. These candles would burn long, almost from the dark till morning. They had been put in new on this night, and there was only a fragment left when the assassin had snuffed them out.

It was some time before my uncle moved, then he took up the snuffers and with the sharp point lifted the bits of candle out of the cups of the candlesticks.

But he did not otherwise disturb them.

He replaced them as they had been, put down the snuffers at their place, and went over to the far corner of the room.

There lying in the corner was a thing that he had noticed but upon which he had made no comment.

It was a small fragment of wood.

At first he had thought it a chip from the table broken off by the impact of the blow that had been directed at Bensen as he fell forward under it. But the table was walnut, and this fragment was some dark wood of a close texture. He did not take it up, nor disturb it where it lay in the corner, but he stooped over and studied it intently.

He arose, went over to the fireplace.

He took up the iron poker and turned it about in his hand.

There was a coating of ashes on the poker, extending from the point halfway to the handle, and over this toward the point was the blood of the man who had been murdered.

Abner put the poker down and remained for some moments by the hearth.

No fire had been lighted in it on this night. But there was a heap of wood ashes where former fires had burned.

Abner looked about him.

Randolph wrote sitting at a corner of the table with his back toward him. The old circuit rider was invisible beyond the open door; the Negroes had withdrawn in frightened groups beyond the house.

There was no one to question the thing he did – for he was not yet ready to be questioned – and kneeling down on the brick hearth he put his hand into the heap of ashes.

Then he withdrew his hand, smoothed the surface of the heap as it had been, dusted the ashes from his hand, and rose.

He went around Randolph to the door and stepped out.

It was early in the morning.

No one had arrived, for the servants when they had found Bensen dead had sent word only to Randolph, through the hills. And Abner and old Adam had come by chance.

Abner did not pause.

He went on across the grassplot to the road. He stopped there and looked carefully about.

Then he walked north in the dust of the road, in the direction of the county seat. He went slowly, pausing now and then, and retracing now and then a step. Finally he stopped, advanced, returned, and stood still.

There was a little wood of scrub oak on his right hand, and a rail fence. He crossed the fence and began to look about in this tangle of scrub oak.

It was some time, perhaps half an hour, before he got back to the house.

There was a haircloth sofa, facing toward a bookcase in a far corner of the room. Abner went past Randolph to the sofa and leaning over the back put down on it something that he had brought with him, concealed under his long coat.

He returned to the table where Randolph sat before his sheets of paper.

The man had been so taken up with what he wrote that he had not marked my uncle's absence.

Abner put out his hand and took up, from beyond Randolph, a law book with a cracked back. It was a volume of early legal reports.

The book fell open midway of the volume where the back was cracked.

And when my uncle saw the page before him his face changed.

He read and his features hardened.

He was about to speak when the voice of a man entering from the road stopped him.

It was Barnes Greyhouse.

He was a big man with a heavy brutal face laid over with a sort of fawning geniality. He walked with a slight limp, for in some drunken brawl, at an earlier time, he had been injured.

Randolph rose as the man came in; and my uncle turned about toward the door.

But he did not move.

The man blurted out a jumble of greeting and amazed expletives at the tragedy.

"Good God!" he said. "Bensen murdered. Who could have killed him?"

My uncle did not reply.

But Randolph made a little gesture as of one who has penetrated to a meaning hidden from other men.

"It is the work of some convict that Bensen has sent to the penitentiary. Such creatures hold always a vindictive resentment against the judge; as though their punishment were his work."

"You are right, Randolph," said Greyhouse. "That's the explanation."

He uttered the words as though the conclusion could not be gainsaid, and was a pronouncement in finality. But there was a sort of eagerness in the voice and manner of the man.

My uncle spoke then.

"Greyhouse," he said, "you were here last night."

The man turned with a gesture of assent.

"Yes," he said, "early in the night. The Negroes passing said Bensen wished to see me, and I walked down. But I was here for a few moments only. The judge had sent for me to say that he and West would decide the case at once when they convened in the morning, and that I should come early into the court. I left the judge as I found him, sitting at his table there, and walked home. It was early: about dark."

"Were the candles lighted on Bensen's table?" inquired my uncle.

"Yes," replied the man, "just lighted, I think, as I came in; it was about dark."

"And the candles, Greyhouse; were they new tall candles, as the Negroes say?"

"Yes, Abner," he replied, "I can answer that. They were new tall candles for I noticed the flicker of the wick where the pointed ends had not yet caught up with the tallow."

Abner leaned over the table and took up Randolph's pencil.

"That is an important fact," he said, "for fragments only of these candles were burning in the sticks when the assassin snuffed them out after the murder. I think a note should be made of your observation to confirm what the Negroes say."

He put out his hand with the pencil in his fingers to write a line on Randolph's memorandum. But he bore too heavily and the point of the pencil broke. He turned toward Greyhouse with the pencil in his hand.

"Lend me your knife," he said.

The man took a penknife from his breeches and handed it to my uncle. Abner opened the knife and turned back to the table. But he did not sharpen the pencil. He put down the knife and pencil on the table and stood up.

My uncle looked hard at Greyhouse.

"You think Bensen was killed, late in the night, by some vindictive assassin who slipped in behind him. Is that your belief, Greyhouse?"

"Why, yes," he said, "that is the obvious conclusion. Here are the candles burned down to the cups and the bloody poker. It is indicated in these evidences. Bensen was murdered by some released convict who had a grudge against him, and slipping in behind killed him with the poker."

He was interrupted by a voice; a voice big and dominant that seemed to envelop and fill up the room.

"Bensen was not killed with the poker."

The three men turned as with a single motion of their bodies.

The old circuit rider was standing in the door. Greyhouse cried out at the words.

"How do you know that?"

The old circuit rider looked hard at the man.

"I know it," he answered, "as God knows it."

Then he closed his mouth and was silent.

It was my Uncle Abner that broke the silence.

"Adam is right," he said, "Bensen was not killed with the poker, nor in the time or manner that these evidences would indicate, for they are false and set up to mislead. There is blood on this poker. But there was no blood from the fracture of the skull that killed the judge and therefore there would be no blood on the implement with which the blow was dealt. There was hemorrhage only from the dead man's face where he lay under the table. But this poker was not there. It lay on the floor behind the chair. And consequently, it was made bloody by design."

He paused and turned toward the table.

"But this," he said, "was not the first thing that puzzled me. The first thing was the aspect of these candlesticks. If new tallow candles had burned down in them to the cups, the shafts of the sticks would have been fouled over with dripping grease. They were not so fouled. The shafts of the candlesticks were clean as you see them. How could that happen? The wicks of the bits of candles had been snuffed out. That was clear. But how could the candles have burned down to these bits, and there follow no drip of tallow?

"There was a reason. And I found that reason."

He took up the iron snuffers and with their sharp point lifted the bits of candles out of the cups of the sticks. The explanation was apparent. The candles had been cut off with a knife.

There was silence and he continued:

"What had become of the candles? I searched the room here. I found a certain thing but not the candles."

He made a gesture toward a distant corner, and went on.

"I looked again at the poker. It had a coating of wood ashes on it, as though it had been thrust into the heap yonder in the fireplace. Thrust in before it had been dipped into Bensen's blood, for the coating of ashes was underneath the blood . . . Then I found the candles."

He crossed the room with long strides, seized the poker, thrust it into the heap of ashes in the fireplace, and raked out the two long candles, cut off at their tips.

He put down the poker and stood up.

"The whole thing was clear now. Bensen had been killed early in the night when the candles were hardly lighted, and with some implement other than this poker, by one who had acted on a sudden determination to thus kill; and after the act endeavored to falsify events. He cut off the candles and snuffed them out. He made a hole in the ashes with the poker and concealed them and then, remembering that an implement must be found, had thought of the poker in his hand, and dipping it in the man's blood laid it on the floor behind the chair."

My uncle turned toward Greyhouse.

"Greyhouse," he said, "you are the one who came here early in the evening!"

The features of the man sagged and sweated. But there was a certain courage in him.

"Abner," he cried, "you go mad with your neat little conclusions. Why should I wish Bensen's death? I of all persons would wish his life; for today he and West would decide this will case in my favor."

Again the room reverberated with a voice that filled it. Again the old circuit rider spoke.

"Greyhouse," he said, "you are a liar! . . . I saw this thing in a dream; not all, but a fragment of it. I saw you and Bensen in this room, in anger. He beat a book, opened on the table, with his clenched hand and, from behind, you advanced on him, with something in your hand . . . not the poker, for it was setting against the chimney. You are a liar!"

The big accused creature wavered.

And Abner spoke, when the old man had ended.

"Yes, Greyhouse," he said, "you are a liar. I understand the whole thing to the end, although I have had no part in Adam's vision. That which was confused and hidden is now disclosed and clear. Bensen coveted these lands and he undertook to force you to a sale; a sale that would be a sort of dividing of the loot."

He crossed to the table and opened the volume of Virginia reports at the page where it fell apart from the broken back.

"Look!" he said. "Look, Randolph. Here on this page is the syllabus of a decision of the Supreme Court of Virginia, holding that a will and its codicil must be uniform to be valid. It cannot be half in one form and half in another. If the body of the will is written by someone other than the decedent and signed and witnessed, then the codicil must be so written and signed and witnessed.

"I understand it. I understand it clearly to the end . . . Bensen found this case last night and he sent for Barnes Greyhouse and held the case over him like a club to force a sale of these lands to him at some little price. He must take the price or Bensen would bring in the case today. And so they quarreled, and Bensen beat the book for emphasis, breaking the back under his clenched hand . . . And so Barnes Greyhouse killed him, knowing that West had no knowledge of this case and would decide in favor of the will, and the girl, with no money, could not take it to a higher court!"

There was utter silence. Then my uncle went on.

"Where is your cane, Greyhouse?"

The man did not reply, but his baggy face began to tremble.

"I will answer for you," continued Abner. "Listen, Greyhouse. I went over your track in the dust of the road. It was a clear track and beside it, also in the dust, was the round imprint of the ferrule of your cane. It was all along beside your tracks as you came here from your house, but on your return it was only to be seen beside your tracks for a certain distance. At the field of scrub oaks, on the right of the road, I could no longer find it. What did that mean, Greyhouse? It meant that at this point you had thrown the cane away . . . And why did you throw it away? Because you discovered, there, on your way from this murder, that the cane with which you had killed Bensen had suffered an injury that you might be called on to explain. Look, I will show you, for I found it in the scrub-oak wood by the roadside." He took up the cane from where it was hidden by the sofa and presented it to the man. It was a big heavy crook-handled cane of black wood like teak, and a split-off fragment at the turn of the crook was missing.

"Look at it, Greyhouse," he cried. "Look at it! A piece at the turn of the crook is missing, split off when the cane struck the table, under the powerful blow that you aimed at Bensen when he went down out of the chair. And that piece of it is yonder in the corner of the room."

He crossed with great strides, picked up the fragment of wood, and placed it on the crook of the cane.

"Look, Greyhouse, how the piece fits!"

He made a great gesture.

"There is other evidence against you. Why, sir, it cries like the blood of Abel . . . your knife, there on the table, has tallow on the blade where you cut the candles!"

Panic was on the trapped man and he bolted past my uncle through the open door.

But his foot tripped at the sill and he fell headlong outside, on the flag-paved path. His head struck a fragment of sharp curb and a thin trickle of blood flowed out. Then he got staggeringly to his feet to escape. But my uncle overtook him and the Negroes hurried up to help pin him down.

In the confusion as they drew near, the two hounds hovering about them paused and began to lick the blood where it had trickled on the curb.

The old circuit rider – sitting motionless in the sun, his white head uncovered, his big body, clothed in its rusty-colored homespun, filling up the chair – put out his hand and pointed to the thing.

It was the fulfilling of the prophecy.

As the dogs licked up the blood of Ahab in the pool of Samaria, so shall the dogs lick up his blood.

THE ADMIRAL'S LADY
Joan Aiken

Joan Aiken (b. 1924) should need no introduction to most readers. She has been producing fantasy and horror stories for both children and adults for over forty years. She is probably most noted for her series about Dido Twite, set in a bleak alternative England where the Stuarts still rule. The series began with The Wolves of Willoughby Chase *(1962) and ran through six volumes to* Dido and Pa *(1986). Her many stories of horror and dark suspense have appeared in over a dozen collections including* The Windscreen Weepers *(1969),* A Harp of Fishbones *(1972),* A Touch of Chill *(1979),* A Whisper in the Night *(1982) and* A Fit of Shivers *(1990). With this combination of dark mystery and twisted history you might think Joan Aiken would have written a historical mystery story before now. But not so. Here is her first: "The Admiral's Lady", written especially for this anthology.*

Having assisted for some seven hours at the accouchement of Her Grace the Duchess of Towcester (and a most unsuccessful business *that* was, rewarded after all the lady's pains and my own by no more than a five-pound female child with not the slightest similarity to either parent, but a fairly marked resemblance to Lord Derwentwater – and no more than a five-guinea fee for me, The Duke of Towcester being as penny-pinching a skinflint as ever wore ermine) I was not best pleased to find myself roused again from slumber only two hours later by a loud rat-tat at my door in Half Moon Street.

"Tell whoever it is to go to the devil!" I ordered my footman Joseph, but he reproved me.

"Oh, no, Mr Donovan, no indeed, sir, and ye can't do that –" Joe, like myself, hails from County Cork but, also like myself, has settled into London life as merrily as a mouse into Stilton – "Indeed we can't do that, sir, 'tis the Admiral himself, Admiral Crawford has sent for ye in the most express and vehement manner; Hobbs the coachman who waits at the door tells me 'tis desprit, desprit indeed, sir, or I wouldn't have made bold to rouse ye."

"Oh – very well – if it is the Admiral – I suppose I must bestir myself."

Admiral Sir Mark Crawford was one of my most regular and remunerative patients, a proclivity for a gormandizing and libidinous way of life, coupled with a gouty and choleric constitution rendering him liable to painful seizures of the most acute and agonizing nature at ever more frequent intervals.

"Well, at least the Admiral is no farther off than Hill Street," I mumbled, hastily re-tying my cravat, while Joseph packed the necessary vials of Urtica urents, colchicine, pulsatilla, and Ledum, besides a bag of ice to reduce inflammation, into my black medicine bag.

I had become the Admiral's regular practitioner after another summer evening some five years previously when, as I walked home through the dusk, a series of frantic yells issuing from an open window in Hill Street had impelled me to thrust my head through the casement and inquire if I could be of any use; which offer the Admiral's nephew, a friendly and well-mannered youth, then aged about sixteen or seventeen, had been only too glad to accept, his unfortunate relative being at that moment so distressed in his nether limbs that he sounded like a victim who was being broken on the wheel. This condition I was able to alleviate, and so gained the goodwill of the family. Even Lady Crawford, a female of a particularly glacial and repellent disposition, did not disdain, at times, to ask my advice on matters relating to her poodle Chowder, a fat, ill-conditioned beast with a nature closely resembling that of his mistress. Though it is true she had much to try her.

(The Admiral's lady being mistress of her own fortune, and that a handsome one amounting to over sixty thousand pounds invested in the Funds, must be considered a person of no small consequence in that family. But I digress.)

"Hey-day, coachman! Where are we going? This is not the way to Hill Street!" I exclaimed after a few minutes in the Admiral's barouche.

"Oo said anythink about 'Ill Street? It's Twit-nam *we're* bound for," retorted Hobbs the coachman. "An' a plaguey long way it is for my poor nags, what had to go round Richmond Park only this arternoon with Miss and her precious Ladyship."

"*Twickenham?* Oh, devil take it, if I'd known that was where Sir Mark expected me to go, I'd not have agreed to come, not though he was halfway through the portals of Dis."

"I dunno anything about Dis. But it ain't the Admiral, Mr

Donovan," Hobbs informed me. "He's all right and tight. 'Tis my lady. She's the one what's poorly. And precious poorly she *be*, by all accounts."

"Dear me, what can be amiss?"

I was surprised, for I had never known Lady Crawford to suffer from the least indisposition. Always upright, haughty, dressed in the impeccable height of the mode, she ignored her husband's cantrips, so far as was possible, and led a life of calm, balanced, acid elegance.

If I had understood that it was for *her* sake that I had been roused from my second slumber and obliged to proceed to Twickenham, I would have put up far more of a stand against losing the rest of my night's repose, for I could not believe there was anything seriously the matter with her. As it was, bowing to necessity, I contrived to slip into a doze between Hyde Park and Putney, while the horses wearily jogged on the second half of their twenty-mile journey.

Hitherto I had not been required to visit the Crawfords' cottage in Twickenham for the family had never, to my knowledge, passed a night there. The Admiral had bought the place some three years previously as a summer refuge. And possibly – I thought – as a refuge from his wife.

"It will make a neat little place enough," he declared, upon first acquiring it. "After I have cleared and opened the grounds to a greater degree, and improved the river frontage by means of a terrace or two, and given the building itself more of a picturesque and interesting aspect, by means of a few arches and a pair of gothic turrets, it will do well enough for passing agreeable summer afternoons."

But it seemed that the work was progressing very slowly.

"The truth of the matter is," Henry Crawford once explained to me, shrugging ruefully, "that my uncle seldom knows his mind for two days together. And, furthermore, since the Peace was declared, and Uncle retired from active service, he has not sufficient occupation elsewhere. So the cottage, where my aunt and sister were supposed to pass peaceful afternoons, is never anything but a perfect maelstrom of dirt and confusion, without a gravel path fit to walk on, or a bench to sit on. Uncle Mark is continually issuing contradictory sets of orders, has dismissed two architects, and my aunt is out of all patience with him. For my part, I am only thankful that I have my own estate in Norfolk where I may take refuge when the confusion becomes unbearable. But I pity my aunt and Mary. I do indeed."

For myself, I did not feel that too much sympathy need be expended upon Lady Crawford. She was never one to suffer in silence, and was at all times quite capable of expressing her dissatisfaction with her surroundings. As for Miss Mary Crawford, she moved in a different sphere from mine. Their own parents having died some twelve years before, the brother and sister had been brought up since then by the Admiral and his wife, an arrangement which had satisfied all parties. Henry and Mary were both young people of fortune, the brother with his estate in Norfolk, the sister with a handsome competence of her own. Both possessed of good looks, intelligence, and high spirits, the pair had many friends and, latterly, had passed less time with their uncle and aunt, more with fashionable acquaintances about Town. Miss Mary I knew principally as a well-gowned, bonneted, and parasol'd figure most often to be seen in an open carriage being driven briskly along Hill Street or through Berkeley Square.

I was not a little astonished, therefore, on arrival at Twickenham, the time being now near dawn, to find Miss Mary quite distracted, hair in dark dishevelled ringlets, beads of perspiration on her brow, her dress somewhat disordered, kneeling by the bedside of the suffering older lady, while the maidservant wrung frantic hands and Chowder the poodle howled dismally and ran unreproved about the room. This was a ground-floor chamber that had evidently been fitted up in haste as a sick-room with jugs of water, basins, a table covered by a towel, and some bunches of mint or lavender to give a pleasant odour.

"What appears to be the trouble?" was my inquiry, entering upon this scene.

"Ha, Donovan, there you are at *last*! Took long enough to make your way here!" declared the Admiral, hurrying towards me; and then remembered, I suppose, that it was his own coach that had fetched me. It did cross my mind then to wonder why Crawford had not sent for some medical practitioner who lived closer at hand; surely there must be several, now that Twickenham was becoming such a popular resort?

"Ar – hum – well, well – now you are here, what d'you make of her – hey?"

I could see that the lady upon the couch appeared to be suffering from some kind of seizure. The complexion of the face was greatly engorged, breath was taken only with the most frightful difficulty. I applied ice to the feet, and called for hot mustard in water to plaster the spine and chest, besides a cold compress on the belly. I had planned to administer arsenicum album in water every quarter of an hour, but it proved impossible to make the patient swallow. The throat and windpipe were swollen and almost wholly closed up. I perceived with alarm that I might have to perform a tracheotomy.

"Can you give me the history of this malady, sir? When did it set in? Did the lady complain of any symptoms at an earlier stage?"

"Nothing wrong with her at dinner," stated the Admiral. "Was there, Mary?"

Miss Crawford shook her head.

"No, my aunt was quite herself earlier. We had come from Hill Street to spend the day and, after our excursion in Richmond Park the servants prepared a scratch repast of cold meat, fruit, and cake, of which my aunt partook; she did complain about the tea, served afterwards – she said that it was not hot enough – "

"Nor it was, hogwash," agreed her uncle. "How you females can maudle your innards with such stuff – if you were content to stick to port, now – "

"And then? Did Lady Crawford complain of any pains – nausea – faintness?"

"No, she merely said she wished to rest a little after tea. She retired with a book to this room, which we have been in the habit of using as a parlour. My uncle went to give orders to the architect, my brother and I decided to take a walk along the tow-path to Eel Pie Island. So we went our several ways – and when we came back we found my aunt as you see her now."

"There were servants in the house? She did not groan – call out – make any outcry?"

"No – or so Maule, her maid, asseverates – "

The hot water came, and I mixed a mustard plaster. But before I could apply it, the patient's face became even more congested, she had a last unsuccessful attempt at drawing breath, and finally expired.

"Dammit, she's gone!" quoth the Admiral, as the body writhed sharply, then came to its final quietus. "All that way for the horses to fetch you, and then you get here too late!"

"I deeply regret, sir – though, indeed, it was hardly my fault – "

The Admiral, to my considerable surprise, now burst out a-crying, and had to be led away by Mr Henry, whose own face was drawn and haggard. It was some months since I had seen him and I thought that he did not look well. I recalled hearing tales that he was in difficulties with gambling debts.

"Come, sir," he said to his uncle, not urgently. "Come, you will do better to rest a while – come, lie down and repose yourself in the conservatory."

They went off to a glass-walled room at the rear of the building.

"She was such a pretty gal – when she was a young thing –" blubbered Sir Mark.

Since there was nothing more to be done for Lady Crawford, I followed the two men and administered a soothing draught to the

Admiral, who soon nodded off to sleep on a wicker chaise-longue. I noticed that the conservatory, where he lay, was extremely dusty and littered with dead insects, bees. There must have been several hundred of them.

Henry Crawford looked about him in disgust and said, "This place is in a disgraceful state. Bartlett must clean it."

He opened the outer door, which led to what would some day be the garden – at present merely rough earth, piles of bricks and debris, builders' pails, and ladders – and shouted, "Bartlett? Where are you? Come here at once and bring a broom."

I was surprised that garden servants should be on the premises already, at such an early hour, but, consulting my watch, discovered that the time was after six. A young fellow soon arrived carrying a broom and, with a murmur of apology, began sweeping up the dead insects from the floor. I noticed that one of his legs was a wooden one.

"This should have been done yesterday, Bartlett," Henry said curtly. "You knew that my uncle was coming."

"Very sorry, sir, Mr Henry," the man answered softly, "but Sir Mark had given orders that the terrace was to be laid afore he come . . . We was hard at it all day yesterday – "

As he turned away with his pan full of dead bees I noticed that his hair was plaited in a naval pigtail.

"He was one of my uncle's seamen," Henry remarked, noticing my glance. "On board the *Thrush*. Discharged unfit, of course, after his leg was blown off at Trafalgar; he came to my uncle asking for work and was taken on as under-gardener."

"Very compassionate of the Admiral," said I.

Henry Crawford threw me a sharp look.

"It was indeed," he said. "For the man was of a somewhat questionable character. He had been flogged at the gangway with thirty strokes of the cat not long before the action in which he lost his leg."

"Indeed? For what offence?"

"He stole a piece of bread from the Midshipmen's Mess."

My brother Jack was a surgeon aboard a man o' war. He had told me about these floggings, which could reduce a man's back to raw pulp, or even kill the victim. And if there was a sea battle shortly afterward, what chance would he have to play his part or keep out of harm's way? He was lucky, I supposed, to have escaped with the loss of a leg. And all this for taking a piece of bread . . .

"Let us step out into the air," said Henry. "My sister has gone to try and make some order among the servants. I daresay they will bring us a cup of coffee by and by. What happens now, Mr Donovan? Must there be an inquest on my unfortunate Aunt?"

"I fear there must – and probably an autopsy as well. It is considered needful, you know, in cases of such sudden and unexpected fatality."

"That will upset my uncle very much."

Hardly more than the death itself, I thought. But that I did not say.

After we had stared in silence for a while at the glum prospect of sand-piles, timber, and builders' rubbish, Henry Crawford went back into the house to hurry up some attempt at breakfast, and I walked down through the confusion to a small rudimentary garden which had been laid out beside the river. A brick terrace – brand-new, presumably the one which had taken precedence over cleaning the conservatory – flanked a few lumpy flower-beds where young roses, lavender plants and rosemary cuttings had been set, not too long ago, to judge from their drooping aspect.

"Those plants could do with a few cans of water," I suggested to Bartlett, the pig-tailed young fellow, who was now hard at work building a flight of rustic steps with logs of wood. He gave me a harassed glance.

"I can't do everything at once, can I? Here, Jem, boy –" he called, "water the roses, there's a good lad."

A small barefoot shrimp of a boy stumbled out of a hut which I had supposed to be a toolshed, finishing off a crust of bread and yawning as if he had just woken from sleep. He took a watering pot and dipped some water from the river, which here ran brown, swift, and silent, to pour over the neglected shrubs.

Returning from this errand he suddenly let out a sharp cry and began to hobble, hopping on one foot.

"I've been stung! I've been stung!"

"Sit down and let us have a look," said I. He sat on the log-step that his father was laying, and I inspected the bare and very dirty foot. Sure enough, a bee clung to the hard sole. Fortunately I had a pair of tweezers in my pocket, and was able to remove both the bee and its sting, which had remained in the tiny wound.

"Come up to the house, and I will put some soda on the sting, which will soon make it feel better," I told the child, who, snivelling, accompanied me.

"I wish those pesky bees had never come here," he grumbled. "Last week they all come down outer the sky like a big black cloud. Dad were main pleased, for, he says, we can sell the honey to Missis Propert for her sweeties – and owd Sir Mark, for a wonder, he don't mind – he said as how they could stay – but that's the third time I been stung – "

"Do you live here, Jem?"

"Ay, in the hut, since Ma died in the work'us, and Dad came home from sea – Miss Maule, as looks after Miss Mary, is my Dad's cousin – "

Up at the cottage a hasty breakfast of coffee, bread, and cold ham had been assembled.

Little Jem, his wound treated, was pacified with a piece of ham wrapped in a slice of bread, and returned, limping, to his labours.

"Jem's mother, I fear, died in the workhouse while Bartlett was at sea," Mary Crawford told me, as she handed me a cup of coffee. "He was taken up by the Press Gang, you know. But after he lost his leg and was discharged he was able to reclaim the boy from the orphanage. He is a hard-working fellow and makes himself useful in many ways, as sailors often can. He even, it seems, has a knowledge of bees, and impounded in a straw skep the swarm that arrived here last week. A swarm of bees in June, you know, is worth a silver spoon!" She laughed, a delightful gurgle. "My poor Aunt was wholly opposed to the notion of bee-keeping and considered them a most noxious addition to this establishment. But my uncle was delighted – it gives him the feeling of a landowner with livestock." She laughed again. It seemed to me that she was recovering from her aunt's demise tolerably well.

Excusing myself I went off to locate and seek the assistance of a fellow medical practitioner who lived, I discovered, in Grotto Road, not very far away.

Events took their course, as events do, and must. An autopsy was held, and, to everybody's astonishment – except mine – a bee was discovered in Lady Crawford's gullet. She must somehow have started to swallow it, the bee had stung her, and the consequent swelling and inflammation of the throat and wind-passage had brought about her death by suffocation.

I myself inspected the oesophagus and windpipe, in the company of Dr Hugh Palliser and Sir Ormsby Murdoch, and, since both they and the Coroner were satisfied as to the cause, a verdict of Accidental Death was brought in.

"The unfortunate lady must, by chance, have accidentally allowed a bee to enter her mouth," solemnly pronounced Sir Ormsby. "It is a rare, but not a wholly unknown fatality. If a person should be, for instance, taking a bite from, say, a slice of bread-and-jam . . . and a bee suddenly alights upon the jam – as bees do – and is taken into the throat before the victim is aware . . ."

Yes, thought I, but we happen to know that Lady Crawford, very shortly before she died, had partaken of a substantial meal of cold chicken, angel cake, peaches, strawberries, and cream. So why – only half an hour later – would she succumb to a craving for bread-and-jam?

Nobody in the household has mentioned that she ate, or requested, anything of that nature?

Lady Crawford's will was read. I do not know if it caused any surprise. A portion to her niece, a portion to her nephew, an annuity to her maid Maule, the bulk of her fortune, as was proper, to her sorrowing husband.

I still felt uneasy, unsatisfied. To me, Lady Crawford seemed the last person in the world to be marked out for such a sudden and violent departure from life. Could her death have been *planned* – somehow intentionally brought about? But by whom? Who would have an interest in such a crime? The sailor, Bartlett? (For it had seemed a little singular to me that he should seek service in the home of a man who had been responsible for his flagellation and subsequent injury – unless he could find nothing else?)

But even if Bartlett bore a grudge against the Admiral and was bent on revenge, how would it be possible to introduce a bee into somebody's throat without their knowledge? I supposed, though, that Bartlett, if anybody, might have the skill and facility for such a deed, since I recalled that Mary Crawford said he had a knowledge of bees . . .

Some days went by while I pondered on the event and wondered where my duty lay. Ought I to investigate any further? Then a name let fall by little Jem floated up to the surface of my mind, providing another possible solution. A week or so after the poor lady's funeral, I made my way on foot to the Shepherds' Market, that nest of little streets that lies in a hollow just south of Berkeley Square. And, in a corner, in White Horse Mews, I found what I sought – Mrs Propert's Candy Corner. Here, in a tiny shop not much bigger than a grand piano, all kinds of juvenile delights were on offer: bulls' eyes, barley-sugar-walking-sticks, treacle candy, lollipops, Banbury cakes, lemon drops, and sugar plums. A warm scent of boiling sugar hung over the establishment.

"Where is Mrs Propert?" I inquired of the old dame who presided over all these delights. I remembered Mrs Propert as a fine, high-coloured female with sparkling blue eyes and gold ringlets – she was not unlike the figurehead on some noble ship.

"Why, she bain't here any more. Why? What d'ye want of her?" demanded the old lady.

"I wondered if you still kept those small candy sweetmeats that Mrs Propert used to make – Golden Bonbons, were they called? – a little shell, no bigger than my thumbnail, made of caramel, with a berry or some kind of filling inside?"

"No," snapped the old thing. "We ain't got them no more. They were Mrs Propert's specialty."

"How did she ever make them? Was it with a hard glaze that she moulded into little cups? And then she put in the filling and stuck the cups together?"

"I couldn't tell yer," brusquely replied the old lady. "They was her own special receipt. She never told no one else."

A girl in a mob cap with cherry ribbons had come from the rear of the shop with a tray of fondants.

"You talking about Auntie Chrissie's candies? Those ones she were so proud of? She'd never tell how she done 'em. The Admiral's lady were main fond of those," the girl told me. "Her maid, Miss Maule, used to come in for a pound of them every two-three days. Regular glutton for them, Lady Crawford was, by what Miss Maule did say. She'd scrunch down a whole bowlful of 'em after dinner, all by herself. If no one else was by."

"Oh, indeed?" said I. "Well – if they were as delicious as I remember – it seems very sad that the secret of making them has been lost."

"Oh well – maybe Auntie Chrissie will let it out to somebody by and by," said the mob-capped girl, carefully laying out her fondants on white confectioners' paper.

"Where is she now, then?" I inquired.

"Oh, she's gone to better herself!" said the girl, with a cheerful toss of her cherry ribbons. "Gone to housekeep for owd Admiral Crawford in Hill Street."

THE EYE OF SHIVA
Peter MacAlan

Peter MacAlan is a pseudonym of Peter Berresford Ellis (b. 1943). When he isn't writing learned texts on Celtic history as Ellis, or producing fantasies or mysteries as Peter Tremayne, he is writing thrillers as Peter MacAlan. Somehow the MacAlan alias seemed appropriate for this story set in the days of the Indian Raj.

The harsh monsoon winds were rattling fiercely at the closed shutters of the British Residency building. The Residency itself stood on an exposed hillock, a little way above the crumbling banks of the now turbulent Viswamitri River, as it frothed and plunged its way through the city of Baroda to empty into the broad Gulf of Khambhat. The building had been secured from the moaning wind and rain by the servants; the lamps were lit, and the male guests still lounged in the dining room, unperturbed by the rising noise of the storm outside.

The ladies had withdrawn, shepherded away by Lady Chetwynd Miller, the wife of the Resident, while the decanter of port began to pass sun-wise around the eight remaining men. The pungent odour of cigar smoke began to permeate the room.

"Well," demanded Royston, a professional big-game hunter, who was staying a few days in Baroda before pushing east to the Satpura mountains to hunt the large cats which stalked the ravines and darkened crevices there. "Well," he repeated, "I think the time has come to stop teasing us, your excellency. We all know that you brought us here to see it. So where is it?"

There was a murmur of enthusiastic assent from the others gathered before the remnants of the evening meal.

Lord Chetwynd Miller raised a hand and smiled broadly. He was a sprightly sixty year old; a man who had spent his life in the service of the British Government of India and who now occupied the post of Resident in the Gujarat state of Baroda. He had been Resident in Baroda ever since the overthrow of the previous despotic Gaekwar or ruler. Baroda was still ruled by native princes who acknowledged the suzerain authority of the British Government in India but who had independence in all internal matters affecting their principality.

Five years previously a new ruler, or Gaekwar, Savaji Rao III, had come to power. If the truth were known, he had deposed his predecessor with British advice and aid for the previous Gaekwar had not been approved of by the civil servants of Delhi. Indeed, he had the temerity to go so far as to murder the former Resident, Colonel Phayre. But the British Raj had not wanted it to appear as though they were interfering directly in the affairs of Baroda. The state was to remain independent of the British Government of India. Indeed, the secret of the success of the British Raj in India was not in its direct rule of that vast subcontinent, with its teeming masses, but in its persuasion of some 600 ruling princes to accept the British imperial suzerainty. Thus much of the government of India was in the hands of native hereditary princes who ruled half the land mass and one quarter of the population under the "approving" eye of the British Raj.

Baroda, since Savaji Rao III had taken power, was a peaceful city of beautiful buildings, of palaces, ornate gates, parks and avenues, standing as a great administrative centre at the edge of cotton rich plains and a thriving textile producing industry. A port with access to the major sea lanes and a railway centre with its steel railroads connecting it to all parts of the sub-continent.

After the establishment of the new regime in Baroda, the British Raj felt they needed a man who was able to keep firm control on British interests there. Lord Chetwynd Miller was chosen for he had been many years in service in India. Indeed, it was going to be his last appointment in India. He had already decided that the time had come for retirement. He was preparing for the return to his estates near Shrewsbury close to the Welsh border before the year was out.

"Come on, Chetwynd," urged Major Bill Foran, of the 8th Bombay Infantry, whose task it was to protect the interests of the British Residency and the community of British traders who lived in Baroda. He was an old friend of the Resident. "Enough of this game of cat and mouse. You are dying to show it to us just as much as we are dying to see it."

Lord Chetwynd Miller grinned. It was a boyish grin. He spread his hands in a deprecating gesture. It was true that he had been leading his guests on. He had invited them to see "The Eye of Shiva" and kept them waiting long enough.

He gazed around at them. Apart from Bill Foran, it could not be said that he really knew the other guests. It was one of those typical Residency dinner parties whereby it was his duty to dine with any British dignitaries passing through Baroda. Lieutenant Tompkins, his ADC, had compiled this evening's guest list.

Royston he knew by reputation. There was Father Cassian, a swarthy, secretive-looking Catholic priest who seemed totally unlike a missionary. He had learnt that Cassian was a man of many interests – not the least of which was an interest in Hindu religion and mythology. There was Sir Rupert Harvey. A bluff, arrogant man, handsome in a sort of dissolute way. He had just arrived in Baroda and seemed to dabble in various forms of business. Then there was the tall languid Scotsman, James Gregg. Silent, taciturn and a curious way of staring at one as if gazing right through them. He was, according to the list, a mining engineer. For a mere mining engineer, Tompkins had observed earlier, Gregg could afford to stay at the best hotel in Baroda and did not seem to lack money.

The last guest sat at the bottom of the table, slightly apart from the others. It was Lord Chetwynd Miller's solitary Indian guest, Inspector Ram Jayram, who, in spite of being a Bengali by birth, was employed by the Government of Baroda as its chief of detectives. Ram Jayram had a dry wit and a fund of fascinating stories which made him a welcome guest to pass away the tedium of many soirées. That evening, however, he had been invited especially. Word had come to Jayram's office that an attempt was going to be made to rob the Residency that night and Lord Chetwynd Miller had accepted Jayram's request that he attend as a dinner guest so that he might keep a close eye on events. It was Jayram who suggested to the Resident that the potential thief might be found among the guests themselves. A suggestion that the Resident utterly discounted.

But the news of the Resident's possession of the fabulous ruby – "The Eye of Shiva" – was the cause of much talk and speculation in the city. The Resident was not above such vanity that he did not want to display it to his guests on the one evening in which the ruby was his.

Lord Chetwynd Miller cleared his throat.

"Gentlemen . . .," he began hesitantly. "Gentlemen, you are right. I have kept you in suspense long enough. I have, indeed, invited you here, not only because I appreciate your company, but I want you to see the fabled 'Eye of Shiva' before it is taken on board the SS *Caledonia* tomorrow morning for transportation to London."

They sat back expectantly watching their host.

Lord Chetwynd Miller nodded to Tompkins, who clapped his hands as a signal.

The dining room door opened and Devi Bhadra, Chetwynd Miller's major-domo entered, pausing on the threshold to gaze inquiringly at the lieutenant.

"Bring it in now, Devi Bhadra," instructed the ADC.

Devi Bhadra bowed slightly, no more than a slight gesture of the head, and withdrew.

A moment later he returned carrying before him an ornate tray on which was a box of red Indian gold with tiny glass panels in it. Through these panels everyone could see clearly a white velvet cushion on which was balanced a large red stone.

There was a silence while Devi Bhadra solemnly placed it on the table in front of the Resident and then withdrew in silence.

As the door shut behind him, almost on a signal, the company leant towards the ornate box with gasps of surprise and envy at the perfection of the ruby which nestled tantalizingly on its cushion.

Father Cassian, who was nearest, pursed his lips and gave forth an unpriestly-like whistle.

"Amazing, my dear sir. Absolutely!"

James Gregg blinked, otherwise his stoic face showed no expression.

"So this is the famous 'Eye of Shiva', eh? I'll wager it has a whole history behind it?"

Royston snorted.

"Damned right, Gregg. Many a person has died for that little stone there."

"The stone, so it is said, is cursed."

They swung round to look at the quiet Bengali. Jayram was smiling slightly. He had approved the Resident's suggestion that if one of his guests was going to make an attempt on the jewel, it were better that the jewel be placed where everyone could see it so that such theft would be rendered virtually impossible.

"What d'you mean, eh?" snapped Sir Rupert Harvey irritably. It had become obvious during the evening that Harvey was one of those men who disliked mixing with "the natives" except on express matters of business. He was apparently not used to meeting Indians as his social equals and showed it.

It was Major Foran who answered.

"The Inspector," did he emphasize the Bengali's rank just a little? "The Inspector is absolutely right. There is a curse that goes with the stone, isn't that right, Chetwynd?"

Lord Chetwynd Miller grinned and spread his hands.

"Therein is the romance of the stone, my friends. Well, how can you have a famous stone without a history, or without a curse?"

"I believe I sense a story here," drawled Gregg, reaching for his brandy, sniffing it before sipping gently.

"Will you tell it, sir?" encouraged Royston.

Lord Chetwynd Miller's features bespoke that he would delight in nothing better than to tell them the story of his famous ruby – "The Eye of Shiva".

"You all know that the stone is going to London as a private gift from Savaji Rao III to Her Majesty? Yesterday the stone was officially handed into my safe-keeping as representative of Her Majesty. I have made the arrangements for it to be placed on the SS *Caledonia* tomorrow to be transported to London."

"We all read the *Times of India*," muttered Sir Rupert but his sarcasm was ignored.

"Quite so," Lord Chetwynd Miller said dryly. "The stone has a remarkable history. It constituted one of a pair of rubies which were the eyes of a statue of the Hindu god Shiva . . ."

"A god of reproduction," chimed in Father Cassian, almost to himself. "Both benign and terrible, the male generative force of Vedic religion."

"It is said," went on the Resident, "that the statue stood in the ancient temple of Vira-bhadra in Betul country. It was supposedly of gold, encrusted with jewels and its eyes were the two rubies. The story goes that during the suppression of the 'Mutiny', a soldier named Colonel Vickers was sent to Betul to punish those who had taken part. He had a reputation for ruthlessness. I think he was involved with the massacre at Allahabad . . ."

"What was that?" demanded Gregg. "I know nothing of the history here."

"Six thousand people regardless of sex or age were slaughtered at Allahabad by British troops as a reprisal," explained Father Cassian in a quiet tone.

"The extreme ferocity with which the uprising was suppressed was born of fear," explained Major Foran.

"Only way to treat damned rebels!" snapped Royston. "Hang a few and the people will soon fall into line, eh?"

"In that particular case," observed Royston, screwing his face up in distaste, "the Sepoys who had taken part in the insurrection were strapped against the muzzles of cannons and blown apart as a lesson to others."

"Military necessity," snapped Major Foran, irritated by the implied criticism.

The Resident paused a moment and continued.

"Well, it is said that Vickers sacked the temple of Vira-bhadra and took the rubies for himself while he ordered the rest of the statue melted down. This so enraged the local populace that they attacked Vickers and managed to reclaim the statue, taking it to a secret hiding place. Vickers was killed and the rubies vanished. Stories permeated afterwards that only one ruby was recovered by the guardians of the temple. A soldier managed to grab the other one from Vickers' dying hand. He, in his turn, was killed and the stone had a colourful history until it found its way into the hands of the Gaekwar of Baroda."

Inspector Ram Jayram coughed politely.

"It should be pointed out," he said slowly, "that the Gaekwar in question was not Savaji Rao III but the despot whom he overthrew a few years ago."

The Resident nodded agreement.

"The jewel was found in the Gaekwar's collection and Savaji Rao thought it would be a courteous gesture to send the jewel to Her Majesty as a token of his friendship."

Gregg sat staring at the red glistening stone with pursed lips.

"A history as bloody as it looks," he muttered. "The story is that all people who claimed ownership of the stone, who are not legitimate owners, meet with bad ends."

Sir Rupert chuckled cynically as he relit his cigar.

"Could be that Savaji Rao has thought of that and wants no part of the stone? Better to pass it on quickly before the curse bites!"

Lieutenant Tompkins flushed slightly, wondering whether Sir Rupert was implying some discourtesy to the Queen-Empress. He was youthful and this was his first appointment in India. It was all new to him and perplexing, especially the cynicism about Empire which he found prevalent among his fellow veteran colonials.

"The only curse, I am told, is that there are some Hindus who wish to return the stone to the statue," Father Cassian observed.

Sir Rupert turned to Inspector Jayram with a grin that was more a sneer.

"Is that so? Do you feel that the stone should belong back in the statue? You're a Hindu, aren't you?"

Jayram returned the gaze of the businessman and smiled politely.

"I am a Hindu, yes. Father Cassian refers to the wishes of a sect called the Vira-bhadra, whose temple the stone was taken from. They are worshippers of Shiva in his role of the wrathful avenger and herdsman of souls. For them he wears a necklace of skulls and a garland of snakes. He is the malevolent destroyer. I am not part of their sect."

Sir Rupert snorted as if in cynical disbelief.

"A Hindu is a Hindu," he sneered.

"Ah, so?" Inspector Jayram did not appear in the least put out by the obvious insult. "I presume that you are a Christian, Sir Rupert?"

"Of course!" snapped the man. "What has that to do with anything?"

"Then, doubtless, you pay allegiance to the Bishop of Rome as Holy Father of the Universal Church?"

"Of course not . . . I am an Anglican," growled Sir Rupert.

Jayram continued to smile blandly.

"But a Christian is a Christian. Is this not so, Sir Rupert?"

Sir Rupert reddened as Father Cassian exploded in laughter. "He has you there," he chuckled as his mirth subsided a little.

Jayram turned with an appreciative smile.

"I believe that it was one of your fourth-century saints and martyrs of Rome, Pelagius, who said that labels are devices for saving people the trouble of thinking. Pelagius was the great friend of Augustine of Hippo, wasn't he?"

Father Cassian smiled brightly and inclined his head.

"You have a wide knowledge, Inspector."

Sir Rupert growled angrily and was about to speak when Lord Chetwynd Miller interrupted. "It is true that the story of the curse emanated from the priests of the sect of Vira-bhadra, who continue to hunt for the stone."

Royston lit a fresh cheroot. He preferred them to cigars provided by their host.

"Well, it is an extraordinary stone. Would it be possible for me to handle it, your excellency?"

The Resident smiled indulgently.

"It will be the last chance. When it gets to London it will doubtless be locked away in the royal collection."

He took a small key from his waistcoat pocket and bent forward, turning the tiny lock which secured the box and raising the lid so that the stone sparkled brightly on its pale bed of velvet.

He reached forward and took out the stone with an exaggerated air of carelessness and handed it to the eager Royston. Royston held the stone up to the light between his thumb and forefinger and whistled appreciatively.

"I've seen a few stones in my time but this one is really awe inspiring. A perfect cut, too."

"You know something about these things, Royston?" inquired Sir Rupert, interested.

Royston shrugged.

"I don't wish to give the impression that I am an expert but I've traded a few stones in my time. My opinion is probably as good as the next man's."

He passed the ruby to Father Cassian who was seated next to him. The priest took the stone and held it to the light. His hand trembled slightly but he assumed a calm voice.

"It's nice," he conceded. "But the value, as I see it, is in the entire statue of the god. I place no value on solitary stones but only in an overall work of art, in man's endeavour to create something of beauty."

Sir Rupert snorted as an indication of his disagreement with this philosophy and reached out a hand.

Father Cassian hesitated still staring at the red stone.

At that moment there came the sound of an altercation outside. The abruptness of the noise caused everyone to pause. Lieutenant Tompkins sprang to his feet and strode to the door. As he opened it Lady Chetwynd Miller, a small but determined woman in her mid-fifties, stood framed in the doorway.

"Forgive me interrupting, gentlemen," she said with studied calm. Then looking towards her husband, she said quietly. "My dear, Devi Bhadra says the servants have caught a thief attempting to leave your study."

Lord Chetwynd Miller gave a startled glance towards Inspector Jayram, then rose and made his way to the door. Tompkins stood aside as the Resident laid a reassuring hand on Lady Chetwynd Miller's arm.

"Now then, dear, nothing to worry about. You go back to your ladies in the drawing room and we'll see to this."

Lady Chetwynd Miller seemed reluctant but smiled briefly at the company before withdrawing. The Resident said to his ADC: "Ask Devi Bhadra to bring the rascal here into the dining room."

He turned back with a thin smile towards Inspector Jayram.

"It seems as if your intelligence was right. We have a prisoner for you to take away, Inspector."

Jayram raised his hands in a curiously helpless gesture.

"This is technically British soil, excellency. But if you wish me to take charge . . .? Let us have a look at this man."

At that moment, Lieutenant Tompkins returned with Devi Bhadra together with a burly Sepoy from Foran's 8th Bombay Infantry. They frog-marched a man into the dining room. The man was thin, wearing a *dhoti*, a dirty loin cloth affected by Hindus, an equally dirty turban and a loose robe open at the front. He wore a cheap jewelled pendant around his neck hung on a leather thong.

The Resident went back to his seat and gazed up with a hard-ened scowl.

"Bring the man into the light and let us see him."

The man was young, handsome, but his face was disfigured in a sullen expression. His head hung forward. Devi Bhadra prodded the man forward so that the light from the lanterns reflected on his face.

"I have searched him thoroughly, sahib. He has no weapons."

"Do you speak English?" demanded Lord Chetwynd Miller.

The man did not reply.

The British Resident nodded to Devi Bhadra, who repeated the question in Gujarati, the language of the country. There was no response.

"Forgive me," Inspector Jayram interrupted. "I believe the man might respond to Hindi."

Devi Bhadra repeated his question but there was no reply.

"Looks like your guess was wrong," observed Royston.

Inspector Jayram rose leisurely and came to stand by the man. His eyes narrowed as he looked at the pendant. Then he broke into a staccato to which the captive jerked up his head and nodded sullenly. Jayram turned to the Resident with an apologetic smile.

"The man speaks a minor dialect called Munda. I have some knowledge of it. He is, therefore, from the Betul district."

"Betul?" The Resident's eyes widened as he caught the significance of the name.

Jayram indicated the pendant.

"He wears the symbol of the cult of Vira-bhadra."

"Does he? The beggar!" breathed Lord Chetwynd Miller.

"Well," drawled Gregg. "If he were after this little item, he was out of luck. We had it here with us."

He held up the ruby.

The captive saw it and gave a sharp intake of breath, moving as if to lunge forward but was held back by the powerful grip of Devi Bhadra and the Sepoy.

"So that's it?" snapped Major Foran. "The beggar was coming to steal the stone?"

"Or return it to its rightful owners," interposed Father Cassian calmly. "It depends on how you look at it."

"How did you catch him, Devi Bhadra?" asked Foran, ignoring the priest.

"One of the maids heard a noise in your study, sahib," said the man. "She called me and I went to see if anything was amiss. The safe was open and this man was climbing out of the window. I caught hold of him and yelled until a Sepoy outside came to help me."

"Was anything missing from the safe?"

"The man had nothing on him, sahib."

"So it was the stone that he was after?" concluded Gregg in some satisfaction. "Quite an evening's entertainment that you've provided, your excellency."

The captive burst into a torrent of words, with Jayram nodding from time to time as he tried to follow.

"The man says that the 'Eye of Shiva' was stolen and should be returned to the temple of Vira-bhadra. He is no thief but the right hand of his god seeking the return of his property."

The Resident sniffed.

"That's as maybe! To me he is a thief, who will be handed over to the Baroda authorities and punished. As Gregg said, it was lucky we were examining the stone while he was trying to open the safe."

Major Foran had been inspecting the stone, which he had taken from Gregg, and he now turned to the prisoner.

"Would you like to examine the prize that you missed?" he jeered.

They were unprepared for what happened next. Both the Sepoy and Devi Bhadra were momentarily distracted by the bright, shining object that Foran held out. Not so their prisoner. In the excitement of the moment, they had slackened their grip to the extent that the muscular young man seized his chance. With a great wrench, he had shaken free of his captors, grabbed the stone from the hand of the astonished major and bounded across the room as agilely as a mountain lion. Before anyone could recover from their surprise, he had flung himself against the shuttered windows.

The wood splintered open as the man crashed through onto the verandah outside.

The dinner company was momentarily immobile in surprise at the unexpected abruptness of the man's action.

A second passed. On the verandah outside, the Betulese jumped to his feet and began to run into the evening blackness and the driving rain.

It was the ADC, Lieutenant Tompkins, who first recovered from his surprise. He turned and seized the Sepoy's Lee Enfield rifle. Then he raised it to his shoulder. There was a crack of an explosion which brought the company to life.

Foran was through the door onto the verandah in a minute. Lord Chetwynd Miller was only a split second behind but he slipped and collided with Sir Rupert, who was just getting to his feet. The impact was so hard that Sir Rupert was knocked to the floor. The Resident went down on his knees beside him. Father Cassian was the first to spring from his chair, with an expression of concern, to help them up. The Resident was holding on to Cassian's arm when he slipped again and, with a muttered expression of apology, climbed unsteadily to his feet. By then it was all over.

The young man in the *dhoti* was lying sprawled face downwards. There was a red, tell-tale stain on his white dirty robe which not even the torrent of rain was dispersing. Foran had reached his side and bent down, feeling for a pulse and then, with a sigh, he stood up and shook his head.

He came back into the dining room, his dress uniform soaked by the monsoon skies. As he did so, the dining room door burst open and Lady Chetwynd Miller stood on the threshold again, the other ladies of her party were crowding behind her.

The Resident turned and hurried to the door, using his body to prevent the ladies spilling into the room.

"My dear, take your guests back into the drawing room. Immediately!" he snapped, as his wife began to open her mouth in protest. "Please!" His unusually harsh voice caused her to blink and stare at him in astonishment. He forced a smile and modulated his tone. "Please," he said again. "We won't be long. Don't worry, none of us have come to any harm."

He closed the door behind them and turned back, his face ashen.

"Well," drawled Foran, holding his hand palm outward and letting the others see the bright glistening red stone which nestled there, "the young beggar nearly got away with it."

The Resident smiled grimly and turned to his major-domo.

"Devi Bhadra, you and the Sepoy remove the body. I expect Inspector Jayram will want to take charge now. Is that all right with you, Foran?"

Major Foran, nominally in charge of the security of the Residency, indicated his agreement and Devi Bhadra motioned the Sepoy to follow him in the execution of their unpleasant task.

Lord Chetwynd Miller turned to his ADC and clapped him on the shoulder. The young man had laid aside the Lee Enfield and was now sitting on his chair, his face white, his hand shaking.

"Good shooting, Tompkins. Never saw better."

Foran was pouring the young officer a stiff brandy.

"Get that down you, lad," he ordered gruffly.

The young lieutenant stared up.

"Sorry," he muttered. "Never shot anyone before. Sorry." He took a large gulp of his brandy and coughed.

"Did the right thing," confirmed the Resident. "Otherwise the beggar would have got clean away . . ."

He turned to Jayram and then frowned.

Inspector Jayram was gazing in fascination at the stone which Foran had set back in its box. He took it up with a frown passing over his brow.

"Excuse me, excellency," he muttered.

They watched him astounded as he reached for a knife on the table and, placing the stone on the top of the table, he drew the knife across it. It left a tiny white mark.

White-faced, Major Foran was the first to realize the meaning of the mark.

"A fake stone! It is not 'The Eye of Shiva'!"

Jayram nodded calmly. He was watching their faces carefully.

Sir Rupert was saying: "Was the stone genuine in the first place? I mean, did Savaji Rao give you the genuine article?"

"We have no reason to doubt it," Major Foran replied, but his tone was aghast.

Royston, who had taken the stone from where Jayram had left it on the table, was peering at it in disbelief.

"The stone was genuine when we started to examine it," he said quietly.

The Resident was frowning at him.

"What do you mean?"

"I mean . . ." Royston stared around thoughtfully, "I mean that this is not the stone that I held in my hand a few minutes ago."

"How can you be so sure?" demanded Gregg. "It looks exactly the same to me."

Royston held up the defaced stone to the light.

"See here . . . there is a shadow in this stone, a tiny black mark which indicates its flaw. The stone I held a few moments ago did not have such a mark. That I can swear to."

"Then where is the real stone?" demanded Father Cassian. "This stone is a clever imitation. It is worthless."

Major Foran was on his feet, taking the stone and peering at it with a red, almost apoplectic stare.

"An imitation, by George!"

The Resident was stunned.

"I bet that Hindu chappie had this fake to leave behind when he robbed the safe. The real one must still be on his body," Lieutenant Tompkins gasped.

"On his body or in the garden," grunted Foran. "By your leave, sir, I'll go and get Devi Bhadra to make a search."

"Yes, do that, Bill," instructed the Resident, quietly. He was obviously shocked. Foran disappeared to give the orders. There was a moment's silence and then Jayram spoke.

"Begging your pardon, excellency, you will not find the stone on the body of the dead priest."

Lord Chetwynd Miller's eyes widened as they sought the placid dark brown eyes of Jayram.

"I don't understand," he said slowly.

Jayram smiled patiently.

"The Betul priest did not steal the real ruby, your excellency. Only the fake. In fact, the real ruby has not left this room."

"You'd better explain that," Father Cassian suggested. "The ruby has been stolen. According to Lord Miller, the genuine stone was given into his custody. And according to Royston there, he was holding the genuine stone just before we heard Devi Bhadra capture that beggar. Then the Hindu priest was brought here into this room. He grabbed the stone from Foran and the real stone disappears. Only he could have had both fake and real stone."

Foran had come back through the shattered window of the dining room. Beyond they could see Devi Bhadra conducting a search of the lawn where the man had fallen.

"There is nothing on the dead man," Foran said in annoyance. "Devi Bhadra is examining the lawn now."

"According to Inspector Jayram here," interposed Gregg heavily, "it'll be a waste of time."

Foran raised an eyebrow.

"Jayram thinks the ruby never left this room," explained Father Cassian. "I think he believes the Hindu priest grabbed the fake when he tried to escape."

Jayram nodded smilingly.

"That is absolutely so," he confirmed.

The Resident's face was pinched.

"How did you know?" he demanded.

"Simple common sense, excellency," replied the Bengali policeman. "We have the stone here, the genuine stone. Then we hear the noise of the Betulese being captured as he makes an abortive attempt to steal the stone from your study – abortive because the stone is here with us. He is brought to this room and there he stands with his arms held between Devi Bhadra and the Sepoy. He makes a grab at what he thinks is the ruby and attempts to escape. He believes the stone genuine."

"Sounds reasonable enough," drawled Sir Rupert. "Except that you have no evidence that he was not carrying the fake stone on him to swap."

"But I do. Devi Bhadra searched the culprit thoroughly. He told us; he told us twice that he had done so and found nothing on the man. If the fake stone had been on the person of the priest of Vira-bhadra then his excellency's major-domo would have found it before he brought the priest here, into the dining room."

"What are you saying, Jayram? That old man Shiva worked some magic to get his sacred eye back?" grunted Gregg, cynically.

Jayram smiled thinly.

"No magic, Mister Gregg."

"Then what?"

"The logic is simple. We eight are sat at the table. The genuine stone is brought in. We begin to examine it. We are interrupted in our examination by the affair of the priest of Vira-bhadra. Then we find it is a faked stone. The answer is that someone seated at this table is the thief."

There was a sudden uproar.

Sir Rupert was on his feet bawling. "I am not going to be insulted by a . . . a . . ."

Jayram's face was bland.

"By a simple Bengali police inspector?" he supplied, helpfully. "As a matter of fact, I was not being insulting to you, Sir Rupert. My purpose is to recover the stone."

Lord Chetwynd Miller slumped back into his chair. He stared at Ram Jayram.

"How do you propose that?"

Jayram spread his hands and smiled.

"Since none of our party have left the room, with the exception of Major Foran," he bowed swiftly in the soldier's direction, "and he, I believe, is beyond reproach, the answer must be that the stone will still be on the person of the thief. Is this not logical, your excellency?"

Lord Chetwynd Miller thought a moment and then nodded, as though reluctant to concede the point.

"Good. Major Foran, will you have one of your Sepoys placed on the verandah and one at the door? No one is to leave now," Jayram asked.

Foran raised a cynical eyebrow.

"Are you sure that I'm not a suspect?"

"We are all suspects," replied Jayram, imperturbably. "But some more so than others."

Foran went to the door and called for his men, giving orders to station themselves as Jayram had instructed.

"Right," smiled Jayram. "We will now make a search, I think."

"Then we'll start with you," snapped Sir Rupert. "Of all the impertinent . . ."

Jayram held up a hand and the baronet fell silent.

"I have no objection to Major Foran searching my person," he smiled. "But, as a matter of fact, Sir Rupert, I was thinking of saving time by starting with you. You see, when there was the disturbance of the Betulese being brought in here, at that time you were the one holding the stone."

Royston whistled softly.

"That's right, by Jove! I held the genuine stone. Then I passed it on to Father Cassian and . . ."

The priest looked uncomfortable.

"I passed it on to Sir Rupert just as the commotion occurred."

Sir Rupert's face was working in rage.

"I'll not stand for this," he shouted. "A jumped-up punkah-wallah is not going to make me . . ."

Major Foran moved across to him with an angry look.

"Then I'll make you, if you object to obeying the Inspector's orders, Sir Rupert," he said quietly.

Sir Rupert stared at them and then with a gesture of resignation began to empty his pockets.

Jayram, still smiling, raised his hand.

"A moment, Sir Rupert. There may not be any need for this."

Inspector Foran hesitated and stared in surprise at the Bengali.

"I thought . . ." he began.

"The commotion started. Our attention was distracted. When our attention focused back on the jewel, who was holding it?"

They looked at one another.

Gregg stirred uncomfortably.

"I guess I was," he confessed.

Foran nodded agreement.

"I took the stone from him and that's when we discovered it was a fake."

Gregg rose to his feet and they all examined him with suspicion.

"You won't find anything on me," Gregg said with a faint smile. "Go ahead."

Jayram returned his smile broadly.

"I am sure we won't. You, Mister Gregg, did not take the stone from the hands of Sir Rupert, did you?"

Gregg shook his head and sat down abruptly.

"No. I took it from the box where Sir Rupert had replaced it. He put it back there when the Hindu priest was being questioned."

"Just so. The stone was genuine as it passed round the table until it reached Sir Rupert, who then replaced it in the box. Then Mister Gregg took the stone from the box and passed it round to the rest of us. It was then a fake one."

Sir Rupert was clenching and unclenching his hands spasmodically. Major Foran moved close to him.

"This is a damned outrage, I tell you," he growled. "I put the stone back where I found it."

"Exactly," Jayram said with emphasis. "*Where you found it.*"

They realized that he must have said something clever, or made some point which was obscure to them.

"If I may make a suggestion, Major," Jayram said quietly. "Have your Sepoys take Father Cassian into the study and hold him until I come. We will remain here."

The blood drained from Father Cassian's face as he stared at the little Bengali inspector. His mouth opened and closed like a fish for a few seconds. Everyone was staring at him with astonishment. If nothing else, Cassian's expression betrayed his guilt.

"That's a curious request," observed Foran, recovering quickly. "Are you sure that Father Cassian is the thief?"

"Will you indulge me? At the moment, let us say that Father Cassian is not all that he represents himself to be. Furthermore, at the precise moment of the disturbance, Cassian was holding the stone. Sir Rupert had asked him for it. Our attention was momentarily distracted by Lady Miller at the door. When I looked back, the stone had been replaced in its holder. Sir Rupert, seeing this, took up the stone, examined it and replaced it. The only time it could have been switched was when Cassian held it, before he replaced it in the casket."

Cassian half rose and then he slumped down. He smiled in resignation.

"If I knew the Bengali for 'it's a fair cop', I'd say it. How did you get on to me, Jayram?"

Jayram sighed: "I suspected that you were not a Catholic priest. I then made a pointed reference to Pelagius to test you. Any Catholic priest would know that Pelagius is not a saint and martyr of the fourth century. He was a philosopher who argued vehemently with Augustine of Hippo and was excommunicated from the Roman church as a heretic. You did not know this."

Cassian shrugged.

"I suppose we can't know everything," he grunted. "As I say, it's a fair . . ." He had reached a hand into his cassock. Then a surprised look came over his features. He rummaged in his pocket and then stared at Jayram.

"But . . ." he began.

Jayram jerked his head to Foran. Foran gave the necessary orders. After the erstwhile "Father" Cassian had been removed, against a background of stunned silence, Foran turned back to Jayram.

"Perhaps you would explain why you have had Cassian removed to be searched. The search could easily have been done here."

"The reason," Jayram said imperturbably, "is that we will not find the stone on him."

There was a chorus of surprise and protest.

"You mean, you know he is innocent?" gasped Foran.

"Oh no. I know he is guilty. When our attention was distracted by the entrance of the captive, Father Cassian swapped the genuine stone and placed the fake on the table for Sir Rupert to pick up later. It was the perfect opportunity to switch the genuine stone for the faked stone. Cassian is doubtless a professional jewel thief who came to Baroda when he heard that Savaji Rao was going to present 'The Eye of Shiva' to the Resident for transportation to England."

"You mean, Cassian was already prepared with an imitation ruby?" demanded Royston.

"Just so. I doubt whether Cassian is his real name. But we will see."

"But if he doesn't have the stone, what can we charge him with and, moreover, who the hell has the genuine stone?" demanded Foran.

"Father Cassian can be charged with many things," Jayram assured him. "Travelling on a fake passport, defrauding . . . I am sure we will find many items to keep Father Cassian busy."

"But if he doesn't have the genuine 'Eye of Shiva' who the devil has it?" repeated Lieutenant Tompkins.

Jayram gave a tired smile. "Would you mind placing the genuine ruby on the table, your excellency?"

There was a gasp as he swung round to Lord Chetwynd Miller.

Lord Chetwynd Miller's face was sunken and pale. He stared up at Jayram like a cornered animal, eyes wide and unblinking.

Everyone in the room had become immobile, frozen into a curious theatrical tableau.

The Resident tried to speak and then it seemed his features began to dissolve. He suddenly looked old and frail. To everyone's horror, except for the placid Jayram, he reached into the pocket of his dinner jacket and took out the rich red stone and silently placed it on the table before him.

"How did you know?" he asked woodenly.

Ram Jayram shrugged eloquently.

"I think your action was one made on – how do you say – 'the spur of the moment'? The opportunity came when our prisoner tried to escape. You instinctively ran after him. You collided with Sir Rupert and both went down. Cassian went to your aid. He had his role as a priest to keep up. There was – how do you call it? – a mêlée? The jewel accidentally fell from Cassian's pocket unnoticed by him onto the floor. You saw it. You realized what had happened and staged a second fall across it, secreting it into your pocket. You were quick-witted. You have a reputation for quick reactions, excellency. It was an excellent manoeuvre."

Foran was staring at the Resident in disbelief. Tompkins, the ADC, was simply pale with shock.

"But why?" Foran stammered after a moment or two.

Lord Chetwynd Miller stared up at them with haunted eyes.

"Why?" The Resident repeated with a sharp bark of laughter.

"I have given my life to the British Government of India. A whole life's work. Back home my estates are heavily mortgaged and I have not been able to save a penny during all my years of service here. I was honest; too scrupulously honest. I refused to take part in any business deal which I thought unethical; any deal from which my position prohibited me. What's the result of years of honest dedication? A small pension that will barely sustain my wife and myself, let alone pay the mortgage of our estate. That together with a letter from the Viceroy commending my work and perhaps a few honours, baubles from Her Majesty that are so much worthless scrap metal. That is my reward for a lifetime of service."

Major Foran glanced at the imperturbable face of Jayram and bit his lip.

"So, you thought you saw a way of subsidizing your pension?" Jayram asked the Resident.

"I could have paid off my debts with it," confirmed the Resident. "It would have given us some security when we retired."

"But it was not yours," Sir Rupert Harvey observed in a shocked voice.

"Who did it belong to?" demanded the Resident, a tinge of anger in his voice. "Was it Savaji Rao's to give? Was it the Queen-Empress's to receive? Since Colonel Vickers stole it from the statue of Shiva in Betul it has simply been the property of thieves and only the property of the thief who could hold onto it."

"It was the property of our Queen-Empress," Lieutenant Tompkins said sternly. He was youthful, a simple young soldier who saw all things in black and white terms.

"She would have glanced at it and then let it be buried in the royal vaults for ever. No one would have known whether it was genuine or fake – they would merely have seen a pretty red stone. To me, it was life; comfort and a just reward for all I had done for her miserable empire!"

Lord Chetwynd Miller suddenly spread his arms helplessly and a sob racked his frail body. It was the first time that those gathered around the table realized that the Resident was merely a tired, old man.

"I have to tell my wife. Oh God, the shame will kill her."

They looked at his heaving shoulders with embarrassment.

"I don't know what to do," muttered Foran.

"A suggestion," interrupted Ram Jayram.

"What?"

"The stone was missing for a matter of a few minutes. It was not really stolen. What happened was a sudden impulse; an overpowering temptation which few men in the circumstances in which His Excellency found himself could have resisted. He saw the opportunity and took it."

Foran snorted.

"You sound like an advocate, Jayram," he said. "What are you saying?"

Jayram smiled softly.

"A policeman has to be many things, major. Let us look at it this way – the stone was placed in the safe keeping of the Resident by Savaji Rao. It is his responsibility until it is placed on the ship bound for England. Perhaps the Resident merely placed it in his pocket as a precaution when the thief was brought in. I suggest that you, Major Foran, now take charge of the genuine stone, on behalf of the Resident, and see that it goes safely aboard the SS *Caledonia* tomorrow. Lord Chetwynd Miller has only a few months before his retirement to England, so he will hardly be left in his position of trust much longer. He is a man who has already destroyed his honour in his own eyes, why make his dishonour public when it will gain nothing?"

Foran nodded agreement. "And Cassian must never be informed of how the stone was removed from him."

"Just so," Jayram agreed.

Sir Rupert Harvey rose with a thin-lipped look of begrudging approval at the Bengali.

"An excellent solution. That is a Christian solution. Forgiveness, eh?"

Ram Jayram grinned crookedly at the baronet.

"A Hindu solution," he corrected mildly. "We would agree that sometimes justice is a stronger mistress than merely the law."

THE TRAIL OF
THE BELLS
Edward D. Hoch

Over the last year I have been catching up on my reading of Edward Hoch's Ben Snow stories and have found them a most fascinating and infectious series. Hoch is the author of over seven hundred mystery stories, amongst them a fair number of historical mysteries. The most consistent series in that respect features Ben Snow, a gunman of the old Wild West, the stories spanning the years from 1887 into the twentieth century. Although not the first written, the following is the earliest setting of the Ben Snow stories.

Ben Snow had been on the trail for two days before he found the dying man by the water hole. He drew his horse Oats up slowly, right hand resting on the butt of his pistol, aware that he might be riding into a trap. But then he saw the bloody bandage across the man's chest and recognized him as Tommy Gonzolas, the half-Mexican gunman who'd ridden with Poder since the beginning. His horse grazed on the sparse grass nearby.

Ben still approached slowly, even after he knew Gonzolas was dying. Although the desert terrain allowed little cover for a rifleman, he knew that Poder wouldn't be above the ruthlessness of baiting a trap with a dying man. "Are you armed?" he asked Gonzolas. "Throw me your gun."

The man barely lifted his head, and the hands that clutched at his chest made no movement toward the pistol that lay on the sand a foot away. Ben stepped quickly forward and kicked the weapon out of reach. Then he stooped to examine the wound.

"I'm dying," Gonzolas said quite clearly. He'd been wounded during the bank robbery back in Tosco, and the only reason Ben Snow had taken on the job of tracking Poder through the desert was the belief that the serious wound might slow down the fugitives. But

Poder had left the man to die beside a water hole with his gun and ridden on without him.

"Tell me about Poder," Ben asked the man. "Where's he headed? What does he look like without his mask?"

Gonzolas tried to laugh, but his mouth was filling with blood. "You'll never get Poder," he managed to gasp. "Nobody will."

"Come on, Gonzolas, he left you to die. You owe him nothing."

But it was too late. The Mexican's head lolled to one side and his eyes closed. For an instant it seemed he was dead. Then, as Ben started to straighten up, Gonzolas uttered his last words. "The bells," he said. "Listen for the bells and you will find Poder. Or Poder will find you."

Whether the words were meant to help or to lead Ben to his death, Ben didn't know. But the bells were the only lead he had, and after pausing long enough to bury Tommy Gonzolas at the water hole and unsaddle and set free his horse, he rode on in search of them.

It was the following day that he came upon the girl with the dead horse. She was dressed in denim pants and a man's shirt, but even from a distance there was no doubt about her sex. She held her head high and proud, with long dark hair hanging halfway down her back, and the rifle in her hands was warning enough that she was not to be tampered with. Still, with no towns or trails in sight, Ben felt an obligation to offer assistance. As he drew nearer, he was glad he had. The dead horse on the ground at her feet fitted closely the description of the pinto that Poder had ridden out of Tosco.

She lowered her rifle as he approached on horseback. "I thought at first it was him coming back," she said.

"Who? What happened here?"

"Masked man stole my horse."

Ben dismounted and went over to inspect the dead horse. It had been killed by a shot through the head at close range. "What did he look like?"

"I told you he was wearing a mask – a cloth bag that covered his head, with holes for his eyes. He was short, about my height, and he knew how to handle a gun."

"What are you doing out here alone?"

She started to raise the rifle again. "Who wants to know?"

Ben smiled, stepped up to the weapon, and pushed the barrel gently aside. "The man who stole your horse is known as Poder, and Poder never would have left you with a loaded rifle to shoot him in the back as he rode away. He took the bullets, didn't he?"

"You seem to know everything, Mr – "

"Snow. Ben Snow."

She seemed to relax a little, as if knowing his name made him more acceptable. "I'm Amy Forrest. My brother and I have a small ranch in the valley about forty miles from here. I was looking for strays – "

"In the desert?"

"Sometimes they come this far, especially the young ones that don't know any better. There are some water holes nearby."

"I saw one yesterday."

"Anyway, I heard a shot and rode over this way. When the man saw me coming, he pulled that hood over his head and drew a gun on me. Said his horse twisted a leg and he had to shoot it, and he was taking mine. He emptied the bullets out of my rifle, just as you guessed, and left me here. I wish I'd seen his face."

"If you had, you'd have been a dead woman. That masked man who calls himself Poder has never been seen by anyone. He's robbed banks and stagecoaches all over the New Mexico territory. Generally he doesn't even speak. A sidekick named Tommy Gonzolas did the talking for him. But Gonzolas is dead now."

"How come you know so much about him?"

"He killed a banker in Tosco a few days ago. I happened to be in town and they hired me to go after him – sort of a one-man posse."

"What makes you so good?"

He smiled at her. "They got some crazy notion I'm Billy the Kid."

"He's dead."

"Don't tell them. They're paying me well to bring back Poder, dead or alive."

"Does he have a first name?"

"He doesn't have any name, far as I know. *Poder* means 'power' in Spanish. It's just an alias he started using. Nobody knows a thing about him. Nobody but Gonzolas ever saw his face, and now he's dead."

"I guess I'm lucky to be alive. Can you get me back to my ranch? It's due north of here."

He stared out at the stark landscape, searching for a clue as to the direction Poder might have taken. "I don't know. I was figuring more on heading west. If you plot the locations of Poder's robberies on a map, they seem to be centered west of here. But my horse could carry us both as far as the next settlement and I could drop you there."

"Well, that's something."

He climbed into the saddle and helped her up behind him, surprised at her quick agility.

They'd barely started their trek when he thought he heard something far in the distance. Something that sounded like bells. "What's that?" he asked her.

She listened, cocking her head to the left. "You mean the bells? That's the mission at San Bernardino. It's only a few miles from here. Is that where you'll take me?"

"I think so," Ben decided. "Yes."

The mission came into view at the top of the next rise, and Ben judged it to be about five or six miles from the spot where Poder had stolen Amy Forrest's horse. He rode down the last dune slowly until he reached firmer ground, then urged his horse forward through the scattering of cactus and sagebrush. The mission itself sat in a small oasis and consisted of a white adobe church with a long, low building at the back. Amy explained that this was a monastery of the religious order that staffed the mission and raised what crops they could. "There are only a few priests. The rest are lay brothers who work in the fields. And there are Indians and Mexicans who have a sort of trading post outside the mission."

"You sound as if you know the place well," Ben said.

"I usually stop whenever I ride this way. Women aren't allowed into the monastery, of course, but I like the peacefulness of the church. It always seems cool there, even on a hot day."

He watched several dozen people emerging from the church. "What's going on?"

"It's Sunday morning. They've been to Mass."

"I forgot. Out here the days get to be the same."

"They have just the one Mass at ten o'clock, and that's the only time the bells ring all week. It's a wonder we heard them at all."

"Perhaps we were being called here," Ben murmured . . .

They dismounted near a paddock where the horses were kept and Amy ran to the railing. "That's King!" she pointed. "That's my horse!"

"The big brown one?"

"I'm certain of it!"

Ben spoke to an Indian standing nearby who seemed to be in charge of the paddock area.

"You there – what's your name?"

"Standing Elk. I am a Pueblo."

"All right, Standing Elk. Did you see who brought that big brown stallion in?"

"No. I do not know him." The Indian wore a suit of fringed buckskin, with a headband but no feathers. He was shorter than Ben and seemed younger.

"You saw no one ride in here about – how long ago, Amy?"

"An hour or so. He stole my horse an hour before you came along. Of course, he might have ridden faster than we did."

"I see no one," Standing Elk insisted.

"All right," Ben said. "Come on, Amy. We'll worry about your horse later."

A priest in Sunday vestments was standing outside the mission church, keeping carefully within the shadow cast by the mission's bell tower. He was young and fair-haired and Ben imagined his skin would burn quickly in the heat of the New Mexico desert.

"Good morning," he greeted Ben. "Welcome to the Mission of San Bernardino. And how are you today, Amy?"

"I'm fine now, Father. This is Ben Snow, Father Angeles."

The priest bowed his head in greeting and Ben noticed for the first time the cowl protruding from the back of his vestments. "I'm sorry you're late for Mass, Ben. We have only the one service here, at ten o'clock. There is also a weekday Mass every morning."

"Ben rescued me from the desert, Father. A gunman stole my horse."

"A gunman? Near here?"

"We think he rode this way, Father," Ben told him. "He's a killer and bank robber known as Poder."

"Power," the priest translated automatically. "I have not heard of him." He turned to Amy. "But, my dear child, you must be exhausted after such an experience – come inside and let Mrs Rodriguez tend to you."

Amy started to protest but Father Angeles insisted. Ben followed along until Amy had been delivered into the hands of a fat Mexican woman with a motherly look. Then he waited while the priest reverently shed his vestments and put them away.

"This is a lovely place to find in the middle of the desert," Ben said. "I don't know these parts as well as I should."

"Where are you from?" Father Angeles asked, brushing the sandy hair back from his forehead.

"The Midwest, originally. But I've been roaming for years now. I guess I don't really have a home." As they passed along a cloistered walkway leading to the monastery, he asked, "How many of you live here?"

"Father Reynolds, Father Canzas, and I. There are only five lay brothers at present, along with a few people to help us out.

Mrs Rodriguez cooks the meals, Luis rings the bells on Sunday, Standing Elk tends to the horses, and Pedro Valdez runs the trading post. The others are passers-by who stop to see us when they're in the neighborhood. Like Amy."

A monk with a boyish face came through the monastery door and Father Angeles stopped to introduce him. "Brother Abraham, this is Ben Snow, a traveler who has paused to rest with us."

Brother Abraham bowed slightly as the priest had done. "A pleasure to have you here. I hope your stay will be a pleasant one."

"I'm sure it will be," Ben told him and the monk continued on his way.

"Abraham," Ben said. "An Old Testament name."

"A presidential name," Father Angeles corrected. "The babies named after Lincoln have come of age now."

"Do you have any trouble with the Indians around here?"

"Nothing since Geronimo surrendered last September. The Apaches were a bother at times, but they seem at peace now. The Pueblos have always been our friends. Large numbers have converted to Christianity, though they cling tenaciously to their ancient rites."

He showed Ben through the monastery with its stark cell-like rooms. "It's almost like a prison," Ben observed.

"In a way, although the spirit is free. The lay brothers like Abraham toil in the fields, and often we're at their sides. One of us says Mass each morning, and generally all of the Indians and Mexicans at the trading post attend."

"A great many Mexicans," Ben observed.

"The border isn't that far from here."

"Do you know a man named Tommy Gonzolas? He would be half Mexican."

"I believe he's been here from time to time. Why do you ask? Are you searching for him?"

"I've already found him."

As they returned to the mission church, they passed beneath a large crucifix and Father Angeles crossed himself. "You wear your pistol like a gunfighter, Mr Snow. I hope no harm has come to Tommy Gonzolas."

"The harm had already been done when I found him, Father. I buried him out on the desert."

"May God have mercy on his soul."

"He was a bank robber and murderer, Father. He rode with the man called Poder, whom I've come to find."

"The person who stole Amy Forrest's horse."

"The same one."

"I know nothing of him."

"Was anyone away from the mission this week?"

"There is no way to tell. As I have said, they come and go. Standing Elk might know better than I do – he tends to the horses."

"Yes. I'll have to talk with him again."

"Join us for lunch first. Your questions will flow with more wisdom after a good meal."

The mission food was slight but tasty, and Mrs Rodriguez seemed to take special pride in cooking for them. Ben was only sorry Amy couldn't join them at the table, but the woman served her a special lunch in the kitchen. Only one of the five lay brothers was Mexican, and since he spoke no English Father Canzas conversed with him in Spanish The third priest, Father Reynolds, had been a Civil War cavalry officer who'd come west to fight Indians and found God instead.

"I decided it was more important to save their souls than kill their bodies," he said. "But you would have been too young to remember the war."

"I was six when it ended," Ben said. "I'm twenty-eight now."

"You look older – or more mature, I should say. And riding in the sun has weathered your face."

Brother Abraham sat across the table from him, between Brother Franklin and Brother Rudolph. None of them were especially talkative but Abraham seemed the quietest. Ben wondered what his story was.

After lunch Father Canzas walked out to the trading post with Ben and introduced him to Pedro Valdez, a handsome moustached man who ran the place with a group of half-breed assistants. He joked with Father Canzas, and the fat priest seemed to enjoy what had obviously become a friendly ritual between them. "You are a friend of the Father's?" he asked Ben. "A new friend, surely, or he would have fattened you up to his size by now."

After more casual conversation Ben asked, "Do you know a half breed named Tommy Gonzolas who often comes here?"

"I know him, yes. I know many people."

"He died recently and I'm trying to get word to his close friends. He told me he had a friend at the mission here."

Valdez lit a thin Mexican cigarillo. "You were with him when he died?"

"I was, yes."

"I know nothing about it. He talked with the others, but had no special friends."

Ben remembered the dead horse. "Who around here might ride a pinto?"

"Mottled or spotted horses are common out here, where wild herds still roam and interbreed. Standing Elk must have a half dozen pintos in his corral right now."

Ben sighed. "I only want to give a message to the friend of Tommy Gonzolas. You're not much help."

"I know of no friend."

Father Canzas had drifted away, looking over some of the blankets and trinkets offered for sale by the Indians. It was a meager trade at best, Ben decided, with only a handful of people even knowing of the place's existence – the mission of San Bernardino was not exactly on the regular wagon routes. He wondered if its very remoteness was the reason Poder came here.

"I'm looking for a man named Poder," Ben said finally. "Do you know him?"

Valdez smiled and his eyes seemed to twinkle. "The people of Tosco have hired you to capture him. Yes, Mr Snow, the word has reached here already. An Indian told me just this morning that Billy the Kid was riding to capture Poder, or to kill him. But you're much too tall for Billy. He was short like me. And besides, he's dead. He's buried over in Fort Sumner, not far from here, where Pat Garrett dropped him with two bullets at his girl friend's house." Valdez studied the burning tip of his cigarillo. "Billy should have taken General Lew Wallace's offer of amnesty if he left the New Mexico territory. He met with Wallace, you know, but he refused the offer."

"Is there a message here for me?" Ben wondered. "Should I get out while I can, too?"

The Mexican shrugged. "Where do you think you might find Poder? Do you think it is fat Father Canzas who rides with the mask over his face? Or one of those Indian children playing in the dust? Do you really care?"

"I've come a long way."

"We have all come a long way, Mr Snow." Valdez turned away as a loud dispute erupted among the children. He shouted something at them in Spanish and they fell silent. Ben turned and headed toward the corral.

There were over twenty horses penned up, but no sign of Standing Elk. Perhaps, he, too, had gone to lunch. Ben wandered back toward the mission and noticed one of the monks hurrying along the cloister. His hood was up and there was no way of identifying him, but there was something about his movements that attracted Ben's attention. He was moving too fast, almost running.

Ben boosted himself over the low cloister wall and followed in the direction the monk had taken. He knew it led to the monastery itself, and as he stepped through the doorway he was aware he was entering forbidden territory. There was no Father Angeles with him now, giving him a tour.

The shadows were deep here, with only an occasional hint of the afternoon sun outside. He moved along the passageway, past the empty rooms where the lay brothers slept. Once he thought he heard a footstep behind him and whirled, his hand on his gun, but there was no one. He seemed to be alone in the building.

Then he rounded a corner and froze.

Straight ahead was a wooden partition, with spiraling bars like a grillwork. A man's arms extended between the bars and then hung down, as if he had been caught in the instant of escape.

It was the Indian, Standing Elk, and he was dead.

Father Reynolds was the first to arrive on the scene in response to Ben's shouts, and he administered the last rites to the dead man. "There's blood," he said as he finished.

"He's been stabbed."

Father Angeles arrived then, with Brother Franklin. "What's happened here?"

"Standing Elk has been murdered," Ben said. "I should have guessed it would happen."

"You can't blame yourself," Father Angeles said.

"My coming here was the cause of it. Poder killed him before he could tell me who rode here on Amy Forrest's horse."

"I cannot believe this person you seek is hiding here," Father Reynolds said.

"There's the evidence of it," Ben said, pointing to the body.

"If the body is here," Brother Franklin said, "does that mean one of us killed him?"

Ben shook his head. "If Standing Elk could enter this building, so could any other Indian or Mexican. Dressed in one of your robes with the hood up, who would know the difference?"

"There is no sheriff within a hundred miles," Father Angeles said. "What shall we do?"

"Bury him. I'll report it when I return to Tosco. You certainly can't leave the body above ground in this heat."

"We must have a funeral Mass," the priest said, rubbing his sandy hair. "But we have no method of embalming here. He must be buried soon."

*

The funeral Mass was held late that afternoon, with Father Angeles officiating. While the mission bells tolled mournfully, the people of the oasis filed into the church for the second time that day. Ben sat near the rear of the church with Amy Forrest, watching the ancient rituals. When the priest had finished, another Pueblo, Running Fox, came forward to add some beads and bracelets to the plain wooden coffin Pedro Valdez and his assistants had fashioned.

After it was over, after Ben and Amy had stood with the others in the little graveyard behind the mission, he studied the faces of the departing mourners. But if one was the face of Poder, there was no sign of it. Ben asked Father Canzas if he had a map of the territory. "There's one in our library," the fat priest answered.

He showed Ben and Amy to a book-filled room near the cloister and left them. On a map Ben measured the distance from the mission to the sites of Poder's crimes as well as he could remember them. As he worked, Brother Abraham came in to watch over his shoulder. "What are you doing?"

Ben glanced up from his task. "The man I seek, who probably murdered Standing Elk, committed a crime at each of these sites. All are within three days' ride of this mission."

The monk nodded silently, and after a time he left. Ben asked Amy, "Do you know anything about him? He seems a bit strange."

"Just that they say his parents were killed by Apaches when he was ten and he's been here ever since."

Ben returned to the map and she wandered over to the bookcases. "They have quite a library here. Melville, Victor Hugo, Dickens, Hawthorne. There's even a copy of *Ben Hur*, the novel by our territorial governor."

"I'm surprised they'd have Hugo. I heard once that the Church doesn't approve of his novels."

"I don't suppose anyone sees it but the priests and brothers. Most of the Indians and Mexicans probably don't read English."

"Do you think that's why Poder rarely speaks?" Ben asked. "Because his English is limited?"

"I had the same idea when you said this Gonzolas person usually did the talking. I wondered if it was because Poder's English was poor."

"But he talked to you when he stole your horse."

"Just a few words, and they were muffled by his mask."

"There is one other explanation of why he rarely spoke," Ben said quietly. It was something that had been hovering at the back of his mind all day. "Do you have your rifle handy?"

"I brought it into the kitchen when we arrived. It's probably still there."

"Let's go get it."

She seemed puzzled by his request but she went along with it. They found the rifle standing in a corner while Mrs Rodriguez worked on the evening meal. "We eat soon," she said. "Do not go far away."

"Just outside," Ben assured her.

They walked into the courtyard by the cloister and Ben pointed the weapon toward the sky. "I was saying there was one other explanation of why he rarely spoke. Poder could be a woman."

"I – "

"You might have been riding toward the mission when your horse twisted its leg. You had to shoot him, and when I happened along you feared I might recognize that pinto as Poder's. So you made up the story of his stealing your horse."

"Do you really believe that?"

"There's one way of testing it. If your story was false, then he didn't empty your rifle at all. It should still be loaded now." He squeezed the trigger.

There was a loud crack as the weapon fired toward the sky.

Amy Forrest stood her ground, staring at him. Neither of them moved for a full minute. Then she said, "I bought some cartridges from Valdez this afternoon and reloaded it. You can ask him if you don't believe me."

He lowered the rifle. "I believe you."

"Poder isn't a woman. It was a man's voice that spoke to me." She turned and went into the house.

Ben stood there for a moment, looking after her. Then he turned and walked out toward the trading post. There were few people around and he went to sit by himself in the shade of a large cactus, drawing letters in the sand.

Presently Father Angeles joined him. "I heard a shot," the priest said. "And I saw Amy. She's very upset."

"It's logical," Ben told him. "She killed Standing Elk not because he saw who rode into the corral this morning, but because he knew no one rode into the corral. He would know she lied."

"Logic is not always the same as truth," the priest said. "If Poder is really here, it is not that young woman."

Ben raised his eyes to stare at him. "You know the truth, don't you, Father? Poder has confessed to you."

"He has not, but of course I could not tell you even if he had."

His eyes strayed to the letters Ben had traced in the sand. "What is this?"

"*Poder* and *Pedro* have the same letters. One is an anagram of the other."

"So you have a new suspect in place of Amy."

"Is Valdez the only Pedro here?"

"Yes. But go slowly this time, Ben."

The priest left him as Mrs Rodriguez summoned them to dinner. But as Ben got to his feet and smoothed over the sand in front of him, he remembered one of the books in the mission library. His education was far from complete, but he had read the classics as a boy in the Midwest. Perhaps part of the answer was in that book.

A sudden movement among the cloisters caught his eye and he saw again the hurrying monk he'd been pursuing when he came upon Standing Elk's body. He broke into a run, intent on catching him this time. The man had been spying on him, and that could mean it was the one he sought.

"Stop!" Ben shouted as the cowled figure pulled open the door of the monastery. His fingers reached out, grasping the back of the hood and pulling it off just as the monk was about to disappear through the entrance. And as the figure turned around toward him, he saw what he'd hoped and feared.

There was no face. There was only a cloth mask with holes cut in it for the eyes.

"Poder! We meet at last!"

From beneath the folds of the cloak a pistol appeared. Ben grabbed it, wrestling at close quarters to keep it from pointing at him. There was a shot as a bullet tore past his head, and he relaxed his grip for just an instant. Too close to aim again, Poder swung the gun hard against Ben's temple.

Dazzling lights and a searing pain cut across his head and he felt himself falling. He clawed at the hooded face before him, managing to catch a finger in one of the eyeholes. As he went down, he pulled the mask with him, praying that with his dying breath he would at least see the face of his killer.

And then he saw it – the face of Poder.

It was the face of a man he had never seen before.

As his vision cleared and he returned to consciousness, Ben recognized Amy and Father Angeles kneeling by him. "Who was it?" Amy asked. "Who hit you?"

"Poder."

"Did you see his face?"

"Yes." He tried to stand up. His head hurt, but otherwise he seemed all right. His pistol was still in its holster. "I have to go after him."

"He'll kill you," Amy said.

"He didn't just now."

"We came running and frightened him away."

Ben leaned against the wall to steady himself and then took a few steps. He was all right. He could do it now. "You two stay here," he said.

"Do you know where he is?" Father Angeles asked.

"I know."

He left them and went to the church. Once inside, he found a ladder leading the way up and began climbing. He kept climbing until he reached the top of the bell tower, some fifty feet above the ground.

Poder was waiting for him, standing behind the two mission bells with his back to the sky.

"I knew you'd come up here," Ben said. "Luis is your name, isn't it? I remember Father Angeles telling me this morning, *Luis rings the bells on Sunday.*' I thought I saw everyone at Standing Elk's funeral, but of course I didn't see you because you were ringing the bells then, too."

"You should have stayed away," Poder said. "You shouldn't have come up here."

"I was hired to bring you back."

"Gonzolas told you, didn't he? I was afraid someone might find him before he died, but I couldn't bring myself to kill him."

"He said to listen for the bells and I would find you. I didn't take it quite as literally as I should have. I thought he only meant you were here at the mission. But your mistake was in stealing Amy Forrest's horse."

"I had to take it."

"I know. Your time was running out. You must have had a moment of panic when your pinto twisted his leg and came up lame. But then you saw her, and took her horse. When I thought about it, I asked myself why. You were only five miles from the mission – certainly not a long walk for a man capable of robbing stagecoaches and banks. Why risk showing yourself, even masked, and then leaving the witness alive?"

"I have never killed a woman."

"But why risk it at all when you could have walked the distance in eighty or ninety minutes? Why – unless you had to be back at the mission for some Sunday morning duty? I asked myself what that duty might be. There was the Mass at ten o'clock, of course. Could

Poder be one of the mission's three priests? No, because they said Mass daily and Poder had been gone all week, riding three days to Tosco and three days back. He'd been away that long, or nearly that long, before. So he couldn't be a priest, nor one of the lay brothers who worked daily in the fields. Nor Mrs Rodriguez, who prepared all their meals. But the Indians and Mexicans came and went at will, and certainly wouldn't be missed on Sunday Mass. Only one person was free the rest of the week, to the best of my knowledge, but had Sunday morning duties – Luis, who rang the bells on Sunday. If those bells didn't ring at ten o'clock, people would ask where Luis was."

Poder shifted slightly and Ben saw the pistol in his hand. He stepped a bit to his right, putting the bells between them. "Draw!" Poder said. "The time for talking is over."

But Ben kept on talking. "I suppose it was the view from up here that did it to you. Looking down on all those little people can give a sense of power. Hugo's Hunchback of Notre Dame was a poor deformed creature until he looked down from his bell tower on the streets of Paris far below. It can make one feel like God up here – invincible, with the power to rob and kill. The mask and the silence were part of the image, adding to your legend."

"Draw, damn you!" Poder shouted, and fired his six-shooter. The bullet clanged off the bell, sending tremors through the air.

Ben drew his gun.

He stared down from the tower for a long time, watching the tiny figure on the ground, seeing Father Angeles and Amy running out to where it had landed. The priest knelt in the dust and prayed over Luis's body while Ben watched.

He could feel the power from up here, the power that Luis had felt, and finally he had to look away, toward the vastness of the desert horizon, until he felt small again.

MURDERING
MR BOODLE
Amy Myers

*One of the enquiries I had after the publication of the first volume was
why I had not made any reference to the Auguste Didier stories by Amy
Myers. You may recall, in the bibliography at the end of that volume,
I had set a cut-off date of around 1870 for my survey of historical
mystery stories, mainly because after that date the volume of Sherlock
Holmes stories would have filled another entire book! But I probably
should have made reference to the many very excellent detective stories
set at the end of the nineteenth century. Some of the most eclectic
of these are the Auguste Didier stories. Didier is a cordon bleu
chef with a penchant for solving crimes. The novels, which began
in 1986 with* Murder in Pug's Parlour *and have now reached
their eighth volume, are written with a tongue-in-cheek humour and
a remarkable eye for parodying Victorian values. They are also very
clever crimes. So now, for the many fans of Auguste Didier, is his very
first short story.*

"Money? My dear Mr Didier!"
Gervase Budd was shocked. Checked in expansive mid-
flow, he was hurt beyond measure. The willow-patterned waistcoat
quivered with emotion, over the incline of Mr Budd's stomach. "My
partner, Mr Boodle, attends to such details."

Had he inadvertently transgressed some unwritten code by enquir-
ing about financial terms, Auguste wondered, a code understood by
any gentleman who entered this sanctum but not by mere maître
chefs such as he? When he had been approached by this venerable
publishing firm he had been given to understand by Mr Budd that
had the sixteenth century been fortunate enough to produce Messrs
Boodle, Budd & Farthing, Mr William Shakespeare would have had
to look no further for a publisher who would have left the authorship
of his work in no doubt whatsoever, and moreover provided his widow

with considerably more financial reward than his second-best bed. On the threshold of the twentieth century, what better home could there be to immortalize Auguste's ten-volume magnum opus, *Dining with Didier*?

"Shall I be meeting Mr Boodle?" Auguste watched him carefully. There had been a certain heartiness in Mr Budd's tone which he was well accustomed to hearing in underchefs who assured him all was well with the entrées, when that was far from being the case.

"Ah, Mr Popple, come in, pray do," Gervase Budd boomed – in relief? – at the entry of a wild-eyed young man of about twenty years, with his hair artfully arranged as to suggest a life of constant debauchery lasting twice that number. "Mr Didier, may I present Mr Clarence Popple, our perspir – ah," Mr Budd mopped his brow with an ornamental red silk handkerchief – "*a*spiring poet."

"A poet can survive everything but a misprint," Clarence smirked.

"Ah yes, I recall dear Oscar did observe that once," murmured Mr Budd.

Clarence eyed him balefully. "Mr Budd is to do me the honour of publishing my thoughts on life."

"A wise decision." Auguste opted for diplomacy, while privately thinking this young man's thoughts would bear as much relevance to life as Francatelli's masterpieces to a soup kitchen.

Gervase Budd rose to his feet, his dark frock coat parting to either side of his paunch. "Shall we take a glass of port wine, gentlemen, while awaiting your fellow prospective authors?"

He flourished a cut glass decanter, much as Maskelyne and Devant might display their magical mysteries. Auguste's heart sank. He had a particular dislike of ruining his palate before the first great adventure of the day, namely luncheon, and regarded the glass that Mr Budd obviously believed contained the nectar of the gods without enthusiasm.

"I shall recite my ode to a golden carp," Clarence Popple announced.

At least he showed some appreciation of cuisine, Auguste thought tolerantly. The carp was the king of fish, a fish of remarkable powers and longevity. It was only as Clarence progressed it occurred to Auguste that he might possibly have misheard carp for harp.

"My muse she sings above . . ."

Auguste promptly lost interest, but Mr Budd smiled brightly throughout, though perhaps his eye had a glazed expression worthy of a dressed carp itself. It only sprang into life at the entry of a third author. Mr Budd however had not appeared bored so much as preoccupied, he thought: he seemed a distinctly worried man. Why?

"Ah, Miss Mellidew," Gervase greeted the new arrival.

Auguste rose to his feet, eager to meet the famous Queen of the Circulating Library, author of (among other delightful novels) *Cecilia's Sahara Sojourn* (3 vols, crown 8vo, illustrated boards, Heart & Whitestock, London, 1875), which had been devoured in enormous numbers by Mudie's Select Library, creating a market for every word penned by Millicent Mellidew thereafter. The three-decker novel might be waning in popularity but not if it had her name attached.

"Dear Miss Mellidew, or should I say Cecilia?"

Mr Budd's archness was wasted, for Miss Mellidew was clearly agitated at entering this masculine sanctum, though now considerably older than Cecilia.

"I am delighted to meet you, Miss Mellidew," Auguste said truthfully, as she nervously pushed back a lock of mousy hair which had escaped from beneath her old-fashioned ornate hat. The artificial robin that adorned it leered threateningly towards him, as if protesting that his nest had been jammed on to her head regardless of his comfort. "I of course know *Cecilia*. Dare we expect a sequel?"

Mr Budd beamed, taking this as a personal tribute to his acumen in persuading Miss Mellidew to change publishers.

"Oh!" Millicent Mellidew gasped breathlessly. "I do so value gentlemen readers." She smiled uncertainly. "But I fear Lambkin thought his Cecilia sadly changed."

In Auguste's opinion, any change to Simpering Cecilia could only be for the better, and years of feasting on Arab cuisine might well have taken their toll even on the magnificent physique of Sheikh Hamed the Shining One, known to his beloved Cecilia as Lambkin.

"Never." Gervase Budd assured the prize so nearly within his grasp. "The truly beautiful triumph over time."

Miss Mellidew looked her prospective publisher straight in the eye. "Provided they receive their just rewards," she whispered modestly. "What terms do you propose?"

Auguste almost applauded. Clarence showed no such restraint. "Bravo, Miss Mellidew," he declared enthusiastically.

Mr Budd was not dismayed. "Generous, dear lady, generous. You may be assured of that. Ah, you have arrived, General."

The meeting had been called for twelve o'clock, and it was now twelve-fifteen. No wonder it had taken so long to relieve Mafeking, Auguste thought irrepressibly, if this was the standard of organization.

"Naturally, I am an Army man, sir." General Eric Proudfoot-Padbury, a tall lean man of fifty-odd, with a fine moustache carefully curled for adorning commemorative china, glared at the assembled company.

"Will you take a glass of port, General?"

"Never touch the stuff. Brandy and soda."

Gloom spread once more over Mr Budd's jovial face, as he reluctantly opened a side cupboard, extracted a bottle, poured a small measure and firmly replaced it. The General snorted. "I trust the money flows more generously than your liquor, Budd. Me memoirs would be a major contribution to history, you told me. *Time Marches to a Drumbeat*", he told Miss Mellidew complacently. He did not bother with Clarence or Auguste. Poets were merely those unfit for soldierly service, and humble cooks, like batmen, did not rank. Armies might march on their stomachs but what went into them was of little importance.

"Naturally," Gervase Budd purred, sitting down, resting his hands proprietorially on his desk, in a vain attempt to imply all was well with himself, the company, its prospective authors and the entire world.

"Old Boodle still holding the purse strings, eh?"

Gervase Budd jumped. "You know of Mr Boodle?" There was a certain caution in his voice. "Indeed, yes, Boodle, Budd & Farthing are still fortunate enough to retain his services."

"Who is Mr Boodle?" Auguste enquired.

"Mr Boodle is *the* Mr Boodle," Mr Budd informed him reverently. "I myself am his junior." Mr Budd's girth and years made the word instantly inappropriate. "The original Budd was my father. I like to think of my little office as the temple to art, but we are ruled by the business acumen and wisdom of Mr Boodle."

"And Mr Farthing?" asked Millicent.

"Mr Farthing, dear man, retired from the business, having made his penny." Gervase Budd chuckled at his little joke, and stopped when nobody else did. "Mr Boodle also likes his merry jest." There was a touch of defiance in his voice. "When as a raw youth of twenty I entered these portals I was guided by the beneficent hand of Mr Boodle. That hand thankfully has been at the helm ever since."

"Then I shall look forward to discussing the details of a contract with Mr Boodle," Auguste told him firmly. Negotiating with publishers, after all, would be no different to dealing with butchers. The quality of meat supplied must determine the price.

"You may rest assured, Mr Didier, that here at Boodle, Budd &

Farthing, we acknowledge our duty to the future. The food of today nurtures England's gentlemen and mothers of tomorrow."

"Bravo," cried Miss Mellidew boldly, overcome with emotion. "I am glad you accord woman her rightful place. It is what I look for in a publisher. I do sometimes sense that lady novelists are not as highly regarded as they deserve. I trust you are not a disparager of womankind in any respect, Mr Budd?"

"I am not, dear lady," he assured her fervently. "Why, our own receptionist is a lady, Miss Violet Watkins. Doubtless you met her when you entered, together with our invaluable doorman, Mr Wallace."

"The bourgeoisie," declared Clarence languidly; he had obviously decided he had been excluded from the conversation long enough. "My poetry shall enrich their lives."

"It shall, it shall, Mr Popple," Budd assured him.

"I have entitled it *Poems for Posterity*."

"Ah." Mr Budd's face clouded over once more. "And might I enquire your proposed title, Miss Mellidew?"

"*Mildred's Missionary*."

"Ah." Gervase Budd looked even more dejected. "A story of passion and frustrated romance?" he enquired with no great hope.

"A priest torn between love and duty."

"My dear Miss Mellidew!" Tears of gratitude appeared in Mr Budd's eyes at this unexpected commercial break. "If I might suggest a change of title, however?"

"You may not."

"Me memoirs," the General shouted as Mr Budd showed no sign of interest in *Time Marches to a Drumbeat*, "centre on the reverse at Isandhlwana."

Mr Budd blenched in alarm. "I thought you were in command at Rorke's Drift," he cried, as sales prospects disintegrated before his eyes.

"Overrated," snarled his prospective author. "Now Isandhlwana, the Sudan . . ." He trumpeted on, as Budd regarded him with increasing dismay. The General seemed to have had a distressing tendency to be present at every reverse of the British army in recent times.

"And you, Mr Didier," Budd turned feverishly to Auguste. "May we hope for glimpses of food favoured by the famous, just a mention of the Prince of Wales, even Her Majesty Herself?"

"I regret we may not," Auguste returned amiably. "My professional code, you understand."

"Ah, but our advance – "

"How much *do* you pay in advances on royalties, Mr Budd?" Miss Mellidew asked. Auguste noted that timid though Miss Mellidew appeared a certain briskness entered her voice when money was mentioned.

"Ah. Mr Boodle has decreed a most democratic system," Mr Budd announced with nervous pride. "Here at Boodle, Budd & Farthing every author receives an identical advance in order that the well established may thus encourage our younger, less experienced authors."

Even as Auguste reflected on his own reaction to this somewhat startling concept (unknown to butchers), he saw Clarence Popple's languid look suddenly readjust to the possibility of receiving a sum far beyond most aspiring poets' expectations. Miss Mellidew, on the other hand, clearly had severe doubts about Mr Boodle's sanity, and the General looked decidedly frosty. Democracy was seldom practised in the British army.

"How much?" the latter demanded.

"Mr Boodle will – "

"How much?" Miss Mellidew's voice was suddenly strident.

Mr Budd recognized defeat. "Twenty-five pounds." He glanced round the stony faces, and cleared his throat. "I will speak to Mr Boodle – "

"I am far from sure I can agree to this," Miss Mellidew announced. "*Mildred's Missionary* deserves as much as Lambkin."

"Art, Miss Mellidew, is art. And there will, naturally, be royalties. On the 31s 6d edition, the 6s *and* the 2s editions," Mr Budd added ingratiatingly.

"I myself," Auguste decided to ally himself with the Missionary, "would expect an advance suitable to meet the considerable expense involved." Indeed his bachelor home life did not include the luxury of purchasing truffles for experimentation. The integrity of *Dining with Didier* must not be compromised by cutting back on quality.

"When shall we be meeting Mr Boodle?" the General asked grimly.

"Mr Boodle is a most reasonable – " Gervase stopped in mid unhappy flow. In the street below directly beneath his window a dull murmur of conversation had suddenly swelled into a vast commotion of shouting voices and banging on doors, unknown in this quiet London Georgian backwater. "What, I wonder, is that?"

Auguste crossed to the window and peered down into the street.

"There appears to be a large number of people attempting to gain entrance to your premises," he said with some interest. "I believe you should investigate, Mr Budd."

"No!" Gervase Budd's face was pale. "No doubt it is merely

a crowd eager to purchase *Steadfast's Last Stand*. A most popular recent publication. By Mr Arnold Hope." His voice trailed off as four prospective authors gazed at him unconvinced. "Our best selling author. At present," he added.

Clarence joined Auguste, all trace of languor vanished. "Wait till I tell Arnold about this," he grinned. "He'll dine me at the Ritz."

"*Steadfast's Last Stand* appears to appeal to ladies and gentlemen, both young and elderly," Auguste pointed out, observing both parasols and walking canes waving like military barley in the wind.

"They're demanding to see old Boodle," Clarence yelled in high glee, as Miss Mellidew elbowed her way in between him and Auguste.

"Mr Boodle?" Gervase Budd laughed lightly. "Dear me, how could I have forgotten? It's Mr Boodle's birthday," he announced triumphantly. "Doubtless these are his admirers bearing due tribute."

The General exerted his authority, pushing Auguste and Miss Mellidew aside at the very moment that some of the better aimed due tribute in the form of rotten fruit splattered on the window pane before him. He withdrew hastily. Behind them the door flew open and a terrified Miss Violet Watkins skidded to a halt at her employer's desk, distraught from her neat brown bun to the buttons quivering on her boots.

"I have been loyal, Mr Budd," she informed her employer, a choke in her voice. "I have been loyal for thirty years. But now our authors are insisting on seeing Mr Boodle immediately. They are causing an affray, Mr Budd. Mr Wallace cannot restrain them. Mr Boodle refuses to meet them since he is occupied on the yearly royalty accounts. But they are *abusive*, Mr Budd. What am I to do?"

Gervase Budd rose magnificently to his feet and the occasion.

"Mr Boodle must be protected at all costs. Kindly request Mr Simmonds of Printing, Mr Jones of Subscriptions, and Mr Catling of Reading to step to Mr Wallace's aid." The services of the red silk handkerchief were once more called upon.

"Oh . . ." Miss Watkins' wail would have done justice to Cecilia in mid-Sahara, as the noise intensified below.

"Lead on, Budd. We're behind you," the General announced, retirement at an end as new battle honours loomed in his sights.

"No!" Gervase's cry was heart-rending.

"Then allow me to go for you," Auguste offered immediately, hurrying to the door. Mr Budd however moved even quicker, forestalling the General, and somehow to his surprise Auguste found himself and Mr Budd outside the door, and the other three still inside. To Auguste's even greater surprise Mr Budd appeared to be locking them in. He caught Auguste's stare of astonishment and attempted nonchalance.

"For their own safety," he explained lightly. "I should not like them to be mistaken for Mr Boodle."

"You mean the due tribute would reach the wrong person?"

Gervase looked blank.

"It is Mr Boodle's birthday," Auguste reminded him gravely, having to shout now to be heard over the hubbub below. The words "police", "the law", "immediate action" and "demand" could be distinguished, amongst some far less polite.

"Bumps," gabbled Gervase wildly, following Auguste reluctantly past the hallowed door and down towards mayhem. "They have come to give Mr Boodle his birthday bumps." There was desperation in his voice.

Below him on the staircase which wound its way up through the four floors of Boodle House, Auguste could see Miss Watkins barring the way as effectively as Horatius his bridge to Lars Porsena, her arms outstretched against the tide. The advance rush of Mr Boodle's admirers crossed the landing of the first floor and were checked as they realized the strength of the defence.

"Mr Boodle is working," Miss Watkins shrieked. "On *your* royalty accounts. He must not be disturbed. The accounts will be with you . . ." She hesitated for a moment, then proceeded firmly, "*tomorrow.*"

From the rear Auguste could see the stalwart form of Mr Wallace already turning back the more faint-hearted of the mob, and the apparently disorganized group first rumbled, then murmured, and finally retreated piecemeal, beyond the hallowed portals of Boodle House.

"It seems to me they lack organized union power," Auguste observed. "Perhaps that might be my role?"

Mr Budd gave him a swift look of pure dislike. "Pray do not jest, Mr Didier." His plump and highly agitated rear proceeded up the staircase again. Hurrying in his wake, Auguste was beginning to feel like the Lighthouse Keeper's Daughter in the old melodrama. Certainly *Dining with Didier* was going to be a more adventurous experience than he had hitherto realized, he decided, as he heard the rumpus coming from behind the locked door of Mr Budd's office.

"Really, Mr Budd – " The door was opened to reveal a hysterical Miss Mellidew. "I am a maiden lady. To lock me in with two strange gentlemen is hardly the action one expects of one's prospective publisher."

"I'm sure Mr Popple and the General are as gallant as Lambkin

– er – Sheikh Hamed the Shining One." Gervase Budd attempted to regain an urbane composure.

He failed. Miss Mellidew turned a cold eye on bohemian Clarence and the apoplectic General Proudfoot-Padbury. She turned an even colder one on Mr Budd.

"Lambkin was a true gentleman, I would remind you; he was almost *English*, educated at Oxford, fully conversant with Shakespeare and Keats, a former officer in the British army, and winner of the VC before returning to duty in his own land, his beloved desert."

"The dashed fellow had several wives. They don't allow that in the British army," snarled the General.

Miss Mellidew turned pink. "That, General, is what parted them. Lambkin, while loving Cecilia truly, passionately, eternally, was forced to marry for duty under Muslim law. He was the flower of chivalry to Cecilia however. And I am glad," she added pointedly, "that you have read my little book, General."

"My wife," the General trumpeted feebly, caught out. "I merely glanced at it. Thought it was Jorrocks."

"In life," intoned Clarence sanctimoniously, "one should experience all, read everything, and meet everyone."

"Including Boodle. *Now*," the General announced firmly.

"I must admit to a certain curiosity myself, Mr Budd," Auguste backed him up.

"Allow me first to introduce you to the rest of our devoted staff," Gervase Budd said hastily, beginning to regain composure. "I will then ascertain whether Mr Boodle might be persuaded to spare a few moments."

"Good of you," the General grunted.

"Publishing," Mr Budd continued forlornly, "is going through a very bad time. Trade has been quite devastated by these cheap sixpenny books. The death of the trade is at hand, I am reliably informed by Mr Jones of Subscriptions."

"Indeed? I understood that the new Net Book Agreement so vigorously requested by booksellers was proving the saviour of the trade," Auguste said mischievously.

"An improvement," Mr Budd conceded hastily, "but a drop in the ocean. We have a long way to go, Mr Didier, a very long way."

"Despite Arnold Hope's *Steadfast's Last Stand*?" Clarence asked innocently, winking at Auguste in a most unpoetic way. "I'm sure he'll be most distressed to hear of your pessimism."

"Ah, Mr Popple, of course you are a *close* friend of his. Naturally I did not mean to imply a lack of future for books of the quality of Mr Hope's."

"Romance will always find a market," Miss Mellidew reminded him sternly.

"As will food," Auguste contributed. Indeed the latter could claim precedence in his opinion.

"Miss Mellidew, if you will permit me to lead the way – " Gervase hastily put an end to this insubordinate talk of markets by prospective authors by bustling from the room. A casual hand flung open the door of the other office on this fourth floor of the tall narrow Boodle House. "The board room where Mr Boodle, the staff and I gather to discuss the running of the company. We pride ourselves on democracy."

It did not seem to be an overused room, to Auguste's eye. It was gloomy, overshadowed by the house opposite it, and its large table had a distinct film of dust. The portrait of Mr Budd Senior stared down at it in distaste, and his son hurriedly closed the door, descending the stairs to the third floor. Here was the hallowed door of Mr Boodle, according to its ornate nameplate. Or what Auguste could see of it, since Mr Budd was standing across the doorway, making it hard to squeeze past his stomach in the narrow passageway. Once Mr Boodle's privacy had been safely guaranteed, Gervase Budd led his flock downstairs and to one of the two offices on the second floor.

"Mr Simmonds, Printing," he shouted, throwing open the door.

He hardly needed to announce its role. The two tables were littered with photographs, rulers, piles of manuscript and compositor's proofs. A Remington typing machine adorned one table, a man with greying hair and moustache worked feverishly at the other. A monocled eye glanced briefly at them before returning to the work before him. "Crown octavo," he muttered cryptically. "Vellum, I must have vellum, Mr Budd. Nothing but the best for Boodle, Budd & Farthing authors."

"You shall have it, Mr Simmonds," his employer beamed. "May I present four new authors to you?"

Mr Simmonds inclined his head. "I trust you have all availed yourselves of the services of a lady typewriter?" he demanded in a high tremulous voice.

"My handwriting is excellent," Millicent Mellidew told him querulously. "I do not hold with such modern inventions."

"And I am a poet," Clarence said soulfully. "My pen is my poetry."

"My wife is my typewriter," the General boomed from the doorway where Mr Budd had kept them in order that the smooth running of Boodle, Budd & Farthing might not be interrupted. "All the Farthings are excellent at that sort of detail."

Mr Budd jumped. "Farthings?" he repeated cautiously. "My dear sir, did you mention the Farthing family?"

"I did, sir. My wife is William Farthing's sister."

Auguste had the distinct feeling from the General's moment of triumph (one of the few in his career) that he had been waiting for the opportunity to drop this in. Generals did not become generals by accident.

"Ah." Gervase rallied, rubbing his hands together with somewhat forced bonhomie. "How is dear Mr Farthing?"

"Dead. Without getting his money from Mr Boodle," the General said grimly.

"I am indeed sorry to hear of his demise," Gervase gabbled. "I had a high opinion of Mr Farthing, and so," he added unwisely, "did Mr Boodle."

"Then he can pay out what he owed him to his heirs."

On the whole the meeting with Mr Boodle bade fair to be spirited, Auguste thought with some amusement.

"I thought Mr Jones of Subscriptions and Trade next," Mr Budd announced brightly, not inviting disagreement, as he led the way slowly downstairs to the room beneath on the first floor.

"Moodie's have placed an excellent order for Mr Hope's next work." Mr Jones's dark hair and sideburns, almost disappearing into the tall white linen collar, were almost all that could be seen of him from their vantage point behind Mr Budd at the doorway; he was buried in ledgers and files that confirmed the age-old reputation and reliability of Boodle, Budd & Farthing.

"Splendid. And we are to be the proud publishers of Miss Mellidew's next novel."

"Delightful." Mr Jones appeared already to be writing up orders for it as he buried himself once more in his ledger. His demeanour suggested the sooner he returned to work the greater the sales. Miss Mellidew, Auguste noted, did not seem quite so enthusiastic at the prospect before her. He also noted one other interesting fact, his eye on Mr Jones's collar.

Mr Budd banged the door shut and beamed. "And now to return to the holy of holies. Reading." He almost tiptoed past the discreetly labelled Bathroom and up the staircase to the next floor once more, the room opposite Mr Simmonds'. He knocked, a courtesy he had not extended to the other staff.

"The muse must not be disturbed without warning," he whispered.

The muse answered readily enough in the guise of Mr Catling, the youngest of the three underlings, judging by his jaunty red hairstyle and moustache.

"I think I have a little gem here, Mr Budd." Mr Catling, it appeared, could no more be wrenched from his duty than his colleagues.

"Excellent, excellent. Mr Boodle will be delighted at the good news," Mr Budd beamed happily. "And that," he concluded with some relief, "completes the tour of our little kingdom with the exception of the stock cellars."

"What about Mr Boodle?" Miss Mellidew asked on Mildred's behalf.

"Luncheon first," Mr Budd told them firmly. "I had thought Romanos – " Clarence brightened with enthusiasm "– but I realized you would think the time more profitably spent discussing the finer details of publication."

"No," the General disagreed tersely.

"Shall we return to my office?" Mr Budd suggested loudly, apparently not having heard the General. "A sherry, and we could if you wish take a pie with it."

"Romanos," Clarence opted.

"I agree," Auguste said, beginning to enjoy himself hugely. "Surely the author of *Dining with Didier* should not be presented with a mere pie?"

Overcome by the prospect ahead, Gervase Budd temporarily neglected his duties as shepherd dog and it was not until they had reached his office that he realized that one of his flock was absent. His eyes glazed over in panic.

"Where is Miss Mellidew?" he shouted hysterically.

The General coughed in amazement, and Clarence sniggered.

"I think perhaps she has merely withdrawn for a few moments," Auguste soothed tactfully. "I am sure she will be with us shortly."

She was, but not in the state Gervase would have welcomed. The door burst open and Millicent almost fell inside.

"He's dead!" she shrieked. Auguste's reflexes stiffened.

"Dead. Dear lady, who's dead?" Gervase Budd squawked, paling slightly.

"Mr Boodle."

"How – where?" Auguste asked urgently, as Gervase Budd was speechless with shock.

"In his office. I opened his door to speak to him, and there he was. Dead."

"My dear Miss Mellidew." Gervase relaxed. "You must be mistaken. A trick of the light, no more. Mr Boodle is in perfect health."

"He is dead, Mr Budd." Her voice quivered, but held no uncertainty.

Auguste rose to his feet. "I suggest I investigate, Mr Budd."

"No, no. You obviously entered the wrong room, dear lady," Mr Budd protested.

"What does the room matter?" Auguste replied impatiently.

"It was Mr Boodle's room and he is *dead*," Millicent repeated adamantly, perhaps reflecting that Cecilia would have received rather better treatment than her creator, had she swooningly announced her discovery of a corpse.

"He can't be," Gervase replied complacently.

"I am going to see," Auguste repeated, walking to the door.

"No," shrieked Mr Budd, hurling his bulk across the room to prevent him.

"Are you mad, sir? Stand from our path," the General commanded. "Have you no concern for your partner's welfare?"

"No. I mean yes. But it can't be Mr Boodle," Gervase moaned.

"I demand you summon help." Hysteria was rapidly overtaking Miss Mellidew.

"There is no body."

"Kindly stand aside, Mr Budd," Auguste ordered. "If Miss Mellidew is mistaken I shall soon be able to confirm it."

"Mr Boodle can't be dead."

"Stand aside, Budd," the General commanded once more, with much the same effect as when he ordered the Boers to give up the siege of Ladysmith.

"I won't. He can't be dead."

"Why not?"

"Because he already is."

"Gibberish, man," snarled the General.

"Explain yourself, Mr Budd," Auguste asked quietly.

"There *is* no Mr Boodle," his late partner moaned. "Mr Boodle died twenty years ago."

"Are you out of your mind, sir?" the General exploded.

"Mr Boodle died in 1880."

"But – "

"What the deuce do you mean, sir?" The General saw no reason to wait for a mere woman's interjection.

Seeing no alternative, Gervase Budd crumpled, giving a fair unconscious imitation of Mr Jingle. "Mr Boodle – very fine man – certain trifling weaknesses – as we all have. Mr Arnold Hope discovered minor discrepancies – most unpleasant – blackmailed unfortunate Mr Boodle into publishing and advertising his books as great works. Succeeded – " he added gloomily. "Books sold – Boodle man of great integrity – driven beyond endurance to depart these shores – with proceeds of autumn programme – lost them all – shot himself – bad for Boodle, bad for Boodle, Budd & Farthing – why tell anyone? So I let everyone continue to believe Mr Boodle still ran the firm." Mr Budd looked round hopefully. "Brilliant idea."

"But – "

"I say – " This time it was Clarence who interrupted Miss Mellidew. "Are you telling us all this yarn about Mr Boodle and authors' royalties was balderdash?"

"But – "

"Bad time in publishing," Gervase said apologetically. "Seemed best. Poor old Boodle. In his grave for twenty years."

"I am sorry to correct you," Miss Mellidew positively shrieked, "but Mr Boodle's corpse is not in his grave; it is in his office and very recently dead."

"It can't be, dear lady," Gervase beamed, much happier now all was explained.

"I fear you are overlooking the point, Mr Budd," Auguste intervened sharply. "Irrespective of Mr Boodle, Miss Mellidew claims to have seen a corpse."

"I did, I did – "

"And I shall investigate *now*."

"By Jingo, I'm behind you, sir," the General bellowed.

"By Jingo, so am I," Clarence declared enthusiastically. Publishing was obviously much more fun than writing sonnets in a garret.

Auguste wished he could share this youthful enthusiasm. Such abilities as he had in detection hung like an albatross around his neck. Alexis Soyer never had to contend with dead bodies while writing his *Gastronomic Regenerator*, nor had Eliza Acton stumbled across a corpse in her kitchen in the middle of *Modern Cookery*. Mrs Marshall's cookery school was not spiced with sudden death, or Brillat-Savarin interrupted in mid philosophical flow by the news that he was to don a detective's hat. He tried to persuade himself that Miss Mellidew was mistaken, that the man was merely stunned, but as he put his hand to the hitherto inviolate knob of Mr Boodle's door Auguste found his heart unaccountably fluttering. Life was seldom as simple as that, and death even more rarely so.

Behind him breathed his seconds in command, the General and Clarence, and lurking behind them the reluctant and ashen-faced Mr Budd and Miss Mellidew. The room was still and quiet. Books with heavy leather bindings stared gloomily from glass-fronted bookcases, dark blue velvet curtains shielded Mr Boodle from too close an inspection by the sun. A grandfather clock stood in one corner, silent now, as if stopped never to go again when Mr Boodle departed. On the floor the dark maroon carpet was alleviated by two skin rugs. Tiger-hunting not, presumably, having been a sport available to Mr Boodle, he had compromised with the skins of two bulldogs, heads and all, to guard their John Bull of British publishing.

Gervase Budd followed the direction of Auguste's eyes. "Mr Boodle's beloved Albert and Victoria," he explained faintly. "Mr Boodle was always one for a merry jest."

Auguste scarcely heard him. If there had been any doubt in his mind over Miss Mellidew's declaration, it had been dispelled. On the carpet by the fireplace was a portly elderly man, lying half on his side, half face down, and with a deep gash visible in his temple.

"I moved it," quavered Miss Mellidew. "I thought he was alive, you see. But there – there was no pulse." The memory overcame her, and she sank into a leather armchair. Auguste knelt over what he was already convinced was a corpse. Millicent Mellidew had been right. He stood up again, trembling slightly, wishing that men too had the privilege of sinking into chairs and being gently revived with smelling salts. Or preferably cognac.

"Miss Watkins" – seeing her with the redoubtable Wallace in the doorway – "pray make a telephone call to Scotland Yard and ask for Inspector Egbert Rose at my request, and the police doctor."

"Police?" shrieked Mr Budd.

"This is a sudden death," Auguste answered quietly.

"Accident. Think poor Boodle committed suicide by throwing himself on the corner of the fender, do you?" the General snorted disdainfully.

Auguste did not reply. Sometimes the albatross weighed heavier than at others. It probably *was* an accident he told himself firmly, fighting back the little niggle inside that had made him send for Egbert. There were tiny spots of blood on the shirt front that might, just might, have a different source than the wound on the temple.

Clarence had nervously come to stand at his side and looked down at the corpse. His eyes widened. His mouth fell open. "It's Arnold! It's not old Boodle at all." He ceased to be a "greenery-yallery, foot in the grave young man" and became the scared twenty-year-old he was inside. The General unceremoniously caught him as he fainted, and deposited him contemptuously in the adjoining chair to Miss Mellidew. With one cautious eye on the body, she waved her smelling salts under his nose and his revival was prompt if ungrateful.

"What did you do to him?" Clarence shouted at the unfortunate Mr Budd.

Gervase Budd shrank back. "Me?" he bleated. "I did nothing. Why should I cause harm to our favourite, beloved author? Our best-selling author," he added glumly, as the terrible truth began to strike home to him.

"He wasn't beloved by you, Budd. He was blackmailing you, he told me. He must have known about Boodle. That's why you've done for him. He was going to organize the protest this morning, unless you coughed up more royalties. Now I know why he wasn't there. Because he came to see you first."

Gervase regarded his budding poet with intense dislike.

"Is it true Arnold Hope was blackmailing you?" Auguste enquired gravely.

"Why else would I be publishing this dear boy's atrocious poems?" Gervase wailed.

Clarence fainted again, though an eye opened quickly at Auguste's next question. He had been delving deep in his memory of old scandals of which he had privileged knowledge from Egbert. "Didn't Hope leave England at much the same time as Oscar Wilde's trial, and on much the same issue?"

"Oh!"

"I beg your pardon, Miss Mellidew." Auguste turned instantly at her faint cry. "I forgot there was a lady present."

"If you mean was I his nancy, yes I was," Clarence shrieked. "I loved him. He loved me." Miss Mellidew's face turned an even sicklier hue.

"Dear Arnold's next work of art," Gervase remarked as if at random, "was to be entitled *My Nephew, My Friend*, a humorous book of recollections of travels on the Continent with his young friend Clarence, an ignorant and foolish young man whom he was able to instruct on the niceties of life. One might almost say the young man was to be held up to ridicule."

"It's not true," cried Clarence. "Arnold would never do such a thing. Our love is – was – too sacred."

"Sacred?" Miss Mellidew sat bolt upright, pink spots of anger in her pale cheeks. "How dare you profane the name of love, you – you – *criminal*." She burst into tears.

"Naturally *you* would say that," Clarence smirked.

There seemed to be remarkably little sympathy being shown for the late Arnold Hope, Auguste thought. Clarence was smug, Miss Mellidew self-righteous, and the General studiedly indifferent. Even the corpse of a stranger should arouse pity and shock, but here there seemed none. And if that were the case, it could only be because those present were thinking not of the corpse but of their own position. He decided not to pursue Clarence's comment for the moment, for he needed to reassess it in the light of his first reactions to his fellow prospective authors. Meanwhile he returned doggedly to fact. "If Mr Hope had been to see you, Mr Budd, what was he doing here, in Mr Boodle's room?"

"It was merely a social call he paid to me," Gervase gabbled, perceiving his drift and disliking it intensely.

"And then he came down here, fell over and died," Clarence jeered.

"I fear my port wine is a little on the strong side," Gervase Budd offered feebly. "No doubt it affected Mr Hope adversely. It is the best Oporto."

"Accident is highly probable," Auguste said diplomatically. "However since there is a slight possibility this unfortunate man did not die by accident, might I suggest we move downstairs, lock the front doors until the police arrive and ask all your staff to join us there."

"Ah. That may be difficult." Mr Budd looked sheepish.

"This poor fellow's dead, Budd. Surely you can afford to stop your staff working for a while?" the General roared. "Common decency, man."

"I think what Mr Budd means is that there is no staff," Auguste explained. "Is that not so?"

Gervase Budd nodded miserably.

"They *all* died twenty years ago?" squealed Miss Mellidew.

"Good God, you didn't murder the lot, did you?" snorted the General.

"They did not. I did not," Mr Budd replied with dignity.

"We saw them," Clarence pointed out.

"I rather think we saw the same man." Auguste glanced at Mr Budd who sulkily nodded. "Mr Simmonds, Mr Jones and Mr Catling were simply Mr Wallace in disguise, nimbly making use of the outside staircase provided for the event of fire, and climbing through windows." He had observed during their tour that while the hair and moustache changed colour, the three gentlemen all had a tiny ink blob in an identical position on their tall white linen collars.

"You run this whole show on your own?" the General demanded, astounded.

"No money for wages," Mr Budd explained miserably. "Publishing is going through a very bad time. Miss Watkins and Mr Wallace – most loyal." His voice trailed off, as he deemed this the appropriate moment to lead his band of increasingly unlikely additions to his future programme from Mr Boodle's desecrated office.

A quick examination after they left told Auguste no one had entered via Mr Boodle's window, which was firmly shut, and had

been these few years from the smell of the room. He forced himself
to look once more at the body, before leaving. In cookery one had to
select ingredients that complemented one another: in detection one
sought those that did not. Here were two such: the corpse and the
location.

Why had Arnold Hope come here? To meet Mr Boodle? Surely
Hope of all people must have been aware the room was untenanted.
Or had Gervase Budd fooled him too? Had there followed a quarrel
with Budd in this very room? And was it accident or murder? Did
his own fear of murder lead him to see it where it did not exist,
Auguste asked himself. Fortunately Egbert would shortly be here
to lift responsibility from him. Then conscience awoke. How often
had Egbert told him that the sight of sudden death often released
talkative tongues that later lost such agility. Now was the time to
lead and to listen. Later was the time for Egbert to judge.

The staff of Boodle, Budd & Farthing (Miss Watkins and Mr Wallace)
sat nervously on the edge of their chairs, unaccustomed to sitting in
the presence of authors, especially prospective ones – unlikely though
it now was that these four would be adding their lustre to the spring
programme.

"While we are waiting," Auguste began firmly, "we should establish our own arrival times, as well as Mr Hope's. What time was
his appointment with you, Mr Budd?" He invested just the correct
amount of authority in his tone.

"Eleven o'clock," Gervase supplied unhappily. "He was on time."

"Five minutes early," supplied Miss Watkins helpfully.

"You escorted him to Mr Budd's office, Miss Watkins?"

"Staffing arrangements did not permit." She avoided her employer's eyes in case he deduced a note of reproach.

"And what time did he leave, Mr Budd?"

"Shortly before you arrived," came the listless reply.

"And that was a quarter to twelve."

Miss Watkins nodded vigorously as if glad to help to exclude
Auguste from suspicion.

"I had a most friendly discussion with Mr Hope," Gervase
volunteered hopefully.

Clarence laughed in triumph. "That's not what he said." Revenge
was sweet, if ill-advised.

"*When* did he say that, Mr Popple?" Auguste asked mildly. Clarence
looked wildly around, as if pondering a further swoon.

"I meant darling Arnold was not *expecting* it to be a friendly
meeting."

"No. He was intending to tell the authors about Mr Boodle, wasn't he, if you refused to publish his next book on moral grounds?"

Sometimes guesswork succeeded, as Mr Budd's silence confirmed.

"And at what time did you arrive, Mr Popple?" Auguste switched attack.

"You should know. You were there."

"About ten minutes after you, Mr Didier," Mr Budd supplied, anxious to be helpful now the limelight had moved.

"I think not," declared Miss Watkins. "Mr Wallace, I distinctly remember this young man was here before Mr Didier. I thought he might *be* Mr Didier."

Auguste was not flattered. Messrs Wallace/Simmonds/Jones/Catling were in agreement, however. "As always you are correct, Miss Watkins."

"So where were you, Mr Popple?"

"In the closet," Clarence declared loudly. Miss Mellidew blushed at such bohemian frankness, then she looked puzzled.

"But – " She paused.

"Yes, Miss Mellidew?" Auguste prompted gently.

"Nothing." She pursed her lips.

"Please. It is necessary we should be frank, no matter the circumstances."

Millicent shut her eyes and whispered: "When I arrived, I visited the bathroom."

"And when was that?"

"She came in just after you," Miss Watkins supplied eagerly.

"Just a moment, madam." The General had been applying his thinking cap. "You went to the latrines after the tour round the house as well."

"Really, sir." Miss Mellidew looked ready to cry. "I am of a nervous disposition."

The General subsided, murmuring something about army manoeuvres and good training. Miss Mellidew stared into a future bleak with disgrace. So did Gervase Budd. At the very least he could expect Mildred's Missionary to escape unconverted.

"And you, General, arrived last. Just before twelve-fifteen, I recall."

"Before that," Wallace supplied gruffly.

"So where were you, sir?"

"Where do you blasted well think I was?" the General growled, caught out. "In the latrines."

Miss Mellidew bridled, her honour somewhat restored.

"So the intervals between your separate arrivals in the building and your entries into Mr Budd's office, were all spent in . . ." Auguste hesitated. How could he put this delicately? He abandoned the attempt. "All spent in the same closet on the first floor. Mr Popple was there from, say, 11.40 to about 11.55, Miss Mellidew from 11.50 to somewhere close to 12.10, and the General from 12.05 to almost 12.15."

"You are indelicate, sir," Miss Mellidew gasped.

"Unusual, to say the least, since I presume none of you noticed the others," Auguste continued regardless. "All of you in theory had time to visit Mr Boodle's office, as did Mr Budd, since we only have his word for it, as to when Arnold Hope left him." A bleat of protest escaped the unhappy publisher. "Now Miss Watkins, Mr Wallace, can you tell me where you were?"

They could. "Here," they said in unison. "Until the abusive mob arrived." Miss Watkins added as a solo contribution.

"And then?"

"Mr Wallace restrained them while I came to see you, and I restrained them on my return. I held them," she added in modest pride.

"And after they had left?"

"I remained downstairs while Mr Wallace – " She broke off, blushing.

"Carried out his amateur theatricals," the General barked.

Mr Wallace folded his arms, on behalf of Messrs Simmonds, Jones and Catling.

"And you were here alone?"

"Yes." Miss Watkins suddenly realized her vulnerable position. "But I would have been seen if I had come up to Mr Boodle's room," she cried in alarm.

"Calm yourself, Miss Watkins. We stood at the doorway to each room. There is no way you could have passed us unseen."

"Wallace could," Clarence pointed out. "He could have gone up to Mr Boodle's room and murdered poor Arnold before we opened Mr Simmonds' door."

Mr Steven Wallace stood up. "I, young sir, was a soldier, a sergeant in Her Majesty's Bloomin' Army, until injury to my health caused me to abandon my profession. In the service of Boodle, Budd & Farthing I have found contentment, even if it does involve jumping through windows like a blasted clown, begging your pardon, ladies. But I am forty-five years old and suchlike cavorting don't leave time for running up stairs and murdering old gentlemen like Mr Boodle."

"But it wasn't Mr Boodle," Clarence wailed.

"Or anyone else," Mr Wallace amended. He sat down, the victor.

"It certainly seems unlikely," Auguste broke the silence that fell, "that Mr Wallace would have any reason to murder – unless for the good of Boodle, Budd & Farthing. I feel, however, that there may be less altruistic reasons for some of us here to have wished to murder Mr Hope – assuming that to be the terrible case. You for instance, Mr Popple. It is quite possible that you saw Mr Hope leaving Mr Budd's office, and went with him into Mr Boodle's room for a private talk, knowing it was empty."

"No, I didn't," yelled Clarence. "And even if I did, what of it? He loved me."

"Hah!" Mr Budd muttered.

"Yes, Mr Budd?" Auguste turned to him.

"Normally," Mr Budd continued virtuously, "I would never publish such cruel, nay obscene material, but Mr Hope, as you pointed out, Mr Popple, was threatening to tell my authors about poor Mr Boodle. Mr Hope mentioned to me that you knew the content of his novel: he had told you yesterday."

"Rubbish. You're lying. It wasn't me. It was *her*," Clarence shrieked.

Miss Mellidew paled. "Goodness gracious, young man, why should I wish to murder Mr Boodle, let alone Mr Hope, anymore than would the General here?"

"Me, madam? I could have you shot for less."

"That would hardly help," Auguste intervened firmly. "And you did have the opportunity to kill Mr Hope. Also, a reason."

"Never met the fellow in my life."

"Not Mr Hope. But you would have assumed you were addressing Mr Boodle. You had no idea that Boodle died twenty years ago."

"Dash it, sir," the General spluttered.

"Mr Boodle had hung on to Mr Farthing's portion of the business, I deduce, thus denying your wife her rights." The General scowled but did not refute it.

"It was *her*," Clarence shouted again. "Why don't you listen?"

"I discovered the body. How dare you take advantage of a maiden lady, young man." Miss Mellidew dissolved into tears.

"You announced it on your second absence, yes. But earlier you had had as much opportunity to go into Mr Boodle's room as the gentlemen,' said Auguste implacably.

"Why should I wish to kill Mr Boodle?" she sobbed. "I had come to find a new publisher. Why should I wish to quarrel with its accountant?"

"Not Mr Boodle." Auguste hesitated, then plunged, taking a gamble. An irritated robin, an interesting use of the past tense where none was called for – trifling details in themselves, but now assuming a vital relevance. "But perhaps you had a reason for killing Arnold Hope."

"Of course she did, the old bat. How he laughed about her," Clarence jeered.

"I think," Auguste said gently, "you may have overheard a quarrel between Mr Popple and Mr Hope while you were on your way up to Mr Budd's office and recognized the voice. It was a quarrel that made their relationship quite clear. You saw Mr Popple leaving, very upset, and took your opportunity to speak your mind to Mr Hope."

"I am not a campaigner for moral purity, Mr Didier, whatever I may or may not have overheard." Tears rolled down her face and Miss Watkins solicitously produced a cambric handkerchief on behalf of the sisterhood of women.

"Not even," Auguste asked, "if heroes turned out to have such terrible feet of clay?"

"Oh." A gloved hand flew to her face.

"He was Lambkin, was he not, Sheikh Hamed, the Shining One, and you were Cecilia?"

She drew herself up. "You may not believe it, but I was considered a handsome girl."

"And the story of Cecilia is your own?"

"It is."

"And the four wives?"

"One wife only. In Balham, he told me. I believed it. But today I overheard the truth. The Lambkin whose memory I had treasured all these years was a degenerate. When Mr Popple left, I hurried in to confront him." She paused, then continued, "He jeered at me, and worse, he jeered at Cecilia, at the Shining One himself. He besmirched my dearest child." She bowed her head.

"So you murdered him," Clarence shouted. "My Arnold. My beloved."

"There is still Mildred, dear lady." Gervase rushed in, in case all was not yet lost.

"No." Her head shot up. "It was an accident. I was standing by Mr Boodle's desk. Lambkin was behind it. He said . . . he said he'd give me a taste of what I'd been missing all these years. I realized he was going to attack me, perhaps even kiss me. I could not bear it. I took out my hatpin, the mainstay of a woman's defence, so Mama instructed me. Keep away, I threatened, as he began to come round the desk towards me.

"He saw, was startled and then it happened. I don't know *what* happened though. There seemed to be a lot of noise and suddenly he fell against me. I moved aside, he grunted and toppled over, hitting the corner of the fender. I realized the hatpin was still in my hand, and, terrified, knew it had entered him. But there was a wound on his head too. My sheikh was dead. I could feel no pulse. Such a predicament, Mr Didier. Even Mildred has never had to face such horror."

"Miss Watkins," Auguste said gently, as she heaved with sobs, "would you attend to Miss Mellidew." He ran quickly upstairs again. Who could doubt her story? But something was still curdling this hollandaise.

He stared round the late Mr Boodle's office, trying to keep his eyes from the body and from Albert and Victoria, whose eyes seemed to follow him everywhere. They mocked him, the room mocked him for he knew the answer was buried here.

If Miss Mellidew had been standing here – he gingerly took his place at the side of the body – and he *fell* towards her, was he already dead? If so, how? He looked up. Death could not have dropped from the ceiling, nor did the dogs' heads stand up sufficiently to cause Arnold Hope to fall against the hatpin quite so heavily.

He walked behind Mr Boodle's desk, imagining himself Arnold Hope. No, not Arnold Hope. He imagined himself Mr Boodle repelling demands from unreasonable authors, at the mercy of blackmailers like Hope.

Mr Boodle was always one for a merry jest.

The bulldog heads . . . in a flash he was mentally in his kitchen with the finest dish in all the land: the boar's head . . . stuffing it with the finest ingredients, bringing it back by art to simulate life.

He was Mr Boodle, a man beset by problems, but who liked a merry jest; his hands reached out, rather as Mr Budd's had done on his own desk. His fingers found two knobs as he stood up. He pressed, he pulled. Suddenly the air was full of growls, dog growls; as he rushed round the desk he was in time to see Albert's head rearing up, full of air, baring its teeth, a fearsome sight. Had he been Arnold Hope, startled, he might well have tripped over the monstrosity, tumbled headlong into Miss Mellidew's hatpin, the weight of his falling body knocking the air from Albert once again.

He was in a world of illusion, Auguste told himself, and like all illusions these would have a practical explanation. No doubt Egbert's men would find some kind of drum and catgut arrangement in the desk to produce the growls, and pistons or compressed air or gas pipes to control the air supply to Albert. Perhaps even a primitive electrical contact.

Even as he studied it, he heard banging at the door downstairs, movement and familiar voices. Egbert had arrived. By the time he reached the doorway, Egbert was already racing up the stairs. He looked up and saw Auguste waiting.

"Accident, Auguste?"

"Murder. There is motive, means and opportunity."

"Got the murderer for me, have you?"

"I believe so."

There was a faint cry from Miss Mellidew below, listening, terrified.

"Who is it?"

"A gentleman called Boodle. Mr Boodle."

PART V
Holmes and Beyond

THE
PHANTOM PISTOL
Jack Adrian

*Jack Adrian (b. 1945) is a journalist and editor with an encyclope-
dic knowledge of genre fiction, particularly in the realms of mystery
and the supernatural. As a novelist he has produced* The Blood of
Dracula *(1977) as Jack Hamilton Teed, and probably more pseud-
onymous stories than you could shake a stick at. As an editor he
has compiled several very worthy anthologies, including* The Art
of the Impossible *(1990, with Robert Adey),* Detective Stories
from the Strand *and* Strange Tales from the Strand *(both
1991) and* The Oxford Book of Historical Stories *(1994, with
Michael Cox), as well as collections of lesser-known stories by Edgar
Wallace, Dornford Yates, Sapper, E. F. Benson, A. M. Burrage,
and Rafael Sabatini. His short fiction is less well known, so it is
a pleasure to resurrect this "impossible crime" story set in a foggy
London of 1912 and including that well-known solver of the impossible,
Mr H. . . .*

On this chill November night fog rolled up from the River
Thames, a shifting, eddying blanket that insinuated itself
inexorably through the grimy streets of central London. It pulsed
like a living thing, moved by its own remorseless momentum – for
there was no wind – great banks of it surging across the metropolis,
soot and smoke from a hundred thousand chimneys adding to its
murk. Within an hour from the moment the faint tendrils of a river
mist had heralded its approach, the fog, like a dirty-ochre shroud,
had entombed the city.

Here, in the heart of the metropolis, in High Holborn, the rattle
of hansom cab wheels, the raucous coughs of the newfangled petrol-
driven taxis, were muffled, the rumble of the crawling traffic stifled
as it edged and lurched its way along, the dim yellow light of street
lamps serving to obscure rather than illuminate. On the pavements,

slick with slimy dew, hunched figures, only dimly discerned, almost wraithlike, groped and shuffled along through the gloom, an army of the newly blind, snuffling and hawking at the harsh, choking reek of soot and coalsmoke.

Yet only fifty yards away from the main thoroughfare, down a narrow side street that had not changed appreciably since Dr Johnson's day, sodium flares fizzed and roared, powerful electric globes thrust back the muddy haze. For only a few feet, to be sure, yet enough to reveal the tarnished gilt portico of the Empire Palace of Varieties, a large poster outside announcing in bold scarlet lettering, two inches high, that here, and only here, were to be witnessed the dazzling deeds of the Great Golconda – illusionist *extraordinaire*!

Inside the theatre the atmosphere was just as miasmal, but here the fog was a blend of pungent penny cigars and the richer reeks of Larangas, Partagas, Corona-Coronas, and Hoyos de Monterrey, for the astonishing variety and ingenuity of the Great Golconda's baffling feats of prestidigitation fascinated the rich as well as the poor.

The Great Golconda was something of a democrat. He had consistently refused to perform in the gilded palaces that lined the Haymarket and Shaftesbury Avenue, preferring the smaller halls of the outer circuit. Thus whenever and wherever he appeared, rich men, dukes, earls, high-born ladies, and even (it was whispered) members of the Royal Family were forced to make the unaccustomed trek away from the gilt and glitter of London's West End to less salubrious haunts, there to mix with the lower orders – not to mention enjoy the unusual experience of paying half the price for twice the amount of entertainment. For certainly the Great Golconda was a magician and illusionist of quite extraordinary ability. It was even rumoured that emissaries of Maskelyne and Devant – whose fame as illusionists was spread worldwide – had endeavoured to lure his secrets away with fabulous amounts of money and, when these offers were spurned, had even gone so far as to try for them by less scrupulous methods.

Whether or not this was true, the Great Golconda stubbornly performed on the stages of the tattier music halls, and all kinds and conditions and classes of men and women flocked to see him, and to cheer him.

But tonight was a special night. The Great Golconda was retiring from the stage. This was to be positively his final performance.

Unusually, the act started the show. Normally, the Great Golconda and his assistant Mephisto came on for the last half hour of the first house and the last half hour of the second. As an act, nothing could follow it.

Tonight, however, the audience – restless at the thought of having to sit through the somewhat dubious hors d'oeuvres of jugglers, low comedians, soubrettes, and "Come-into-the-garden-Maud" baritones before getting down to the main course – sat up in eager anticipation as the curtain rose at last to reveal a totally bare stage with a black backcloth, from the centre of which stared two enormous eyes woven in green and gold.

For several seconds there was utter silence, a total absence of movement – on the stage and off. Then the lights dimmed and the glowing figure of the Great Golconda himself could be seen – in black silk hat, long flowing cloak, arms folded across his chest – descending slowly from the darkness above the stage, apparently floating on air. Simultaneously, two more Golcondas, dressed exactly alike, marched towards the centre of the stage from both left and right wings. Just before they met, there was a flash of white light, a loud bang, a puff of red smoke, and all three figures seemed to merge.

And there, standing alone, smiling a mite maliciously, stood the Great Golconda. The audience roared.

From then on, for the next twenty minutes, wonders did not cease.

White horses cantered across the boards, to disappear in a dazzling firework display; doves, peacocks, birds-of-paradise soared and strutted, all, seemingly, appearing from a small Chinese lacquered cabinet on a rostrum; a girl in sequinned tights pirouetted in midair, had her head sawn off by the Great Golconda's assistant Mephisto, then, carrying her head beneath her arm, climbed a length of rope and slowly vanished, like the smile of the Cheshire Cat, about thirty feet above the ground.

Part of the performance was what appeared to be a running battle between the Great Golconda and his assistant Mephisto. Mephisto made it plain he wanted to do things his way but invariably, like the sorcerer's apprentice, failed, the Great Golconda smoothly but sensationally saving the trick – whatever trick it happened to be – at the very last moment. Penultimately, Mephisto became so incensed at the Great Golconda's successes that he knocked him down, crammed and locked him into a four-foot-high oak sherry cask, and then proceeded to batter and smash it to pieces with a long-handled axe.

Triumphantly, he turned to the audience, his chalk-white, clown-like face (its pallor accentuated by the skin-tight black costume he wore, leaving only his face, neck, and arms below the elbows bare) leering malevolently – to be greeted by gales of laughter as the Great Golconda himself suddenly appeared from the wings behind him to tap him on the shoulder.

At last the stage was cleared for the final act. Mephisto was to fire a revolver at the Great Golconda, who would catch the bullet between his teeth.

Members of the audience were invited up to the front of the stage to examine the .45 service revolver and six bullets and vouch for their authenticity. Among them was a stocky, moustachioed man in his late forties, in frock coat and bowler hat, who clearly, from the professional way he handled the gun – flicking open the chamber, extracting the bullets, testing them between his teeth – had more than a little knowledge of fire-arms. The Great Golconda noticed this.

"You sir!"

The stocky figure acknowledged this with an abrupt nod.

"You seem to know your way about a pistol, sir."

"I should do," admitted the man.

"May I enquire of your profession, sir?"

"You may. I'm a superintendent at Scotland Yard."

The Great Golconda was clearly delighted. Seen close up he was younger than the Scotland Yard man had supposed – perhaps in his mid-thirties. Something else he noted was the distinct resemblance between the Great Golconda and his assistant Mephisto, now standing to one side, his pasty white face impassive.

"And your name, sir?"

"Hopkins. Stanley Hopkins."

The Great Golconda bowed.

"A name that is not unknown to me from the newssheets, sir. Indeed, a name to be – ha-ha! – *conjured* with! And what is your professional opinion of the revolver, Superintendent?"

Still holding the bullets, Hopkins dry-fired the gun. The hammer fell with a loud "click", the chamber snapped round.

"Perfectly genuine."

"Pree-*cisely!*"

With a flourish of his cape, the Great Golconda handed the revolver to his assistant Mephisto and ushered the half dozen or so members of the audience off the stage.

The lights dimmed. Twin spots bathed the two men in two separate cones of light. They stood at the rear of the stage, against the black backcloth, about ten yards apart. All around them was utter darkness. From his seat Hopkins watched intently.

Mephisto, wearing black gloves now and holding the gun two-handed, raised his arms slowly into the air, high above his head. Hopkins, following the movement could only just see the revolver, which was now above the circle of radiance surrounding Mephisto – then light glittered along the barrel as the assistant brought his hands back into the spotlight's glare and down, his arms held straight out. The revolver pointed directly at the Great Golconda.

It seemed to Hopkins that the Great Golconda's expression – up until then one of supercilious amusement – suddenly slipped. A look of mild puzzlement appeared on his face.

Hopkins glanced at the right-hand side of the stage but could see nothing but darkness. At that moment there was the oddly muted crack of a shot, and Hopkins, his eyes already turning back to the Great Golconda, saw the illusionist cry out and throw up his arms, then fall to the floor.

There was a stunned silence.

Even from where he was sitting, the Scotland Yard man could see plainly that around the Great Golconda's mouth were scarlet splashes, where none had been before.

Then the screaming started.

Mr Robert Adey, the manager of the Empire Music Hall, looked as though he was on the verge of an apoplexy. His face was red, his mouth gaped, his mutton-chop whiskers quivered with emotion.

He stuttered, "It . . . it *couldn't* have happened!"

"But it did," Superintendent Stanley Hopkins said bluntly.

They were on the stage of the now-empty theatre. Even with all the stagelights up and the crystal chandeliers blazing over the auditorium, there was a desolate air about the place; shadows still gathered thickly in the wings, and above, beams and struts and spars could only just be glimpsed.

Since the shocking death of the Great Golconda – whose body now lay under a rug where it had fallen – nearly an hour had elapsed. During that time an extraordinary fact had emerged: although the Great Golconda had been shot, his assistant Mephisto (now detained in his dressing room) could not have shot him. Of that, there seemed not a doubt.

And yet neither could anyone else.

Adey – with a slight West Midlands twang to his voice – gabbled, "It . . . it's utterly inexplicable!"

"This is 1912," said a sharp voice behind him. "*Nothing* is inexplicable."

Adey turned. The man who had spoken – a tall, thin, almost gaunt individual of sixty or so, with a high forehead, dark hair shot with gray, an aquiline nose, and eyes that seemed to pierce and probe and dissect all that they looked upon – had accompanied Hopkins up to the stage when the theatre had been cleared. Adey had no idea who he was.

"A colleague?" he muttered to the Scotland Yard man.

"Just a friend," said Hopkins, "a very old friend. We're both interested in the impossible – why we're here tonight. The Great Golconda's illusions had certain . . ." he glanced at his friend ". . . points of interest."

"Although many, I fancy, were accomplished with the aid of certain kinematic devices," said the older man. "The girl in the sequinned tights, for example – a lifelike image only, I take it."

Adey nodded uneasily.

"Of course, I know very little about how he managed his tricks. Magicians are a close-mouthed bunch. This one in particular. He was adamant that during his act both wings should be blocked off, so no one – not even the stagehands – could see what he was doing. Always worried people were trying to pinch his tricks. Of course, he had to have some assistance in erecting certain items on stage, but all the preliminary construction work was done by him and his brother."

"Mephisto," said Hopkins.

"Yes. Their real name was Forbes-Sempill. Golconda was Rupert, Mephisto Ernest. They were twins – not identical. Rupert was the elder by fifteen minutes . . ." Adey's voice sank to a worried mumble. "That was half the trouble."

"The reason why the Great Golconda was retiring from the stage?" said the gaunt man. "The baronetcy, and the £200,000?"

Adey stared at him, open-mouthed.

"How the devil did you know that?"

"Ah," Hopkins said waggishly, "my friend here keeps his finger on the pulse of great events – don't you, Mr H?"

The older man permitted himself a thin smile.

"Now *you* tell us about the baronetcy, and all them sovs," said the Scotland Yard detective.

Adey shrugged his shoulders.

"Both Rupert and Ernest had a row with their family years ago. Left the ancestral home – somewhere in Scotland, I believe – never," he smiled faintly, "to darken its doors again. But their father's recently died, and Rupert succeeded to the title, estates, and money. It's as simple as that, although it wasn't generally known."

"I take it," said the gaunt old man, "that Ernest disliked his brother?"

"Ernest *hated* Rupert. Made no secret of the fact. One of the reasons their act went down so well – Ernest communicated that hatred to the audience. Rupert didn't object. Said it added spice to the performance. I don't see it myself, but it seemed to work."

"Doubtless the new Viennese school of mind analysis could explain that," said the older man dryly, "but for the time being I am far more interested in why Mephisto should for no apparent reason have donned black gloves to fire his revolver tonight."

"So he did," said Adey, in a surprised tone. "But how . . .?"

"This is not the first time we have seen the Great Golconda perform. As Mr Hopkins implied, his act was an unusual one, and I have always had an interest in the more sensational aspects of popular culture." The gaunt old man's eyes took on a faraway, introspective look. "On previous occasions Mephisto fired his revolver bare-handed. That he did not this time seems to me to be a matter of some significance."

"But the *weapon*, Mr H.!" said Hopkins, almost violently. "We now know what ought to have happened. The real revolver is shown to the audience. It's stone-cold genuine. But when Golconda hands the gun to Mephisto – flourishing his cloak and all – he's already substituted it for another gun – one that only fires blank shots. The real gun is now hidden in his cloak. Mephisto fires the fake gun at him and he pretends to catch the bullet, which is already in his mouth, between his teeth. Simple!"

"Except that this time he falls dead with a bullet in his head."

"*From a phantom pistol!*" exploded Hopkins. "The gun Mephisto held in his hands didn't fire that bullet – *couldn't* fire that bullet! The real gun was still in the folds of the Great Golconda's cloak – so that's out, too! He wasn't killed by someone firing from the wings, because the wings were blocked off! Nor through the backcloth, because there ain't no hole! Nor from above or from the audience, because the bullet went into his head in a straight line through his mouth!"

Here Adey broke in excitedly.

"It's as I said – inexplicable! Indeed, downright *impossible*!"

The gaunt old man shot him a darkly amused look.

"In my experience, Mr Adey, the more bizarre and impossible the occurrence, the less mysterious it will in the end prove to be."

"That's all very well, sir," said the manager a mite snappishly, "but facts are facts! The entire audience was watching Mephisto. When Golconda fell dead, all Mephisto did was drop the revolver he was holding and stand there gaping. Let's say for the sake of argument he had another weapon. What did he do with it? Damm it, sir, he didn't move an inch from where he was standing, nor did he make any violent gesture, as though to throw it away from him. We've searched the entire stage. We've even searched him – not that that was at all necessary because his costume's so skin-tight you couldn't hide a button on him without it bulging."

"Perhaps," said the older man slowly, "he didn't need to throw it away."

"Didn't need?" Adey's voice rose to an outraged squeak. "You'll be telling me next he popped it into his mouth and ate it!"

"By no means as outrageous a suggestion as you might imagine," said the gaunt old man sternly. He turned to the Scotland Yard detective. "You will recall, Hopkins, the case of the abominable Italian vendettist, Pronzini, who did just that."

Hopkins nodded sagely. The older man began to pace up and down the stage, gazing at the sable backcloth.

"Notice how black it is," he murmured, gesturing at the curtain. "How very black . . ." He swung around on Adey again. "Apart from the incident of the gloves, is there anything else to which you might wish to draw our attention?"

"Anything else?"

"Anything unusual."

Adey's honest face assumed a perplexed expression.

"Well . . . no, I don't believe so."

"The placing of the Great Golconda's act, for example?"

"Oh. Why, yes! Right at the beginning, you mean? That was unusual. They did have a bit of a barney about that. It was Mephisto's idea – begin the show and end it, he said. Golconda finally agreed."

"Nothing else?"

"Not that I can . . ."

"I noticed that tonight they both stood at the rear of the stage. Did they not normally stand at the front?"

"Well, yes. Now you come to . . ."

"You will forgive my saying so, Mr Adey," there was a touch of asperity in the old man's voice, "but your powers of observation are somewhat limited."

"You believe Mephisto killed Golconda?" said Hopkins.

"I am convinced of it."

"Then we'd better have a chat with him."

The older man smiled frostily.

"That will not be necessary. You have a stepladder?" he enquired of Adey. "Bring it on."

"Stepladder?" muttered Hopkins. "You think there's something up top?"

"Of course. There has to be. A second gun. Golconda was killed by a bullet. Bullets, for the most part, are shot from guns. Golconda's revolver was incapable of shooting anything, only of making a noise. Thus . . ."

The Scotland Yard man interrupted. "Ah. But. Wait on, Mr H. These two were masters of illusion, am I correct?"

"Certainly."

"But when you get right down to it, their illusions, like all illusions, are fake. Created. Constructed."

"To be sure."

"So this here Mephisto needn't have used a gun at all. He was a clever fellow. Could've built some kind of weapon that fired a bullet, and . . ." He stopped as a thought struck him. "Here, remember the to-do you once had with that tiger-potting colonel. Now *he* had a special shooter."

"Indeed, an air-gun constructed by a German mechanic, who, though blind, had a genius for invention." The old man smiled a skeletal smile. "But you miss the point entirely, my dear Hopkins. It matters not *what* the weapon is, but *where* it is. That is the nub of the problem. We have searched everywhere, eliminated everything, on this level. As we must inevitably strike out from our enquiry any suggestion of magic, the inexorable conclusion we must come to is that the weapon – whatever it is – must be above us."

Hopkins struck the palm of his hand with a clenched fist. "But it can't be! Mephisto stood stock-still the whole time. We *know* he didn't chuck anything into the air."

"As I remarked before, perhaps he did not need to . . ."

By this time the heavy wheeled ladder had been trundled on and heaved to the centre of the stage. A stagehand climbed into the darkness above.

"Merely look for anything that seems out of the ordinary," the old man directed.

In less than a minute the stagehand was calling out excitedly.

"Something here . . . wound round one of the spars on – why, it's elasticated cord!"

"Unwind it. Let it drop."

Seconds later a small object fell through the air, then bounced upwards again as the cord reached its nadir. The old man stretched up and caught it before it could fly out of reach. He turned to the watchers.

"What do you see?"

Hopkins frowned.

"Not a thing."

The old man opened his fingers.

"Come closer."

The Scotland Yard detective stepped forward, his expression turning to one of amazement. Gripped in the gaunt old man's hand – clearly seen against the white of his skin – was a miniature chamberless pistol, perhaps five inches long from grip to muzzle, painted entirely matt-black. The old man pressed at the bottom of the stock and the barrel slid forward, revealing a two-inch cavity.

"A Williamson derringer pistol, capable of firing one shot only – quite enough to kill a man," said the old man dryly. "Hand me the false pistol."

He held the blank-firing pistol in his left hand with the derringer gripped in his right, levelling both at an imaginary target. From the side all that could be seen was the massive bulk of the service revolver. Then he clicked the triggers of both guns and opened his right hand. The derringer, at the end of the taut elasticated cord – totally invisible against the black backcloth – flew upwards into the darkness above, whipping round and round the high spar to which it was attached.

Adcy looked utterly at sea.

"But how did you . . . what made you . . .?" he babbled.

"When three singular variations in a set routine – the black gloves, the change of position not only of the act itself but of the two principals on the stage in that act – take place," said the old man a trifle testily, "one is tempted, to use the vernacular, to smell a rat. After that, it is a matter of simple deduction. The gift of observation – sadly lacking in the general populace – allied to intuition. Believe me, there is really no combination of events – however inexplicable on the surface – for which the wit of man cannot conceive an elucidation."

He began to pace up and down the stage again, his hands clasped firmly behind his back.

"Mephisto tied the derringer to the spar, letting it hang down just within reach of his outstretched arm. It could not be seen because he had painted it black and hung it close to the black curtain. In any case, the lighting was subdued. Even so, there was the risk of someone spotting it, so he persuaded his brother that their act should start the show. Came the climax of the performance. The two spotlights only lit up the area within their twin beams. Mephisto raised his arms, holding the false revolver, until his hands were just above the spotlight's glare. He had positioned himself perfectly – no doubt he rehearsed the entire sequence thoroughly – and the hanging derringer was now within inches of his right hand. If his hands had been bare, one might possibly have noticed that he was holding something else, but he took the precaution of wearing black gloves, thereby making assurance double sure. Grasping the derringer, he pulled it down on its elasticated thread, pressing it to the side of the much larger weapon, as his arms dropped to the levelled-off position. He was now holding not one, but *two* guns – one hidden from the audience's view and in any case virtually invisible. Except to the man at whom he was pointing them."

"Yes!" snapped Hopkins. "That's what made Golconda look surprised. I thought he'd seen something *behind* Mephisto."

"Mephisto then fired the derringer, releasing his grip on the gun, which shot up into the air. All eyes were on Golconda falling to the floor. The derringer wound itself round the spar to which its cord was attached. In the confusion afterwards, doubtless, Mephisto meant to get rid of the evidence. What he did not reckon on was the presence of a Scotland Yard detective who would immediately take charge of the proceedings and confine him to his dressing room. But in the meantime there was absolutely nothing to show that he had just murdered his brother in cold blood. It was as though," the old man finished, shrugging, "the Great Golconda had indeed been shot with a phantom pistol."

"And being next in line," said Hopkins, "Mephisto would've stepped into the baronetcy and all them lovely golden sovs. Nice work, Mr H. Nice work, indeed!"

THE ADVENTURE OF THE FRIGHTENED GOVERNESS
Basil Copper

In 1929 the young August Derleth wrote to Sir Arthur Conan Doyle to enquire whether there would be any more stories featuring Sherlock Holmes. When Doyle replied that there would not, Derleth determined to write some himself, but to avoid any charge of plagiarism, he created his alternative Holmes and Watson, Solar Pons and Dr Lyndon Parker. Pons operated out of lodgings in Praed Street, London, and the stories are firmly set in the 1920s. Because they were contemporary with Derleth's original creation they are not classed as historical detective stories. However after Derleth's death, the Solar Pons stories were continued by British writer Basil Copper. Copper has been a prolific writer of American private-eye thrillers, with his long-running series featuring Los Angeles detective Mike Faraday. But he is also a noted writer of horror stories, and has blended the themes before in his wonderfully gothic mystery novels Necropolis *(1977) and* The Black Death *(1991). Copper has now written six volumes of stories about Solar Pons and the wordage probably exceeds Derleth's. The stories are usually longer and more menacing, and are an even closer imitation of Holmes than Derleth's originals. In my previous volume some readers queried why I had drawn the line at the end of the last century and not included stories from the start of this century. Strictly speaking I did. My definition of a historical mystery had been a story set in the years before the author's birth. Well, most of the Pons stories are set in the early 1920s and as Basil Copper was not born until 1924 they just squeeze in. So we end with a rousing tribute to Sherlock Holmes.*

I

"Wake up, Parker! It is six o'clock and we have pressing matters before us."

I struggled into consciousness to find the night-light on at the side of my bed and Solar Pons' aquiline features smiling down at me.

"Confound it, Pons!" I said irritably. "Six o'clock! In the morning?"

"It is certainly not evening, my dear fellow, or neither of us would have been abed."

I sat up, still only half-awake.

"Something serious has happened, then?"

Solar Pons nodded, his face assuming a grave expression.

"A matter of life and death, Parker. And as you have been such an assiduous chronicler of my little adventures over the past years, I thought you would not care to be left out, despite the inclement hour."

"You were perfectly correct, Pons," I said. "Just give me a few minutes to throw on some things and I will join you in the sitting-room."

Pons rubbed his thin hands briskly together with suppressed excitement.

"Excellent, Parker. I thought I knew my man. Mrs Johnson is making some tea."

And with which encouraging announcement he quitted the room.

It was a bitterly cold morning in early February and I wasted no time in dressing, turning over in my mind what the untimely visitor to our quarters at 7B Praed Street could want at such a dead hour.

I had no doubt there was a visitor with a strange or tragic story to tell or Pons would not have disturbed me so untimely, and as I knotted my tie and smoothed my tousled hair with the aid of the mirror, I found my sleepy mind sliding off at all sorts of weird tangents.

But when I gained our comfortable sitting-room, where the makings of a good fire were already beginning to flicker and glow, I was not prepared for the sight of the tall, slim, fair-haired girl sitting in Pons' own armchair in front of the hearth. The only indication of anything serious afoot was the paleness of our visitor's handsome features. She made as though to rise at my entrance but my companion waved her back.

"This is my old friend and colleague, Dr Lyndon Parker, Miss Helstone. I rely on him as on no other person and he is an invaluable helpmate."

There was such obvious sincerity in Pons' voice that I felt a flush rising to my cheeks and I stammered out some suitable greeting as the tall young woman gave me her cool hand.

"A bitterly cold morning, Miss Helstone."

"You may well be right, Dr Parker, but I must confess my mind is so agitated that I have hardly noticed."

"Indeed?"

I looked at her closely. She did not seem ill but there was an underlying tension beneath her carefully controlled manner which told my trained eye there was something dreadfully wrong.

There was a measured tread upon the stair and the bright, well-scrubbed features of our landlady, Mrs Johnson, appeared round the door. She was laden with a tray containing tea things and as I hastened to assist her I caught the fragrant aroma of hot, buttered toast.

"I took the liberty of preparing something for the young lady to sustain her on such a cold morning."

"Excellent, Mrs Johnson," said Pons, rubbing his thin hands. "As usual, you are a model of thoughtfulness."

Our landlady said nothing but the faint flush on her cheeks showed that the deserved praise had not gone unnoticed. She hastened to pour out the tea and after handing a cup to Miss Helstone with a sympathetic smile, quietly withdrew.

"Will you not draw closer to the fire, Miss Helstone?"

"I am perfectly comfortable here, Mr Pons."

"You have come from out of London, I see?"

"That is correct, Mr Pons."

Pons nodded, replacing his cup in the saucer with a faint clink in the silence of the sitting-room.

"I see a good deal of mud on your boots which means you have been walking on an unmade road."

"It is a fair stretch to the station, Mr Pons, and I was unable to get transport at that time of the morning."

"Quite so, Miss Helstone. You are not more than an hour out of town, I would surmise. Surrey, perhaps?"

Our client's surprise showed on her face as she took fastidious little sips at the hot tea.

"That is correct, Mr Pons. Clitherington, a small village on the Redhill line."

Solar Pons inclined his head and favoured me with a faint smile as he bent forward in his armchair.

"That light, sandy soil is quite unmistakable, Parker. You no doubt noticed, as did I, a distinctive sample on the seams of the young lady's right boot."

I cleared my throat, caught unawares with a piece of toast halfway down.

"Now that you point it out, Pons, certainly."

"It is obviously something serious that brings you to us at this hour, Miss Helstone, and you have already told me it is a matter of life and death. You are equally obviously agitated beneath your calm manner. Please take your time. You are among friends."

The young woman drew in her breath with a long, shuddering sigh.

"That is good to know, Mr Pons. It has indeed been quite unbearable this last day or two. And affairs at the house . . ."

"You live there with your parents?" interrupted Pons.

The young woman paused and made an engaging little contraction of her mouth.

"I beg your pardon, Mr Pons. I am telling the story very badly. I am engaged as a governess at The Priory, Clitherington, the home of Mr Clinton Basden."

Solar Pons tented his thin fingers before him and gave our fair client his undivided attention.

"So far as I know, Miss Helstone, there is no train on the time-table which leaves a remote place like Clitherington at such an hour as 4.30 a.m."

Miss Helstone gave a faint smile, the first sign of returning normality she had evinced since I had entered the room.

"That is correct, Mr Pons. I came up on the milk train. There are always two carriages used mainly by railway staff and I found an empty compartment."

"So that the matter is one of the utmost gravity. Pray continue."

"My full name is Helen Jane Helstone, Mr Pons, and I come of a good family originally settled in the West Country. My parents were killed in a local uprising in India some years ago and after I had completed my schooling in England it became necessary to earn my living. I enjoy the company of children and so I became a governess with a view to entering a teacher-training college when I am a little older."

"What is your age now, Miss Helstone?"

"I am just turned twenty-one, Mr Pons."

Solar Pons nodded and looked thoughtfully at the girl, who had now recovered the colour in her cheeks. She looked even more handsome than before and I found the contemplation of her most engaging but turned again to the tea and toast, aware of Pons' glance on me.

"I give this information, Mr Pons, so that you shall know all of the salient circumstances."

"You are telling your story in an admirable manner, Miss Helstone."

"I had two positions, Mr Pons, one in Cornwall and another in Cumberland, which I held for several years, but I decided to move nearer to London and when I saw Mr Basden's advertisement in a daily newspaper, Surrey seemed ideal for my purposes and I hastened to answer his announcement."

"When was that, Miss Helstone?"

"A little over three months ago, Mr Pons."

Our visitor paused again and sipped at her tea; her face was thoughtful as though she were carefully contemplating her next words but my professional eye noted that her breathing was more regular and she was becoming calmer by the minute.

"There was something extremely strange about my engagement as governess, Mr Pons. I have often thought about it since."

"How was that, Miss Helstone?"

"For example, Mr Pons, it was extraordinarily well-paid, though the duties are somewhat unusual."

Pons nodded, narrowing his deep-set eyes.

"Pray be most explicit, Miss Helstone."

"Well, Mr Pons, I have no hesitation in telling you that the salary is some five hundred pounds a year, payable quarterly in advance."

Pons drew in his breath in surprise and I gazed at him open-mouthed.

"That is indeed princely for these times, Miss Helstone. I should imagine there would have been quite a few ladies in your position after the appointment."

"That is just it, Mr Pons. There were literally queues. I met some people on the train who were answering the advertisement. Apparently it had been running in the daily newspapers for more than a week."

"That is highly significant, Parker," put in Pons enigmatically and he again resumed his rapt study of Miss Helstone's face.

Our client went on breathlessly, as though some reserve had been breached by the confidence my friend inspired in her.

"My heart sank, Mr Pons, as you can well imagine, but as the train stopped at Clitherington, my spirits rose again. You see, I had heard one of the girls say that though the announcement had been running for some time, the prospective employers were very fastidious and no-one had yet been found to suit them."

"And as you already had experience of two similar appointments, you had high hopes?"

"Exactly, Mr Pons. But my spirits were dashed when we arrived at the house. A large car had been sent to the station to meet applicants and we were taken to a vast, gloomy mansion, set in an estate whose main entrance was locked and guarded by heavily-built men."

"An odd circumstance, Miss Helstone," said Pons, glancing quizzically at me.

"You may well say so, Mr Pons. But though the grounds, with their great clumps of rhododendron and pine plantations were gloomy and sombre indeed in that bleak December weather, the interior of the mansion was extremely luxurious and well appointed, evincing the most refined taste. It was evident that the prospective employer was a man of enormous wealth."

"And of fastidious nature if it took him so much time to select a governess for his children, Miss Helstone. How many were there, in fact?"

"Two, Mr Pons. A boy and a girl, aged nine and twelve respectively. But my heart sank again, when we were shown into a sumptuously furnished drawing-room to find between twenty and thirty young ladies already there."

"It sounds more like a theatrical producer's office, Pons," I could not resist observing.

Solar Pons gave me a faint smile and his eyes held a wry twinkle.

"Ah, there speaks the sybarite in you, Parker. The lover of night life, good wine and chorus girls."

"Heavens, Pons!" I stammered. "What will Miss Helstone think of me?"

"That you are a poor recipient of waggish remarks at your own expense, my dear fellow. But we digress."

Miss Helstone had smiled hesitantly at this little exchange, revealing two rows of dazzling white teeth.

"Well, there is a great deal of truth in Dr Parker's remark, Mr Pons," she said earnestly. "It did in truth look like a theatrical agency, though they are a good deal shabbier as a rule. But the most extraordinary thing was the proceedings. A hard-faced woman in black beckoned to the first girl as I sat down and she disappeared through the big double doors. In less than a minute she was back, with an angry shake of the head."

Miss Helstone put down her cup and leaned forward in her chair, regarding my companion with steady grey eyes.

"Mr Pons, five of the applicants went in and out of that room in five minutes and it was obvious by their angry expressions that none of them were suited. But even more extraordinary – and I learned this afterwards – each and every one was given a new five pound note for her trouble, a car to the station and a free railway ticket to London."

Solar Pons clapped his hands together with a little cracking noise in the silence of the sitting-room.

"Excellent, Parker!" said he. "This gets more intriguing by the minute, Miss Helstone. There is more, of course."

"Much more, Mr Pons. Of course, I got most intrigued as the minutes went by and the girls disappeared into the room. Those of us who were left moved up and fresh arrivals sat down behind us. Now and again there would be loud exclamations from behind the door and it was obvious as I got closer and closer to the double-doors guarded by the woman in black, that none of the girls had been found suitable by the mysterious advertiser. I did not, of course, at that stage, know the name of my employer, Mr Pons, as it was not given in the advertisement."

"I see. It was a box number?"

"Exactly, Mr Pons."

I got up at Pons' glance and re-filled the tea-cups for all of us.

"But I was within three places of the door before a girl came out with whom I had travelled down from London. She was angry and had a heavy flush on her cheeks. She came across to me and had time for a few words before the woman, who was letting in a new applicant, came back. She said she was not asked for references or even any questions. A tall, dark woman was sitting at a desk and she looked at someone obviously sitting behind a heavy screen who was concealed from the applicant. He must have had some method of observing the candidate but in every case the answer had been no, for the woman merely nodded and said that the interview was closed. My informant said she was merely asked her name, address and if it were true that she was an orphan. It was obvious that even these questions were a mere formality."

"An orphan, Miss Helstone?"

Solar Pons had narrowed his eyes and on his face was the alert expression I had noted so often when moments of great enterprise were afoot.

"Why, yes, Mr Pons. That was one of the stipulations of the advertisements. I have one here in my handbag. Another requirement was that applicants should be single or widows."

"Sounds most peculiar, Pons," I put in.

"Does it not, Parker?"

Solar Pons glanced at the newspaper cutting Miss Helstone had passed to him and read it with increasing interest.

"Just listen to this, Parker."

He smoothed out the cutting on the table in front of him and read as follows:

YOUNG GOVERNESS REQUIRED FOR TWO SMALL
CHILDREN IN HOME OF WEALTHY SURREY WID-
OWER. LARGE MANSION, CONGENIAL SURROUND-
INGS. DISCRETION ESSENTIAL, MANY ADVANTAGES.
SALARY £500 PER ANNUM. NO-ONE OVER THIRTY
NEED APPLY. REPLY INITIALLY IN WRITING AND
WITH TWO REFERENCES. THE POSITION IS FOR
THE BENEFIT OF ORPHANED YOUNG LADIES ONLY.
BOX 990.

Solar Pons frowned and looked at me quizzically.

"Extraordinary, is it not, Parker? I am obliged to you, Miss
Helstone. Despite my enthusiasm for bizarre cuttings, this is something I missed. There are a number of unusual points, Parker."

"Indeed, Pons. The orphan stipulation is strange, to say the
least."

"And tells us a great deal," said Solar Pons slyly. "Coupled with
the lavish inducements it indicates a certain line of thought. What
happened at your own interview, Miss Helstone?"

Our visitor put down her tea-cup and wiped her mouth fastidiously
with a small lace handkerchief, waving away my proffered plate
of toast.

"That was the most extraordinary thing of all, Mr Pons. Within
thirty minutes of my arrival at The Priory, thirty applicants had
passed through those doors and then it was my turn. It was a large,
though quite ordinary room, except for a circular window high up,
which made it a dark, shadowy place. There was a desk underneath
the window and a desk lamp alight on it, which threw the light
forward on to a chair placed in front of the desk.

"A dark-haired, pleasant-looking woman with a Central European
accent asked me to sit down and then put to me some perfunctory
questions. I naturally observed the large, heavy screen to the right of
the desk and was then startled to see, in an angled mirror placed so
as to favour my place on the chair, the reflections of a man's bearded
face, with eyes of burning intensity."

II

There was another long pause which I employed in re-filling my
tea-cup. Miss Helstone leaned back in her chair and put out her
hands to the fire, which was now blazing cheerfully.

"Some signal must have passed between the two because the woman at the desk gave a relieved smile and, as though making the decision herself, informed me that the position was mine. She called me over to another table in the corner and asked me to sign a document. I just had time to see that this asserted that I was an orphan, specified my age and verified my references, before I heard a door close softly somewhere. I was sure that the man behind the screen had quitted the room, Mr Pons, and when we went back to the desk I could see that a chair placed behind the screen was empty."

Solar Pons rubbed his hands briskly.

"Admirable, Miss Helstone. This is distinctly promising. I may point out, by the way, that the document you signed has no legal standing whatsoever."

The girl smiled.

"I am glad to hear you say so, Mr Pons. But that is the least of my worries. You may imagine the consternation and dismay among the young ladies in the ante-room when they heard the position was filled. I was astonished when Mrs Dresden, the dark-haired woman, whom I then learned was the housekeeper, said I should start on my duties at once. But I prevailed upon her to let me return to my old employers to collect my luggage and to inform them of my new post, though even then they insisted on sending me by chauffeur-driven car in order to save time."

"You did not think this at all strange, Miss Helstone?"

"Strange indeed, Mr Pons, but the salary was so princely that I did not hesitate, I was so excited."

"So you left The Priory without seeing your future charges?"

"That is correct, Mr Pons. I was told the children were on holiday and would not be back until the following Monday.

"When I returned I was a little perturbed to see that the grounds were patrolled by similar men to those at the main gate and I realized then that I would not be free to get out and about as I had hoped and in the manner I had become used to in my other situations."

"You met this mysterious Mr Basden?"

"Almost at once on my return, Mr Pons. He was quite an ordinary little man, an Englishman obviously, and rather ill at ease, I thought, among the foreign-sounding employees among his retinue."

Solar Pons tented his fingers and stared at me sombrely.

"Does not that strike you as strange also, Parker?"

"Perhaps he had served in India, Pons?"

Solar Pons shook his head with a thin smile.

"I believe the young lady referred to Central Europeans, Parker."

"That is correct, Mr Pons. There were other extraordinary requirements in my new duties also. For example, I was asked by the housekeeper to leave my own clothes in my room. She supplied me with a new wardrobe. They were very expensive clothes, Mr Pons, but I had no objection, of course."

"Indeed," I put in.

"But then Mrs Dresden asked me to put my hair up in a different style and gave me expensive jewellery to wear. I was a little apprehensive in case I lost any but was told not to worry as Mr Basden was a very wealthy man. I was given the run of the magnificent house and was told I would be treated as a member of the family.

"I dined with Mr Basden that evening and my impression of him being ill at ease in his own house was reinforced. He said little and after two days at The Priory I knew very little more about the post than when I arrived. I noticed one other odd thing, also. I could go almost anywhere I liked in the house, but there was a wing stretching off the main landing. I was forbidden to go there by Mrs Dresden, as it was private.

"But I could not help seeing what went on, Mr Pons. There were disturbances in the night once and I have seen what looked like nurses with trays of medicine. One morning also I surprised a tall, dark man on the stairs, with a little black bag. He looked grave and I was convinced he was a doctor."

Solar Pons leaned forward and his deepset eyes stared steadily at the tall, fair girl.

"Just what do you think is in that wing, Miss Helstone?"

"Some sort of invalid, evidently, Mr Pons. I did not enquire, naturally."

Solar Pons leaned back again in his chair and half-closed his eyes.

"And you have not seen the bearded man again since that first accidental glimpse at the interview?"

"Not at all, Mr Pons. I had another shock when my two charges arrived. The children were attractive enough, but their voices were low and husky and I was told by Mrs Dresden they had colds. They seemed rather odd and sly and I was completely non-plussed when I found that neither spoke a word of English."

Solar Pons gave a low chuckle.

"Excellent, Miss Helstone."

The fair girl stared at my companion with very bright eyes.

"And what is more, Mr Pons, I am convinced their father cannot speak their language either!"

"Better and better, Parker."

Miss Helstone stared at my companion in astonishment.

"I do not follow you, Mr Pons."

"No matter, Miss Helstone. What was the next thing that happened in this extraordinary ménage?"

"Well, it was obvious, Mr Pons, that I could not begin to conduct any lessons. When I pointed this out to Mrs Dresden she said it was of no consequence as they had a tutor in their own tongue. I would be required for companionship; to take them on walks in the grounds; on motor-rides and to control their deportment."

"An unusual list of requirements and one which apparently commands a salary of five hundred pounds, Parker," said Pons, a dreamy expression on his face. "It gives one pause to think, does it not?"

"My words exactly, Pons."

"And when you hear that the walks were mostly conducted at night in the floodlit grounds of The Priory, you will begin to realize my perplexity, Mr Pons."

My companion's eyes had narrowed to mere slits and he leaned forward, an intent expression on his face.

"The grounds were floodlit, Miss Helstone? And the walks were how many times a week?"

"About three times on average, Mr Pons. Between ten o'clock and midnight."

"Unusual hours for small children, Parker."

"There is something wrong somewhere."

"For once you do not exaggerate, my dear fellow."

"The last three months have been strange ones for me, gentlemen," said our visitor, whose paleness had gone and whose natural vivacity had evidently returned, for her eyes were sparkling and her manner more animated.

"I took occasional meals with my employer; walked or drove with the children; read and played patience. I soon found that I was not allowed outside the gates alone, but I have learned that the art treasures in the house are so valuable that Mr Basden is scared of burglars. I myself think he is afraid that his employees will be approached by criminal elements, for he insists that if one goes outside, then one does not go alone."

"Another curious circumstance which gives one much food for thought," observed Solar Pons.

"This was the odd routine of my life until a few weeks ago," Miss Helstone continued. "The people in the house were kind to me and I was well treated, but I felt circumscribed; almost imprisoned. The sealed wing was still barred to me and medicines and medical staff were in evidence from time to time, but nothing was explained and I did not think it circumspect to ask. But there was another peculiar circumstance; my employer does not smoke, or at least I have never seen him do so, yet I have on several occasions smelt strong cigar smoke in the children's room when I go to collect them for their walks. On one occasion there was a half-smoked cigar end on the window sill and the little girl looked distinctly uneasy. I myself think that the bearded man had something to do with it."

Solar Pons looked searchingly at the girl.

"You think he may be the real father and not Mr Basden?"

Miss Helstone looked astonished.

"Those were my exact thoughts, Mr Pons! You see, there is no genuine resemblance to Mr Basden and the man with the beard had a foreign look."

"You may have stumbled on to something, Miss Helstone," Pons went on. "It is a most intriguing tangle that you have described. But you mentioned life and death?"

The girl swallowed once or twice and her eyes looked bleak.

"Twice in the past fortnight we have been accosted on our walks abroad, by strange, bearded men in a car. They spoke first to the children and then became very excited when I approached. I could swear they were all speaking the same language together. Yesterday a big black car tried to force ours off the road near Clitherington when we were out driving. Our chauffeur accelerated and drove back to the estate like a madman. We were all considerably shaken, I can tell you."

"Mr Basden was informed of this?"

"At once. He looked white and ill and came down to apologize to me immediately."

Solar Pons pulled once or twice at the lobe of his right ear and looked at me quizzically.

"Which brings us to the early hours of the morning, Miss Helstone."

"I was walking in the grounds with the children last night, Mr Pons. They sleep much during the day and their parent does not seem to mind their nocturnal habits. We had left the floodlit portion and followed the drive as it curved around. It was nearly midnight or a little after and we were about to turn back when there was a shot. It gave me such a shock, Mr Pons! The bullet glanced off a tree-trunk only a few feet from my head. I could hear guttural cries and I told the children to run."

"Highly commendable, Miss Helstone," I put in.

"Unfortunately, in their panic to escape they ran toward the voices," the girl went on. "Naturally, I had to go after them as they were my charges. We all got lost in the darkness, blundering about. I heard two more shots and then the same guttural voices I had heard from the men who had questioned the children on the road. I was so frightened, Mr Pons, that I hid. I must have been in the woods for hours.

"I found myself in an unfamiliar part of the grounds; it was dark and cold and I did not know what to do. I was in an absolute panic. I had abandoned my charges, you see, and I did not know what might have happened to them. I could not face Mr Basden. I found a small wicket-gate in the wall, which was unlocked; it may even have been used by the men to gain entrance to the grounds. Anyway, Mr Pons, to bring a long and exceedingly rambling story to an end, I ran from The Priory and caught the milk train. I had read your name in the newspapers some months ago as being the country's greatest private detective so here I am to put my destiny in your hands."

III

Here our client paused and looked so appealingly at Pons that I could not forbear saying, "There, do not distress yourself further, little lady," while Pons himself looked at me disapprovingly.

"While deploring Parker's sentimental way of expressing it, I am in great sympathy with you, Miss Helstone. I have no hesitation in saying I will accept your case."

"Oh, thank you, Mr Pons."

Helen Helstone rose from her chair and shook Pons' hand warmly. Pons looked at me interrogatively.

"Are you free, Parker?"

"Certainly, Pons. I have only to telephone my locum."

"Excellent."

He turned back to Miss Helstone.

"We must make arrangements to get you back to The Priory as soon as possible, Miss Helstone."

"Go back?"

Dismay and apprehension showed on the girl's face.

"It is the only way. We all want to know what went on there and I must confess I have not been so intrigued for a long while. And Parker and I will be with you."

"How are we going to manage that, Pons?" I said. "Considering that the estate is so well guarded."

"Tut, Parker," said Pons severely. "We have found Miss Helstone upon the road in the early hours of the morning when we were driving through the district, brought her home with us and are now returning her to her employer. The man Basden will have to see us. If there are such strange goings-on at his estate he will deem it imperative to discover just exactly what the outside world knows."

"Of course, Pons. I follow you."

Pons turned to our visitor.

"Do you feel up to it, Miss Helstone?"

"If you gentlemen will accompany me, Mr Pons."

"That is settled, then."

The girl looked ruefully at her bedraggled coat and her muddied boots.

"If you will give me an hour or so, Mr Pons, I must get to the shops and purchase a few things."

"Certainly, Miss Helstone. If you will give me your parole?"

"I do not understand, Mr Pons."

"If you will promise to come back within the hour."

Our visitor flushed and glanced from Pons to me.

"Of course, gentlemen. I am over my fright now and am as anxious as you to know what is happening at Clitherington."

"Very well, then."

Pons looked at his watch.

"It is a quarter past eight now. Shall we say ten o'clock at latest."

"I will be here, Mr Pons."

When I returned from showing our visitor to the front door Pons was pacing up and down in front of the fireplace, furiously shovelling blue smoke from his pipe over his shoulder.

"This beats everything, Pons," I said. "I have never come across such an extraordinary story."

"Does it not, Parker? What do you make of it? Let us just have your views."

"Well, Pons," I said cautiously. "I hardly know where to begin. There is something curious, surely, about the high salary being paid to this young lady for her purely nominal duties."

"You have hit the crux of the matter, Parker. Inadvertently, perhaps, but part of the central mystery, certainly."

"Ah, I am improving then, Pons," I went on. "But I confess that I cannot see far into this tangle. The children who speak a different language from their father; the nocturnal habits of such

young people; the invalid in the sealed wing; the heavily guarded
estate; the floodlit promenades. And who is the bearded man who
sat behind the screen?"

Solar Pons took the pipe from between his strong teeth and looked
at me with piercing eyes.

"Who indeed, Parker? You have retained the salient points
admirably and isolated the most important. You are at your
most succinct, my dear fellow, and it is evident that my little lessons in the ratiocinative process have not been entirely
lost."

"Let me have your views, Pons."

"It is foolish to theorize without sufficient data, Parker. But I
see a few features which must resolve themselves with determined
application. It is obvious why Miss Helstone was engaged but I
would rather not speculate further at this stage."

"It is far from obvious to me, Pons," I said somewhat bitterly.

"Well, well, Parker, I am sure that if you employ your grey matter
to good advantage, the solution will soon come to you."

And with that I had to be content until Pons returned from some
mysterious errand of his own. I had just telephoned my locum when
I heard his footstep upon the stair.

"I have hired a car, my dear fellow. If you will just step round to
the garage in the next street and familiarize yourself with its controls,
we will make our little expedition into the wilds of Surrey. Ah, here
is Miss Helstone now."

Our client's step was light and she looked transformed as
Mrs Johnson showed her into the sitting-room.

"I am quite ready now, Mr Pons."

Pons looked at her approvingly.

"Good, Miss Helstone. There are just a few preparations more. I
have our plan of campaign mapped out. Parker, you will need your
revolver."

"Revolver, Pons?"

"Certainly. I do not think the danger lies within the house. But
the gentlemen who broke into the grounds appear to me to be an
entirely different quantity altogether. Is there a tolerable inn in this
village of Clitherington, Miss Helstone?"

"The Roebuck is very well spoken of, Mr Pons."

"Excellent. We shall make that our headquarters, Parker."

I fetched my revolver and packed it in my valise. When I returned
from the garage with the car, Pons and Miss Helstone were at the
door of 7B in conversation with Mrs Johnson, Pons well supplied
with travelling rugs, for the day was a bitter one indeed. There

was the usual tangle of traffic in town but I think I acquitted myself rather well, losing my way only once at a major junction, and we were soon well on the way to Surrey, the engine humming quietly while Pons and Miss Helstone, in the rear seats, conversed in low tones.

We arrived in the village of Clitherington about midday, smoke ascending in lazy spirals from the chimneys of the cluster of red-roofed houses which comprised the hamlet. As Miss Helstone had told us, The Roebuck was a comfortable, old-fashioned house with roaring fires and a friendly, well-trained staff. When we had deposited our baggage Pons, Miss Helstone and I repaired to the main lounge for a warming drink after our journey while Pons put the finishing touches to our strategy.

As we sat at a side table he looked sharply at a tall, cadaverous man in a frock-coat of sombre colour, who was just quitting the room.

"Memory, Parker," he said sharply. "Quite going. Once upon a time I should have been able to recall that man in a flash. A doctor, certainly. And a Harley Street man if I mistake not. You did not see him?"

I shook my head.

"I was attending to the inner man, Pons. Is the matter of any importance?"

Pons shook his head.

"Perhaps not, Parker, but the name is struggling to get out."

"Perhaps it will come later, Pons. In the meantime . . ."

"In the meantime we have much to do," he interrupted, draining his glass and getting to his feet. He smiled reassuringly at our companion.

"And now, Miss Helstone, to penetrate your den of mystery."

IV

A drive of about twenty minutes over rough, unmade roads, the traces of which Pons had already noted on our visitor's boots, brought us up against a high brick wall which ran parallel to the highway for several hundred yards.

"That is the wall of the estate, Mr Pons," said our client in a low voice.

"Do not distress yourself, Miss Helstone," said Pons warmly. "I would not ask you to go inside again if I did not think it necessary.

And, as I have already pointed out, you are in no danger from the occupants of The Priory unless I miss my guess. The shot came from the men who broke into the grounds; therefore the peril is from without."

Miss Helstone gave a relieved smile.

"Of course, Mr Pons. You are right. But what could those men have wanted with me?"

"That is why we are here, Miss Helstone. Just pull over in front of those gates, Parker."

It was indeed a sombre sight as we drew near; the sky was lowering and dark and it was so cold that it seemed as though it might snow at any minute. The road ran arrow-straight past the high walls of the estate and two tall, gloomy iron gates with a lodge set next to them framed a drive that was lost among dark belts of trees.

I drew up at the entrance lodge and sounded the horn. Almost at once a roughly dressed, dark man appeared, a sullen look upon his face.

"Open the gates," I called above the noise of the engine. "Inform your master that Miss Helstone is here."

As I spoke our client showed herself at the rear passenger window and the big man's jaw dropped with surprise.

"One moment, sir. I must just inform the house," he said in a marked foreign accent.

He shouted something and a second man whom I had not seen set off at a run along the driveway and disappeared. I switched off the motor and we waited for ten minutes. All this time Pons had said nothing but I was aware of his comforting presence at my back. The sentry at the gate – for that was his obvious function – stood with arms folded behind the locked portals and stared impassively in front of him.

Then there was the sound of running footsteps on the drive and the second man re-appeared, close behind him a tall, dark woman whom Miss Helstone immediately identified as Mrs Dresden, the housekeeper. A short conversation followed, in a language with which I was not conversant, and then the first man unlocked the gates and drew them back. I drove through and Mrs Dresden, who at once introduced herself, got into the rear of the car with Pons and our client.

"My poor child!" she said, obviously moved, and embraced the girl. "We thought something dreadful had happened to you."

"These gentlemen found me on the road and took me to their London home," Miss Helstone explained. "I was exhausted and incoherent, I am afraid. I explained the situation this morning and they kindly brought me back."

I was watching Mrs Dresden closely in the rear mirror as I negotiated the winding driveway and I saw her look sharply at Pons.

"That was very good of them, my dear. Mr Basden has been frantic with worry, I assure you. The children are quite safe."

"Thank God, Mrs Dresden. I have been so concerned. What will Mr Basden think? And what could those evil men have possibly wanted?"

The housekeeper faltered and I saw a look of indecision pass across her face.

"Do not trouble yourself further, Miss Helstone. Mr Basden will explain. He is waiting for you. And he will certainly want to thank these gentlemen."

I drove on for some way and then the estate road widened out into a gravel concourse. I was prepared for an imposing building but the fantastic folly which rose before us in the darkling winter morning was a Gothic monstrosity on the grand scale, with turrets like a French château and crenellated walls grafted on. All surrounded by sweeping banks of gloomy rhododendrons, interspersed here and there with groups of mournful statuary, which seemed to weep in the moist air.

I stopped the car before a massive flight of steps, at the top of which another bulky, anonymous-looking man waited to receive us. I felt somewhat apprehensive but Pons looked immensely at home as he descended from the vehicle and looked approvingly about him with keen, incisive glances.

"You have not exaggerated, Miss Helstone. The Priory is indeed a remarkable piece of architecture."

Our client said nothing but took Pons' arm timidly as he mounted the steps after the hurrying figure of the housekeeper. She paused at the imposing front entrance to the house.

"Whom shall I say, sir?"

"My name is Bassington," said Pons in clear, pleasant tones. "And this is my friend, Mr Tovey."

"A ridiculous name, Pons," I whispered as Mrs Dresden disappeared through the portals and we followed at a more leisurely pace.

"Perhaps, Parker, but it was all I could think of at the moment. It is not unpleasing, surely? The name of a distinguished musician came into my mind."

"As you wish, Pons," I said resignedly. "I only hope I can remember it."

We were being ushered into a vast hall floored with black and white tiles now and we waited while Mrs Dresden and our client hurried up the marble staircase to the upper floors.

I looked round curiously, only half aware of the bustle in the great house; it was evident that Miss Helstone's return had caused quite a stir and I could hear a man's voice raised in tones of relief. The mansion itself was magnificently appointed and all the strange circumstances of our client's story came back as I took in the details of our opulent surroundings.

We stood there for perhaps ten minutes, Pons silently observing the dark-coated men who scurried about the hall on furtive errands of their own, when a man came hurrying down the staircase. From his appearance and his timid air, I recognized the figure described so eloquently by Miss Helstone as Basden, the head of this strange household.

"Mr Bassington?" he said in a trembling voice. "I am indeed indebted to you for the rescue of our little Miss Helstone. I have been distraught with worry. Mr Tovey, is it? Do come into the drawing-room, gentlemen. Miss Helstone will join us once she has removed her hat and coat."

He led the way into a large, pine-panelled room in which an aromatic fire of logs burned in the marble Adam fireplace.

"Please be seated, gentlemen. May I offer you coffee or some stronger refreshment?"

"That is indeed good of you, Mr Basden," said Pons blandly. "But speaking for myself I require nothing."

I smilingly declined also and studied Basden closely while his conversation with Pons proceeded. He did indeed look furtive and ill at ease, and constantly glanced about him as if we were being observed, though we were quite alone in the room.

"And how are the children?"

Basden looked startled and then collected himself.

"Oh, quite well, Mr Bassington. They were merely frightened and ran back to the house. But I am not quite sure how you came across Miss Helstone . . ."

"We were on our way back to London in the early hours when we found the young lady bedraggled and half-conscious, lying by the side of the road. We got her into our car and as my companion is a doctor we thought it best to take her straight to my London house, where my wife made her comfortable overnight. In the morning, when she was sufficiently recovered, she told us her story and so we brought her immediately back."

Basden licked his lips.

"I see. As I have already indicated, that was extremely good of you both. If there is any way in which I could defray your expenses . . ."

Pons held up his hand with an imperious gesture.

"Say no more about it, Mr Basden. But they sound a dangerous gang of ruffians about your estate. Ought we not to call in the police?"

The expression of alarm that passed across Basden's features was so marked it was impossible to mistake, though he at once attempted to erase it.

"We have had a good deal of trouble with poachers, Mr Bassington," he said awkwardly. "My gamekeepers have dealt with the problem. We called the police, of course, but unfortunately the rogues got clean away without trace. The neighbourhood has been much plagued with the rascals."

"Oh, well, that would appear to dispose of the matter," said Pons with a disarming smile. "I am glad it was no worse. And now, if we could just say goodbye to our young companion, we will be on our way."

"Certainly, Mr Bassington. And a thousand thanks again for all your trouble."

We had just regained the hall when our client came hurrying down the stairs, the worry and strain of the past time still showing plainly on her face.

"Going so soon, gentlemen? I had hoped you would be staying to lunch."

"We have to get back to London immediately, Miss Helstone. But we leave you in safe hands, I'm sure."

Basden beamed in the background, one of the dark-coated men holding the hall-door ajar for us.

"You may rely on that, Mr Bassington."

Pons bent his head over Miss Helstone's finger-tips in a courteous gesture. I was close to him but even I had difficulty in making out the words he breathed to the girl.

"Have no fear, Miss Helstone. You are not in any danger. The doctor and I will be just outside the estate. Make sure you show yourself in the grounds tonight at about eight o'clock."

"Goodbye, gentlemen. And thank you."

There was relief on Miss Helstone's face as she and Basden said goodbye. The latter shook hands with us briefly and the two of them stood on the front steps watching us as we drove away. I had noticed previously that there were other cars in front of the house and Pons seemed to show great interest in a gleaming Rolls-Royce Silver Ghost which was parked near the steps. As soon as we had been passed through the entrance-gates by the guards and were rolling back toward Clitherington, Pons became less reticent.

"Well done, Parker. You played your part well. What did you think of The Priory?"

"Miss Helstone had not done it justice, Pons. But I judge it to be an elaborate façade."

"Excellent, Parker! You improve all the time. If Basden is master there I will devour my hat in the traditional manner. Just pull into the verge here like a good fellow, will you. I have a mind to engage in conversation with the owner of that Rolls-Royce when he comes out."

"But how do you know he is coming this way, Pons?" I protested.

Solar Pons chuckled, his face wreathed in aromatic blue smoke as he puffed at his pipe.

"Because, unless I am very much mistaken, the gentleman concerned is staying at the very same hostelry as ourselves. I assume that he would have remained at The Priory in order to let us get well clear."

"What on earth are you talking about, Pons?"

Pons vouchsafed no answer so I pulled the car up in a small lay-by at the end of the estate wall, where the road curved a little. We had not been sitting there more than ten minutes when Pons, who had been studying the road keenly in the rear mirror, which he had adjusted to suit himself, gave a brief exclamation.

"Ah, here is our man now. Just start the engine and slew the vehicle round to block the road, will you?"

I was startled but did as he bid and a few seconds later the big grey car glided up behind us and came to a halt with an imperious blaring of the horn. An irate figure at the wheel descended and I recognized the tall man in the frock coat whom Pons had pointed out in the bar of The Roebuck.

Pons bounded out of the passenger seat with great alacrity and beamed at the furious figure.

"Good morning, Sir Clifford. Sir Clifford Ayres, is it not? How goes your patient's health?"

The tall, cadaverous man's jaw dropped and he looked at Pons sharply, tiny spots of red etched on his white cheeks.

"How dare you block the road, sir? So far as I am concerned I do not know you. And I certainly do not discuss the private affairs of my patients with strangers."

"Come, Sir Clifford, you are remarkably obtuse for a Harley Street man. If you do not remember me, you must recall my distinguished colleague, Dr Parker?"

Sir Clifford made a little gobbling noise like a turkeycock and stepped forward with white features, as though he would have struck Pons.

"By God, sir, if this is a joke I do not like it. My presence here was confidential. If you are Press you will regret printing anything about me. I'll have you horsewhipped and thrown into prison. Clear the road or I will drive to the police immediately."

Pons chuckled and motioned to me to remove the car.

"Well, well, it does not suit your purpose to remember the Princes Gate reception last month, Sir Clifford. No matter. We shall meet again. Good day, sir."

And he politely tipped his hat to the apoplectic figure of Ayres at the wheel and watched him drive on in silence. He was laughing openly as he rejoined me.

"Sir Clifford is noted for his fiery temper and bad manners and he is running true to form today. Either he genuinely did not recognize me or it obviously suits his purpose to plead ignorance. But it merely strengthens my suspicions about his patient."

"What is all this about, Pons?" I said as we drove on. "I must confess the matter becomes more confusing by the minute."

"All in good time, my dear fellow. I must contact Brother Bancroft when we get back to the inn and then I must purchase a daily paper. We shall have a busy evening if I am not mistaken."

And with these cryptic utterances I had to be content for the time being. We lunched well at The Roebuck and though Pons was obviously on the lookout for Sir Clifford, the tall doctor did not put in an appearance. We were eating our dessert before Pons again broke silence.

"Come, Parker, I need your help. You are obviously more au fait than I with Sir Clifford. Just what is his forte?"

"In truth I have never met the man, Pons," I said. "Though you seemed to think he should know me. I do not move in such exalted circles. As a humble G.P. . . ."

"Tut, Parker, you are being too modest. My remark was merely meant to inform him that you were a fellow physician. We were introduced at the reception I spoke of but there were many people there; we were face to face for only a few seconds; and I relied on the traditional obtuseness of the medical profession and felt confident that he would not recall me."

"Come, Pons," I protested. "That is a definite slur."

Solar Pons chuckled with satisfaction.

"You are too easily ruffled, my dear fellow. You must practise indifference in such matters. But you have not answered my question."

"Sir Clifford? I know of his work, of course. He is one of the country's foremost specialists in heart disease and strokes."

"Indeed. I find that singularly interesting. This may not be so difficult as I had thought. If you will forgive me, I must telephone Bancroft. I will rejoin you for coffee in the lounge."

V

"Now, Parker, let us just put a few things together. In addition to the other small points we have already discussed, we have an eminent Harley Street specialist staying in this small place and in attendance on someone within The Priory. Does not that suggest a fruitful line of enquiry?"

Solar Pons sat back in a comfortable leather chair in the coffee-room at The Roebuck and regarded me through a cloud of blue pipe-smoke. It was early evening and the place was quiet, only the occasional rumble of a cart or the higher register of a motor-vehicle penetrating the thick curtains.

"Certainly, Pons. The invalid in the sealed wing suffers from heart trouble."

"Elementary, Parker. But why?"

Pons' brows were knotted with thought and his piercing eyes were fixed upon a corner of the ceiling as he pulled reflectively at the lobe of his right ear.

"I do not follow the question, Pons."

"It is no matter, Parker. Things are becoming clearer and I should be able to arrive at some definite conclusion before the evening is out."

"You surprise me, Pons."

Solar Pons looked at me languidly, little sparks of humour dancing in his eyes.

"I have often heard you say so, Parker. I have spoken to Brother Bancroft and he has given me some interesting information on affairs in Eastern Europe."

"I should have thought this was hardly the time for it, Pons."

"Would you not? However, it is no matter. My thoughts were directed to the subject by the events of the last day's newspapers. Apparently things in Dresdania are not going too well. Her Highness is out of the country and there is a concerted effort to unseat the government in her absence. Bancroft is most concerned."

"I must confess I am completely bewildered by your line of thought, Pons."

"Perhaps this will clarify matters."

Pons handed me a bundle of newspapers, among them The Times and The Daily Telegraph. I perused them with mounting puzzlement. In each case Pons had heavily ringed or marked certain items in ink. I caught the large heading of The Daily Mail: PRINCE MIRKO APPEALS FOR CALM. Apparently things in the state Pons had mentioned were in serious disarray.

"I must admit that the Balkans has increasingly occupied the world's thoughts, Pons," I observed. "Matters are constantly in ferment there and it is certain that our own Foreign Office has a definite interest in maintaining peace in that area of the world. But I know little about such affairs . . ."

Solar Pons chuckled, holding his head on one side as he looked at me.

"Do you not see the connection, Parker? Oh, well, there is really no reason why you should. All will be made clear to you in due course. Now, you have your revolver handy, I trust?"

"It is in my valise in my room, Pons."

"Good. Just run along and fetch it, there's a good fellow. We may well have need of it before the night is out."

He paused and stared at me sombrely.

"Pray heaven we are in time, Parker. Either she is already dead or so ill that she cannot sign documents."

"Good Lord, Pons!" I cried. "If anything has happened to Miss Helstone through our neglect . . ."

To my astonishment Pons burst out laughing.

"Do not distress yourself, my dear fellow. I was not referring to Miss Helstone at all. You are on entirely the wrong tack."

He glanced at his watch.

"It is only just turned six o'clock. We have plenty of time. It is a fine night and we will walk, I think. As long as we are at the estate by eight we shall have ample room for manoeuvre."

It was a long and lonely walk, on a clear, moonlight night, though bitterly cold. As Pons and I, both heavily muffled, walked along the grass verge at the side of the road, with the wind whistling through the leafless branches of the trees which came down in thick belts of woodland close to the highway, I could not help reflecting on the anguish and terror which must have animated Miss Helstone when she ran along this same thoroughfare to catch the early morning train to bring her to Pons.

It wanted but a few minutes to eight when we arrived at the high wall of the estate belonging to The Priory. Pons' eyes were bright in the moonlight and his entire form seemed to radiate energy and determination.

"Now, Parker," he whispered, looking about him keenly. "We will just cast about for the side-gate Miss Helstone mentioned. I have a feeling that it may be in use again this evening."

"I do not see how we are to get in, Pons. Basden's people may be watching the entrance there."

"We shall have to risk that, Parker. And I daresay I can get over the wall at a pinch, with the aid of your sturdy shoulders. But come what may, we must get inside The Priory tonight."

I followed Pons as he stepped off the road and we skirted the wall for something like a quarter of a mile, beneath the dark boughs of overhanging trees.

"We must go carefully now," Pons breathed. "It cannot be far. I questioned Miss Helstone carefully about this gate and it should be somewhere here, according to her description."

As he spoke the moonlight shimmered on a gap in the wall; a few strides more brought us to the gate in question. I looked at Pons swiftly but he had already noted what I had seen. The portal was slightly ajar. I had my revolver out and we crept forward quietly. Pons bent to examine the chain and padlock.

"Our friends are already in the grounds," he whispered. "Cut through with a hacksaw. They must have made some noise. It is my opinion, Parker, that Basden's employers mean to bring the game to them. Which merely substantiates my conclusions."

"I wish I knew what on earth you were talking about, Pons," I murmured irritably.

Solar Pons smiled thinly.

"Just keep your revolver handy, friend Parker, and follow me."

He disappeared quietly through the small gate which pierced the massive wall and I followed him quickly, finding myself in almost total darkness, the shrubbery grew so thickly and so close to the boundary the other side.

But as we went farther in, treading carefully and taking care to see we made as little noise as possible, the trees fell away and soon we found ourselves near the estate road along which we had driven earlier in the day. There was a strange light in the sky ahead and as we rounded a bend, skirting the drive and keeping well into the thick undergrowth, the façade of The Priory suddenly sprang sharply into view, clear-etched in the flood-lights.

"The little charade seems to be successful," said Pons drily. "Now, just keep a sharp look-out, Parker. You are an excellent shot and I should not like the men who have preceded us through that wicket-gate to come upon us unaware."

I knelt by his side and looked round somewhat uneasily. We were well concealed here but through the fringe of leafless branches we had a good view of the house with its lawns and statuary. Even as we settled, the slim figure of Miss Helstone and two small children were descending the steps.

"Ah, they are early this evening, Parker," said Pons with satisfaction. "It seems that things are expected to happen. If I were you I should just throw off the safety-catch of your revolver, there's a good fellow."

I obeyed Pons's injunction, secretly puzzled at his remarks. Our client, after pausing initially at the foot of the steps, was now coming toward us across the grass, while the children shouted and ran in circles about her. Their shadows, caught by the glare of the floodlighting, cast long replicas before them across the lawn.

I was shifting my position when I was almost thrown off balance by my companion seizing my arm.

"There, Parker, there! We are just in time to avert tragedy."

I followed his pointing finger and saw the bushes move at the other side of the drive. Then I became fully aware of what his keen eyes had already discerned. A thin, dark man with a pointed beard, down on one knee, crouched over a black rectangle which glinted as he moved. Pons was up like a flash and running back down the verge, away from the figure in the bushes. I was only a yard away as we crossed the roadway behind him.

"Your bird, I think, Parker," Pons called as the bearded man turned. The flare of light was followed by the slap of the shot and I heard the bullet whistle somewhere through the bare branches. I was cool now and sighted the revolver carefully as I squeezed the trigger. The rifle went off in the air as the man dropped.

The night was suddenly full of cries and noise; heavy bodies blundered about the bushes. I saw Miss Helstone frozen in mid-stride, the two children running from her. I dropped to the gravel as more shots sounded. Then Pons was beside me and urging me up.

"We must get to the young lady, Parker."

A group of dark figures had debouched from the terrace and were running across the grass; I heard a whistle shrill. Miss Helstone's face was white as we drew near. But the children were before her. The little girl's face was twisted. I saw the knife glint and was astonished to see Pons fell her with a deft blow from the flat of his hand. The knife fell on the grass and I levelled my revolver at the little boy who was barking orders in a strange, guttural language.

He sullenly let the barrel of the pistol in his hand sag toward the ground.

"What does all this mean, Mr Pons?"

Helen Helstone's face was white, her eyes wide in astonishment.

"That the charade is over, Miss Helstone. You are quite safe now and have nothing to fear."

"I do not understand, Mr Pons. The children . . ."

Solar Pons smilingly shook his head and went to help the little girl up. She was quite unhurt and kicked him on the shin for his pains.

"Not children, but midgets, Miss Helstone," said Pons gravely. "Evidently to guard your safety. I will give the Prince that much, at any rate."

"What is all this, Pons?" I began when a sullen ring of dark figures closed in on us. Others appeared behind, bringing with them three roughly-dressed men with beards; one was wounded and had a blood-stained handkerchief clapped to his wrist. A tall man detached himself from the group which had come from the terrace. He had a commanding air and his eyes glittered.

"Drop that revolver!" he ordered me. "You will find it is a good deal easier to get in than to get out."

Solar Pons smiled pleasantly.

"On the contrary. I beg you not to be foolish. Just inform Prince Mirko that we are here and that we have averted a tragedy."

The big man's face was puzzled. His English was almost perfect but his sudden agitation made him stumble over the words as he replied.

"Who are you?"

"My name is Solar Pons. Just give the Prince my card, will you, and tell him that the British Foreign Office knows we are here and will hold him responsible for our safety and that of Miss Helstone."

The tall man stood in silence for a moment, studying the card Pons had given him, while the floodlights beat down their golden light on the melodramatic tableau on the broad lawn, turning the faces of ourselves and the guards into ashen masks.

"Very well, Mr Pons," the tall man said at last, lowering his pistol. "We will all go into the house."

VI

"I think you owe me an explanation, Mr Pons."

The tall man with the quavering voice took a step forward and regarded Solar Pons with indignation. The big room with the opulent appointments seemed full of people; apart from ourselves there were a number of armed guards and the sullen captives. Only Solar Pons seemed supremely at ease as he stood, an elegant, spare figure, and regarded our host thoughtfully.

"On the contrary, Mr Basden, it is you who must explain yourself."

"I do not know what you mean."

"Oh, come, Mr Basden, if that is really your name. Shots, a murderous attack, threats, armed guards. To say nothing of the danger to Miss Helstone, a British subject. His Britannic Majesty's Government would not take kindly to a Balkan enclave within a friendly sovereign state."

Basden stepped back, his face turning white; he looked as if he were about to choke.

"Pray do not discompose yourself," said Solar Pons. "My guess is that you are an excellent actor, hired for the occasion, but a little out of your depth. Now, if you will kindly ask Prince Mirko to step out from behind that screen in the corner, we will proceed to hard facts."

Pons turned a mocking gaze toward the screen in question; now that he had directed my attention to it I could see a thin plume of blue smoke rising from behind it.

"How is Her Royal Highness's health this evening, Prince?"

There was an angry commotion and the screen was flung violently to the ground. A huge man with a thick beard stood before us, his eyes burning with rage.

"Why, that is the gentleman I glimpsed at my interview, Mr Pons!" said Miss Helstone in surprise.

"Allow me to present His Highness, Prince Mirko of Dresdania," said Pons. "Your real employer and the instigator of this elaborate farce."

Mirko had recovered himself.

"Hardly a farce, Mr Pons," said Mirko levelly, regarding Pons with a steady gaze from wide brown eyes. "You have unfortunately penetrated to the heart of Dresdania's secrets and you may find the price a high one to pay."

"I think not," said Solar Pons coolly. "My brother Bancroft holds an eminent position in the Foreign Office. If anything happens to us, troops will be here in short order."

He broke off and glanced at his watch.

"In fact, you have an hour to give me a satisfactory explanation of this affair."

There was an air of grudging admiration about Prince Mirko as
he stared evenly at Pons.

"You do me a grave disservice, Mr Pons," he said quietly. "I
wish you no harm and I have certainly done my best to protect
Miss Helstone."

"After first putting her life at peril."

Mirko shrugged his massive shoulders.

"Politics, Mr Pons. Dresdania must come first with us. I implied
no physical threat by my remark about paying a high price. Merely
that the British Government will find the Balkans aflame if my efforts
fail. Let us lay our cards on the table, shall we?"

"By all means," said Solar Pons equably. "Will you start or
shall I?"

The Prince smiled grimly and led the way across to the far door.
He said something in a foreign tongue to the big man who led the
guards and they trooped from the room with their prisoners.

"We will be more comfortable in the library, Mr Pons. Will not
you, the lady and the doctor sit down? Ah, I think you already know
Sir Clifford Ayres."

The tall, sour figure of the Harley Street man uncoiled itself from
an armchair and came down the room toward us. He held out his
hand stiffly, embarrassment clear on his face.

"I must apologize for my earlier rudeness, Mr Pons, Dr Parker. I
could not breach the code of professional conduct, as you well know.
I did remember you from the reception, Mr Pons."

"Good of you to acknowledge it, Sir Clifford," said Pons smoothly,
as we seated ourselves. "This is an unfortunate affair but events
appear to have taken a turn for the better. How is the man Dr
Parker shot?"

"Dead, Mr Pons," said the Prince.

He waved me down as I started to get up from my chair.

"You need not distress yourself, Dr Parker. Krenko was one of the
most murderous scoundrels who ever walked in shoe-leather. You
have done Dresdania a great service tonight, doctor, for which she
cannot thank you enough."

I cleared my throat.

"Thank goodness for that, anyway, Pons. I should not like the thing
to lie heavily on my conscience. And then there is the little matter of
the police . . ."

Pons smiled.

"That is the least of our problems, Parker. You must just content
yourself with knowing that you have saved Miss Helstone."

"At your instigation, Pons. I am completely baffled."

"And yet the matter was a fairly simple one, Parker, merely requiring the key. I am sure Prince Mirko will correct me if I am wrong, but it was obvious from the moment Miss Helstone consulted us that she was not required for duties as a governess; neither was she being paid five hundred pounds a year for her undoubted skills in that area."

"But for what, Pons?"

"For a masquerade, my dear fellow. For her remarkable resemblance to the Princess Sonia, the ruler of Dresdania. Everything pointed to it. And as soon as I saw the Princess's picture in the newspapers, the whole thing became clear. The interview with Mr Basden – he is an actor in your employ, is he not? – the man behind the screen who was making the selection; and the quite extraordinary way in which Miss Helstone alone from all the hundreds interviewed suddenly fitted the bill. She could not even speak the same language as her charges.

"But it was crystal-clear that the sole object of her employment was her unwitting impersonation of an absent person, even to changing her hair-style; wearing unaccustomed jewellery and expensive clothing; and to being seen late at night beneath the floodlighting outside this house. The whole thing smacked of the stage, Parker."

Prince Mirko gave a wry smile and studied the tip of his cigar.

"I can now see why Mr Pons is spoken of as England's greatest consulting detective," he observed to Sir Clifford.

Helen Helstone's eyes were wide as she turned toward Pons.

"Of course, Mr Pons. It is so simple when you put it like that. I had not thought of it."

"Exactly, Miss Helstone. And there was no reason why you should. But it is at least to the Prince's credit that while tethering you as a decoy he at least provided you with adequate bodyguards."

"It was a regrettable necessity," said Prince Mirko. "Dictated by the inexorable requirements of the State."

"And a most original method," said Pons reflectively. "They looked exactly like children. And they are potentially deadly."

He rubbed his shin with a slight grimace. Prince Mirko's smile broadened.

"They are the Zhdanov Twins, circus and music-hall performers. Boy and girl. They specialize in the personation of children and both are expert at ju-jitsu, knife and pistol. You were lucky they did not shoot you first and ask questions afterwards. We have several times used them in our secret service operations."

"But how could you know this, Pons?" I cried.

"It was a fairly rapid process to the trained mind, Parker. I soon came to the conclusion they were midgets. The harshness of voice; the fact that they stayed out so late at night, which no real children would do; their peculiar actions when the attempt was made on Miss Helstone's life."

His smile widened.

"You remember they ran toward the source of danger when Miss Helstone's life was attempted. That was significant. To say nothing of the male twin's cigar-smoking in their rooms. The lady suspected that you were the parent in the case, Prince."

The bearded man bowed ironically to our client.

"That was most careless and I will see that the guilty party is reprimanded."

"Your prisoners, Prince," put in Solar Pons sharply, as though the idea had only just occurred to him. "No Dresdanian summary justice on British soil."

"It shall be as you say, Mr Pons," said Prince Mirko. "In any case, Dr Parker has despatched the principal viper. And with the imprisonment of the others, the threat to Dresdania's internal politics is entirely removed."

"If you would be kind enough to elucidate, Pons!" I said hotly.

"My dear fellow. Certainly. If you had taken the trouble to read the newspapers properly this morning, they would have told you most of the story about Dresdania's internal troubles. It is Princess Sonia, is it not?"

Mirko nodded gravely.

"Her Royal Highness was in England incognito, on a short holiday. She is only thirty-eight, as you know. To our alarm and astonishment she had not been here more than three days when she was laid low by a crippling stroke. That was some four months ago. When she was well enough to be moved from a small, private nursing home near Epsom, we brought her here to this mansion, which belongs to the Dresdanian Embassy. Our own personnel surrounded her and we had the world's finest medical attention and nursing staff."

Here Sir Clifford bowed gratefully in acknowledgement of his services.

Solar Pons turned his lean, alert face toward the Prince.

"And how is Her Royal Highness at this moment?"

"Much improved, I am glad to say. It was a freak condition, I understand, and rare in one so young. I am assured by Sir Clifford that she will make a complete recovery. She will be well enough to sign State documents within the next few days."

"I am still not quite sure that I follow, Pons," I said.

"I see that you do not understand Balkan politics, doctor," said the Prince.

He held up his hand.

"And there is really no reason why you should. But Dresdania's internal stability is a vital element in the uneasy peace in that part of the world. Dissident elements have long been pledged to opposing the Throne and tearing it down. Vilest of them was Krenko; bombings, murder, political assassination and torture were only a few of the weapons he employed. As you know, the Princess is a widow and she has ruled as Regent, with me to guide her, on behalf of her son. He is now fourteen and of an age when he may soon be able to assume his responsibilities. Princess Sonia is anxious that he should do so, as the last decade has been a fearful strain. Indeed, it was probably this which precipitated the stroke. Her medical advisers prescribed complete rest and she came to England.

"But there was an attempted coup within a week of her arrival and unfortunately she was already ill. It was imperative for the country and for the sake of the young Crown Prince, who knows nothing of his mother's condition, that all should appear to be well."

"Hence the masquerade!" I put in.

I stared at Pons in admiration.

"And you saw all this at a glance?"

"Hardly, Parker. But it was not too difficult to arrive at the truth, once all the threads were in my hand."

Prince Mirko cast a regretful look at Miss Helstone.

"I must confess that I did not really think I would have much success with my ruse but I inserted the advertisement which Miss Helstone answered. I was in despair when I saw her at the interview but then realized what an astonishing likeness she had to the Princess."

Here he indicated a photograph in a heavy gilt frame which stood on a piano in one corner of the library.

"I determined to take a chance. It was a desperate act but the only card I had left to play. It was imperative that the Princess should be seen behaving normally. Hence the deception; the flood-lighting and the nightly promenades. We had heard that Krenko and a band of desperadoes had arrived in England. He would either make an attempt on the Princess's life, in which case we would be ready and try to eliminate him; or, he would merely report back to his political masters that the Princess was well and carrying out her normal duties. Either would have suited us, because there is no fear of a coup while the Princess is alive – she is so popular among the common people. All we wanted was to stabilize things until the Princess should be well enough to sign the Instrument of Succession on behalf of her son. But Krenko evaded our vigilance and made an attempt on her life; we knew he would try again."

"For which purpose you put on a visible show of guarding the estate, while deliberately leaving the side-gate vulnerable," said my companion. "And you required an orphan in case of any tragic developments."

"Exactly, Mr Pons. We had hoped that the presence of so distinguished a heart-specialist would pass unnoticed in the district – Sir Clifford insisted on staying at the inn where he could obtain his peculiarly English comforts – but we had not reckoned on your deductive genius."

"You are too kind, Prince Mirko."

Pons consulted his watch.

"I shall need to telephone Brother Bancroft, unless we wish the military to descend upon us."

Mirko nodded thoughtfully, the smoke from his cigar going up in heavy spirals to the library ceiling.

"It would be helpful if you would ask him for a responsible officer from Scotland Yard to attend to this affair, in conjunction with your Home Office and our Foreign Office, Mr Pons."

"Superintendent Stanley Heathfield is your man, Prince," said Solar Pons, with a conspiratorial nod which took in myself and Miss Helstone. "If you will just excuse me."

He paused by the door.

"It occurs to me, Prince Mirko, that Miss Helstone has been in considerable danger while under your roof. Now that her duties are prematurely ended, do you not think that some compensation is in order?"

"I had not overlooked that, Mr Pons," said Mirko gravely. "My Government's cheque for twenty thousand English pounds will be paid into any bank of her choice."

"Twenty thousand pounds!"

Helen Helstone's face was incredulous as she gazed from me to Pons.

"The labourer is worthy of his hire, my dear young lady," Solar Pons murmured.

"And it is cheap for the security of the state," Prince Mirko added.

"I hardly know what to say, Mr Pons."

"Take the money, Miss Helstone. I assume that Mr Basden has been well looked after?"

"You may rely upon it, Mr Pons," said Mirko gravely. "Though an admirable actor he is hardly ideal when called upon to play a part in which reality may intrude at any moment. His behaviour under stress has made him an unstable tool at times. And though we coached him carefully in the language he forgot even those few phrases when under pressure."

Solar Pons returned from telephoning within a few minutes, rubbing his thin hands together.

"Excellent! Superintendent Heathfield is running down with a party of selected officers just as soon as train and motor-car can bring him. In the meantime I think our work here is ended, Parker. No doubt you will wish to come with us, Miss Helstone?"

"If you will just give me a few minutes to pack, Mr Pons."

"Certainly. And I must emphasize that you must exercise the utmost discretion as to what you have heard in this room tonight."

"You have my word, Mr Pons."

Mirko looked on with admiration.

"Mr Pons, you should have been a diplomat."

"I leave all that to my brother, Prince Mirko," said my companion carelessly. "But I think that under the circumstances you would have done better to have taken our Foreign Office into your confidence."

"Perhaps, Mr Pons," said Prince Mirko, studiously examining the glowing red tip of his cigar.

Sir Clifford Ayres rose to his feet and stiffly shook hands.

"A rapid convalescence and a complete recovery to your patient, doctor. And my congratulations."

"Thank you. Good night, Mr Pons. Good night, doctor."

"Good night, Sir Clifford."

We waited in the hall as Miss Helen Helstone descended the stairs, her face still bearing traces of the excitement of the night and of her unexpected good fortune. Prince Mirko took the paper bearing her address and studied it beneath the chandelier in the hallway, his bearded face enigmatic.

"Dresdania is grateful, young lady."

He brushed her hand with his lips and bowed us out. The Princess's car was waiting outside and conveyed us back to the high road.

"A remarkable achievement, Pons," I said, as soon as we were driving back in the direction of Clitherington.

"A case not without its points of interest, my dear fellow," he said with tones of approbation.

He smiled across at our fair client.

"They do things a great deal differently in the Balkans, Parker, but by his own lights Mirko has not done badly by Miss Helstone. By the time she marries – and providing she has handled her funds wisely – she will be a well-propertied woman."

And he lit his pipe with considerable satisfaction.